This book is dedicated to the memory of my father, Victor, who was present with me throughout the entire writing process.

Acknowledgements

The first lines of the *Keepers of Terra* passed through my keyboard in the summer of 2022, though I had written down a few short-stories that took place within the same setting over the course of the last ten years. In the months since I began working on the book, the story went from something I would pursue as either a quirky hobby or a form of therapy (depending entirely on what mood I was in), to something more.

Then, one evening in late fall, as I got into my car after work and prepared for my drive home, I was overcome with this very familiar feeling. I believe it is the feeling one experiences when they come across a great television series that they get really into. It is a feeling I've been fortunate enough to have many times and it often comes accompanied by a very distinct thought: 'I can't wait to get home and find out what happens next!'

It was in that exact moment that I knew I had something special on my hands.

It might sound obvious for an author to feel that way about their book, but you'd be surprised by how elusive that emotion can be. I've scribbled and doodled words and stories for most of my life and I could've sworn that they all came from somewhere deep within my heart. Such an origin would entail that I, at least, would find them to be (to put it mildly) 'pretty good'. However, I never really found myself becoming enthralled by these early forays into creative writing and most of my stories were left abandoned and lifeless somewhere on my hard-drive, to be forgotten, as only things that were never truly alive could be. They had no *soul* in them. *This book*, however, has *a lot* of heart and it has been its pounding beat that has compelled me to turn it into the first story I would write to completion.

Thus, the story itself is what carries most of the merit for its own creation. I often find myself flipping through the pages and remembering a line from Cersei Lannister in *Game of Thrones*. After learning of the death of her only daughter, the notoriously unlikeable Queen of the Seven Kingdoms declares: 'I don't know where she came from! [...] She was nothing like me!' Though here-and-there I see the familiar notes of my own past experiences and passions, the story frequently ventures into realms I never really knew I had an interest in. Throughout its creation, I often found myself feeling less like an author and more like an editor, as I continuously ended up engaged in the act of taming a wild story, trying desperately to stop it from going feral. Often I succeeded, yet frequently I did not. I don't know if I am more thankful for the wins or for the losses.

In those cases where (I can tell) I draw from my own life experiences, I can only indirectly thank the great many people who've had an impact on me, whether large or small. In most cases, that impact was quite small, yet apparently it was potent enough for its ramifications to warrant presence among the following pages. Some people, however, require a more direct 'Thank you!'

The first would be my fiancé, who – despite thinking that the setting I chose is rather silly – frequently encouraged me to go as far as I needed to go and at whatever pace I needed to go at. I suspect she enjoyed how my incessant ramblings about topics that one could only describe as 'geeky' disappeared, as I channelled them into the story gushing out of me. I also stopped being an embarrassment at dinner parties, as I would no longer derail civil conversation into the wilderness of niche pop culture, casual existentialism and my fervent disdain of political correctness. I think this provided our friend group with some much needed respite.

The second would be my mother, who thought that the reason why I insisted on coming back home to virtually lock myself up in my childhood bedroom was because I was working on finishing some very serious project for some very important clients, and that I thus needed to isolate myself for two months, so that I could fully immerse myself in my work (which was *technically* what I was doing, though perhaps not in the way she pictured in her mind). I believe that by the time this novel is published, she has likely learned of what I was up too and has likely proceeded to explain to me (at great length and in painful detail) why being a writer is the shortest path to financial ruin, career suicide and medically diagnosable mental illness.

Which *is* true (I guess) but, what the hell, I've had the time of my life making it happen and I'll take any price charged as fair payment.

Lastly, I'd like to thank my two editors, Caesar and Oscar, whose input has proven to be truly invaluable. If you think the finished product is something of a mess now, you wouldn't imagine how it looked like before they came on board. They also served for the inspiration for one of the characters present within the pages that follow.

Preface

There is a balance which I believe should be struck between producing a story that is true to itself and a story which can better the reader. A story which is true to itself will often fight with its writer over the right to pursue its own destiny. This, at least, has been my experience.

Whether or not that balance has been struck by this tale is not in my power to determine.

I have, for better or for worse, allowed the story to win and become what it wished to become. This decision has produced a text which is, first and foremost, near and dear to my heart.

My hope is that you will discover a book that is easy to read, yet hard to finish.

My hope is that you will often step away from its pages in a flurry of thoughts, or in an outburst of rage, or a moment of wonder, or a fit of laughter. Hopefully, the story will unfold both on the pages before you, yet also in the room you find yourself in, after you push away the text or pause the audio and you pace around angry, or amazed, or annoyed, or alarmed, or anxious.

My hope is not that you agree or disagree with any subject, decision or theme the story touches upon, I am most concerned with there being something to agree and disagree with.

Before we proceed with the story of Thomas Muller and his fellow Keepers, I must make a small suggestion. It concerns the appendixes you will notice at the end of the book. I have never been a fan of books that require other books in order to make sense. However, I have also never been a fan of books that regard ambiguity as some pinnacle artistic excellence. In some instances, a little mystery can be beneficial to the story. Yet, most of the time I find such decisions to be motivated primarily by lazy writing, a fear of inconsistency or (worst of all) a belief that such restraint is something cool that only 'the real writers' do.

Thus has emerged my decision to include the appendixes within the book. I must underline the fact that the story is written in such a way that there is virtually no need to ever even look at the appendixes. They are there solely for the purpose of clarification and immersion. If you finish the story and found it to your liking, I wholeheartedly recommend you continue by reading the appendixes for a more in-depth look at how the world functions in the aftermath of the *End Times*.

With that out of the way, below a quick overview as to what you may find in each appendix. I wish only to give a quick outline of what they contain, so that you may always know where to go if you have some question or another regarding the story's setting.

The first appendix presents almost every character featured or referenced in the book. That way, if you ever find yourself in Act V and all of you find yourself wondering 'who the hell is "Sorbo Falk", again?' you may look to this appendix. It contains information such as name, rank, species, nationality, relationship to other characters, as well as some quick overview of who they are at the beginning of the story.

The second appendix is a historical timeline of the fictional world in which the story takes place in. As a point of reference, the First Battle of Terra takes place sometime in the middle to late twenty-first century CE (or AD; I personally don't care which abbreviation you use). You will likely never truly feel the need to consult this particular appendix while reading the text. It exists solely as an instrument for immersion.

The third appendix is essentially a glossary of words and expressions specific to the story. If you ever wonder what a 'dushman' is or why Thomas refers to both male and female superiors as 'sir', this should be your first stop. If you don't find any specific word within this appendix, then it is likely explained in either Appendix IV or V.

The fourth appendix explains certain particularities of *Terran* civilization. If you ever find yourself wondering why Thomas can hear a cat's heartbeat from several feet away, why 'oldtimers' are treated with so much reverence or what the difference between a 'citadel' and a 'holdfast' is, this is where to go. Each story-specific term is written in **bold** if it is included in a title and in *italics* if it is described within the explanation of another term. You will find this appendix to be an exercise in creative anthropology, sociology, political science, economics and biology.

The fifth appendix does for the Universe of Terra, what the fourth appendix does for Terra itself. If you ever find yourself wondering what a 'remani' is, how the 'Hyperborean' economy works or what the 'Republican Alliance' is, this is where you want to go. In other words, this is the extraterrestrial appendix and should be consulted accordingly.

The sixth appendix explains worldbuilding decisions that are almost never referenced within the story. It exists solely because I personally don't like it when science fiction writers without degrees in theoretical or practical physics explain how intergalactic travel works. As such, it functions primarily as a disclaimer to be read by any reader that might have some legitimate qualms with certain liberties taken with the laws of physics within the setting. That being said, the story's genre is a mix of science fiction *and* fantasy, with the latter offering a lot of freedom in terms of worldbuilding, which I have shamelessly exploited on numerous occasions.

On that note, whenever you notice some similarity between the setting of the story and other fictional universes, as well as our own actual reality, just know that the answer is: 'yes, you're right, that *is* where I got the idea from!' I am deeply passionate about the works of Raymond E. Feist, J.R.R. Tolkien, Frank Herbert, Glen Cook, G.R.R. Martin, Liu Cixin, Stan Nicholls, David Eddings, Paul Stewart and Chris Riddell, as well as the creative teams behind the settings of *Warhammer 40k, Warcraft, Starcraft, Star Wars, Stargate* and even *Star Trek*. To be honest, I actually feel bad about the previous sentence, since I had to narrow it down to my all-time favourites and had to exclude a whole host of storytellers that have had a profound impact on me, as well as on the development of this books' setting, such as C.M. Kosemen, Harlan Ellison, George Orwell, Aldous Huxley, Cormac McCarthy, Fyodor Dostoyevsky, Albert Camus, Søren Kierkegaard, Ibn Tufail, Quentyn Tarantino, Martin Scorsese, David Chase, Akiro Kurosawa – ok, I'll stop now.

I am not including this final disclaimer as a safeguard against plagiarism, since I would be personally offended if anyone ever found themselves in such a moment of bad taste that they would suggest that my petty scribbling bears too much of a similarity to the work of the above giants of storytelling and world literature. On the contrary, I think such works as mine are built on the shoulders of giants as a labour of love and admiration for the creations of those blessed to bear a creative light much brighter than my own little sparks of imagination.

Regarding the actual background of said imagination, I have decided to include the 'About the Author' section – typically found at the beginning of such texts – right after the last appendix. I always found it a bit pretentious when this section was included at the beginning of the book. The author is simply the vessel through which the story wills itself into existence and the two, though inseparable, are not one and the same. Moreover, one is not truly ever responsible for the other's existence, for it has been my experience that the two simply meet each other during the course of their existence, much like how a parent is not the same person as their child.

Lastly, I am forced by common decency to point out that the style of this book is to traditional science fiction and fantasy what gangsta rap is to pop music. Thus, an explicit content warning is required. This story contains colourful language (including, yet no limited to, profanities, ethnic and racial slurs, as well as crude humour), descriptions of violence (particularly war crimes, instances of terrorism and torture), references to self-harm, in-depth descriptions of mental illness, descriptions of drug use (including alcohol and tobacco), as well as content that might be considered blasphemous by anyone with a loose grip on theology. The above behaviours are neither encouraged nor glorified, yet they do form an important thread which is essential to the story's course. If at any point you somehow get the feeling that any of the traditionally unsavoury elements this book touches upon are presented in too much of a positive light, I am apologizing now, in advance, for what I can guarantee is nothing more than imperfect storytelling. Though, I would recommend that you simply continue reading, if you ever get such a feeling. The world of *Terra* is neither grimdark, nor noblebright. It's somewhere in the middle and occupies a particularly grey area of morality.

Finally, I would never take the liberty of instructing a parent as to the best way to raise his or her children, yet in my most humble opinion this book is most definitely not suitable for children, regardless of age. Reader discretion is most definitely advised.

Prologue

We count years since the First Battle of Terra. Years were counted years differently before, just as how they counted years differently before Jesus of Nazareth was born, lived or died. Just as Jesus was not born on December twenty-fifth of the first year AD, the First Battle of Terra didn't take place in Year 1 AB either, but the year before. We just chose to start counting on January first of the next year.

That doesn't mean everyone in the Universe counts time from the year in which some small skirmish took place on some world in a galaxy only just discovered. No one remembers exactly who began counting first and starting from which moment in time. Yet, people keep track of time as a compulsion, with the tracking place now being more important than any tracking taking place at any time other than now.

What is known is that a long time ago, in a galaxy, very much like our own, on a world very much like Old Earth, people, very much like us, awoke under stars that were very different from our own. They used fire, they told stories, they counted things that were and things that could be, they wondered, they loved, and they kept track of time. At one point, they even left their world to find new skies. We should not wonder as to why they did this. After all, would we not have gone on to do the same? Are we not human too?

They were the first. Yet, not the only.

They found life on countless worlds. And on countless worlds, they found other human life.

So began the great irony of human life among the stars, as it would appear that what makes human beings special is that there was nothing special about us at all. Humans, it seems, are a naturally occurring phenomena within the universe, albeit with relative prevalence. What was to be expected happened and the oldest among these early people were also the most advanced, the most powerful and the most imitable. Those that were the finders would unite the early disparate flowerings of

2

new humanity and would plant the seeds of old humanity among the many places of the Universe where humans had not yet emerged.

Thus began the Age of Bliss.

And there was peace. And time was being counted. For it is that we were all mortal then, as we were now.

Again, one may understand why these people wished to vanquish death by thinking first as to why we would wish the same. They had conquered death by ageing and were, for lack of better terms, functionally immortal and forever young. Yet accidents still could happen. More importantly, accidents had happened, and there was not one person alive that had never known the loss of a beloved human life.

So it was that a plan was born. A Great Plan. A plan which may be explained only through metaphor, simplification and, especially, omission.

If the Universe were a sleeping giant, or a child, it would leave an imprint on the mattress beneath it and the sheets around it. On this bedding, every single crease of the sleeper's body could be recorded, allowing for a map of the Universe, not just through space, but also through time. Every single cell in the sleeper's body that ever was, that had been and ever would be, could be seen upon this imprint.

And if it could be seen, it could be grasped and replaced with an identical, yet inherently broken copy. At the right moment, that is. The moment in which the universe would have broken it anyway in what we call 'death'. It could then be taken somewhere else. To a better place. To a human place. Made by humans.

For humans.

Or people in general.

Thus began the Age of Strife in which we have been born and will also inevitably die in.

Since, as you may have noted, we are dealing with people, conflict arose as to what Heaven was supposed to be like. Mankind had long struggled to make the Universe into a Heaven in itself, a task which they eventually achieved only at the cost of much effort and sacrifice. Yet, they could not have anticipated what sorrow would flow from the wounds of disagreements long-neglected, as the Old Realm tore itself apart.

It would perhaps be best to leave the speculated intricacies of the War at the Gates of Heaven for a more focused *Ancient, Unclear and Unknown Histories* lesson. Suffice to say, the Shattered Heavens were born. Instead of one single, certain and secure home for all mankind that ever was and ever would be, several very different heavenly realms are believed to have been crafted. It is at this point where it must be mentioned that the Universe had the last laugh, since we will never truly know which Heaven, if any at all, lays on the other side of our life, until we make the crossing.

Every so often, a new Heaven is supposedly made, whether through the use of knowledge passed down from the Age of Bliss or otherwise independently developed. Such is the setting of our story.

For so it was that, in the year 45 BT, we Terrans were working on crafting our own, very special, Heaven. As we had been instructed by our friends from amongst the stars, we appointed a number of our most gifted individuals the duty of working on this great project. We are the Keepers of Terra and what follows is the story of how we learned from death what life is about.

Chapter I
Minarets of Dust

It was snowing moondust outside.

Luna had not been terraformed the same way Mars had been. Instead of being turned into a lush green and vivid blue world, Luna had simply been covered in a layer of construction, dotted frequently with shipyards, hangars and towers. Some air had made its way outside of the lunar habitats of Selena City and had created something akin to a rudimentary atmosphere. Though it rarely rained (in the classic sense of the word) it frequently 'snowed', as primal currents and the passing of ships stirred up dust which ultimately made its way back down.

Thomas didn't mind. He actually liked watching the grey lunar snowfall. Every so often, he counted himself lucky to witness a dust storm. He remembered the last one he had seen, a few weeks before. He realised that, if he didn't get the chance to see another one tonight or tomorrow, it would likely be some time until he got to experience another one.

'Thomas! Your tram is arriving!' his operator's voice rang out in his mind.

'Thank you, Clara,' he replied.

'You're welcome, Thomas.' Clara was his personal basic operator. Primitive artificial intelligences, though incredibly advanced in their own right, 'operators', as they were known, were designed to be emotionally stunted. Their personality was simplistic, their sense of self basic, more akin to that of a primitive mammal, like a cat, than to an actual person. She was a far cry from the fully sentient and conscious artificial intelligences which operated entire starships, stations and systems. Yet, like all personal operators, she was essential to the smooth operation of modern Terran technology. As a result of this duality, most people treated their operators as a cross between an assistant and pet.

Thomas turned away from the window facing the lunar landscape towards the tracks behind him, just as his tram came to a stop. He waited for the doors to open, walked in and took a seat in one of the free cabins.

'How many stops?' he asked.

'Nine. I'll let you know when you should get ready to disembark. Would you like some music?'

'No, thank you. There'll be plenty of that later. Right now I want to spend some time by myself.'

'I understand, Thomas. I'll keep quiet. Enjoy the ride!'

Clara was 'located' on the watch he wore on his left hand and was connected to an implant coating his wrist bones. From there, she communicated with his brain via the nerves of his hand, giving him the impression that his watch was talking to him. Other, more invasive, forms of artificial intelligence did exist, yet were not available for use by most people, due to their susceptibility to being hacked. It was a very unlikely possibility, yet Terrans didn't like taking any chances. Having an assistant helping you around and playing your favourite playlist all day was all fair and dandy. Having a potentially hostile entity being able to interact and influence your mind directly... not so fair and dandy, as the orcs had learned less than a decade before.

Having peace of mind was something Thomas could finally grasp now and he planned on enjoying it unperturbed. At least for a brief moment.

He had just finished his mandatory five year service with the Allied Host. It was the culmination of his first twenty-five years of life. Five years in school, followed by five years in the gymnasium, followed by five more years at the Terran Academy, then, finally, his mandatory Allied Host service. All that remained was his Terran military service and that was something that would last for a lifetime.

After those first twenty-five years, each Terran chose which military path they wished to pursue: either continue service in the Allied Host or begin service in the Terran Military. The former was the united armed forces of what was known as the Republican Alliance: a union of several peoples, with a shared history, the same enemies, common interests and similar worldviews. The latter was the military-industrial complex that passed for modern Terran society.

In theory, upon finishing mandatory military service, each Terran had an equal choice between the two. Yet, there was a quota which had to be met. Moreover, the results of careful examination and analysis were what dictated which career path each young Terran citizen could pursue. If you scored high in the areas you were interested in, you were allowed a choice regarding your future.

All in all, the system worked well, with each Terran ultimately ending up with more-or-less the position they desired. Thomas was no different. Starting next week, he would be free to begin his service in the Terran Logistics Corps, the segment of Terran society which dealt with fuelling the Terran war machine. Frontline combat was virtually guaranteed, since the Terran military had a very hands-on approach to warfare.

This didn't really bother Thomas at all. He had seen quite a fair amount of combat during his time with the Host and had fought with all the ability expected of him both by his comrades and by his people. War was the way of Terra. Growing up in a world that had survived the Apocalypse, only to find itself in a universe which seemed intent on their extermination, could do that sort of thing to a people.

Life was somewhat grim and mostly a struggle. However, Thomas enjoyed this. Proving himself worthy had long been all he had focused on. Now, he could finally be allowed to relax and enjoy the fruits of his labour.

It was in this state of blissful self-satisfaction that a voice in Thomas' mind spoke out. It was a voice he had never heard before in his entire life. A voice which did not belong to Clara or any other operator for that matter. Yet, somehow, it was a familiar voice. A voice he somehow knew spoke the truth.

Enjoy this moment. For there will come a day when you will die.

Immediately, Thomas felt himself tense up in primal fear and great panic.

No! No! No! No! Don't think about that. He tried fighting it, but it was too late.

He knew now. There was no going back.

But he had always known that he would die, hadn't he? Death was all around him. It had been all around him growing up. At first, it had been the knowledge of death. His parents and friends and family – the very society he had been born into was obsessed with death. How could they not be? Theirs was a society built upon the ashes of an apocalypse. Though he had not seen death in front of him or taken a life until he had grown into a young man, death had always been everywhere around him. He had thought that he understood what it was.

But, he hadn't. He may have understood his death, but not *the end of his existence*. That moment in which he would cease to be. When he would not build towards anything. When he would have no hope. When he would not think. When he would not feel. That moment after which he would... *end* and be no more.

Revelation coursed over him in a flurry of thoughts and in waves of emotion. His body had gone cold as he sat there, clenched in his seat. He had to find a way to calm his mind. He was clearly having some kind of panic attack, which was something he had trained for.

Exactly! Remember the training! You know how to do mental conditioning! Do breathing exercises!

He closed his eyes and focused on his body. His feet first. He felt how tense and clenched they were. Slowly, he focused on relaxing them. He then moved up his body, soothing muscles along the way, all the while focusing on his breathing – it was important to keep breathing! He eventually reached his chest, where he felt his heart race and his lungs struggle to breathe coherently.

If I would stop breathing I would die.

That kind of thinking was all that was needed for him to start feeling a slight choking sensation, as if he was about to suffocate.

Ok. Breathing exercises and mindfulness aren't really doing the trick. Let's try a mantra. That should work.

He recalled the Herbert mantra. It was standard Terran military training and it had worked for him in the past when he had feared for his life.

> *I will not fear.*
> *Fear is the mind-killer.*
> *I will face my fear.*
> *I will let it pass through me.*
> *When the fear has gone,*
> *There shall be nothing.*
> *Only I will remain.*

He recited the words in his mind in conjunction with a continued focus on his breathing. After about seven or eight internal recitations, he paused.

Did it work? Did it pass?

It would appear that it had. He looked outside. He saw, in the distance, how it had stopped snowing. Moreover, the tram had stopped as well. He checked the station's name, only to realize that the next stop was his.

The dust on Luna was very light and, with gravity being very weak and the atmosphere being very thin, the dust had a tendency of piling up on top of itself, forming long towers of dust, similar to how stalagmites formed in caves. One such minaret had formed outside his window. A pretty thing it was. Thomas could tell that this was a particularly tall one. He then felt the tram move, ever so slightly, letting loose subtle vibrations as it picked up speed again. Just that, somehow, those little tremors were enough to topple the little tower of dust, despite having not disturbed it when the tram had first arrived in the station.

As he saw the minaret topple into a heap of grey powder, to be picked up and played with by the lunar wind, Thomas couldn't help to think about his own condition. He felt that he himself was little more than a fragile construct of dust and water, which could at any moment be toppled by forces outside of his control.

Oh no. The mantra didn't fucking work at all!

'Clara?!'

'Yes?' she responded. 'I was just about to talk to you myself. Are you alright?'

'Wha-what do you mean?' *Is something happening? Am I dying now?*

8

'You appear to be experiencing some type of psychosomatic stress. Elevated heartbeat. Hyperventilation. Stress hormone secretion.' At least he wasn't imagining things.

'Yes. I feel it. Is… is everything alright?' Normally he would have asked in a much insightful manner, but his only insight was that things weren't at all normal.

'None of your vital or auxiliary functions seems to be threatened or malfunctioning. You seem to be alright. You have received no information since when we last spoke. I assume you are just having troubled thoughts?'

Well, there's an understatement. 'Yes… Something like that.'

'I see. Well, you will be arriving in one minute. I recommend you get ready.' Clara didn't have time to get her recommendation across, as Thomas had already gotten up from his seat and was waiting by the exit for the doors to open.

I'll snap out of this. All I have to do is get moving, meet some people, and put a few drinks in me. I'll snap out of this real quick. It's just a weird moment in my head.

Thomas was quite sure that he was lying to himself, which added a sense of betrayal to go along with his dread. As the tram stopped at Eileithyia Station, he immediately got off as soon as the door opened, only to stop for a moment to recall where he was going.

You finished the service. The brigade is throwing a party for the officers at the Reacher Pub. You've been there before. Exit the tram station, walk down the street, you'll be there in three minutes.

So that's what he did. All the while, the feeling of dread walked right behind him, which was probably why he ended up making the three minute walk in less than one minute. He heard the party before he saw it. Normally, this would have triggered excitement and a sense of expectation in him.

The sound of music, conversations and laughter. The clinking of glasses. The sound of furniture being bumped into. It meant fun. It meant he would get to hang out with his friends, talk, drink, laugh and love. But, this was different and, as he neared the entrance to the pub, he didn't even bother to look around. No one seemed to notice him anyway.

I just need to find Motley, Liaco or Hampstead – or all three – and I'll sit with them for a bit, get some drinks from the bar, and then I'll get better.

Motley was easy to find. The hobgoblin was doing what hobgoblins always did when they got a few drinks and smokes in them: arguing with random people about random shit in a clearly friendly and somewhat charming manner.

It appeared that he was explaining his family tree this time. 'Kimmie Jimmel is my mother's sister's ex-husband, which means I know what I'm talking about when I –'

'– you mean your uncle?' Ketamy was, as always, very perspicacious.

Motley was confused for a moment 'What? Yes! Glad to see you're following! Which, as I was saying, means I know what I am – no! It actually means he's my ex-uncle! See, Bethany, this is why you should shut up when the grown-ups are talk…'

'Ketamy,' his reluctant conversation partner corrected him once more.

'Ketamine? I mean... maybe... I dunno... Fuck it! I mean it's a special occasion…' the hobgoblin began talking himself into doing hard drugs.

'*Ket-a-my*… it's my name ya gibby cunt!' Ketamy emphasized.

Motley raised a bushy eyebrow. 'Oh… I thought your name was Sebastian.'

'Then why'd you call me "Bethany"?'

'It means "distracting bird chirping in the background" in my language! I never told you, but it was always in the back of my head! Thought I'd tell you now that I ain't gonna see ya for a while!' As always, Motley's good-natured insults and banter managed to get him out of trouble.

He was, nevertheless, unable to articulate his initial idea and Thomas was quite sure that this would be the case for some time, having noticed how the initial point always had a tendency to get lost in the banality of such conversations.

If we all died right now, how would it be if their final thoughts had been of such simple things? This is what it means to be sentient. To be consumed with such little thoughts, hiding from the inevitable truth our meaninglessness and mortal –

'Hi, Motley!' Thomas decided to cut the thought short. He wasn't going to have a panic attack here.

'Oh! Hey, Thomas. Fashionably late, I see! That's a bit atypical for you, ain't it? Being a Lieutenant's suiting you well, I see?'

'I … I talked to my mum before coming over –'

'Oh, please don't drag your mother into your lies!' He wasn't lying. He actually had been talking to his mother. She had seemed so proud. *Such a sad thing that she was proud over such a small achievement as this, when it was something so insignificant in the vast expanse of time and…*

'Have you met Ketamy? He was asking if we wanted to do ketamine!' Motley continued.

As Thomas took note of his dilated pupils, the glass of whiskey in one hand and the peculiar smoke drifting up from the cigarette in the other hand, and concluded that perhaps additional stimulants might not be recommended for either of them.

'He wasn't. Hi, Ketamy. Hi, everyone!' Thomas shook hands with Ketamy and the rest of the little crowd which had assembled around his ever-ranting goblin friend.

The group continued their conversation. Normally, he would have enjoyed taking part in it. He had always thought these conversations were fun. Growing up on Terra, life had always felt so focused on trials, tribulations and tests. It had only been in the Allied Host that he had discovered the simple joys of communication.

It didn't have to be so utilitarian. Conversations didn't need to have a direction. They didn't have to be about learning something or impressing someone or proving something or earning something. No! Conversations could be fun! Not in the way conversations in old Terran films were. They didn't have to advance some plot or prove some point. They could just be something distracting. A distraction from the inevitable fact that they would all die at one point, whether it by the sword, by accident or when the end of the universe ultimately came –

It's happening again. This isn't doing it. I need to move. It goes away when I move and when I distract myself.

'Hey!' he blurted out awkwardly. 'I'm gonna go get a drink!'

'Sure, mate! You've got some catching up to do. Don't miss Liaco and Hampstead on your way in!' Motley got back to arguing some 'very relevant' nonsense with Ketamy as the song switched to a Terran song and Thomas entered the pub.

'*Ra-ra-rasputin! Lover of the Russian Queen...*'

'Thomas!' Liaco had a very high-pitched voice for an orc. Yet, it still carried with great difficulty across the Terran disco music. What helped was the fact that her and Hampstead were sitting together at one of the tables closest to the exit. This was likely the influence of his fellow Terran, as orcs and goblins usually gravitated towards the centre of the room.

Thomas faked a smile and waved as he made his way over to their table. 'Hi, Liaco! Hello, Hampstead!'

'What up, mister? Talked to the mum, yeah?' Hampstead quizzed him.

'Yeah. All good.' *With my mother, at least.*

'Yeah. Me too. I cut it short. Wanted to get here quick and get a buzz going.' Hampstead emphasized his words with a variety of hand gestures.

'Is this some weird Terran thing?' Orcs were curious by nature, even sullen Ersatz orcs like Liaco. It was one of the many things about them that were complementary to Terrans. Orcs loved learning about other people's cultures and Terrans were obsessed with offloading their identity onto typically oblivious bystanders.

Hampstead answered, 'What? Having a healthy relationship with your parents?'

'No! Every Terran I know talks to their parents regularly – if they're still alive, that is. By "regularly", I mean at official times, as if it's some task on a to-do list,' Liaco explained.

'Yeah, well,' Hampstead was smirking now, though not at Liaco or Thomas, but at himself, 'Terran mothers are… dotty.'

'What is dotty?' Liaco inquired. She had an English-Orcish dictionary downloaded into her memory, yet the dictionary couldn't translate words that didn't exist in the other language.

'Dotty? Uhm... they're like... hmmm... very vigilant birds. Like hawks. They always want to make sure their hatchlings are fine. You know... force of habit... and history.' Thomas and Hampstead shared several struggling looks, as the latter tried to explain how post-apocalyptic mothers were like.

'I see. Our mothers love us too. Just that, like hawks, they do let us leave the nest at one point and live our own lives.'

'Oh, yeah? How often do you talk to your mum?' Hampstead continued.

'As often as I can, but that's the thing! My mother is my friend. I talk to her because I love sharing my life with her. Not because I have to report back to her!' Liaco seemed befuddled by the idea.

'Yeah, well, it's different with us.'

She did seem to understand; just that she thought it was a bit strange. 'I see...' she said.

'No, I mean... Come on, Thomas, back me up!'

Thomas had been following the conversation, yet he had forgotten how he would usually participate in it.

'Yeah... It's what they've been through. They know that you can die at any moment and want to make sure that you are fine.' *Ah crap… it's spilling out. I should go get a drink. Minimize exposure.*

'*Amen*. See, he's good with the words, Thomas, I'll give him that!' Hampstead slapped him on the back, as he struggled to keep it together.

'Thank you! I'm gonna go over to the bar and get something to drink.' He made to sit up, yet both Liaco and Hampstead immediately protested.

Hampstead looked confused. 'We already ordered for you?! We got you a pina colada. There's shots, wine, whiskey, whatever…' Thomas had thought all the drinks laden around the table belonged to some of their other friends who might have been away at that moment.

Crap, I can't go to the bar and be by myself for a second.

'Oh, well, that's very nice. How much do I owe you?'

'Nothing. It's on the brigade's tab.' *Ah, good, I can drink myself out of it.*

He did shots with the two of them and then began sipping his pina colada, just as Liaco began tapping the table. 'Well. I see Thomas has some catching up to do. I'll leave you both to it.' With that, she got up from her seat. 'I am off to the bathroom. I'll be back in about fifteen minutes.'

'OHHHH!' Hampstead let out a roar.

While Thomas bumbled in astonishment, 'What the..?'

12

'What?' Liaco's eyes opened wide in surprise at their outbursts.

'Too much information!' Hampstead was adamant.

'We didn't need to know that...' Thomas was also quite firm, yet mostly weirded out.

Liaco raised a bushy eyebrow. 'I don't understand. You've even seen me do it a few times. What ...'

'... *in the trenches*!!!' Hampstead cut her off.

'Well, what's the difference between the trenches and here?' Liaco was smiling now. Her early look of surprise was gone. Mild amusement and curiosity had replaced it.

'Here you don't have to do it next to us. You don't even have to declare or hint at it! You could've just said you're going to the bathroom!' Hampstead explained.

'I don't understand. What if something happens to me? I was only letting you know where I was supposed to be and for how long. Some things were implied, yes, but I didn't *tell you* I am going to take a shit –'

She didn't pause as the two rolled their eyes, averted their eyes and mentioned the names of various ancient Terran prophets and deities.

She did continue though, 'You just assumed that and now you're revolted at *me* for trusting *you* to notice if anything was to go wrong and I didn't come back.'

'You're going to the loo, not enemy positions...'

'I can't predict what's in there!' *Well, no one can, that's how life is really, when continuous trek into the unknown, with the only certain destination being the grave –*

– Fucking stop it!

'Well... there's a sink, some towels, a mirror, sanitizer, maybe the toilet has one of those built-in bidets –' his fellow Terran began explaining.

'– Oh, shut up!' Liaco was the one rolling her eyes now.

Thomas tried to act normal and chip in. 'You could've just said you were going to the bathroom and just that. It's all we're saying!'

'Yes. But, if the acknowledgement of my bodily functions is inadequate in this context, does mentioning my intent to go to the bathroom alone not imply that I am doing so for only a certain selection of reasons? All of which imply some degree of body waste management?'

'No!' both Terrans responded.

'But, why else would I be in the bathroom?' She had a point.

'I don't... please don't... just go!' Hampstead was pinching the top of his nose now, eyes closed, while Thomas had actually started giggling to himself. *Damn Liaco... You probably have no idea, but I needed this moment...*

'Very well. I will leave the table and return later!' Liaco smiled, mostly to herself, at this point. 'Goodbye! Momma's boys!'

As Liaco left for the bathroom, to return in fifteen minutes, Hampstead stopped massaging away his embarrassment and turned to Thomas, raising his glass. 'Well, you know what they say: "*An orc in a trench is like an Orc on a park bench and an orc on a park bench thinks he's still in the trench"*!'

They both laughed, yet Thomas' laugh came from his mouth, not his heart. 'Ersatz orcs. The Vigilant orcs, they're always... *civil*, aren't they?' He tried to move the conversation in whatever direction was possible. He was afraid of the silence. Thoughts might come in the silence.

'Yeah, but even them, they're civil in a fight too. It's still the same as with Liaco's creepy fucks: they only know one lifestyle. They're just civil all the time and it makes it look like they know what "off-duty" means.'

'Well... don't we also?' Thomas, only at this moment, realised that, in five years of always being in the same unit as Hampstead and after countless hours of conversation, both profound and banal, he had never spoken with him about anything critical of their own lives as Terrans.

'What do you mean?'

'Well... "never again", "ever watchful", "siege mentality"... Don't we also know of only one lifestyle?'

Hampstead's eyes flickered between what Thomas could tell was a perfect understanding of his point and a clear confusion as to why he was only now bringing it up. 'Yeah... I know what you mean... I mean we have Leisure Time.'

'With capital letters, mate, and... why do we even have Leisure Time?' Thomas felt he was being a bit weird at this point. Not necessarily with his choice of topic – though he was going places with it – but with his tone.

He felt himself more... erratic and... almost desperate to talk and get words out. Being coherent was secondary. Somehow, he began to think that he shouldn't have been so frustrated by Motley's constant digressions outside. Keeping a point was quite difficult. Particularly when your mind is running around in your head hiding from itself.

Hampstead looked down and smiled. 'So that we can focus better on what we have to do when it's not Leisure Time.' He turned to stare off in space for a second, seemingly looking out the window in Motley's general direction. 'Orcs have Leisure Time too.'

'Yeah, that's where we got the idea from. But it's not the same. Orcs always do stuff together. Meditate. Cook. Paint. Sculpt. They do all of it together. There's structure even in that. Our Leisure Time has no structure.'

'Yeah. I know. I mostly sleep during Leisure Time... and hang out sometimes.'

'And what do we do when we hang out?' Thomas himself wasn't even sure as to what his point was.

14

'Well, watch movies. Listen to music. Dance sometimes. Read. We used to go fishing with my mum and dad back in Baikal.' Hampstead had over twenty brothers and sisters. He was ethnically English, though he had been raised in northern Mongolia.

His parents were part of the Gardener. They raised not just their own children, but also clones, orphans, cyborgs and the salvaged. Hampstead himself was salvaged. His father and mother's reproductive cells had been recovered from the wreckage of a British egg and sperm bank and been mixed together as part of the Terran High Command's repopulation drive. The only information to have survived the End Times, and the only information he had, regarding his biological parents was that his mother had been born in a place called Hampstead, hence his first name. His last name was Tsedenbal, after his Mongol parents.

'Yeah but, we don't do anything… we don't *create* anything during Leisure Time. We're mostly resting and relaxing before we go back to work, or training, or studying, or war. It's just another form of staying busy. Just that we're staying busy by taking a break before we get busy again.'

'Hey! I draw!' Hampstead protested. Drawing was his 'art', as Terrans called it. Every Terran had an 'art' and a 'science'.

'I know. What do you draw?'

'Well… you know… comic book superheroes.'

'From *Old Earth*. From *before* the End Times. You draw things because you enjoy it, yes, but you're just drawing things from before. When was the last time you made or even saw artwork that was Terran, original *and* new?'

'I… Phew… If you put it like that, I haven't really.'

'My point exactly.' Thomas was lying. He was ranting his way towards his point, happy that he was caught up in a conversation outside his own head, no matter how incoherent. Surprisingly, he had actually stumbled upon something.

'It's all a distraction.' *Here we go again.* Turns out he had a point after all. Just that it wasn't a point he wanted to have.

Hampstead jumped in at this. 'Yeah… I did think about that!'

Thomas' eyes opened wide. Had Hampstead been having these same thoughts?

His fellow Terran continued, 'It's the oldtimers! Everyone is too busy and tired to make new art. However, the oldtimers miss the shit they had growing up. They're the ones who perpetuate it. I mean… don't get me wrong. I grew up with Lion King, Bugs Bunny and Spongebob Squarepants and I love that shit. But, yeah, you're right. There's no new things. We're just recycling things from the past.'

This was a very valid point, yet not really what Thomas felt. He felt that everything, regardless if it was Duty Time or Leisure Time, was just a distraction meant to keep people's minds away from their inevitable death. He felt that it was because of these distractions that he himself hadn't had these thoughts before. In this moment, at the age of twenty-five, when he had perhaps had his first moment without these distractions, the terrible truth of his condition had come to him.

He failed to notice Hampstead's eyes following someone across the room. 'This was a good chat mate! I wish we would've gone into this before. But,' Hampstead got up from his seat, 'I need to cut it short and go figure something out.'

'What?' Thomas followed his friend's gaze to see Varna Koraline, a high elf lieutenant. 'Varna?'

'You know what they say mate: "*Make love, not war*"! Gonna go talk to her before she goes back to Gondolin.'

'She's not staying?'

'No. All the good people are leaving.' He turned to wink at Thomas. 'I always wanted to know if she had the eye for me. Now's probably the last time and I say it's probably the best time!' He began fixing the collar of his shirt. 'Oh, yeah mate! One more thing.' He looked Thomas in the eye now, a cheeky smile across his face.

'Did you and Liaco ever... you know... do the thing?'

It appeared that Hampstead really was covering all the loose ends in the eleventh hour. Thomas paused for a second, wondering what Liaco would think of him telling Hampstead about what had happened a few years before. She hadn't explicitly told Thomas not to tell anyone, yet she hadn't told anyone herself. That he knew of, at least.

On the other hand, Hampstead could keep a secret. He didn't want to lie to him and he reckoned Liaco wouldn't mind anyway. But, then again, he didn't know what Liaco –

'Ah, shit! Knew it! When?' Hampstead's words made Thomas' mouth move, yet no words came out at first. He had failed to realise that a long pause was an answer to the question all in itself.

After Musspellheim,' he conceded, looking down in shame, his secret now revealed.

'That makes sense. Well...' Hampstead's genuine smile was now ear-to ear. He raised his fists in front of his abdomen. 'You fucked an orc!' His thumbs shot up from both of his closed hands.

'Nice!' he declared, before turning around on his heels and setting out towards his crush.

Thomas stood there, speechless, as he watched Hampstead leave the table and head out to try his luck with Varna.

Yes, he had slept with Liaco after Musspellheim and on a few other occasions. It had been a distraction, like many others in his life. Now, somehow he wondered if Liaco had sensed that. What if she had wanted something more?

16

But what more could she want? Even if they had spent the rest of their lives together and raised children and lived somewhere on some lush farm on some ambient planet, it would have still been a distraction in its own way. What was the difference between that and any other distraction? The amount of time invested into each type of distraction? In the end, death would have claimed both of them and what would they have achieved in doing? Bring into the world new souls, without their consent, to either spend their limited existence in superficial ignorance of the futility of their condition, or to be struck by the terrible revelation of aforementioned futility, as he had been just now?

Thomas felt the pina colada glass slip from his hand and onto the table. He initially thought that it was because the glass was cold and the cold liquid had condensed on its outside, making it wet and slippery. However, his other hand, which had never held the glass, was also wet with his own chill sweat. He also realised that he was shaking slightly and he suddenly became aware of the fact that he was likely going to have another panic attack. Immediately afterwards, his mind was flooded by a fear that he would somehow lose control and faint.

Not here! I need air. Sitting up and walking would do me good.

He got up in one quick, jerky motion and walked outside.

It was not an 'outside' in the classical sense. The actual outside was Luna's dusty thin atmosphere. The lunar settlements, known under the collective term of 'Selena City', were all located in enclosed habitats. The outside, as it were, was simply a large boulevard lying beneath the transparent material which kept out the near-vacuum of Luna's surface.

Smoke a cigarette! It's weird to just go outside to sit by yourself not doing anything.

As he pulled out a cigarette, Thomas found a quiet place in front of the pub, keeping a distance from other groups of partygoers. He found an empty table where he placed his glass, as he sat upright, with his back to the crowd. He closed his eyes and started attempting the breathing exercise again.

'*Nobody wants to be lonely. Nobody wants to cry. My mind is longing to hold you, so bad it hurts inside. Time is precious and it's slipping away...*'

Another Terran song. This one also had words that bothered Thomas, in an even more strikingly sharp manner than the ones before.

'Do you have a spare cigarette?' a thin, waifish voice startled him.

He turned to see Toph Pamento of all people.

The elf had sneaked up to his side. She was quite short, even for a low elf, barely reaching Thomas' shoulder. He was surprised he had even heard her over the loud music and the sounds of revelry behind him. Thomas hoped she hadn't seen his hand instantly reach for his pistol, only to drift to the pocket where he kept his cigarette pack.

'Hi, Toph!' Thomas didn't know Toph that well. Terrans, in general, kept their distance from elves, which was something the elves themselves seemed to appreciate. They served together in the Allied Host, sure, but old wounds seemed to hurt the worst when close to their cause. It was why it hadn't actually surprised him that much that Hampstead had waited five years to make a move on Varna.

Quite frankly, now that he thought about it, bar a few formal discussions concerning work, Thomas was more-or-less certain he had never spoken to Toph before.

'You smoke?' Thomas forced himself to not sound aggressive. However, he had kind of overdone it and he ended up asking the question with a tone that sounded shocked.

'No. I just... I've watched you smokers for five years now. You seem really into it. I thought I'd smoke one now. It is an occasion after all. Please?' She had that monotone, yet sing-song accent typical of low elves from Menegroth. Coupled with her particularly soft voice, she sounded like a small human child trying to sing very softly, so as not to bother any adults.

'You know it's addictive, right?'

She smiled slightly. 'I do. I just want to try one. You're a Terran. Wouldn't you enjoy getting an elf addicted to something?' *Edgy. Very edgy for an elf.*

He faked a smile. 'By that logic, I'd argue that a Terran wouldn't enjoy doing anything that would give pleasure to an elf.' Those weren't his words, but words he heard overheard long ago and had kept in his mind. In truth, he didn't really feel them in his heart.

As a feeling of shame overcame him, he took out his pack and his lighter, and passed it to the young elf. Thankfully, Toph seemed to think he was being funny, as opposed to just being rude for no reason. She gingerly took out a single cigarette, closed the pack and passed it back to him.

Thomas saw her wet her lips before putting it in her mouth, driving home the point that she had, clearly, never smoked before. 'You'll get dizzy.'

'I know. Isn't that the fun of it?'

'No.'

'Oh. I'll get dizzy because it's the first time?'

'Yes. Breathe it in slowly. Don't even inhale from the first puff. Let your mouth get used to the smoke before breathing into your lungs or else you might –'

Toph had lit the cigarette and Thomas saw her cheeks pull inwards as she drew in a lungful of nicotine. She immediately started coughing as she choked on the smoke.

He waited for the choking to subside. '– choke...'

Toph took a sip of her own drink, made a strange swallowing sound, and then took another puff. Thomas saw her play with the smoke a little, as she felt it move around in her mouth. She then took another puff, this time slowly, and breathed the smoke in.

She didn't choke and proceeded to sit there next to him, staring forwards towards nowhere in particular. After a few more puffs, she turned to him, eyes on the cigarette in her hand and said, 'I am getting a little dizzy.'

'Hmmm...'

'Not too dizzy though.'

'Hmmm.' Thomas saw that she wasn't going to leave. Likely she didn't want to smoke in front of the other elves or maybe she thought it was polite to smoke the cigarette with him.

Anxiety washed over him first. The dread followed and then the thoughts. What were any of them doing here? Was it just to distract themselves from the futility of their existence? Was this distraction the very reason why their existence was futile? Was he the only one who knew that? Was he the only one who now suddenly found it unbearable? He felt so alone. He wanted to ask for help. But, asking for help meant explaining the problem and what if explaining the problem would cause someone else to feel as horrifyingly bad as he did?

Thomas didn't want that. He felt as if he would have to bear this burden whilst forever alone. He couldn't tell his friends. His parents might not even understand. It might hurt them. Or it would hurt him if they misunderstood the way he felt.

Thomas glanced at the little elf next to him, still puffing on the cigarette as she watched the smoke dance from the tip of the cigarette.

Oh, fuck it.

'Hey!' he started.

She turned to meet his eyes, yet his gaze was now fixed somewhere on the ground. 'Yes?'

'Do you, ever, like, bump into random people you don't know at parties and talk to them about things you would never talk about with your friends?'

She giggled. 'Yes. I do sometimes.'

Thomas smiled a forced smile. 'Me too. Not often, but I do.'

'Because, unlike your friends, you don't care if it will change some stranger's opinion of you for the worse?'

'Exactly.'

'So, do you want to talk about anything in particular?'

'How old are you?'

'Thirty-seven Terran years.'

'Ah, I'm twenty-five. How old is the oldest elf?'

'Like... the oldest in the Commonwealth?'

'No. Anywhere.'

'Oh... There are elves among the Tribes who are said to have been alive during the Age of Bliss, in the days of the Old Realm.'

'So, how long? And what do you mean by "said to have been"? They might be lying about it?' Thomas was puzzled and it showed on his face.

'Well, no one knows how long ago that was. That is the answer to your first question. Not even them. That is the answer to your second question.'

Toph's eyes glazed over slightly. 'You can only store so many memories in a mind. The mind forgets things often, even during a natural human lifespan. Over the aeons, most is forgotten. Even that which is essential.'

'What about soulkeepers?' Thomas had heard of the fabled artefacts of the elven races. They were used to store memories and even consciousness when needed

'Soulkeepers conserve the mind in a single moment either as a copy or as a transfer. They can also conserve memories, if that's what you were asking.'

'It is.' Thomas wanted to ask the next question, yet he already knew the answer. Yet, there was no reason to ask, as Toph explained regardless.

'Soulkeepers can work very well. Even indefinitely. In theory. In practice, they can get lost or degrade. The mind can also change, over time, into something so different from the mind which lived the memories from before that it would become impossible to understand, or even interface, with its own memories. If a consciousness is transferred to a soulkeeper and mind is allowed to live an existence within the soulkeeper, than that mind would also become radically different to the original consciousness.'

What a terrible thought to consider. Even if your body somehow managed to survive and you could live forever, your mind never could. You would never be able to store all the memories needed to be yourself. Even if you did, could you truly be a person if you could always remember millions, billions or even trillions of years of experience? What about an infinite experience? If a mind wished to live forever and aimed to live forever, then the goal would be to have a mind which could comprehend and recall an eternity of experience. Was that even possible?

How cruel it all was.

Every fibre of his existence wanted to live and – more importantly – didn't want to die. Yet, even if a vessel for his mind, his soul or just his very essence could be made to exist forever with absolute certainty, his actual self would die. His identity and his 'self' would be devoured and recycled in the never-ending process of change that was life.

20

Eventually, it was inevitable. Anyone would become as those ancient elves Toph spoke of now and of which Thomas had heard of before. The only way they could avoid complete insanity was if they changed to such a degree where they had nothing in common with their minds of millennia before.

He thought about his own life. His dreams, his aspirations, his thoughts, his character. All would be lost. Even if the memories could be stored, if he were to access them, would he still see the memories as being *his* own past thoughts? Or would it seem he was reading the autobiography of someone else's life?

'Why are you asking me these things?' Toph's whisper of a voice cut through the whirlwind of thoughts.

Lie to her. She must not know. No one should know. 'I've just been thinking about what comes next after this.' Thomas caught himself speaking the truth and turned to her, about to spin a tale different to his own experience that evening. Something about his career plans in the Logistics Corps, maybe.

'After this life?' As Toph's lips moved, Thomas' mouth went dry and numb.

Maybe she knew. Maybe Toph knew. Maybe elves thought about these things more often. After all, wasn't that the hallmark of their kind? Elves evolved from humans that lived on blissful, perfect worlds in utopian societies which mastered medicine and science. They evolved to be naturally long-lived and healthy. Given the right environment, elves could, in theory, live forever without the need for any artificial augmentation.

Humans were not like that. If left alone, humans would just expire one day, no matter how much they exercised, no matter what they ate or drank, no matter how much they cleaned themselves or stayed out of trouble. Thomas knew how, in the days of Old Earth, the oldest people lived was just over a century old and those were very rare exceptions, not the norm.

Nowadays, technology and knowledge, both gifted and stolen, had allowed Terrans to become functionally immortal. Then again, how old was the oldest Terran? Maybe a hundred years old? The End Times had culled many of the old, with most of the survivors being well under the age of fifty and that had been almost a half century ago. How many other End Times were lying in wait on the path before them? How many other times would they be culled by the carelessness of existence?

A feeling of impending doom within Thomas began to pulse. He had to say something or he might risk losing his mind in silence. 'Yes. After this life. How did you know?'

'Humans often think of death. I've noticed you don't often speak about it. However, it is always implied. Your goals in this life always seem to be linked to prolonging it. I have only ever seen you, Terrans, and now the Hyperboreans, the

Aesir and the Vanir. You Terrans, in particular, bring death with you wherever you go.' Toph's eyes locked onto Thomas' and he knew why. She was tiptoeing dangerously close to the unspoken connection their two peoples shared.

After meeting his gaze and determining that his eyes spoke of more than threats and rage, she added, 'It almost looks like death *follows* you everywhere you go. It weighs on your heart and forces your hands. You run from it with every step you take and, yet, it always lurks in your shadow.'

'Is that just not what it means to be a person?'

'Maybe. But it is not the way of other peoples.'

'Elves do not think of death?'

'Oh, we do. But not like humans. We know that all of our time we have in this universe will be spent living, not dying. Why make the entirety of that time be about that one moment that is to come at the end?'

Maybe because, if you don't, it might come faster. That was what he wanted to say. Yet, he felt there was no point in doing so. He had not wished to push these thoughts on Motley, Liaco and Hampstead for fear that he might hurt their spirit. With Toph, he could tell that she simply would not understand. The dread had subsided, somewhat, to be replaced by anguish at finding yet another person with whom he couldn't speak about what was happening to him.

Toph had finished the cigarette and was putting it out in an ashtray on the table next to her. 'Before the Revolution, do you know what most elves died of?'

Thomas met her eyes. He did have an answer and she could tell.

She continued, her voice now carrying the melancholy of a sad lullaby. 'Sadness.'

Her words cut into his very soul.

Yes, of course, it was sadness. He had heard of this before. Though, he had never considered it the way he did now. It was, after all, something of a joke among Terrans: elves had everything they ever wanted and, yet, they committed suicide more often than any other species. Part of the reason was, perhaps, the fact that there was no stigma attached to the act. At least none that he knew of. For Terrans, even the suspicion of suicidal thoughts was sometimes enough to strip a Terran of all their rights and privileges. Such pariahs would be condemned to live the rest of their natural lifespan in exile and poverty. Suffice to say, said natural lifespan was usually cut short by the thoughts themselves. Nevertheless, despite happening, it was incredibly rare and such instances were drops in the ocean compared to what occurred in elven society.

Another reason was, perhaps, the fact that elves just, sometimes, lost their will to live. Such stories were strange to human ears, yet not to the pointy ones of elves.

22

Thomas had heard stories of elves just sitting down on an armchair in their house and... passing away. Perhaps that was the inevitable end of life extension. After all, humans did not evolve with the goal of living forever and – no matter how much both species may deny – elves still carried the hallmarks of their human ancestry. Humans had evolved to survive just long enough to pass on their genes to their offspring. Their minds had grown, evolved and advanced, as a tool to be used towards that single goal. Contemplation was nothing more than a by-product of the awareness our ancestors cultivated to succeed in not dying of hunger, cold or predation.

Perhaps our minds simply were incompatible with an eternal existence. The end of the self might be more unavoidable than the death of the body. Perhaps not for all living beings but, then again, had there ever lived a creature for long enough to prove otherwise?

'Goodbye, Thomas. Until we meet again!' Toph broke the pensive melancholy which seemed to have overtaken both of them. She lingered only ever so slightly, before turning around to rejoin her friends.

'Do you believe that?' Thomas had not turned to face her, yet saw her pause in her stride as he spoke.

'I do not believe that anything is certain in this world.'

She's right.

Damn her.

Chapter II
A Crisis of Faith

Thomas had left the party shortly after his cigarette with Toph.

He had made his way to his room in his battalion's barracks and had done his best to fall asleep and ultimately failing spectacularly, as he was still awake when he heard Hampstead come back home in a drunken stupor in the late morning. The following evening at dinner, he realised that no one had even noticed his early departure. Everyone had just assumed that he was simply somewhere else in the Reacher Pub and that they simply hadn't crossed paths.

The second night after the *thoughts* had come had not been much better than the first. Thomas had spent the day performing pointless tasks he could have easily left for a later time, whilst unsuccessfully trying to take his mind off what was bothering him. Clara had told him that he had finished a weeks' worth of tasks in one day, yet she had not congratulated him, as she insisted he attempt to get some sleep and to relax, as eighteen registered panic attacks within twenty-four hours, some of which lasting for over half an hour of continuous palpitations, profuse sweating and hyperventilation, was in no way conducive to his health.

The next morning, he said his goodbyes to Motley, Liaco & Hampstead in a strange haze. Motley had insisted that, on his first vacation from the Allied Host intelligence wing, he would come visit him and Hampstead on Terra. Liaco's goodbye was much more heartfelt, as she had insisted that they continue to keep in touch and continue their group chat, no matter the distance between them. She would be returning to Ersatz, where she would rejoin the martial society of her people, not unlike Thomas himself.

Hampstead accompanied Thomas on the flight back to Terra, as he would also enjoy a month-long vacation, before returning to Luna and the Host. He had been quiet the entire flight, much like Thomas himself, though the satisfied grin on his face told him that it was for completely different reasons.

24

He had tried to enjoy the view of Terra as they neared the planet, attempting to echo the childish wonder he had felt when he had first gazed upon the world of his birth years ago. His father had taken him with him during one of his assignments to Luna. This time, unlike all those years ago, he saw for the first time the fragility of his home. He now saw his world as the oldtimers saw it.

Very vulnerable before the capricious nature of the universe, no matter how hard they tried to turn it into an indestructible fortress.

Grey lines crisscrossed Terra's surface along the ancient lines of longitude and latitude. From a distance they looked as though some cosmic giant had laid a steel mesh around the world, with two massive plates covering the two poles. Closer inspection revealed the lines and plates for what they were: the giant superstructures known as the Spines and Shields.

They were Terra's most ostentatious line of defence. The Shields were gigantic fortresses which covered the entirety of both the lands beyond the Antarctic Circle, as well as the seas beyond the Arctic Circle. Rocket batteries, communication towers, weapons platforms, solar panels and more, littered the surface of the Shields. Beneath them, a vast network of hangars, bunkers, warehouses, factories and who-knew-what-else spread out along the entirety of the superstructures.

From each Shield, the twenty-six Shadow Spines jutted out at regular intervals only to be intersected by the nine Horizon Spines which circled the globe. The Spines served a variety of purposes.

They served as gigantic fortresses, in their own right.

They housed the tracks of the Terran train system.

They could provide emergency housing in the eventuality of an attack on Terra.

They also controlled the weather, which was one of the main reasons why they had been chosen, as opposed to other proposed defence systems. The technology employed by the Spines split the planet into two hundred and eighty different quadrants with each quadrant being, to a degree, separated from the others. If one quadrant was, say, devastated by a nuclear strike, the others would be insulated from the ensuing fallout and shockwave.

In the places where the Spines crossed Terra's oceans, they doubled as gigantic filters, making sure that nothing passed from one quadrant to another without the Terrans' approval.

This was a world born out of the trauma of the past. When the End Times began, the opening act had been a period of time known as the Fimbulwinter. This had not been, as the name might suggest, some new ice age but a series of global catastrophes, as the extraterrestrial invaders had employed geomancy to break both the world and its people. Earthquakes, volcanic eruptions and landslides had torn the earth apart. The seas had spewed forth tsunamis, monsoons and hurricanes with unimaginable intensity and frequency. Tornadoes, thunderstorms, hailstorms and sandstorms had been commonplace. Fire had rained from the sky and wildfires had scorched the world, leaving behind the ashes of what had once been.

The Spines would prevent that from happening again. The Terrans would make sure of it.

Their ship docked at Prime North Station, where Thomas and Hampstead parted ways. Hampstead would take a train to Severnaya station, travelling along the rim of the Northern Shield, and from there he would take another train and travel south towards his parents' estate in the Mongolian steppe. Thomas would just board the first train from Prime North to Aquitaine Station. From there, he would use one of the many public shuttles to get home.

Rosenheim had been a small German city before the End Times, located at the foot of the Alps, just south of Munich, in the land of Bavaria. More than fifty years later, Rosenheim was, by modern standards, a large German city, second only to Berlin, the recently rebuilt German Holdfast.

The northern European coast had suffered heavily in the End Times, with entire lands, such as the ancient lands of the Dutch, falling beneath the waves, as the dikes burst and sea levels rose rapidly. The lands south of the coast had also suffered, as never-ending storms had whipped the land for months on end. All the water pouring forth from the sky had led to mudslides and unimaginable flooding. Then, when the volcanoes of the Mediterranean had erupted, shockwaves shook the very roots of the Alps, which partially collapsed, leading to rockslides that buried entire countries. Many Terrans insisted that one could hear the rumble of tumbling mountains of rock all the way in the lands of old India.

What had remained of Berlin, Hamburg and Frankfurt had been completely destroyed when the invasion had begun in earnest and their Enemy, or 'dushman', as they were known in the early days of Ragnarok, was revealed. Munich had fared better, in part due to geography, but in no small measure due to the fact that Munich had been the place where half of the old Bundeswehr had chosen to regroup. The other half had joined up with surviving elements of other Eurasian armies and refugees in Prague. Though Prague had survived Doomsday, Munich had fallen in the waning hours of the Hour of Twilight, with the last pockets of human resistance managing to carry on fighting in the Bavarian countryside. Rosenheim itself had been the last true bastion of German resistance, holding out until the Hour of Twilight had passed and the day was won.

As a result, Rosenheim had become the Holdfast of the German Nation, meaning that it was viewed as a type of capital, a title held for over two decades, until Berlin had been rebuilt. Being a Holdfast mattered little from an administrative point-of-view, since the centres of power of Terra now lay beneath the two Polar Shields.

Holdfasts existed only as cultural artefacts, functioning only as symbolic cultural centres of the Nations of Terra. Some, like Moscow, Kampala and Jerusalem, had been the site of bitter fighting on Doomsday, with some, like Delhi, Gandhinagar and, most famously, Prague, even managing to hold out until the very end. Others, such as Berlin, Cairo and Mecca, had been completely destroyed during the Day of Reckoning, when the invaders made landfall. Many former capitals, such as Jakarta, Tokyo and Tenochtitlan had been completely destroyed during the Fimbulwinter, as many had been located on Terra's coasts or other areas vulnerable to the wrath of nature.

All of this history mattered little to Thomas now though, as all he could see now, flying over the verdant countryside, was a reminder of how vulnerable life was. He had learned that before the End Times this corner of Europe, over which he was flying, had been home to over twenty million Terrans. At one point in the last fifty years, there had been less than twenty million Terrans alive in the whole universe.

Official records stated that over 99% of all Terrans had died during the events of the End Times and the War of Vengeance. The tragedy had continued, as many had died in the years after in the other conflicts Terra had taken part in. It so was that, in the year 45 BT, less than twenty million Terrans born before the End Times remained alive. Of these, less than a quarter were true oldtimers, men and women who remembered Terra before the apocalyptic events of the invasion of their world, with the rest being the Yin, babies and children that had been stowed away in the dark places under the world, as their parents, and humanity as a whole, did battle for the fate of their world.

Terra's current population was just about to surpass one hundred million, in part due to the Gardener Corps and its many programs. This was the name given to the policy of repopulation instated by the Terran High Command during the War of Vengeance and was not a single program, but an entire family of programs. Terran couples could pursue the path of becoming *gardeners*, if they so chose, like Hampstead's parents had done. The Gardener Corps, though still part of the Terran military, consisted of couples which raised large groups of children with the help of the Terran High Command. However, only a small percentage of these children were usually the biological offspring of their parent guardians, with most of them being conceived and gestated in Terran breeding pods, to be then distributed to gardener families upon birth.

Many of them were clones of dead Terrans, whose genes had been 'reused' (usually at the request of friends or family). Others were 'salvaged': humans produced by splicing together various gene codes by whatever means had proven possible in each specific case. The genetic material involved belonged to either Terrans who had died in the End Times (whose genetic material had somehow been preserved) or to oldtimers that had donated their gene code to the Gardener programs. Many more were orphans and a large number were cyborgs placed in the care of human parents, to raise them as their own and to help grow their own human identity.

Thomas did not come from a gardener family. However, this did not mean that he had no experience of being part of one. When Terran parents were away offworld on duty, they left their children as *wards* to gardener families. Thomas had spent a total of around five years of his own childhood as a ward in various foster families, at first in Germany, then in Bulgaria, America, Nguni, Brazil and Melanesia.

He had been lucky. First, to have had his parents be away for so little time and, secondly, to have them return at all. His parents, both of them Yin, had been away on their first war when he had been only eight years old, returning only three years later. He had kept in contact via the Terran messaging system, yet it had been a rough period of time for him. He loved his parents and they loved him. Their absence had caused much turmoil within him, despite the excellent treatment he had received from his foster families.

How would they take their news that their son had a broken mind?

This was the dark conclusion he had reached. That must have been what was happening. He must be going insane. He wasn't able to focus on anything else, other than an extreme and continuous fear of death. That first night on Luna, he had fought with the thoughts for the first time in his life. They all boiled down to one simple hope.

Was there any way for him not to die?

The answer – though remarkably difficult to comprehend – he had at least accepted. No, there was no way not for him to experience death. Even if he managed to die and be resurrected, like some had succeeded in the past, his luck would eventually run out. Whether it be by explosion or vaporisation or a gunshot to the head or even just having his brain rot out in the dirt for too long, he would eventually die in the classical sense. Even if Terra managed to stay out of any war from then to the end of time, death would certainly claim him in the end. There was simply no way he could be certain that he would live forever and that, in itself was proof enough of the certainty of your own death.

The next question had come almost immediately after he had acknowledged this inevitability of the first. *Is there a way around that?*

Having his consciousness transferred to some server was, also, not going to guarantee his eternal existence, because the server itself would be located in the physical world. It would be just as exposed to the chaos of the universe as his current body of flesh and bone was.

No. That wouldn't work.

Perhaps there was another way?

Perhaps there was a way to live forever while still dying here, in this world.

The ways of Old Earth had shifted into something very different, yet still somewhat recognizable, when it came to religion. True believers of the faith (whichever that faith may be) were few and far between. Those that still clung to the old ways frequently did so in a type of open secrecy. They had to, since religion was partially outlawed.

The Terran legal code split the definition of religion in two.

There was *cultural* religion, which was mostly unchanged and recognizable. Terrans still celebrated events such as Christmas, Ramadan or Diwali. Mosques, churches, temples and shrines of all faiths still dotted the Terran landscape. Though most had been rebuilt upon the foundations of lost temples of Old Earth, a few had been built upon grounds where no religious edifice had ever stood before. People still wore religious symbols, such as crosses or karas. Most Terrans still had at least one religious icon in their house, whether it be a menorah, a kamidana or an ikon. Religious words still permeated modern Terran languages, as people frequently took the Lord's name in vain. In its most extreme form, cultural religion included even the acknowledgement of the existence of historical religious figures, such as all the Buddhas, Jesus Christ or even Hercules. Albeit, with the strict insistence that there was nothing divine about these people. They were just special thinkers and doers of long gone times, who had been confused with gods, demigods and prophets.

Cultural religion was not just tolerated, but celebrated in the otherwise pragmatic world of Terra. Yet, a certain aspect of it did tend to walk the thin line between accepted practice and forbidden dogma, when historical context was taken into account. Oldtimers in particular were often guilty of flirting with certain ideas and beliefs which they themselves would usually decry as problematic, to say the least. The issue, in question, had to do with the dead, of which there were many.

Cemeteries were everywhere on Terra. Pictures of long gone loved ones littered rooms and screens in houses all across this post-apocalyptic world, as oldtimers fought vehemently to keep the memory of the dead alive. A subtle, yet palpable, type of ancestor worship had emerged in this society that struggled to cope with the overwhelming grief whose sombre shadow stood engraved deep within the Terran psyche.

It had been by way of such thinking, that the colour of mourning had become the colour of Terra.

Thomas was reminded of this as he passed over Rosenheim, during his descent towards madness and his parents' place. Alongside the black, gold and crimson of the German tricolour, the black flag of Terra flew, a small white circle, symbolising Terra itself, laying in the centre of a sea of darkness. His was a society of black-and-white, of death and of life, and of right and wrong. The trauma of past suffering had become the foundation of their very identity and was now inextricably linked to their vision of the future.

Never again.

Those words, written in a thousand Terran languages, lay etched on uniforms, weapons, door frames... everywhere Terran hands had claimed something as their own, they left the mark of their worldview. Every aspect of this society was a result of what they had been through, what they had lost and what they had discovered as their world had collapsed around them. The days of the End Times were legend, particularly to sunrisers such as Thomas, who had learned of the many great deeds, bloody battles and untold suffering endured by their forefathers, not just in classrooms, but also during many a fireside chat.

As he signalled the Muller Estate's security system that he had arrived and would be landing in front of his parents' hangar, he gazed over the woodland that covered the mountains behind his parent's house. Thomas remembered those woodlands. He remembered them as they had been when he was but a small child: a vast sea of saplings atop a bed of endless broken rock, a testament to the days when the Alps had been torn asunder. Now he could see an actual mature forest behind him, different from the one he had last seen over five years before. The colour was a deeper and darker shade of green than he had ever seen on Terra before. The trees themselves seemed to have grown enormously in the last few years, as acorns littered the forest floor. Acorns which seemed... different, not just in size, but in colour and somewhat in shape.

Where have I seen those before?

Oh...

He realised what had happened.

These trees had received Askr treatments, like the trees of the Aesir and Vanir worlds. He had heard that this would be done. He had even helped load the necessary reagents, manuals, machinery and... 'workers' required onto cargo ships himself. Sure enough, as he landed and looked into the distance, he could see one of those little hard-working cunts.

Askr squirrels were much larger than Terran squirrels, reaching about half a meter in size. They weren't even truly squirrels, being more akin to emaciated beavers in appearance and temperament. They were only called squirrels due to their great bushy tales and were comical creatures to behold both in body and behaviour. They had skinny limbs and walked upright, seemingly caught in a continuous drunken wobble as they always appeared to struggle to keep their balance. One might even find them pitiful, were it not for the absolutely astonishing athletic feats they were capable of in their preferred environment: the canopies of forests. While their limbs were hilariously skinny, their belly was spectacularly bloated, since it held within the reason why these squirrels were such good caretakers of the woods.

Askr squirrels were scavengers, with their ideal diet consisting of dried leaves, pests, weak plants and anything else not serving any purpose at any given time. They would take the forest's waste and quickly transform it into their own nutritious fertilizer.

They also helped spread the seeds of a myriad of trees, brushes and grasses. Some, such as the acorns of oaks (like the ones before him now) they would compulsively hide in areas where no other oaks stood, whilst only attempting to be discrete in the most superficial of ways.

The particular squirrel before him was exhibiting one of the main behaviours that made them so annoying: they felt compelled to bury acorns in places no one wanted acorns to be buried. This one was somewhat atypical, since it was light outside and Askr squirrels usually preferred doing their 'gardening' at night. Many an Askr squirrel had been shot by a startled Allied Host soldier during their tenures on the worlds of the Aesir and Vanir. Yet, their obsessive night-time activities were nothing in comparison to their absolutely maniacal reaction to pollen, which was when their annoying nature was truly made manifest.

When exposed to any type of pollen, they would be overcome by a compulsion to cover themselves in as much pollen as possible, then run around maniacally looking for new places to spread said pollen. They also seemed to be aroused by the pollen, as two speeding balls of furry pollen would always find themselves on a collision course, from whence they would only disentangle after joining together into the most psychotic copulation presented by the entire animal kingdoms of several planetary ecosystems. The noises they made during such entanglements were horrifying, especially at night, when they were most likely to occur. When Thomas had first heard them back in the Triangulum Galaxy, he had pictured a gorilla beating a horse to death.

He found the idea of hearing the same noises through the open window of his childhood bedroom to be in no small part dreadful and depressing.

After all, he was now looking at one in his own backyard, seemingly scouting out a future dig site, right in the middle of his parents' lawn. It seemed to have decided upon a place where neither the shade of the house nor that of the hangar would ever reach it. It was likely thinking about its midnight digging session when Yeats bit its head off.

Yeats was a two hundred kilogram direwolf who enjoyed playing fetch, humping shuttles and decapitating average-sized members of invasive species in single bites. At least, Thomas hoped the squirrel had been decapitated, since that would have guaranteed a quick death. Thus, it would have spared it of the trauma inflicted by Yeats, as he began bashing its convulsing body over the rocks and tree trunks of the forest's edge, jaw clasped on its torso, as it head dangled from a mangled neck.

All of this happened as Thomas waited for the public shuttle to leave and as he prepared himself for the task of hiding his existential dread from his father and mother. Then, the latter opened her living room door and rushed across her lawn to hug her son. His father followed her out and strolled towards them, with a bright, big smile on his face.

Thomas could tell his mother was about to cry. 'Welcome home, my boy! I was worried! I knew you were on Luna and were almost home and safe and sound and yet I still worried. For a week!' she managed to blurt out.

'Hello, mom!' He hugged her. Tightly. Tighter than he could ever remember hugging her. How he wished it could have been for the longing for her presence alone! How many times had he worried that he might never see her again? How many times had he wished he could have told her he loved her? How many more had he wished he could have said his 'goodbyes' to her better? He found himself holding onto her as a small child: clinging to her, knowing – or at least *hoping* – that she would make the bad go away.

She'll know something is wrong. Stop!

He let go of her to see that she was, indeed, weeping. He smiled, trying to act normally. As normally as one could act when seeing loved ones after returning from war.

His father said something clever as he clasped his hand and hugged him.

Thomas believed he said something back. Yet, he couldn't be sure, as he could hear Yeats beginning to feast upon the squirrel. He had to say something.

'I see you've done some gardening!' *Because that's what parents walk to talk about when they have not hugged their child in five years.*

'What? Oh, yes, we askered the forest.' His mother replied, while looking him up-and-down, as if checking that he had returned in one piece.

'I… I see Yeats doesn't seem to agree with the change in scenery.' Yeats broke one of the squirrel's thin arms and proceeded to lick the bone shards, likely looking for marrow.

His father had also noticed Yeats snacking on the poor little woodland creature. 'What are you talking about? Look at him! He loves hunting those things.' Maximillian Muller seemed very pleased with Yeats' ferocity, as he gestured towards his beloved pet as it currently enjoyed a snack.

Thomas had shot several Askr squirrels himself on several occasions. Yet, whether due to Yeats' brutal glee or his own current mental state, he was definitely disturbed by the carnage of nature on full display right in his family's backyard.

32

He figured out a way to walk inside with his parents. All the while they bombarded him with a thousand questions. To most, they already knew the answer to, as they had many calls together, linked across the vastness of space through Greyspace communication. Thomas could tell that they just wanted to talk to him, in the flesh again, for so they had missed his actual presence, as he had theirs.

Thomas felt a deep shame inside of him throughout the entire day and into the evening. He had missed them so much. He tried really hard to show them how much he had missed them, yet he did not *feel* the joy of seeing them *now*. Such was the turmoil of his mind, that he did not even remember most of the day. They had dinner together and he believed that his mother had made for him his favourite beef pho, yet he could not guarantee that had been the case. It could have been schnitzel or shrimp fried rice, he couldn't really remember.

He believed that he had answered their questions. Questions about the war – *his* war, the Ayve War of the Triangulum Galaxy – must have been answered by Thomas, of that he was sure of. The memories those answers brought back had come forth naked into his mind, their regalia of glory & gore, valour & violence, trickery & tribulation now removed. Only the cold darkness of their true nature remained, revealed to him now for what the experience had actually been: a mad dance at the edge of death.

It didn't help when his father would interject to bring up his own war, the Senoyu War of the Andromeda Galaxy. Thomas had heard the tales before. Whilst his had been a war of planetary invasions and naval engagements in the deep void, his father's war had been much different. It had been a war of shadows. Sabotage, ambush, assassination, reconnaissance and partisan warfare had been the staple of that conflict. His father had always spoken with much awe of his time spent fighting alongside the likes of Djibril al Sayid and Kimmie Jimmel. Yet, he had never hesitated to insist that the Senoyu War had been little more than one prolonged skirmish, when compared to the War of Vengeance fought by the oldtimers.

This insistence on the grandeur of the War of Vengeance now continued as he spoke of his opinion of his son's Ayve War. Normally, he might have been annoyed by his father's thinly veiled hints that the titanic galactic conflict that had seen him travel to the Triangulum Galaxy to do battle against demigods was little more than a small strategic move on a much broader chessboard. However, he found himself unable to entertain himself with such petty concerns. He wasn't even saddened by his father's refusal to acknowledge the fulfilment of his rite of passage as a man. He couldn't even feel joy at the fact that his mother did acknowledge it.

His father had insisted that he join him on a stroll through their garden to see his newest crops. Yet, Thomas had discovered that the presentation of his father's agricultural skills had been little more than a ruse to get him outside alone, so that he could lecture him as to what the next steps of his military career should be. Usually, Thomas would've paid attention to his father's words, since they tended to be an unpredictable mix of profound wisdom and general ignorance. Yet, though he recalled participating in the discussion and being both congratulated for his decisions and berated for his choices, he couldn't really remember that much of it. His father seemed to both agree and disagree with his decision to join the Terran Logistics Corps, likening it with his own decision to join the newly formed Engineering Corps over twenty years before, as well as his mother's decision to join the Gardener Corps. This similarity seemed to be both the reason why he disapproved of his decision *and* why he applauded it.

He could have confronted, or at least pursued, this idiosyncratic view. Yet, his mind and heart weren't in it. After exchanging a few pleasantries with both of them, he returned, at last, to his childhood bedroom, seemingly left untouched by his parent's recent renovation spree. Whilst the rest of the house had seemingly grown, accumulating new, unfamiliar tools and decorations, his own room had remained just as he had left it. He passed by his old bookcase, filled with his beloved collection of tomes and tales.

He dropped his suitcases and backpack next to his wardrobe before walking back towards the stacked shelves and running his hand across his favourite titles. These were but a fraction of his collection, with the majority being located on data drives neatly stacked underneath his desk and uploaded onto his internet server. Yet, he had always enjoyed the feeling of having a real book in his hand. He used to love running his fingers across the rows of books. He did so now and his fingers slid across books whose names he knew not by the words printed on their backs but by the colours of their covers.

The favoured books of his childhood: *Freeglader, Harry Potter & the Prisoner of Azkaban* and *The Lion, the Witch & the Cupboard*.

Then came the books of his youth: *The Chronicles of the Black Company, Magician* and *Dune*.

Then came the books of his adolescence, when his curiosity had shifted to the real world of Old Earth, as opposed to the imaginary worlds of the days of old: *Guns, Germs and Steel*, *Imagined Communities* and *the Fall of the Ottomans*.

Further on down the line were the books he had collected before going off to join the Allied Host: *1984, Brave New World & Slaughterhouse Five*.

And those were just the Terran books. The other shelves were littered with original copies of goblin and troll literature, as well as printed versions of orcish & elven literature.

It was only then that he remembered that he had brought home books from the war. Some had been gifts from comrades. Some had been bartered for on the worlds he had visited. A few were even stolen from the Aesir libraries he had passed through. He placed these new additions on one of the lower shelves and stopped, stepped back, and looked over his library as a whole, rather than as a collection of individual texts.

How many nights had he spent reading away into the wee hours of the morning, only to have to wake up for school the next day? How much had they nurtured him over the years? How much comforting energy had he drawn from these tales in hard times?

How little comfort they would offer him that night.

That night was dark and so were many others after it. That first night had been the most restless though, for he was visited by ghosts.

Ghosts he had realised would visit him from the moment he had seen Yeats savage the Askr squirrel at the forest's edge.

His first kill had been a human boy, likely not much older than himself. He had shot him in the back of the head as the young Aesir warrior had charged at one of Thomas' comrades, after exhausting his ammunition reserves in one swift detonation of energy towards the Allied Host position. He had seen his eyes as the body hit the ground.

His second had been another boy, albeit this one was of higher rank. He had also shot him – this time in the ear – during an ambush.

The third, fourth, fifth and sixth he didn't know much of. That was quite a typical outcome of a successful grenade toss into a bunker.

The next eight he had been quite proud of, since they had been earned during a real battle. He had slain three of them during actual melee combat, with the other five falling to his rifle rounds within the chasms of Musspellheim.

He had slain seven more by the time of Battle of Astarte, the climatic peak of the Ayve War.

It was at Astarte where he had, as the orcs would say, 'crossed the veil of presence'. There were four he remembered, in the early stage of the fight, then who knows how many during the bloody fracas that had formed during the battle's main phase. In the last stage of the battle, after the King of the Aesir was felled by the blade of Quentyn Andromander, the surviving Aesir had collapsed into those who would surrender alive and those would surrender only in death. Thomas and his platoon and had gunned down dozens of their number. He remembered only his last kill clearly, for it had been his mightiest.

The proud Aesir Einherjar had stood atop the corpses of a dozen of his companions and a score of Thomas' comrades, his force shield still active and his physical shield still intact. A great warhammer lay in his right hand, seemingly so heavy that only the strongest of Terrans might have been able to wield it two-handed, yet this Aesir would swing it with only one as he hewed humans, orcs, elves and goblins alike into the ground. In the end, his warband had been obliterated, with only he remaining, his back now against the wreckage of an Aesir gunship. The Allied Host soldiers before him had fallen trying to bring him and his Einherjar down. It was now Thomas' platoon which stood against him.

Thomas hadn't understood then, as he did not understand now, how he had stayed so calm. He had been trained to strive for such clarity, thought he did sometimes fail and lose his focus during moments of extreme violence. Yet, in his mind, in that moment, all that was present was standard military tactical guidelines. Specifically, his mind had narrowed down on the fact that there was only one reaction he could have when faced with such a clearly fearsome, yet enticingly lone, opponent. Without thinking, he had executed what he had assessed to be the proper approach to the issue before him.

He had walked, calmly, towards the Einherjar. When he had been close enough, he had lunged at his opponent's feet, rifle first. Once he had passed through the force shield, he shot through his opponent's ankle, severing his foot from his leg. He had then dropped his rifle, stabbed the Aesir in the groin in the place where he had seen his force generator connect to his belt and thus destroyed his force shield. The Aesir warrior had thrown his physical shield and swung his axe, missing him by a hair's breadth with both. Thomas had rolled away, brought out his pistol and shot him in the temples until the jarl collapsed. He finished him off with his dagger.

They had promoted him to Lieutenant that night. His pride had overwhelmed any ability to reflect on how close he had come to dying that day – not just with the Einherjar, but on all the other occasions presented by the Battle of Astarte. It would appear that he had kept that terror within him and it flowed over him now, together with another felling.

Shame.

Shame at his own lack of empathy. Shame of not ever pausing to think – for just one second – how he had ended so many lives. Warriors they had all been, yes. Humans just like him. Individuals just like him.

And he had sent them to the void that lies beyond; the great sleep from whence none came back.

It was in the wee hours of the morning that the god of sleep took mercy on him and allowed him a rest, only for Thomas to find himself visited by the god of nightmares.

In the dream, he was once more a child at his old school and he played a game with his fellow pupils. Yet, this was not some innocent children's game. His classmates were in some kind of death cult, with Thomas himself being a member. They would dance with knives in their hands. Whoever would stop dancing would be stabbed to death by the others. The victim would try to defend himself, yet the dancers would always overwhelm him. In the end, it came down to a dance of two of which Thomas was one and a girl – whose face he recognized and whose name he did not remember – was the other.

He had pleaded with the girl to stop dancing and their torment, yet she had refused. In the end, Thomas had stopped and insisted that the girl not fight him. None of the stabbing was even necessary. They could stop and end this strange death cult game. The girl had refused and attacked him. He defended himself, accidentally slicing the girl's neck open. Thomas dreamt of rivers of blood gushing through a tiny cut on her neck and, at that moment, the school bell rang and Thomas knew that within the mad world of the dream the next recess would see another dance.

It had been then that he had woken up in a cold sweat. Such were most of his nights that first week back in Rosenheim. His waking hours were merely visions of a clear nightmare. During the day, he alternated between avoiding his parents and attempting to think his way out of his problem, which refused to limit itself to simply being a case of overthinking things. He had scoured the Terran internet for answer to his questions, for that is how the thoughts (as he had taken to calling them) presented themselves.

What happens after death?
What if there is nothing after death?
If there is something, is it permanent or only for a further limited time?
Would that 'something' be a 'good something' or a 'bad something'?

Each question would have an answer which, Thomas found, had to be a *fact*, not a *belief*. He knew this, for his mind appeared to refuse to *believe* anything. 'Belief that there was life after death' was met only by the wailing winds of his mind, as they screamed for the justice of a truth, not a hope. Thomas had obliged himself to honour this demand.

He knew not what came after true death, when a person's brain had gone past the point of recoverability. Many claimed they did. Yet, none could provide proof for their beliefs. At least, not proof Thomas found convincing.

If there was nothing after death, then the only way to avoid the nothingness was to avoid death. Many had attempted this. A few were still alive. None could truly guarantee that they could keep it up forever.

If there was something after death, then spiritual immortality was almost certain, at least while this universe still existed. It did not matter whether or not they would die after their afterlife, since the cycle would likely commence once more, if the first death was little more than a door to another place. If no 'afterdeath', as it were, occurred, one could expect to be immortal in the afterlife.

Yet, what if life after death was a terrible thing? What if the afterlife was simply one continuous tortuous existence? It mattered not if one would come to experience 'hell' as a result of his own actions or by the whims of some cosmic entity. The thought that a hell could even exist was terrible to behold in its dreadful entirety, even if he could count himself as one of the lucky few to be spared such a fate. After all, what kind of 'virtuous' person could enjoy heaven if they knew their brethren burned in hell? With what type of people is heaven populated with, exactly?

Every time he would answer a question, he would gain some relief for the slightest of moments, before another thought would come and a new question had to be answered. All the while, it would feel as if his mind was a flimsy wooden house in the midst of the fiercest storm imaginable. The howling gales would threaten to tear the very structures of his house out of the ground and scatter them away on crazed winds and Thomas did not want that to happen.

So, he had to make his house stronger, find another house or build a new one.

He poured over vast amounts of literature, as he treated each question as an assignment, for which he would have to acquire new knowledge in order to complete. He started out by reading about physics and how the universe worked, only to realise that the rules of the universe allow for infinite possibilities and almost no certainties. Then he switched to rigid philosophy, as well as its more flexible brother: theology. While philosophical arguments were very much like encountering different people dressed in the same clothes, theological beliefs were much more akin to encountering the same person dressed in different clothes.

Philosophy had a million schools and theology a million sects. Philosophers and priests, it appeared to Thomas, attempted to behold the same darkness, yet saw two completely different things lurking beyond and within it. The philosopher seemed to be obsessed with wondering what the darkness was. The priest, on the other hand, seemed to focus much more on where the darkness came from. In the end, the philosopher would provide a definition of the darkness, just as the priest would begin to tell the tale of the birth of the darkness.

Religion frightened Thomas deeply.

How could it not? He had no religion.

It was not as if he had never thought of himself as religious. He somehow believed in God – or at least *had* believed– in some form. He had always taken the existence of a higher power for granted. Sure, no one went to church, no one truly believed the tales of the old holy books and no one claimed any faith in any deity anymore. At least not on Terra.

Yet, somehow, among his people, he had always felt an unspoken agreement that some 'God' existed. Most wouldn't even describe it as such; rather, they would use terms like 'higher power', 'spirit of the universe' or 'an energy'.

Ancestor worship required at least some degree of belief in the supernatural. In any of the Shrines of the Lost on Terra, did anyone question those mourning within? Did anyone ask them if they were simply remembering the dead or praying to some god or another? Their whole society was based on this unspoken agreement that they would be secular in public and religious in private. Believing in 'God', though publicly denied, was privately taken for granted.

His parents were not Christians and yet they celebrated Christmas. His mother had told him that she would pray for him before he left to join the Host. His father always spoke about how only 'God' knows some things. Thomas himself had never questioned whether he had a religion or not. He had just assumed that his religion was the unspoken religion of Terra.

His exploration on the internet had revealed to him that this religion even had a name, with some scholars now referring to it as 'Ambiguous Terran Monotheism' (or ATM, for short).

The core tenets of this religious movement apparently were:

(1) Belief in the existence of an afterlife where one would be reunited with lost loved ones,

(2) Belief in the existence of an intelligent being that was omniscient,

(3) Belief that all life is actually one single entity, and

(4) Belief that the survival of the Terran people was an act of religious duty.

It was a religion with neither a church, nor a text, nor even a congregation yet, it now occurred to him, Ambiguous Terran Monotheism was a religion with a state, a law and an army.

And what a petty religion it was.

Time had given the Humans of Terra many friends and those friends had granted them the tools needed to traverse the vast darkness of the most distant stars. To eradicate illness and disease. To harness energy on a scale that was truly cosmic. To dream of survival in a Universe that had decided that they were a threat to the natural order of things.

They lived in an age of heroes, as the Humans of Terra showered themselves in glory in battle against gods, emperors, monsters and men. Yet, why did they fight? Just to survive? Could they only survive if they fought?

Did any people do more than just fight to survive? What had happened to the great arts of Old Earth? What had happened to music? Thomas knew of no songs sung by Terrans that were not of Old Earth's making, except those taken from other peoples, or birthed by the carnage of one conflict or another.

Their allies fared no better.

Orcs believed in a Great Free Will, a type of energy that flows through all things, bending the flow of time into ways only it understood and which one would be wise to accept.

The elves believed in nothing more than the pursuit of a continuous existence of vast cycles of reinvention, until one individual was either truly dead, confined to a soulkeeper or if they succeeded in the impossible task of being the same ideal person over and over again.

The demani pretended to hide their belief in some Infinite Architect of Infinity whose works were the entirety of creation, akin to how their ancient ancestors could boast that their galaxy was their own creation.

The remani believed in a Great Pride that lay behind the tapestry of our own universe, free to roam wherever it pleased, in much the same way as they themselves aspired to within our own universe.

For the trolls, God had better be dead, for if he were not, he had a lot to answer for.

The same person in different clothes, each one opting to favour one accessory over another, yet all bearing the same body beneath. All were beautiful outfits in their own way.

Yet, not all fashion choices were so tasteful.

The Continuum of Humanity lay across the table from the Humans of Terra and their Republican Alliance; one single leviathan shadowing over the united front presented by the ants before it and the dwarves around it. In the Alliance, they liked to tell themselves that the giant was kept in check by the dwarves that stood ready to lay into the goliath with blades the size of the giant's cutlery. A death by a thousand dwarven cuts would end the behemoth if it dared overextend itself to crush the ants across from it.

In truth, the giant hadn't really bothered itself with something as small, distant and benign as their little alliance. It was the Continuum's complacency and self-absorption which kept the Terrans safe, not some wondrous alignment of intergalactic geopolitics. For that is what the Continuum did: it sought to make all of humanity within its borders the same and it did so in ways which the harshest communist of Old Earth recoil in horror.

Thomas had heard the stories and seen the tapes. After all, what empire had ever existed that did not have propaganda? It was the madness of all empires to reach a point where they assumed that life within the empire was by default better than life outside of it. Surely all those beyond the empire's borders would envy what the empire was if they saw how amazing life was within its borders?

That's how they knew what life in the Continuum of Humanity was like: they boasted about it. They could all witness the boring world where everyone was the same, for nature 'wanted' everyone to be the same. Nature had produced perfection when it had produced the human body and one could not improve upon perfection, hence all artificial change was only the malevolent degradation of the human body and mind.

Yet, each human body was part of the greater body of humanity and in every body there are many organs and tissues. Some tissues provide the body with nourishment, others keep it pure and immune, while others – not too many though – direct the body's actions. All of these tissues had to be made of many separate cells and each of these cells had to be of the same quality. After all, was that not how things were within the human body? If the body of humanity was to be as perfect as the human body, each cell was to be produced over-and-over again, aspiring to fulfil exactly the same function as the expired cell it had been made to replace.

How convenient it was that the Emperor of Humanity and his family had achieved immortality, for the Emperor himself had to be perfect in the execution of his role within the body of Humanity. The obvious conclusion that followed from this line of thinking was that the only perfect Emperor is He who is also a God and God is immortal.

He did have heirs though – just in case. After all, shouldn't the perfect system of government come with spare parts?

If ever there was a cell within the body of humanity that chose to pursue any activity other than the one chosen for it, the cell would be 'recalibrated'. If that didn't work, the cell would be recycled, for the perfect system was also perfectly efficient, with nothing ever going to waste.

Mind control was one thing, yet mental recalibration was another entirely, particularly when one could not disturb the perfection of the human body. The only way the 'thought police', as Terrans referred to it, could recalibrate the mind of a cancerous cell was to make the citizen understand, accept and shun his own morbidity as an aberration. What was terrifying was not the fact that some minds found themselves beyond the point of repentance and were simply extinguished.

No, what was terrifying was the fact that the *thought police* almost always got the job done!

They had to. It was their divine duty to. They were not just immune cells of the living human body, but also of the human body that lay beyond the veil of death.

So it was that the Continuum of Humanity had something the Humans of Terra didn't: an afterlife.

Aeons in the distant past, in a time before elves, orcs, trolls, goblins or many other branches of the Tree of Man, all of humanity allegedly stood together in the Old Realm. Among all the recorded histories of mankind tracing back to the twilight years of the Age of Bliss, the Old Realm was described as truly being Heaven-on-Earth.

The only thing missing from this paradise were the dead that had passed away before the last brick of the kingdom of Heaven-on-Earth had been set. So it was that work commenced on a Great Plan: a plan for all of humanity, from all times, past, present and future, to be reunited in one true heaven, beyond the borders of our own universe.

Much has been lost and even more is debated of what transpired next. What was known was that the Old Realm was torn asunder as conversations turned to debates, debates turned to arguments, arguments turned to fighting, and fighting turned to war. This War at the Gates of Heaven, as it came to be called, had resulted in both the birth of the orcish race and the Schism of Mankind, as the two major surviving sides of this great conflict would be the Continuum of Humanity and the newly arisen Others Unaligned, with the latter factions continuing to fracture and grow into the various branches of the *Tree of Man*. History, however, begrudgingly admits that it was the Humans of the Continuum which managed to carry the Great Plan to fruition.

Yet, this was not the Great Plan that was laid out at first, in the times before horrors of war had twisted the souls of men into demons of intolerance.

No, this was an abomination.

The Continuum's afterlife was a horrid place, where no individuality truly existed, for individuality would breed selfishness and selfishness would sow chaos and chaos is anathema to heaven. It was merely an infinite continuation of the same repetitive hell that was life within the Continuum of Humanity itself.

Thankfully, the Humans of Terra, of which he was one, had been deemed heretical and beyond repentance almost immediately upon their discovery. Hence, Thomas could hope, with a reasonable degree of confidence, that he would not be cursed with such an afterlife, if such an afterlife indeed existed. According to Continuum dogma, Thomas' soul would be given over to the cold void of inexistence.

But what if there had been a Heaven before the Old Realm? What if there had been a heaven built for all mankind before there had ever been humans to speak of anywhere in the universe? What if there was a greater heaven which would save them all from both the empty void and the Continuum's hell? A *true* heaven, for lack of a better term?

What could a *true* heaven, even be?

This question had been what had brought Thomas to the minds of Terra's past: the Humans of Old Earth. Thomas' reasoning was that, if a true heaven did exist, then the bloodlines of Terra would link up with the bloodlines of the people of Old

Earth. It was the only way in which all the people of both Old Earth and Terra could meet their lost loved ones. This bloodline would also have to lead into the future, seeking out a potential infinite line of descendants.

Yet, Thomas did not know the future. But, he did know the past. That was his *art*: chronicling. His specialty was Terran history; specifically the lives lived by those humans of Old Earth centuries before the End Times. If the lines of love went back far enough, which they did, in this scenario, there would be thinkers on Old Earth who would've struggled to comprehend a heaven. Such attempts would yield different images of heaven, not all of which would overlap with his.

Yet some would and these ones he could grant more attention to.

His research revealed many results of such attempts to visualise an afterlife. Some were better than others. None satisfied his mind's hunger for certainty on the matter. What was worse was that, along the way, he had come to realise that a truly rational conclusion would be that heaven itself, might be inherently unattainable.

At least a heaven for truly everyone seemed to be unattainable. Thomas' thinking was that several levels of heavens and hells might be a more pragmatic visualisation (an idea he got from reading Dante's *Inferno*). Yet, even this was a flawed idea, for a bad man might suffer adequately in hell, while a good man would never be capable of enjoying absolute heaven whilst knowing that others suffered in hell. After all, wasn't empathy a virtue one might expect of their neighbours in heaven?

His mind spun back to death and wondered why life itself existed. If heaven was to exist forever, why bother with this short thing called life? Was something happening now? Was this existence necessary? A quote from Mark Twain haunted him from the moment he first read it.

'I do not fear death. I was dead for billions of years before I was born and suffered no inconvenience from it.'

His quest eventually led him to read Fyodor Dostoyevsky's The Brothers Karamazov. He recalled opening the book on the first page, then closing it after finishing the last. What transpired in between those two moments was not clear to him, though Clara informed him that three days had passed. It was an astounding text, but what bothered Thomas about it had been that he hadn't understood why the author had felt the need to present his views on existence over the backdrop of what was, essentially, a whodunit detective novel.

He found himself on the porch outside the living room, patting Yeats' on the head, as they both sat at the top of the steps leading down towards the garden. It had been a week since his arrival in Rosenheim. At one point during the day, the dread had grown too restless for him and he found himself unable to abide within his room any longer. So, he had come outside for some fresh air. Yeats had been waiting for him there. The direwolf had been bred from Rottweiler genetic stock and still possessed the boxed head of its lineage, which now rested in his lap.

He used to despair when Yeats would do this, for he would excessively drool when excited or comfortable. Thomas could already feel a pool of wet slob begin to seep through the fabric of his trousers and onto his leg. Though he would normally be grossed out, he now cared very little for the goo pooling in his lap as Yeats happily grunted in joy at being petted. Once, Thomas had enjoyed scratching him behind the ears, pulling at his jaw or wrestling with the direwolf on the lawn before him. He had done so ever since Yeats had been a puppy. Yet, now, just as he did not care for the drool, he did not care for the satisfied grunts either.

He felt as though he couldn't enjoy anything. All was *terror*. Terror at the vast array of likely horrors that might wait beyond the certain horror of death.

It was in this state that his mother found him.

'Oh, I didn't know you were here,' she said, a plate of leftovers in her hand, which Yeats immediately detected, lifting his head from Thomas' lap and licking his snout in excitement.

She moved to throw the contents of her plate out onto the grass of the yard, as the direwolf sprinted towards his dinner.

She smiled, though she avoided eye contact with him. 'I left a few bites for you as well. We made schnitzel and kimchi. It's very good. I thought you might like it.'

He realised he had missed today's dinner, just as he had likely missed the dinner of the night before. Or did he have dinner then, but not three days before? Had he even been having lunch with them? Were they even home the whole time? Where was his father now? Could he be away with work? Had his mother been away with work?

They had spoken since his arrival, yet Thomas had not really been... *there* for most of the time.

All of a sudden, yet not unexpectedly, waves of shame and loneliness came over him. They began as a longing. A pull. A need to share with another that which he was going through in the hopes that perhaps the other could do for him what he could not do for himself. Bring him the peace he had somehow lost.

'Thank you, mom. I'll come have a bite later,' was all the profoundness he could utter at that moment.

Again, his mother smiled a half-smile, not bearing herself to look at him directly; though Thomas did feel her eyes following his when he was not looking at her. She turned and made her way back towards the inside. It was just when she had crossed the threshold that Thomas could take it no longer.

'Mom! Wait…' He didn't know what he wanted to say to her.

44

Neither did she, yet she swiftly took a seat on a chair next to him. 'Of course, Thomas!'

He paused, at a loss of words. Where could he even begin?

'I... I am unwell, mom.' *Might as well start with the truth.*

'I noticed, my son. Talk to me. What is wrong?'

Thomas looked at her, not knowing if he was supposed to feel shock, panic or relief.

Of course she knew. She must have noticed how absent he had been the whole week. If she knew though, then how bad was it? How bad was he that it was noticeable from the outside? At least he wouldn't have to explain how he felt, thus he could focus on trying to explain *why* he felt the way he did.

'After we came back to Luna, there was a party to celebrate the end of our service'.

'Yes. Yes you told us, with Hampstead, Motley and.... What was the name of that girl –'

'Yes. That one.' He cut her off.

'Did something happen at the party?'

'No. But, before it...'

He choked up. He felt a lump in his throat and choked. He felt so happy to finally share his struggle with someone that he started to weep. He told her as much as he could, as coherently as he could. He told her about the first thought that had gripped him. He told her about those that came after. He told her about the feeling of impending doom that haunted him now. He told her of his searches through his books and across the internet. He told her everything. The whole damned incoherent mess.

He had done all of this while crying and ranting away into the darkness of the woods beyond. In the end, after exhausting his words – but not his besieged mind – he remembered that she was there and turned to look at her.

He knew his mother's face well, yet he had never before seen it formed the way it was at that moment. It was definitely a look of concern, albeit her confusion was also palpable. Right as he had turned to see her, she had seemed to have been piecing together thoughts of her own. Yet, the look had changed somewhat as she saw him look at her.

Tears still lay in his eyes. It was only then that Thomas realised that she had likely not seen him cry since he had been a small child. Moreover, he realised that the last time his mother had seen him cry had likely been the last time he had ever cried.

Panic flooded him, filling the space only recently relieved of anxiety by the outpouring of tears. He was a Terran, a warrior citizen of the Bastion of Terra.

Furthermore, he was an officer now, a commander of men. He had seen war. He stood now not just before his mother Lisa Muller, but also before Master Sergeant Lisa Muller and she had seen war also. Likely somewhere in the house was Master Sergeant Maximillian Muller. They had seen war, just as him. They showed in themselves the resilience blossomed into strength by adversity which was the expected norm of all their people.

Weaklings cried at the foot of things not worth the attention of warriors. He did not want to be a weakling. He did not want his parents to think their son was a weakling. Yet, perhaps this was how weaklings showed themselves. Perhaps all weaklings had been brave before they had been able to see the world for the horrifying place it truly was. Perhaps that is why weaklings feared death so much…

'Mother, I am sorry!' he burst out.

His mother stood up. 'Thomas! No!' She didn't come to hug him though. She somehow seemed too shocked to show affection through touch. However, she seemed to still be able to show it through a smile.

'Thomas, you don't understand! This is horrible. What is happening to you is horrible. But… darling…' She choked up now also and Thomas saw in amazement and terror that she had tears swelling into her eyes.

'Thomas, darling, I am so sorry for you. But – *please* understand – I am also happy. I thought you were... I thought you were stuck. I thought the war… Never mind, Thomas!' She paced around the porch now. 'My darling son… The thoughts you are having now... I have had as well.'

Thomas' felt his heart skip a beat and so did his mother.

'No! Wait! No! Thomas, my darling, I do not know the answers to your questions!' She was sobbing now, yet she fought hard to say her words properly. 'I do not have a cure. No one does! But, I… I understand and – Thomas, *listen to me*!'

She walked over to him now, Yeats had returned to lie next to Thomas, yet as she neared he sat at attention, likely expecting another snack.

She sat down next to him. 'I've had these thoughts… and so did your father. I was younger than you, though, and your father was younger still, but we had them. I know they are terrible!'

Thomas, for one instant, felt the flicker of hope inside of him grow into a promising flame. 'They… they are. Do you still have them?' he asked.

'No. No, I don't. I mean I still do sometimes, but they're mostly gone now…' she confessed.

'How did they go away?' he begged.

'Oh, but I don't know!' Her voice had turned to rage. Motherly rage. As if she was angry that she had not recorded the tools with which the thoughts were defeated, since she could have given them to her son now in his hour of need.

'Your father's thoughts just... just went away one day. He has no idea how. With me... I just forced myself to not think about it. In the end, it worked.'

And that's what he tried to do for a few days, before all the bottled-up existential dread exploded and almost pushed him towards the precipice.

For three whole days he tried doing everything he could to push the thoughts away. He helped his parents around the house. He travelled to the Northern Polar Shield to arrange his future service with the Logistics Corps. He then went too Berlin to formally join the Army of Germany. He taught Yeats how to play fetch. He even tried to finish watching *Game of Thrones*.

Ultimately, while training with his sword and rifle in the woods, he broke down. Yeats had been his only witness, as the direwolf had joined him on his trek through the woods of his youth, towards a great meadow he remembered from his childhood. He had found that the Askr squirrels had made short work of it, transforming it into little more than just a collection of small clearings. Instead of the sweet pain of nostalgia, he felt only the cold stab of entropy. He realised that nothing would last forever. Just as the forest had changed now, the forest would change again in the future, as it had before in ages past. The old trees would, in the end, die, as new trees would take their place.

In the end, death would claim all.

In the silence of the woods, he broke down and cried for the second time since his childhood. He had failed in keeping the thoughts away. If anything, the suppression had built up pressure inside of him. A pressure he now released by weeping on the forest floor, as Yeats went from brutally murdering Askr squirrels, to tenderly licking away Thomas' tears.

When twilight had neared, his father had called him to ask if he was alright. Furthermore, he had insisted that Thomas not shoot himself in the face, since his mother would be disappointed if he didn't look good at his own funeral. Thomas had laughed nervously at Maximillian Muller's morbid humour. Truthfully, he had enjoyed it as a child. Yet, now, he could definitely understand why his mother often thought it to be a bit off-colour.

He was reminded that evening that his father was undeniably a peculiar man. He had arrived home to find his mother worried, untouched food lying in front of her, whilst his father gorged on a roast lamb with couscous.

'You alright, son?' He asked Thomas as he took a seat at the table.

'What? Yes!' he lied.

'Huh? You sure you're not rattled by what you told us about a few nights ago?' He had told his father, albeit in a more composed manner, what he had told his mother, after Maximillian Muller had arrived on the porch to ask what all the weeping noises were about. Lisa had made her husband confess that he had eavesdropped on the entire conversation.

It would appear that it had been his father that had noticed that something was wrong with him before his mother. Whilst Lisa had feared PTSD, Max had put his money on heartbreak. Suffice to say, they had agreed that they had both been wrong.

His father had given the same instruction as his mother. 'Try not to think about it. Some people even go a little mad if they think about it too much!' his father had said before insisting that they make some fondue for dinner the next day.

Now his father asked him if he was still rattled. What could he do? Lie? Could he pull it off? No! Not in the state he was in.

'Yes. Yes, I am,' he confessed.

'I understand, son. When I had them, I would wail and scream into the night at the horror of it all. I guess it helped, though I don't advise you to startle the neighbours! The squirrels do enough wailing!' He paused to giggle.

Thomas pretended to find him humorous.

'But, you do need some help. Help you won't find by reading shit online. Help we can't provide. Help someone else might provide.'

They're going to do it. They're sending me away to the crazy house to get mental reconditioning like the people who get stuck get at the Medical Corps.

'I told you about Ronan, right? You know who he is?'

Thomas was puzzled. He knew who Ronan was and he was pretty sure that he did not work for the Medical Corps. He had never met Ronan. Yet he knew much of him, for Ronan had been his father's commanding officer during the Senoyu War. His father often spoke of how the Irishman was the greatest warrior he had ever seen, rivalling the likes of Djibril al Sayid and Thomas Ashaver. Many a time his father had castigated Thomas' failings, yet he had never given himself as the ideal to which his son should aspire towards. He had, however, at least during Thomas' early childhood, given Ronan O'Malley as an example.

Then, one day, the stories stopped and Maximillian Muller had replaced Ronan with other oldtimers as his chosen examples of paragons of Terran valour. Quite frankly, Thomas wasn't sure if he had heard the name in over ten years. Nevertheless, remembering his father regaling the great deeds of Ronan O'Malley was one of his fondest childhood memories, as he remembered not only the awe he felt hearing his father's stories, but also the awe his father had felt while reliving through the times he spoke of.

'Yes. I remember you telling me stories about him.'

'Me too… I… I think it would help if you were to meet with him.'

Chapter III
Pater Noster quoth Cuchulain

Thomas had never been to Ireland before.

He had *flown* over Ireland before and could remember looking out towards the bright green hills and meadows of Ireland from afar with wonder in his eyes. He remembered his father pointing towards a spot on the window and proclaiming: 'That's where Ronan lives!'

That memory brought him here. He hadn't even had to plot a path or ask for an address. His destination was outside a village called Drogheda, in what was now still Heath County, atop a hill, surrounded by dense woodland. It was not Terran trees that grew here, but trollish heartwood. These were truly giant trees, akin to the giant sequoia trees of Old Earth, yet far swifter in their growth.

This part of Ireland had been one of the grants of land received by the troll refugees of Kalimaste. In their twenty year tenure here, they had populated the region with various plant and animal life from their homeworld, as they had in many other places they had been granted. Giant trollish elephants still roamed the savannas and tundra of Terra, while trollish sea turtles still grew islands on their back in the oceans of this new, hybrid ecosystem. The Heathwood, as it was now called, stretched from Dublin to Belfast, penetrating inland as much as the village of Cavan. The Irish had taken a liking to it, vowing to never remove the forest, only to contain it, lest it overtake the entire island. It would be one of many ever-living reminders of the brotherhood of the Humans of Terra and the Trolls of Kalimaste.

Yet, within this forest lay many large clearings and Thomas now stood at the edge of one such opening. Before him lay a lone hill, from atop which one could only just begin to see above the tips of the massive trees. On the hill lay one large building next to a much smaller house. He had been told by his parents to be courteous and not fly right next to Ronan's dwelling and to most certainly not park his shuttle in his yard. These were Terran standards of politeness; though his parents had been particularly strict in the way they had advised him to respect them. He had no actual fear that Ronan might hurt him in any way, even if Thomas did startle or disrespect him. Just that, this Terran was an oldtimer, a man who had lived through the End Times, and that was reason enough to be extra polite and cautious.

Though he was a very strange type of oldtimer.

Oldtimers occupied all of the top positions in the Terran military and also formed a large contingent of the Allied Host leadership. Thomas was a rather young Lieutenant, given that most officer positions were filled by either oldtimers as well as a few Yin. In the Allied Host, he knew of a handful of sunriser Commandants, with young Terran Captains and Lieutenants being relatively rare as well, despite the fact that Terrans, as a whole, were the largest minority group present among Lieutenants. In the Allied Host, the rank of lieutenant had valued much, on Terra, it mattered less. Next to an oldtimer, it counted for very little.

And in the grand scheme of things, it counts for nothing.

Thomas was swiftly reminded as to why he was here. However, he couldn't say he understood why he had been sent here of all places. Ronan was something of a hermit and an outcast, for he had committed one of the cardinal sins of modern Terran society: he didn't want to fight anymore. This sin was more prevalent among the oldtimers than among the Yin or the sunrisers. However, even among their kind, it was exceedingly rare. Ronan was the only such oldtimer whose name Thomas knew and that alone was due to his father.

His father had never introduced him to Ronan; he had just told stories about him, like how he had served under him during the Senoyu War, what a hero he had been and how much he had fallen from grace. For though there was no official shame in refusing to fight, the punishment was severe. Those that refused to fulfil their martial duties benefitted from only a fraction of the rights and privileges granted to regular Terran citizens. They were basically allowed only to have a small plot of land of their own. They received only a very limited salary, wielded virtually no authority beyond that granted by their rite of passage as oldtimers and, most importantly, they were not allowed to extend their lifespan using modern technology. They were to die the old way.

Of old age.

Was this his death sentence? Did it take one to know one? Is this how it would be decided? He felt his heart begin to pound as he contemplated his fate. Perhaps his parents just wanted to scare him out of this, to make sure he would not be viewed as a coward. After all, the truth was on his side. It wasn't that he didn't want to fight or that he didn't want to live. It was just that it broke him that at least one of the two was a certainty.

Just remember that when you talk to Ronan.

50

As Thomas neared the house, Thomas saw it for what it was: the most basic Terran housing unit. It seemed smaller than his parent's entire living room and was built in an old Terran fashion: red brick and glass windows. Many oldtimers stuck closely to the old designs, yet this was much more than that. The windows didn't just look like glass. They were made of *actual* glass. The brick walls weren't just blastproof bunker walls with bricks layered on top for the sake of nostalgia. No, they were actually made from salvaged red bricks! The door wasn't sculpted to look like wood, it *was* wood. It wasn't even Kalimasti heartwood, which could stop most bullets on its own, but what looked like old Terran oak.

The large building next to the house was made of the same wood. He realised what it was as he drew near it, searching for the Irishman who dwelt in this strange place.

A church. He's building a church.

Thomas had never seen a wooden church before. He could tell that the foundation was in the shape of a cross and the structure itself was roughly twenty meters at its longest and ten at its widest. Where the two sections met, an unfinished tower rose. *That's where he'll put the bell, I suppose.*

It wasn't just the bell tower that was unfinished, but also the windows. He assumed they were windows, yet, at this stage, they were just large three-sided holes scattered along the building's walls through which the morning sunlight could have peered in, had they not been covered with shabby wooden panels. He heard a strong buzzing and a heavy boiling sound coming from within. He could also feel a subtle heat coming from the inside as he neared entrance.

He knocked on the wooden door, left somewhat ajar.

'Oh, don't linger now! Come in! I heard ya coming a mile away!' The voice was still strong, yet somehow frail; as if it was a weak wind blowing through what had once been a great iron corridor.

Thomas opened the door and walked in. It would have been quite dark inside, had it not been for the light of several light bulbs strewn out across the ceiling. The building was packed with construction materials – particularly lumber and woodworking tools – as well as what seemed to be an oven at the very centre of the room, right beneath the incomplete tower. The room itself had a strange feeling to it. He was reminded of the halls of the Aesir he had lived, worked and fought within during the Ayve War.

It seemed to be designed to be both calming, yet stirring. The latter aspiration felt oddly comical given how there were vaults beneath the Polar Shields which spanned the length of entire old Earth countries. Even Rosenheim had a Shrine of the Lost which felt at least ten times the size of this apparent place of worship. Yet, it was not just the construction that seemed out of place in his world, but the constructor himself.

Thomas had never seen an old man in real life before.

The closest he had come had been the Aesir jarls and some of the Vanir wizards, which kept long grey beards and shaggy white hair, as they nestled faces which bore the marks of many battles and studies. He had seen old people in Old Earth movies and documentaries. However, Thomas had never before seen up close what old age could do to a man. As he walked towards Ronan O'Malley, he could see that it was not just his face that was old, but his entire body. The old man extended his hand to him in greeting and Thomas was struck by how frail it was in his grip.

Now right next to him, he could gaze upon Ronan in all of his antiquity. His frame was small, with clothes too large for him clinging to his body like rags on a scarecrow. His face was a bizarre earthen colour, speckled by brown freckles and areas of bright red, where the sun had likely lingered on him for more than he could handle. The same small brown spots dotted his hands as well and what hands they were! Dotted with hundreds of cuts, crisscrossed by a thousand wrinkles and covered in paper-thin skin they were. Beneath, Thomas could make out wry muscles – *like those of a cat!* – moving slowly as Ronan worked the machine next to him.

He lay bent over the oven Thomas had seen as he had entered the room, leaning with his left hand on a handle which he seemed to be gently manoeuvring. With his right hand he had shaken Thomas' hand, only to immediately bring it back to the edge of a large tray which jutted out from the oven. On the tray, beneath a protective layer of thermal glass, Thomas could just make out the image of another old human white man with a strange haircut.

'Do ya know who that is?' Ronan's voice was feeble yet, somehow, he spoke in the style of the oldtimers, despite his thick Irish accent. It was a voice of authority, though softly spoken, almost as if it were half-forgotten by the speaker.

'No. No, I don't, sir,' he confessed.

'Oh… "sir"!' The old man giggled a strange sound; more a choke than a chuckle. 'Of course ya don't know who that is. Ya don't even know who *I* am! I'm Ronan, an old man and a fool! There's no need to "sir" *me* around!'

'I… apologise. I meant it out of respect.' Thomas felt so strange talking to him. His body was old, which triggered feelings of pity in him, yet his mannerisms were those of the oldtimers, which stirred a sense of obedience in him. In some way, Ronan's demeanour was more oldtimey than that of any oldtimer he had ever met before. It was as if the oldtimers had copied him, as the Yin and the sunrisers had copied them.

'I know ya did, lad. But there's no point in it. As I said, I'm Ronan, and *you* must be Thomas?'

'Yes. Thomas Muller. I'm Maximillian Muller's son.'

'Hmmm... I can tell from the eyes. Yer face is yer mother's face, though. Which is quite a blessing, I must say.' Ronan smiled to himself again. 'I miss Max. He never comes to visit anymore. Is he well?'

'Yes? He's working on –'

Ronan cut him off before he could give updates on his father's career, '– does he have a happy life? Does he smile often?'

'I ... I assume.' Thomas was a bit taken aback.

'Well, don't. When you go home, ask him! Parents want to speak of these things with their children. Believe me, it'll give him joy.'

Ronan pressed a button next to the tray, making the humming noise of the oven cease. 'It needs to settle now.' He reached towards the stool next to him, covered completely in old tools encased in grime and grease and dust and dirt, and pulled out a pair of gloves from one of the piles of metal and cloth. He used them to gently remove the thermal glass, slowly allowing the hot air to escape and fully revealing the stained glass icon beneath.

'That, young Thomas, is another Thomas. Thomas Aquinas, though he was more like me than like you,' he turned from his creation to smile at Thomas, 'another old man and a fool, ya see!'

'I... I assume I do... What did he do?'

'Do?' Ronan shook his head. 'Not much.'

'Oh... was he...?' Thomas had long learned to be careful with the question he wanted to ask.

'Oh, no! He died around eight hundred years ago! No connection to me by blood or bond.' Ronan smiled to himself, lovingly admiring his work. 'Is that what warrants memory? To have done things or to be related to someone who is still alive?'

'I... no. I mean I don't know.' He thought he did, yet Ronan's question made him question his assumption.

'Good. I feel that you are here precisely because there are things that ya don't know.' Ronan took his gloves off and tossed them back onto the pile. 'Tea?'

'Hmmm? Oh, no, there's no need.'

'Oh, no, but I insist. Come lad! Let me help you to a cup of Irish breakfast tea. It's delightful!' Ronan made his way to another worktable and turned on an old electric kettle. From a cupboard to the side of the kettle, he took out one teapot, two teacups, two saucers and one teaspoon. 'Milk?'

'No, thank you!' *Who the hell takes milk with their tea?*

Ronan threw the teaspoon back into the cupboard. 'Good lad! What do you think of the place?' Ronan asked, as he began brewing.

'Oh, it's lovely!' It did have a certain charm to it, in a rugged way.

'Not done with it yet! I reckon I'm gonna need about three more years to finish it. But it's a labour of love. Took me a long time to set up the stained glass machine. It's not how they used to do it back in the day, but it works well enough for a beginner like me!' The water in the electric kettle had begun to hiss and whirl as it boiled. 'Oh!'

Ronan proceeded to pour the hot water into the mixture of tea he had placed inside the teapot, before covering it with a lid and bidding Thomas come take his cup and saucer. As Ronan carried the teapot and his own cup and saucer, Thomas noticed how his hands shook. As the old man made his way outside, he followed not just by his visitor, but also by a continuous clicking sound. He sat down on the wooden beams that passed for stairs at the entrance of the church. Thomas proceeded to sit down next to him.

'I was very happy to get Max's call. He told me that his son is going through a… a "crisis of faith" was how he put it. There again, that was how *he* put it and Max always had a… special way of saying things. I think it best if you were to use your own words, Thomas.'

'So, what *does* bring ya here, lad?'

'I…' Thomas had dreaded this moment.

His father had bid him speak only the truth to Ronan. His mother had not shown her face to him, bar only in passing glimpses since the night before, when Maximillian Muller had made his pronouncement that he was to come visit Ronan the next day. Thomas had initially attempted to protest, yet his father had already taken the liberty of calling his old commander and asking him if it was alright if Thomas came to visit him the next day. He hadn't really slept the night that followed. A million scenarios had crossed his mind, most of which he had forgotten by now and all of which mattered little as he sat next to the old man he had come to visit.

In the end, he decided to ask for help. 'I had a thought. I was feeling very good about my life and what had become of it. In that moment a voice in my mind told me…' He gulped, seeking not to choke on his words.

'*Enjoy this. Since a day will come when you will die.*'

His heart had been beating anxiously ever since Ronan had asked him why he had come, yet now, as the words left his mouth, the pounding reached a climatic crescendo and Thomas could hear it in his own ears.

'I have been… not myself ever since.'

Ronan had listened intently to every word. 'The Lord often speaks words of reckoning to those with ears to hear them.'

Thomas was taken aback for a second. *Did he just bring up 'the Lord'? I mean, he is here building a church and all, but… the 'Lord'?*

His surprised expression was not lost on the Irishman. 'What lad? You've never heard the name of the Lord brought up before?'

'N-not often,' was all he could confess to. In truth, he had never heard it from a Terran before. At least not seriously. He had heard 'the Lord' referenced in the texts and recordings of history, yet never in his life had he heard someone refer to any Terran deity as 'the Lord'.

'*Shame*! "Shame" I say! And it is because I say "shame" that I find myself here, all alone! Though we may have forgotten the names of our Lord and His written Word, He Himself has forgotten neither our names nor our stars. He still watches over us, lad. He still has us in His guard.'

'He does?' *I can think of a few moments when we could've used some divine intervention.*

'Yes, lad! God does not turn away from us. He is our Father, who art in Heaven. He sees all and He wishes to see all, for He loves all His children.' Ronan spoke these words not as some fanatic, but as someone speaking of their own loving father to their oblivious siblings.

'Then…' Thomas would never have dared ask an oldtimer this under normal circumstances. Yet, for some reason, Ronan's quirkiness put him at ease. He felt as if he could ask him things he would never dare ask an oldtimer. He felt as if he could ask a question never before posed to a Christian Terran before, though it may have been a question posed to many Christians of Old Earth. He couldn't help himself, the question burning him. 'Then why –'

'– did the End Times come?' Ronan looked off towards the sky, a peaceful smile upon his face as he spoke the name of the apocalypse. He turned to look at Thomas, the honest smile seemingly hiding a certain glint in his eye; a glint much like an old ember that still burned.

'Y-yes. I… I've been reading about the old faiths. Christianity, which I see you are… a *practitioner* of, was one of them. I understood that it was, at its root, a religion under a… *benevolent* God. A… "good shepherd" to his flock.' Ronan had allowed him to speak his piece, as Thomas had rushed to make his statement as candid and polite as possible.

'True. The faith of our Lord Jesus Christ is a faith of kindness and compassion. Why would God allow such suffering to visit his flock, if He were so full of love for us, you ask?'

Thomas nodded.

'I guess the answer is a different one depending on who you ask. For me, I believe the answer to be self-evident. God brought the End Times upon us to test us. To train us. For what is to come.'

'What... what is to come?' *Death?*

'The ways of our Lord are mysterious. I do not know what. I only see! I don't know what He intended, though I see the result.' The old man let out a sad sigh, as he gazed above the tree line. 'Earth was not a perfect place, though it was definitely not a godless place. This new Terra... I do not know what He intended, yet now I would advise Him to stay away from us, since most would hold Him accountable for the suffering that was brought down upon His people.' *The clothes of Terra take much after the fashion of Kalimaste.* Or so the saying went...

'You think it was God's will that the elves come?' Thomas pushed his luck, now more curious about Ronan's worldview than of what the old man could do for him and his own understanding of the universe.

'Aye! And by His Will the remani came upon us decades before and took us under their watch. By His Will the orcs arrived in our hour of greatest need, when all seemed lost. By His Will everything that transpires is willed. To what end? That I do not know.'

'I... I understand.' Thomas didn't really.

'I believe you do. Such understanding is within us all.'

'As Terrans?'

'As people. The Lord has many flocks. The one raised on Earth is naught but one of many.'

'So... our Lord, is also the Lord of other peoples?'

'The answer to your question is both "yes" and "no".' *Mysterious are the ways of the Lord indeed, aren't they?* 'What do you think came before the Universe?' the old man asked.

A cold chill crept up Thomas' spine as that dreaded question had come upon his heart just a few days before. It was one of those lucky questions he thought he had come up with an answer to.

'It is known that our universe is much like Swiss cheese. Some parts are melting and expanding, others cooling and contracting. That which melts will one day cool, while that which cools will one day melt. It goes ever onwards, infinitely in all directions and across all times. It is unknown how the cheese came about in the first place, if it ever did.'

'Do you believe, in your heart, that it has always been here?'

He struggled to speak both accurately and truthfully. 'In my heart... *No*, I don't believe it was always here. Yet, my mind struggles to accept that there once was *nothing* and from that endless, timeless nothing came *something*.'

'Hmmm... timeless nothing, aye?' A smile crept into the corners of the Irishman's mouth.

'A nothingness where no time passed, yes. Isn't that what there was before there was God?' Thomas asked, puzzled.

'No. Such a nothingness never was, since there has always been God. He was there before the Universe, alone in the nothingness. All the Universe was within God and by His will did it begin, as it will one day end, only to begin anew.' He turned to Thomas now, giving him another smile, this one cheeky.

'He made all the cheese and, one day, He will make it milk, once more.'

'Then what's the point?' Thomas snapped. He didn't know if Ronan had any more praise for divinity prepared to be unloaded upon him. Yet, he intended to cut straight to the point. Oldtimer or not, he couldn't bear hearing how his God was the only God present in an infinite universe of humans, orcs, goblins, elves and a thousand other sentient species he could think of and a trillion he couldn't.

Thomas' brusque tone had seemed to fly right past him, as Ronan answered his questions calmly. 'God's point? His goal? I think we both know that such understanding is beyond us. However, I think your question is... much closer to home? You are, perhaps, asking, why *you* are here? What the point of *your* life is?'

'Not just mine, anyone else's. Why do we live? Why... do we die?' It managed to come out, just as Thomas felt a tear swelling up. He quickly, yet discreetly, wiped away.

'Ah... He prepares us for what comes after, of course.'

'And what comes after?' *Now we're getting to the point.*

Ronan breathed in and then gazed dreamily off into the distance as he answered. 'White shores, and beyond, a far green country under a swift sunrise.'

Did this motherfucker just quote Gandalf?

'For... all of us? All peoples?'

'The halls of our Lord are many, with room enough for all.'

'Even... even the elves?' He wanted to hear it. He wanted to hear him say it. He wanted to hear him match his beliefs with his experience, in a manner only one who had lost so much could.

Thunder could be heard in the look that crossed Ronan's face. After it had subsided, he answered. 'Those unworthy of salvation go into another room, reaping what they have sown in life.' Thomas didn't hear it. He didn't hear the forgiveness of a man that had overcome his past and now loved his enemies. He just heard the answer he expected. Hell awaited those misguided in life.

Perhaps another question, in the same neighbourhood, albeit on another street. 'Is there even room in God's realm for those righteous of heart, regardless of whether or not they heard his name?'

'Oh, I see you have studied the old texts.' Ronan put his hand on his shoulder. It felt as if a small bird had gently perched upon his jacket. 'Good. I'd suggest you spend more time reading the Holy Book.'

Thomas had been trying to study several holy books for the last few days. It hadn't helped.

'Now, to answer your question. Yes, there is, though it is not as great a room as that of the faithful. Yet, the Lord rewards those that act as instruments of good faith to His Will. Think of the orcs, who came to us from the heavens themselves upon a bed of light in our hour of greatest need. Think of the remani who toiled in the dark to help guard against the Enemy. Yes, lad, even the elves! Is Daw al Fajr not an elf? Was she not the one to banish the wicked before her?'

Thomas had qualms with this particular point. 'She did. But did she do so knowingly in God's name? Or was it just, an alignment of interests? If it were just an alignment of interests, that would mean that one's virtue in the eyes of God is little more than an issue of luck. The luck to be one of the virtuous.'

The old man's face seemed to shift into an old sadness. 'Aye, lad, there is such luck to speak of.' He seemed to recollect himself. 'I take it I am the first of my kind you have met?' He turned to face him. 'The first believer? The last of the faithful?'

Thomas nodded.

Ronan nodded back. 'There are not that many of us left. Most hide their faith or – I should say – they hide the slivers of faith. There was once a time, when I was young, when there were many worshippers in the world. I should know since, well, I used to belittle them. I used to wonder how so many could be deceived by such a lie. You see... I found my faith much later in life. In the old days, I was what you'd call an *atheist* – there's a word you don't hear often anymore either. Why would there be any need for such a word in a world where everyone is godless?'

'But, you believe now?' Thomas could hardly reconcile the idea of the man before him having ever not believed in God.

'I was with your father in the Andromeda Galaxy, during the Senoyu War. It was there that we both served under a man... *the* greatest man I had ever met. It stunned me to be in his presence. There I was fighting men born in another galaxy than my own. Their abilities and their technology made us look like drunken children flailing sticks before them... and yet they did not match him. I had also seen great men that were orcs or trolls or remani or goblins and, aye, I had even seen great men that were elves and ursai, and still I had not seen a man greater than he.' Thomas already knew of whom he spoke.

'His name was Djibril al Sayid and his wife was Sarasvati Singh. Now, I will not hide from you, that to spend time with him was one of the great honours of my life. Your father was too young to have been allowed anywhere near him, for we would all fight for the chance to spend time in his shadow and we would push our rank in the faces of the younglings, as we left to bask in his presence. His wife was a creature of myth for us. When he spoke of her, it was as if one was hearing a giant speak of an angel. And then...'

'They died. The angel died in Antarctica and the giant on some wretched world whose name I have succeeded in erasing from my memory. I believe the world is now called *Suqut Albatal* – the Hero's Fall, in his native language.' Thomas recalled the events of Hellsbreach and stood in awe of this man who had met – *and once been, believe it or not* – one of the legends of old.

'... and I lived. As did so many others far less than them in worth and valour. It was... it was not fair to me you see? That I should live and they should die...' Ronan's voice seemed to crack a little.

He struggled, his lips shaking. 'I spent a long time lost and I was not alone in my waywardness! The world was full in those days of people who looked upon the lives they had and wondered why it was they that still lived while many more far more deserving of the gift of life did not. My... my mind could not understand it! I couldn't wrap my head around it.'

'Then... then it came to me, lad. I do not know when. I do not know where. I do not even know how it came or why it did when it did, but I *knew*! I *understood*.' He smiled now, once more, his lord's light seemingly returning to his eyes now, as he had to his heart so long ago.

'It was God's Plan. It was He who kept me alive. It was He who stayed the bullets. It was He who made the aim of my enemies weak. It was He who made my body strong, so that it may withstand the plagues. It was He who kept me safe from sea and storm. It was He who had kept me alive. The Lord *did* answer my prayers when I begged for life, for I was to be His instrument with which He would work.'

'But, why, you might ask?' Thomas nodded and Ronan continued. 'I asked myself that very same question. I looked around and saw only a world which did not trust God anymore. It mattered not what faith they had before the End Times: Christians, Jews, Muslims... the Lord had no church left. His Words we now saw as little more than the scribbling of primitive men. His Works we now saw only as that to be taken for granted. His Church... we had allowed the Enemy to tear down the Lord's Kingdom and to scatter his flock and, in our arrogance, we said "good riddance"! We sought to build a world without God in denial of the truth that God had placed before us self-evident!'

'That the Kingdom of God does not live in one man, nor a group of men, but in all men! And as long as men walk, his Light shall forever be with us! And as long as His Light is within us we must be thankful for it! And if we are thankful for it, we should praise Him and do Him honour and live as He would have wanted us to live!'

Ronan's voice, though weak and tired, now roared with an inner flame that made Thomas fearful for the old man's wellbeing.

'Yet, the other members of the flock have grown ever wayward. They see themselves now as wolves, with little need for a shepherd which, they claim, never came to their aid! So, I decided to be a wolf no longer. Hence, I returned here!' He gestured toward his humble abode.

'When they came to ask that I relinquish the powers bestowed upon my body, I welcomed it. I welcomed a return to a way of life that God would have wanted for me! I did it gladly! And for that I am an outcast... as you fear that you will be also.'

Thomas snapped out of his contemplation of Ronan's journey in life. He dared not look the Irishman straight in the eye, yet a subtle tilt of his head gave away his admittance of guilt. *How did he know that?*

'It is the nature of the young to shun the old and look down upon those cast out. Don't worry, lad, it's not contagious.' Ronan's eyes left Thomas' worried face and return to the trees before them. 'I feel coming from inside of you the yearning of our Lord's embrace, yet I do not feel faith within you, lad. Do you feel His Word beckoning you towards Him?'

Thomas knew the answer, yet he did not know how to say it. How could he say that he had never felt anything of the divine in his life? How could he say that he had always simply taken for granted the idea that everything would be alright in the end? How could he say such a thing to a man for whom things were very clearly not alright in the end? He had never felt God or any god for that matter. Nor had he even *asked* himself whether or not he had felt god. He didn't even know why he was here. He didn't even know what Ronan could say that would make him feel better. He did not feel as if this man had any answers.

He felt as though he had merely an attitude. This was just a man who seemed to have convinced himself that he knew what lay beyond the realm of understanding. Thomas wasn't even sure if this man would be interested in knowing the answers he craved, even if such things even existed.

How Thomas would have wanted to feel the same!

He actually wondered if this was but a simple show. Perhaps that was how the people of Old Earth became religious? Perhaps some charlatan came to them in their hour of need with words they knew were false or whimsical and they bought them out of simple desperation.

Then again, this old man seemed to be aware of the fact that Thomas was not a believer. Far from it, Thomas was experiencing the revelation of the fact that he did not truly believed in anything spiritual of any nature. He never had. His entire life he had taken concepts such as 'God' or 'Heaven' for granted. He had always functioned on a deep assumption that these were not things to be *believed*, but rather to be *known*.

He had always known it was an assumption. Yet, somehow, it was only now that he was aware of that assumption and something within him had decided to begin torturing him with the fact that he didn't really know much of anything. Within this swirl of thoughts, he saw a choice: to answer Ronan's question honestly or to merely assume that the old man had no satisfactory answer within him.

Thomas decided to take a chance: 'No. I don't. I... always took God for granted. Yet, somehow, now I find myself troubled by the idea that I have lived my entire life for things whose finality I did not understand.'

Ronan sipped his tea. 'Go on, lad.'

'I risked my life for this... ' Thomas used his hand to point to the ground, the forests around them and even the sky. 'I didn't really question it. It was what my life seemed to be all about. Train, learn, study, work, fight... It just all seemed to be one straight line forward. I thought I knew what that line was and I felt like that line was set in stone. Right now, I'm twenty-five years old, and I feel like my entire life I've been driving a car towards a destination I couldn't see and I was fine with it the entire way. Now, I see that no matter what destination lies at the end of my road, death will surely be in front of me at one point or another.'

Thomas struggled not to shed tears as he reached his point. 'And, now, all I would like to do would be to get away from the death, but I know that's just not possible. So, no matter what, it shall be inevitable for me. Somehow, I never really realised I was living under the assumption that my life would never truly end and that, after my body died, I would simply go on to live elsewhere. In a place I cannot see from where I am right now. And now...'

His lips trembled but he did not shed any tears before the oldtimer. '... and now, *knowing* that was just an assumption and knowing that it might actually be something unlikely... all the joy has been sucked out of my life. I live scared and tormented by *thoughts* and questions to which I have to provide answers and I do not *feel* that there is any end to it. I feel as if I am doomed to a short life spent like this: miserable.'

'... and you don't want that.' It wasn't a question. It was a statement from the old Irishman.

'I wouldn't want it for anyone.' *Not even my worst enemy.*

'Hmmm...' Ronan's eyes drifted off once more. However, for one instant, Thomas saw him thinking not of the glory, word or church of God, but of something else. Then his face changed, revealing the face of someone who had reached some inner decision. 'Thomas, you strike me as a young lad with a lot of potential in him.'

'Thank you!' *I don't give a shit about my potential. I just want all of this to be over so I can get back to my life. Just that I don't think that's possible anymore.*

'I think... I think I don't have any answers for you. Quite frankly, I think no one does.' Thomas' heart sank, as he now heard the answer he had feared and hated. 'Faith is not truly something that is pushed onto those that have no desire for it. The Word of God reveals itself only to those that have ears to hear. From what I can tell, you are not one blessed with such hearing. Though, I would say, that it is through those that do not seek God's favour that come some of the greatest of God's works, yet also the vilest deeds of the devil. Your abilities should be put to good use. Maximillian tells me you are now a war hero?'

Thomas' throat filled up with shame. *A war hero I might have been, yet now I feel like a coward.* 'I... I did my duty during the war in Triangulum, yes.' His decorations seemed like marks of shame now, not the trophies of valour they had been when he had received them.

'Ah, I see! Modesty is a noble virtue! You strike me as a thoughtful lad, to say the least. Have you given any thought to what you will do now? I understand that you have finished your Allied Host service.'

What does that have to do with anything? 'Y-yes. I have. I, eh, I was going to join the Logistics Corps here. I am currently on vacation.'

'I see...' The Irishman's eyes met his now and within them Thomas saw a question being prepared. 'Would you consider, perhaps, another career path? You see...' Ronan paused, as he seemed to choose his words carefully. '... I know a thing or two about soldiers and fighting... and all sorts of military matters. Call it the arrogance of an old man who still thinks the world might have some use for him, but I think I could suggest something that you might find quite... challenging, yet also fulfilling. I think it would be something that could really suit you. Would you be interested?'

A job recommendation... Really? 'I... for certain! Of course!'

'Good.' Ronan seemed to have figured out that would be his answer. 'Have you ever heard of woman called Shoshanna Adler?'

Who hasn't? Shoshanna Adler was a Terran General, the commander of the Marines, one of the Terran Avenger Legions. One of the younger oldtimers, she was nevertheless one of the most powerful Terrans alive.

'Yes. Yes, I have.'

'Good! Well, you see, she recently reached out and told me that she was looking for some experienced and thoughtful young officers – such as yourself – for a certain project she was working on. Now, I don't know about you, but to me that sounds a lot like you. Plus, it'll give you a good chance to spend some time and recover from this turmoil you're having now before you go ahead with your Logistics Corps career.'

What you're describing is so ambiguous, it could be a good match for most people my age. 'I... I would be open to it!' *I didn't come here for that.*

'Good. Well...'

The old man rose from his steps. Thomas was startled by the sound of cracking joints, for he had never heard the sound before, at least not outside of combat.

'... as you can see, I have a lot of work to do and not that much time.' He gestured both toward the structure behind him and to his own frail body.

Thomas got his meaning and, not wanting to be rude, followed suit. *It's actually great that he's cutting this off, since all its done has been to drift me further away from what I was looking for.*

'Say "hello" to Max and Lisa, for me! Tell them I wish them well! It wouldn't bother me to have them around here from time to time!'

With that, they shook hands and Thomas left for home.

Shaken and demoralized.

He didn't even remember the way back to Rosenheim. He only truly woke up when he walked through the door of his house and his father greeted him from his seat at the living room table, where he sat getting some work done. 'Hey, where are you going?' Thomas stopped in his tracks. 'How did it go?'

Thomas had thought about a lot things on his way back, but not about the way back itself, nor what he would say to his parents. 'Eh, it was alright. He, eh, he didn't really help that much. But, he pointed me in a few directions! At the end, he even said he might recommend me for a job!'

Maximillian Muller leaned back in his seat, seemingly descending into thought. 'Oh, well. It was worth a shot...'

Thomas' heart sank. *Oh, I don't want him to suffer because of me...* 'He said you and mom should drop by!' He did. It was as good as anything to say to change the subject.

'Oh, well... we'll make some time!' His father didn't really seem convinced that such time could be made any time soon.

There was another thing Ronan had told him to say to his father. 'Dad, are you happy?' Thomas blurted out.

'Me? Yeah. I'm happy. Why shouldn't I be? I have a nice big house. I have you! I have your mother... I...'

Oh shit! Something's there! Something's coming.

'...I just wish I could help. It bothered me too, a bit. When I was younger. What you have now.' Thomas froze, expecting something. Expecting some solution.

None came.

'You did?' His mother had told him he had, though Maximillian Muller had never really gone into that much detail about the event.

'I did.'

Again. Silence.

'... and what happened? How did it go away?'

'Oh... I dunno. It just did one day.' His father's face was transparent; his father's memory was notoriously faulty.

Oh, thanks dad! 'Do you still get it?'

Maximillian Muller rubbed an eye, as he seemed to want to say one thing and mean another. 'When you get older, death doesn't bother you as much as it does when you're younger.' He turned to face his soon. 'It's how things work. It's part of the order of things. It's how I know you're going to be alright.'

Thomas nodded and smiled. He knew his father meant that. He hoped he was right and, yet, he doubted him. He found his mother in the hallway leading to his room and he told her something similar to what he had told his father. Her pain seemed to be no less and no more than that of his father, albeit it was expressed in a different way. With a warm smile, she bid her son goodnight, as he made his way to his room.

He sat there, in his bed, looking up at the ceiling as the thoughts came to him once more. He closed his eyes, readying himself for another night of nightmares. Now would come, once more, the mental torture of his *thoughts*, as they pounced on him like –

'Thomas?' Clara's voice rang out through his mind, startling him.

'Yes?' *What does she want now?*

'You have a message. It's "High Priority"!'

'Oh, who is it from?'

'General Shoshanna Adler.'

What the fuck? Thomas stood bolt upright in his bed. 'What is it about?'

'You are invited in two days time to Baffin Citadel for an interview. It is for a position to which you were recommended by Ronan O'Malley.'

Chapter IV
Surreal Times with someone from the Old Times

He had never experienced the way waiting rooms felt.

He knew oldtimers still employed them or, at least, he had heard that they did. He hadn't known that Shoshanna Adler was one of those people. His father had once told him it was a power play of sorts, with the goal being to make you mentally weaker. As if, in all that time you had to wait and, supposedly, prepare for what you were waiting for, your mind would somehow turn on itself and you would overthink yourself into self-sabotage. As a result, when the person you were about to see finally saw you, you'd have less of a stable façade to charm them with.

Quite frankly, Thomas had never really taken the idea to heart. Maybe some people were just busy. Maybe some people were bad at sticking to a schedule. Maybe it was just a freak coincidence that people broke under the non-existent pressure of simply having to sit in a room and do nothing.

It so was that he himself, at that very moment, didn't feel nervous at all. Though he wished he did. Nervousness was good. It was a good feeling, despite not being a feeling that felt good. He knew how it felt, as he had felt nervous many times. In time, he had come to realise that feeling nervous about something meant that you were invested in the outcome of said something. An outcome which could be good or bad, but which he would prefer to be good. Nervousness is simply thinking that, maybe, you hadn't done everything in your power to assure a good outcome. Nervousness meant you thought that a good outcome existed to begin with.

The absence of any nervousness was not due to some belief that all the possible outcomes were bad. Just that he didn't really feel inside himself the hope that a perfect outcome existed anymore. Everything was just various degrees of irrelevant. If you set a goal and achieved it, either you had aimed too low or had been lucky. If you didn't achieve it, well, it was just one of many things you had set your mind too and hadn't achieved. Over time the growing mountain of failures made each individual failure matter less and less, as there was so much failure to go around. Maybe that's where confidence came from: the knowledge that, regardless if you fail or not, it ultimately won't matter since –

'Thomas Muller?!' an American voice asked.

Thomas was startled. He realised his mind had been wandering and had become oblivious to his surroundings. He was in the waiting room of Shoshanna Adler's office. There were three people in the waiting room with him. There had always been four of them in the room. All were there to be interviewed. Each time one of them was called in, they would enter a small hallway. To the right was the staircase which they had all used to reach the waiting room. To the left, an old wooden door with a gold plaque bearing the inscription 'General Shoshanna Adler' indicated the entrance to the actual office.

Thomas rose from his seat. He looked in the general direction of the other three people in the room and muttered a 'Good day!'

One of them, the black guy, nodded back.

The black girl looked up politely from the pistol she had been neurotically disassembling, cleaning and then reassembling over-and-over-again, and smiled quickly in his direction before returning to her compulsion.

The fourth person (the white girl) wished him a loud 'Good luck!' as he went out the door and came face to face with the Marine guarding General Adler's office.

Thomas glanced to his right to see the previous interviewee leave down the flight of stairs he had climbed up himself earlier. He saw the Asian man he had shared the waiting room with earlier. He had learned that he was a Yin Master Sergeant of the Hwarang Avenger Legion and a physician with twenty years of frontline experience battling spawn and Aesir.

As he reached the bottom of the stairs and turned towards the exit, Thomas noticed the hardened veteran's look of outright perplexion and worry on his face.

Well, that settles it. I guess I am fucked.

The black guy inside was a medical officer, the girl fidgeting with her pistol was a codewriter working with the Intelligence Corps and the white girl was a member of Representative Joji Higashikuni's Avenger Legion. All were of officer rank and all were in elite positions.

Yes, sure, he was an officer too, but he was a very junior Allied Host officer, only recently transferred to the Army of Germany. He was a good one, yes, and had seen frontline combat, yes, but these guys were different. The man that had exited Shoshanna's office as he had arrived had been none other than Commandant Albrecht Hausser of the Jaegers, the Hero of Calaiad himself, who, just like the Hwarang, also had worn a look of shock and awe on his face.

He glanced back towards the Marine sitting at the desk next to him.

The Marine looked back at him.

Thomas looked at him more.

The Marine, a round-faced man of East Asian heritage, looked at him with a slightly more curious face than the one he had when he had instructed him to enter the waiting room earlier.

Thomas pointed towards the door.

The guard's eyes opened in even more apparent confusion. He raised his hand from the desk he was leaning on and gestured for Thomas to go in already, humour visible on his face.

Thomas proceeded to knock on the door –

– which resulted in the guard letting out an exasperated sigh and opening the door for him and gesturing with his outstretched palm that he could just go in already without all the knocking!

As Thomas took the hint and walked in, he heard angry footsteps, which he could tell were coming from the bottom of the staircase. *Probably the next interviewee.* He granted himself a quick glance back to see who the next person much more qualified than him was.

Despite all of his cynicism and wild imagination, he was not prepared to see who it was. Since, just as the annoyed guard shut the door behind him, making her way up the stairs was Mira al Sayid.

I am going to waste her time so much...

As the door shut behind him, thoughts began to race through his mind.

How did I apply for this position?

I didn't. I was selected.

Recommended actually.

This was supposed to be something like a demotion. Ronan said it'll be something I could go through to help me recover, not some high performance elite program for the damned best-of-the-best that Terra had to offer –

– Why are you still looking at the door?

Thomas quickly turned around, on his heels, like on the parade ground. The floor, he realised, was made of polished wooden floorboards, and he made a loud squeaking noise as he turned to face a black-and-white painting of four men on horses, with an angel above them, and their terrified victims beneath them. He recognized the four as the Horsemen of the Apocalypse, an Old Earth myth about the end of the world.

Oldtimers, he had noticed, had a tendency to surround themselves with apocalyptic imagery. After all, for them it was basically like having an old photo album from their youth. Had they not seen the Apocalypse come and go?

Armageddon. Ragnarok. Apocalypse. Day of Reckoning. Rapture. Skyfall. Doomsday. The Hour of Twilight. There were literally hundreds of names for what they had lived through. Thomas was twenty-five years old, born in the year twenty BT, more than two decades after the end of the Fimbulwinter which marked the beginning of the cataclysmic End Times of Old Earth. He had been born almost a full decade after the end of the War of Vengeance, when the surviving humans of Terra, together with their allies had brought bloody vindication to Gondolin itself.

Thomas knew this all very well. He had heard the stories his entire life. The Three Deaths of Thomas Ashaver. The Charge of Djibril al Sayid. The First Battle of Terra. The Second Battle of Terra. The Crimson Trek across the Stars. Those and a thousand more stories had echoed around him his entire life. He loved those stories. They were the reason why he became a chronicler. It had been his reasoning that, even though he couldn't choose his first profession – as being a warrior was the first fate of all those born on Terra in these times – he might as well choose a second profession he truly loved.

And he loved stories.

Not just the stories of the oldtimers and their discovery of the worlds beyond the skies of Terra, but those that had come before, when their world had been a much smaller place. It had always been his fascination as to how people had lived before the End Times. Not just in the nearest history, but beyond: Ancient Rome, the Rise of the Mongols, the Sengoku Jidai, the Crusades, the Mafia in America, the Sagas of the Vikings, the Islamic Caliphates, Jesus Christ and a thousand other stories from the World-Which-Was.

It was then that he remembered the real reason he had agreed to Ronan's proposal. The real reason why he had wanted to be interviewed by Shoshanna Adler. The real reason he had been willing to give it a shot, despite being in no real capacity to take advantage of any career opportunity.

The presidents of the old United States would preside, in days past, from a desk: the *Resolute Desk*. Reagan, Kennedy, even Nixon and the Bush presidents had sat at that desk, had conversations over that desk and delivered messages over the desk to their people and beyond. He had first read about it in an old wiki article he had found as a teenager. He had used to daydream about it. He had made the mistake of telling his friends and family about it. They smiled at his 'ambition' even though he had made no statement of it. They had assumed that he had been enamoured by the prestige that came with the desk. That he wanted to be the man who sat in the chair behind that desk.

He wanted no such thing.

His ambition – nay – his *hope* had always been that, one day, he might be able to touch it. Just touch it. Just to feel beneath his fingers that the stories were not just true, but also real.

In the aftermath of the End Times, the desk had come into the possession of General Shoshanna Adler. It was her desk now. It was in the office in front of him. Job or no job, he had come here to touch that desk.

He saw that he was in what he presumed was an antechamber. To his right, he could see the gold artificial light of several old lamps give way to natural sunlight, coming from an open door. Thomas made his way towards the door and finally entered the General's office.

Shoshanna Adler was a dignified woman of average build and bright, fiery, brown eyes framed by a friendly, yet stern face. She sat in an old-style office chair made of light brown leather. Behind her, one could see the sun above Baffin Bay through a large window, which basically took over entire the wall behind her. They were about five hundred meters above sea-level, facing south, located on one of the middle sections of the Northern Shield, one of two gigantic military structures that covered Terra's polar regions.

Most Avenger Legions opted for a Citadel located somewhere in their Nation's territory, such as the Kamayuk Citadel of Ancohuma, the Hajduk Citadel of Bâlea or the Jaeger's Citadel of Heidelberg. Yet, those whose territory bordered the Polar Shields would sometimes lay claim to one of the neighbouring sections of the great megastructures. Such had been the case of the Vikings, whose citadel towered over the Svalbard Islands and the Marines, whose Citadel lay watching over Baffin Bay.

Adler gestured for him to take a seat across from her. Thomas was ready for this. It had actually been his plan all along. After he saluted her, he made the nine steps needed to reach the seat across from her.

He had a chance to look at it.

The White House had burned, just as it had in 1812 AD when the Canadians had last assaulted Washington. Yet, this time it had also been levelled by an aerial bombardment delivered by the dushman's warships in orbit far above Terra. For a while, it had been presumed that the desk had burned to a crisp as the sundered Americans exchanged gunfire outside. The story went that a stray IED, set off in nearby Farragut Square, had set the trees and the porch of the White House on fire. Carried by the hellish winds of those times, the fire had reached the Oval Office itself, with the curtains being the first to catch flame. In the ensuing chaos and subsequent evacuation, the desk had been lost, presumed either to have been burned to cinders during the fire, destroyed during the looting or blasted into oblivion by the dushman.

It was later revealed that the last president of the United States, with the assistance of the remani of the Dark Knight, had long left the White House for the supposed safety of Cheyenne Mountain. Within the underground facility, the desk had also been stored and as the mountain crumbled under the shockwaves sent out by the explosion of the Yellowstone Volcano, the desk was buried beneath the literal mountain of rubble, only to be found intact years later.

And there it was.

Shoshanna had famously refused to fully recondition it, with only a simple layer of lacquer being applied to its surface, thus protecting the wood from further erosion. One could still see small specs of grey concrete embedded in the oaken timbers. The old seal of the American presidency lay almost intact, with the exception of the eagle's beak, which had been broken and never fixed.

When Thomas got within a hand's width of the desk he enacted the final part of his plan. He extended his right hand, as was customary, and as Shoshanna leaned forward to clasp it, he leaned with his left hand onto the desk, fully touching it for just enough seconds to be able to fulfil his little teenage daydream.

'*Shiiiiiiit…* He's here for the desk Shosho!'

Thomas was startled and he could feel Shoshanna clasp his hand just tightly enough to feel his instinct to reach for his pistol, as his left arm rushed near his thigh, near where his shortsword lay. He saw both annoyance and reassurance in her eyes, with the reassurance addressed to him, and the annoyance to the man sitting on the couch to her right.

He turned towards the source of the voice and, for one second, Thomas couldn't believe his eyes. *This is why the Korean and Hausser were shocked!* His first instinct was to assume that it was simply someone with cosmetic facial modifications. Some truly dedicated and awestruck Terran – probably a sunriser youth like himself – who had also gone through the trouble of modifying his voice to sound like that of his idol. Lots of people even carried shortswords modelled after Berlo, albeit this one, hanging from the man's belt, would have been too much of an absolutely perfect replica of the blade of legend.

But the uniform wouldn't lie. At least, no one would misappropriate *that* uniform, especially in the presence of an oldtimer like Shoshanna Adler.

There was only one uniform like it in the entire Terran military and only one man who had the right to wear it. The fully black uniform of the Terran Old Guard, with the smiling silver skull of hid legion pinned on his chest, next to his Hierarch badge and the Polish flag.

Thomas Ashaver.

First Warchief of the Alliance and current Hierarch of the Terran Old Guard.

'You want to touch me too? Or are you mostly a fan of inanimate antiques?' the legend joked.

'My apologies, sir!' Thomas made the few brisk, yet wobbly, steps needed to shake hands with the most famous Terran to have ever lived and introduce himself, as he had just done with Shoshanna.

'Lieutenant Thomas Muller, sir!'

The touch of Thomas Ashaver was as strange as the legends said it would be. The Hierarch's grip was relaxed, though Thomas could feel the strength it kept in check. It felt like an orcs' hand. The skin was rubbery, the flesh beneath felt hard, like a rock, as if his hands were those of a statue wrapped in leather. It was a strange thing to experience if one had never felt the touch of an orc before. Nevertheless, Thomas had felt the touch of an orc before, so that aspect, in itself, did not unnerve him. Yet, he had never been touched by a human with the hands of an orc before and the strange sensation did manage to unsettle him.

'Like the football player?' Ashaver asked, his eyes wide.

'I beg your pardon, sir?'

'Yeah, see, I've been wonderin' ever since I saw your name on the list.'

Thomas let go of his hand before it got awkward. 'Wondering what precisely, sir?'

Ashaver turned to Shoshanna. 'Guess that's a "no"!' He gestured for Thomas to sit down across from Shoshanna, as he sat back onto the couch. 'German Football player. Golden Boot at the 2010 World Cup. I reckoned they named you after him – your parents, I mean.'

'Oh. No, sir. They named me after you.' Thomas Muller was shocked at his own lack of self-control. The words had fled his mouth before any thought of polite censorship had ever entered his mind.

'Oh… I see… Well… it's better than "Timothy", I guess. Except when people call you "Tom"… like the fuckin' cat. Which I suppose is better than being called "Jerry", eh? Shosho?'

General 'Shosho' Adler rolled her eyes as she lay back in her seat, pouring herself a glass of tea from a pot located on her desk. Thomas saw to his horror that she didn't use coasters, and the teapot had left a heat imprint on the desk.

Her face was visibly tired of the Hierarch's shenanigans. 'A little bit of anti-Semitism to get the ball rolling, Tommy?'

'Now, ya' see? "Tommy" is even fuckin' worse. It always sounds as if you're a naughty little kindergarten boy. Which I guess is entirely adequate in this situation? By the way, the poor lad's right, Shosho. Get some fuckin' coasters! You're fucking up the desk.'

Shoshanna looked up at both of them in annoyance, albeit her gaze lingered more on Ashaver, who continued 'Nah, nah! This ain't about no respect for ancient artefacts and whatnot. It's just messy! Ask Xian to get you some coasters! Don't give me that loo…. fine *I'll* tell Xian to get you some coasters. Fuck it! I will get you some coast –'

'Thomas, would you like some rooibos tea?' she cut him off.

'Yes, please!' both Thomases answered.

Ashaver decided to address the issue, 'Well, now that's gonna be confusing... Look – I'm Polish – my name's actually "Tomasz". Pronunciation is just different enough, eh? I'll go by that, for the sake of this interview – and whenever else we may meet. Would that be alrigh' Shosho?'

'That's fine by me.' Shoshanna proceeded to pour Thomas his cup of tea and stated that, 'He has been like this all morning and I am literally beginning to think it's the caffeine in the tea. Just that there is no caffeine in this tea.'

'And you've been saying "literally" *literally* all morning, dear Shosho, and I'm beginning to suspect it's *literally* a verbal tick. No, I mean, seriously, like Tourette's or some shit –'

'What were you thinking about in the waiting room?' General Adler had to literally cut him off again or he would have gone on forever.

'I beg your pardon, sir?'

'In the waiting room. We organised the interview like this to make you overthink things as you sat there. It is a *power play* of sorts. It's also why we didn't allow you to use any external communication. That and the fact we didn't want you finding out from the other interviewees what the questions we had and who exactly was in attendance.' Her head tilted towards the living legend sitting on her couch.

Thomas was quiet for one second. First, he had to admit to himself that he had to give his dad a bit more credit. Second, he decided to do just that, and follow another piece of advice his father had given him.

When you find yourself in a tough spot, being asked questions by someone who expects you to lie, just speak the truth. Most of the time, they'll think you're lying and they'll dismiss the truth as irrelevant. On the rare occasion you manage to encounter someone with any semblance of character, you'll earn their respect.

'Well, at first I started thinking that I'm underqualified, given how you had me in there in a room with decorated war heroes –'

'– you are also a decorated war hero,' she interrupted.

'Yes, sir. But not like Albrecht Hausser or… I saw *Mira al Sayid* come in just as I was told to go in... and in the room with me there was one medical officer who's seen twenty years of frontline combat and surgery, a Captain who worked on the Hyperborean template implementation, there was this guy who knew actual magic –'

'We know Master Sergeant Park's, Captain Mapupu's and Chief Master Sergeant Sikorski's credentials quite well, thank you! Though we do appreciate your additional input and praise! That is not the purpose of my question. Though, you have said something interesting. You know those things about them because you talked to them?'

'Yes... well... I also *listened* to them talking among themselves... '

'... and it made you feel out of place?'

'Well, yes. But not due to their achievements.'

'Go on.'

'... to answer your question – as frankly as I can, General – I felt out of place due to their excitement. I mean I know these interviews are not set up for you to see if we are qualified for the job – whatever that may be – since you already *know* we can do the job. That's why you had us come here to begin here. You must be looking for certain character traits. I mean, correct me if I am wrong but, isn't that how interviews worked before the End Times?'

'They did work like that. You are correct. Is this your first interview?' Adler's face stood immobile.

'Yes. But I've read about them. If I may return to my point, I felt out of place, not due to their achievements or rank, but due to their attitude.' Thomas paused for one second, his blank face betraying the rush of thoughts and the indecision in his mind.

The General's face softened upon noticing this. She tilted her head, in a motherly fashion. 'Please tell us the truth, as accurately as you can.'

'I used to be like that. I used to have dreams and aspirations and ambitions. And – don't get me wrong – I have achieved many of them. But many I have not. And that has cast a weight on me... and an apathy. To be honest, for a moment, I thought this was some type of disciplinary hearing on the grounds of my recent poor performance.'

'Poor performance? Your record could hardly be described as poor.' Adler's hand pointed towards a screen on her desk.

'Yeah, I know, but this is kind of a recent phase I'm going through.'

She raised an eyebrow. 'A "recent phase"?'

'I've been feeling a bit under the weather recently,' he confessed.

The eyebrow went down. 'You're depressed?'

'No. No. Not at all. Like I said, I'm apathetic. What I mean is that I feel that, no matter what I set my mind to, I either fail at it, in which case I try again, or I succeed, in which case I become happy. Then I move on to the next objective, the happiness wears off, and I just feel myself caught in this endless… cycle.'

Ashaver had been quiet up until for the exchange, with Thomas purposefully avoiding looking at him, so he wouldn't become awed to the point of paralysis. '... like you're rolling a boulder up a hill, just to have it roll downhill and sit there waiting for you to roll it up the hill again and again?' the Hierarch asked.

'Yes. The "labour of Sisyphus", I believe it is called.'

'It has many names,' this was General Adler again. 'You've read about it?'

'Yes, sir. I have.'

Ashaver interjected, 'The actual myth or the book?'

'Book, sir, initially. I read about the myth after.'

Ashaver was visibly studying him now. 'I see. Well, that allows for a great segway, Mister Muller. Shosho, I think you can do the thing.'

'Lieutenant Muller. Do you know exactly what the position you are here for entails?'

'No, sir.'

'Why did you apply?'

'I didn't, sir. The position was recommended. To continue to be frank...'

'Oh, please do, lad. It's downright outstanding how frank you got so quickly,' Ashaver quipped in.

'Thank you, sir.' *Thanks, dad!* 'When I came back from the Host, I wanted to join the Logistic Corps. But, then, I sort of hit this rough patch. When this position was brought to my attention, it was advertised as something I might do until I got my bearings back.'

'... and you'd get to see my desk.' Shoshanna's stern face had switched to a cheeky smile.

'Oh, well, yes, that to.' *I should've listened to you, dad. If I would've said the whole truth it would have been better.*

'Why?'

'Why did I want to see the desk?'

Shoshanna nodded.

Tomasz nodded too without taking his eyes of Thomas.

'Well… it's a bit of history, from before the End Times...' he caught himself '... not like an oldtimer...' *Ah crap… some of them don't like being called that.* 'I mean...'

'We know what you mean. Go on!' Adler spurred him on.

'All right.' Thomas was trying really hard to compose himself. He had become a bit too confident upon realizing that he had earned their trust by blurting out the truth. Now, he had to remind himself that Tomasz was actually Hierarch Thomas Ashaver and Shosho was still General Shoshanna Adler. They were some of the most powerful people on Terra and in the whole Alliance. He had daydreamed about meeting Ashaver his entire life. The fact that he was suddenly right here, a few paces away from him, languishing on a couch should not take away from the fact that he had unimaginable power over Thomas' life.

It would still be best to make a good impression.

Adler noticed his thoughts. 'Stop telling yourself that you still need to impress us, Thomas.'

'Pardon, sir?'

She moved forward: 'Look, we've been interviewing people – extraordinary people – not just all day today, but for the past three days. They've all impressed us thoroughly. They've all been charming and we enjoyed the presence of each and every one of them. However, the point of these interviews is not for us to be awed by the war stories of younglings or to catch up on the latest slang. The point of these interviews is to determine what kind of person you are, how you interact with others in a non-combat capacity and to see exactly how much time you've spent working on the subject matter of this position,.'

'And, Thomas, in a couple of minutes you've achieved more than almost all the others did throughout the entirety of their interviews. You've allowed us to jump directly into the conversation we actually wanted to have with you. Now, *don't* fuck this up by trying to tell us what we want to hear. Just tell us, in as honest manner as you can, why you wanted to see the desk.'

'... was that the "thing"?'

'I beg your pardon?' Adler looked a bit confused.

'Hierarch Ashaver, earlier, told you to "do the thing".' Thomas finally let go of the armrests he had been clutching white-knuckled to gesture, somewhat erratically. 'Was that... the "thing"?'

Adler's initial confusion once again gave way to a cheeky smile. 'No. He meant to describe the position. Which I was going to do, after you got about explaining why you wanted to see my desk.'

'Oh, ok.' *Alright, dad. Let's go at it again.* 'I don't want to sit behind it – just to get that out of the way. I... like stories. I like stories about things that *actually* happened the most. Hence, I like history. Our recent history is... everywhere around us and – if I may be open – for us born after the Battle of the Terra, it is literally at the forefront of our lives. Every day. We all work and train and study, driven either by our duty to Terra and to our people and to our families, and out of... the desire to prove to you, the oldtimers, that we are worthy of *our* legacy. Of *your* legacy. With the End Times being the central storyline of that narrative. All that we are told of the World-Which-Was is what you, the survivors, tell us, as well as what we can learn from what records remain. It would appear to me that things were... *good* and that there were a lot more people around – if you'll pardon my lack of tact?'

'Pardoned and agreed with. Go on!'

'Yes. Well, I idolised you all and I would read and listen and watch the stories of what happened and what you achieved and how you survived and how we won the war, over-and-over again as a child. But, I then started wondering, well, why did you survive? Why was it you? And then, in the other direction, I wondered why we were so vulnerable to begin with. What world was there before the End Times? How did that world come to be the way it was? And, to be honest, General Adler, it is a rich, fascinating history, which I have spent much, much time studying and looking over and... well... archiving and chronicling, since that is my art.'

'It is a fascinating history, yes. What do you find most interesting about it?'

'How small the world was, even with all the people living it. I mean... I was on Luna two weeks ago.' Thomas paused as he waited for the impact of his idea to hit him, so that it would be able to hit Adler and Ashaver with the impetus of his own amazement.

There was, however, no need for such theatrics, as an old, knowing and subtly melancholic smile made its way into the corner of their mouths.

He continued, 'That's just something *I* can do which I just take for granted. But, to my parents, to the oldtimers, to you, that's something that happened *during* your lifetime. There was a time in your lives, when you would look up at the moon and think: 'I'm never going to be up there.' And now, you can – *we* can – have fresh pizza, baked on the Moon, while sitting in the spaceport lobby, waiting for our shuttle back to Earth.'

Ashaver was fixed upon him at this point. 'Damn fine that Pizza Dragheta, I agree. But go on lad! How do you think we were different back then?'

'You seemed to not worry about survival at all, sir. Nowadays, that's all we talk about. How not to fade away before the near-continuous onslaught of horror the universe seems to throw at us. It started with the elves, yes. But now the elves are part of the Alliance, and all we talk about now is how to defend ourselves if the Continuum attacks. It seems to me that back then we spent very little time thinking about death or our own existence, as a people.'

'We weren't one people back then, lad. And we couldn't even comprehend how much death could happen in just a few years.'

'I know, sir. I understand. What I find fascinating about the World-Which-Was is the way it must have *felt* to be alive during those times. To not know about... the Continuum, or the Vigilant or... everything.'

'Which is why you wanted to see this desk?' Adler tapped said desk with her forefinger.

'Yes! Quite frankly, sometimes I wonder if it was all real. For me, it doesn't feel real. It's not my reality. My reality is so different. This desk, and other artefacts like it, make it all feel real.'

'Do you regret not being born back in those days?'

'No, sir.'

'Because you would've had to live through the End Times at one point?'

'No, sir. With all due respect, maybe we all have to deal with our own End Times.'

This was the first time Adler and Ashaver reacted in two completely different ways. While Adler looked genuinely shocked and on the verge of exploding with rage, Ashaver's eyes merely drifted away for a few seconds as his face showed the faintest smile.

Thomas continued, 'I wouldn't wish to have been born back in those days, because I wouldn't have become *myself*. I would have been someone else.'

The General seemed to slowly recollect herself. '... and do you want to be the person you are today?'

'Not always, sir. But it is who I am. I guess we all feel the need to conserve our sense of self.'

'Conserving your "self" and your "sense of self" are two entirely different things, lad.' Thomas felt his face flush and he realized that his shirt collar squeezed his neck a bit too tightly. He knew which events Ashaver was referencing. 'No need to worry, lad. It was a long time ago.' Ashaver's eyes seemed to have fixated on the missing beak of the desk's eagle. Albeit, the unfocused stare hinted at a recollection rather than at an inspection. 'Truth be told. I often forget the experience myself.'

His gaze shifted towards Thomas once more. 'Was it a thought about death?'

'Sorry, sir?'

'This thing you're going through. The thoughts you're having.'

Thomas paused. Due to shock and… an unexpected and almost overwhelming sense of… relief.

No one had guessed that until that moment.

The Hierarch needed little time to draw an answer from Thomas' silence. 'I'll take that as a "yes".'

'Yes!' Thomas confirmed.

'You know what a hamster wheel is?'

'Sir?' *What does that have to do with anything?* 'Yes. Pet hamsters run in a wheel to exercise and stay healthy.'

'Well, that we know of. Who knows what the fuck is going on in their heads while they do that? But that's another discussion. The reason why I mention it is because that's how it felt for me when I had the thoughts you are having. Like my "self" was the hamster and the constant need to answer, well, homework questions from my own mind about the nature of existence – and my place in it – was the hamster wheel. Every time I would come up with a pertinent answer my mind just lobbed over a new impossible question for me to come up with an answer for.'

Thomas couldn't take it anymore. He burst out talking now. 'For me it is like living in a house while a storm rages outside threatening to tear *it* down and *me* apart at any moment while I search in books for a magic word to make it stop and make it be how it once was!'

He stopped himself, realizing he sounded like a madman

Shoshanna's eyes were fixed upon him now. 'Don't stop. How else would you describe it, Thomas?'

He looked into her eyes for reassurance. She granted it with a nod. 'I… feel as if I am shaking. At my core. Sometimes my body itself shakes but it is mostly an internal feeling. I… think about the questions. But, I still have to go about my day and I can't focus properly on the thoughts or the day. It feels like my vision shakes.'

'Do you feel afraid that you might lose your mind? Like it would snap? And you might lose yourself?'

A slight trembling in his legs began, as Thomas began to feel his own sincerity. 'Yes?'

'Sober?' Adler's eyes narrowed down upon his now, seeking the certainty of an honest answer.

'What?'

'You smoke weed, son?' Ashaver offered clarification.

'...'

Adler nodded. 'I'll take that as a "yes". How often? Did the thoughts come while you were sober or high on anything, even alcohol?'

'Sober. It happened… It started a week ago. I was sober.'

'Describe how it happened.'

Thomas took a deep breath as he prepared to relive the initial trauma of his existential crisis. 'I was on the tram on Luna. I… felt like I had finished the part of my life that was all about training and testing. That I was going to be an actual adult. A citizen. A Terran. I was content. Happy even. For the first time in my life! And then…'

Thomas had begun a rant. His stream of consciousness had slipped into his speech and in the rush he had forgotten what he had been saying. He paused to gather himself. He tried to clear his mind and stop the incoming storm. The relief of knowing he was not the only one to have ever felt like this was overwhelming. He wanted to tell them everything. As if speaking would make the poison and the terror and the anxiety go away. But he had to be coherent. He had to stop thinking so much and focus.

What did I want to say? Which part was I at? Oh. Yes. The Thought.

'... and then I thought – and I've never had this thought before, at least not like this. *'Concentrate'*

'Enjoy this moment. Because there will come a day when you will die!'

The words came out.

Just like they had come out with Ronan. He was looking down at his legs. He focused heavily on staying coherent. Taming his mind had taken all his concentration and he had neglected his eyes. He had stopped looking at Shoshanna at one point. He knew he should look up. Yet, he was afraid. What if, once more, he would not see understanding and comprehension in another's face? What if he would look up and see nothing? What if Shoshanna would babble off-topic in discomfort? Not understanding? Not being able to help?

He mustered the courage to look up because he still had some hope left in him.

Shoshanna was not looking at him. She was looking straight at the other Thomas in the room. As Thomas glanced over towards Ashaver, he saw his eyes jump from Shoshanna to him and then back to Shoshanna.

The Hierarch smiled. 'Ronan's still got it!'

'The luck of the Irish.' Adler bent forward in her seat, hands clasped together, almost in a soothing motion as she leaned on top of her desk towards Thomas. 'Which question are you at?' General Adler's voice was much colder now that it had been at any point in the conversation.

'I'm sorry?'

'You're not at your own mortality anymore, are you? You have passed through some of the questions. But it's not over isn't it? Which one is it now? Which one is bothering you now? Which brick are you laying in your defence against which madness?'

This was too much for Thomas. He felt his throat close up in complete anxiety. He was as tense as a man could be while still sitting in a chair. He took in an audible breath of air before immediately blurting out the truth.

'That even if I never die. Eternity would be boring and I would get depressed and I might kill myself in the afterlife.' Panic set in as he realised what he had just said. He felt himself go cold, pale, the blood left his head, arms and legs. His limbs went numb almost instantly.

General Adler raised a palm towards him, her wrist still on the desk, her other palm still spread out on the table. 'No! None of that! No fear! Don't worry. You're doing great. I promise you, you're doing great!

Now, Thomas, bear with me. Why are you afraid of suicide?'

What the fuck do you mean 'why'? It's fucking obvious, isn't it?
'Because it might fade to black. It might fade to nothingness.'
'And why is that bad?'
'Because I like living.'
'And there is no life after death?'

'*I don't know!*' the words came out of his mouth as if he was crying. He blinked to check his eyes. No tears (yet). But he was shaking a little. He was barely focusing now. Silence gripped the room.

'Thomas.' Adler's eyes were on her desk but her mind was somewhere else now.

'Yes, sir?'

'Do you remember being born?'

'NO and I DON'T CARE about that Mark Twain bull*shit* about existence after death being the same as existence before life! That's vague *bullshit* and answers nothing!'

He caught himself. At one point during his outburst he had started waving an erratic finger towards Adler. People had been demoted to Corporal for much less.

However, instead of outrage at his outburst, he saw something else in Shoshanna's wide eyes. The brief coldness from earlier had passed. She looked like someone who had just scored a jackpot.

'He's still in the First Act.' Shoshanna's eyes never left the young lieutenant's, but her words were meant for Ashaver's ears.

'Aye… Aye, he is.' Ashaver's voice was disconnected. His gaze fixated on Thomas as he leaned forward on the couch. 'Lad…. A week ago, you said? This started a week ago?'

'Yes, sir.'

'You're slow…' Ashaver leaned back as he looked out the window towards the restless icy sea outside. 'That's good!' He looked back towards the General as he pulled at his nose and exhaled. 'Shosho...'

'Thomas… *Thomas*!' She tapped her fingernails on the desk.

Thomas had been digesting what being "slow" and the "First Act" meant. Blood pumped in his ears as his mind panicked, both due to what he had been dealing with for a week and how he had been behaving in front of two of the most important people on Terra.

'Yes, sir?'

Adler went on. 'You are here in a hotel room, aren't you?'

Thomas nodded.

'Your essentials are there?'

Thomas nodded again.

'Excellent! Go straight there and pack. You will receive a message from your assigned Army unit containing your detachment from your current force –'

Oh no! They're demoting me to a frontline grunt and sending me to die.

'– and reattachment to mine. Specifically, you are now part of Project Kralizec, though I will ask you to refrain from using that term. You will relocate to your new, designated lodgings. A team will drop by your home and pick up your belongings. Where is your permanent residence?'

What the fuck?

'Rosenheim, sir. My parents' place. It's where my belongings are. I brought them there after I left Luna. I haven't picked my own place yet.'

'You've had too much on your mind to pick one?'

'Well... Yes.'

'Well, you won't have to worry about that. You're moving to Jerusalem, which is where, at this stage, Project Kralizec is being executed and you will do so immediately. We expect you to be there in four hours. Upon arriving in Jerusalem, you will head straight to Golgotha hospital, where a medical officer will perform an assessment of your overall health. You didn't perform a medical assessment when you arrived from Luna, didn't you?'

'No.' *But, I don't understand what's going on.* 'General?'

'Yes?'

'Did... did I get the job?'

Shoshanna began tapping her fingers on the desk in a rhythmically impatient manner. 'You're right. He is a bit slow.'

'It's understandable, Shosho.' Ashaver got up from his chair and walked towards the desk, his hands gripping the sides of his tabard. 'Yes, lad. You got the job and we are going to tell you why. Since we don't do that ol' "we'll get back to you with our decision and feedback" thing you might have read about in them history books.' He moved to sit beyond General Adler as he nudged her chair forward with his knee.

'You do the honours, Shosho! You love yourself a good revelation now don't ya?'

Shoshanna was far too fixated on Thomas to care about Ashaver's antics at this point. 'As you have probably figured out by now, Thomas, you are having an existential crisis. A profound one. The revelation and, more importantly, comprehension of your own mortality is forcing you to reassess and reassemble the way you see yourself and the world around you. From what I can tell, in the coming weeks and, possibly, *months*, you will struggle acutely with the profound questions of existence, until you decide upon a worldview which will dictate how you will proceed in the aftermath of the revelations you're having. All of that makes you the perfect person for the task at hand.'

Shoshanna looked down once more as her hands moved from clasping each other to gripping an imaginary sphere. ' It's not the fact that you're having this existential crisis which is important, though it is paramount for everyone involved in Project Kralizec to have contemplated such thoughts at some point in their lives. Rather, it's the fact that you're having one right now which is important. Your role will become clear in Jerusalem, in time. But, before we proceed, there is something I must stress, Thomas, and I need you to muster up all the focus you can. I need your absolute attention for this next part.'

'Yes, sir.'

'Henceforth, you will never speak about Project Kralizec to anyone. You will not even mention the name to anyone outside of Project Kralizec. If anyone asks, you're working on a superweapon based on stolen Continuum technology.'

Shoshanna saw the confusion in his eyes. 'Yes, Thomas. It's that important. It is so important, in fact, that you will be required to consent to a potential mindwipe, if you ever disclose, intentionally or otherwise, information pertaining to Project Kralizec to anyone outside of Project Kralizec. Do you understand?'

'I… Not yet. But I understand that it is important.'

Ashaver intervened. 'It is lad, and, to be honest, it won't be a hard secret to keep – once you wrap your head around it, at least. Plus, the plan is to share Project Kralizec with everyone – and I mean *everyone* – at one point.' The Hierarch seemed to be willing to deny Adler some of the 'honours', apparently.

Thomas had figured out what they were talking about at this point.

Though he couldn't believe it.

His mouth was half-agape, as he stood there motionless, about to ask the question which was burning his mind at this point.

'Yes, Thomas. *It is that.*' As Shoshanna Adler spoke those words, the blood in his ears began to pump so loudly he feared he would go deaf or faint. 'Do you understand the implications?'

Thomas felt alternating waves of anxiety and disbelief wash over him in a vortex of thoughts and emotions. In the end, he decided to follow his father's advice to the end

'No. But, then again, I think no one does.'

Shoshanna did not smile, her face was still stern. 'Good answer.' She drew a deep breath. 'After your physician's appointment, if you pass the medical assessment, you will be directed to meet with someone from the Intelligence Corps the next day. That person will assess your ability to stay quiet about what you'll be working on. Now, bear in mind that if it is assessed that you are not fit for Project

Kralizec, you will receive a mindwipe. You will sign a consent agreement during the medical examination and, from that point onwards, if anything problematic happens, you will receive a mindwipe. Do you understand?'

'Yes.' He wasn't certain he did. He had heard of projects which were subject to potential mindwipes. *But I've never met anyone who had actually had been... ohhh. That part is a bit obvious now, isn't it?* 'Is the mindwipe... a limited one?'

'Yes. Specifically, it will be a complete memory wipe starting from two days ago, right before you met Ronan. Do you understand?'

'Yes.' Thomas didn't say a 'but', yet it was implied on account of the horrified expression on his face.

Ashaver provided an answer. 'You see, regardless of whether or not this whole thing works out or not, an existential crisis is something you'll find beneficial in the long run. It came when it came for you. There's no changing that. We're just gonna exploit it. You're still gonna experience it and we don't want that bit of personal growth to be wasted or otherwise adulterated. At least... not in an *exceptionally* intrusive way.'

'I... I see. That was only one of my questions though...'

'Yeah, we're not gonna get into all of 'em. That's what Jerusalem's for.'

'No. I mean... I know about Project Kralizec now. If I am a liability, am I not a liability *now*?'

Ashaver's famous ear to ear smile showed itself in all of its glory as General Adler's eyebrows fused together in an angry frown.

It was she who responded, 'Not very slow apparently.'

'The ones that are that are slow don't look like him. No, Thomas, you're not! We have plausible deniability. You came in here, went off-topic, started babbling nonsense and misconstruing our words. We let you go. You didn't understand what happened. You started ranting random crazy talk to someone close to you about how you came to this interview and sat in a waiting room and touched the *Resolute Desk* and talked to Thomas Ashaver and Shoshanna Adler about some super secret project and shit...'

Ashaver couldn't contain his giggles anymore as he gesticulated the described scenario. 'But, that isn't gonna happen isn't it? Because telling those around you what this whole thing is about isn't gonna make *your* actual problem go away. It never will.'

The Hierarch paused after this last sentence, the fingers of his right hand no longer waving around in the air, but now soothing each other as he rubbed his palms together in a circle. 'But this thing *can* help you and you can help us. And by *us* I mean everyone. I'll leave it at that. Now...' Ashaver took out a handkerchief from one of his inside pockets, lifted Shoshanna's teacup and began whipping the wet imprint it had left on the table.

'Now go back to your hotel. Pick up your things and hop on a train to Jerusalem. If you get the green light in Jerusalem, you'll be smoking cigarettes and pondering existence erratically in no time.' Thomas finished wiping the table, placed the handkerchief under Adler's teapot and made his way back to his seat on the couch, all the while ostentatiously ignoring the General's glare.

With his back still towards Thomas he lifted one finger. 'One more thing. You mentioned you happened to see Mira al Sayid walking in as you came in?'

Thomas needed a few seconds to remember the events of less than five minutes ago. 'Yes, sir. Yes, I did, sir.'

Ashaver groaned as he slouched back onto the couch. 'Relentless now, ain't she?' he said towards Shoshanna. 'Mira had her existential crisis when she was nine years old. I was there to see it. It was... mind-blowing and what's even more mind-blowing is that she has somehow managed to figure out *on her own* that we are working on... *what we're working on*.'

'She even managed to convince someone to recommend her as a candidate despite the fact that I, and everyone around her, insists her place is elsewhere.' Ashaver's words began to drift as he looked out the window again.

'She probably bullied her way into finding out where we've been conducting these interviews and showed up without an appointment…Typical… gonna try and cut the queue and everything…'

He let out a long breath as he looked blankly at the air in front of himself. 'Lad?'

'Yes, sir?'

'We gave you some direct orders now, didn't we?'

'Right, sir. Apologies, sir.'

'None needed. I'll see you in Jerusalem sometime. Shosho you'll likely see more often. Now go! Time is of the essence.'

Thomas got up from his chair and almost forgot to salute.

'Thank you!' he said to both of them.

'You're welcome, Thomas. But, just so you know, Tomasz is not exaggerating. We will be, for lack of a better term, *exploiting* what you're going through. We don't want to put you in too much difficulty. We're not really going to help you either. It'll be challenging at times. More so than how these things usually are.'

'I understand. My gratitude still stands.'

'Good! So does ours! I'll see you in Jerusalem soon.'

Chapter V
Within normal parameters

In order to get to Jerusalem, Thomas had to go through Egypt.

He had gone back to his hotel room, as instructed, to get his backpack. He then boarded a train from Baffin Station to Svalbard Station. From there, he had boarded the 2E line which would take him to Egypt Terminal. At least he assumed that he had, since it was only when he had passed Terminal Euxinus that he managed to slip out of his erratic, dreamlike trance.

He checked the time to see that less than three hours had passed since he had left Shoshanna Adler's office. *Good, Egypt is about five minutes away.* From there, he would take a shuttle to Jerusalem and report to the physician's office. He'd make it just in time. He checked the time again to see what time it would be in the Eden Quadrant at the time of his arrival. *Eight in the evening. We're in June. It will still be light outside.*

He remembered that he hadn't eaten since the day before, when his mother had insisted that he come down for breakfast. *Hopefully I won't look too unhealthy.* He looked around to see if there were any mirrors in his cabin. There was a screen fixed to the table next to him. He opened it and selected the mirror function.

It was surprising to him how parched his face looked, especially given how sweaty his palms were. He studied himself for a moment, only to realize that he didn't recognize himself. He remembered being a child and knowing what his face looked like. He remembered knowing who he was. But now, he saw just the face of... *someone*. He could have had any other face. It just happened that fate had made this one his. Now, it was as if he saw himself for the first time.

Somehow, that same feeling of not being understood or comprehended – a feeling he had seen so often in the faces of others since this whole thing had started – he now saw within his own reflection. It wasn't just his face. His whole body felt alien to him. Only his mind felt as if it was... not necessarily *his*, but at least *him*.

How strange and banal it felt to have a body. What *was* his mind after all? His consciousness? Was it anything other than his brain? What was a brain? He knew what a brain looked like. He knew how a human nervous system looked like. It was almost as if some eerie squid-like parasite had commandeered the cells of another species and had made those cells build a bone dome around it and feed it the things it wanted, processed in the way it wanted. The body would fetch it water. Give it the oxygen it needed to fuel itself. It would get rid of its waste. It would even breed with other infected bodies and produce a whole new symbiote which would proceed to do more or less of the same thing.

Yes, of course, the parasite would take care of the body and manage it, as best as it could, but, ultimately, the body was little more than a tool for the parasite. The body never granted the mind its consent. It had no control over its own fate. One might think that the body and the brain were on the same team, since they both wanted to live and to breed. However, on closer inspection, the brain frequently seemed willing to sacrifice both the body and itself in order to fulfil some thought or achieve some goal.

Thomas had seen combat. He thought about it often now. Over the course of his life, he had become desensitised to it, as was the Terran way. How cold was he now? How uncaring had he become? How parasitic was he towards his body? How many times had he risked his life, knowingly, to achieve something his mind had decided was good enough to die for? He still remembered all the times he had risked his life during his years with the Allied Host. He remembered the explosion that had killed two men next to him just because they were in the way of shrapnel. He remembered the assault in which his entire battalion had been shot at with lasers and bolts and shells. Yes, they had shields and an EMP at the ready. Yes, they had a plan and, yes, it had worked, but *dammit*! If anything would have gone slightly different, they wouldn't have lost only sixty men in the whole operation.

They could have lost sixty-one.

Or sixty-two.

Or two hundred.

Or a thousand.

What if they would have been wrong in their assessment of the situation by some marginal, yet catastrophically sufficient, degree?

Yes... His body *and* brain would have died.

Yet, his brain had factored that in. It had judged the risks and the rewards, and every possible consequence it could comprehend, and it had decided that it was better to possibly die, as opposed to almost certainly live.

And for what?

To be a Terran? To be accepted? To be respected? To be loved? To not be a loser? A traitor? A coward? A weakling?

Why?

Thomas knew exactly and precisely why.

Yet, he could not put it into words. Not even into words spoken *by* and *only for* his own mind. Yet, that question, at least, did not require an answer he would have to construct from scratch. He knew the answer and it was cheap in its simplicity.

Because it felt good.

Because it felt good to be as good (or better) as everyone else. To have those you've loved, those you've admired, those who raised you, those who you were raised with, those who taught you, those who protected you, and those who provided for you... it felt good to have those people be proud of you. To accept you as one of their own. To be worthy of such a thing. Now that Thomas thought about it, nothing had ever felt so good in such a consistent way.

It was... to be happy, to have achieved – not joy – but happiness. His mother had explained that to him once.

Joy is feeling very good for a very short time. Happiness is feeling good for a long time.

What other way had Thomas ever known of being happy? He only knew how to be happy by doing what others expected of him. Or, at least, he had mostly felt happy when he knew he was on his way towards becoming someone who *was* what others would have wanted him to be. How often had he longed for his father to tell him he was proud of him? Not in passing, for some slight achievement, but for *who he was*? For who he had become? Or his mother to trust him? To have her acknowledge that he was a capable man? A man able to take care of himself?

His colleagues in the Host whose acceptance he had sought? His comrades? Most of them weren't even Terran and he cared about their respect for him deeply. He had been willing to risk his life for every single one of them and for what? So that they would do the same and also hang out with him in between the battles? So that his commanders would make *him* a commander one day? Because that was the thing everyone wanted; at least every Terran. To be a Captain, then a Commandant, a General, maybe become a Representative, then maybe become the Marshal, then become the Warchief, then become a Hierarch with your own Legion like Thomas Ashaver. Terran Military or Allied Host, whichever one you liked, it didn't matter. Either that or get chosen to be in the Legendary League and be acknowledged as an actual superhero.

And what was all of that for?

To keep Terra safe?

Against... *everything*?!

Against the Sun ejecting a solar flare? Against the Continuum? Against some spawn? Against some surviving dark elves? Against who-knows-what?!

What for? The Universe itself might end one day and perhaps there's no way of stopping that. Maybe it didn't matter if your group of people had an afterlife set up for them beyond the darkness of oblivion, since it just might not work. It might all fade to black anyway and then nothing would matter. Maybe nothing would have ever mattered at all?

What would happen to him if he just didn't fight? If he didn't want to risk anymore? Yes, of course, there were people like that. Ronan was one such person and he lived alone in an alien forest in the middle of his homeland, building a church for no congregation.

What kind of life is that?

But your father would trust Ronan with his life and fucking Thomas Ashaver and Shoshanna Adler knew who Ronan was and they even seemed to admire him.

Yes, but even they ignored him. Ronan was never invited to dinner at his parent's place. Ronan never married, despite donating his DNA to the Seeding Program... regarding that last bit, who would want Ronan's seed?

If he hadn't been an oldtimer... *Oh, yes. He is an oldtimer. That's tried-and-tested genetics right there...*

But if it weren't for that...

Could he live Ronan's life? He wasn't an Oldtimer. He wasn't even a Yin like his parents. He was a sunriser. Born after the end of the War of Vengeance. His generation had not earned their rite of passage through the horrors of the Apocalypse itself! The Ayve War had been a fair fight. Quite frankly, in retrospect, losing the Ayve War would've been embarrassing. What kind of laurels could a sunriser even rest on? Even the Yin had the Senoyu War, a true example of asymmetric warfare.

He had never heard of a Yin retiring either. They all lived like his parents. They spent every day working on the defence of Terra. Every moment of rest they took was simply something they had to do to continue to be capable of protecting their people. A debt they had inherited from the oldtimers when they had been children, unable to even comprehend what was going around them as the world fell apart.

His was a generation that had spent its entire existence in knowledge of the fact that the worst thing you could do in life as a Terran was to not participate in the eternal war effort that was Terran society. Everything was about war. Since war was unavoidable in the Terran mind.

How could it not be, when the greatest military superpower the Universe had ever known wanted their complete and utter annihilation?

Oh... the Continuum. What did they live for in their Orwellian society?

'Welcome to Terminal Egypt. This is your declared destination, Thomas,' Clara's voice rang out.

Thomas shook away the nihilism. He picked up his backpack and opened his cabin door and proceeded to exit the train.

He hadn't been here in years. Last time he had been here had been on vacation with his parents. They had come to meet some of his parents' old campaign buddies, Salman and Aadila. They had a villa on the banks of the Nile, near Qena, he recalled. One night, he had left the villa after dinner to sit on the banks of that old storied river and feel its waters as they coursed through his fingers, all the while looking around for crocodiles.

During the End Times, the Nile had alternated between catastrophic bouts of flooding and periods of extreme drought when the river had dried up completely. Sandstorms, wildfires and famine had plagued the Egyptian countryside. The Burning of Cairo was one of the first actual battles the Terran Nations had fought against the dushman, who had only just announced themselves on the Day of Revelation. It was still mourned as the first battle humanity had lost against the invaders.

The Egyptian military, already weakened by years of famine, infighting, plague and the raw fury of the elements, had converged on Cairo to meet in battle an elven warband that had recently began slaughtering the old Garden City district.

The Egyptians had been obliterated by orbital bombardments, the arrival of enemy reinforcements, as well by the initial warband itself, which meet the Egyptian vanguard on the outskirts of the city. The actual battle lasted for a little under an hour before the elves began their aerial assault.

As Thomas walked out of the Terminal's inner hall and into the shuttle hangar, he looked out towards the lush countryside that stretched out beyond. It was strange to think about how, just fifty years before, almost all of Egypt had been an actual desert. He had always known it as a green place, even though the last arid patches were supposedly still present when he was eight or nine years old. Using technology stolen from the elves, gifted by orcs or otherwise developed by Terrans with the help of their allies, the entire Sahara had been converted into a vast green grassland, peppered with young forests and even jungles in the far south, in the lands of the old Chad, Sudan, Niger, Mali and Mauretania. Most of the grassland was put to use as farmland, yet some pockets dedicated to leisure still remained, particularly on the banks of the Nile, where the Egyptian Terrans had built new homes in the rubble of the old.

Thomas found a shuttle to his liking (meaning that it was the one closest to him), checked its availability, opened its door, dropped his backpack in and got inside.

The shuttle's operator commenced its inquiry as soon as he sat down. 'Hello, Lt. Muller! Where are we going?'

'Hello…' he looked at the controls to see the operator's name written on the steering wheel '... Edric. We're going to the Golgotha Hospital in the Jerusalem Holdfast. Golda Meir Street, number …'

'As you know, sir. I don't need to know the exact destination, just the general area, so that I may clear your airspace. In this case, I understand that's Jerusalem Holdfast?' The operator had one of those deadpan monotone voices.

I'm being awkward with computers now. 'Yes. That's correct. Do I have clearance or do I have to –'

'You don't have to do anything, Lieutenant Muller. You're already cleared for a Category 3 airpath. Please proceed to take off and follow the route marker on your screen.'

Category 3? That's fancy shit. I haven't had Category 3 before. Category 3 meant that only ambulances and Terrans trying to stop an invasion had more right of way than him.

'Sure thing. Can I see the route too?'

'Of course. It's located to your right.' Thomas could see that it was essentially a *crowfly* route. Which was great, because it meant that in about two minutes he would get to see the pyramids. He had seen them before several times, but it never got old. Maybe they would help him silence his thoughts even more than the shuttle ride would.

Terran public shuttles were free to use for everyone and the driver was legally obliged to pilot it himself, unless he was unable to due to injury, exhaustion, intoxication or if he was otherwise occupied with something deemed serious. In that scenario, the shuttle could drive itself without any issue. The whole rationale was that it counted as practice for combat, since all of these shuttles were basically lightly armed battle shuttles, with the capacity of carrying around four people comfortably, though the space could be stretched to as many as ten in case of emergency. They were even designed to fly in space and were sometimes used, albeit rarely, to reach Luna, though it would take a shuttle around a day to achieve such a feat, while it would take a starship going at comfortable sublight speeds around five minutes to cover the same distance.

But flying for twenty minutes up to Jerusalem didn't bother Thomas at all. He liked driving. He had always found it relaxing since it always helped take his mind off things. Throw in a little sightseeing and he had a proper road trip in front of him to help take him off the edge.

Thomas looked to his right as he passed them.

The Great Pyramids of Giza had been shattered by the aerial bombardment wrought on by the elves during the Burning of Cairo. After the Burning of Cairo, the nuclear warheads launched by Israel and Russia caused the stones to melt and boil into lava. After the War of Vengeance, three obelisks, each one with a tip the size of each ancient pyramid of Giza, were erected in their place, each reaching two kilometres into the sky.

They were plated with a smooth mix of white marble, black obsidian and gold. The marble had come from the rubble of Old Earth. The obsidian had come from the numerous craters left by the erupting volcanoes, asteroid impacts and nuclear explosions of the End Times. The gold had mainly salvaged from elven otarc plating, the material the Svart elves had coated their bones with, in a manner similar to Terran honeybone. The symbolism evoked by the three obelisks was quite commonplace on Terra, particularly when it came to the reconstructions of old monuments.

Terrans would not forget the memory of Old Earth.

Terrans would build a new world from the ruins and rubble of Old Earth together with their inhuman allies.

Terrans would take the tools of their enemies, make them their own and turn them against their foes.

This last bit of imagery was clearest at night, when the three obelisks were light up with white light, making them shine in the darkness as they had during the day. They were powered by the sun's rays, harnessed each day as they heated the obelisks' plating and charged the massive batteries housed within each structure. The batteries also powered the heavily armed defence platforms that stood ready to turn each tower into an unassailable fortress at a moment's notice.

This last detail bothered Thomas.

Very utilitarian we Terrans are.

Everything new seemed to be so centred on practicality. Even the aesthetic appeal of these three obelisks was meant to be intimidating to Terrans, their allies and their potential opponents. No art existed merely for the sake of beauty anymore. No matter how many Renaissance or Fimbulwinter paintings they placed in their offices and homes and museums and libraries... the fact was inescapable.

Terra was rooted in its past. The future was likely as barren as the present.

His entire life, he had seen that mentality in action. Perhaps it had been most obvious to him only after he had joined the Allied Host. He had met orcs, elves, trolls, goblins, demani, remani, ursai, and even other humans such as the Vanir, the Hyperboreans, and the Aesir. With the obvious exception of the trolls, which had also seen their world destroyed in a perhaps even more cataclysmic event than the

End Times, no other people of the Republican Alliance was as fixated on keeping their past alive as much as the Terrans were.

The elves he had met were compelled by some inner shame of the past. High elves for having consented to the genocides of Kalimaste, Terra and, potentially, Moria. Low elves for having allowed the other elves to force them into a subservient caste over millennia of ever increasing segregation and subjugation. Primal elves lived in shame of having allowed the high elves to proceed with their plans – not due to groupthink or a sense of national solidarity, as the low elves had – but out of fear. Thomas had often had the feeling that all they had in common were the pointy ears and that inner shame. A shame they seemed to feel that only they understood.

The orcs were also atoning for some sin of their people. Albeit this one was so ancient, only the insistence of the orcs themselves that it existed to begin with was what gave meaning to what would have otherwise been just some myth.

The remani origin story was also so ancient even the remani themselves doubted its veracity.

The hobgoblins, being goblins, were mostly concerned with the future, with the present being just a stepping stone and the past being little more than a reservoir of potentially useful (yet currently out-of-fashion) ideas.

Those demani he had met were still so overwhelmed by the joy of having earned their freedom after untold generations of apartheid that their entire cultural identity seemed to revolve around a sense of optimism for the future.

Other peoples had their own distinct cultural identities, but they either revolved around an ancient objective or some yearning for a bright future coming out of the darkness of the past.

Yet, Terran cultural identity revolved around proving that the past was worthy of having the future be dedicated to its memory.

Of course we're building our own heaven now. It's a way of keeping the past alive forever.

It was at that exact moment that, for the first time in his life, he experienced genuine pride at being a Terran. Not in the traditional jingoistic way, no! Rather, he saw how fortunate he was to have been born on this world at the time he was. He was part of a long line of Terrans which had struggled to survive and prosper on this world for millennia, only now having earned the tools needed to go head-to-head with Death itself, after having gone head-to-head with the Apocalypse.

That short moment of elation and ethnic pride immediately gave way to despair and desolation, as he realised it was all a great gamble which would probably lead to war with the Continuum and, potentially, their annihilation in the very near future.

That's what all the secrecy was about.

Secrets are surprisingly rare in societies which are truly obsessed with keeping secrets. Yes, of course, they supposedly shared all their actual secrets with their allies, but said allies just kept the information amongst small groups at the tip of their leadership structures. Everything else, meaning anything they did not consider to be a secret, was not something they felt obliged to share. That was official Terran policy and it moulded perfectly onto a society of people defined by their struggle against a Universe which they perceived as potentially hostile.

Sure, they shared their books, their films and their culture. But, that was just another way by which they ensured their survival, albeit in a much more subtle way. That had been something he, and his fellow Terran comrades, had struggled with in the Allied Host. Right before they got shipped away to Luna to commence their service, he remembered the speech given to them by the then Terran Marshall of Terra.

'Those you will serve with are your brethren.
In your eyes, see them as Terrans in war.
You all know what that means.
See them also as Terrans in peace.

Eat with them. Show them your songs. Listen to their songs. Dance with them. Love them. Embrace them. Go to their homes as friends and see their worlds alongside their eyes. Bring them to Terra and let them see your world alongside your eyes.

But, never forget that you are Terran and that they must earn the right of your friendship. You have nothing to prove to them other than the fact that the legends are true.'

The duality of that order had led to both the most valiant and the most petty behaviour Thomas had ever seen in his life. On the one hand, every non-Terran in the entire Allied Host knew he could entrust any Terran with his life in complete confidence. On the other hand, Terrans were stereotypically seen by their allies (with the notable exceptions of orcs, remani and trolls) as arrogant homicidal maniacs.

On the one hand, Terrans were particularly dedicated to exposing others to their culture and were known to be genuinely curious about the cultures and lives of others. On the other hand, having someone continuously insist that you listen to Drake or Jimmi Hendrix, or watch *The Godfather* or *The Dark Knight*, or read the *Quran* or *the Grapes of Wrath* all day, had a tendency to become tedious and exhausting.

Yet, with the exception of their culture, Terrans stayed quiet about everything else. No one shared information about the day-to-day events or the ideas circulating around Terra during current times. Which was quite easily explained by the fact that, when you obsess over creating a militarised society engaged in either an ongoing war or preparing for a future war, the development of new cultural artefacts begins to take a backseat to survivalism and utilitarianism. Contemporary Terran culture being a heterogeneous mix of the cultures of the old Terran Nations and what they had copied from other societies.

No one spoke about the Terran military unless asked or, sometimes, *ordered* to do. No one talked about Terran weapons factories. No one talked about the defences of Terra. *Especially **NOT** about the defences of Terra.*

This Project Kralizec, however, was the first Terran project he had been part of where he had been ordered to keep its existence secret including and especially from other Terrans. Which meant it came from the High Command and the Marshal of Terra himself.

Terrans, being Terrans, followed orders with remarkable fanaticism. Which meant that no Terran was ever involved in ongoing secret operations, despite it being an open secret that secret operations took place all the time and were ultimately revealed to the general public when declassified.

This conundrum clashed with another interesting aspect of modern Terran life: it was technically illegal, yet frequently tolerated, for Terrans to lie to *one another* (they could lie to non-Terrans unless ordered not to). A lie was only ever punished if uncovered *and* deemed to be serious enough to be punished.

Thus, people lied openly about being in secret operations, only for it to be ultimately revealed that they were lying. Of course, Terrans were frequently caught lying about other things, both trivial and serious. Yet, the toleration of small lies, the harsh punishment of big lies, and the insistence that one should not lie to begin with, had (more-or-less) led to the emergence of remarkably honest society. It had also hindered the development of an open one.

The secrecy, particularly having to consent to a mindwipe, did mean that this Project Kralizec must truly be something serious. He remembered Adler's words: *If anyone asks, you're working on a superweapon based on stolen Continuum technology.* Stealing tech was grounds enough to court open hostilities with the Continuum. After all, the Continuum knew they were stealing their technology, even if they couldn't prove it. Which was part of the reason why they were openly hostile to Terra and the Alliance.

But, if this was worse than that, then meant that it was something which would certainly lead to immediate all-out war.

There are only 3 separate things which are guaranteed to lead to war with the Continuum.

1. *Being Human and refusing to be part of the Continuum,*
2. *Allying with non-humans, and*

3. *Heaven-building.*

They had been doing the first two for about forty years now and maybe the Terran leadership decided to start going for the hat-trick.

'Lieutenant Muller, you will be arriving at your destination in under two minutes. I see you have a permanently assigned personal shuttle waiting for you at the destination. Please park next to this vehicle to receive confirmation of receipt of your vehicle. Also, Lieutenant Muller, congratulations!' Edric's voice was, once more, deadpan, though the news was startling.

I... I get my own work car?

A public shuttle was just a shuttle. But a personal shuttle was a *car*. He hadn't bought a car yet, since he had been saving his money to buy his own villa. He thought he wouldn't care for a car that much since he would be on military duty so often and, with public shuttles being everyone, there wasn't any real need for one.

But, he had always thought it would be nice to have your own car. It was a luxury, really, and luxuries were not necessities... but some cars were really nice.

And this one was *too* nice.

A Mercedes Falke model. Stylish in a deep and dark ultramarine. *A fucking fortune.* Only Captains and above could even think of affording one.

Permanently Assigned. Oh, no... their expectations for me must so be fucking high! And so it was that Thomas was so caught up in his own head that he was completely unable to enjoy the fact that, out of nowhere, he had just received his dream car. Not loaned, but permanently assigned. This was his permanent property now.

'Don't forget your appointment, Lieutenant. Muller. Have a good day!' Edric said as he closed his door.

'Bye, Edric!'

No time to look at it. He checked his watch. The appointment was in five minutes. Ahead of him lay the entrance to a hospital. He glanced at the name above the gate: Golgotha Hospital.

Thomas had always found Christian mythology to be one of the more boring topics he had to study in school. It was the only reason why he had failed to score a 10/10 on his Abrahamic mythology exam. Christian theology, on the other hand, had been one of his favourite topics. Thus, he wasn't sure if Golgotha was the hill Jesus was crucified on, or if it was the name of some ancient sinful city.

4 minutes.

He opened the Mercedes' door and dropped his backpack on the left passenger seat. *That's new car smell. What the hell have I signed up for? Is this really what I think this is? Ashaver and Adler suggested as much... but, now, it feels real.*

'Hi, Thomas!' Clara was already integrated into the car's system.

'Hi, Clara!'

'The doctor is Commandant Opera Bokha. Don't be late!'

'I won't,' he said as he shut the door.

He walked in and made his way to the central hall, where he asked the hospital's director at the reception where he could find Commandant Opera Bokha's office, got the directions to her office and was instructed to enter her office and wait. She would attend to him shortly.

He entered Commandant Bokha's office precisely four hours after leaving Adler's office. He only had enough time to sit and breathe a sigh of relief for being on time before Bokha herself entered the room from a balcony he had not noticed going in. She was a black woman with long, curly hair and very probing eyes, more so than most Terran doctors. He realized that the assessment had begun the moment he had entered the room.

'Lieutenant Muller?' she spoke with a Yoruba accent.

'Yes, sir.'

'I'm Commandant Opera Bokha. And none of that "sir" with me, you can call me Opera or, if you insist, *madam*.' A common request from oldtimers, though a bit more uncommon with Yin. Thomas glanced quickly around the room to see if he could gauge her exact age. Perhaps she had some plaque somewhere... *A commandant tends to be an oldtimer though.*

However, she continued speaking '... and, yes, I am a Yin.'

'Pardon, madam?' His eyes now fixed now upon hers.

'You're looking around the room to tell my generation. I am a Yin. I'm forty-eight years old.'

'That's not... I didn't need to know that, madam.' *Oh, shit now she'll think I'm some cunty kid.*

'Yes, you did. Most people your age do it. It's alright. We've all become quite used to it. The thing about you though, is that you're bad at masking it. Likely, due to some internal frustration, confusion or lack of focus.' She sat down opposite Thomas. 'You definitely seem to be having an existential crisis. It started about a week ago, correct?'

I can't believe it's that obvious. Maybe Ashaver told her. How many other people could see how distressed he was? He nodded

'Not that many people can see it, Thomas. Don't worry. I am a doctor. A psychiatrist, to be precise. It's my job to see it. So relax!' He had been finding that to be impossible for quite some time now. 'As best as you can, that is. I've looked through your medical file already. You're as healthy as a doctor or a medical operator can tell just from looking at your body. So I know you're not sick, I am here to determine if you are sane or not.'

Oh, no. They think I am going crazy. Maybe I am going crazy. Maybe Ashaver was a hallucination…

'… which I don't think you are. So, again, relax!'

Thomas forced a smile. 'How can you tell?'

'I can't yet. I just know that Thomas Ashaver and Shoshanna Adler know a thing or two about assessing people's mental health, despite not being psychiatrists themselves. If they say you're having an existential crisis, I am inclined to assume they know what they're talking about. That being said. No one is perfect and they might be wrong. I will not be. So…'

She leaned back in her chair and balled her fists as she seemed to measure him out. 'How do you feel?'

I see we are very specific with the questions. 'It's hard to put into words…'

'You just did. Next question: have you ever thought about suicide?'

Holy shit. Holy shit. Holy shit.

'Now you're not even using words and you're still answering my questions. Have you seriously considered killing yourself?'

Oh shit, no! 'N-no! That's just it! I don't want to die!'

'You're scared of dying?' Her face never really moved; just her eyes when he spoke and her lips when she spoke.

Thomas paused as he thought about his father's advice again. 'Yes. Yes, it all started from that. Now… there are other things that bother me too. But that is still the main issue.'

'Are you scared of the act of death itself? Or what comes after?'

'What do you mean?'

'When you think about this *death* that worries you, do you visualise ways you might die? Burning alive? Drowning? Being crushed alive? Anything?'

'I mean I think about all the times I've been in mortal danger in the past... But, it's not about how I could die. It's about the fact that my existence would end with my body's death.'

'I see. So you fear the end of your existence?' Thomas nodded. 'Good. We all have good reason to be afraid of that. Do you fear it may be inevitable?'

'Well, it seems like it is.' *I mean I'm not delusional.*

'That's an assessment that shows you're still rational. In this last week, have you experienced feelings of choking or suffocation? Do your palms sweat? Are you finding it hard to focus on things you see or things you are thinking about?'

'Yes! Yes, I do. I also get hot flashes! I haven't been able to sleep. Sometimes things hurt, like my liver and my pancreas, even though I know I am healthy. I –'

'– That's enough. I get it! None of those things matter. You're having panic attacks. Has there been a drop in exercise in the last week?'

Had there been? I think there has been. 'Y-yes, there has?' He hadn't really thought about there being some causal relationship between the two. At least not seriously.

'There you go! The crisis started, you stopped exercising, your body felt that drop in physical exercise and it wasn't accustomed to it. Plus, there's a reason why we say that exercise is good for the mind. Start training or just exercise again and the panic attacks will go away.'

'Really?' *I doubt it's that simple.*

She turned her head sideways. 'The *panic attacks* will go away. The crisis will likely persist. So don't get too excited. Any regular psychoactive substance use?'

Now she sounds like a medical practitioner. 'I mean I sometimes smoke pot and drink, but…'

'*Regular*. I'm asking if you're a *regular* user. I'm not asking you if you get wasted at the Academy or in the Host. I am asking you if *you* believe that you are a regular consumer of anything with a psychoactive effect.'

'I mean I don't think I am, but what if I am and I can't comprehend it?'

'Good question! Do you drink or smoke or get high in any way every day?'

'No.' *I'm not some fucking savage...*

'Do you ever get high by yourself?'

Well... I might be a little savage '...sometimes.'

She rolled her eyes. 'When was the last time?'

'Like… a few months ago.' *I think?*

Opera nodded, as if in agreement. 'You're not a drug addict. If you don't trust yourself in that assessment, then trust *me*, I'm a doctor. Moving on, feelings of dissociation?'

'Yes.'

'Do you feel trapped in your body?'

'What? No!' *I am the fucking body. For now, at least. If it dies. I die.*

'Then just an awareness that your body and mind are in a way separate, though not *separated*?'

'Yes.' *Yes. I am a living human being. That's usually how that works.*

'That's alright. What do your loved ones – parents, friends, lovers, the people close to you – what do they think? Have they noticed a change in you in the last week?'

'My parents I told. My friends couldn't tell what was happening.' *At least I hope they couldn't.*

'No lover?'

'Not… not now. No.'

'Have you recently exited a long-term relationship?'

'No.'

'Alright. Regular sexual interactions?'

'I… I wouldn't call it regular.'

'Ok. I do not need to know all the details. Are you having enough sex?'

'I… What's enough?'

Bokha rolled her eyes. 'Would you like to have more sex?'

'Well… well, I mean ever since this started I haven't wanted to have sex at all. But, before I wanted to have more.'

'Much more or a little more?'

'Somewhere in the middle, I guess?'

'Normal sexual impulses and normal sexual regularity for a bachelor of your age group, then.' She looked to him for confirmation, as if she didn't already know the answer.

'Yes – wait! I mean... that's your assessment? You don't even know if enough sex for me is daily, twice a day or once a week!'

'I don't really need too. You told me you have more-or-less *irregular* sexual interactions and that you would like to have more sex. All I can say is: get a lover! It's great for both of those problems. Hell, it's better for the other person's problems too! From a medical perspective, you have the normal urges of a bachelor of your age. So, please, can I move on?'

'Wait. So – about the drinking – I am not an alcoholic because I don't *think* I am and I don't do it every day? What if I do it every other day but I go really hard on that day?'

'Well... do you?'

'No! But that's not what I am asking.'

'I know and the answer is: "basically yes". You don't exhibit any signs of a particular pattern of addiction or pathology. However, those pathologies that have no outside signs tend to result in the people suffering from them being honest with their assessment of their situation.'

'But what if I'm lying to you or myself?'

'If I couldn't tell, then that's just how some things are. Everyone makes mistakes and nothing is certain. I assume you've been thinking about the last part quite a lot in recent days, haven't you?'

'Yes. Yes I have.'

'Before you went to Ronan O'Malley, the man who recommended you to General Adler…' She was about to ask another question, but she stopped upon noticing the confused look on his face. 'I've read your file – your *whole* file – and Shoshanna also called me after your interview to brief me on you. That's how I know these things.'

'You... you read my file?'

'Yes.'

'My whole file?'

'Jesus Christ… Yes! What do you think I've been doing for the last four hours?'

'Oh… nothing… I … and you assessed from my whole file that I am… medically and psychologically fine?'

'A bit narcissistic. Very subtly autistic. Some antisocial tendencies. Neuroticism is a little high, but reasonably within normal parameters.' She raised a hand in the air, indicating his position between respective parameters whilst also giving him a funny look. 'Mentally sane. Perfectly capable of sound judgement. Just going through something which looks a lot like a mental breakdown, but seems to be entirely different.'

'How could this not be a mental breakdown?'

'Well, it could be. I just don't think it is. Mental breakdowns can only truly be identified after they occur. They also can't truly be stopped; just delayed. As it unfolds, the acute phase of an existential crisis can just look like the person is merely dealing with some inner turmoil. Which you *do* look like you are.'

'So, I *could* be having a mental breakdown?'

'Oh, but everyone could. Just that most people don't really get them out of nowhere and you don't really look like you are.'

'Yes, but how do you *know* that?'

'I don't. I'm just reasonably sure of both the fact that it's neither what is happening now, nor something that will happen in the future… Do you ever hear voices?'

Thomas' face went pale, but he felt as though he had to plough through this thing at this point. 'It all started with a voice.'

'You hear one voice? Other than your own?' Bokha actually looked a little surprised now.

'Yes. I did once.'

'When?'

'When it started. It started with a voice telling me: *Enjoy this while it lasts. Because one day you'll die.*'

Bokha was not impressed. '*Tsk*… A voice in your head said that?'

'Yes.' He had also come to believe that he was becoming a schizophrenic.

'*Inside* your head! Not outside? Like you heard a voice with your ears?'

'No. Of course not!' *Who the fuck hears voices outside their... Ohhh...*

Bokha put her hand to her head. 'Oh my God! Muller! Having *a thought* does not qualify as an auditory hallucination!'

She put her hand down and started looking through him. 'Yeah. There's no need to go on with this. You're ok. You're mentally apt,' she started typing on a screen next to her, 'and. Of. Sound. Judgement... Experiencing... Existential... Crisis... In the acute phase. *Good!*' she pronounced. 'Sign here, please.' She handed him her screen. 'This is the mindwipe agreement. It applies for both the selection procedure and the entirety of Project Kralizec in perpetuity.' She stared off into space for a moment.

'Or at least until it is declassified.'

Thomas held the screen. The document was quaint. No more than a few paragraphs on a single page. It didn't attest to anything more than what Bokha or Ashaver and Adler had said. He saw that, if the Terran High Command, together with the leadership of Project Kralizec, agreed to mindwipe him for selected memories pertaining directly to Kralizec, he consented that they had his acknowledgement and agreement to proceed.

Pfff... this whole thing is so surreal, I still haven't decided if it's all just my imagination. So, fuck it! Who gives a fuck if don't remember any of it. That might even be for the better.

Thomas allowed the screen to scan his bio signature and clicked the 'consent' icon.

'Excellent. Accommodation has been allocated to you in Jerusalem. You'll receive the address in a few minutes. However, your things have likely not arrived yet. Which is great, because you have somewhere else to be.'

'I... I do?'

'Yes. Dinner.'

'Oh...' Thomas was startled.

'With Laur Pop.' She said the name so casually.

WHAT?!?!?! 'Now?' *Did she really just say Laur. Fucking. Pop?*

Bokha was surprised 'You thought it was tomorrow?'

'General Adler said I had an interview with someone handling security was tomorrow morning.' *But she didn't mention it'd be with the fucking Lord Inquisitor himself.*

'Yes, well... not even Shoshanna Adler can convince Laur Pop to wake up early in the morning. You're having dinner with him in... forty minutes, at his villa in Harnof. Are you experiencing any loss of appetite? Not now, I mean in the last week or month?'

Fuck you! 'I... a little.' *I feel like I'm gonna throw up.*

'Oh, you'll be fine then. Laur makes great food.'

He's also the scariest man on Terra.

Chapter VI
Riddles in the Dark

Laur Pop's house was on a hill overlooking Jerusalem.

It wasn't as much a house as it was an actual villa built in the Italian style of a masseria, seemingly more in place in the Apulian countryside, rather than atop the hills of Palestine. The two storey building had white colonnades all around and a courtyard observably nestled within, which Thomas drove through, as directed by Silvia Murărescu, one of Laur Pop's centurions, who had sent him the formal dinner invitation after he had left Bokha's office.

He parked the shuttle in the courtyard, which surrounded a white marble water fountain depicting statues of crying baby angels and galloping horses. *As oldtimey as you'd expect.* As he got out, he realised that there was loud music coming from somewhere in the house. He recognized Pink Floyd's *Dark Side of the Moon* instantly. He also noticed a selection of luxury cars, parked throughout the courtyard. His own Mercedes looked cheap by comparison.

After closing the car door, he made his way to the balcony where he had seen Laur Pop and his entourage seated as he had descended to land. *Thank God I was going slow! I almost fainted when I saw them. I actually fainted a little when they turned to look at me.* He had recognized some of them as members of Thomas Ashaver's Old Guard, as well as Pop's own Hajduks.

Laur Pop, unlike Thomas Ashaver, was not a Hierarch, meaning that he had never been Warchief of the Republican Alliance. Yet, he still had his own Legion, just that it was of the Avenger variety. The Balkan Hajduks were an Avenger Legion of Terra, one of almost a hundred elite warbands which acted as the elite of Terra's military. They stood above regular Terran society (which was one giant warband to begin with) and were commanded and formed to protect either Terran Generals, Representatives or the Marshal of Terra himself. Though technically outranked by Hierarch Legions (such as the Old Guards), it was tradition that they informally see themselves as equals, since both groups were part of the very pinnacle of Terran martial skill and experience.

As was standard for an Avenger Legions, the Hajduks had an identity based on the ethnic make-up of its members. About a third of the Hajduks were Romanian, with the rest being members of the old Terran nations of Yugoslavia, Hungary Albania, Bulgaria, as well as a large contingent of Kalo. The initial Hajduks were formed when Laur Pop pieced together a guerrilla force composed of the surviving members of the intelligence communities of the above nations, coupled with some of the surviving elements of the Greek, Turkish, Ukrainian and Russian militaries, after the First Death of Thomas Ashaver at the Battle of Bicaz. In the weeks leading up to Doomsday, this force proved to be mildly successful in hindering the elven takeover of Central Europe. After the end of the War of Vengeance, the Ukrainian members had formed their own Cossack Legion, with the Russians formed the Druzhina Legion. Years later, following the Senoyu War, the Greek contingent also departed to form the Cataphracts and the Turkish contingent had formed the Akinjis naught but a few weeks later.

The commander of the Hajduks was the man who got up from his dinner table to greet Thomas. Laur Pop was one of the few people alive whose name ignited more fear in the hearts of Terrans than it did for outsiders. That was not to say that he wasn't held in great regard and love by his people, just that his past deeds carried a certain weight which could not easily be forgotten.

He was a friendly man and remarkably down-to-earth, particularly for an oldtimer, though his dark brown eyes did have a certain menace about them; a menace which he hid with a charismatic charm. Before the End Times, Laur had been a Romanian Domestic Intelligence officer. Unlike Ashaver, who tracked down Islamic terror cells for a living before the End Times, Laur was a product of counterintelligence, something that had carried over into his new life, as his infamous nickname, *the Lord Inquisitor,* attested too. He had earned this title by being one of the chief architects of the event known as the Last Fitna, the great purge which occurred on Terra after the War of Vengeance's conclusion and the last time in history when Terran had slain Terran.

The legends spoke of how Thomas Ashaver, Djibril al Sayid, together with the rest of the Terran High Command had met in a dark bunker on the island of Tristan da Cunha, to hear Laur Pop read out loud the names of those that were to be purged. A list he himself had compiled. Some say that though some changes were made to the list by those in attendance, the final list was more-or-less the one the Lord Inquisitor had presented to the conspirators. Laur Pop was also the one that had proposed the rule which would later become the First Law of the Terran Constitution.

'A Terran shall never kill another Terran. The penalty is imprisonment in isolation for the duration of natural life.'

He had also followed this up by being the champion enforcer of this policy, to go with his participation in the purges of the Last Fitna.

These two actions stood at the core of Laur Pop's image in the eyes of other Terrans. On the one hand, perhaps no one had dedicated more of their life to assuring Terran unity. On the other hand, he was a living grim reminder of the dark and treacherous nature of life on Old Earth before the End Times. A nature he himself had helped extinguish with a particularly cold brand of savagery.

Though the man who smiled at him now, as he shook his hand, did not seem to be a treacherous savage. He made a joke about how he knew Thomas' mother was Vietnamese and how they had luckily chosen not to make Vietnamese pho that evening, and had opted for a Spanish paella. He said he wanted Thomas to tell his mother about how he had eaten an amazing paella, as opposed to a mediocre pho. He insisted that he sit down and eat with them before the interview, which they could conduct privately in his study.

This was how Thomas found himself having dinner next to Marco Acosta and Silvia Murărescu. Any other man would've been awestruck and overwhelmed to find himself of such a beautiful and legendary warrior as Centurion Murărescu, yet Thomas found himself much more transfixed on Sergeant Major Acosta.

After being seated, he had received little more than a nod and a handshake from Acosta and (maybe) Murărescu had also nodded. Maybe she had even smiled slightly as he had sat down; he was not sure. They had only started eating a few minutes before his arrival and Pop had insisted that he join in while the paella was still fresh off the heat. Thomas had smiled awkwardly and had proceeded to fill his plate from the giant metal plate on which the paella had apparently been cooked on from start to finish.

Not too much. He didn't want to seem like a scrounger.

Not too little either, he didn't want to seem ungrateful.

When asked from across the table by one of the Old Guards, whose name he knew to be Abhijoy Mukherjee, if the food was good, he politely responded that it was great. Murărescu had poured him a glass of sweetened wine and Acosta had even passed him the condiments (without saying much, not even asking Thomas if he even wanted condiments to begin with).

Right after this quick introduction, the table, occupied by Pop, eight of his Hajduks and three Old Guards, proceeded to talk about how Orcish rugby was like American Football, but with beach volleyball equipment and less people. Someone proposed that they should organize an Alliance Cup for something athletic. The general consensus was that Orcish rugby would make a great Alliance Cup. Then arguments began over how ursai couldn't participate, since having ten bear people – weighing at least four hundred kilograms each – chasing humans and orcs so that they could take their balls away, was downright ridiculous.

This was what they talked about?!

Thomas had expected tales of old battles, debates on the current state of the military and serious strategizing regarding potential defences against future threats. If not that, then perhaps they would discuss history, the world of their childhood, or debate modern policies or politics. Perhaps the most recent scientific revelations?

But no, for over half-an-hour Thomas watched these martial champions talk about goblin sitcoms, elven food, orcish sports and Vanir music. They spoke about seeing remani eating with forks and it being hilarious. They told jokes about demani and debated the best orcish mantras. They discussed the films of Roberto Rossellini and goblin neo-noir cinema. They argued about whether or not Volvos were still the safest cars manufactured on Terra, as they had apparently been before the End Times. One explained why he was growing a vineyard and another why he had decided to raise chickens. There were jokes about hobgoblin steroid use and about English food still being terrible. All the while, they laughed, and ate, and drank, and excused themselves to go to the bathroom, and smoked, and argued about what music they should listen to and they did all of this throughout the *entire* evening.

Though he had at first followed the conversation, Thomas found it hard to focus on the continuous stream of pop culture references and commentary, no matter how witty, well-articulated or informed it may have been. It was hard, particularly when something else had captivated him from the moment he had sat down. He had rather quickly become aware of the fact that, at this very table, there was someone who had come back from the dead. Several, actually.

The initial Terran Old Guard had been formed by Thomas Ashaver in the aftermath of Doomsday (also known as the First Battle of Terra). The initial membership was limited to those who had come to be known as 'death knights', with the first name of the warband which would become the Old Guard being the *Death Knights of Terra*.

These men and women were those Terran soldiers and warriors which had waged war with such ferocity against the elves that the invaders had decided that they were likely to provide genuine entertainment as reanimated corpses, despite varying degrees of memory loss and the suppression of their free will. Upon their death, their bodies had been swiftly collected by the elves, placed in stasis and transported to their flagship, the *Marlafior*. There, elven biomancers had healed and enhanced their bodies, reversed their neural decay (with the notable exception of some memories which had been forever lost) and connected them to what the death knights would refer to as 'Evil Wifi', the elven telepathic web which had negated their sense of self. Under its direction, the elves had played with them as gladiators, pitching them against one another in the lounges of elven officers, as their world burned beneath them.

But, at the climatic peak of Doomsday, when the orcish Worldship Vigilant had arrived to join the great battle, some death knights succeeded in breaking free from the grip of the web and fought alongside the orcs that had successfully boarded the elven flagship. Together, they deactivated the modem which was generating the Evil Wifi, allowing the other surviving death knights to regain their senses. When Doomsday ended, over four hundred death knights had rejoined their people on Terra.

More than half of their number had died in the decades that followed, and one of the surviving one hundred and sixty-nine lay next to him, putting extra hot sauce on his shrimp paella. This was a man who had died and had returned bearing the terrible truth of death. Some had seen their lives flash before their eyes, a few claimed to have had some vision of an afterlife.

A vision which then had faded to black. They hadn't come back from an afterlife. They said that it had been like sleeping and waking up to a dream: inhabiting your body, but with no control or even comprehension of one's own actions. Nonetheless, it had been a dreamless sleep before that rudest of awakenings.

Nowadays, the original death knights made up slightly over half of the Old Guard. The other two Old Guards, Abhijoy Mukherjee (known as the 'Bonegnasher', due to reasons pertaining to an event involving a mandrake and a hammer) and Xing Ye (more commonly known as 'Yellow River Charlie'), though recent additions, were still both oldtimers.

Abhijoy was well-known amongst Terrans for his exceptionally good-natured and joyful personality. He was known for frequently using a thick Bengali accent during combat situations, despite speaking perfect English and knowing full well that confusing language was explicitly against regulation during battle. He did so for so for no strategic reason whatsoever, other than to raise the morale of his comrades, who had come to find his shtick to be quite entertaining. He had been a commercial airline pilot before the End Times and, as one of the Old Guard, his role had become that of a shock trooper.

Yellow River Charlie's origin story involved hiding for over a month in the actual Yellow River of China, deep in occupied territory. When the ruins of Yuncheng were liberated, he had emerged from the river and had almost been shot on sight. This would have been understandable since he had somehow managed to acquire a full set of elven armour and weaponry. In the World-Which-Was, he had just finished high school, right as the Fimbulwinter had forced schools to shut down all over the world. Both he and Mukherjee had experienced both death and reanimation, for that was the one essential prerequisite for being invited to be a member of the Old Guard.

Marco Acosta had been a Mexican police officer in the state of Guerrero with a freelance career working for the Sinaloa Cartel. He had died ambushing an elven column in the jungles of Central America, but not after warranting resurrection for a rampage which had claimed dozens of elven lives.

Does he still have it? Does he actually wear it?

Thomas moved forwards ever so slightly. Acosta was wearing a plain white Terran shirt, the seal of the Old Guard etched on his chest, a subtle silver on white. Yet, it wasn't this icon which Thomas was dying to see. No. He wanted to see if Acosta really did wear a...

'It's not a Santa Muerte anymore.'

Thomas was shocked. Acosta had noticed him. The Old Guard turned to look at him and smiled. He put his hand beneath his shirt collar and pulled out a black cloth necklace. On it was etched the image of a small child, dressed in blue and red. He gestured for Thomas to hold it and look at it.

'My son, Esteban, has the Santa Muerte one now.' Thomas, awestruck, held the escapulario in his hand and studied it intently now. Acosta's escapulario of Santa Muerte had been a famous artefact of legend. He had fashioned it himself in the months following Doomsday. Death symbols were common on Terra. After all, in a society obsessed with the past, when the past was so full of death, the present became saturated with macabre imagery and dark colours. The capital ship of the Old Guard themselves, the *Naglafar*, was plated not with smooth darkplate, like other Terran warships, but with ebony weirdplate, with skulls and bones encrusted across the entire surface of the ship. By comparison, Acosta's old escapulario of a white skull etched on a black background had seemed almost cheerful.

'What is this one?' Thomas asked.

'This one? Santo Nino de Antocha. My old escapulario. Well. Not the old one itself. This is a new one I made. You have bad luck. I gave Santa Muerte to my son last week. He finished his Allied Host service. He joined the Otomi Legion. Like you, he always looked at it and asked questions and wanted to know more. I told him that one day, if he earned it, it would be his. And he earned it last week. Like you.' Acosta raised his hand and pointed at Thomas. 'I will make you one. If I see you again, it will be yours.'

'I...thank you! I mean there's no need...'

'Never there is "need"! Sometimes there is "want". I look at you. I see you. You deserve one too. You would like it.'

And that was it. Acosta didn't speak to him for the remainder of the evening. He went back to arguing that next time they be allowed to make chimichangas, taquitos and maybe even some 'actual Mexican food which we eat in Mexico' since 'Spanish food was just boring Mexican food for white people'.

How? Was he mad? Had he always been mad? Had he gone mad? This was a man that had died and who had seen that there was nothing after death. And here he was wearing a religious talisman on his neck. This was a man that had not only seen the skies rain down hellfire, but had danced among the flares of hellfire in orbit across dozens of worlds. He had seen demani tech so advanced it looked like actual magic and had fought *demons* and *spawn*. He had seen the infinite expanse of civilizations and life across the universe and knew it ranged so far and wide across the stars that none knew where the edge lay, *if* it lay.

That knowledge didn't seem to matter to him here. The law didn't seem to matter that much to him either. Oldtimers insisted that they were not true believers but, then again, it was always they who wore the crosses and the arm bracelets. They were the ones who had statues of fat men and blue people in their houses. It was they who got upset if a black cat crossed their path and if you didn't wash your hands before touching some book in their library. *They* always celebrated Christmas and Diwali. But could *they* possibly actually believe?

Did they think about it? If they didn't, how was it possible for them to not think about it? How could they be so cheerful if they thought about it? Thomas spiralled in and out of these ideas, until Laur Pop placed a hand on his shoulder and said that it was time they spoke.

They left the merry assembly below and entered the villa, stopping by the kitchen. Pop insisted that Thomas have a drink. After several polite refusals, he finally succumbed to another glass of sangria, while Pop made himself a cappuccino.

His office lay on the first floor overlooking the city. A wide balcony with pillows, screens, a water pipe and small table laden with fresh fruit lay outside the office. In the distance, one could see the flickering lights of Jerusalem as the city tucked itself into bed. Laur Pop bid him take a seat at his desk, as he closed the balcony doors.

His office was very disorderly. It was the exact opposite of Shoshanna Adler's immaculate minimalist design. While her office had been centred around one large piece of Terran history, Pop's was littered with smaller mementos of the past, present and future. Books, screens and artefacts of hundreds of cultures of dozens of worlds lay scattered all around. Thomas saw an orc houseblade crossed with a Japanese katana and an elven razorblade on a wall above what appeared to be a demani pensive plate. The head of a great buaram, from the forests of the Primal Elf world of Pandora lay on another wall, next to a bookcase full of tomes, grimoires, dictionaries and manuals. Everything was scattered all across the room, with the exception of the floorboards in the middle, where Pop's desk and chairs lay.

Yet, the room, overall, was also somehow harmonious. This last aspect was lost on Thomas, as the flurry of thoughts evoked by all the things within the office, coupled with his overall sense of uncertainty regarding his circumstances, gave him neither peace nor the ability to enjoy this place. It didn't really occur to him that he would have otherwise been overjoyed to explore and linger among Pop's artefacts.

'So, did you enjoy dinner?' Pop sat down in the armchair that served as his office chair and began clearing a corner of his desk by shifting what was in excess to a distant corner, thus making room for one lone screen which he placed before him.

'Yes, sir. It was great.' *I don't remember any flavour but I'm certain it was wonderful.*

'I didn't ask if it was great, though I am glad it was. I am asking you if you enjoyed it.'

Oh, ok. He's another one of these weird mind-reading people I've had been seeing for the last six hours. Fuck it. Lemme skip the bullshit. They all seem to appreciate that.

'No, sir. It was hard to enjoy the dinner given that I have no idea what I was doing attending it. I honestly don't even know I am here. Do *you* know why I am here?'

Laur Pop smiled a strange smile upon hearing Thomas' words. He had initially seemed annoyed, yet his eyes switched to a wide-eyed... wonder, almost. He did, however, answer swiftly.

'Yes. You are here, because you do not know why you're here. And,' Pop opened a drawer to pull out a cigarette and a lighter, 'that makes you important.' He lit his cigarette and continued. 'So, how has your day been?'

This wasn't a question to Thomas though, since the General began speaking before he had a chance to answer. 'You woke up – probably freaking out over the immortality of the soul and whatnot – in your hotel room in Baffin. You met Shosho and Tomasz, expecting to meet only her and interview for some job working on some minefield or portal works or whatever – you probably didn't care that much anyway, so why should I bother making something up?'

'After all, you only went there because your father and mother told you to listen to Ronan O'Malley's advice. You had no *other* solution to what you're dealing with so you said: "Come on. Fuck it. Let's try this. Maybe it'll be good for me". At worst, you might just distract yourself long enough to make the whole thing you're dealing with go away for a little while.'

'Then, all of a sudden you're pulling dicks with Tomasz Ashaver, you're being sent to Jerusalem under orders of extreme discretion, and now you're having dinner with Old Guards and Hajduks.'

'I guess that's a good summary of how you ended up here? On a step-by-step basis?'

'Y-yes.' Thomas didn't know what 'pulling dicks with Thomas Ashaver' meant, but he assumed it was just some Romanian expression that got lost in translation.

'Alright. Now let me explain why all of that happened and – just so you know – I'm not going to explain *why* you are here, just why we did what we did –'

'– Project Kralizec.' *Please let's just cut it to chase. I literally can't bear it anymore.*

Laur Pop balled his right hand into a fist, causing ash to fall from his lit cigarette onto his closed hand. 'Well… fucking shit, has *everyone* forgotten the meaning of fucking discretion?' He looked around, spotting an ashtray, then proceeded to throw away the ash from his hand.

His tone wasn't angry. Just very aggressive. He looked up to see Thomas' worried look.

'Yes! Yes, goddammit, Project Kralizec – though the idea was that you wouldn't know that name until tomorrow. Well,' he placed his cigarette in the ashtray and pressed a symbol on his screen, 'no point in beating around the bush any more than we have to...'

He got up from his seat in one quick motion and moved towards the bookshelves on Thomas' right. At the same moment, to Thomas' left, shutters descended over the windows facing the balcony, obscuring the city beyond.

'Do you read, Lieutenant Muller?' Thomas couldn't see what Pop was doing, though he did seem to be rummaging around through the mess on one of his shelves.

'Yes, sir.'

'Ah! Fiction? Or just manuals and that sort of thing?'

'I… yes, fiction too.'

'Good. Terran?'

'Sometimes.'

'Russian?'

'I have, yes.'

'Really? What was the last Russian book you read?'

'I… I read *The Brothers Karamazov* last week.'

Pop had stopped his rummaging. He turned his head slightly. 'Oh. Have you read *The Idiot*? Also by Dostoyevsky?'

'No, sir.' Thomas heard a click behind him. Normally, he wouldn't have given it much thought, but a heavy silence had descended upon the room after the window shutters had locked in position and Pop's rummaging had stopped. At first he thought it had come from the door, yet when he turned, he saw the door still sealed shut.

Pop had not continued his questioning.

As he shifted to face forward towards Pop's, now empty, desk he saw something out of the corner of his right eye. He slowly turned, only to look down the barrel of a handgun.

A Berretta style Terran handgun, with Laur Pop's emotionless face behind it. Thomas saw Pop flick a screen on his hip and heard a very low humming sound. He looked down to see, to his horror, the marble floor begin to subtly glow.

A stasis field.

'You know what a stasis field is?' Thomas twitched at Pop's words. He met the General's eyes.

'Yes.' *They're many things.*

'You know what they're used for? In this context?'

'Yes.' *They're used for blowing my brains out without any evidence of you doing it remaining. Even the sound of your gun going off would be absorbed.*

'Good. Now, listen to me very carefully, Thomas. I am only going to say this once: all that you have to do is convince me that you know that I am not going to shoot you and, if you do, I won't shoot you.'

'...w-what?'

Pop cocked the pistol as he saw Thomas tensing up. 'Eh! Eh! Don't move!' Thomas still had his own handgun, as well as his sword. 'I would kill you way before you'd even have time to twitch a single muscle in the slightest direction of your gun. Do not move!' Pop had never raised his voice. 'Now, what did I say about listening carefully?'

'Convince. You. That I know. That you. Are not going to kill. Me.' Thomas wasn't gonna try quoting him exactly.

'Good! Almost word-for-word. Now, take your time – but not *too* much time – and explain why that's not going to happen.'

Thomas looked up in horror at the Romanian.

'Pop stared back coldly.

'It's illegal?' Thomas knew it was said as an answer but meant as a question.

'Because it's the law? What is the law? Our law? No! 2 plus 2 is 4. Objects attract each other. $E=mc^2$. Those are laws. *True* laws. Our *human* law isn't true! It's not real. It is something we made up. No! Not because it's illegal. Try again.'

'You'd get caught.' He wouldn't.

'That's what the stasis field is for. You're not giving good answers. Focus, Thomas. Actually. Let's do it like this. You have one more chance to convince me that you don't believe I will kill you and if you fuck it up we find out the other way what I'm going to do.'

Thomas could tell from the way Pop held the gun that it was loaded. The slight sheen of a metal round was visible down the barrel. He had been trained to see such details, yet he never thought he would be applying that knowledge in this kind of situation.

Pop was right. There was nothing stopping him from killing him.

Somehow, he bought it. He bought that Pop was willing to murder some lowly sunriser lieutenant in his office for the sake of some test. Maybe he and the other oldtimers did this all the time. Maybe they were great at it and that's why no one ever found out. He looked the oldtimer in the eye and saw the coldness there. About half of oldtimers were known to be at least slightly sociopathic, yet Pop seemed to be far over the edge of morality. His reputation, though propped up by his dedication to Terran unity, was nevertheless shadowed by the knowledge that he was a dark man who had written death lists as those named had celebrated their triumph against the Enemy.

If there was ever a Terran who would kill another Terran, it was Laur Pop.

In that moment, a ray of hope flickered in Thomas' heart.

It was all too perfect. It was all too staged. This whole situation didn't make any sense outside of this room. Why give him the personal car knowing there was a chance he might not be around to drive it? Why give him a check-up to see if he was sane? If this was some test and he failed, couldn't they just mindwipe him and get it over with?

Then again, perhaps this was the punishment for the thoughts he had been having. Maybe this was why he felt so alone and why no one seemed to understand. Maybe this was what happened to Terrans who had these thoughts. There might be no Project Kralizec and it might all just be some elaborate execution.

But, then again, *why*? The only thing that seemed to make sense was the fact that he was in danger at this moment. Yet, everything before that seemed to have been part of a completely different story. Why make him go through all of this? *Why all the lies?* Every fibre of his being told him to trust the people that had guided him down this journey. What they had all had in common was that they all had good reason to care for his well being. His mother and father loved him. They trusted Ronan absolutely.

Why would Ashaver want him dead? Ashaver wasn't like Pop. He had participated in the *Last Fitna*, yes, but he was one of the few who spoke publicly about how it haunted him. He had spent the last forty years, together with men and women like Pop, making sure that their people would survive in a cruel and cold universe and not tear themselves apart, as they had in the World-Which-Was.

For perhaps less than an instant in time, a sense of calm flickered in his mind. Yet, it was all that was needed for Thomas to piece together an answer.

'There is no reason for me to be alive, yes. Yet, there's also no reason for me to be dead,' he blurted out.

'Maybe the reason is that I would take pleasure from it.' Pop answered back quickly, his face showing no emotion.

'Well then shoot me and be done with it!' Thomas was shocked at the words coming out of his mouth. 'Because if Thomas Ashaver and Shoshanna Adler and Ronan O'Malley and my mother and my father sent me here to die for your pleasure then, truly, nothing makes sense anymore!'

Pop had taken a slight step back as Thomas had begun to lean forward in his seat. He had almost bumped heads with the pistol as the rage had overcome him.

Thomas leaned back, slowly, into his chair. 'Yes. You can kill me. It wouldn't make any sense to me. But, what the fuck do I know? Nothing makes sense anymore!' he repeated, as he looked down, aghast.

His words rang true. Perhaps not to Pop, but for sure to himself. Nothing made any sense. The world, as had known it a week ago, was gone; perhaps forever. In this new world, he understood how he understood nothing –

His thoughts were cut off as the window shutters began to lift. He turned to see Pop re-rummaging through the shelf, with his back to him.

Without turning to face him, the General spoke. 'If you would've known me better, you would've known that I don't like waste. If you would've known that, you could've just said that I wouldn't have fed you if I knew there was a chance I'd put a bullet in you later. But, I know you don't know me and – more importantly – I was looking for a different answer.' He finished his work on the shelf, as the pistol now once more lay hidden behind a copy of Cormac McCarthy's *The Road.*

He turned to Thomas. 'Which you gave,' he said, as he made his way back to his seat. 'Let me explain what this was for.' Pop sat down in his armchair and picked up his cigarette, now almost burnt out. It was only then that Thomas realised that, while only a few seconds had passed for him, several minutes had gone by in real time.

'Up until this moment, you were just the right person at the right time. Now, you're also special. At first there was nothing distinct about you, other than circumstance. Now you've also been selected. Let me explain to you how.' Pop took a sip of his coffee, licked the foam off his upper lip, and then placed the cup back on its coaster.

'We have been working on Project Kralizec for over two years now. Six, if you count all the deliberation and preparation that had to be done to get the ball rolling. A few months ago, we decided that we needed people who were undergoing an *acute* existential crisis. We wanted to test certain assumptions we have by bouncing them off minds which have not yet undergone the entire process that comes with overcoming such a crisis. Minds which that have not yet decided upon a worldview. Minds that are not asleep, yet not fully awake either. Minds in the exact moment of awakening. Minds like yours.'

'A week ago, we started screening and searching. Certain people – such as your friend Ronan – were told to report to High Command if they came across anyone who fit the criteria we were looking for. Tomasz and Shosho volunteered to conduct the first week of interviews. Their role was to make sure that the subjects were, indeed, going through an actual existential crisis. They found you and, hopefully, you won't be the last one they find.'

'After Tomasz and Shosho confirmed your acute phase, we sent you to the good Dr. Bokha, to make sure that you're not *actually* going crazy. This was not something we expected to be the case, but, we had to be sure. And then, it was my turn.'

He leaned back in his armchair. Thomas had been listening to every word transfixed.

Pop lit up another cigarette. 'You see. We estimate that, given enough time and the adequate context, most people will develop an existential crisis; at least in some form. However, what we need for Project Kralizec is someone who can trust us and whom we can also trust. I determined that you were trustworthy rather quickly. Yet, I needed to be certain that, no matter how much what you've been going through might have affected you, you still knew the baseline reality you inhabit. A reality in which you trust those around you.'

'You and your entire generation have been taught to trust those around you. Hell, I would even go as far as to use the word "indoctrinated". However, when pondering the mysteries of existence, some people find themselves... *detaching* from what makes them... *people*. There is a chance for some people to lose themselves in their struggle against revelation. Such people, we have determined, should not be part of Project Kralizec. At least, not at this stage.'

'Your answer was that your world would not make any sense if those you trusted betrayed you. Which means that the love of those you hold dear, your trust in those around you, and your faith in our way of life are your last line of defence against the void of nihilism and despair. And that line of defence still stands.' Pop let his words linger in the air as he studied Thomas' wide-eyed expression.

'Welcome to Project Kralizec. You start tomorrow at nine am. Noah Street, number 314.'

Chapter VII
Happily Ever After in the Hereafter

'Good morning everyone! To those of you new to Project Kralizec, perhaps you might be wondering why we chose to conduct the most secretive project in Terran history out here in Jerusalem.' General Adler's voice was the same pitch and tone it had been during their meeting overlooking Baffin Bay. Yet, it carried the same weight in the amphitheatre they now found themselves in, as it had in her spacious office. Hardly impressive, given the eager and, remarkably, tense, silence that filled the room.

'After all, one of the use cases put forward when the construction of the Polar Shields was first proposed, was that they could help hide that which was most important to the survival of our people. I know, having spoken with each of you, that you would all agree, that this is perhaps the endeavour most essential to the *eternal* survival of our people.'

Adler paused. At first, Thomas thought she did so to let the importance of her words sink in. However, he quickly remembered who her audience was and how they had come together.

Around three dozen people lay scattered around the amphitheatre, built to seat around a couple of hundred. Adler spoke from the stage at its centre, sitting behind a podium bearing the seal of the Nation of Israel, a six-pointed star, on a white and blue background. In the semi-circle located in front of her were scattered around thirty Terrans, including Thomas, who had picked out a place for himself in the seventh row. He had arrived twenty minutes early, thanks to another sleepless night. His existential crisis and Laur Pop's eccentric interview methods had shown him no mercy, as Thomas' heart would begin to pound every few minutes or so, as his mind reminded him that his eyes had looked down the barrel of a gun.

Just as General Adler had entered the room and began walking towards the podium, he had been startled by a loud *thump!* next to him. Someone had picked the seat right next to him, out of all the many other empty seats in the room.

Well, it looks like Ashaver hasn't succeeded in convincing her to stay away from Project Kralizec.

He had never been so close to Mira al Sayid before. He had seen her before, not just outside General Adler's office, the day before, but on many different occasions in the past. Sometimes in peace and sometimes in war. He had first seen her at the Janeiro Carnival, almost eight years before. They had shared the same German beer hall during an Oktoberfest almost seven years ago. They had trained on the same arena on the Vigilant naught but six years before.

They had walked past each other after the Battle of Astarte, during the Ayve War. She had entered the fray first, as one of the Ghazis, together with Thomas Ashaver's Old Guard and Sorbo Falk's Wildriders. Thomas' Allied Host battalion had followed, meeting the Aesir host after the Old Guard, Ghazis and Wildriders had borne the brunt of the fighting. He remembered the look on her face. Free of any shellshock, she scoured the battlefield for any signs of remaining resistance, her eyes blazing with a cold savagery which had taken Thomas aback. She hadn't spared him anything more than a passing glance, looking more at his uniform than at his face.

This time, after abruptly slouching on the seat next to his, she had performed a more pensive review of him. Recovering from her sudden appearance, Thomas had quickly blurted out a 'Hello, sir!' to which she hadn't replied. Moreover, she hadn't even moved a single muscle beyond those of her eyes, which simply locked with his own and immediately began picking at his mind. She had the gaze of an oldtimer, despite being a sunriser, like himself, albeit a little older, born on July thirtieth 19 BT.

Stop looking at her, she'll figure out you even know her birthday! Don't fanboy out for fuck's sake. Particularly now is not the time for that... Why do you even care? She's someone just like you. Her existence is meaningless and the significance you attribute to her due to her fame is little – nay – nothing more than –

He stopped himself.

Goddammit, that type of thinking is why we're here. Please shut it down and focus, at least for now. Look around the room, centre yourself.

And that was what he did, he looked around the room, to see who else was in attendance, all the while attempting to coyly ignore Al Sayid's glare. Though he did feel some relief when he saw, out of the corner of his eye, her head turn as she proceeded to do the same.

He saw the doctor from the day before, Opera Bokha, take a seat in one of the middle rows to his left, next to another doctor. To his astonishment, he recognized

Bokha's companion as the black guy from Adler's office. *It would appear he also made the cut. Is he going through the same thing?*

The front rows were populated by men and women bearing the seal of the Terran Engineering Corps, the flaming black cog on a white background proudly displayed on their shoulders. Thomas knew the symbol well, for he had grown up seeing it often around the house, since it was his father's Corps. Thomas could tell that most were not oldtimers, in part due to their attitude and in part due to the fact that the old timers seemed to have congregated in the back of the room. He had scouted them out as he had entered the room.

He had also recognized Abhijoy Mukherjee and Marco Acosta as he had walked in, with the Bengali waving towards him as he had entered. He had waved back, but now a moment of worry came over Thomas as he had realised that perhaps he should have sat down next to them, as the wave could have been an invitation.

The worry had quickly switched focus from the denial of the Bonegnasher's possible invitation, to the people who took their place behind the podium in front of him.

Of the four Terrans he saw, he recognized only Ruben Zaslani, General of the Sayeret. The oldtimer was well-known on Terra, having been the highest-ranking survivor of the Siege of Eilat, during the End Times. He had largely disappeared from public eye afterwards, with his name surfacing only in relationship to the Sayeret. The legion had maintained a quiet, yet active role, in Terra's many conflicts over the years.

The other three he didn't recognize, though he could tell from their demeanour and uniforms that they were also oldtimers. One, a Persian Colonel, also bore the emblem of the Engineering Corps. He sported a great black beard which did its best to hide a face which was very used to smiling. The contrast to the more stern-faced Zaslani sitting next to him was striking, if not downright humorous.

The third was another Colonel, a Gujarati woman, also an Engineer. Of the four, she was the most casually dressed, the only elements of her military uniform she had brought with her that morning being her standard melee weapon, which, in her case, was a dagger, and her service pistol. Her clothing was a standard Terran cotton tracksuit, of purple and ultramarine, with gold lines dividing the two. She had, however, had the seal of Gujarat and the logo of the Engineering Corps emblazoned on her shoulder, together with another symbol. Thomas recognized it immediately: a plain black circle, with two drops, (one red, one blue) situated within and strewn across a white background. It was the symbol of Sarasvati Singh's old Hierarch Legion: the Pandavas. During the End Times, the Pandavas had proven to be the most successful human force when it came to hacking into the elven systems. The team had survived the End Times, only to be almost completely destroyed during the events of Hellsbreach. The few survivors, of whom this Colonel appeared to be one, had been reorganised as part of the Engineering Corps, the Akali Legion and the Sepoys Legion, with the Pandavas being disbanded as a unit.

Thomas fought against the urge to look to his left, where he could see, at the edge of his vision, the young Arabian Captain take out a pair of small scissors. She then began trimming the tips of her long brown hair. She made no noise, but the flashing metal must have caught the eye of the Gujarati Colonel, who turned to stare right at her (visibly stifling a laugh) and winked slyly. Mira raised a hand to let out a subtle, yet cheerful, wave.

Well, I guess she's how Mira managed to work her way into this thing.

The fourth and final Terran was a Scandinavian Colonel of the Medical Corps. Fully bald, Thomas could see a series of runes adorn his bald white head, tattooed in bright blue. He was quite peculiar, in no small part due to the fact that he chose to be bald, but also because he wore eyeglasses. What need he might have for those, Thomas could not fathom. He had heard of some oldtimers having their glasses augmented and using them as a primitive user interface. Allowing oneself to have poor vision was illegal, as the Terran legal system explicitly forbade allowing one's combat ability to degrade in any way whilst being on duty.

Normally, Thomas would have pondered this question much more, had it not been for the fact that the three other people sitting behind Adler's podium were not human. At least, not one of them was a Terran human.

Sitting together, flanked by the four Terrans, were a remani, a troll and a Vanir human. Thomas instantly recognized Sorbo Falk, Hierarch of the Alliance. The old troll languished in his seat as he ostentatiously smiled and eavesdropped on the conversation between the Gujarati Colonel and the Vanir human to his left. To Falk's right, Thomas believed he could identify Basenji.

At least he thought he did; he always had a hard time telling remani apart.

If he speaks, it's not Basenji and I am lost. If he doesn't speak... probably Basenji.

As he tried to determine if it was indeed the legendary Basenji, he realised that the remani was looking at him. He saw his tail begin to wag, as he raised his hand to wave.

Thomas panicked.

He didn't know this remani. He was jet black and had an average length coat. No scars crossed his snout. He wasn't sure.

Why is he waving at me? Do I know him? Fuck it. We'll figure it out later. Wave back!

Thomas had raised his hand to awkwardly wave back, only to see the remani immediately lower his hand. His tail had also paused, but then it had wagged again.

Yet, it did so differently this time. Whereas it had first wiggled excitedly, now it just slapped the seat between his legs.

Thomas then heard Mira al Sayid snort.

This time he had been compelled to look towards her, only to see the young Captain covering her face, barely hiding a giggle.

Well, it is Basenji, but he wasn't happy to see me! He was waving at Mira, since he's known her ever since she was a baby.

I have just made a jackass of myself.

Mercifully, it was at this moment that Adler had begun to speak and he didn't have to bear the awkward moment for too long.

Thomas' recollection of the embarrassment was cut short as Adler finished gathering her words and continued speaking.

'Project Kralizec is only partially located here, in Jerusalem. The technological facilities necessary for the success of this operation are actually located twenty kilometres under the surface, throughout the Styx tunnel network, with the main facility, to which we will refer to as the Orpheus Chamber, being located beneath the Northern Shield.'

'I am the current Managing Officer of Project Kralizec. Behind me, are four Section heads. Colonel Zaslani is the Head of the Security Section. Colonel Hosseini is Head of the Translation Section. Colonel Patel is Head of the Inception Section. Colonel Rasmussen is Head of the Transient Section.'

She now addressed the room before her. 'Captains Diaoxing, Nguyen, Tsihisekedi and Mokokoane, together with Lieutenants Nakazawa, Kim, Tanaka, Ubuntu, Achebe, Chang, Arapovian, Kowalski, Moro, Ignatieff, Christchurch and Musonda, you are to report to Colonel Hosseini.' Adler surveyed the front row of engineers as she pronounced the names. Thomas could see heads nod as each officer acknowledged his assignment.

'Captains Lupo and Mapupu, together with Lieutenants Jackson, Hjalmar and Kendri, you will be reporting to Colonel Rasmussen.' Thomas saw those in the room bearing the emblem of the Medical Corps nod in acknowledgement.

'Captain al Sayid and Lieutenant Muller, you will be reporting to Colonel Patel.'

What the...? Thomas swiftly nodded. Captain al Sayid only gave a curt nod of approval, as her new colleague turned towards her, a look of confusion on his face. She swiftly nudged his elbow with her own, urging him to look towards Adler and spare her his questions, for now.

'As you all know at this point, Project Kralizec reports directly to the High Command. Our cover is that we are working on the repurposing of Continuum military technology. The subtext is that these are weapons of mass destruction. If anyone asks, that's your answer. However, in order to not raise suspicion, you will be provided with an entire legend detailing your cover story. You are allowed to employ this cover story at your discretion in circumstances where your silence could raise suspicion among your peers. Though you should bear in mind that you will be regularly interrogated concerning such instances. Colonel Zaslani will cover that more in-depth later on.'

Adler moved forward, resting her hands on the podium, as she had done the day before on the *Resolute Desk*. 'Now… onto the essence of things.' She let out an audible *pfff* as she blew a strand of hair from her face.

'I don't know if this is common knowledge among you but… *Everyone dies.*' Thomas felt his heart skip a beat as nervous laughter echoed from his half of the amphitheatre. *It's happening.*

'I was born in a time when that was evident. Albeit, in a different way than it is for you. When I was young, before the world changed, people died of old age, disease, car accidents, a sizable number died violently, but' she raised her eyebrows before continuing 'nothing like what was to come. We were restricted by our technology, but blessed by our ignorance. It was estimated that around one in fifteen people that had ever lived on Earth were alive when the Fimbulwinter began. That means that fourteen out of every fifteen people who had ever lived, were dead even before the End Times started.'

'As you all know, after the end of the War of Vengeance, only a fraction of our number survived. An unnumbered many were gone; taken from us by the hand of our Enemy and delivered onto the inescapable grasp of death. I look at you now, having just spoken with some of you and I feel the weight of the future you have before you. You will not die of strokes, cancers or plague. You will not die at the hands of an enemy which you will not be prepared to face. However, there will always be enemies we will never be able to prepare for. Some enemies, no matter how much we may deny, have a chance of ending us.' Thomas' heart skipped more beats.

'You've heard this all before. You understand the implications of what I am saying and, furthermore,' Adler let out a long exhale, 'even if we do deter every aggressor, our sun itself will die one day. Even if we manage to keep it aflame, one day our corner of the universe will ultimately become uninhabitable. Even if we flee that inevitable death of our environment, we can never guarantee that we will forever escape our Great Enemy: *death.*'

'Death will forever be present with us here, in this Universe. As it has been for humans all across this Universe, since times immemorial or so it is that we have come to learn.' Adler turned slightly towards the inhumans located behind her. 'It is the great struggle at the end of all our paths, as it has always been. Perhaps sentience itself walks in the footsteps of this awareness.'

'As such, it should come as no surprise to anyone that this is not the first time people have come together to find a way out of this predicament. As you all know, the Continuum of Humanity claims to have in operation an afterlife program exclusive to humans. The catch is that in order to be a part of that program, one must meet certain criteria, among which are certain requirements most of us Terrans – most of our friends, most of our ancestors, most of our loved ones and, hopefully, most of our children – will never meet. To put it better: requirements they *should never* meet. The penalty for this is the *allegedly* either oblivion or the damnation of our very souls.'

'I know that I have glossed over much and left much unsaid. As have many figures of authority during your lives. I did this on purpose. To my great shame, I must confess that, I believe that we have indoctrinated you, the youth – the... the Yin and particularly the sunrisers – far more than we should have with such overreaching statements.'

Wow...

Wow...

To have Laur Pop say the very same thing to him in private had been one thing, yet to hear it said out loud in public was another thing entirely.

'I want you to understand *that*. I want you to understand that *that* is something which has marked who you are. A major part of Project Kralizec is the process of critical, yet constructive, reflection and discussion. Despite all the talk about cover stories and silence and mind wipes, I want you all to understand that no one – let me be clear: <u>no one</u> – doubts your loyalty. We will only ever question your discretion. Failure to accept and comprehend that will be viewed as direct insubordination, and is one of the very few things which will lead to your expulsion from Project Kralizec and the execution of those mindwipes you all signed off on.'

'If you are not *open*. If you are not *frank*. If you withhold any observation or idea which you believe, in your mind, warrants any degree of consideration, no matter how minuscule... Please, understand, that is the seed of failure. Not just for you, but for all of us.'

Adler paused and Thomas saw, for one second, the glimmer of something he had never noticed before. He saw someone who was struggling with something.

'We are building an afterlife for Terrans alive today, yesterday and tomorrow. This afterlife shall communicate with the existing afterlives of our friends,' she waved behind her, 'whether they have been established now or will be established in the future.'

There it is. Finally said out loud.

'If our people die out, this afterlife will survive our extinction, ensuing our survival somewhere in the multiverse, forever beyond the reach of death and all those who would deliver us to oblivion.'

'So, onto the plan itself,' she announced, seemingly more to herself, than to her expectant audience.

'I will explain the great themes and tools of Project Kralizec. My colleagues will go into a more in-depth overview of their respective sections. There are ten sections in total. Five sections are not represented here. This is due to the fact that their onboarding has either ceased or is yet to begin. I will explain in due time.'

'The first section is the Security Section headed by Colonel Zaslani in collaboration with General Pop and several other members of the High Command. You may notice the Hajduks shadowing you, as you communicate and interact with those that are not part of Project Kralizec. The Sayeret will assure more direct security. They operate the various checkpoints littered throughout our regions within the Styx Network. They also conduct regular interviews with you, to assure your reliability and operational awareness. Regarding security, the Sayeret and the Hajduks merely represent the most dedicated line of defence. You are all expected to act in a defensive capacity, at all times. Furthermore, you might encounter members of other legions, particularly the Old Guard, but also the Ghazis, the Keshik, the Akali and others during your time in the Styx.'

'The second section is the Collaborative Section, headed by Colonel Ramirez, who is currently away off-world. His section deals with the exchange of technology, information, expertise and resources needed for Project Kralizec, all of which are being provided by our friends in the Alliance. Bear in mind that this section deals primarily with assuring the access of all the other sections to this exchange. Once the exchange occurs, all non-Terran technology, information and assistance provided immediately falls under the jurisdiction of the respective section. Furthermore, as you can tell from those behind me, you will also interact with certain members of the Alliance assisting us in an advisory capacity. After all, none of this could have been possible without their help. *Remember that.* Remember that they are here, risking the survival of their own peoples, to assure the survival of ours. Let the weight of that soothe away any possible shred of doubt regarding their competence or loyalty.'

'The third section is the Entropy Section, headed by Colonel Gonçalvo, who is also currently not here. This section deals with two major issues. The first is assuring that Project Kralizec always has access to the energy needed to power every aspect of this operation. The second is to assure that the use of said energy goes unnoticed to the rest of the Universe.'

'The fourth section is the Exploration Section, headed by Colonel Xhisa; also absent. It is at this point where I will begin explaining the mechanics of Project Kralizec.' Adler raised both hands to pull away all the hair from her face. 'In the early days of Kralizec, we spent most of our time looking for a specific pocket universe to suit our exact needs. Eventually, Colonel Xhisa and his team succeeded in finding one. We refer to it as the "Aether" and it is currently empty. The Exploration Section now works primarily on the "Orpheus Chamber".'

'The fifth section is the Translation Section, headed by Colonel Hosseini. First and foremost, the Translation Section deals with the actual process of "extraction". That is to say, the *extraction* of *consciousness* at the *exact* moment of death from the body. The Translation Section also deals, in no small measure with the Orpheus Chamber, in preparation for "Theogenesis". "Theogenesis" is how we refer to the moment Project Kralizec goes live. I will let Colonel Hosseini explain further in greater depth later on.'

'The sixth section is the Inception Section, under the command of Colonel Patel. This section is dedicated to the construction of the artificial intelligence – to which we refer to as "Olorun" – which will act as the builder and maintainer of "Satya", the name we generally use around here to refer to the end goal of Project Kralizec.'

Adler paused and raised a calming hand to her audience. 'I know: it's a lot of terms. "Olorun" is God. "Satya" is Heaven. "Aether" is the place where Heaven will be built. Olorun is going to build Heaven. In time, you will get used to these terms. For now, it's best if you just keep up with the main ideas. Also, in regards to section names and numbers, it helps to know that each section is numbered in the sequence of its founding. In other words, the first section is the first section that was founded, the second was the second, so on and so forth.'

'I will continue with the seventh section: the Transient Section headed by Colonel Rasmussen. This section deals primarily with issues pertaining to the mind-body question. I don't have time to get into that now, I will leave it to Doctor Rasmussen to go into greater detail later on.'

'The eighth section is the Elocution Section, headed by myself. My section is focused on the issue of preparing the Terran population and, indeed, the rest of the Known Universe for the revelation of this endeavour. I say preparation, since the actual execution of said revelation shall be undertaken by the future tenth section, which is aptly named the Revelation Section.'

'For those of you still able to keep track, I commend you, and I inform you that, yes, there is a ninth section, which will handle the actual process of Theogenesis. Said section, is to be referred to as the Alignment Section.'

'On that note, I will yield the floor to my colleagues. Each will give a brief overview of what it is that their respective section deals with and how you will be assisting them.' Adler moved aside and gestured towards Zaslani, who was already rising from his seat.

As he neared the podium, he cleared his throat and began to speak in a fast, yet soft manner, almost as if he disliked having his words being heard by so many and he was trying to get it over with as quickly as he could.

'I will keep things brief, since most of what concerns me has already been said and I don't want to keep you away from the good stuff.' Nothing resembling a smile ever went near Zaslani's face.

'All I have left to say is this: you will encounter a great many people during your work on Project Kralizec. Amongst yourselves, you may refer to them as "keepers", with those of you that are Terran, being referred to as "keepers of Terra". Use this nomenclature extensively. At this point, there are so many Keepers of Terra you might find it difficult to remember who is and who isn't a keeper. In that regard, never forget the *Cosa Nostra* rule which applies here. A keeper will never introduce himself. A keeper will always be introduced to you by another keeper.'

'Suffice to say, look around the room and submit the faces to memory, for I am now introducing you all to each other.' Zaslani stopped talking, but he did not leave the podium. His eyes scanned the room as he noted turning heads. Thomas could swear he saw his lips move slightly, as if he were counting.

'Excellent. We randomly execute interviews to make sure everyone is alright. These interviews will occur at times which may be described as *regularly*, yet *unexpectedly*. Don't waste time worrying about their outcome. That is our job. In regards to checkpoints, our goal is to be always *along* your way, yet never *in* your way.'

'That's it from me. Hos-Hos, you're up!'

Before he had barely finished the sentence, Colonel Hosseini was already up and gingerly making his way to the podium.

'Well. Good morning to all of you. My name is Hossein Hosseini. As you've probably guessed, my friends, of which Ruben is one, 'the Colonel paused to smile and gesture towards Zaslani (who forced a smile as he sat down), 'call me Hos-Hos. I must first apologise for my colleagues' rudeness and offer you a belated welcome to Project Kralizec, on behalf of the whole Section Council, of which Shosho, Ruben, Lakshmi, Lars and myself are all a part of. I must inform you, against the advice of the head of security – which I admire much – that this is the first time we've done an onboarding in this manner. As such, bear in mind that this is a first for us, not just for you. Though, I can tell that you're a lot more shaken than we are judging from your faces, all of which are a mix of shock and awe.' Hosseini paused to make a show of looking across the room.

'Yes. We can see you. It's not just young Thomas over there – sitting next to dear Mira – who looks like his world is in a maelstrom.' Thomas gulped and struggled not to choke on his own throat, as confused faces turned to him in amusement. Thomas felt his pulse rise so sharply, he could swear his heart was knocking into his throat. Embarrassment, terror and shame flooded him in waves, engaging the maelstrom of existential dread and hope within him in a riptide of emotion.

Bullshit. I am certain they look more balanced than me right now.

Hosseini wasn't done with the seventh row in front of him, however. 'Even you, Mira! I know you well enough to see when you're thinking so fast you fail to think at all. 'Thomas saw the eyes of his fellow keepers switch from him to his neighbour.

He joined them to see the cheeks of the stone-faced Mira begin to darken from rage.

'Such feelings as those you are experiencing – all of you, I must emphasise – are normal given the profound implications of what you have just been introduced to by Shosho'. He turned to General Adler as she began to smile.

'You did a fine job dear, do not worry! No one's head has exploded – yet – so I would count that as a definite victory!'

'So, after Themba – meaning Colonel Xhisa's team – succeeded in identifying the Aether, which is the field on which Satya is to be built and, more importantly, *can* be built *and* cannot be *unbuilt*, we set about figuring out how to get there. Meaning how we would transport the Olorun sourcecode there.'

'You see, the real issue is getting Olorun - and *only* Olorun – there and making sure no one can follow him there *without* his *permission*. After all, the whole point of eternity is the fact that it is, well, *eternal* and cannot be undone by unwanted visitors.'

'With the assistance of our friends, and I speak now specifically of our orcish, demani, Vanir and, yes, elven allies, we were able to overcome this issue simply by virtue of the attributes of Aether itself. That is to say that, we found a universe which can be observed and entered without permission *only once*.'

'Think of it like this: you know there is a specific cavern in a specific mountain, but there is no tunnel to that cavern. Furthermore, you know that there is only one way to build a tunnel leading towards this particular cavern. So, you build this tunnel, reach the cavern and then you turn around and blow up the tunnel behind you, ensuring that no one else will ever be able to repeat the feat.'

'It is from this point forward that things begin to get truly weird. Why did you make your way to this cavern to begin with? To construct a paradise for our people? Well, how will our people get there? Do we all just kill ourselves and make a break for it? *Of course not!* Furthermore, what of all the people that would have lived before this massive self-genocide? They weren't even alive when construction of the tunnel would have begun!'

'The solution to this issue is, once more, something solved by the attributes of the Aether itself. Normally, at this point I would branch off into the finer points of Multitude Science, i.e. the study of the multiverse and multidimensional space. However, since not all of you are students of this specific branch – or, rather, root, as it were – of physics, I will explain it like this: imagine our universe as a sleeping giant, located on a giant bed of … does everyone here know what "hay" is?'

Hos-Hos paused and looked around, his hands suspended in the gestures he had been employing to help his audience visualise what he had been describing.

'I am being serious; some of you are quite young, as Shosho pointed out earlier. So, please, if you may, snap out of your existential crisis for one brief instant, just so that I can be sure you all know what "hay" is!'

This time, the room did react, with everyone, including Thomas and Mira, nodding expectantly.

'Good! Now, imagine our universe as a giant sleeping on a giant bed, on a mattress made of *hay*. This mattress is filled with a remarkably large number of individual *strands* of hay. For every position the giant lays in, each hay strand has a unique position of its own, due to the forces exerted on it. Hence, every possible position of the giant can be determined by knowing the position of a single strand of hay. Now, understand that this mattress has infinite strands of hay in it. The Aether is one of these strands of hay. The Orpheus Chamber is currently open towards the Aether. Once the day of *Theogenesis* comes and Olorun is sent into the Aether, the entrance shall be collapsed, thus guaranteeing insulation.'

'Now, it's time you started earning your keep. So, question time! What issues do you see with everything I've just said?'

Immediately hands shot up in the front row: 'Yes, Kenji! Go ahead!'

'How do we know that no one has selected this strain before and that no one will select it in the future?'

'Excellent question! You see, we have built the tunnel to the Aether, with our end of the tunnel being located in the Orpheus Chamber, and the other end being located… well, nowhere, since the Aether is… its *formless*! It's *empty*! Which raises the rational follow-up question: how do we know it's empty?'

Kenji's, and several other heads, began nodding in agreement.

'We know it's empty because we dug a tunnel leading to an empty cavern. If the cavern wouldn't have been empty, we could not have reached it.' Hos-Hos paused to let the absurdity of his words sink in.

'EXACTLY! If you understand my words, yet not the possibility of what I am describing then, I must congratulate you! It means that your mind is fully capable of understanding Multitude Science!' Genuine laughter exploded from the Vanir human behind him and several keepers in the front row.

'Suffice to say, the way that works can be explained and, in my opinion,' he turned to Shosho, '*should be attempted* to be explained to every Terran.'

He turned back towards his audience. 'But, for now, the aforementioned metaphors should be enough... Next question! There, in the back row! Captain *Alessandro* Lupo, I believe?'

'Yes, sir! If the tunnel leads to the Aether now, in our timeline, and the Aether is an empty universe, with no spacetime, does that mean that —'

'Yes, it does! Excellent Alessandro! What are you doing being a physician, you have the mind of a physicist! Lars!' He turned to the Head of the Transient Section behind him. 'Please, be particularly mean to him, so that he will quit and I can take him on my team!'

Colonel Rasmussen smiled and Hos-Hos turned back towards Lupo.

'It means that, right now, the tunnel has *always been open* into the Aether, even though we opened it only about two months ago AND THIS!!! – I am getting excited now! If I become maniacal, please restrain me – and this means that the Aether has a property which can be used in a very special way. It means that the Aether can communicate, at all times, with different moments in our universe!'

'To be more precise, and I will not go into the exact calculations by which we have arrived at this conclusion, the Aether has the property that it can communicate – at all times – with *every single moment* and *every single place* within our own Universe.'

'Now, I will not be rude and ask for your next question. I have already realised that your minds are capable of observing the next logical conundrum: what is this communication? Because, "if it is just achieved by opening new tunnels, then you are contradicting yourself, Hos-Hos! You just said we would be collapsing the tunnel toward the Aether, thus sealing the Aether!" No? Is this not the logical fallacy that immediately arises?'

Thomas hadn't noticed this fallacy but, sure, he did now.

'Well, a tunnel is different from *vibrations* within the mountain. It's even more different from vibrations within a mattress. These vibrations are – or, rather, *can be* – a form of communication. However, they are different from downright access! Moreover, because of the nature of these things, from the Aether you can *hear* our universe. However, from our Universe, we cannot *hear* the Aether. Not because it is silent, but because the, the, the, the... the *waves* only travel in one direction'

'Now that you have received your crash course in Multitude Physics, before I hand you your PhD,' no one laughed, likely because probably no one knew what a

PhD was, 'there is one more aspect I will go into, just so that you understand, at a basic level, how this technology works.'

'How do we get the consciousnesses out of our universe and into the *Hereafter*, once it is ready?' A tentative hand slowly went up from one of the middle rows to Thomas' left.

'Yes, Kai!?'

'A bait-and-switch –' Captain Diaoxing didn't even have time to finish his sentence as Hosseini slapped his hands and started pointing at the Han keeper.

'– ALHAMDORELAH!!! YES!!! Exactly, Kai! Shosho, we need to have these things more often! They are a brilliant bunch, aren't they? Yes, Kai! A bait-and-switch!' Hosseini, who had begun to pace erratically around the stage, came over to the edge of the platform and continued gesturing and speaking.

'We take the brain – Lars, will explain what the brain *is* by our working definition – and, in the exact instant of death in our universe, when a Terran is in *before* that first moment of death and right *after* the last moment of life, Olorun senses the vibration, decides that the end is nigh, responds by reaching out and opening a tunnel into our universe. He takes the brain out, replaces it with an *already dead* copy of the same brain, seals the portal, the brain, still alive, is fixed and made viable once more, and it is now in the afterlife in Satya. From the point of view of our universe, no change has occurred. But the dead get to live happily ever after in the Hereafter. Next question? Yes, Katarazyna! You want to ask something?'

'Yes, sir, if it's possible.'

'Asking any question is possible, it remains to be seen if answering it is also.'

'Yes, sir. Such technology exists...' she paused, trying to articulate.

'Is that a question? Because the tone was –'

'No, sir. It wasn't. This is the question: If it's possible for us to do that – to find a strain of hay out of an infinity and to put something there that can reach out and pull things out of our universe at whatever time, now and in the future – wouldn't that mean that any civilization – if it were at least as advanced as ours – would be able to do the same? Couldn't they have an entity similar to Olorun in another Satya that was ready at-all-times to alter our own Universe in a manner of its liking?'

'Though I love that question and would love to answer it by addressing various aspects of time travel and its many wild paradoxes, I am afraid that the best answer is much more mundane and –'

Hos-Hos turned to one of his colleagues. '– Lakshmi, if I may apologise for entering your territory, ever-so-slightly?'

Colonel Patel waved his concern away.

'So, I have permission?'

She smiled and nodded.

'Excellent. In short, it's because of the way *soulkeeper* technology works. You all know that elves, orcs and others use soulkeepers?'

The room nodded.

'Good! Fabulous bits of technology they are! However, what you may not know is that soulkeepers know which souls they are responsible for. In other words, we can teach Olorun who is a Terran and who isn't. We can have him only select individuals over which he would, in essence, have jurisdiction over.'

'Now, that is all the time I am allowed, I leave you with Lakshmi – I mean *Colonel* Patel – and she will tell you more about... about Olorun... you have a question, Thomas?'

Thomas could not believe what he was doing, but he couldn't control himself. The compulsion was that strong. The question burned that brightly.

'If we collapse the tunnel and cease communication, how will we ever know if this thing works?'

Towards the end of his point Hos-Hos had begun to smile. He did not address Thomas' question immediately, choosing to leave a long pause between them

'Shosho?' Hos-Hos never took his eyes from Thomas.

General Adler had to snap out of staring into the distance directly midway between her and Thomas. 'Hmm?'

'I have always seen your administrative abilities as sublime. But, up until this point, I never realised what an amazing judge of character you are!'

Adler smiled slightly as she let out a soft sigh that was audible over the deafening silence. Her smile joined that of Sorbo Falk, Colonel Patel, and several others seated behind Hosseini.

'Good job, Thomas! Questions like that are exactly why you are here. Questions like that have answers. However, I will ask that you not honour me with the answer, at least not now. Listen to Lakshmi and the others and I promise you that soon, but not today, your question shall be answered.'

Colonel Lakshmi Patel was already making her way towards the podium by the time Hos-Hos had turned his smiling gaze away from Thomas. It was barely then that he noticed Mira had been looking at time for some time as well. He turned to face her, only to see her pokerface turn into a smirk, followed by an exaggerated nod of approval, as she turned to face their new commanding officer.

'Hello, everyone. My bit will be quick and easy, as opposed to what my section deals with, which is arduous and complicated. To summarise, my section is designing Olorun, the artificial god of the Terran afterlife, which we will implant into the Aether on the day of Theogenesis. I am thankful for Hos-Hos' bridgehead toward my field and I will meet it by pointing out to you a basic issue we address within my section: memory space.'

'The Aether, though currently empty, is infinite, much like our own universe. Furthermore, our universe likely contains, at any given time, an infinite number of souls. These souls can be human, elven, orcish, goblin, troll, as well as an unknown number of other sentient life forms. Some are known. Others are not. Many are animal souls. Think of dogs or cats, or birds and mice, but also of fish and even ants. All these creatures are conscious living beings. Now, understand that this is only an infinitesimally small snapshot of all the life that has ever existed in our universe and an even smaller snapshot of all the infinite moments in time throughout the universe's infinite expanse.'

'It is at this moment that you will begin to feel your head swirl. That feeling is due to the fact that your mind, though able to rationalise infinity, is unable to comprehend processing it in its entirety. Yes, I mean the *entirety* of infinity. This issue is actually, not due to the quality of your rational thinking, though it helps to be as rational as one can be. Rather, it is due to the fact that your mind simply does not have at its disposal enough space in which to develop the resources to process all that information.'

'An artificial intelligence, such as Olorun, given an infinite amount of time and space, such as that present in the Aether, would be able to eventually develop the capability to process an infinite amount of information, by virtue of being, itself, infinite.'

Patel spoke in a well-paced voice, often introducing pauses and always focusing on her audience, making sure she was understood. One could tell that she knew the words coming out of her mouth very well and she seemed to focus far more on making sure she wasn't losing the room, rather than on reciting her script. In a sense, though similar to Hos-Hos' erratic lecturing, the delivery of her speech was a stark contrast to the whirlwind of information from earlier. She had paused after the last idea, giving Thomas enough time to comprehend beginning to understand what she was describing.

'However, the ability to process the *entirety* of our universe, across all space and time, within only one single universe, is simply impossible. At least, to our knowledge.'

'This creates a conundrum from the perspective of Project Kralizec: how can Olorun observe all of spacetime and know when it should intervene and where? The answer, it would appear, is actually fairly intuitive and, ironically, is in line not just with our opposition to being part of the afterlife of the Continuum, but also with our goal of joining together with the afterlives of our friends.'

Patel smiled frequently yet, now, as she brought her fingers together in a web, her smile had reached its broadest point and stars began dancing in the corners of her eyes.

'Olorun will only be able to track those sections of spacetime where those he judges to be Terran are located. Now... we know that the number of Terrans that lived in the past was finite: likely well under one hundred and fifty billion, as Shoshanna mentioned earlier. We know how many Terrans are alive right now: slightly over one hundred million. However, we have no way of knowing how many Terrans will exist in the future. This is the current impasse we have reached on this topic. However,' she smiled again now, albeit in a more timid fashion, 'you should understand that, ever since Project Kralizec has begun, we have encountered many hurdles on our way that have threatened to push us over into the depths of despair and we have come up with solutions to all of them.'

'For this specific issue, we believe that we have found a solution, though we have yet to officially conclude that we have solved the issue. If we're wrong, don't worry, we'll figure something else out!'

'You see, there are three possible destinations to our path as a people: extinction, assimilation or expansion. Extinction is, in a way, the most predictable outcome. I know that statement clashes with the usual bravado with which modern society faces the future. However, from the perspective of aeons and factoring in the vast and unknowable expanse and volatility of this universe, it is the most rational outcome. Remarkably though, from our perspective, it is also the easiest outcome for Olorun to address: if we do go extinct, Olorun will be able to know when our existence is snuffed out and the process of catering to a *finite* number of souls is something he will be able to do quite easily.'

'Assimilation is, in many ways, also an easy question to answer, if you understand what it refers to in broad terms. However, it becomes a difficult question to answer, when you attempt to understand the *exact situations* to which it refers. Assimilation is how we call the scenario wherein the Terran genetic lineage extends further into the future than our awareness of our cultural identity. What that means is that it is possible and – to the continuous worry of the Terran High Command – *probable* that sometime in the future, near or far, our descendants will either reject or forget their identity as Terrans. This can occur either en masse or on an individual basis and will have the outcome of us having descendants who do not *want* to be part of Satya and would rather be part of another afterlife, perhaps one that is not even part of *Yggdrasil* – which is a term you have not heard before now, at least to my knowledge, which refers to the network of afterlives of which Satya will be part of.'

'Since Hos-Hos', in his inexhaustible and ever-present excitement, omitted to mention –'

'– I didn't "omit", I "forgot"!' Hos-Hos raised a hand from behind Patel to acknowledge his mistake.

Patel chuckled without turning. 'Yes… Glad *you* said it.'

'Yggdrasil is the name of the network of afterlives we are constructing together with our allies, some of which already have functional afterlives, while others are currently within the process of establishing ones, much like ourselves. You will recall the metaphor used by the previous speaker which described the Aether as a hay mattress. I will build upon that metaphor.'

'Think of other afterlives as other strains of hay, different from the Aether, some of which are, to our knowledge, being employed much in the same way as the Aether is. These strands of hay are located within the same mattress, or, to build upon another metaphor used by my colleague, in the same *mountain* as the metaphorical cavern of the Aether. This means that they obey different rules, when interacting with one another, than the rules which govern the relationship between the strands of hay and our universe.'

'These rules allow for communication among the strands of hay which is more permissive than that between the mattress and the giant. Said communication allows for souls located in one afterlife to communicate with souls located in other afterlives, as if they were part of the same universe.'

Thomas felt as if he was about to throw up.

'This communication is essential for what we, as Keepers, refer to as *experiential veracity*, which is a fancy way of saying "making sure that the heaven feels like heaven for those in it".'

'Take the following example: a child born by one Terran parent and one non-Terran parent. The Terran parent, upon death, will fall under the care of Olorun, while the other would fall under the care of their own respective afterlife administrator. Who takes care of the *child's* soul when they pass away?'

'This would be the scenario under which I will fall under with my husband Fiol, sitting over there, behind me.' The Vanir human waved. 'When he will die, his caretaker shall be Ashun, who presides over the Vanir afterlife of Folkvangr, while I, if everything goes according to plan, will reside in Satya, and be looked over by Olorun. Our daughter will be able to choose between Satya and Folkvangr and be part of whichever afterlife she chooses. However, no matter which afterlife she will choose, all three of us and, hopefully,' she turned to smile at Fiol who smiled back, seemingly knowing her thoughts, 'all of her brothers and sisters, cousins, nephews, grandparents and friends, will be able to enjoy each other's presence.'

'Within this scenario, assimilation is not difficult to resolve as, basically, even if a time came when no one would choose Olorun's afterlife, the residents of Satya would still be able to communicate with their descendants, no matter the afterlife. However, in order to maintain *experiential veracity*, one must account for those scenarios when loved ones will choose afterlives outside of the Yggdrasil network.'

'This is an uncomfortable topic to discuss. Yet, if we were to be hindered by uncomfortable topics, Project Kralizec wouldn't have gotten very far. So far, we haven't come up with any solution to this issue, beyond simply hoping that, somehow, Yggdrasil and other networks like it manage to spread to encompass all afterlives.'

'This leads to the third issue of our future as Terrans, in relation to Project Kralizec: expansion. Specifically, I am referring to the potential for infinite expansion of Terran culture and genetic stock throughout the universe and, indeed, even the multiverse.'

'Remember the computational problem: no afterlife could ever harbour enough processing power to service the entirety of our own universe, yet alone the whole multiverse. Hence, the logical solution would imply that Olorun, like Ashun, Easpirac, and other afterlife administrators, continuously seeds other strains of hay – other *Aethers* – with new afterlife administrators, responsible for new branches of Terrans.'

'Remember the words of Shoshanna from earlier: no one questions your loyalty. However, as I see you have noticed, this assumption runs counter with current conceptions of what it means to be Terran. Namely, this assumption is in direct violation of the principle of Terran unity which, as you all know, directly prohibits any splintering of the Terran people. I know that it will be uncomfortable to consider, and downright unpleasant to discuss such futures among yourselves. However, once more echoing Shoshanna's words: refusal to comply is considered failure.'

'The assumption that it is impossible for Terran society to fracture in the future, no matter how hard it may be to digest, is foolish and, worse, *irrational* to presuppose. As such, remember that though we currently must under work under the assumption that Yggdrasil might be able to spread and include all possible afterlives, we must account for both scenarios. There is a scenario in which Yggdrasil forever remains separate from certain other specific afterlives and a scenario where Yggdrasil encompasses all possible afterlives, including different Terran afterlives, not just that of Satya.'

'This is because of the fact that even if the Terran people never fracture and endure for something resembling eternity, this would force Olorun to create new afterlives regardless, simply because Satya would not be able to harbour both the entire Terran population and the computing power required to keep track of every single Terran in our universe. Hence, splintering of the Terran afterlife is not only a possibility, but a best case scenario.'

Patel stopped and surveyed her audience.

She seemed comfortable with the silence in front of her. Thomas felt her gaze upon him at one point, right after the Colonel had locked eyes with Mira. Her face was friendly, yet behind her bubbly personality he felt a deep seriousness. One which she revealed only with her eyes. Her happy, yet solemn face somehow reminded him of how all human faces were merely soft, excitable faces, atop hard, expressionless bones.

'The scenario in which Yggdrasil never joins with other afterlives directly challenges our goal of *experiential veracity* which is, as it were, not actually my primary focus, but that of my colleague Lars, who will take it from here.'

Patel gave them all one last smile before returning to her seat next to her husband, while Lars got up and began approaching the podium. He took his time adjusting his glasses and arranging a screen before him on the podium.

'Good morning. I know you have a lot to digest. I will tell you now that my words will be more similar to Ruben's, as opposed to those of Hos-Hos or Lakshmi, meaning that I will be short.' He spoke very slowly. Thomas had the feeling that he might say as many words as Ruben, yet take as long as Patel.

'My section, the Transient Section, deals with two major issues.'

'The first is the issue of experiential veracity. As Lakshmi has already explained wonderfully, this term encompasses our struggle to understand what heaven is like for those experiencing it, while we ourselves are currently locked out of heaven. On a more fundamental level, it deals with the question of *what does it mean to be happy?*'

'The second involves a deep collaboration with the Inception Section, since it deals with the task of making sure that even though we, as people, do not understand what happiness is, Olorun, the *artificial* – and I place great emphasis on that word – intelligence which we are designing, will understand happiness. At least, Olorun *must* understand what a happy eternal existence means for us. Furthermore, also in collaboration with the Inception Section, we share the task of designing Olorun in such a manner that he can feel empathy, which is the most crucial personality trait of his character. You must understand, just because you understand how someone feels, doesn't mean you want to make them feel good. You need empathy, in order to feel the drive to make someone feel good.'

'Both of these issues are heavily linked with what is called the "mind-body question". That is to say, how much of who we are is our mind. How much of *us* is our body? Is the soul a third, separate element? Is it part of both? Is it only in the mind? Which parts of the mind make up the soul? Is the conscious, the subconscious or the unconscious part of ourselves an inseparable component of our souls? Does the soul of a person change from one moment to another?'

'The answers to these questions are, strangely enough, not an issue of discovery, as much as they are an issue of definition. Our friends have already shared with us which parts of the body and the mind we need to, eh, *teleport* to Satya, in order to assure them of the – and I am certain you are familiar with this concept – *truthful relocation* of one's soul. The reason why we must wrestle with the body-mind question is actually due to the fact that there lies the challenge of organising a heaven where one can interact with others experiencing the same heaven.'

'Take this question: consider yourself and a child rapist from 1890s London stealing food from the mouths of mothers struggling to feed their starving children whom – just to be clear – the rapist is *also* rapping, while being their landlord and their biological father (since he raped the mothers as well). Would you be comfortable sharing heaven with this person? Would you be happy, knowing that this person is in heaven as well? The answer, I am certain, you all feel in the pit of your soul.'

'No! You wouldn't be. Clearly such a person should not experience everlasting bliss, especially if they are to be your neighbour in heaven.'

'I think that's a reasonable statement. However, where is the line drawn? When is one unworthy of sharing an eternity of happiness with you? That is a question which we must *decide* an answer to. Once we decide what the answer to that is, we must ensure that Olorun makes the same assessment. Why is this important?'

'It is important because we must *decide* when it is moral for Olorun to employ his greatest power.' Rasmussen paused now, no longer surveying the room before him, but looking down at his screen.

'*Alteration*. You see, souls are malleable. They can change. The issue emerges as to when a soul *should* be changed, since it is incompatible with a heaven. All keepers of all afterlives must face this horrific moral dilemma: when is it right to knowingly change someone so that they, *and* those around them, can enjoy each other's presence for all eternity?'

'I will not bore you with the solutions arrived upon by the keepers of the Continuum of Humanity, since I am certain you have heard of the… *liberties* taken by their afterlife administrator. Suffice to say, our solution will be different, not just from theirs, but also from that of the Vanir, the Aesir, the orcs and, I am certain, in due time, the trolls and goblins.'

'However (and this is the final thing I wish to clarify before leaving you) perhaps you might be wondering why everyone needs to be thrown together into the same heaven? Perhaps, you might be wondering why we place so much emphasis on the Yggdrasil network and why we want to be certain that, in the afterlife, we will actually be interacting with the actual souls of the people we knew in life.'

'The answer, once more, is concerned with experiential veracity.'

'*You need to know the truth in Heaven.* That is something you *expect* to happen in heaven. If you were interacting with a copy, an *imitation* of a loved one, no matter how credible the simulation would be, you would still *know* that it was a simulation. This would take away from your ability to appreciate the closeness of this person's presence. Thus, this would not be "heaven", in your experience. It would just be a different type of mundane existence, which you would be condemned to endure for all eternity. Thank you for your time. Shoshanna?'

'Thank you, Lars. I will finish this off briefly as well.'

'You've heard a lot today and you all deserve some time to absorb it. Please feel free to enjoy our facilities here, for the time being. I recommend you spend time processing everything, as well as getting to know your colleagues. We've organised a dinner in Eilat at eight pm tonight. You are all expected to attend. General Zaslani has also confirmed that you have received your mission statements in your inbox.'

'Welcome to Project Kralizec! Best of luck!'

Mira immediately got up from her seat once Shosho formally closed the introductory session. Where she went, Thomas did not know. He barely remembered getting up from his seat, as well as where he planned on going. He didn't even notice how someone had moved to block his path as he made his way out of the amphitheatre.

He felt Acosta's hand on his chest before he saw him sitting right in front of him.

'You did not get any sleep last night, didn't you?' the Old Guard said, his hand not leaving his chest. Thomas could tell he was feeling his heartbeat.

'Not much, no sir!' he babbled.

'It's "Marco".' He still did not take his hand away. 'I have a feeling that you are going to go back to your room and, this time, you will fall asleep from exhaustion,' he pronounced sombrely.

'I… I suppose so.' *After all this? I doubt it.*

'It's ok. You will have help.' With that, he brought his hand away from Thomas chest. With his other hand, the Mexican lifted Thomas' right hand, grasping it between his own two hands. Thomas felt something being pressed into his palm.

'I started this morning. I finished it here. Making them helps me relax. What they speak about here... It is… complicated. I need to focus always. You cannot focus if you are not relaxed.' Acosta withdrew his hands and Thomas gazed upon what the Old Guard had placed in his palm.

Unlike the red and gold scapular Acosta sported now, or the black and white one he had before and which now belonged to his son, this one was blue. He turned it around in his hand. On one side was the image of a woman dressed in white and blue, whom he assumed must have been Mary, the mother of Jesus Christ, while on the other he could discern a strange symbol, seemingly a combination of the letter 'M' and a cross.

'The Blue Scapular of the Immaculate Conception. It is not common in Mexico. But you are not Mexican.'

Thomas was at loss for words for one second.

First, he was taken aback by this encounter to begin with. Second, he was taken aback by how Acosta had not just forgotten or cast aside his promise, but actually spent time knitting something for… *for him*?!

'Thank you!' He looked up from his hand. 'It is very beautiful and… well-made.'

'Will you wear it?'

'Of course!' Thomas quickly put it around his neck.

'The blue looks good on you.'

Chapter VIII
A Great Many Tears

Thomas stood there alone on the rocky outcrop overlooking Eilat.

The afternoon sun had begun its descent across the Sinai Peninsula to the west. Not that he had spent any time taking in the scenery. His world was shaking. He himself had only just stopped shaking a while ago though; at least according to Clara.

I must be losing my mind. This must all be some type of hallucination since I am losing my mind. I am going crazy.

He didn't really believe it was all a hallucination since everything his body felt... *it felt so real.* Everything his eyes saw and his ears heard felt... right; compatible with a faithful experience of reality. Even from where he stood, almost a hundred meters above the sea, he could smell the subtle taste of salt drifting up on playful winds from the waves below, as the fruit trees behind him, in full bloom, seemed to peddle their wares with wisps of scintillating perfumes.

Marco had been right. He had gone straight to his room, tried to read all the materials sent over by the Security Section. Failed. Paced around the room in a panicked frenzy at the weight of what was being revealed. Then, somehow, when he had sat on the bed, he had passed out. Upon waking up, he found that he still had two hours to go until the planned dinner with the other new keepers was to take place. Not suffering the thought of spending those two hours maniacally pacing around his room, he had gotten into his car, flown past the restaurant and parked on a rocky cliffside overlooking the Gulf of Aqaba.

Thinking about Acosta reminded him of his gift, which he now wore under his uniform. He brought it out to look upon it once more, only now realising that he had never owned a hand knit item before. Items of clothing were all made by machinery. Some of the oldtimers still wore things from the old days. Many more adorned museums and places of remembrance. His parents even kept a few old pieces of clothing from the past in their house. One was a shirt his father had been using as a blanket in the Yin nursery he had been found in. It was a woman's shirt, made by a company called Zara. His father didn't know if it belonged to his mother, his sister, or merely one of those women who had helped hide him and the other children.

His mother, Lisa, still had her old baby clothes, neatly packed in the small suitcase she had been transported in. A folder inside the suitcase had also contained her travel history. It was how she had known her birth name, Chi Nguyen, and how she knew that she had been born in a place called Dien Bien Phu in the year 2 BB. It chronicled her evacuation to China while 'attended,' followed by her evacuation to Kazakhstan while 'unattended', then her passage through the Pass of Bicaz into old Europe and, ultimately, her placement in the same nursery as his father near Stuttgart. Thomas remembered how one night he had found her, sobbing and sniffing softly at her most prized possession: the worn leather wristband of a broken watch, which she had always believed had belonged to Thomas' grandfather, a man she had no memory of.

Yet, to own something knitted by a Terran hand, let alone an oldtimer, let alone an Old Guard... that was something Thomas never thought he would be worthy of.

But, was he worthy?

Was he worthy of any of this?

Does it even matter?

These questions and many more gnawed at different parts of his mind and, what's worse, he couldn't really ever tell which part of him was being gnawed at any given time. In some ways, it felt as if his very sense of himself was being chewed up, yet never swallowed, as if his conception of the world would just soon drip from the fangs of two great beasts, concerned more with dissolving him, rather than consuming him.

Before walking into Adler's office, he had felt the weight of revelation only upon himself. He would have given his very essence for the chance to be able to have some command over his destiny. At the very least, he would've given anything to just have a few answers. He had felt the weight of being alone and had been wracked by the deep desire to not feel so alone anymore.

Now, he found himself regretting what he had wished for, since it would appear that there were others working on resolving the very same issue that had stripped away all joy from his life. With that reveal had not come a sense of camaraderie, but terror at the responsibility laid before them all.

A responsibility only he felt he was aware of.

How could they treat everything so... mundanely?

A few days ago, he had thought about a room like the one he had found himself in today. A room of people working on that very same problem. Yet, the room he had thought of was something which he hadn't even dared visualise. Attempting to do such a thing would have done that which being in the actual room had done to him: make him lose faith in the possibility of such a group of people succeeding in such an endeavour.

For they were just people, like him. People of the same flesh and blood as himself. Even the inhumans. Did it matter that they had different skin colours and different noses and different hair? No. Of course it didn't. They were creatures of the very same existence as him, not gods. Yet, there they were: wearing clothes, scratching themselves, concerning themselves with appearances and engulfed in petty social interactions. Their minds would wander. They assumed too much and seemed to understand very little. They didn't know some things. They would forget other things.

Worst of all, they made mistakes. The worst of which was relying on him for anything at all. For this was the second beast which tore at his faith and which silenced all those places in his mind where hope could be forged: disbelief that he could contribute in any way at all.

Perhaps he could cling to that.

Perhaps in not understanding he could find solace. Perhaps he could just surrender himself. Maybe that's what they wanted: for him to surrender himself. Fully. Why shouldn't he? His despair was making him lose himself which, in turn, drove him to despair; a vicious cycle he had stumbled into like some fool and from whence he could not escape. A cycle which ended with his obliteration at the hands of his own mind.

The fools... the poor fools... To believe that they could *fix* something like that which was going on inside him... They really were doomed. They really all might be little more than insects flying aimlessly above a muddy lake at twilight, assuming that they understood the whole world. Perhaps even the flies around a cow's arse sometimes think of constructing their own afterlife. Some might even be delusional enough to start drawing-up action plans and organising committees–

'It's at eight... PM.' Mira's voice brought him out of his darkness.

It also brought his hand to his pistol. He paused when he saw it was her. She was walking towards him, a white Agnelli Bisono shuttle parked behind her, beneath the shade of a fig tree, the driver's door closing as she drew closer to him. She didn't pause, despite seeing him reach for his sidearm.

'It's also a social event. A party, of sorts. At least to my understanding.' She took a seat next to him, on the hood of his shuttle. Not that Thomas was still sitting on it. He had risen, startled by her, and had followed her nonchalant canter with his eyes. He did not sit down though, which was something she didn't seem to take note of.

She did take note of his silence though. 'Do you ever speak?'

'Y-yes!' he blurted out, slightly choking on the salty sea air in the middle of the word.

'You're not going to comment on being almost an hour early or as to why you're still in day uniform? Albeit, even if it's a casual day uniform?'

Thomas realised what she was talking about. He was dressed in standard Terran military clothing: short boots, straight pants, belt, pistol, blade, white shirt and jacket. It was perfectly fine, utilitarian clothing, with no formal or professional pieces present. However, it wasn't exactly what one would wear on a night out. Mira, on the other hand, wore a more adequate outfit: crisp white sneakers, beige pants strapped tightly around her legs, as well as a white dress shirt tucked into a black belt. Attached to that belt Thomas could see the only military decor she had chosen to keep: a broad bowie knife and a Colt 1911 handgun lay strapped to her belt, as they had that morning.

On her jacket she displayed her colours and he was surprised to see that, alongside her Terran and Arab colours, she had also swapped her Ghazi insignia with those of the Logistics Corps. His commitment to their cover was remarkable. After all, her desire to join the Ghazis had been the stuff of legend among the Terrans, particularly the sunrisers, who had followed closely to see if she would be the first sunriser to join the legendary unit, which she had been. To see her leave the unit, after only two years of service, was surprising to him.

'I... I like being comfortable. How did you know I was here?'

'You crossed national lines. I get a notification when that happens,' she said, as she tapped her watch to emphasise this fact. 'Jerusalem, Eilat and Sinai are part of Israel.' She pointed across the gulf towards the lush farmland beyond. 'Over here it's Arabia.' She pointed both towards the ground and the rolling forests spreading out to the southeast.' I got a beep like an hour ago. Decided to come check up.'

'Oh. That's nice... Uhm... if I may ask, why?'

Mira stared at him blankly. 'Did you read the mission statement?'

'Y-yes.'

'What did it say?'

'It... it said to be discreet concerning my role.'

'Cute. Did it mention that I am a Captain and you're a Lieutenant?'

'Yes, sir.'

'No, it didn't. That's what the lines on the arms are for.' She gestured to his single line and her double line. 'I outrank you and we operate within the same operational unit. In our case, the Inception Section. Which means that there's no need to be cute with me. I know what you know. Also, please don't use rank words with me.'

'Oh-kay.'

'Good. Now what did your mission statement say?'

'That I would analyse various assumptions made by the sections and give clear feedback as to…' the words felt like lumps of cold shit in his mouth '...as to what my *opinion* was.' Thomas' answer was dutiful and dry, as was both his intention and the norm when reciting orders.

'Excellent! And who's going to help you with that?'

'A… *mentor* officer?'

Mira put on a fake smile as she gestured towards herself with both hands, palms outstretched towards her closed mouth. 'Reporting for duty!' she proclaimed.

'Oh.' *As if things weren't weird or insane enough.*

Thomas had read the mission – correction: Thomas had *attempted* to read the mission statement. He had succeeded in getting through the first pages, only to progressively begin spiralling towards madness in a whirlpool of ideas, terms and concepts. He thought the part about having mentor officer was somewhere in the middle of the document, yet he couldn't be sure, since he couldn't even remember the last few pages, bar the last sentences:

'Project Kralizec is the highest priority on the agenda of the Terran High Command, in accordance with its capacity as helmsman of the Terran people, with only the imminent survival of our people outranking its urgency. Its strategic importance is <u>absolute</u>. This endeavour will continue regardless of your capacity to further its objective.'

The words had been the final nail in the coffin of Thomas' sanity, since he felt them meant for him and only for him.

How could he be important, as Adler had insisted, if even in the limited scheme of this faithful endeavour of absolute strategic value he was ultimately irrelevant? It was a sad thought to be at the right place, at the right time, yet not be the right person. It was an even sadder thought to think that there was no right person at all.

How could there be? After all, they were all… people. People attempting to fill the role of an absent God. How could he trust himself given his status as one such person among an infinity? The only way he could even fathom to trust himself was to trust in the judgement of those wiser than him. Yet, after seeing those wiser than him and having heard their assertions of his worthiness, he felt only the failings of their own judgement, akin to his own.

These thoughts crossed his mind now in mere specs of a single second, as they had a thousand times today, each time having danced across his field of thought in a maddening waltz of profound movements and pirouettes of abandon. For the thousandth time, he flooded the dance floor with the muffling waves of the present and his current circumstances.

He couldn't recall understanding what having a mentor officer meant. Perhaps Mira did. Certainly he would appreciate the relief of hearing someone else's musings over his own repetitive ruminations.

He sat down next to her on the hood of his shuttle and began putting words together.

'What is your understanding of your role?' the words came out, uncaring to the answer. He just wanted to get her talking so he could listen.

'Do you know what a "therapist" is?'

'... I... you mean in the sense of Old Earth?'

'Yes. I take it you do.'

'I do, I think.'

'Good answer. I thought you might answer like that. Your science is chronicling, right?' Thomas nodded. 'Causal research? History? The study of the past.' Thomas nodded some more. 'Well, my science is…'

Mira paused. She looked blankly in the space before her for a fraction of a second before looking back at Thomas.

'Do you know what my science is?'

'I… think it is computer science?' *Of course I know. Everyone knows.*

'Yeah, you see, that's what we have to address if this thing is gonna work.' Mira brought out a cigarette case. Thomas noted it had a strange design. He could only tell that it was a cigarette case from the fact that Mira kept cigarettes in it.

She caught him staring. 'You want one?'

'I… yes. Thank you'. Mira extended the case to him.

'No, I mean...' Thomas began rummaging in his jacket. '... I have cigarettes too… but, thank you!' He showed her his pack.

Mira looked at him with the same critical gaze she had irradiated him with that very morning when she had sat down, before returning to her point. 'You don't *think* you know my science. You *know* my science. As you probably know my art. What's my art?'

Caught red-handed, Thomas only paused in embarrassment for just a few seconds. 'Cooking.'

'Excellent! So, we need to address *why* you know that. Which is…?' she gestured towards him, wiggling her fingers.

'You… you… pffffuck….'

'There we go, we're getting there.'

'You're Mira al Sayid.'

'It's not pronounced like that, but let's go with baby steps for now. Pleased to meet you! And you are…?' She cupped a hand to her ear and leaned closer to him.

'Thomas Muller.'

She extended her right hand, in a clear handshake gesture. 'Thomas! Pleased to meet you!' Reluctantly and awkwardly, he shook it. To be accurate: Mira did most of the shaking.

'Thomas. I know nothing about you, Thomas, bar only what I read in this morning's report.' Thomas didn't mind her rude tone and neither did she.

'You, on the other hand, know a lot about me. As do a lot of other people. If us two are going to work together in a productive manner, there's a couple of rules we are going to have to set between us. Would you like to hear them?'

'Y-yes.'

'Great! The first rule is fairly simple: don't pretend you don't know who I am. You get me? None of this… "I think" business, unless it's honest. Are we on the same wavelength?'

Thomas thought they were. 'Yes.'

'The second rule can also be easy, if you follow it properly.' Mira took a deep breath. 'Don't treat me differently than you would if I was anyone else who happened to be your mentor officer. Got it?'

Thomas paused for too long.

'Yeah. You see, let me clarify that. In order for me to do my job, you're going to have to treat me as you would anyone else. Not as an equal. Just as another person. Any other person. You need to get over the fact that you know who I am because I'm famous and everyone knows who I am. Do you understand that? At least the concept?'

'Y-yes. I think I do.'

Mira gave him a sarcastic look. 'Do you respond to everyone else with "y-yes"?' She also did a mock imitation of his accent, not just his speech.

'As of late… I do… frequently.'

Mira's violent eyes froze for a second. She smiled a careful smile. This time, Thomas saw no mockery in her eyes. 'That's better. I think you get what I'm saying now.' She turned to face the sea and after a few moments she continued, 'One more rule – and this one's a bit more structured.'

'Ignore our ranks when it's just me and you. Pretend we're both lieutenants or that we're both captains. I don't care. But, when other people are present or are listening, unless I tell you not to, it's "*Captain* al Sayid*"*. D'you catch my drift Thomas?'

'Y-yes,' he said and she was about to continue, yet Thomas had something to add. '…Mira.' He stood up straight as he exhaled. 'Yes, Mira! I understand the rules.'

She gave him the same face she had given him after he had asked Hos-Hos how they would know if Project Kralizec was successful. 'You catch on quickly. That's good. Now...'

'Now that that's out of the way, yes, my science is computer science, also known as cognitive science, neuroscience or – my personal favourite – translated logic. I study how natural cognitive systems work and implement what I learn into artificial systems, thus making them intelligent.'

'– like your mother.'

Mira paused, her eyes coming aflame for a long moment. 'Do you treat every new person you meet as if you've known them your entire life?' she said, without looking at Thomas.

'I... ehm... no. I don't.'

'*Oh*,' she responded sarcastically and continued coldly 'well then what makes me so special?'

Thomas saw his mistake and felt ashamed for his presumptuousness. 'I apologise.'

'Accepted. Baby steps. Now, getting back on track, your science makes you akin to a historian of Old Earth, since your toolkit is virtually the same, despite a few fancy tricks, the overwhelming amount of information you have access to and the fact that you can now study different histories. Am I right?'

'You... are making a few generalisations but, yes, you are right.'

'Oh. Well don't mind me as I make a few generalisations about my own science. As long as I'm right, of course.' Thomas nodded, his insistence on accuracy having been parried tactfully.

She continued: 'Just like how you'd be a historian on Old Earth, I would be a therapist or,' she began waving her hand around in circles, 'a computer programmer. But that must have been boring as fuck. Therapy sounds pretty cool though. They still have therapy in Moria. Do you know what a therapist did or does? '

'They... something similar to what a priest would do during confession?'

Mira now froze completely, looking at the space right in front of her, with the cigarette in her mouth, her lungs not drawing any smoke in. 'Yeah... Actually, yeah. Shit... you really are having one aren't you? An acute episode.'

'So they tell me. Just that calling it "acute" makes it sound like it will go away at one point. It might be chronic, but... I guess I'll know in time.'

'*Pfff...*' Mira scratched her head. 'Well, then I guess there's no need for any additional clarifications on that front.'

'There is, actually.'

'Huh?' Mira sounded genuinely surprised.

'What qualifies you to be a therapist?'

'I just told you. I know how minds work because I need to in order to make other minds work the same way, but better, in some regards.'

'That's what qualifies you to be a scientist – a neuroscientist, to be more precise. I'm asking you what qualifies you to be a therapist? To practise therapy?'

It was Mira's time to err now. 'I, eh –.'

'Have you ever had a patient or, I think, they're called clients?'

'... I mean I have friends and I listen to their problems...'

'... Pfffuck.'

'Ay yo, *fuck you*!' Mira jumped from the hood of the car, immediately squaring up in front of him. She stood at the same height as him and, though he was male and heavier, Thomas felt intimidated, not by her stature, nor by her reputation, but by how palpable her rage was.

Oh my God... This must be what her father's rage must have been like.

The rage of Djibril al Sayid was the stuff of legend. In some strange way, Thomas felt the same echoing nostalgia now as he had felt touching Adler's desk. Just that, this time, he felt as if he were in a play, with words written long ago by someone of a past age being rendered before him by one with a masterful presence.

He gave in before the demon of old before him.

He looked up and dared himself to meet her glare. 'I'm sorry. I apologise.'

Mira began to relax almost instantly, yet Thomas did see her reconsider the de-escalation before finally giving in. She did not break eye contact, waiting for Thomas to avert his gaze by once more looking towards the sea. Only then did she return to her place next to him and not without letting out a loud grunt as she slouched aggressively, making the shuttle wobble slightly.

She really is a beast or, at least, she acts like one quite convincingly.

After visibly struggling to finally relax, she continued, 'I knew they were working on something like this. It was clear as clean glass. I spent months trying to confirm it until I knew for certain that this was going on. Ever since that moment, I have been knocking on every door I know to be a part of it.' Her voice had gone from a rambling frustration to a solemn confession.

Now *that* caught Thomas' attention.

He turned to see Mira, still furious, yet, he could tell, no longer at him. 'And, when I finally got a deal, *you* came along with it.' *Ok, well, she's still primarily angry at me.*

She pulled out another cigarette. The first one having flown out of her hand into the sea below during her fit of rage. 'That's what Thomas and Shosho offered me after you left their office: that I could be part of this, if it was as your mentor. It's not what I wanted. But, hey, you have to play the cards you're dealt.' She didn't strike him as someone keen on folding, that was for sure.

'I... I don't understand. How could you know about Kralizec, while not being part of Project Kralizec?'

'That's a pretty easy question to answer. Hopefully, the next ones won't be.' She turned to look at him again. 'How does one become a keeper? Ruben told you this morning.'

Thomas thought about his own experience over the last few days. 'You get recommended. Apply. Then you get selected for whichever role you can fill in.'

'That is, by and large, correct.' Mira sparked her second cigarette. 'It took a while but, in the end, I finally got someone to recommend me.' Mira paused, seemingly gathering her thoughts. However, she seemed to drift off at one point, which was not something Thomas wanted her to do at this point.

'But, how did you figure it out?' What he really wanted to was to ask who recommended her or, more exactly, how did she convince that person to recommend her. Yet, he felt that it was not something she was willing to share.

'I've spent some time wondering how I figured it out myself. It started out as a hunch. A feeling. Something more at home at night, in the world of dreams. It finally grew into a question: how far are they willing to go down the rabbit hole? You see... there's no other way to say this without sounding arrogant, but... I grew up around the most powerful people in the Alliance. They were my caretakers, my tutors, my guardians, my playmates, my friends, my...' Thomas saw something strange happen to her as he was saying these words. She seemed to be forcing herself to say them. '... my family.'

None of this surprised him. She was, after all, the Terran equivalent of a princess. 'When someone is family, you get to know them in a very deep way. Little things they do carry meanings neither you nor they can put into words. Mostly because, most of the time, you don't even consciously know you're observing those little things to begin with.'

'They would hide. They always hid things. They always left the room when the conversation had to turn to sensitive matters. I got used to it. I didn't like it at all, though. In time, they stopped leaving the room. When I came of age, they would speak of things, things they would not speak of in front of a child, for fear that the child wouldn't keep things to themselves and, yet...' for a moment it seemed as if she was about to give up.

'... and, yet, I still felt that they were hiding things and it ate at me. This particular thing, I think I managed to figure out by virtue of the fact that, well, I know these motherfuckers.' Her smile, cheeky now, had returned. 'Tomasz, Laur, the other Hierarchs, Representatives, Generals... they are obsessed with survival and security. Ironically, it was Tomasz who told me that "men, in their madness, seek certainty, not understanding that within that impossible certainty lies only certain misery".'

She turned to face him now. 'If you ever get to know him, you'll notice that Tomasz Ashaver is dead to his own wisdom. '

Thomas had managed to keep the thoughts at bay, yet, now, despite no words drifting into his mind, he felt the cold despair tear at his essence again, as he struggled against the certainty of his own uncertainty. He shifted, ever so slightly, like an animal caught in a hunter's crosshairs. This hunter's eyes, however, also shifted, revealing that she had noticed the subtle movement.

'That,' she pointed her chin in his direction. 'Turns out that, in the end, *that* is why I was allowed to be here. I got recommended, but Tomasz shut me down immediately. Gave me shit as to how I am too well known. How I'd attract suspicion from the outside. How I was better suited elsewhere. But, in the end, he told me the real reason.' She stood up straight and scratched her hair as she looked out over the horizon.

'I couldn't "contribute in any meaningful" way to the whole thing.' Mira's voice, he had noted, was usually adept at only ever transmitting one emotion at the time, usually boredom, rage, interest, mockery or just a cold emptiness. Yet, as these last words left her lips, they had blown forth with sadness, disappointment, shame and, yes, quite a hefty dose of anger.

'I guess you and him have more in common than your first names.' He had shifted her head to look at him, once more, beneath a furrowed brow and fiery eyes. 'But, in the end, I decided to give it one more shot. That shot was two days ago, when I stepped into Shoshanna's office after you. I spent some time there and in the end, there was a breakthrough.'

'I would be allowed to take part in Kralizec, yet my role would be a very specific one. Which is where you come into play.' Mira stopped herself. Thomas could tell that she knew what she was going to say. It just seemed to him that she was doing her best to put it into words as best she could.

'I understand your situation, in broad terms. Tomasz and Shoshanna gave me… a high level breakdown of what your problem is. There is a report in my inbox, outlining and detailing absolutely everything about you that could be recorded: your medical record, your examination results, your service record, analysis of your friends and family… everything. Now, have no doubt, I will read every single line with great care and consideration. However, I think it is best if we had our initial discussion with me knowing that much about you. That way, we can have a conversation, as opposed to me just analysing you.'

She turned to look at him. 'Do you agree?' Thomas felt that the question came from a place of honesty, yet he felt no choice other than to respond with a lie. 'Yes'.

'Good.' This time she didn't take his eyes off him. 'You wanna… give me a rundown? We have a few minutes before courtesy dictates we get going.'

Thomas looked at her. He felt the mix of doubt and despair that raged throughout him pause in anticipation... It was almost as if it waited to see if he dared to still hope for a good outcome to things. Thomas had learned the difference between doubt and despair all too well these last few days. Doubt was the double-edged blade which stood above the throat of reason, its edge so sharp, one could imagine a throat being slit without the body even realising it had been cut. Despair was what one felt when the hope that flowed through the veins of any living being gushing out into oblivion. In these last days he had struggled to stop the torrent of hope seeping out of him, as doubt cut at his capacity to seal the open wound which had started all of this back on that tram on Luna.

What little hope he had drawn from telling himself that everything would turn out alright, that there might be a benevolent God of the whole Universe, that the problem might be solved by men and women much wiser than he in a future far far away, that perhaps a solution had already been provided, had been drained away that very morning in that amphitheatre in Jerusalem. What a curse it was to meet your heroes and see how flawed and *human* they were. This was, in all certainty, yet another mistake. How they had decided to let his girl – this troubled, angry girl – act as a guide and a mentor to him, was just more proof of their well-meaning incompetence.

How could she help him? She was a berserker, an avatar of rage and fury. She, at least, was exactly as he had pictured her: a creature of the battlefield, an instrument of Terran vengeance and 'a bull in a china shop', as the old saying went. Tomasz and Shoshanna – and who knows who else – had seen fit to let this bull loose in the china shop of his sanity? The shards of his faith in the infinite potential of his life already lay strewn across the floor. There was no need for someone to barge and stomp on them.

What did they know of these things? What qualified them to play God? Their survival? That they had lived through the Apocalypse? If anything, that alone was reason enough to disqualify their judgement from consideration. What could anyone who had seen the world shatter around them know about helping someone who felt their world shattering *inside* of them? After all, they were the ones going on about how it had been their inner strength that had kept them alive during the dark days of the End Times and the War of Vengeance.

His problem was the exact opposite: he had no inner strength anymore. The barriers that had kept away the madness in his mind – as they likely stood in every other sentient mind – had fallen and now the demons were loose. Even now, he felt numb and defeated. He would have liked nothing more than to stay here, curl up under his shuttle like some wretched slithering creature of the muck and sit there until the despair would stop. The only thing that stopped him was the even clearer knowledge that the demons would not stop their dance as long as they had their dance floor. It would be only oblivion which could end the suffering now.

Thus, the cycle of torment, for the thousandth time in the last days, reached full circle again. He feared death. The fear obsessed him. He only thought of the fear. He couldn't live like this. He wanted the fear to go away. He knew only death could take the fear of death away.

IT'S ALL SO FUCKING MADDENING!

Fucking joke. A sad, certain joke.

He smiled. These words had acted out in his mind before. Right before he had decided to tell his mother about the thoughts. Right before he had gotten into his father's shuttle to go see O'Malley. Right before deciding to tell Adler and Ashaver about his actual situation. He had even had these thoughts right before he had signed Opera's paperwork and sealed his fate as a keeper. Perhaps not the same words, but definitely the same feeling.

Somehow it had been the hope presented by the unknown path lit up before him that had spurred him to action. His ignorance of what lay outside the realms of possibility he was familiar with had been where he had found the hope to move on. He turned to look at the girl next to him and saw not her eyes, boring into him questioningly, obviously held back by her decision to be agonisingly patient with him. Rather, he saw something else.

He saw a 'maybe'.

If I thought that this path was worth it before and if this is where the path has led me, I will stay on this path.

It was by the power of that commitment, not by the signature in Opera's office, nor by his honesty in Adler's office, and definitely not by virtue of O'Malley's recommendation, that he had become a Keeper of Terra. He may not be a believer in the mission, but he wasn't much of a believer of anything anymore, other than the possibility that there might be some hope out there. That there might be an angle to things he hadn't seen before. That there might be some golden nugget of information which might fix him somewhere.

If he acknowledged that he did not know everything – which he knew he didn't – then moving forward might reveal the way out of the labyrinth of dread that was his mind.

In the end, he nodded and collected his thoughts to speak. 'It happened more than a week ago, on Luna. I… I was so happy to finish my Host service. I was going to be a Lieutenant in the Logistics Corps, which was all that I ever really wanted. In that moment of joy, I heard a voice say: "enjoy this moment, for one day you shall die".'

'I... been like this ever since.'

Mira was not looking at him anymore, yet he could tell she was listening. 'Go on.'

'I... I thought it was a passing thought, but it wasn't. I... tried to fix it by myself. I couldn't. I asked for help. The help I got wasn't that great. The questions have multiplied ever since. It's like I'm getting homework. That voice – that part of my mind – sends me questions to which I have to come up with answers. Once I do and I turn the homework in, I just get new questions!' he confessed, though acknowledging it out loud hurt him.

'Tell me more about the thoughts themselves. What questions bother you?'

'Death. Is there anything after death? Where does... all of this...' he gestured vaguely '... the Universe, the Multiverse, everything... Where does it come from? How did it come about?' he paused, waiting for a reply, as if she was going to tell him where the universe came from.

'What else?' she asked, after seeing that he would not go on.

He smirked, though he didn't find anything to be funny. 'Isn't that enough?'

Mira, remarkably, did not get angry at his sarcasm. 'No. Is that it?' she asked calmly.

'Well... thinking about those things goes very deep. I'm not sure if I understand what you're asking?' he confessed and looked to her, begging her for some understanding, at least.

Mira met Thomas' candid question with her own distant silence. 'You have, somehow, *progressed*. It was probably the meeting in the amphitheatre which moved you to the second question.' Her face changed, as if she had made up her mind about something. 'Well, I guess that's the first thing we could set up.'

Mira began to rummage around in another pocket and pulled out another case, this one smaller. This one he could tell was of trollish design. He recognized it as a traditional hill troll woodworking pattern, reflecting a sea of moving leaves across a forest floor. Mira opened it to reveal cigarettes inside, seemingly the same as those in her other box.

'What's that?' he asked, surprised that he somehow knew the answer already.

'Pot.'

'W-what?!'

'Marijuana? Weed? Cannabis? Ganja? I'm good with synonyms.' She raised the case to him. 'You want?'

'No!'

'Didn't think you would. *That* I could tell already!' she said, as she lit a cigarette from the second box.

Thomas' spirits once more sank. She wasn't taking this seriously, wasn't she? He really was doomed.

Mira noticed his appallingly abandoned look. 'Yeah, look, here's the thing: I'm going to be honest with you. If things go according to plan, me and you are gonna end up discussing some wild shit during these sessions. Now, I'm not going to lie, I'm really into this deep, existential crisis shit. However, it's one thing to be into something, and quite another to be in the midst of it. You're going to go places far away from my usual thoughts. At least, hopefully you will. After all, that's the point of all of this. It's why you're here. By some strange twist of fate, it's also why I am here.'

'If I am going to sit here and listen to all of it, *I'm gonna be high*. It'll make it easier to get to your level. It will, also – and I want you to appreciate how candid I am right now – allow me to get through with it without getting mad at some of the shit you're going to come up with. It is very important that, at the end of the day, I – and I quote the higher-ups – "not pollute the results with [my] know-it-all bullshit".'

'So, as I was saying…' she paused to take a deeper puff '… you have only been struck by two facts,' The first one,' she exhaled, 'on Luna, was the certainty of your death. The second, today, was the absence of any inherent structure to the universe. These questions have no rational answer, at least not in the traditional sense. They're not even questions to begin with. They're simply axioms, at the end of long streams of questions. And they're only two, out of a total of four.' She paused to look at him. 'You ever hear of a guy called Zapffe?'

'No, I haven't.' He knew a sergeant named Ziffer though.

Mira seemed surprised 'You haven't been googling philosophers? Camus? Nietzsche? Fucking Kierkegaard?' Mira paused as Thomas took in the wave of existential dread coming over him.

She would've gone on, yet Thomas interrupted her, 'I have! Yes. I have. I haven't heard of Zapffe though.'

'Ah. Ok. Well, you see, Zapffe was a Scandinavian philosopher in the nineteenth century AD… or twentieth… I dunno; whatever. The point is that he boiled down all of these existential questions into four major end-of-the-road facts about existence.'

'These are:'

'(1) The certainty of the end of one's existence – i.e. you're gonna die one day;'

'(2) The absence of any inherent structure of the universe – i.e. there ain't no God, at least not in the traditional sense;'

'(3) The unavoidable loneliness of the individual – i.e. you're alone and always will be, unless if you're a spawn, but that's a whole different can of worms;'

'(4) The absolute freedom of the individual in the pursuit of one's own destiny – i.e. whatcha gonna do given the aforementioned three things?'

'Now, have you thought about all four?'

Thomas had to struggle not to throw up, as each of Mira's words had fallen on him like a hammer, striking at every tender bit of his soul.

'Tangentially,' he managed to whisper.

'I suppose that's to be expected. But have all of them obsessed you? As the first one does and how the second one seems to be now also?'

'I don't...' he paused to gather his thoughts and decide how best to put it. Within this process, he realised that he did not even know how to put it to himself. 'I don't know. I would say the first two are the most pressing matters, though the other two have crossed my mind.' It sounded as true to him as it could be. The vagueness bothered him. Something else bothered him. 'Doesn't telling me these things pollute my experience?' He meant no jest. The question was honest.

Mira smiled now, once more. 'I'm not giving you any answers. Nor am I suggesting any answer. I'm merely presenting questions to you. The answers are yours to give.'

'But, the fact that you've told me this… *categorization*... it will affect me. I mean it rings true to me! These are, indeed, the four questions with no answer and, yes, I have thought about how the only thing to be done about it is to make up my mind as to what I'm gonna do now that I'm aware of them, but… won't it influence me?'

Mira paused and looked blankly forward. 'Which Terran philosophers have you come about?'

'Jesus Christ…'

'I guess he counts as one too. More of a religious figure, though…'

'No, I mean –'

'Have you googled religious things too?'

'Y-yes.'

'Good, tell me about that.'

'I… I'd rather talk about the philosophers first.'

'Good. We'll save that for later. Go on then.'

'I read *the Brothers Karamazov* by a Russian called Dostoyevsky a few days ago.'

'I didn't read that one. Have you read the *Stranger*? By Albert Camus?'

'I read the resume… and I watched some videos about what the meaning is.'

'I see. Well, if you do, read it in French. It's much better than the English version. So, other than Dostoyevsky, what else have you been getting into?'

'I've read a lot about Nietzsche, Kierkegaard, Sartre, Kant, Hegel, Jung –'

'– dayum. Ok. We get it, you're German. Chill! What do you think about what they had to say about things?'

'That… that existence is inherently meaningless.'

'It is.'

'You said you won't give any answers…'

'I'm not. That's just my opinion. Anyway, go on.'

'We are responsible for attributing meaning to it.'

Mira paused and looked confused. 'Well, then it's case-closed. Why are you still freaking out?'

'Because, in the vast totality of things, no meaning attributable to my life will survive the entropy of the universe! Nor is it relevant or impactful in any way to anyone or anything other than myself.'

'Ah… Ok. Why does that matter to you?'

'Because the meaning I want to attribute to my life is to figure out a way to live forever, *goddammit*!' Thomas caught himself yelling just as he finished his outburst.

Mira seemed nonplussed. 'Why?'

'Because I love life! I love living. Life is great. Every day is a new adventure and I don't want to stop living it.'

'Good. Did what you hear today reassure you?'

Thomas wanted to reply with the truth, but his nature urged him to lie. His thoughts went to Adler's words from earlier in the day.

'No one questions your loyalty, not adapting to that constitutes failure'.

He may not grant them the credit needed to carry out their most ambitious of projects, but he did grant them the competence of understanding that he, a Terran sunriser and a lieutenant, would follow commands to the letter. If they wanted him to find holes in their plan, then he would, especially if they appeared to be so glaring to him.

'No. No it did not.' *I am not a bad lieutenant.*

'Why?' she pressed.

'Uhm… *pfff*… huh… I … pictured it differently in my head. I didn't picture... I didn't visualise it at all. In many ways, I think I never wanted to see it with my own two eyes. Seeing it makes it… *vulnerable*, since it makes if feel like a goal and not all goals are reached. Goals are things people set and people are… imperfect.'

'You dare doubt the Terran High Command?'

He turned to look at her properly, not even bothering to hide his shock. Mira's tone carried a light sheen of humour, yet her face was the epitome of a poker face. To tell if she was being playful or dead serious would be a difficult task under normal circumstances. Given Thomas' awareness of his affected mental state, he wasn't going to bother to figure out her intent.

'How old am I?' It was his turn to ask questions again.

'... twenty... six?'

'I'm twenty-five. What is my rank?'

'You're really cocky for someone on the edge, you know that?'

'Maybe that's why I haven't tipped over yet. What is my rank, *Captain* al Sayid?' He might be pushing it again, but fuck it. If he was getting mindwiped, he might as well justify it.

'You are a Lieutenant.' Mira seemed to have decided to play along. For now.

'How many sunriser lieutenants are there?' Thomas realised that maybe he shouldn't have said the word 'sunriser' out loud. Some sunrisers saw it as derogatory, particularly ones who carried themselves the way she did.

She smiled. 'Not that many. I should know.' She had been the fifth sunriser Lieutenant in Terran history, the first to be promoted as a member of an Avenger Legion. She had also been the second ever sunriser Captain. *She told you not to fanboy! State your point and forget the career highlights.*

'Well, there's more than there was when you started out, but not that many. Last time I checked there were less than two hundred of us, most hushed far away from Terra, so as not to risk the terrible travesty of having a youngling give orders to an oldtimer.'

'You… "check"? You check the rankboard?' Mira seemed genuinely surprised.

'Yes, goddammit! But that's beside the point. My point is that I'm not some fucking idiot! I'm fairly competent and intelligent –'

'– and modest –' she felt the need to add.

'– and now is not the time for mincing words and beating behind bushes! Yes, by and large, I am a competent, intelligent, reliable *and* modest person.' He paused artistically, wanting her to understand exactly how what he was about to say contrasted with what he had said thus far.

'... and I make mistakes.' *Yeah, I said it!* 'It hurts me to say it. My very nature is against me saying that out loud, but it's true. I make mistakes all the time. It is something, which I was taught – *we* were taught –' he raised his head to look straight at her, seeking to make sure that she remembered the same lessons he knew she had been taught 'that to make mistakes is to be expected, yet not accepted.'

He saw her slowly nod, understanding seemingly dawning on her. He continued. 'When it comes to this thing which is … the greatest objective I could possibly imagine, any mistake is – not "could" – *is* the unmaking of the entire endeavour. And it is a goal undertaken by men and women just like me. People just like me who can have lapses in judgement, just as I do. Moreover…' he paused, looking, once more, deep inside himself for the strength needed to say what he had to say.

He didn't have too. 'Perhaps your very presence here is a sign of their lapse in judgement.' He saw that there was neither ill will, nor anger in her as she spoke. Her eyes lingered on him, a sadness looming over them now.

He nodded. 'Yes. It all seems so... *basic*. So mundane. So prone to the ever-present failings and vulnerabilities of people. Yes. Yes, I did imagine that maybe someday, somewhere, someone would go ahead and do what we appear to be trying to do here now. Just that... I imagined *gods*. I imagined beings of incomprehensible wisdom and ability. Not *people*! Seeing that it is just *people*, fills me with so much doubt and it's worse now! I told myself that I might be able to take solace in the fact that I will never know whether it could be done or not. As if I was wounded now and I was about to have surgery performed on me sometime in the future. I took solace in the thought that I would not be there, at least not awake, to see the surgeon stitch me up. For if I were, I might see the surgeon be little more than a person: prone to distractions, susceptible to biases, tiredness and other such failings. I may not know how to perform surgery, yet I do know other things. Difficult things. I know that I – and others much more able and experienced – can make miscalculations.'

He stopped now, as he felt he had gone too far. His eyes had drifted away from hers again. He turned to focus on her.

The wind had picked up slightly and tendrils of smoke made their way from the burning tip of her cigarette into her eyes, which did not water or blink. She didn't even squint. She seemed to notice him observing the smoke and lifted the cigarette to her lips to puff absent-mindedly, as if she had been reminded that it was something she had set out to do.

Eventually she spoke. 'I think you're not the first to think about things that way. I actually think that's the entire purpose of having you on board. I think people have become too confident and too cocksure of themselves here. I think they've noticed it themselves and recognized the fact that arrogance is the root of all mistakes made by otherwise competent people. Your role here is to point out any crack in their thinking. Which seems to be something you're more than willing to do. From what I can tell so far.'

She puffed her cigarette again. 'Also, like... like that was back-in-the-day, you know? Surgeons? I mean most surgery now is done by operators. So that's a bad example.'

Thomas made to speak but she cut him off. 'No, I mean, I get it. Just that, that example, in itself, shows how advancements in technology can help avert human error and, at the end of the day, that's what the administrator is. It's an artificial intelligence... with feelings.'

'Which could make it as prone to mistakes as any other regular person.'

Mira paused and looked off into the distance or, perhaps, the past. For a second Thomas believed that he might have finally crossed a line. Mira's life had been marked, after all, not by the actions of one, but of two different artificial intelligences. One had changed her life for the worst, the other, for the best. His statement had been an expression of his doubt, not an attempt at intimacy. He wondered if the message had reached her in the way he had intended.

'You ever seen the movie *Casablanca?*' she asked suddenly.

'Yes. Yes I have.'

'Well then, "I guess this is the beginning of a beautiful friendship".' Mira got up from the hood of the car and began walking towards her own shuttle. 'Let's bounce! We're late. I like getting to these things on time. Plus, I'm dying for a drive.'

'But… but you're high!' Thomas babbled after her.

'I've got perfume in the car. No one will know.' She stopped walking. 'You ain't no snitch now ain't ya?' She turned and gave him the sarcastic look of a (hopefully) mock interrogation.

'No. Just that … it's against regulation to drive high.'

'Is it illegal?'

'No. But there's a reason why it's against regulation.'

'Yeah. So that you don't put yourself in situations where you might break the law.' She gestured to the cigarette, still lit in her hand. 'Driving high *isn't* illegal. Driving bad *is*. Come! Let me show you how well I drive!'

Thomas felt all the blood rush from his face to his skull. 'It's fine. I'll dwe… d-d-drrrive… eh…' He raised his hand, slightly, pointed towards his car.

'Dwe-d-d-d-du-du-duive? Nah, Elmer Fudd! What's your operator's name? Casper, what's his operator's name?' *Was she talking to her operator? Out loud? She must be high!*

'C-C….' Thomas gulped his stammer away. 'Clara?'

'Ok. Well, tell Clara to take your shuttle home. Me and Casper will drop you off later.'

'But… but why don't you tell Casper to drive?' which was what he had initially thought she was going to do, until she specified that *she* would be the one doing the driving.

'Because I feel like driving. Come on! Don't make me give you an order!' She had reached her shuttle now, opening her door. As she stepped inside, she left her left hand outside, as she gestured to him, cigarette in hand, to hurry up.

Thomas stopped himself for one second. He told Clara to take the car back to Jerusalem, then pretended to make sure he was checking to see if she was listening to his command. As Clara turned on the shuttle and began lifting off, he asked himself why he was so terrified.

He had been scared like this before, also in situations pertaining to means of transportation. His platoon's tank had crashed through the orbits of four different worlds, crashing in fiery flames to the surface below, where thousands of Aesir warriors had waited to bring great battle to the fabled Republican Alliance which had come to rain down the terrible fury of its Allied Host upon their realms.

Their tank pilot had been a high elf Sergeant named Guilisier, nicknamed "Speedy" for both his love of high velocity and amphetamines. That must have been definitely against regulation albeit not illegal (for some reason). Being a bit scared then had been a sign of sanity. Being scared now actually pointed in the other direction.

What the hell? I've driven high myself. What the fuck?

Why was he scared? So suddenly? For nothing?

The answer came swiftly: he wasn't comfortable with the risk anymore. He realised now the tendency of the universe to loom a small amount of risk over every waking moment. One could live in constant struggle to decrease that risk, yet one could also learn to live with a level of risk which they could deem acceptable and, most importantly, ignorable. Somehow, it had always felt so natural for him to choose this second worldview. Yet, now, he found himself knowing that something had shifted inside of him. The risk was no longer tolerable.

Therein Thomas saw the path to cowardice and the scorn of all Terra for one as wretched as himself. To be worse than even poor Ronan, for he had *chosen* to not fight, rather than having been revealed by circumstance to be a coward. He stopped himself from tripping down the path of cowardice by tripping in real life, as he turned and sprinted towards Mira's shuttle with more fake bravado in his step than was sustainable.

He barely remembered getting into Mira's shuttle, as he had spent most of his way concentrating on telling himself that it was all going to be alright and that he was just overreacting. What did succeed in bringing him back to reality was the sound of Mira spraying coconut & patchouli perfume all over herself and the cockpit.

She caught him looking. 'What? It's fine! It's a unisex smell or at least most people seem to think it is, so you won't smell exclusively like a girl.'

'No. No. It's ok. I like the smell,' he replied politely.

'Oh. Really? You want some?' Mira was offering him the bottle, whilst manoeuvring the shuttle into the air. One-handed. Without looking at what she was doing or where she was going.

'No. No. It's fine. I have my own. I've got enough fallout over here.'

'Great!' She wasn't wearing her seat belt.

It's not illegal, but it is very against regulation.

Her speed was also legal while also being against regulation. The trip to Eilat should have taken about two minutes from parking spot to parking spot, at reasonable speed. Yet, Mira made the trip in less than sixty seconds. The first admirable thing about the ride was that she had attempted to make small talk about perfume trends amongst the Terran population by gender, nationality and age, whilst comparing them with the much better perfumes of the goblins, ursai and, yes, even the elves, but not the demani, the orcs and the remani, whom she insisted were mediocre, except the macadamia-smelling one used by some remani.

All Thomas could coherently remember as he fought through his anxiety attack was how her favourite perfume was an ursai scent that smelled like Christmas.

He was much more concerned with the second admirable thing about Mira's driving. Even though she drove like a maniac, she did make extensive use of her signalling lights… by igniting the 'Warning! Collision possible!' lights almost continuously.

That being said, Mira wasn't a bad driver. His father was a much more erratic driver. In fact, at one point, in a moment of clarity, he even realised she might be a better driver than him. She was also one of those people who just pressed the on/off button to stop the car, instead of following adequate protocol.

'Here we are! Let's go!'

The restaurant was located on the upper battlements of Eilat, facing the Gulf of Aqaba to the south. Thomas had never been to Eilat before, yet had heard of the old city's fame during the End Times. At the Hour of Twilight, when all had seemed lost and humanity's flame on Terra had almost flickered out, it had been only Eilat that had survived the final battle of the End Times, of all the cities of old Israel. Tel Aviv and Haifa had been wiped out by the volcanic activity that had torn the Mediterranean apart, along with all the other cities of the old coastlines. Nazareth and the other cities of northern Israel had fallen in the days leading up to the Battle of Armageddon. Jerusalem itself had held out until Doomsday itself, only to fall in the early hours of the morning, the last IDF soldiers and Arab militiamen burning together as the elves lit the city aflame, not bothering to take on the defenders, after their orders had switched from extermination to destruction.

Israel had fared much better than most Terran nations, only losing half of its population during the End Times. However, this had the unfortunate effect of having the Israelis becoming one of the largest contingents of the old Warhost of Terra. As the Terrans had sewn their vengeance in red letters across the stars, they also experienced loss of human life which would have shocked even the most stone-hearted warriors of Old Earth. Yet, compared with the obliteration experienced during the End Times, casualties numbering in the millions seemed mild by comparison. Such had been the callousness and savagery of those times.

Eilat had become the home base of Army of Israel and, later on, the Sayeret, with the Terrans having focused on fortifying the city, pending the reconstruction of Jerusalem and Haifa. A shipyard was the most distinguishing feature of the inner city, with Terran cruisers still docked in the vast hangars, hidden beneath green parkland. From above, the great citadel of Eilat Nahal watched over the blue sea to the south and the green seas of the Negev to the west, north and east. From the fortress, a great circle of masonry spread out in a circle, encompassing the city within.

Mira had left her shuttle beneath this encircling wall, in an area of the city designated for parking. She was already making her way up a flight of stairs leading up to a doorway with the words *Ethil Akerdil Eilatrae* etched above its frame. Thomas recognized the words as orcish for *The Beloved Esplanade of Eilat*. The Orcish influence was recognizable as elegant blue and gold met with stern Terran black and white along the walls of the hallway within. The hallway led to the esplanade itself, which lay situated on the battlements facing the sea. Several tables ran along the wall's edge, many of them packed with the establishment's patrons, likely having just arrived for dinner.

Thomas had just caught up with Mira as he identified their table, situated on one of the few towers which jutted out from the fortress' walls towards the sea. As they turned the corner towards the tower, he glanced quickly at the table and recognized some of the keepers from the meeting in the amphitheatre, including the doctor, Opera.

He followed Mira as she made her entrance. Though most of the keepers attempted to act nonplussed by her presence, the sounds of their conversation had changed as she had drawn near. Words were spoken differently, faces flashed as they glanced her way only once, never twice, and more than one back straightened, as she had come closer. Seeing this, Thomas realised something about Mira.

This was her life. She had spent her entire existence as someone known by all of her peers. He remembered how during his time with the Allied Host he had heard goblins, elves and demani utter the name of al Sayid in reverence. It was a name known on Terra, Vigilant, Moria, Gondolin, Menegroth and a hundred other worlds, spoken in the same breaths as the names of Ashaver, al Fajr, Braca, Falk, Uhrlacker, Andromander or Jimmel. All had heard the story of the child found in the snows of Terra's poles, as a galaxy away her father died a warrior's death alongside hundreds of enemies while in the broken halls that lay before her makeshift crib, her mother denied an empire with one hand, and a demigod with another.

Child of heroes, sister to a god, raised by legends, tutored by paragons and friend of demons. Here she walked amongst them high as a kite and with her stumbling charge skittering behind her.

He was surprised to see her wave to Opera, as her fellow captain waved back and gestured to the seats next to her. The doctor moved to her right, highlighting the two vacancies to her left. Mira turned to gesture for him to follow her, as she greeted the table and took her place next to Opera. Thomas followed suit, finding himself next to…

Sorbo Falk?!!!

He hadn't noticed him. He had been too busy following Mira's sprinting stride, following her gaze as she had waved to Opera and acting all cool as he had greeted the table without making eye contact with anyone seated.

The old troll was over two and a half meters tall and hard to miss, sitting slouched on an armchair, shisha pipe in one hand and a glass of brown bourbon in the other. He was dressed, as he had been in the morning, after the fashion of his people, in an outfit closely resembling an old Terran three-piece suit, with his blazer's collar turned upwards, as was the style of the military of Kalimaste, revealing the inverted 'A' of a Hierarch. So it was that Thomas found himself, for the second day in a row, sitting next to a Hierarch of the Republican Alliance. Yet, this troll was so different from Ashaver. Being in the presence of the great Terran warlord had been a bizarre feeling, as he had been so gregarious and playful in his temperament. One could likely be in the same room as Ashaver for hours and not feel the greatness of the man before him. Nor the trauma or hardship behind his greatness.

This was not the case with Falk. He had long, green eyes, bearing the hallmarks of a quiet melancholy deep within. Whereas one might look upon Ashaver and behold a madman blissfully unaware of the terrific violence, horror and tragedy of the life he had lived, one could not bear Falk's presence without feeling the presence of loss and, beneath it, in the bright centre of his eyes, the bright beacons of hope and resilience. Thomas saw the dignified lights beneath the troll's dark eyebrows before he had even realised that they were looking right at him.

'Sir!' he said quickly, not knowing for how long he had been staring at the old troll.

'Do you hear that, Mira? I am not his godfather and yet he still finds it civil to greet me.' The troll smiled now, his gaze lingering on him a second longer, before turning to his goddaughter.

'Well then you'll have to pardon him. He doesn't know he's being impolite.' Mira spared one of the greatest men in the entire Milky Way Galaxy only a passing glance and the corner of a smile.

'Aha? And why is he impolite?' The troll had not stopped smiling.

'Because he doesn't know that you don't like it when people greet you first.' She turned to smile at him now. It was a true, honest smile, broader than Thomas would have thought possible of her. 'It makes you feel old.' Almost a bit too big of a smile it was.

'Eh... it does.' He stopped slouching in his chair and leaned towards her, his head now looming over Thomas' measly two meter frame, as the troll gestured with two fingers the size of bananas for her to lean in towards him.

Which she did. 'I think you didn't say hello because you're – how Tomasz would say – "high as giraffe pussy"?' Mira drew back slightly, breaking eye contact with Falk, her lofty cool flicked away on a passing sea breeze by the troll's words. Her godfather continued. 'What are you doing?'

He didn't give her the chance to answer.

'For weeks all I hear from you and of you is how you've been going about raising hell in your quest to be assigned a role within this endeavour. It tore at my heart to know that you had come to understand that which was happening without your knowledge. I went against the judgement of men whom I admire more than you may ever imagine when I told Tomasz that, if you keep pushing, he should relent and God bless him, he did! He heeded an old friend's advice and gave in to your relentlessness. How overjoyed I was just yesterday to learn that you would join your brethren on this road. I looked forward so joyfully towards the thought that you would find within this journey the great trial of your life, from whence you would emerge a better woman than you were when you first embarked upon it.'

'Only for me to come here and see you to not take it seriously? Do you now, perhaps, understand everyone's reservations?' Mira now meant to speak, yet a hand the size of a frying pan rested on her shoulder. She took the hint.

'I know you're doing this to numb yourself, child. You've likely steeled yourself into thinking of it as being necessary for you to maintain your distance from the task at hand. However, I was hoping that you aspired to contribute more than empty space to things. It hurts me to see that you have opted to not even grant this task the bare minimum of your capacity.' His tone was fatherly, as was the melody of many expressions of disappointment uttered across the universe.

He drew back and puffed his shisha pipe. Thomas felt a familiar odour escape his flaring nostrils as he exhaled. Pineapple and... pineapple express?

The tell-tale scent was not lost on Mira as she smirked.

'You're a hypocrite.' Yet, she didn't meet the troll's eyes.

'No. I am not. I am here enjoying stimulating conversations with some future friends over fresh hummus, good bread, good bourbon, some "aromatics" and, later on, hopefully, some babka.' He quickly turned to look at Thomas. 'I really like babka.' He felt the need to emphasise this love of babka, while Thomas felt the need to nod in agreement, despite not knowing what 'babka' was.

Turning back to Mira. 'Surrounding myself with youthful energy helps me stay young. At least, it keeps my heart young. I did, however, also think I'd drop by this specific establishment, to make sure you're not doing what you appear to be doing, which is being a terrible child.'

He pointed at Thomas with his pipe. 'The boy needs your help and guidance, Mira. Not your abuse, nor your neglect. Some argued that you would not be capable of providing the former, only the latter. I argued otherwise. As did others –'

Mira interrupted. '– There were other ways I could –'

'– No! There weren't!' Falk did not raise his voice. He turned to Thomas now, as Mira's eyes sought to set the grey hair of the troll's temples aflame. 'She was nurtured with love for the kindness of her nature, which we all could see with a naked eye, ever since she was old enough to smile and laugh. She was nurtured with care, for fear of the burning flame raging inside of her, which one could feel from the moment she was old enough to wrestle with your fingers.' He pointed said fingers at Mira's eyes.

'There! It has always been there, as part of her as the flesh clinging to her bones and even more! She was also nurtured with hope, for you could see the flashes of wit forever in her. She made us all cry in wonder as only a child's wisdom can. The expectation that her mind would blossom into a wisdom of the ages quivered the hearts of men who could've sworn they had no pulse left in them.' He turned to Mira again.

'You were kept away because you're a protector, Mira. We wanted your talents to bloom around that facet of your nature. That you would grow into a leader of men.'

Mira scoffed. Falk scoffed too, before turning to Thomas once more. 'Yet, there is another dragon within her. One which she hides very well yet is clear to see for all who know her. You see, young man, Mira, if given her way, could spend an eternity indulging her curiosity. Ever since she was a toddler, this was her way! All children are blessed with the virtue of curiosity yet, with her, one could say it was more a vice than a virtue. All day, all she did was explore and ask questions. She would rage like a demon if one ever dared enforce slumber upon her.'

The troll's eyes drifted now, the melancholy of his eyes mixing with the tender tones of nostalgia. 'Eventually, we just stopped telling her to go to bed and we would find her the next day, cuddled up like a cat next to some book with her hands around some contraption she had gotten a hold of'. He paused now, once more, appearing to take in one such image in and smiling to himself. He spoke after a while, to both of them.

'A force of nature, we wanted you to be and you are, Mira. What everyone omitted was how all you wanted to do was see the world for what it was and understand it for what it was. Now…' He began fidgeting with the waterpipe, as he looked down upon it in his hand. 'If you were to be taken away from your place at the gates, it would have to be in a capacity where you could truthfully contribute. You could contribute by watching over this young lad during the dark times he has to go through, as the guardian of his spirit, and by helping him explore the dark edges of his own mind. Two things which you could have had the decency of treating with respect for him, for yourself and for those of us who believe in you…'

He turned to Thomas and placed his gigantic paw over the entirety of his chest, tapping him twice, before resting it above his heart '... and in you, young man, we believe in you too.'

The babka arrived later and was excellent.

Chapter IX
The Hellish Realms of Eschatology

'How long were they in for?' Thomas wasn't even sure he wanted to know the answer.

'Depends on the person and, of course, that's what's interesting about it.' Rasmussen flicked a few symbols on the screen in front of him. Details concerning the human in the tank in front of them appeared on the glass which separated the cold air of the outside and the seemingly warm liquid within. 'This one, Elia Duquesne, spent the equivalent of eighty years. A relatively lengthy period, yet nothing in comparison to Attila Kocsis over here. He spent the equivalent of four thousand years in Para-Satya. 'The Colonel gestured to another tank, twice removed from Duquesne, where a white man's body lay in stasis, suspended in the same green liquid.

'Is he the record holder?' Mira asked.

'For the single longest session, yes. However, for the largest total period of time spent in Para-Satya, the record holder is Deng Xi Cheng.' Rasmussen was still surveying Duquesne's record, yet he pointed towards a currently empty tank, closer to the entrance to the chamber they found themselves in. 'Seven thousand years, roughly, over three sessions.' Rasmussen let his words sink in, as he continued to browse Duquesne's file. He did so in a slightly bored manner, making his perusal seem more of a habit as opposed to a need. Thomas was quite certain that it was likely not his first encounter with the file's contents.

The room they found themselves in was deathly quiet. They were deep within the Styx Network, the underground web of tunnels which lay right above the molten core of the planet's asthenosphere. The Styx served many different purposes. It fused together Terra's tectonic plates, which massively decreased the likelihood of any earthquakes occurring. The tunnels gathered geothermal energy from the melting lava which lay beneath them. In the event of a siege, the underground network would serve as a reliable logistical hub and a last line of defence against any invader. Lastly, yet most importantly for the purpose of Project Kralizec, the underworld housed various facilities whose nature was deemed of absolute importance.

It was within the Styx, almost a hundred kilometres beneath the surface of Terra, that some of the most eldritch, abominable and downright abhorrent of Terra's many contingency plans were located. If the surface resembled the obvious evolution of a society that had survived an alien invasion, then the Styx was a reflection of the dark horrors which a society obsessed with stopping history repeating itself was able to concoct. No one, bar perhaps only the highest echelons of Terran society, such as the High Command, the Terran Hierarchs and, likely, the majority of colonels knew of all that lay at the root of the world, ready to unleash untold horrors upon the enemies of Terra. The rest knew only of what they had seen themselves, what they had heard rumours of, the little they had overheard others discuss and, in all honesty, what they could only imagine.

The most infamous feature of the Styx was Tartarus, Terra's only prison, home to almost twenty Terran murderers. Since it was forbidden for a Terran to harm another Terran, there had emerged a conundrum in that those few that had gone down the dark path of fratricide could not be executed by neither their brethren nor outsiders, since the latter were also explicitly forbidden from taking Terran lives. Extenuating circumstances such as friendly fire meant little to Terrans: if you kill a Terran and you're not Terran, you were dead. In the aftermath of the Ayve War, the Terrans had sought out every single Aesir that had ever taken a Terran life and summarily executed them, even if their faction had surrendered unconditionally and was no longer a threat. Such absolutism was a hallmark of Terran thinking and had some merits, as many potential foes were indeed deterred from attempting to raid some Terran outpost, commandeer some Terran vessel or even argue with some Terran in a bar.

So it had come to be that those who had committed that most atrocious crime of kinslaying were locked deep within the dark pits of Tartarus, kept alive only by the ability of their own bodies, their superhuman alterations removed, as had been done with Ronan. Yet, unlike Ronan, these men and women were not allowed to live out the rest of their lives building some church in the Irish countryside. Their fate was a dark one, as they were kept in total isolation and allowed to go mad in the endless darkness of the deep world. They were fed only a tasteless liquid mix of nutrients, which frequently had to be administered by force. Their bodily waste was removed immediately by drones, so as to deny them death by infection or poisoning. Rumour had it that their cells, once sealed, never opened. At least, that what was commonly believed to have been their fate and, according to Rasmussen, that *had been* their fate up until a few months ago, when the Transient Section had announced their need of test subjects for Para-Satya.

Para-Satya was essentially a type of near-heaven, which the Transient Section had designed to work out the bugs of the eventual, true, Satya. There were many inherent problems with Para-Satya, with Rasmussen half-jokingly referring to it as the 'Paradise of Kitsch'. The main issue was the fact that the absence of experiential veracity was not only *not* a possibility, but a certainty. The subjects knew they were in Para-Satya, which meant that they knew that everything they experienced was a simulation. They could not observe their own universe, across all times, as was a key element of any perceived heaven. They also did not have access to any knowledge beyond that available to the administrative entity, thus denying them the possibility of 'enlightenment-by-omniscience', another element of experimental veracity absent in this near-heaven. The only beings they could interact with were simply simulated entities, created and manned by an artificial intelligence called Nurkai, named after the orcish god of mistakes.

Nurkai was a very basic copy of Forseti, which was the Terran name of the artificial intelligence which supposedly governed the Aesir afterlife. According to Rasmussen, they had deemed it necessary to test the artificial intelligence's code, to make sure that it would work adequately on Terrans. Initially, they had volunteers undergo the process of having their sentience transferred to Para-Satya. Volunteers would be kept inside Para-Satya for a maximum period of a few days at first and gradually progressed to weeks, months, years and, eventually, decades and each decade spent by someone in Para-Satya, went by as just a few seconds for someone on the outside. Most importantly, volunteers were able to exit Para-Satya at will. However, they were strongly discouraged to do so, with the goal being of seeing how much one could spend enjoying Para-Satya, before succumbing to the urge to return to the real world.

This had been where issues had begun to emerge, as had been foreseen by the Aesir and the Vanir themselves, when they had passed their technology over to the Terrans. Volunteers never got past fifty years in Para-Satya, as the longing to return to the real world and their real loved ones overcame even the greatest pleasures or the most absolute of comforts that could be offered by the Paradise of Kitsch, with their orders to delay their return always coming to their unavoidable finality. When they returned, they spoke of the great wonders Nurkai had managed to construct for them to enjoy, all of them meant to delay their departure. However, in the end, whether it be of boredom or longing, all would succumb and return to their dear reality.

The prisoners had been brought in to bypass such longing. They were offered the same deal, with one caveat: if they ever wanted to leave Para-Satya they would be allowed to do so, yet they would have to spend an equal amount of time in the 'Olive Garden'. The Olive Garden was a hauntingly Terran creation. Rasmussen told them they had set it up in one short afternoon. The idea behind it was simple: it was a simulation which mimicked the conditions of Tartarus itself. The only difference would be that one could not die in the Olive Garden. If they managed to stay within Para-Satya for over ten thousand years, they would be spared the Olive Garden and simply be returned to Tartarus, to live out the remainder of their lives.

Thomas noticed a discrepancy. 'If Deng was a convict, then how did he have three different sessions? You said prisoners would only enter Para-Satya once.'

'I did. And Deng did spend a long time inside Para-Satya on his first try. More than eight hundred and eighty eight years, to be precise. Which was enough for Nurkai to be able to *alter* him.' Rasmussen closed Duquesne's file and turned to face the group behind him. Mira and Thomas were joined by Opera Bokha, as well as the black guy from Adler's office, whom he had learned was named Ifeanyi Mapupu.

It was Opera who took over from Rasmussen, to explain that, 'We use the term "alteration" for the process by which afterlife administrators are able to permanently change an individual in a positive manner, albeit potentially changing who they are fundamentally as a result. The only certain way to alter someone is only achievable in a true afterlife, where an individual can be healed by the administrator with the assistance of people of importance: loved ones, family members, mentors, historical figures, descendants, victims… anyone within the community which can in some way contribute to the healing in a meaningful way.'

She stopped, seemingly remembering that she should just be brief and answer the simple question posed by Thomas. 'However, altering can occur, much more rarely, in artificial simulations, such as Para-Satya. This happened to Deng. He was altered and, even though he is the man who committed the crimes for which he was imprisoned here – he would actually agree with you that he is – he is no longer the same *person* he was before,' Bokha explained.

'How long does that take? In standard years?' Mira asked.

'It varies greatly for subjects in Para-Satya. No volunteer went through any significant alteration, bar a few minute changes in personality and mannerisms. The prisoners experienced significant time in Para-Satya,' Opera explained.

'That could simply mean that the volunteers didn't spend enough time in Para-Satya,' Mira put forth.

'Well, that and the fact that Para-Satya has a very an imperfect level of experiential veracity by default and subjects know their time in Para-Satya is limited. This provides an incentive to not change.'

Opera paused once more, as she appeared to ponder the best way of explaining something. 'A good case study is combat prowess and technique. Combat style suffered in some cases and prospered in others. Yet, no true difference occurred. We've had volunteers spend forty years in Para-Satya, of which the last ten were dedicated solely to combat simulations and training modules. We have also had subjects for whom Para-Satya resembled something of a gladiatorial arena, as opposed to the seaside resort one might imagine.'

'Seaside resorts are a good example,' Rasmussen interjected. 'In the old days, many people pictured the sea when thinking about Heaven. They imagined some Greek or Caribbean island with clear blue waters, cocktail glasses which never went empty, and a soft sea breeze under a gentle sun. Some sunrisers and a few Yin volunteers experienced a Para-Satya with this type of scenery. However, those of my age group – *oldtimers*, as you might refer to us – rarely experienced such simulations. I believe you can understand why.' *The sea claimed more lives than any elven blade during the End Times.*

'The fact that such differentiation exists is a good sign that Parra-Satya is nevertheless *functional*, despite all its flaws. However, returning to your question regarding time spent in Para-Satya, volunteers, for this exact reason, proved to be unviable test subjects.' Rasmussen had taken a seat on one of the office chairs littered around the chamber.

'I think that would conclude things for today. I think it's time you met Themba,' he continued, referring to Colonel Themba Xhisa, the Head of the Exploration Section. 'Ifeanyi, go with them. I trust Opera told you the exact location. But come back once you're done. We have to perform some preparations so that we wake up these guys properly.' He pointed to the occupied tanks.

Rasmussen had been very detailed about how difficult it was to wake subjects up. Their brains would develop completely different structures while in Para-Satya and forget exactly how they connected to their physical bodies. In the centuries they experienced, time went by very slowly for them, allowing their minds to change beyond recognition. Their brains would reach such a level of differentiation that entire teams of operators and doctors had to be dedicated towards their incarnation.

The Orpheus Chamber was located apparently located under an entirely different continent than Rasmussen's tanks; hence they had to take the subway. As they found themselves in their respective railcar capsule, Mira took the opportunity to interrogate her fellow captain. 'Opera isn't coming?'

Ifeanyi didn't seem surprised. 'No. She seems to be busy with other matters,' he answered.

'Huh...' Mira turned to look at Thomas, then back at Ifeanyi. 'I read she's your mentor, for the purpose of this,' she pointed around them, 'thing of ours.'

'She is.' *What? So he really is also–.*

'Well, she seems to be taking her job *very seriously...*' Mira slumped back and likely reminisced about a conversation she had a week before in Eilat with her godfather.

'Oh, she does.' Ifeanyi smiled as he looked down onto a screen he used to take notes.

Not a care in the world... 'Did you snap out of it?' The words sprung out of Thomas' mouth, hope kindling in his heart.

Ifeanyi looked up, still smiling. 'I did and right after I did, I figured out that it was only me and you in Adler's waiting room that looked like we were getting ready for the chopping block. Everyone else was just trying to get a good job. Which is why it's just me and you here, not Hausser or the other.' He winked at him. 'My new duties include helping Opera keep track of the progress of everyone we currently have under observation for the acute phase.'

All of the words coming out of his mouth hit Thomas' ears like a train plummeting into sealed tunnel, with each wagon pilling up on top of the other. He wanted to speak, but Mira beat him to it. 'Huh... You reckon there's a cure? Because my lieutenant is about to beg you for one.'

'I am!' Thomas managed to say.

Ifeanyi's smile continued. 'I know what cured me and if that cure would've worked on him, he would already be doing other tasks for Kralizec, not just acting as a proof-reader.' He saw Thomas' intent gaze and met it. 'The cure was administered to me during our introductory session in the amphitheatre. It came in oral form and was delivered via the voices of the speakers.'

What the fuck is he talking about?

The Hausafulani Captain saw his confusion and leaned in his seat. 'The fact that other people were not just thinking about what I was thinking, but also actively working on a solution. That was the cure. It snapped me out of it then and there. Opera saw it at dinner that very evening, when Falk chewed you out.' He spoke the last words to Mira.

Who smirked. 'Nice one... I particularly liked the part where you danced on the razor's edge and wagered that my guy here isn't a fucking moron and that he had the same thought as you, just that it didn't work for him.'

He taped the screen in his hand. 'Oh, he's no moron! I can tell you that much, but you knew that already. He just has a different mental landscape.' He turned back to Thomas. 'Which doesn't mean you are going crazy, Thomas, but Opera told you that already! It just means that what snaps you out of it is going to be different that what snapped me out of it.'

He leaned back in his seat and raised his eyebrows as he gazed into the distance. 'Plus, I spent two months dealing with that shit. You're barely in your first. There's ways to go and paths to tread!'

'I don't remember Opera telling me you were cured at the dinner.' Neither did Thomas.

'I know. I guess you could call it patient-doctor confidentiality. Not that you would notice, since you were busy getting scolded.' Ifeanyi got up as they reached their destination. 'However, it was in a memo you should have received at least five days ago...'

As their railcar arrived at their destination Mira had to tap Thomas on the shoulder to take him out of his revelry.

What had just happened? There were others like him? Some had been cured already by something that happened a week ago?

Mira was keen on offering her own interpretation of what had occurred. 'He's too cocky, this one. Of course he snapped out of it. He's too cocksure of himself to take the thought that he's gonna die seriously!' she whispered to him, as they followed Ifeanyi down a long corridor to reach Xhisa and the Orpheus Chamber he dwelt in.

It was a great grey chamber. The walls were at least fifty meters tall, with the floor being fifty by fifty meters square. They had emerged on an observation deck roughly midway up the walls. There were no other observation decks to their left or to their right. Directly opposite them was a great black screen that covered almost the entirety of the wall. Thomas had never seen something like it. It seemed to be made out of darkness itself. It was how the night sky would look like if there were no stars.

No suns.

No moons.

No worlds.

Nothing.

Just an endless, timeless, formless, empty...

'It's not the Aether itself,' a voice rang out from below.

A single figure lay within the chamber below. He was a black man, like Ifeanyi, but whereas the captain was merely dark of skin, the man below seemed to be made out of the darkness of the screen before him. He was almost gaunt in his build, reminding Thomas of Ronan O'Malley. One could tell that his body was still benefiting from the advantages of a genetic template, yet he seemed to have omitted to maintain it in any capacity. His uniform lay loose around his body, bereft of any decorations or markings, even those of rank or nationality. It wasn't even much of a uniform, as he simply wore a black T-shirt with long sleeves, as well as dark pants and dark working shoes. His face was almost regal in its structure, with high cheekbones and a strong jaw line.

His eyes however, were not those of a king, but those of monk. They were haunting, in their intensity. Thomas felt as if the man below saw his soul, not his face. He lowered them rather quickly, returning to what he had been working on.

A great white semisphere lay in the middle of the room. It lay atop a pedestal of black stone, at the base of which sat the speaker next to an open compartment. It was not the only open compartment within the room, as Thomas quickly realised that the walls were not actually walls, but simply panels. Behind them likely lay great vaults of knowledge far beyond his comprehension. He could tell, since there were a few panels opened, revealing their contents.

Soulkeepers.

It was an ancient technology. The elves made use of it, as did the orcs, Aesir, Vanir and Hyperboreans. The elves fashioned them in such a way that they resembled long white poles of crystal, while the humans fashioned them in the shape of massive slabs of milky marble and the orcs moulded them into forms resembling eggs. The ones he could see in their open compartments were more similar to the human design, as they resembled sheets of white marble in their appearance, arrayed along the walls like the many pages of some great library.

If they were to look upon an elven vault of soulkeepers, Thomas would know that each long crystal pole would have been a collection of little disks placed in sequence. Each little disc would have been placed within the newborn head of a baby elf, which would then carry the disc for their entire life. The disc would merge with their brains, allowing for no true separation of the elf from it. When the elf died, if their body was lost but the disc survived, their consciousness would be transferred into it. The disc would then be placed at the end of one such soulkeeper, along with many other thousands of such discs, to be connected to their afterlife program. Their afterlife program was essentially a virtual reality, from whence some elves could be brought back, if needed, so as to assist the living in one way or another.

Elves could still experience the *true death* which occurred when their body *and* their disc was destroyed. It actually happened quite frequently, for if something could destroy an elven brain, then it likely could destroy a soulkeeper disc as well. It was actually believed that, one day, when the universe would somehow cease to exist (if such a thing was possible) every single elf in every single soulkeeper vault would experience *true death*. If ever an elf was to die in such a way, then the elves passed into their true afterlife and fell under the rule of the Dancer, the great afterlife administrator believed to be the god of death of all elves in the cosmos.

Yet, this was a vault clearly more heavily inspired by *human* soulkeeper vaults. The greatest human civilization in the entire Known Universe was the Continuum of Humanity and they kept no such vaults, for they were considered an abomination. Within the Confederation of Humanity, the distantly second largest conglomerate of human civilizations, soulkeepers were also absent since peace between the Confederation and the Continuum was based around an agreement that stipulated that the Confederation would never deploy soulkeepers *en masse* throughout their entire population. Given the fact that most humans employed a remarkable degree of care for their central nervous system, since its survival guaranteed their survival, this was not necessarily an issue. If some humans still wanted to have soulkeepers, they could not be part of the Confederation and they would have to be ever watchful against the Continuum, which hunted such peoples fanatically.

The Aesir, Vanir and the Hyperboreans were examples of such a people, having fled towards a distant backwater of the Known Universe, in the galaxy of Triangulum, right next to the Milky Way. They still had afterlife programs, much like the humans of the Confederation, just that they also had the forbidden benefit of potentially being able to bring back the dead, among other things.

The Terrans were considering developing soulkeepers for their own use in such reanimation schemes but, this... this thing Thomas was looking at right now.

This was different.

This was an afterlife initiation set-up of soulkeepers, not an afterlife maintenance one. These soulkeepers had been brought here empty, and filled with the *Olorun sourcecode*. This code would be what they would broadcast into the Aether, the empty plain on which Satya would be built. An empty plain which lay beyond that black screen.

It's not the Aether itself.

'Colonel Xhisa!' Ifeanyi, Mira and Thomas all saluted.

'Just "Xhisa" will be fine!' he said, continuing his work.

As they made their way down the stairs of the observation deck, to the location of the Colonel himself, Thomas saw the full extent of the preparations underway. Several operators moved around the chamber. Some resembled metallic spiders, chitterling away at one soulkeeper sheet or another. Others resembled smooth floating spheres, with a myriad of small limbs emerging from within. These spheres spent most of their time immobile around certain open panels, likely editing the information within.

'Colonel Rasmussen sent us here to be briefed on the role performed by your section, sir.' Ifeanyi continued.

'The past tense of that verb – *performed* – is the valid one here.' Xhisa remained intent in his work. He gestured around the room. 'All we are doing here right now is superficial in nature. I mean, yes, I guess you could say we are optimizing but, in actuality, our task was finished almost a year ago.'

Mira had been staring at the black screen in front of them. 'When you found that?'

'Yes.' He interrupted his work to look at her properly. 'You have your mother's voice, yet your tone is your father's. You have her eyes, yet behind them I can see his fire. Last I saw you, you were little more than a newborn.'

Mira studied his face. 'I take it we've met before?'

Xhisa returned to his work. 'I was there when Daw brought you back. I saw her put you into the arms of Çingeto Braca. I was on the Vigilant, being taught by the orcs the nature of their ship's technology.' He paused, glancing towards the rest of the group. 'I must apologise, I do not read the recruitment reports anymore. In all frankness, I don't read that much of anything anymore. I just sit here and make sure everything is ready for when the time comes.'

He turned towards one of the nearby spheres. 'Thot, are they keepers?'

The sphere turned towards them. 'Captain Amira al Sayid, Captain Ifeanyi Mapupu and Lieutenant Thomas Muller are Keepers of Terra, indeed!'

Xhisa spoke almost to himself. 'I guess if they got this far, it really wouldn't matter now, wouldn't it?' He turned to Ifeanyi. 'You weren't introduced to me. Neither were any of you. Yet, they kept quiet. You spoke! You divulged information. Don't do that ever again Captain Mapupu. Do you work with Opera?'

'Yes, sir!' Ifeanyi confirmed.

'You see? You just did it again!' Xhisa turned now to look at Ifeanyi directly. 'I can see in your eyes that you have traversed the *dark tunnel* and have only just recently been returned to the sweetness of the light. Do not forget that we are a people under siege! Now and forever! Never divulge information to anyone who is not a keeper!' His voice never rose above a cautionary whisper, as Ifeanyi seemed to sink into the ground.

'Colonel Xhisa?' Thomas asked.

Xhisa turned slowly, looking him up and down. 'Yes?'

'What do you mean it's not the Aether?' he asked, speaking towards the Colonel, as his eyes glanced towards the black screen before them.

Xhisa smiled. 'You would have me make the same mistake as him?'

'No, sir!' He hadn't even thought of that. 'But, you mentioned it the moment we walked in. Keepers or not, I'm assuming you would've said that to anyone you didn't recognize up there in that balcony.'

Xhisa continued smiling, albeit now his eyes were downcast, as he pondered the lieutenant's words. 'I would have, indeed! Especially if they would've had your look on their face.' He now turned to stare at the black screen also. 'The Aether is not a thing that *is*. It is not a thing that can be seen either. It cannot be observed in any way, for simply observing it would change its properties, making it useless for our purposes.'

'Shira!' Xhisa shouted.

Footsteps could be heard, as the massive doorway behind them spun open. Thomas had not even noticed it, as it had been covered by the same panels as the rest of the walls. A Terran Chief Master Sergeant bearing the livery of the Sayeret appeared. Thomas recognized her from the amphitheatre. 'Yes, Themba?' she asked.

'Do you know them?' The Colonel asked.

Shira gave them all a quick look. 'Ifeanyi Mapupu... Thomas Muller... Hi, Mira!' She waved at Mira, as she still sat in the doorway. Mira smiled and waved back. 'Yup, they're all keepers of Terra.' She looked at Thomas and Ifeanyi. 'You two recognize me?'

They both nodded. 'Good!' She pointed at Xhisa. 'That's Colonel Themba Xhisa, commander of the Exploration Section of Project Kralizec. You guys got that?'

All three nodded again, as Xhisa smiled out of the corner of his mouth.

'Good! I'm out. It's almost dinnertime. I'll be outside.' She turned to look at Xhisa as she prepared to exit. 'Food today?'

Xhisa responded without looking at her, for he had returned to his work. 'I already ate!'

'No, you didn't!' Xhisa did not seem to care. Shira turned to the three Terran officers. 'Intro session, right?'

'Yup!' Mira responded.

'Nice! You got five minutes – probably less – before I come in here and ram some chicken tika masala and some lemon sherbet down his throat. I'm not letting him go for a week without eating,' she turned towards her superior officer, raising her voice slightly, 'again!'

'It was only six days.' Xhisa responded quietly.

Shira heard him. 'You're not God!' she shouted back and closed the door behind her after waving goodbye to the three officers.

Xhisa whispered quietly, 'None of us are... though He might be here... right now.' Xhisa drew a quick breath as he got up to his feet from the position he had been squatting in. 'I wouldn't want to appear lazy...'

He turned to face Thomas, once more. 'You are experiencing it now, aren't you? The sickness of the soul?'

Thomas shivered slightly, overwhelmed by the moment and the question. 'Yes!' he whispered almost.

'I could tell.' He looked towards the black screen. 'It is a design choice, really. We could have made it any colour. The Aether doesn't have a colour, for even darkness cannot exist within it. We cannot allow anything to enter it either. The screen you see stops anything and everything from going through.' He pointed towards the very centre of the screen, right opposite from the semisphere atop the pedestal next to him. 'The entrance itself is right there and it is of such small size that only a photon could ever pass through it.'

'Which is all that will be needed. So we hope, at least. This...' He pointed at the white semisphere atop the black pedestal. 'This is what will channel that light. It is called a "Genitrix" or, rather, such is the name we have chosen for it, for it has many names across the stars. Upon the day of Theogenesis, the Genitrix will move towards that exact point where the tunnel to the Aether lies open and the veil shall be lifted, allowing only for the light of the Genitrix to enter the Aether, before the veil shall collapse the tunnel behind it. Thus, the act shall be done.'

Xhisa gestured towards the walls around them. 'Within the soulkeepers we have built here, lie the entirety of all that we have ever documented as a civilization, both from the days before the *dushman* came and in the years after. Much has been lost, but Olorun must know with absolute precision which people he is to select for what the Aether is to become.' He looked down, seemingly speaking to himself. 'Else some souls would be lost...'

'Is it really light?' Mira asked, a slight tone of scepticism in her tone. 'The sourcecode?'

Xhisa smiled. 'Yes and no! It is something else entirely, though it does behave in a similar fashion to light. That similarity warrants its description as *a light*.'

'Is it an energy?' she continued.

'No! Not at all. Though it is something that requires a great amount of energy to produce. You've probably heard that there's an entire section dedicated to hiding that energy signature from our enemies. You see, it *cannot* be an energy, for to transfer energy from our universe to the Aether would be impossible. If the Aether is empty, it cannot transfer anything back. If it is full, it would reject anything we would send towards it, for it would be sealed shut.'

'*Full?*' Mira asked. 'Shouldn't it be full now?'

Xhisa smiled. 'Yes. It is "full" now also. Such is the nature of it. For us, now, it is empty because we haven't sent anything into it. However, after Theogenesis, we will say that it is "full". Though these are just the words we would use as beings used to the passage of time. In the Aether, from our perspective, there is no time. At least, not the way we would imagine it.'

A pause followed, as they all pondered the incomprehensible. Thomas had more questions, however. 'What's so special about this one?'

Xhisa smiled. 'This specific Aether?'

Thomas nodded.

'Not much. All such spaces are the same, at least until they are enlightened. There are many doors beyond which an Aether could lie, though we had to choose one which could connect to Yggdrasil, thus assuring our eternal kinship with our friends. We had to go knock on each door until we found this specific one. Once we opened the tunnel, we knew what lay beneath and knew we had our match.' He turned to look straight into Thomas' soul. 'What other questions do you have?'

'I... I have many...' He just didn't know where to even begin.

'Save them. There will be time.' Xhisa smiled, not just with his mouth, but also with his eyes.

'How do we know it is connected to Yggdrasil?' Mira, apparently, was in no mood for patience.

Xhisa, however, was willing to oblige. 'When the War at the Gates of Heaven sundered the Old Realm, the primordial Aether that was first scouted out by the necromancers of old was claimed by those which would go on to lay the foundation of the Continuum. Neither they nor we know with certainty if this primordial Aether was as insulated from the other Aethers as the Continuum claims it is. That was what set that Aether apart, you see, and why it was chosen: it was insular in nature.'

'Other Aethers had been found, yet had been dismissed on account of their potential for interconnectivity. The founding fathers of the Others Unaligned, upon realizing that the battle was lost and the Continuum's triumph was inevitable, decided to repurpose the other Aethers by using them as fields to plant their own Heavens. These Aethers were different in nature, for they could communicate with each other.'

'Yggdrasil is naught but a sapling in a much greater garden within the realm of many Aethers and Satyas. Every one of its branches grows in a specific space and the space is limited. If too many branches grow, they will get in each other's way. Thus, each network such as Yggdrasil has a finite number of constituent Aethers.'

'When we set out to add our own branch, we received from our friends a list of places where we may find a space for our branch to grow. It was among these places that we found *our* Aether. After Theogenesis, we will destroy all records containing the exact whereabouts of this specific Aether, thus ensuing its safety and its perfect integration within Yggdrasil. When the time comes for others to craft their own branch upon the trunk of Yggdrasil, they will receive the same list of potential locations we did. They may then knock upon each door, as we did and find one chamber that is open, as we did.'

'*Safe*?' It was Thomas who spoke. He wasn't sure if Xhisa was done or not, but he couldn't help it.

The oldtimer smiled at him, yet it was Ifeanyi Mapupu who spoke next. 'We were told that the Aether would be kept safe by virtue of the collapsed tunnel alone,' he clarified.

Xhisa's eyes remained fixed upon Thomas', as if he sought to see exactly how the young keeper would respond to that which he was about to reveal.

'From our universe, all Satyas are safe. Even if someone from our side would simply enter an empty Aether without collapsing the tunnel entrance, they could not access the other branches of Yggdrasil while the initial entry was still open. However, if one was to know the exact location of Satya and its Aether within the Great Realm that lies beyond, one could access it from their own existing branch of Yggdrasil,' Xhisa turned to look once more upon the black void before them.

'We do not know what might happen if that would ever come to pass. Perhaps Yggdrasil and Satya might be able to stop any unwanted interaction, though we know this not for certain,' he turned towards the three Terrans before him.

'It is why we guard this place and what lies beyond this tunnel with so much care. If an enemy was to learn the true location of our Aether, they could potentially disturb its harmony or even destroy it if they have their own branch within Yggdrasil.'

'Themba! It's dinnertime!' Shira's voice announced.

Chapter X
The Desolation of the Self

'Did you always suck so much?' Mira was playing with her axe, juggling it absentmindedly, as her fingers flexed over and over again in between tosses. Thomas lost his footing as he tried to get up, the cut to his forehead throbbing his brain into a dizziness of the body.

'You…' He decided to lay on his back and rest a little, waiting for his blood to clot the wound shut and for his head to stop hurting. '… fight… weird.'

'Weird' was a fucking euphemism if he'd ever said one. Mira's fighting technique was downright animalistic. This was their fifth sparring session and the first one where she had informed him that her weapon of choice would be an axe.

And I thought her swordsmanship was savage.

It had taken him ten sessions to finally stand his own against the flurry of thrusts and swings and blows and throws and kicks and punches and even biting that was Mira al Sayid's idea of *practice*. The day before, he had managed to catch her chin with his the tip of his blade. It had been the first time he had managed to draw blood. He hadn't even had time to enjoy the accomplishment before Mira's blade had gone in between his teeth and out his right cheek.

Now, as he felt his forehead muscles clench the wound together, the pain brought him the clarity needed to realise that it was the first time Mira had spoken during their sparring. All that usually came out of her mouth were grunts, shrieks, moans and flurries of base vulgarities. For some reason, today was the day she had decided to grace their training sessions with complete sentences. Either that or she had struck him a bit too hard and he was just hallucinating a conversation.

Mira answered, 'I do. But you fought against the Aesir, like I did. I even read that you had, and I quote, "substantial melee experience". You're not dead. How did you survive?' Had Thomas heard those words a few months ago, back when the blood of the Aesir was still fresh on his hands, he would've made her wonder how she survived her fucking nerve. Now, he couldn't help but join her in contemplation.

He managed to sit upright on the floor. 'The Aesir… fight with discipline.' He reached to his side to pick up his sword. 'They're perfect in movement.' He got up from the floor and began making his way to the medical capsule at the edge of the sparring arena.

'Every action is perfect. Decades, centuries of experience behind each decision. Countless hours of training. A warrior culture spanning back millennia, back when our people were just monkeys frightened by sudden changes in the wind.' He finally reached the capsule and slumped into the seat within.

As the machine began healing his forehead, right before his metal skull began to vibrate, Mira asked. 'My point exactly. I remember what it was like. I don't need a history lesson, particularly not one that's so bland.'

As he felt his nerves go numb and the metal of his bones begin to shake, he opened his mouth to speak, since he knew it would help. 'You could rely on them to do everything perfectly. That made them predictable. If you just always expected them to do the best possible thing from their perspective and the worst from yours, you could guess what they would do. After a while you usually see a pattern–'

The sound of Mira slurping down her hot coconut macadamia latte with whipped cream interrupted his reminiscence.

Why do I even…

'See, that's bullshit now, innit? Sure, from a certain skill level upwards, you're right: you know reasonably well what the better fighter can do. But, if you suck, you still don't stand a chance, no matter how well you can guess what the opponent will do.'

Mira walked with her coffee to the window overlooking the Jerusalem barracks' courtyard. One could see almost a hundred Terrans training, socialising and relaxing outside. They found themselves on one of the middle levels of the southern tower of the Jerusalem Holdfast. Opposite the barracks and across the courtyard, one could see the Israeli skyport and the Keep of Jerusalem rising from atop the old Temple Mount. The blue and white colours of the Israeli Nation overshadowed even the typical Terran black masonry of the fortress walls, as thousands of small white and blue triangles hung on long ropes across the courtyard.

'Oh, sounds like you have a lot of experience with that sort of thing.' Thomas had learned that it was best to taunt Mira when she was in this bored state. If she went without some object of focus for too long, her boredom would suddenly switch to a particularly mischievous form of anger. Having her respond to being offended or annoyed was far preferable to that. By far.

'I do, as do you... allegedly.' She didn't turn around from her study of the combatants below.

'*Allegedly*, hmphhh...' Thomas squinted as the healing machine reactivated his senses. His mind once more had to deal with the strange reality of having tissue that was utterly destroyed naught but a few moments earlier, be completely healed in just a few moments. 'I didn't know you had so much experience fighting opponents so much above your own ability.'

Mira understood his meaning. 'I don't.'

'Ah... well you seemed to be very knowledgeable about the dynamics of asymmetric combat. I just assumed–' Thomas didn't have time to close his sloppy attempt at a verbal jab as Mira interrupted him.

'I'm used to other people fighting against me the way you say you fought against the Aesir and how you *attempt* to fight against me now.'

Typical Mira bullshit...

She turned to him. 'D'you know you could die during training?'

Thomas froze a little as he got up from the medical capsule, then proceeded to walk off the onset of his anxiety. 'No one's ever died in training.'

'Not yet they haven't,' she replied accurately.

Thomas' walk became a wobble as he struggled to keep the weakness in his knees from turning into a collapse of his legs. 'There's the capsule and the blades aren't sharp enough. We can't exert enough force with our muscles to break plated honeybone–'

'– and yet it still can happen.' Mira turned away from the window and made her way slowly towards him, eyes fixed on his. 'During the Ayve War, there was an attack on the Janissaries while they held Vorenie. Sergeants Papastathopoulos and Dogan were engaged in a sparring session. The Aesir EMP hit them just as Papastathopoulos managed to stab Dogan in the heart. Dogan couldn't heal the wound. No medical capsule was functional.'

'The new template heals those wounds...' *It was supposed to, at least.*

'Still. It can happen.' Mira sat down, squatting, axehead in one hand, while the other ran the nail of her thumb across the edge. She gestured for him to join her on ground level.

He obliged, collapsing to the floor as gingerly as he could. It was no small effort to hide how relieved he was to catch a prolonged break. Their sparring sessions were as exhausting as they were educational. Mira was a good teacher, in her own way. Thomas had fought 'controlled berserkers' before, yet none that matched her ferocity and certainly none as masterful as her in the art of dancing at the edge of the bloodcraze. At times during their fights, he was afraid that she would actually go berserk and lose control over her senses. She sometimes did seem to struggle to regain her composure, yet there was nevertheless a graceful, yet brutal, reasoning behind her every action.

His fighting style was that of a 'focused fighter'. He focused on staying calm during combat, concentrating on understand his opponent. He would often be intentionally passive, allowing his adversary to divulge their own weakness. He would leverage his strength and stamina against the skill and ferocity of an adversary, bidding his time until an opponent made a mistake. If he ever came across an opponent more passive than him, he was quite adept at taking the initiative, albeit in a more straightforward manner focused more on securing a victory efficiently, rather than swiftly.

In theory, he could allow a more proactive and aggressive opponent, such as Mira, to eventually overextend. In the meantime, he could just scout out her weaknesses, until the moment came to go on the offensive. At such a time, he could use his superior strength and greater bulk to overpower her, with her speed, skill, endurance and initiative being negated by the drawbacks of her own fighting style.

In practice, what ended up happening was that Thomas would have to struggle to figure out her rhythm first, and then dance with her until she grew overconfident. Only then did he ever have a chance against her. The only problem was that confidence seemed to be Mira's perpetual state of mind, with the moments in which she overextended into arrogance being few and far between. What's worse was that these moments were almost indistinguishable from her usual self.

'I think you're holding back. I think you've been holding back with me this entire time.' Her eyes had locked onto his from the moment she had begun to speak.

And she was right.

In a way.

'I'll... take that as a compliment.'

'Don't be evasive. Are you?'

Why did I even try... 'I... have been unable to focus, yes,' he conceded. He knew it would not be enough though.

'I could tell. The thing is, right,' she began to wave a finger at him, 'it's more than that. In the beginning, I think we both used to think it was that. You saw I go near-berserk and you started looking for a rhythm. It took you a long time to see it even though – to keep it real with you Tommy – I've kinda been keeping it as basic as I can with you. But, now, it seems to me like we both know it's not just that. It seems to me like you are neither willing to focus, nor able to.' She went back to grinding her fingernails on the axehead.

'Now, you see, I like that because it means that you're still in the acute phase, plus that I get to try out some new moves. You know... I get to work out some bugs. But, what I find surprising is that you don't seem to mind how things are going either. It's like you prefer being nothing more than a training bot taking hits to the head on the regular.'

Thomas was taken aback. Sorbo Falk's lecture in Eilat had clearly made an impact on her but this was truly remarkable coming from her. Ever since that first, fateful diner, Mira had fully embraced her role as Thomas' caretaker. Yes, her curiosity and interest in the inner workings of Project Kralizec often got the better of her, yet she never did falter in her duty in keeping an eye on Thomas' mental state. Her vigilance had birthed these strange little moments, when she would seem to see right through him, seemingly spotting things at work inside of him of which even he was only vaguely aware of.

But still, this particular observation was particularly impressive. Thomas had only slightly begun to even acknowledge the fact that, yes, he was indeed holding back. Not for fear of hurting Mira, but for another, far more shameful, reason.

'I don't want to make it real,' was all he could muster.

'Me neither. I don't want to kill you. You don't want to kill me either. But, there's a difference between not wanting to hurt me and not wanting to get hurt yourself. It's two entirely different perspectives. On the one hand, it's insulting to assume you could. On the other hand, it's concerning that you'd think I would.'

'...and you've figured out it's the latter?' He could tell she had.

'Of course I have. I just haven't figured out if it's just me you don't trust or the world, in general.'

Oh...

He had figured out which one was the case. He had just avoided confronting it.

Apparently, today was the day Mira had decided to *make* him confront it.

'It's the latter,' he smiled, nervously, 'again.'

'I thought so.' She smiled, at first to him, then at her hands, as she began to rub away at some speck of dirt she'd uncovered. 'You think not striking back at the world will make it hit you less?' Her tone was humorous, yet not mocking. He felt her genuinely want to hear his answer.

'No... No, I don't. Quite the contrary, I think it will make every hit more damaging. It's... I don't do it on purpose. It's more like I don't want to treat fighting you as if it was a real fight, because...' *How can I put this without sounding like a coward?* '... because, if I do, and you win, I'll be reminded of the fact that sometimes, usually only once, someone else will win in a real fight against me.' It came out of him with as much dignity as was applicable.

'Don't you already know that?'

'I guess I do. I just don't want to feel it.'

He was so tired of feeling so much. All the anxiety and the stress and the despair and the dread. It felt so hard to be alive. Ever since he had joined Project Kralizec, it hadn't gotten any better. If anything, things were much worse now. What's more, he now worried that the whole point was that to make things as difficult as possible for him.

It had taken him a few days to get into a parody of a rhythm. Every day, Clara would wake him up from the feverless fever dreams that were his nights. He would then make his way to Mira's room to wake her up, as had been her insistence. They would then spar together and proceed to have their morning briefing with one of the section heads. For the first two weeks, what would follow would be a tour or a lecture on some specific aspect of Project Kralizec. He had found that each section head had a very specific way of going about introducing their area of work.

Rasmussen was a big fan of guided tours and Para-Satya subject interviews. Hosseini would gather groups of over a dozen people into his office and combine their sessions with brainstorming rounds with his staff. Patel would organise little tea parties with her husband Fiol and her young daughter, Sara. Ramirez had left them with an entire library of inhuman texts they were to read in his absence, for he had yet to return from his off-world endeavours. Gonçalvo and Zaslani were both extremely secretive, with their briefings being more akin to the brief summary training sessions of his early adolescence. Zaslani was actually the more talkative of the two, as he would also interrogate them, ever seeking to assure himself of their discretion. Xhisa had been perhaps the strangest of them all, as he never left the area surrounding the Orpheus Chamber. They had only encountered him on that one occasion in the first week.

Lastly, there was Adler herself, who acted as something of an aggregator of knowledge, especially after the first weeks of instruction had passed. She and Patel were now the two section heads they interacted most often with. To be more precise, they were the ones who were truly dedicated to probing Thomas' troubled mind.

Every day, Patel and Fiol would introduce world-shattering concepts to him, then wait for him to successfully enunciate how he felt about said revelations. Once a week, Adler would ask Thomas to report to her what inconsistencies he may have spotted within the grand plan of Project Kralizec, an experience which usually left Thomas weeping, which was something of a relief, as the daily sessions with Patel often left him shaking and sweating, on top of the crying.

He and Mira would close off the day with a dinner together, during which time Mira was supposed to help him structure his thoughts and centre himself. The dinners were supposed to be moments of reflection and relaxation. Mira would insist that they would scout out different restaurants, not just in Israel, but also in Turkey, Kurdistan, Alawiyah, Hauran, Assyria and even as far as Persia, Greece, Sudan and Ethiopia. She would pick charming places which usually would have been the perfect place for sweet contemplation and stimulating conversation.

What actually happened was that she would bombard him with her own speculation and introspection. The dinners were perhaps the most shocking part of the day, for Thomas would often sit across from her fully consumed by the cold flames of existential dread, as Mira would wax on-and-on about the hopeful potential and the potential hopelessness of what they were working on, all the while completely unfazed by the depth and impact of what was coming out of her mouth. She would work him up into such a frenzy of angst that, by the time they got back to their quarters, he would fall asleep due to the trauma alone.

Said sleep was not something Thomas found in any way rejuvenating. Somehow, in the two months he had spent working on Project Kralizec, he had come to feel as if he had been simply living the same long day he had started back on Luna. The sparring sessions with Mira, though stressful in their own right, were actually the most relaxing parts of his day, as Opera had predicted. As Mira al Sayid assaulted him with a flurry of blows and jabs, he could actually find some peace in the simple act of staying in one piece. He didn't really want anything more than that. When the sessions would finish, he would be overcome by the terror of what would follow.

Of course he held back. He didn't want to win. He just wanted to stay within that moment, no matter how dangerous or challenging it may have been, for it was the only moment when he felt neither dead nor alive. Everything outside of that moment was burdened by the awareness of his own mortality and his weakening grip on reality.

'You know... Laur Pop put a gun to my head.' He looked up at Mira, her pokerface returning to adorn her eyes. 'He asked me to tell him why he wouldn't shoot me.' He paused, pondering why he hadn't shared this with her before and why he had chosen to share it now. 'I told him that if he did, my world wouldn't make any sense for me anymore. So, he might as well put a bullet in my head. That was the right answer... apparently.'

Mira smirked as he finished. 'Of course it wouldn't make sense, you wouldn't be part of it anymore... he's also not big on waste.' She smiled to herself. 'Dead Terrans are very wasteful.'

He's also consistent, apparently.

'Why are you telling me this?' she asked.

He thought he had pinned down the answer. 'I trust other people. Our people I trust most of all. I trust you, Mira. I just... I wonder if what we are doing here is enough. If we are all... enough.' *In the face of a universe which appeared, at best, uncaring and, at worst, hostile.*

He felt relieved to share this with her. Somehow he knew she would take it well.

'You still fight like a little bitch.' Thomas snapped out of the moment of closeness to realise that Mira was smirking at him. After a moment's pause, she tilted her head to the side and raised her shoulders slightly, emphasising how obvious her statement was.

'Well, you can keep on pondering how likely we are to transcend existence as much as you want during practice. It's fine by me.' She pointed at the axehead. 'Tomorrow I'm gonna try and see if I can bludgeon you with the shaft, while the head's in your ribs.'

She got up and extended her hand towards him. 'Come on now! Let's go rock your world! We've got Lakshmi and Fiol in thirty minutes.' Thomas took her outstretched hand and lifted himself back up.

Lakshmi and Fiol had a house by the Dead Sea. As always, Mira drove her shuttle with an anxious Thomas squirming in the passenger seat. He had, *once*, suggested that *he* drive. After all, he was of lower rank than her. Junior officers were expected to double as chauffeurs when accompanying their seniors. Mira's reply had been curt and blunt. She could've said it was a nice drive, even if the sun was in their eyes on the way towards the Colonel's mansion and on the way back to Jerusalem. She could've said it was a short drive; little more than five minutes, given Mira's cruise speed. She could've even just said she liked driving, which she clearly did.

But, no, Mira had just told him she knew that not driving would get him even more worked up, which would help them on their assignment.

Moreover, she always insisted on going the extra mile and always had Casper play orcish death metal at just the right tempo and volume to make sure Thomas got to experience both the fatalistic verses and the delirious beats.

At the end of each morning trip, she had him ask Clara what his stress levels were on a scale of one to ten, with any answer under nine being met with pretend surprise and an enforced conversation about the inevitability of one's own death, the inherent loneliness of the human condition, the pointlessness of existence and the vast cold expanse that was the oppressive universe they had been born into without their consent.

As they neared the Colonel's villa, Thomas felt the nervousness return, as he rehearsed, in his mind, the points which they would cover today. The rehearsal was cut short by Mira's traditional rough brake as she parked the shuttle. On cue, Clara's voice rang out in the shuttle's speakers.

'Lieutenant Muller's psychological stress level can roughly be estimated at around 7.9, a score 1.6 points below his average over the last month. This is a new record. Congratulations, Lieutenant!' Thomas could feel the stress jump to at least

8.5 as he closed his eyes, not daring to meet Mira's glare. He began to exhale slowly, readying himself for what was to come.

He heard the sound of her tapping the steering wheel, as it did every time he managed to get through this far in the day without a debilitating panic attack. However, this time, it took a bit longer than usual for her words to begin their methodical stirring of the pot that was his soul.

'Am I your friend?' Mira asked. *I wasn't expecting that course of attack.*

He wasn't sure. Quite frankly, he hadn't really thought about things like that. The Mira he had known of before all this – the 'public' Mira, as he thought of her – was a gorgeous woman he had been infatuated with ever since the first stirrings of his manhood. Somehow, the real Mira had come into his life at a moment when romance of any nature or seriousness was not exactly on top of his mind.

She was intimidating. She had always been. Not just to him, but to those around her as well. Even some oldtimers treated her with a degree of reverence usually reserved for the heroes of the End Times. Heroes like her father.

Thomas knew nothing of Djibril al Sayid other than the legend sown into the wide eyes of young Terran children for decades; a legend he himself had consumed in awe. Yet, he could not deny that within this woman burned a fire of old which he found to be sweltering. A fire which had somehow passed down through blood into the veins of the young captain next to him.

The truth was that he had never even wondered what she was to him. At least not on a personal level. At an existential level he thought of her both as his caretaker and his tormentor. He found in her intensity both a comforting flame and a burning rod, ever willing to seek out his most tender doubts and fears. At times he found her selfish and almost childish in her relentless pursuit of her own curiosities. Other times he thought of her as an elder out of whom would blossom the most profound of insights. She could be infantile in her humour, yet, also sage in her wisdom.

Alas, he did find that she was, much like the legend of her father and mother, more of a force of nature, rather than a mere mortal, as he himself knew so painfully, that *he* was.

But, a friend?

Mira interrupted his line of thought. 'Because you can't think that.' *The fire decides when the kindling is to burn.*

Thomas couldn't help but feel hurt. The pain of being rejected a relationship he hadn't even considered until a few moments before caused more pain than it did confusion at her choice of words.

She was still clutching onto the steering wheel, the shuttle now fully parked now, with the engine little more than a subtle tremor now. She pressed a button, turning off the power entirely, then reached into her tobacco case and sparked a cigarette, as she always did before the sessions with Lakshmi, as smoking was not allowed in her house.

'I don't know how you accept this.' Mira turned to face him, anger in her eyes. An anger directed right at him. An honest anger. An anger which, somehow, Thomas knew would not burst forth any danger to his being.

'I know you're afraid. I know you're desperate. I know you want to cling onto whatever hope you still can. It is so clear that that's what you're doing. But, for the love of life, I do not understand how you tolerate this. Do you ever think about what is being done to you?'

Thomas didn't have time to answer. 'You are being used. You are being used as a tool. Not even for an experiment. You are literally being used as a *resource*. I know you're going along with all of this because you see it as the only path towards getting back some semblance of peace, but – *dammit, Thomas* – I don't understand how, how, how you let me walk right over you and your own intimate, personal path towards, towards, towards your place in this world!'

She opened her door as if to exit the shuttle. Thomas, despite being taken aback by the topic of her rant, habitually followed suit, only for her to seemingly change her mind and loudly shut her door back closed. Thomas had seen this sort of thing before with her and quietly followed suit again.

'This should be a private thing for you. The only people allowed on your journey should be those you deem worthy of sharing this intimacy with. It should be people whose clear, vested interest is your own peace and wellbeing. Mentors, guides, shoulders to fucking cry on. Not me. Not Lakshmi. Not Shosho. Nor everyone else.' She paused to take an angry puff of her cigarette.

'I mean, bless their hearts, they're good people and they mean well. This whole thing means well. But, for fuck's sake, Thomas, do not believe we are acting in your best interest here!' She turned to look at him. Up to this point, her rant had been delivered whilst facing the windshield.

'Have you figured it out? Have you figured out that it is in everyone's interest that your existential crisis goes on for as long as possible? Except yours?' She paused, waiting for a reply and looking for an answer.

Thomas was certain she was left empty-handed. He had pondered this topic as a passing terror; one of many that had plagued him. He had thought about it, yet, up until now, he had reached no conclusion.

Mira slumped back in her seat. 'You're not gonna get mindwiped when you snap out of it. You know too much now and that makes you useful. Both you and I will get new assignments within the project. When you'll snap out of it, it'll be the end of it and you can get on with your life and everyone will be happy. You won't have to deal with anyone's bullshit anymore. Just… phew…'

She let out a long exhale, then paused to focus on calming down. 'Just remember what happened here! Remember that you were *used*! Deal with that as you wish. Just don't go around fucking oblivious to what was done to you. Alright?'

Thomas didn't really have time to ponder the meaning of Mira's words, or even nod in agreement, as she opened the shuttle door and immediately barged off towards the entrance to Lakshmi's home. Thomas barely had time to reach her side before she had reached the doorbell. She took a few quick tokes of her cigarette, before proceeding to throw the butt into the ashtray the Colonel kept outside her door for visiting smokers.

'It's Freudian death drive today. You got the homework?' She asked, while rummaging through her jacket.

The very thought upset Thomas' stomach. 'Yes.'

Mira finally found what she was looking for. Thomas instantly recognized it for what it was: an Old Earth fidget spinner. 'Is… is it that bad?' He managed to put on a fake smile.

'What? No! This is –' Mira's answer opened the door and greeted them cheerfully.

Sarasvati Patel's Vanir heritage was not immediately obvious. One would only realise the child's peculiarity if they knew she was less than two years old. At only twenty Terran months, she was already walking steadily, had fully grown teeth and spoke as a child three times her age. As she stood in the doorway, her short arms barely reaching the handle, she let out a happy squeal of excitement, as she did every morning they arrived at the Patel household.

She turned around and shouted through the open hallway into the room beyond. He could not see them, yet Thomas knew that almost certainly her mother and father were already sitting around their living room table, which was likely covered with drinks, snacks, screens and notes.

'Daddy! Mommy! Auntie Mira and Thomas are here!'

Fiol responded from inside the house. 'Let them in! The samosas are getting cold!'

'Hello, Sara! I got you something!' Mira was not really one to smile, at least not fully sincere smiles. She mostly smirked. Yet, she smiled ear-to-ear as she presented Sara with her gift, held in both hands, as she tilted her head to the side and leaned back slightly.

The little girl let out another happy little squeal of excitement as she picked up the toy. Her look of pure joy gradually shifted to one of wonder and then, suddenly, confusion. 'What is it?' She asked, puzzled.

'It's a fidget spinner!' Mira seemed pleased with herself.

'Wu…Wa… What do you do with it?' Sara held the item in her hand as if it were some strange artefact. It was that manner specific of children blissfully oblivious to the nature of the mundane.

'Well, let me show you!' Mira picked up the toy from the little girl's hand, held it between thumb and forefinger, then began spinning it with her other hand. She gingerly began to balance it on her fingers. Thomas was quite surprised to see that she was very much adept at handling the spinner, as she proceeded to show off a variety of tricks, before gliding the present back into Sara's palm, whose face was still puzzled. 'What is the purpose of learning how to do that?'

Now it was Mira who was a bit puzzled. 'Well… it's in the name: you spin it when you fidget.'

'But, do I have to fidget?' The little one always asked the right questions.

'I mean no, but… it's fun to play with it.'

'So, *you* have fun playing with it?' Sara had moved out of the doorway, still studying the item gifted to her. Mira and Thomas entered the house.

'Well, not anymore but, I used to. Quite a lot.' Mira flashed Thomas the most passing of angry glances, as she saw him raise an eyebrow from the corner of her eye.

'Why did you stop?' Sara continued as she closed the door behind them.

'What?' *It didn't take long this time…*

Were it not for the main purpose of their visits to the Patel household, Thomas would have positively been fascinated by the ease with which Sara managed to make Mira uncomfortable. It was the only time when he got to see the young captain behave awkwardly. Her normal persona was usually either one of boiling rage, annoyed boredom, jubilant curiosity or stern seriousness. All were states she navigated with an air of authority which was always airtight, with nothing truly ever getting to her.

Yet, this little girl had an almost supernatural ability to throw her off-balance.

The root cause of this unease had become evident the very first instant Thomas had first met Colonel Patel's daughter and had learned her name. No one had felt the need to say it out loud, yet he had immediately realised the origin of the little girl's name. She was named after Mira's mother, Sarasvati Singh.

Mira clearly cared for the child yet, somehow, the bond they shared was just heavy enough to weigh on her mind. Coupled with the child's inquisitive and peculiar nature, this awareness seemed to result in instances of full-blown comedy, as the usually assured and aloof Mira struggled to not be excessively awkward around a two-year old.

'Why did you stop playing with it if you enjoy it?'

'Well, I got bored of it.' *Typical.*

'So, you don't like it anymore.' This was a statement, not a question.

'No, little one, I do still like it. Just that, you see, sometimes you can enjoy doing something very much, only to get bored of it. Then, after some time, you begin to miss the feeling you would have when you would do it in the past. At that moment, you should do it again, since you will enjoy it once more. It doesn't mean you ever stopped liking it, just that you're sometimes in moments when you don't enjoy it anymore.'

'Did you learn that from the elves?' the little one asked.

Thomas paused in his stride. *Of course she fucking did! I didn't think about that before.* He shot Mira a quick glance, which she ostentatiously ignored.

She never talked about what she had learned during her time spent among the elves. Not just in conversation with him, but in general. She was always quiet about that one topic.

After her parents' death, a deal had been struck between the surviving al Sayids and Daw-al Fajr. Mira, then only a few days old, would spend her time split between Terra and Menegroth. Her first six months she spent at the Arabian Holdfast of Mecca, together with her father's family, followed by another six months spent in the gardens of Irulan Palace, under the close care of Daw herself. This pattern was repeated until, as agreed, upon reaching the age of fifteen, she passed entirely under the care of Terra.

She frequently visited her stepsister on Menegroth, even after commencing her education on her parents' homeworld, and they frequently travelled together to the other worlds of the Milky Way, be they elven or otherwise. Whenever Daw would visit the Solar System, she would immediately beeline towards Mira, with the two frequently visiting and exploring the many corners of Terra, Luna, Mars, and the rest of the Terran Dominion together.

Elves were just the most remarkable childhood companions of the Terran princess. Mira and Daw's famous sisterhood had been one of the most potent signs of Terran and elven reconciliation, bar perhaps only the actions of Daw herself during the War of Vengeance, as well as those of Quentyn Andromander and Vorclav Uhrlacker. However, whilst Quentyn and Vorclav had increased their standing among the Terran population by the bloody edges of their blades, Daw and Mira had proven something else. Something far more remarkable.

Love could still bring people together. A friendship of the ages could be born among the unlikeliest of individuals. Two children playing games in the grass could mend the deepest of wounds.

This had not been the limit of Mira's dealings with elves, or inhumans in general. Her godfather, Sorbo Falk, had spent many a month by her side during the troll's time on Terra. One of his sons and Mira were known to have been inseparable playmates as children, with Mira famously insisting that the little troll join her during one of her stays on Menegroth. A remarkable occurrence, albeit much less remarkable than Sorbo's acceptance of the idea.

As was the tradition of the orcs of Vigilant, following her parent's death, Mira passed under the wardship of Çingeto Braca, her father's bloodbrother. As was typical of his people, the orc had taken his duty as the guardian of the young Mira very seriously, with Braca spending many a day tutoring and playing with her, as well as many a night telling her stories of the wandering city of Vigilant and the many heroes of times long gone, yet not entirely forgotten.

These were just the highlights, with Mira's relationship with many other inhuman peoples being well-known and documented.

'*Mira had her existential crisis when she was nine years old. I was there to see it.*' Ashaver's words echoed in his mind as Thomas suddenly realised the implications.

Mira's crisis must have been heavily influenced by her time spent with the elves. It must have been why it had come so early. A human child raised by elves thousands of years old with an immortal god telling her that she was her stepsister… of course her thoughts had drifted towards eternity and the endless.

The elves, Daw al Fajr, and likely many other inhumans must have been there to lend their wisdom during Mira's time of need, let alone her own Terran family, with their own fair share of esoteric knowledge. Who knows what they would have shared with her? Who knows what paths they had walked her on? Who knows what balms had cared for her during the dark night of *her* soul?

And, yet, she never spoke of it.

Camus, Nietzsche and, of course, Zapffe.

Fyodor, Soren & Jean-Paul.

Moses, Jesus and Mohammed.

All Terrans of Old Earth.

Never some elven thinker, or at least an orcish muser, not even some goblin writer.

He had never noticed that before.

If it weren't for the fact that she was clearly deeply interested in Terran philosophy, he never would have questioned her continuous omission of inhuman philosophy. Sure, inhuman philosophers would occasionally come up during their many discussions with the other members of Project Kralizec, particularly Lakshmi & Fiol. However, Mira would just seem to wait out those moments in the conversation, only to jump right back in when the discussion turned back to the great thinkers of their own society.

He started feeling anxious, betrayed and surprisingly angry. It was the type of anger one feels when they hit their nose. The fury came from a conscious revelation yet the darkness and the depth of his rage came from something close to his very core.

This spoilt brat doesn't give a single shit about me or what I'm going through. She's not here to help, that's for sure. She doesn't even give me the courtesy of telling me she cares, She'll only do it when she feels like that her own goals require it, like she just did earlier in the car.

The fury overcoming him was like a hot storm blowing over the cold sea that where his emotions. For months he had been caught in a flurry of terrors and revelations which had left him feeling either paralyzed or spinning. He was still anxious now, yet he also boiled. The anger which came over him made him entirely forget how he ended up sitting across from Mira at Lakshmi and Fiol's living room table. The hosts, as always, sat together on a couch to his left. Little Sara would either play with her toys on the floor to his left, perturb Mira with a flurry of peculiar inquiries, cuddle up next to one of her parents or, quite frequently, disappear somewhere in the house or the garden outside. This time, she had decided to investigate the appeal of her new toy in one of the seats near the exit to the house's many terraces.

Colonel Patel was pregnant, a fact which had been barely noticeable during their first encounter in the Jerusalem amphitheatre, yet had started becoming more apparent in recent weeks. Over the course of their sessions, she had gone from her traditional Terran officer tracksuit outfits, which were quite comfortable in their own right, to more loose fitting and colourful dresses. Today she wore a yellow, pink and green sari, with the latter colour matching her husbands' garb.

Vanir outfits were remarkably few and far between in number, which was strange for a galaxy-spanning civilization of almost a thousand worlds, each one populated with a variety of independent-minded cultures. Independence was a concept which stood at the heart of Vanir identity. Yet, strangely enough, this agreement on the importance of personal freedom actually resulted in a remarkable degree of uniformity in thought and dress among the various Vanir subcultures. Over the course of their meetings, Thomas had seen Fiol experiment with different Terran styles, such as jeans, bomber jackets, headscarves and even a Scottish kilt. However, today, he had apparently retreated back into more familiar costume, as he wore an outfit that was almost ostentatiously Vanir.

It could only be described as a very tight-fitting Robin Hood outfit, bar only the feathered hat. He wore no shoes, as was the custom of his people yet, upon his wife's insistence, he would wear socks when outside the house. Hence, the Patel household had an entire cupboard of socks of various shades of green, brown and yellow near the entrance. Lakshmi would frequently scold both her husband and her daughter when the latter would insist upon going barefoot outside, since it was 'what daddy did'.

These details had been scarred into his mind in the kind of detail only trauma can carve. For what had felt like years he had stayed here with them in this set-up, pouring out his thoughts, trembling, squirming and, yes, crying. It had been a strange thing to weep in front of them on so many occasions, yet somehow it had felt expected of him. The very first session they had together, their living room table had been adorned only with a wooden box, whose contents always jutted out from its top.

Tissue paper.

Napkins.

A not so subtle hint that tears were to be accepted here.

It had not taken long for Thomas to start crying. It had come whilst discussing whether or not the moment of death itself should be expected to have an impact on the type of afterlife Olorun constructed for the departed. It had been during their jump from Valhalla, an expected destination for those norsemen who had met death in battle, to Tlaloc, an expected afterlife for those Aztecs who had died drowning, that Thomas had honoured the topic with a gush of wet tears.

Yet, he had never reached out to grab the paper before him.

It was his very own little vow. A remnant of his pride. Somehow, in his mind, an idea had formed that he could retain his dignity, at least in his own eyes, if he did not succumb to the offer to wipe away his tears. He used his hand, sure. His sleeves often were still wet when he had dinner, yet not the napkins. This small act of rebellion was the way by which he retained some level of respect, even if it was just in his own eyes.

But today, he found himself in his typical seat full of more than just this single small rebellious streak. Patel was staring at her screen, setting-up what he knew would become a report of the meeting, which would later by processed by the operators designing Olorun, together with countless other pieces of code and data. Fiol was perusing an old Terran book; Thomas could barely make out the title 'Maitreyi' on the cover, but not the author, as it was obstructed by the Vanir's hands.

Not that he cared, as he was busy glaring openly at Mira, who looked back at him with her blankest of expressions. Neither Lakshmi nor Fiol seemed to notice the staredown going down in their living room.

'So, Thomas, have you done the reading?' Lakshmi began with her usual question.

Jenseits des Lustprinzips, Die Destruktion als Ursache des Werden, The Ego in Freud's Theory and in the Technique of Psychoanalysis, and seasons I and II of *Casa del Papel.*

'Yes. I have.'

'Excellent!' He always did the readings and she always thought it was excellent. 'How did you find it?' She didn't look up from her screen.

'Poor.' *I can't believe I just had the balls to say that.*

And that definitely got everyone's attention. Mira froze completely. Fiol did not look up from his novel, yet stopped playing with the pages. Lakshmi immediately looked up from her screen.

After a short pause, she asked. 'You... you found Jacques Lacan to be a poor read?'

'Not a poor read; poor in scope.' The pause that followed was atypical, since Lakshmi had a love of follow-up questions matched only by Fiol's passion for dissecting minutiae. Thomas didn't need a prompt though. At this point, he was fine with going off the reservation on his own.

'I wish there was more information, really. Or, perhaps, a more comprehensive approach to things.'

Lakshmi seemed to recollect herself. 'Ah, I see you're concerned once more with theories which have a limited set of tools by which they tackle a topic.'

'No, this is more than that. This was just plain bland.'

'... you found Lacan... to be *bland*?' Lakshmi seemed to have been, once more, taken off-guard.

'By no fault of his own! Don't get me wrong, he was working with the tools available to him. That's the problem, really.' He moved forward in his seat and got into his ranting position.

'Old Earth philosophy is all we discuss here. Mostly because there are no Terran philosophers and partially because we focus on the *known* subjects of Olorun, not the *unknown* ones, which will come in the future. Now, to this end we've gone through the two main schools of thought, which are philosophy and religion. With religion we break it down between mythology, which we ignore, and theology, which we use as a starting point for what Satya and Olorun are supposed to be. Hell, the names are taken from Hindu and Yoruba mythology, respectively.'

'With philosophy, what we do is make sure all our expectations of Satya and Olorun are rational and possible. Experiential veracity, inter-eschatological communication, cyclical Epicureanism, that sort of thing. And we start out with Western philosophy, which mostly builds on Greek philosophy and Christianity, and we follow-up with Eastern philosophy, which starts off from Confucianism, Islamic philosophy, mysticism... so on and so forth. At first, they start out from similar places, then a lot of them branch out, then they intermingle again a little, and now we're trying to reconnect and reconcile all of them in one grand thesis – or, should I say *theosis,* – no! *Theogenesis*!'

'But the sample size is so limited! We only focus on Old Earth philosophy and we just input what we learn from that into our new technologies. We make sure the two work together, then what we spit out becomes the Olorun sourcecode. What I am saying is that: of course it's poor, we are only drawing from our own body of work on the topic of existence, while we have dozens of other – far more advanced – civilizations from which to draw upon.'

Lakshmi found a moment to interject: 'Because there is a lot of overlap – '

'–of course there is! Everything our predecessors have thought about, their predecessors had *already* thought about. Now, you see, there *is* a lot of overlap. I know that. You know that. But, at the end of the day, Albert Camus died at forty-seven. *Forty*-seven! A few lucky ones got to live almost twice that long. But the orcs, the remani, the demani, the elves,' his gaze switched and became fixed upon Mira, 'their Camus lived for forty-seven *thousand* years and he's just the one they remember having. How many thousands more Camus' did they have and forget about?'

He would've gone on but was interrupted. 'You just answered your own question. The elves forgot–'

Thomas interrupted Lakshmi back. '– the elves forgot their names, but not their work! The work was integrated and snowballed and preserved in the works of thousands of generations after them...'

The sequence of interruptions continued. 'How many names did we forget? How much knowledge have we integrated without knowing?' Lakshmi didn't have the moment needed to follow-up on her point, as Thomas once more fired back.

'It's all just knowledge accumulated in singular lifetimes perhaps eighty years in length! How old are you Colonel? Seventy? Maybe almost eighty? How much more do you know now than you did when you were fifty? That was when Lacan wrote the book we are supposed to go over today. Fifty!'

'You want non-Terran wisdom?' Fiol's voice was soft and naturally melodic. He had one of those singsong voices which never said anything off-pitch. In some of the earlier sessions, Lakshmi would play jazz in the room. Not loudly. Just as a soundtrack. The practice had ceased when Thomas had reluctantly pointed out that every time Fiol spoke, it sounded like he was part of the music and it made it difficult to focus. Yet, now, that musical voice had a certain... frequency, which gave Thomas some pause.

Though not enough to fully stop him in his tracks. 'Yes! I would, actually.'

'Fine' Fiol hadn't looked up from the pages of the book in his hands up until now, when he closed it with a loud *pop!* 'We even have a name for it: *Uliel's law*. It states that, the total volume of contribution one makes to a body of work is directly proportional to his lifetime, while the impact of his contribution is inversely proportional to his lifetime.'

Thomas needed a second to process the math, yet Fiol would rather explain it himself. 'The longer one spends working on something, the more he is able to advance the borders of knowledge in his field. However, there is a peak. When the young come into a field, they do not master it. They have to learn to master it. They spend a long time mastering it, but not centuries. In the end, they are able master their field. When that happens, in order for progress to be achieved, those that were once young must push the line of knowledge further. However, they can only push it so much until they are stopped by either their own demise, the rise of those younger than them or by their own success.'

Fiol threw the book on the table with a loud thud to which no one paid attention.

'In your society or – to be more precise – in the society of your forefathers, it was usually death that stifled progress and, yes, as was the case with your Camus and many others, death likely turned future advancements into unfulfilled potential. However, I ask you this: if Camus knew not that he was coming towards death, would he have lived the same life? Would he have had the same intensity or passion or obsession for the borders of knowledge which he was pushing?'

'I ask you more: if Camus would have known of a hundred other Camus' in past, whose work he would have studied in order to become a master, could he have become someone that would push the borders of knowledge further? Was it not precisely the dissatisfaction with the knowledge that existed so far in his world that compelled him to push forward?'

'I give you now my answer, Thomas, as to why I do not tell you more of Uliel, or of deterministic counter-integralism or of the Bukayo School of neo-rebuttalism.'

'It is not physics that we discuss here, but *metaphysics*.'

He put his hand forward, thumb and forefinger outstretched, as if he was holding an invisible cube. 'Between these two fingers lies all the information needed to understand the physical universe: particles, energy, matter, empty space, forces of attraction and repulsion... I can go on for a long time, just as the study of what I have between my fingers can go on for a long time. But, nevertheless, all the materials needed to understand the universe, the multiverse and even those things beyond, lies now between my fingers. It would be hard, yes, but certainly not impossible to discern everything that we have come to know about existence from so little.'

'There is no hidden vault on a world far away guarded by some eldritch demon of another dimension which hides some key to understanding physics. It is all right here.'

'The understanding of *meta*physics – if one can even imagine such a thing – can be achieved solely with that which is found right here!' Fiol brought back his hand to his head, which he touched gently with the tips of his fingers. 'It would be very hard to do it alone, but it would, nevertheless, be entirely possible. What we discuss here is actually all related to consciousness.'

'Not *sapience*, mind you, for there are many things out there that are definitely conscious, yet not sapient. If you have this,' he patted his head with his fingers, 'you have everything you need to approach the task we have come here to complete.'

Fiol formulated his closing statement. 'The wisdom needed to fulfil the task at hand exists already in all civilizations of sufficient technological advancement. The exact structure may vary, yet the contents are one and the same.'

Thomas was quiet only enough for the time needed to structure his point. 'Then why restructure it? That is what you're doing after all, right? Olorun needs to be able to construct Satya in such a way that every consciousness in it obtains experiential veracity according to its own understanding. Right?' Their silence was a positive answer which Thomas didn't really need.

'Then why bother restructuring it?'

Lakshmi responded. 'Thomas. You know why. The theology needs to make sense to Olorun. It needs to be structured in such a way that will help Olorun become the type of administrator that provides experiential veracity. It can't do that if the information is structured badly.'

'You don't know that.'

'We don't, but –'

'– then why not copy what someone else did? Like the Continuum,' he turned to Mira, 'or the elves?'

Lakshmi did not get mad, yet her tone did become irritated. 'I am starting to believe this whole conversation has nothing to do with some desire to broaden our horizons.'

Finally, Mira spoke. 'No.'

Which was just what Thomas wanted. 'Oh, yes, it does! Because every time I ask a question, none of you ever answer it! Which, to be fair, is understandable given what my questions are. But, you do *respond* and when you respond, it's always with Terran thoughts. Never with non-Terran ones, unless if I push for it.'

Fiol (who seemed to have figured out that Thomas' unusual behaviour had something to do with Mira) intervened, '*You* are Terran, Thomas. Satya is for Terrans. It must be compatible with *Terrans*.'

This almost drove Thomas towards apoplexy. 'A-all... *all... all Terrans?!* My grandparents – whomever they were – didn't do tequila *shots* with *goblins* in *another* GALAXY!' He was shouting now.

This was enough to illicit a response from Mira. 'This isn't all about you, Thomas.'

'It isn't all about you either!' he shot back.

'Alright I'm really confused now.' Lakshmi was being honest. He turned to her daughter. 'Sara! Go to your room!'

'But it's getting interesting now!' the little girl complained. Thomas noticed that she had at one point sat up on her chair and was now spinning her new toy absent-mindedly as she stood all ears, listening to what the grown-ups were going on about.

'Go!' Colonel Patel didn't raise her voice, yet a subtle shift in tone was enough for a disappointed little girl to leave the room.

All four of them stood quiet, until they all heard the distant sound of a Sara's door closing.

The moment they heard the door shut, several things happened all at once. Thomas began to speak. Mira switched from lounging in her seat to sitting forward, mirroring Thomas' own position. Colonel Patel stood up and began pacing with one hand on her showing belly. Fiol took advantage of the now empty seat next to him to stretch his legs and the chaos began.

'You're a fucking hypocrite, you know that?' *Oh boy... the cat's out of the bag... No going back now.*

Mira's eyes flashed with a white hot rage that almost made Thomas go blind. 'I beg your fucking pardon?'

'You talk all this talk about how I'm being fucked with and used and exploited but you're part of it! You go on-and-on-and-on *all day* about "death this!" and "death that!" and you put the fucking grey death chant music in the car every morning and spit out every fucking murder and bloodbath grim shit story you know all the fucking time. Y don't even let me eat in some piece of piss peace–'

'– I thought the problem was that I don't talk about my childhood.'

'That's part of the same fucking issue!' He started wagging a finger at her and it seemed to move in tandem with the flaring of her nostrils. 'You're not her to fucking help! If you were, you'd tell me things I don't know every now and then! Maybe that would make me feel better, if you really gave a shit!'

Lakshmi intervened now. 'Thomas, Mira's role is to help you structure your thoughts, not help you!'

Thomas did not relent. 'I know! I've been told. That's everyone's task, you know? That's what I've noticed. That's what I'm *told*. I know I am alone in this.' Lakshmi's upper lip quivered, ever so slightly, as she choked on a response.

He pushed forward. 'I'm fine with that. I'm fine with all of it. I get it! Everyone tells me I'm going to snap out of this and you're all just here to observe my journey towards the other end. Just that I can't *see* the other end! And I'm tired of hoping I see the light at the end of the tunnel. It's exhausting to have hope, if over and over again what happens is that your own mind crushes that hope. And I want hope. And I want help. I want to stop feeling like this. And I feel alone in this. And everyone keeps telling me that that's all that's needed–'

Mira spoke with all the composure she could muster '–and you will–'

'...and you're delaying it, on purpose –'

'– because it's my job!'

'You're like fucking Tokyo in *Casa del Papel*!'

'Are you calling me a whore, now?' Her eyes were shooting cinders now.

'No, I am calling you a *cunt*!' Silence filled the room for a minute. The only thing to be heard were four (and a half) very accelerated heart beats.

Thomas continued, 'You're fucking selfish! You only see things from your own perspective. "What can *I* get out of everything? How am *I* undermined by this? How is this thing or that thing to *my* advantage?" You spread fucking bullshit drama everywhere you go and... and this is what hurts Mira! You have *the balls* to act like you're by my side and that you're helping me to be better and *I hate that*! Just don't give me hope! Just let me be alone and spare me your bullshit drama advice, when you won't even help me with the fucking homework!'

That was it. That was the end of the rant. He was spent and Mira could tell.

She sat forward in her seat a few seconds longer, then sat back in the armchair again, hands outstretched over the wide arms of the chesterfield leather. All of a sudden, her mouth opened and her lips began mouthing the beginnings of letters. Yet, she stopped herself from talking. At one point, she even looked towards a corner of the room, mouth half open, her jaw moving, as she began tapping her fingers on the armchair.

I've never seen her this angry before...

This is some Robert de Niro rage right here.

'*Advice*?' It was Lakshmi who spoke. '*Help to be better*?' Mira's eyes moved as she looked towards the Colonel, her mouth still half open. 'Mira, I swear to God, every morning I wake up I see the face of my daughter, followed by the face of my husband, whom I love very much. Then, Mira, I see your face. Every evening, before I go to bed, I see the face of Eliafas, Cantor and all of those fucking *bastards* whom I hate from the bottomless pit that is my heart! In between I see the faces of everyone else in my life whom I've met. Some that are still alive and a great many that are not. Now, you've moved down the ladder in recent times on account of the birth of my own child. I would rather any subsequent steps you take down the ladder be the result of future childbirth, not of your own foolish actions.' Thomas was startled by Patel's cold fury. He had never seen her like this before.

Mira began shooting back. 'I thought our role was to make sure Project Kralizec–'

'– Your role was to make sure that what we were doing wasn't too much for the boy!!!' Patel had finally snapped. To be his therapist! Do therapists, in your experience, give *advice*? Do they tell their patients *what to do*?' Mira answered with her silence.

'What did she tell you to do?' Thomas was struck by the intensity with which the Colonel questioned him.

Don't lie.

That would be difficult to do, so he took a deep breath. 'She told me not to forget how you exploited me. How... how this thing was supposed to be personal and how you're taking advantage of me... and...' Thomas paused, wanting to say the next part, for a variety of reasons, yet not sure if it was in good taste.

'And?' Lakshmi would be the one to judge the flavour of his words.

He surrendered. 'That you all mean well. That you're good people.'

'Hmphhh... Good advice... At least the first part.' Lakshmi conceded.

Her mind seemed to wander for a second as she seemingly fell upon her own thoughts; possibly even her own memories.

In the end, she smiled.

The moment Lakshmi's lips curled upwards. Mira stood up, her eyes returning to lock with Thomas'.

'I'm taking a leave of absence tomorrow.' She made her way towards the door.

'On what grounds?' Lakshmi inquired.

Her response came without her head turning. 'Operational exhaustion.'

After the door shut behind her, they heard her shuttle door open softly and close loudly, followed by a very aggressive lift-off.

'Well...' Fiol began.

'Well... well... well...' Lakshmi continued, still smiling slightly. They both looked at Thomas at the same time. Somehow, with Mira gone, Thomas' rage immediately subsided, to once more reveal the anxiety lurking beneath.

Both Lakshmi and Fiol caught on rather quickly that Thomas' mood had changed.

'We're going to conclude today's session earlier than usual, Thomas. Which is something I think we would all welcome. Right?' Thomas nodded quickly and confused. 'And if Mira's going to get a day off tomorrow, so will you. Me and Fiol have been putting off a day trip to Sardinia for quite some time now. If the opportunity has presented itself, then we will take it.' She looked to her husband as he nodded in agreement.

Thomas realised that they might want him to leave as well and got up. 'Apologies, Colonel!'

'None needed, Lieutenant. It's understandable given the circumstances. Quite frankly, I'm happy your relationship with Mira has progressed to the point where it upsets you when she doesn't have your back.' Lakshmi's words took him so off-guard that he legitimately didn't know how to answer them.

'I... I'm glad, sir. Am I... Am I free to go?' He didn't even know what that meant. *Did I just earn my mindwipe?*

'Well, of course you can. Though,' Lakshmi chuckled and broke into a fit of laughter, ', it's a long walk to Jerusalem!' As Fiol joined in, Thomas realised what they meant. Mira had taken her shuttle with her, leaving Thomas an infantryman.

'It's... it's fine. I'll summon a shuttle.'

'Oh my God, Thomas, calm down! Fiol can drive you.'

'Of course I can. But first, Thomas, are you familiar with the game *Settlers of Catan*?' Fiol's words made Lakshmi burst into another fit of laughter.

'I... the... the board game?' His mother and father used to play *Catan* at the orphanage where they had met as children.

'Yes! Do you know the rules?' Fiol was genuinely excited now.

'I... Yes. We had one at the house...' His parents had taught him the game.

Fiol snapped his fingers, in a Vanir gesture signalling excitement. 'Excellent!' He got up from his seat. 'I'll get Sara – she is just now learning, so we go easy on her. Thomas, you set up the board. Honey, let's have an atmosphere with music and snacks!'

'Calm down there, my guy, you don't even know if he wants to play!' Lakshmi was all cool now, yet Thomas could see that she was still occasionally touching her belly.

'Ohhh, but you're a Colonel and he is a Lieutenant. Perform some abuse of office! We need four people to play with all the extensions!'

'Oh, my! Thomas, are you ok with this?' she asked genuinely.

'I...' *will not be able to focus at all and I will probably play embarrassingly bad but, hey, as long as I am not getting mindwiped* '... would love to.'

The series of games that followed were, as Thomas had predicted, disastrous for him and terrific for little Sara, who didn't even really seem to need any help to win.

He spent the remainder of the day at the Patel household. They even had a short pseudo-session in their garden where they had discussed whether or not sentient Terran animals should be catered to by Olorun in the same manner as Terran humans, a thought which little Sara had passionately supported because 'there's puppies with better souls than people'. A discussion revolving around getting a new family pet quickly followed, with a Samoyed being the agreed upon as the ideal breed of the new family member. Promises were made that one would be acquired once they moved back to Gandhinagar after Theogenesis took place.

Not that Thomas could follow the conversation properly since, between the board game, the afterlives of pets and the morning's events, he could barely keep two thoughts together in his head.

After dinner, which, upon Lakshmi and Fiol's insistence, Thomas had with them, Fiol had kept true to his word and had driven him back to Jerusalem. Right before leaving the Patel household, little Sara had pulled Thomas aside and explained to him that he and Mira should make up, since 'she is angry at you differently now and everything that's changed is that she knows you better now!'

The first couple of minutes of the shuttle ride with Fiol were rather quiet. He drove much more sensibly than Mira, so the ride took twice as long. However, at one point Fiol started telling him about some of his other interviews; the ones him and Lakshmi held with test subjects of Para-Satya, both volunteers and prisoners.

And then he said something which took Thomas by surprise.

'You know me and Lakshmi met only a week before we went in and tested Para-Satya?'

No, he did not. 'You and her... went into Para-Satya?'

'Oh, yes, that's where we began our relationship.' Fiol paused a second, as he frequently did when trying to say something with simple words. 'We fell in love in the dream. We spent decades there in love. When we came out, we returned to a world where we had met but days earlier. We planted the seed of our first daughter, Sarasvati, that very evening.'

'I... I didn't know that.' Fiol's candid retelling of his love story was quite touching. Yet, oddly enough, it felt out of place.

The Vanir continued. 'The thing about falling in love in a simulation of Heaven is that... you learn that love is something of *all* existence, you know? When you are in love, you go from Heaven to Hell *and back* in a moment and you are happy for the entire journey!'

Wha-what the hell is he on about?

'You go from being in love to also loving the other person. In the beginning, you do not love the other person, since you do not know them, yet. You love the image of that person in your head. You love the way they make you feel. As you transition from being *in* love to *loving* the other person, your relationship becomes a partnership. In a partnership, a balance must always be struck between freedom and equality. Now, if one person thinks that there is an imbalance, that can lead to conflict. But, you must remember, communication is key in all things and, well, good interactions are needed. You need to have more good interactions than bad interactions.' *Oh...*

'Sometimes that's hard but, you just have to remember: there's no reason to feel bad in a relationship – '

'– Mira and I do not have a thing together.'

'Oh...'

'Yeah...'

'Oh. Well... it's still good advice I just gave. I'd stash it away for future use.'

Chapter XI
Against Regulation

The message had come during the night.

Thomas saw it in the morning when he woke up. It was short and to the point, as Mira's texts frequently were.

'Lunch at my place. 15:00. You have access.'

So, here he was, in front of Mira's door, as he had many times before to wake her up. He had never actually been inside of her apartment before. Usually she just came to the door after getting ready. The whole process would take about ten to fifteen minutes. Now, she seemingly wanted him to come in.

On her day off.

A day off that had com about due to his actions the day before. The day after she had stormed away from their duties, too angry to speak.

He had considered calling his mother and telling her he loved her. He had even considered informing Patel or Adler of the request. For it was a request. It was not formulated as an issued order. He had the right to refuse. Yet, it was not bravery that had brought him to her door. Guilt had kept him awake until late in the night. He had fallen asleep only a mere hour before Mira's text had come in, which likely meant she had not been able to sleep either. Likely due to what Thomas could only assume was daylight rage.

He felt guilty for his outburst. After much thought, he had realised that Sara had been right and Mira was only being true to herself. He was her charge and she had made a commitment to take care of him, yet she also had her orders. Orders which she had respected, as best as she could, until his words had put her orders at odds with who she was. The day before, Thomas had revealed to her his trust and appreciation of her. Not of Captain Amira al Sayid, but of her: Mira.

When he had done that, it had clashed with her sense of justice, which Thomas hadn't realised applied not only to the betterment of her own standing. That's what she had meant when she had asked him if he was her friend. She had been telling him that she now knew that he saw her as a friend, while also confessing that she had not felt like one up until the moment when Thomas had told her he trusted her.

That was when she had flipped. She had gone from taking care of him, to telling him to take care of himself, something which she generally only seemed to expect of herself.

Thomas took a deep breath as he rehearsed his apology in his head, then rang the doorbell before inputting his ID. The door opened to Mira's antechamber, which he had seen before, yet had never been inside of. He closed the door behind him and noticed that today the door before him, leading to what was likely Mira's living room, had been left slightly ajar. He took a deep breath and quietly opened it further, revealing the chamber beyond.

Mira had not finished unpacking. Which was strange as she had likely been here for two months. The living room was a standard Terran officer's living room, with several couches, a dinner table, chairs, screens and, in Mira's case, several elven cushions strewn across the room, all of which were covered by an assortment of weaponry, trinkets, clothes and books. Every table was covered in empty coffee mugs and tea cups, usually next to automated ashtrays, three of which were currently indicating that they needed to be emptied. There was an automated sisha pipe, smoke still drifting slowly from one of its ends, and a huge screen across almost the entirety of one of the walls, with an old Terran TV show running on mute.

The room was dimly lit by a few scented candles and Mira seemed to keep the room on 20% luminosity, with the artificial lighting making one feel as if they were late in the afternoon. He did not recognize the music that played melodically in the background, yet he could tell it was goblin EDM of some kind, the soft beats being *almost* the only sound one could hear.

This was what caught Thomas' attention.

There was a heartbeat in the room.

Small. Much smaller than that of a human, yet much faster.

He focused on it and quickly determined the source, which was a black-and-orange cushion perched up next to the door leading to what he assumed was Mira's bedroom.

I didn't know she had a cat.

The small creature had not noticed him, as it seemed to be transfixed upon the door. Thomas entered the room, just as quietly as he had done so far. He decided best to close the door to the antechamber much more loudly than he had the entrance to the apartment, so as to alert the animal to his presence. Some people had their cats altered with guardian instincts and augmented muscles, claws and teeth. He was in no mood to have some startled feline attack him.

The sound had some of the desired effect, as the cat turned around to reveal one eye which was a bright blue and another one of a golden yellow. The pupils of both immediately dilated as the animal immediately jumped several feet into the air.

Which was to be expected. What was not to be expected, however, was that it started to speak.

'Milady! Milady!!!!!! Milady! There's a yellow nigger in the house!' *What the fuck?*

The cat began rushing around the room, shouting obscenities and racial slurs. Thomas could tell that the animal was indeed augmented, as it had the eggshell white teeth and claws typical of modified Terran pets. It did not, however, attack him on-sight, which Thomas realised was a sign that the animal had not been modified for protection purposes. However, what it lacked in physical aggression, it more than made up with verbal abuse.

'Milady! Milady I AM ALONE! He is coming! He is in the house! He didn't ring the doorbell and he came in the house! Milady, he is putting things in my arse! He is touching my ass! Milady! Stay away slit-eye! Go eat dog dick!'

He had definitely rung the doorbell and he had never been closer than four yards from the hissing little beast.

Finally, after the most uncomfortable ten seconds of Thomas' life, Mira's voice rang out from the bedroom. 'It's fine, Lorgar. He is supposed to be here! Thomas?'

'Hello, Mira!' he replied, eyes still focused on the bigoted feline puffed up on the couch in front of him.

'Feed him!' Mira's instruction raised every eyebrow and whisker in her living room.

'*What?*' they both asked tentatively, albeit for different reasons.

'I don't want to deal with this shit! Feed him!'

'What if he poisons us, milady?' Lorgar asked suspiciously, yet also expectantly.

'He won't! Thomas, there's a leftover a chicken carcass in the phaiser. Box 18. Set it to poultry body temp and–'

Her pet cut her off, as it jumped from atop a couch and trotted towards the kitchen door. '– and put the bowl next to the water tank! Come, Thomas! I will show you!' The cat stopped in front of the closed kitchen door and turned around to the house guest. 'Come, Thomas! Come! I can't open door*knobs*. Only door *handles*. She always changes from handles to knobs. It's against regulation, but she does it against me! Come! Come!'

Equally intrigued and annoyed, Thomas made his way across the room while dodging luggage and martial equipment, until he reached the doorknob in question, which he turned, allowing Lorgar to squeeze through the opening door as he rushed into the kitchen, which was much more orderly than her living room.

'Phaiser's here, Master Thomas! Here! Here!' He tapped his claws on the phaiser, which Mira had also, apparently, modified with doorknobs.

Thomas opened the phaiser, found box 18 and set it to poultry body temperature. After a few seconds, the device let out an audible *ping* and opened box 18's door, revealing the remains of an expertly butchered chicken within. The carcass lay within a white ceramic bowl, with the name 'LORGAR' etched in black letters on the side facing its namesake, as well as his very irritated temporary caretaker.

'Yes! Yes! That is it, Master Thomas! Give it! GIVE IT TO ME! HERE!' The cat began circling a specific spot on the floor.

Well, I hope you choke on it...

Thomas lowered the bowl down next to Mira's water tank to the sounds of ecstatic feline jubilation. Lorgar immediately got to work devouring the chicken. One could hear cracks of bone, tears of tendons and very loud moans of gluttonous pleasure.

There had been a craze, of sorts, more than a decade before. Elven animal biomancy, once used purely for military purposes by the Terran population, had become so widespread, that people had started augmenting common pets. The practice, initially considered to be nothing more than an affectionate luxury, had quickly spiralled out of control. At first, people simply made dogs, cats, horses and all matter of common Terran companions more physically imposing and dangerous. Dogs grew huge and wolf-like, like the Muller's own family pet, Yeats. Cats received enhanced claws, far sharper and sturdier than their original murder mittens. Horses grew even more in size, speed and endurance. In a matter of months, Terra's cute and fury family members became roided-up killing machines.

Which was all fun and games, at the end of the day. The government had nothing against an extra line of defence, but then people started making them talk and everything went to shit.

The process was quite simple: the animal would receive modifications to its throat, facial muscles, tongue and lips, allowing it to articulate human sounds, but without noticeably changing their appearance. Yet, all of that was quite useless if the animal's mind did not have the capacity for language. The early procedures were straightforward enough: their brains were modified, with language libraries, as well as basic speech centres being etched within their existing cerebral structures.

It was in the aftermath of the procedure that things got truly hairy.

The expectation was that the animal would not become much more intelligent than an unaltered counterpart, which was usually the case... for a few weeks. However, very quickly, Terrans began to figure out why their orcish, elven, demani and, particularly, remani allies had warned them against the practice. The simple fact was that the development of a capacity for language was not a one-off boost to the animal's intelligence. Rather, it was merely a spark, setting in motion the flames of cognitive development.

Some developed depression and sought out the end of their lives. A few had gone into fits of rage, attacking their human companions, whom they now viewed as oppressors. The vast majority just became very weird and dysfunctional, with only a select few continuing to be charming creatures of wild nature and human recklessness. The most impactful evolution occurred in various gorilla, chimpanzee, orangutan and other simian populations, which developed outright human sentience and sapience, albeit of a very primitive nature (at first).

In the end, the Terran High Command had intervened: horse-sized pitbulls were 'ok', but talking chickens were not. There were exceptions. One was for animals which had already gone through the augmentation process, like the little cunt in front of him. Another was for animals which received a much more comprehensive mental augmentation, allowing for the development of a more stable intelligence comparable to that of humans. Yet, this was only allowed for new organisms, with augmentation of existing entities becoming illegal. The caveat here was that these animals received person rights and were no longer considered mere fauna.

Person rights were not the epitome of human rights on Terra. Those would be Terran *citizen* rights. Thomas, Mira, Lakshmi and little Sara had citizen rights. Fiol had citizen rights since he had renounced his Vanir citizenship, married Lakshmi and had passed through the very rigorous screening process of Terran immigration. Clara, his operator, only had person rights. The fluffy arsehole in front of him had person rights.

The difference between the two was complicated to formulate, yet easy to exemplify: if there was a famine, Thomas could eat the feline prick munching erratically beneath him with no questions asked. The pathetic asinine arsewipe would be put down if it even looked at him funny and made him feel offended enough to bother convincing a judge that his life had been at risk.

How the hell Mira had come across this dreadful little shitstain was beyond him. He could tell that Lorgar was quite old, both from his appearance and his grasp of offensive English, meaning that he likely originated in the first round of Terran pet augmentation.

'Clara, how many Category 2B felines are there alive now?' he asked out loud.

'Thirteen.'

Lorgar couldn't hear Clara's answer 'I am the oldest one!' he said proudly between mouthfuls.

'You don't say...'

'Ask your headvoice! The rest are dead or younger.'

'I wonder why...' Thomas mumbled. 'Clara, is he the oldest category 2B feline?'

'What's his ID number?'

'What's your...' Thomas didn't have time to ask the question.

'69-420-13' *and proud of it.*

'Are you ser...?' He didn't have time to finish, as Clara's voice rang out in his head.

'Lorgar Erebus Aurelian. *Terrani Felix Catus Sapiens Inferior Adulteratus* Species. Maine Coon Breed. Male. Intact. Tortoiseshell Coat. Born April 20th 13 BT. Second of a litter of five altered kittens. Designated citizen guardian: Captain Amira Parvati Al Sayid.' *This fucking thing is older than me...*

'You really are the oldest one aren't you?' He didn't wait for Clara to confirm.

'I tell no lies!' the dumb twat insisted during gulps of chicken skin.

'There's more,' Clara informed him.

'Huh?' Clara didn't usually bring up things unless she knew they would be of interest.

'Disciplinary record citations: while assigned to Saskatchewan orphanage, was caught preaching Old Earth white supremacist ideology and verbally abusing non-white children with slurs of ethnic nature.'

'What?' *He should have been put down for that.* Verbally abusing an adult was one thing, but Terrans took childcare very seriously. His mother had once shot a dog sight for just growling at a child.

'He was granted a Hierarch pardon.' *The plot thickens.*

'Which Hierarch?' he asked.

It was the cat who replied, 'The Master!!!'

'Djibril al Sayid.' Even Clara felt the need to make her tone more reverent.

'*Oh...* Any notes?' *There'd better be fucking notes on that...*

'Hierarch pardon text reads: "Banter". Guardianship subsequently transferred from Saskatchewan orphanage to Djibril al Sayid.' *Well, that explains it.*

This ancient little beast hadn't come into Mira's care by her own choice. He was an heirloom. His previous guardian had been her father. It actually made perfect sense. Djibril was known to have been a man with a great, albeit peculiar, sense of humour. He likely would have thought the cat's antics to have been just that: antics. Now, how Lorgar's predicament had come to the attention of one of the most powerful men on Terra was a mystery, yet Thomas couldn't deny that pardoning and adopting an imbecile racist cat for the sake of a good laugh was perfectly in line with everything he knew of the second Warchief of the Republican Alliance.

Djibril al Sayid was known to have been a man of contrasts. He was in equal parts kind and cruel, forgiving and vengeful, friendly and foreboding. He had been a rare breed among Terrans and of an even rarer kind among the peoples of Old Earth. What else could one expect of a man who would come back from the dead, triumph over the greatest of warriors, lead a war of vengeance across the stars, make peace with the bitterest of enemies and defy the greatest of empires?

Thomas found himself gazing upon the fluffy fiend enjoying lunch next to him. This was Djibril al Sayid and Sarasvati Singh's pet. He had likely met Thomas Ashaver, Çingeto Braca, Kimmie Jimmel, Quentyn Andromander, Vorclav Uhrlacker and, yes, even Daw al Fajr herself, to not even mention a hundred other heroes, both living and dead. Lorgar had likely frolicked through the gardens of Menegroth, the halls of Barlog or down the avenues of Moria.

How many times had he sat perched on some ledge in the same room as legends? How many plans and tactics had been laid forth as he napped on some pillow in a corner? To what secrets had he been privy to? How many legends had given him a good back scratch?

And now Thomas found himself feeling it again.

The feeling he had felt in Shoshanna Adler's office. That yearning to touch the desk of the American presidents of old now manifested itself anew. This time, it was as an itch to scratch the fur of the feline below. Ethnic slurs or not, this creature had been in the presence of greatness unfathomable to Thomas' own mind, let alone its own pitiful senses. As if in a dream, he began to reach down.

A threatening hiss stopped him. 'Fuck off, gook!'

All right that's enough. Seeing is a form of touching too.

He turned around and made his way back into Mira's living room. Sitting across from Mira's widescreen was a particularly comfortable looking cream couch. Dodging random ammunition and combat boots, he made his way towards it. As he began to lower himself, the door to Mira's bedroom swung open.

Mira had gone for a casual outfit today. It was a somewhat traditionally elven outfit, far more at home in the terraced lounges of Menegroth than in the barracks of Terra. Her shoes were traditional Terran sneakers, yet her close-fitting pants and shirt were those of an elven bodysuit, being of a sandy cream colour to match her couches. At her waist lay no combat belt, which was not surprising, since enough weaponry to start an insurgency lay scattered thorough her apartment. Lastly, she wore a light elven leather jacket.

Thomas had seen those jackets before, though not in real life. They typically brimmed with various tech and trinkets, yet Mira's was quite a plain light brown jacket, with no remarkable characteristics beyond the insignia strewn across the jacket's middle.

The crest of the Brightguard was the symbol of Daw al Fajr personal retinue. Warriors, engineers, scientists, diplomats, sages and attendants of all paths of service made up the Urizen's formal inner circle. Typically, they were all elves yet, apparently at least one Terran made up the Urizen's informal inner circle.

Now, how Mira had come into the possession of such a prestigious uniform was no mystery to Thomas (she probably asked for one and got it). However, what was surprising to Thomas was what wearing the jacket meant. Mira had never before worn any item of clothing bearing the distinguishing marks of her upbringing outside the Solar System. At least not in public. She would sometimes wear things in a certain way which was... odd... uncharacteristic for a Terran. However, going as far as to wear elven garb on Terra itself... Even elves avoided such acts and for good reason.

Is... is she... is she apologising?

Before he even had time to say something, she spoke. 'I know you've rehearsed what you want to say to me. I just want to remind you that things rarely go according to plan during arguments.'

Holy shit, that took me off balance. 'So, is that what we're going to do? We're going to argue?' *Gonna try and regain my footing here.*

'I am going to make garganelli pasta with pesto sauce. You can ask me questions while I do that and I will give elven answers. Then we can eat.'

And just like that, Mira made her way to the kitchen, leaving Thomas confused on the living room couch.

He got up to follow her back into the kitchen just in time to see her pull out a bowl of dough out of the phaiser. As she removed the cover, she gestured for Thomas to take a seat at the dining table, which Mira had placed next to the window overlooking the Mitspe Kerem. She pulled out a box of what turned out to be flour and began dusting her work area, which happened to be the entirety of her marble top.

'Tea? Coffee?' she asked, her eyes fixated on the areas that had escaped her dusting.

'I, uh... tea is good.'

'There's some villist in that cupboard over there!' She pointed with her pinkie finger towards a specific area of her pantry. 'Make more. I want some too. No milk, though!'

Not even giving me a choice, but ok. He went over to the cupboard to find that Mira had an entire selection of teas; some Terran and many non-Terran. He selected the vilist tea, since she had apparently decided that lightly caffeinated Elven tea was what went well with what she was cooking up. Hopefully, it would also go well with the food.

Thomas found that she was quite traditional, as she gestured that he prepare the tea in a Japanese metal kettle and use any number of an eclectic assortment of cups.

Mira seemed to have a pretty expansive collection of Avenger Legion cups, including many from some of the smaller legions, such as the Khevsurs, the Cataphracts or the Tuareg, and even some from the younger ones, such as the Irregulars, the Caudillos or the Sardaukar. He was surprised to notice that she did not have an Ill Ghazi cup, though she did have a cup from the original Ghazis, which she picked out for her, and a Vietcong cup, which he set aside for himself.

A tense silence descended as Thomas waited for the water to boil. Mira began stretching out the pasta dough into one large sheet with a long wooden stick she had taken out from one of her cabinets. Eventually, it was Lorgar who broke the silence, when he clumsily jumped onto Mira's work top, only to receive a gentle, yet firm, tap on the head from the aforementioned rolling stick.

'You'll shed hair, Lorgar. It's not for you, anyway.' Mira's eyes never wandered from the sheet of dough.

'Milady always says that!' Lorgar began complaining.

'Milady knows what she is talking about. Get off! Go sit with Thomas!' Mira reached out into a drawer to pull out a long knife.

'Ok. Ok. I'll sit with Thomas!' He clumsily jumped off the top and onto the kitchen table, then proceeded to stare down the dough as Mira began cutting it into long strips.

'I think the water is done,' Mira said out loud.

Thomas took the hint and poured the water over the tea bags he had set inside their respective cups, then placed Mira's cup next to her on the top. She glanced towards it out of the corner of her eye, then noted Thomas' own cup while cutting the pasta strips into single squares.

'The Jaeger cup is in the living room. The Landsknecht one is in the cupboard. I used to have a Rittebruder cup, but I broke it.' Thomas understood her meaning.

'It's fine. I'm making a statement.' Thomas eyed Lorgar, as the cat seemed to prepare a hiss.

'I see. You made a lot of statements yesterday.' *Here we go.* She continued, 'But, today, like I said, I should be making statements. So, go ahead, ask me anything.' She pulled out a small, thin wooden stick, as well as a little ridged square and began the long and tedious task of rolling each individual square into finished pieces of garganelli.

I wasn't really expecting this. Though I did hope for it.
Fine.

Thomas took a seat next to Lorgar, who continued to leer at him. He ignored the cat and began, 'When elves get an existential crisis, what is the treatment?'

'Depends on the elf. Primal elves don't even really get existential crisis. At least not the way we do. They're much more in tune with nature and the universe. They spend their lives in a manner which they would describe as "free", yet is actually quite rigid. It is common and somewhat expected among them that, during a hunt – particularly after a long, difficult hunt - if the elf is alone, he might fall into what they call the "swirling sense". We would say that their world was "spinning", like you often describe it.' She seemed to nod to herself.

'In the moment of the kill, the hunter understands the environment around him. He feels nature begin to redistribute the matter of the animal. Bacteria begin to overrun the body. The smallest insects begin to stir in anticipation. The wind begins to carry the movements of carrion birds. The very ground itself begins to prepare to participate in the process of matter redistribution.'

'And the hunted. The prey...' Mira paused. 'There is no word for "victim" in the primal elf language. Everything just *happens*. Everything that happens to anyone is merely that: a happening. An event among others. An event caused by other events, going back in time endlessly. Everything that "is" and "was" will one day "no longer be". The dead animal is not a victim, it is merely a one-time participant in an event that has always been; that always was supposed to happen in that exact manner.'

'Primal Elves grow up in an environment that instils this way of looking at things deep inside of them. They get the swirling sense only in moments of extreme exhaustion, when they push their senses to the very limits of their capacity. When that happens, typically the elf enters a trancelike state. This state frequently comes when they are alone, so no one is usually around to assist them through it. Their conditioning, their lifestyle, they beliefs are usually enough to process the swirling sense and they tend to emerge from it the same as before. Albeit, with a mind both aware and immune to it.'

'If they do not, well,' Mira's eyes widened a bit, as if she was admitting something to herself, 'the use of psychedelics is common. Elves that do not overcome the swirling sense alone undergo psychedelic therapy and assisted hypnosis, with the elf's...' her faced switched to one of pure disdain, '... *incompatibilities* being regulated.'

'If you were a Primal Elf, Thomas, an incompatibility would be your inability to enjoy life whilst knowing that it ends.' Thomas squirmed a bit in his seat. 'Where that incompatibility comes from, I do not know. Probably some childhood shit we can't really get into right now and likely never will. At least not in this life.' She paused to apply more flour to her hands.

'The high elves are similar, yet different. Whereas primal elves are a society that highly values freedom, yet enforce a great degree of discipline and conformity to norms on a near-continuous basis, the high elves are a society that claim to greatly value discipline and conformity, yet ultimately provide wide windows for personal choice and neurodivergence. Unless among their servants, that is. But, there aren't a lot of those going around today, due to obvious reasons.'

'They have their own version of *wanderlust*, like you Germans, which they enforce rigorously, as is typical of them. Most acute existential moments among high elves emerge during such times; which is, I think, the whole point why they have them. If the elf cannot overcome the crisis on his own, the most common treatment is... well, that's just it, there is no treatment. High elves are expected to deal with it whatever way they can. Much like us. Low elves, at least, used to be able to get mandatory mental reconditioning back to their baseline. But, nowadays, it's illegal to *enforce* mental reconditioning and the practice itself is frowned upon. So, they end up doing basically what we –'

'Why is it frowned upon?' Thomas interrupted.

Mira paused her rolling of the garganelli and looked up at him confused. 'You know why it's frowned upon.'

'I do, but why not do it anyway?' Thomas' words were flying out of his mouth again.

His host seemed to oscillate between slight annoyance and earnest confusion. Eventually, she seemed to find an answer to his question. 'Daw would often describe it as "having a mind that was born and raised for change, as opposed one which was born and raised for rhythm".' She went back to her artisanal pasta before continuing.

'The elven mind is raised from cradle to tomb in a rhythm. Changes in the rhythm are slow and subtly gradual. There are no great milestones in elven life. They do not have... pfff.... "Adulthood" itself is a gradual step-by-step process with around three thousand different steps, with each step being quiet and small. Adulthood itself is broken down into the various lifepaths they will cycle through to deal with... you know... the boredom and the madness.'

Thomas interjected. 'A madness they could avoid with mental reconditioning. But they don't. Just like how they don't avoid acute phases, they don't avoid the madness at the end. Why?'

Mira fucked up a piece of pasta. 'It's about rhythm, dammit! I just told you!' She stopped and paused to recollect herself from her failures as both a chef and a teacher. 'The whole lifepath cycling is a form of mental reconditioning. It's just slow. It also follows a slow *rhythm*, where the switches are slow and gradual and every little detail is controlled, predicted or, at least, predictable. *Unless...*' She stopped, looking for the same words she had sought out earlier.

She found them. 'Unless something unforeseeable and catastrophic is suddenly registered by the elf's psyche. Something that leads to a complete world-shifting paradigm. Something like what Daw did to them. Something like what *we* did to them.' Mira glanced towards Thomas before going on. 'The high elves enslaved them slowly. It took tens of thousands of years. When they came into the Milky Way, they had been a caste-based society for ten thousand years! A hundred thousand years! That's generations of domination. They had diverged into two fucking different species for fuck's sale! That process took place in an elven manner; i.e. *slowly*! So as not to disturb their rhythm. Because everything that fuck's with their rhythm also fucks with their minds!'

'Daw broke all of that in a matter of months! When she did that – no! *The way she did that* – broke tens of thousands of years of mental conditioning. Their minds, though seemingly healthy from our perspective are in *deep* distress. That's why they're so fucking weird and random and chaotic and awkward and strange. That's not what low elves used to be! They used to be mindless drones in a fucking Orwellian nightmare of which they absolutely adored being part of. They were meek and boring and they all looked and said and dressed the same.' She paused.

'Or so they tell me, since I wasn't alive when they used to be like that.'

She spoke those words as she finished her last square of pasta and began to pull ingredients out of her phaiser. 'Their minds want rhythm and naturally tend towards the instalment of a rhythm much more insistently than those on any other branch of the Tree of Man. They're... *pfff*... they're basically the type of minds we want to be developed in Satya by Olorun,' she conceded, as she gestured towards the thin air in front of her. 'But, the way they stay like that is by having minds that seek rhythm and repel change. So, when change is unavoidable or simply occurs unexpectedly, they go a little crazy. Or – and this is what Tomasz always obsessed about too – if the rhythm itself becomes too "good", that also makes them become depressed. Because that's what those two extremes are like. When Daw broke their rhythm, it made them manic. Living for too long with a rhythm, that will make them depressed... which brings me to the main existential topic the elves obsess about, which is chaos versus order.'

She took out a basil plant from beneath the kitchen top and began harvesting its leaves. Thomas just now realized that she had an entire capsule garden full of plants set-up beneath her work station. Whilst separating stem from leaf, she continued her explanation. 'Elves believe that the universe is both chaotic and ordered, just that an individual should strive for order. Eventually, the elves become bothered by the fundamental clash between their nature and, well, the nature of the universe, and they break off in one of the two directions. In that moment, you can't mentally recondition them, because their minds will reject any reconditioning.'

This is where Thomas had a question. 'The same way as ours does?'

'What do you mean? You mean us as humans or... you know... the mental conditioning *we* get? Terrans?'

'Both.' Thomas' mouth had gone a little dry as Mira had rushed through a lot stuff that bothered him in a manner he found particularly bumpy. He took as sip of his tea as she answered.

'Well, human minds don't seek a *rhythm* as intensely as elves do, so our minds are much more malleable than theirs, which makes us more susceptible to both slow- and fast-paced forms of mental reconditioning and mind control. However, Terran mental conditioning is good enough to keep out most known fast-paced forms of mental reconditioning – which, by the way, happens to be why we know that what you're going through had no nefarious external factors that triggered or maintain it. It also makes it difficult for anyone or anything to read our minds. But, other than that... we're just regular humans. Our minds are plastic and have no real problem changing. They'd rather not change too abruptly, but they have no real preference. Quite frankly, humans like changes. Elves are not like that. Elves abhor change. Humans kinda even enjoy it when life sucks a little.'

She concluded, 'So, no. Not the same way as ours. Much more obsessively than ours.'

'And what happens in their Satya?' Thomas knew the story, but didn't know how it fit with what Mira was telling him.

'Well... in the perfectly ordered world of Anait, the wisps of the Dancer perfectly control every strand of existence, allowing the Dancer to allow every elven soul within to follow that which is called the "perfectly changing path". Which – I, for one – only ever understood by using math.'

Oh. 'Go on.' Thomas urged.

'Think of the life of each elf as a number. Some numbers are simple, like 5, 36, 448 or whatever. Others are a bit more complicated, like 3.5 or 7.5 or 98.3867, but they still all end. Well, some numbers don't end. Pi, for example, never ends, and each individual section of pi is different and. Within pi, every single number that has always and ever been is located, by the simple laws of mathematics. And there's only one pi. Thus, pi is kinda like Anait: it is a place where all elves are one and achieve a type of perfect rhythm by always cycling through a new life; many of which were lives lived by some elves in the past, but an infinite number of which are new, different lives produced within Anait.'

'It's how they motivate themselves to lead good life. If they live a great life, it might be one of the lives that will be part of the "perfectly changing path" within Anait. It's also why they'd rather die than live a bad one.'

'But... will they want to live *every* elf's life? Even the shitty ones?' *What about the evil ones?*

'Well, no.... *pfff*.... Thomas, you're not remembering what elves are: they're humans that have lived under awesome conditions in which they flourish for generations. If humans live amazingly for a couple of tens of thousands of years in a row they turn into elves. If they keep on having more-or-less awesome lives beyond that point, they stay elven. Their entire species exists only when people are doing amazingly well. Their very idea of what life *is* is that it is something amazing by definition. Of course the Dancer fixes the bad choreography when it happens. It's why the Svart fought so bitterly to the very end: they knew that if they lost, then they would for sure unrecognizably edited in Anait.'

Thomas slouched back in his seat. Anxiety flowed through him once more. *This is all* Satya *stuff. It's all incorporated into the Olorun sourcecode.* Fiol seemed to be right. Everything Mira was telling him was simply a reinterpretation of what they had been discussing over the last weeks. Nothing truly new could be discerned from what she was telling him. In the end, it seemed like the dynamics of timeless consciousness didn't really change across the peoples of the universe. At least not for the ones whose existence was even remotely comparable to that of humans.

Mira had finished harvesting the basil and had now moved on to a mint plant, which she gingerly studied. *She seems oddly at peace.* He had never really seen her like this. This cooking thing seemed to be a strange refuge for her. He had initially thought she was preparing lunch as a form of apology. Now, after getting to observe her for some time, he began to realise that it was actually more akin to a soothing mechanism for her. She finished harvesting the mint quite quickly, mixing the leaves with the basil in a large blender, then pulled out two hard cheeses from her pantry, which she began grating into a large bowl.

He couldn't help it. He had to ask.

'Mira, what happened to you?' The words came out true, yet ambiguous.

Mira paused her grating. 'You gotta be a bit more specific,' she said, smiling out of the corner of her mouth, then resumed her grating.

'Ashaver said you had your existential crisis when you were very young and he was there to see it. He said it was mind-blowing. I... I was wondering, what bothered you?'

Mira didn't pause her grating. Not for a long time. It was only after she finished grating one of the cheeses, that she continued, 'It started with questions about how people were in the past. I would ask about my parents a lot. People were always very willing to answer. There were all the stories about my father and mother you'd expect: the War of Vengeance, The Fimbulwinter, Skyfall, the Battle of Tbilisi, the Bahr Aldhabh, and, yes, even Hellsbreach.' Her voice changed for the slightest of instants and in the subtlest of ways upon mentioning the event that claimed the lives of her parents.

'It was all very impactful. However, I wanted to know *who they were* more than *what they did* and I always wondered who they were before the End Times. My father's family had the most survivors from the old times. My mother only had Lakshmi, who she met during the Fimbulwinter, and Uma Kaur, who was like her fourth-degree cousin – I think. Tomasz, Laur and Shoshanna had heard of my father, yet they only met him during Ragnarok. So, one time in Mecca, I asked them who they were. What did they believe? How did they view life? What did they want from life? Things any child would want to know. I asked them what kind of world was the one in which they were born into.'

'So, they told me. They told me how people lived before the End Times. They told me how almost no one ever left Terra. If they did, it was rarely further than the atmosphere. It would take two whole days to circle the world and you did so in a plane which ran on chemical fuel. People had "phones" which they could use to access any information they wished to better themselves and to communicate with whomever they knew anywhere in the whole world. Yet, they used the phones to waste time and make enemies. People had no idea that there were other peoples beyond their own sky and they bickered constantly among themselves in their small little corner of the universe in petty arguments about clothes and music and sports teams and the little politics of men much bigger than them but small in their own right' Mira finished grating what Thomas realised was parmesan cheese, and began roasting some pine nuts on a gas stove she had installed in her worktop. The smell made Lorgar stir a little from the sleep he had fallen into after his lunch.

'It was so... so *small*. People were so ignorant in comparison to what I saw as a child. And then...' Mira flipped the roasted pine nuts into the blender and began looking through a selection of various oils she had stored in a cupboard. '... then it hit me.' She found the perfect bottle of olive oil. 'We are all the same now as we were back then.' She began pouring a copious amount of olive oil into the blender.

'Operators instead of phones. Shuttles instead of cars. Ships instead of planes. Gene templates instead of aspirin. Elves, orcs and trolls, not Germans, Arabs and Russians. The list goes on and on, but the bottom line stays the same. Everywhere you look, there are conflicts among people as to how we should live our little lives in our little corners. People still take shits, even if they get one of those rectum portals and rent out some cesspool. They can dress it up in as much grandeur as they want, we're still bickering over menial shit while we ignore the grand scheme of things.'

After tossing in some expertly peeled garlic, peppercorns and salt, Mira finally turned the blender on, creating a smooth green paste, similar to a thick yoghurt. She tasted the mixture, then proceeded to add about a half a lime to the blend. With the sauce finished, for now, Mira began boiling some heavily salted water.

'That hit me hard as a child. Because I always assumed, unconsciously, that the world was being kept in order by forces outside my understanding. I knew about the

Continuum and I knew that place was a bad place to be. I knew that there were forces at work which kept us safe. That kept a good order in place. The issue was that the forces who kept the world in order were the very same people in whose houses I lived. Which meant I got to see them every day and, believe me, when you see them every day, all the veneer of superiority goes away.' Mira brought out two bowls, setting them aside, as well as one large ceramic bowl.

'Now, as an adult, I'm fine with it. I'm fine with being one of those people keeping the world in order. Keeping everyone safe. But, as a kid... phew...'

She began throwing the pasta into the water. After she finished throwing in the garganelli, she bent over the bowl and gazed at the boiling water for a couple of seconds.

And then she snapped, for some reason.

'You *fucking* soft *shit*! It wasn't the trust. It was you questioning if we were good enough!' Mira had closed her eyes as she began slowly shaking her head in rage. 'You've been going *on-and-on-and-on* about that fucking low self-esteem *bullshit*!' Though she did emphasise some of her words, she didn't really raise her voice. 'At first I thought it was cute that you're so down-to-earth, but... fucking hell, Thomas! Can't you see that fucking *doing is being*?!' She turned around to glare at him.

'I'm sorry I have to do my best to balance my goal of taking care of you with keeping you within this thing for as long as possible. It's fucking difficult, ok? But, dammit, please understand that your constant scepticism – though fucking expectable and appreciated – fucking wears me down! I didn't get pissed off because you stopped trusting me and questioning me. That was the very advice I gave you in the fucking shuttle! That you understand that this isn't about you! It's about using what you're going through to *assure* – remember that fucking word – *assure* ourselves that Kralizec is abso-fucking-lutely airtight! 'She brought a cup down into the boiling pasta water and, for a second, Thomas thought she was about to throw scalding hot water at him.

He flinched and Mira threw the cup's contents into the blender, before turning it on once more. She poured the now fluid paste into the large bowl, coating the white bottom in green pesto. '*Assure*, Thomas! You know why that verb is important?'

She didn't wait for answer. 'Because we are copy-pasting something everyone else's has done! The elves have an afterlife program, the orcs have an afterlife program, the remani, the demani and, yes, even other fucking humans! Even if the oldest and biggest human afterlife is shit! Soon the goblins will get one and then it's the trolls who are next!' She scooped the pasta out of the pot, drained it, then threw it into the large pesto bowl. She immediately began mixing the two, whilst throwing in additional cheese and... lavender?

'You know what the War at the Gates of Heaven was over?' she finally asked, as she began preparing the individual portions.

Thomas had to snap out of the thought storm she had triggered. 'There was a debate as to whether or not individual freedom was more important than the experience of the whole group?' he answered.

'Exactly... Like couples going on vacation together...' She passed him his bowl, a fork sticking out of the mass of green paste and pasta, with a hefty sprinkle of cheese on top. Thomas was in the process of pushing a sleeping Lorgar away from the table in front of him, when he noticed that Mira had made straight for her living room, leaving him alone.

She continued speaking as she could be heard moving things around in the other room. 'It wasn't about the whole thing being impossible! It was about how it should look like. That's why making sure that everyone thinks it looks functional – including people having an acute existential crisis – is of the most absolute importance. Whether or not we can pull it off – even if everyone else has – is not!' There was a pause. 'We don't eat in the kitchen!' Thomas took the hint and followed her into the living room, to see that Mira had freed up about half of the coffee table, but not the dinner table. She sat down on her couch just as he came in and immediately began eating.

Thomas followed suit. The dish before him had an interesting, lively, yet heavy, fragrance, somewhat unexpected given its appearance. Somewhat sceptically, he scooped up one of the pieces with his forks and tasted it.

A comforting warmth spread from somewhere in his mouth to the rest of his body. It was as if an invisible, friendly, soft giant had come to hold him. Though the food warmed him, the fragrance of the mint and the basil filled his lungs with a chill, refreshing mountain breeze. He hadn't eaten that day, but what now lay between his cheeks, playing with his tongue, made him question if he had ever eaten before in his life.

In a beautiful moment, Thomas forgot where he was, what he was doing, where he was in life and what discomfort meant. Discomfort of the body, discomfort of the mind, restlessness of the soul. In a single beautiful moment, without knowing it, he found that which he could not even remember feeling ever in his life.

Peace.

There was no death. There was no fear. There was no anxiety of the thinking mind.

He found muscles long ago clenched finally relaxing. He found feeling in his fingers and toes and in his shoes he wiggled them in pure childish joy. He found his hair tickling him playfully, as one strand fell from his forehead and giggled across his forehead in smiles and breezes.

Words lost meaning as he just felt.

He felt his tongue dance with spirits of flavour. He did not know if his eyes were open or closed, as he felt them rush across meadows of warm green and crisp dew. His nose trembled softly, like a lover's legs in the aftermath of great pleasure. He felt how the bones of his body were friends with his spirit and how the tendons of his joint yearned for the touch of his muscles.

As if from a vision of ecstasy, he awoke, his eyes returning from their adventure, only to gaze upon tragedy.

There was very little of the food left.

'Mira?'

'Huh?'

'Mira, this is extraordinary.'

'Thank you!' She sounded genuinely pleased. No sarcasm.

Her smiles always worried him. 'Mira. Mira did you put something in this?' It wouldn't be like her but, who knew at this point?

'As a matter of fact I did.' She put her bowl down. 'Flour, egg yolks, salt, pepper, basil, mint, parmesan, a little pecorino, garlic, pine nuts, a dash of chilli powder (poblanos, no seeds, just the pepper itself, I dry them myself), olive oil, lavender and a hint of lime juice, to taste. I usually also add a little bit of honey to the sauce, but today's mint was sweet enough.'

'I. I saw...' Thomas felt no deception from her. *This really is how this woman cooks.*

He finished the bowl longingly, then said goodbye to it as he placed it on the table. He saw that Mira was only about a third of the way there and looked at her. Really looked at her. She genuinely meant to ill will towards him. The morning beatings, the constant fanning of the flames of his anxiety, her incessant insistence on his need to both distance and immerse himself within his feelings to be able to see things as rationally as he could...

She had never lied to him. Of course, he couldn't really know; same as he couldn't really know if Adler, Ashaver, Pop, Bokha, Patel or the other section heads had lied to him. Yet, for the first time in quite some time, he felt as though he *felt* that she never lied to him. She didn't put him down either. She only worked to uncover and correct his worst impulses. Yes, she was hard on him and she could be remarkably cruel in concordance with her orders and personal objectives, yet...

She stuck to her principles. She had wanted to be part of Project Kralizec and that meant taking care of him. So, she took care of him. She also saw him as a friend now and that mattered to her. As long as those two things didn't clash she was happy and content; in her own way. If they did, then she would rage. But, beneath that rage, she actively fought to keep the two in balance.

I believe that during the days of Old Earth this would be called 'Stockholm syndrome'.

'Thank you!' he told her.

She looked up, a bit confused. 'Huh?'

'The food. Thank you!' It was all he needed to say and she seemed to understand.

She smiled, looking off into the distance. 'You're welcome, Thomas! It was my pleasure!' She turned to look at him and continued. 'Thomas, I don't know how to snap you out of this. There is no lore on neither Terra, nor Menegroth, nor any other world that I know of to which you have not been exposed to already. If I did know of a way to bring you out of it, I think I would do it. I would let you know. But, if it means anything, I do think you have all the pieces in your head already, you just have to put them together.'

Thomas recognized what she was saying from somewhere. 'Are... are you quoting Zapffe again?'

She nodded, still smiling. 'It's not quoting if it's the conclusion of my own rational assessment, no matter how influenced it may be by the teachings of old Norwegians.'

The quiet sat between them, at first slightly tense, then completely calm. Thomas ultimately sat back in his seat and attempted to relax his body. Mira, on the other hand, reached towards her large waterpipe, which she proceeded to activate and begin smoking what his nose told him was some kind of coconut-watermelon mix. The smell was sweetly calming, yet not in a narcotic way. It seemed to match the lighting, as well as the colours of Mira's cream, brown and black furniture. He found himself comfortable, both within his body and the presence of Mira.

His mind, however, had started racing again. He found *thoughts* returning to him. Unresolved thoughts, yet thoughts he had become accustomed to. Just as Mira had said, he knew everything about them. All that was left was to resolve them and report his resolution to Mira, as he had before.

'What's your favourite book, Mira?'

'1984. No! Brave New World.'

'... cute.' *Typical grim shit. All her literature is grim.*

'What's the last book you read?' She seemed to have picked-up on the exact nature of his criticism.

'The Brothers Karamazov.'

Mira burst out laughing. 'You read it like two months ago and it's your favourite book of all time?'

'Well, it's had an impact on me!' he began explaining.

They talked for hours until the evening came. They only knew that the sun had set when Jerusalem's night signal, imitating the sound of an ancient muezzin, could be heard announcing the coming of darkness. Lorgar, who had, at one point, transferred himself from the kitchen to his living room seat, stood up and yawned at the noise.

'Milady, it is dinner time!' he declared casually.

'Oh, is that so?' Mira replied, while beginning to play with his tail. Lorgar immediately rolled over and began battling her hand with his death mittens.

'Milady, I know you put lamb to marinate yesterday! Milady, you know how much I crave the tajine!' He protested as she began wrestling with his little arms. *She makes lamb foods too?*

Mira looked up at him and immediately noticed his hopeful expression. 'You want some lamb tajine?'

He had wanted to start nodding in agreement from the middle of her sentence, yet his mother had taught him good manners. 'I'd love some!'

'Great! I'll go prep the meat. While it's cooking, I'll come back with scraps and cutlery.' With that, she got up and made her way to the kitchen.

Lorgar, happy to hear that he would soon be receiving food, began to lounge in self-satisfaction. 'She makes it with prunes and almonds and makes it really gross. But the clippings! Milady is generous with the lamb clippings. She gives not just *whites*, but also the *reds*!' The glee with which the cat pronounced colours unnerved Thomas.

He studied the cat now, once more noting its peculiar nature. Lorgar was quite stupid by talking-animal standards. Did he ponder existence? The cat had slept through most of their conversations, but had occasionally stirred, yawned, then adjusted his position. If he could understand language, could he also comprehend what they spoke of? Normally, he never would have wanted anyone else to go through what he was going through, yet he could make an exception for this cunty fuckwit.

'Lorgar?' The feline ignored him and proceeded to clean one of its paws. 'What happens to cats when they die?'

The cat let out a strange squeal, matched in its weirdness by the sound of laughter now coming from the kitchen, as Mira audibly stifled giggles in glee. Eventually, the cat answered his question and cleared up his confusion.

Lorgar let out a little choke as he cleared his throat. 'Milady mentioned you might ask that.'

There was a long pause which Thomas eventually broke. 'Well?'

'I do not know, but I like how things are here and I don't want to find out.' *It appears we have something in common.*

'Mister Thomas? *'Oh... 'Mister' Thomas now?'* Mister Thomas, I would like to thank you for the chicken!' *Oh, would you look at that.* 'You are much nicer than all the other men that come and stay here.'

What the fuck? 'Lorgar!!!' Mira roared from the kitchen.

'Apologies, milady!' The cat shouted towards the open door. He returned to face Thomas 'Milady has been under a lot of stress recently! She comes here and complains about you mister Thomas, but I think she is exaggerating. I see you are a nice man! Much nicer than everyone else who comes here and grabs me and strangles me and chokes me and calls me evil names.' *What the fuck is he on about?*

'It is so pleasant to enjoy a full day in good company. Milady is busy with work all day here. It is the first time I live with her alone, you know? I was milady's companion among the long white men in the green place and they were so nice and good and caring and also I was with milady's family in Mecca. Ohhh!!!' The cat placed a paw on its forehead. *'Ohhh!!!* What food they gave me there! I get chills thinking about it. I was never alone there! Milady leaves me alone and I like it, but I hate it! I go hungry for half the day, since milady does not let me among the Hebrews outside –'

'– he calls them "jerryies" and denies the Holocaust!' Mira interrupted from the kitchen.

'Milady means well! But I am still so alone! And I go hungry so often. Might you know of some sweet someone who could perhaps drop by a few times throughout the day and feed me?'

Ah... so that's what this is about?

'Why don't... the men who come here feed –'

Thomas was interrupted by Mira as she returned from the kitchen with Lorgar's bowl, packed to the brim with lamb clippings. '– because there are no men that come over here. Other than Tomasz, who tortures Lorgar by snuggling him excessively. Sorbo, who just smirks at everything he says and makes him say more-and-more horrendous things. And Basenji, who scares him because he is a remani. Everyone else is female or soldiers coming in for reports and orders.'

Thomas was surprised. 'You,' he gestured around the room, 'you receive soldiers here?'

Mira was also surprised now. 'I am an officer and this is my housing unit. Why would I not receive soldiers here?'

'It's... well, Mira, it's a mess!'

'It's a mess now. I had an exhausting day yesterday.' Her look was both one of mock annoyance and genuine fury.

'I... I'm sorry about that.' He really was.

'Don't be. It's fine.' She looked off into the distance. After a few moments, she seemed to remember something. 'We've got Adler tomorrow. You up for that?'

Thomas knew what she meant. 'Yes.'

'Good. Well, dinner is ready. Let's eat and then off you go. We need to get some sleep in! Adler is an early morning type of person.'

Mira's lamb tajine was one of the most riveting experiences of Thomas' life. After dinner, he and Mira went through what they would be reporting the next day to Adler. The General would have almost certainly learned of the previous day's event at the Patel household. Once they finished aligning their narratives, the day's informal therapy session was concluded and Thomas got up from his place on Mira's couch and made his way towards the door. Just as he was passing through the antechamber, Mira called out, 'One last thing Thomas.'

'Hmmm?' he hummed back.

'That thing you said when we met in Eilat. About "mistakes being expected, yet not accepted"?'

'What about it?'

'I would argue that it's best when mistakes are accepted, yet not expected.'

Chapter XII
Things Fall Apart

You could make the journey from Jerusalem to Baffin in three hours with public transport, yet Mira al Sayid was a firm believer in the privileges conferred by a Category 3 permit. Thus, their journey to Adler's office took about an hour's worth of very aggressive driving.

As always, they found Sergeant Major Xian Shang guarding the entrance to Adler's office. The veteran Marine had at this point gotten used to both Thomas and Mira, though he greeted the German Lieutenant with a cheerful salute and the Arab Captain with an irritated nod. Thomas had learned that Mira and Shang had had something of a small argument during Mira's first trip to Adler's office. Ashaver had apparently intervened, as the two had come close to blows.

The General's office was as simple and elegant as it always had been. During their sessions, she and Thomas would stand across one another with the *Resolute Desk* between them, as they had on that faithful day of their first encounter. Mira would typically lounge on the couch Ashaver had sat on when Thomas had first and last seen him. He had been quietly pleased to notice that Adler had followed Ashaver's advice and had acquired a set of coasters, on which now sat a tasteful selection of white and black tea.

Today, they found Adler near her gigantic window, gazing out over the sea beyond, arms crossed across her tabard. Deep grey clouds could be seen in the sky, covering up the sun and shifting the ultramarine seas to a dark grey brackishness. Thomas and Mira had passed above the clouds as they arrived and had felt the howling gales outside for themselves, as the wind had clawed angrily at their vessel during their descent. No such noise could be heard here, as Adler's office lay hidden behind a meter of blastproof glass, which managed to dull out most of the outside noises.

Adler nodded towards them as they entered the office and ,after they both saluted (Thomas diligently and Mira casually), she gestured for them to take their usual seats. Whilst still looking over Baffin Bay, she spoke, 'I heard from Lakshmi that you two had a little scuffle a couple of days ago.' Her tone, thankfully, was neutral.

Both Thomas and Mira were ready for this. They had prepared their answers the day before after dinner. Thomas, as planned, responded first. 'Yes, sir. We did. It has all been resolved now.'

'Oh, has it?' Adler turned to look at them.

'Yes.' It was Mira who answered now. 'Thomas and I worked it out yesterday.'

'On your day off?' Adler turned her head to look at the sea once more.

Mira sensed something. 'Yes. On my day off. I asked Thomas to come over by my place and we sorted everything out.' ... *which was the truth, after all.*

Adler smiled slightly now. 'Your place?' she turned to Thomas and looked him dead in the eye. 'Her place?'

Thomas, now a little uneasy, nodded. 'Yes, sir. Mira cooked lunch and dinner and we worked things out and caught up with our sessions.'

'Hmmm... Wasn't really a day off for you now wasn't it Mira?' *Is she... is she also thinking what Fiol was thinking?*

'I take my duties very seriously, *General*.' Thomas had never heard someone address a superior with such a sarcastic tone. Mira managed to sound both peaceful and threatening, as if she was stating the obvious and anyone who didn't agree with the obvious would be shot. For a moment, Thomas began to worry that their little agreement would not really matter that much in the end and that a mindwipe might be inevitably incoming.

'Oh, I never questioned it.' Adler paused and was quiet for quite some time. Eventually, she turned to Thomas and asked, 'Does she still have that Nazi cat?' Adler's question sounded funny, but her tone was dead serious.

'Yes, sir.' There was a tense pause. Thomas knew not if he should let it endure, but ultimately decided against it. 'It... eh... called me a "gook", sir.'

The comment had the desired effect, as Adler let loose a snort. 'It called me a "kike" the first time I tried to pet it.' She uncrossed her arms and made her way towards her seat. 'I don't know why he was so fond of the damned thing. Then again, Djibril was a complicated man.' She reached her desk and began leaning on it while still standing up. 'We'll get to the exact nature of your argument soon enough. First, there is something else that must be discussed.' She turned her head towards Mira, who had shifted, ever so slightly, upon hearing the name of her father. 'Did you know?'

Mira's pokerface returned with a vengeance. 'That my father was a complicated man?'

Adler mumbled to herself in a mockery of Mira's voice. '*Dat mai fadr uasa complecatd men.* No, Mira!' Adler didn't raise her voice, yet something was definitely stirring within her. 'High Command just informed me that we are to have a very special guest come over in a matter of weeks.'

Mira didn't move a muscle for a long while. In the end, a twitch in her cheek gave away both her understanding and her satisfaction.

'Did. You. Know?' Adler was very, very stern now.

'Up until this very moment, no.' *I guess she sounds honest enough.*

'Swear it...' Adler paused, thinking. 'Swear *wallahi*!'

What?

'I can't.' *Ok. Mira's not helping...*

'So you did know?!' Adler pushed.

'I *hoped.* I didn't know.' Mira and Adler began a staredown, the tension between them quickly building. However, Thomas needed no additional stress, as he was already agitated at this point by all the ambiguity pilling up on top of his existing existential dread.

'I'm sorry, but what is happening?' he asked anxiously, as a small animal in the woods, hearing the rapid sounds of pouncing predators. The staredown continued for a few moments until Adler answered.

'We are moving forward with Theogenesis.' *Mother of God...*

Adler ceased her staredown competition, as Mira's wide eyes counted as a win for the General. She sat down in her seat, her arms beginning to unwind and her palms stretched out over the lacquered wood.

She continued, 'It shall take place on Diwali Day. The festivities on the surface should serve as a cover for any potential energy escape.' Thomas was stunned; Diwali Day was less than three months away. 'We have already selected the members of the Alignment Section headed by Representative Higashikuni. Preparations are underway to assure that the process takes place in perfect order. Part of those preparations included the arrival of Daw al Fajr, for a final review of the Olorun sourcecode.'

Adler leaned back in her seat, arms now resting on the seat's handles, her eyes studying one of her fingers. 'However, we have just been informed that Daw has decided to arrive early.' She looked up at Mira. 'She'll be here – and I quote – "the day before July thirtieth".'

Now Thomas looked over towards Mira to see something he had never truly seen in her eyes up until this point: genuine joy.

Adler's chair made an audible noise as Adler leaned forward and grabbed her desk. 'This is not funny, Mira!'

The Terran princess replied, 'Oh, it's not funny! But, it does make me happy!'

Adler couldn't take it anymore. She got up from her seat and began pacing.

'Do you have any idea what this could mean for us? For Kralizec? We've spent years – *years!!!* – working on this in *absolute* secrecy! Every single action guarded and hidden under every single layer of security available. Have you noticed how many Avengers Legions there are on Terra? Haven't you noticed that we have sent most of them off-world? To stir up trouble elsewhere? To draw the Enemy's attention away from Terra? Do you have any idea how many have perished so that we could sit here and drink tea, discuss philosophy and daydream about the end of all our suffering?'

She came close to Mira now. 'Do you even understand what we are working on here? Do you even understand that everyone that has ever lived on this little speck of wet dust couldn't hope, even in their brightest dreams, that one day mere mortals could actually have a legitimate chance of achieving that which we are on the cusp of grasping? Do you understand that, right now...' Adler began pointing at the ground.' RIGHT NOW, MIRA!!! There is *nothing* beyond this...' Now her finger began circling the room '... this thing here? *Nothing*! Only dreams and hopes and fairytales and oblivion! And Hell, Mira! *Hell*! A Hell of ignorance and soullessness!'

'And we have a chance to make things right. To save every single soul! Your mother! Your father! Your family! Your people! My people! *Every* people! From times immemorial to futures incomprehensible! *Do you understand, Mira?*'

Mira's pokerface switched from one of thinly veiled insolence to one of outright outrage. 'Oh, I understand that you always bring up my parents when you want to prove a point.'

Adler slapped her so hard she drew blood. Mira stood in shock, managing to brush away some of the blood off her check before the cut sealed. The slap had been so audible that it had startled Thomas and he had knocked over a cup of tea, spilling its dark contents all over Adler's artefact desk. Not that he cared anymore at this point.

The General's words had caused him to tremble. Adler stared Mira down. In the end, a miracle occurred.

Mira relented.

'I had a feeling she might want to come earlier. She told me, last time I saw her, about Kralizec.'

Adler, though having remained somewhat immobile since the slap, now completely froze. Thomas saw her chest cease all movement. Only a subtle pulse could be seen upon one of her neck arteries.

Mira continued, 'After the war ended, I took a leave of absence to visit her in Menegroth. There, in a dream, she told me, in a way only I would understand, about Kralizec. I didn't even figure it out at first. It took me a while. I was already back here when I put the pieces together. But, before I left, she told me that...' Mira gulped, a sign of a nervousness completely atypical of her. '*For every dream you bring to life, I will match you with another one.*'

Thomas and Adler both stared at her blankly, expecting more.

She offered clarification. 'A few days before leaving I told her I wanted her to come to my birthday.'

'*Oy vey...*' Adler seemed to have received a knockout blow. She made her way to her desk, poured herself a glass of tea, then noticed how Thomas had made a mess and began cleaning it up with a washcloth she kept in one of the drawers.

'Why are you telling us this only now?' the General eventually asked.

'Because it's what she would have wanted. She would have wanted me to only tell you once you knew she was coming over anyway. That moment... is now,' Mira confessed.

Adler spent some time thinking, and then turned to Mira. 'You weren't there Mira.' She let Mira's absence sit in the air, before being more specific. 'You weren't there when we decided that we were going to do it or when we went to Daw to make sure it was possible. She told us it was, but it would have to remain a secret for as long as possible, for when the news would come out...' Adler paused, and turned her seat to face Mira and the waves below. '... there would be war. A war on a scale that would make the War of Vengeance, the Senoyu War, the Ayve War... it would make them all seem like nothing...' Adler paused in the middle of her sentence, drawing in a sad breath of air.

'... and still we did it, simply because war...' She sighed and Thomas could see a thousand battles fought twitch beneath her closed eyes.

'... is inevitable.' She opened her eyes and looked upon Mira again. 'We've spent resources beyond imagining keeping this secret. I can think of very few things that would attract more attention than her presence here.'

'A presence that would have happened either way in a couple of months.' Mira countered.

'She was supposed to be here for *two* months, Mira. Not *three months*!' Adler countered.

'What's the difference between two and three?' Mira began to bite again.

'Oh, hell, Mira, shut up!' Adler insisted as she hung her head in her hand. 'Why must she be here for your birthday?'

'Because I asked her and she never did!' There was a pause in the room as both Thomas and Adler both had the same though.

Seriously?

Mira continued, 'My birthday was always during my Terra time. When I grew up we spent some birthdays together, but never on Terra, always on Menegroth or Barlog or wherever! Not home! Not here!' Adler's frustration gave way to giggles, as she began to snort in disbelief.

'Well,' Adler seemed to recollect herself, 'she sure as hell chose a great time to make amends.'

'She always knew how to make an entry.' Mira was smiling now.

'Truth is, Mira... We just always assumed that she wouldn't stay here beyond the time we knew we needed her here for. Which was about two months, meaning she'd arrive by late august. When she told us it would be the day before July thirtieth, we immediately knew two things. The first was that she would be staying for an extra month beyond what we had planned for. The second was that you had something to do with it.'

A quiet gripped the room. One could hear everyone's rapid breathing revert to a more normal pace. 'Giving us a heads-up would have been nice.'

'A heads-up would've been simply speculation. Speculation which Daw would not have appreciated me making.' Mira drove her point forward.

The General paused and then asked. 'Are you happy she is coming?'

For a moment, both Mira's pokerface and her angry scowl left her face open and a little girl was free to smile. 'Yes. A lot!'

'I'm happy...' For a moment, peace seemed to breeze through the room, as Adler and Mira seemed to reach a truce. Outside, another change in tension had occurred, as the heavy clouds broke and the rain began. Ever so quietly, one could even hear the sound of thunder in the distance, as lightning began to assault the waters below. Bereft of all noise beyond the lowest of murmurs of waves, thunder, wind and raindrops, the scene was remarkably peaceful.

Thomas, however, could find no such solace. A single question burned through him. A question that made his mind boil as it begged to be spit out.

'What was the dream?' The words had barely left his mouth and he could tell he wouldn't like the answer, as Mira's face, just before becoming angry, became worried, for just a fraction of a second.

Adler likely observed the same shift. 'What *was* the dream?' she repeated.

Mira's face gradually gave in as she drifted towards a pleasing thought. 'There was a tower.' Adler leaned forward in her seat. Mira continued, 'This tower rose high. Very high. Higher than anything I've ever seen. Taller than the Spines, taller than the platform on Gondolin... Huge! You couldn't see its tip. It was in the clouds and the whole tower is under construction, with scaffolding and ladders and ships buzzing everywhere. And people – a lot of people – all over the tower. Some, near the top, like little ants. And I was an ant in front of it. I was right next to the walls...'

Mire stopped and seemed to visualise the setting. 'In front of me there's small crack in the tower. I go up to the crack and I see that it's exactly the size of my hand. So, I put my hand in. All of a sudden, Daw is right next to me and, without speaking, she tells me that there's too much noise coming from all the people working there and that it's what caused the crack I've just put my hand in. She tells me I have two choices. The first is that I keep my hand in the crack and that will stop the building from collapsing. The second, is that I pull my hand out, but that might cause the tower to collapse.'

'Now... I keep my hand in the crack, because I don't want the tower to collapse. I realise Daw disappears. What I don't realise is that the crack merges with my hand and now the hand is part of the walls of the tower. I pull my arm and what's left is just my arm as a stump with no hand attached. The tower has no cracks now, but I have no hand. Just before I woke up, I grew back a new hand.'

Though Thomas was happy that Mira got her arm back, he couldn't help but shiver at the image, for he understood exactly what the dream's likely meaning was.

'*The Tower of Babel*.' It was Adler that gave voice to his thought.

'That was my interpretation also, in the end. That's when I realised that my suspicions were right and that there really was something big behind everything. And... there was only one thing that could have been big enough to be that well hidden.' Mira confessed.

'Big enough for you to not know about?' Adler's face had twisted to a neurotic smile.

'*Big enough for me not to know about.*' Mira seemed to want to balance honesty with pride. 'I knew that Lakshmi and Fiol had gotten together. I went to meet them and ... something felt off. It was as if they were bound together by more time than they openly admitted to have spent together. I did some digging and... it pains me to say it, but...' She paused, letting out a breath of air. 'Lakshmi is something of an open book sometimes and I immediately figured out what was going on. Why her and Fiol spent so much time together. How they spent it together. What they were working on together. I confronted Tomasz about it. He denied it. Then he confirmed it after Sorbo recommended that he hear me out. I told him I wanted to be part of it. When he said "no" again, I figured out from the position postings on the rankboard that you were recruiting for Kralizec. That's when I came to your office.'

Adler nodded. It was a solemn little nod. She followed it up with a moment of silence. 'So... have you found the crack?'

'I found a place where my hand was needed.'

A moment of anticipation followed Mira's statement. Thomas expected her to pummel them with some dark revelation. It took a while for the silence to give away the answer.

Holy shit. I'm the crack.

Adler broke the silence. 'Indeed you did, Mira. Indeed you did. Your versatility never surprises me. There's one thing I still don't get. Why didn't you tell us about this? That Daw basically told you in a dream? That it wasn't entirely you who figured it out.'

Anger returned to Mira's eyes, but not her voice, as she answered calmly. 'If Daw wanted me to tell you that she wanted me to be part of the Project, she would have done just that: she would have told me. She didn't tell me about the project itself, she just made it that I had a dream which, together with what I already knew, would help me connect some dots. Telling me about the Project would have been something she wouldn't be able to tell me about, likely due to other commitments made. Yet, she still wanted me to know about it and have the chance to be part of it. Thus, she found a loophole. She made sure I'd realize by myself what was happening, without her having to tell me.

'You didn't know she made you had the dream?' Adler seemed genuinely curious. Thomas felt more than a small dose of concern for planetary security behind her words.

'I sleep next to her on Menegroth. Sometimes I dream alone. Other times her dreams come to me without her wanting too. Other times they come when she wants them too. Most of the time, I can tell. But, if they're very subtle, it takes me a while to know for sure.'

Holy shit.

Thomas had heard tales of how Mira and Daw would sleep together like little baby sisters, though he had never realised the implications. Daw was likely one of the most psychically active individuals in the entirety of the Known Universe. Sometimes, her mere presence was enough to (unintentionally) drive someone a little mad. Mira, a mere human, would *sleep* next to Daw when she 'slept', if one could even call it 'sleep', since Daw didn't really sleep. She just had moments in which she would have to replenish her body and would output enormous amounts of psychic emanations as she performed maintenance on one of the most complex entities in the Known Universe: her nervous system.

Terran honeybone plating on her skull. Lamecular membrane coating her nervous system. Later on, Terran military mental conditioning... Yeah, sure, Mira's mind always had some degree of protection, but... the poor girl's mind must have been like an armoured vault next to a nuclear explosion every night.

No wonder she's so stubborn. That's what half a childhood spent making sure that you knew which dreams were yours and which were not probably does to someone.

Any chance for a follow-up from him was cut short by a loud *pfff* as Adler let out a long breath of air. 'Well, I am certain Daw will make great use of her time here. For you at least she clearly will. For Kralizec too, hopefully.' She seemed to realize a few things. 'For Tomasz too. Basenji. Sorbo. Çingeto...' Her eyes flashed to Thomas. 'Maybe even for you Thomas. How would you like to meet Daw al Fajr?'

Thomas suddenly remembered he was technically part of the conversation. 'I... I think it would be little more than what we discuss here on regular basis.'

Adler seemed intrigued by this new opinion, while Mira tilted her head slightly. 'What do you mean?' the General asked.

'Well, that's just what Mira and I were talking about yesterday and the day before. I... questioned why we focus only on Terran philosophy and theology, while generally ignoring non-Terran philosophy and theology.'

Thomas' words seemed to confuse Adler for a moment. 'Thomas, we're not. You have sessions with Fiol almost every day.'

'Just because Fiol is in the room with us doesn't mean we discuss Vanir philosophy or *any* philosophy, for that matter. He only brings it up when it's truly necessary. My point is that we focused a lot on Terran schools of thought and that gave me the impression that it's simply something that's done to keep me in this... "acute phase" for as long as possible.'

Adler seemed to be taken aback. 'Thomas, though we do avoid any outright attempt to snap you out of this, we're not stopping you from doing it. Quite frankly... we're actually, at his point, rather curious to find out what *does* snap you out of it.'

What? 'Why?' Thomas asked his favourite question.

'Well, because we want to know what kind of person you are, really. That's actually what prompted us to go ahead and commence Theogenesis.'

What the... I am the reason?

Adler noted his wide-eyed expression. 'Look, Thomas,' she drew in closer, 'we've told you everything there is to know about Project Kralizec. You know the physics behind it, the biology behind it, the reasoning, the psychology... I could go on. We've bounced everything we have on the project off you and – to be honest with you – from our perspective, you haven't really poked any real holes in it.'

WHAAAAAATTT??? 'What?' he whispered.

'We've told you all there is to know. You've told us that it makes sense, just that you can't believe it. You have not pointed out a single remediable flaw. Believe me, I've read every single report and I have regular meetings with Lakshmi, Fiol, Mira, Opera and everyone else you interact with during your sessions. You've never found any fault in the plan. Which is – to be honest – a good thing!' Adler sat back in her chair.

'You're not the first line of defence, Thomas. Quite frankly, you're one of the last ones. There have been many, many other minds, eyes, and ears before you. Albeit, you are the first Terran mind to have analyzed Project Kralizec whilst undergoing an acute existential crisis for the *entire* duration of said analysis. Though there were others before you who fulfilled the same role and there have been others since you, you have insofar been the most... *resilient* one, if that's a good word.'

It might have been. 'The... the others... I'm the only one who hasn't snapped out of it?'

'Of the batch of about a dozen we've identified so far, yes. You are the first and the last. All the others eventually snapped out of it. However, none of you ever found anything.'

'Then... then why am I still...' His mouth was dry and he was at a loss of words. He just gestured towards his head.

'Still experiencing it?' Adler asked.

Thomas nodded.

'Well, our understanding is that – to put it bluntly – you're just more neurotic than the other ones.' She paused, seemingly wrestling with something. 'At this point...' she looked towards Mira. '... at this point, any more time you spend reviewing Project Kralizec is just an added layer of security and, well, a form of training for you.'

'*Training*?'

'Well, Thomas, no one who joins Project Kralizec leaves the Project ones their initial task is complete. For you and Mira here, once your current task is finished, which will occur when you do ultimately snap out of it, your next assignment will completely shift towards preparing the world for the moment it learns that Project Kralizec has transpired. When that day comes and revelation takes place, we will have to be ready.'

'I... but...' Thomas leaned forwards in his chair and extended further than he had ever been over Adler's desk. '... so... you can't end it?'

'Not that we know of.'

'Could... could Olorun end it?' The thought sent chills through him.

Adler smiled a sweet, bitter smile. 'I don't know, Thomas. I think Olorun and Satya could, but I cannot and never will be able to say for certain. At least not as long as we find ourselves within this universe.'

The room, once more, grew quiet, with both Adler and Mira fixated upon him as he began to squirm. *What the hell is she saying?* Earlier she had been berating Mira over potentially endangering the most important project ever attempted by the people of Terra. *Now, she doesn't know?*

It was Mira, oddly enough, who spoke. 'He hasn't figured it out, yet.' Adler's eyes rushed to meet hers almost faster than Thomas'. 'It's actually funny, really. It's all around him. Everyone around him knows. Everyone around him speaks of it openly towards him. He hears everything. Nothing has been kept from him. He knows everything. He just hasn't admitted the finality of it, just like he hasn't admitted his own finality.'

That was the last straw, as Thomas couldn't take it anymore. '*What?* Figure out *what?*' Mira didn't have time to answer, as it was Adler who had formulated an answer.

'That, in the end, we'll never know if it works.'

The bricks that held together the house of Thomas' reasoning, all of which he had so carefully placed these last weeks, began to fall out of their slots. Adler explained things further.

'No one knows, really. Many who understand every minute detail of the science claim to know, but we can never know for sure. The moment Theogenesis goes live and Olorun is cast into the Aether, the Oculus Chamber will close and we will never have the ability to verify the results. It *has* to be like that. If it is not like that, then things fall apart. Not just that, but the only way anyone has ever figured out it can work *is* like that.'

Of course he knew. But, how could he admit that to himself?

How could he admit that, in the end, there was a chance it would all be for nothing? Worse, they'd never know if it was for nothing? Yes, he understood why it was the only way. If the portal to the Aether was not sealed shut, destroyed and discarded, then there would always be a danger that some malevolent entity might be able to reach Satya and destroy it. If Olorun succeeded, the Aether itself would have to change and become a place which only communicated with the Multiverse only in the exact moment of a Terran's death. A moment so thin, it could only be described as the smallest possible piece of time possible.

But would it work?

Neither he, nor anyone else, would ever know.

Ultimately, there wouldn't really be any difference between him and anyone else that had ever lived. Nor would there be between those of the past and those of the future, for they also would never truly know if what they did here today would even count. If they did, it would be because they had faith, yet what a difference there was between faith and certainty!

Thomas didn't completely grasp the science. But, then again, not even Hos-Hos grasped the science. Yet, within that office of his, sometimes enough people were gathered that one could argue that between all of them there might be just enough understanding to put together a claim of certainty. There were legends of 'certainty' among the ancient scientists of the *Age of Bliss*, on the worlds of what was now the Continuum, the Enemy. Legends alone claimed that some among their number understood the entirety of the science employed in their Great Plan. However, as far as Terrans could tell, there might be no one within the entirety of the Known Universe who could say for sure if heavenbuilding actually worked.

And yet, they had trudged on and decided to have their own heavenbuilding project, knowing full well that there was never a chance that such an endeavour would grant them that one thing yearned so much by so many: certain immortality. A people that had survived the apocalypse, which had passed through the Hour of Twilight and then the nightmare that had been the War of Vengeance had *of course* been driven to achieve that one thing they could not have: ultimate security.

Now, he stood across from Shoshanna Adler, just as he had done on the day he had first walked into her office, and found himself still stuck in the same colour of terror as he had been then. Yet, now the shade was darker and there was another shadow which tore at his mind. *They're doing all of this, knowing this whole thing is not certain... but, the fact that the Continuum will come for us is certain... so... might as well give them the perfect reason to come for us?*

Of course they would find out.

There were just too many people. Terrans could be secretive, yes. The gravity of what they knew would incentivise them to keep secrets, yes. But, eventually, it would come out. No matter the quality of Terran honeybone skulls, lamecular membranes or good ol' Terran mental conditioning, someone would inevitably give something away. A word here, a look there, an odd brainwave way over there...

As long as people knew, the knowledge was discoverable.

'Why... why not just mindwipe everyone?' Thomas spoke, in the end.

Mira seemed confused for one second, but then understanding dawned on her. Adler understood his meaning immediately. 'To still do it and stop the Continuum from finding out?'

Thomas nodded.

'We thought about that for a long time. It was actually the first solution proposed. But... it's just too many people. Too many computers. Too many places. Too much energy. Too much missing time. There was no way of making sure we could pull it off. In the event we did manage to pull it off, there was still a chance that the Continuum would find out and then we would be at an informational disadvantage of our own creation.'

'No, Thomas, we can't do that. Just how we will not be able to keep it secret forever.'

Thomas knew her reasoning to be sound and pure. *Then war really is inevitable.* So, that was it, they would undoubtedly, at one point, go head-to-head against the most powerful civilization in the Known Universe. There was no going back.

But, why? What was so bad about it? He had never dared to ask this question out loud but... this time... somehow it felt right. 'Is it really that bad?'

This time, Adler did not immediately understand Thomas' meaning. 'What do you mean?'

'The Continuum's afterlife? I know that it's basically as likely for them as ours will be for us. I'm just... I've always taken for granted how horrific it is but... I learned to have that opinion before I really had the judgement needed to uphold it. You... the ones who were there... on Karnak... when the Continuum came to parlay...'

Adler interrupted him. 'Do not lecture me on the details of history that I lived through, *Thomas*. What do you mean?' He had never heard her be well and truly menacing until that point. Her voice never rose above the limits of conversation.

Taken aback, Thomas momentarily reconsidered his question. However, in the end, his obsession with closure came through. 'When you first saw it – what it had to offer, I mean – was it really so... bad?'

Adler's face never moved. Not even her eyes. She stared back at him. Quietly. When she did speak, it felt as though aeons had passed on account of her intensity. 'At first... No, it didn't sound so bad. News of an afterlife of bliss was like the sweetest water for us.'

She took a deep breath, her eyes drifting away towards distant memories. 'Twenty years of hell. Twenty years of war, disease, hunger, famine... loss, mourning, desperation... That was who we were. We were not like you. In my life... more than half my life had been that, with the other half being nothing more than a distant memory... A dream of childhood happiness and carefree joy.'

'To hear that that happiness and that joy would be the norm of our existence, with those dark times being little more than a single moment in time... of course we yearned for it. But, then we asked the cost and the cost was... well... it was too great for our comprehension.'

'No control over our own destiny in this life or the next. No true free will. No ability to hold on to our free will. No right to befriend or love anyone who was not human – or a Continuum citizen, for that matter. To abandon those who had saved us and join those who judged us for what we had to do to survive...' Her voice was now somewhere between a snarl and a cry. She smiled bitterly. 'There would be no true experiential veracity for us... *only* adulteration.'

'Tomasz snapped first. Then Hydeyuki, just before Ronan. Then Sara and Djibril. I think the disgust, the horror, the shame to even consider it, hit me just as I could see Manda's fist clench around her sword and I could begin to hear Hernan breath heavily, the way he did before every fight...'

Her words drifted away as there was no need for them. Thomas knew what happened at Karnak in great detail. Every Terran did. The bloodbath that followed had claimed the lives of a dozen Terran heroes, yet three New Enemy paladins had lain slain before them, next to a couple of hundred Continuum soldiers. The Continuum had sparred them immediate open war. Yet, they had made a promise.

A day would come when the New Enemy would come for them.

That day, those hundred men and women who had arrived on Karnak, and who had rejected the Continuum's proposal, had sealed the fate of their world. Adler had, just now, echoed the reason. A reason which Thomas had always taken for granted.

'I... I guess it won't matter after Diwali.'

Adler's tone switched to one of complete empathy, as she seemed to understand how Thomas had drifted towards this conclusion. 'It wouldn't have mattered before Diwali either.' Her eyes drifted towards a place on the wall behind Thomas. 'We had a choice and we made it. Free will over control. Choice over destiny. We were always going to make that choice. On Karnak, both we and the Continuum realised that which had always been true: we were never going to join. They had done too much.'

She recollected herself, returning to the present. 'They couldn't attack us immediately because of events unfolding elsewhere. Leviathan is a huge thing. It borders the Tribes of Elvandom, the Clans of Ork, the Confederation of Humanity, the Goblin Corporation, as well as a thousand other realms whose names and peoples we know nothing of. If they made a move against us then, they would risk overextending and their enemies of aeons past would pounce and tear at the great beast.'

She concluded, 'They needed time and so did we. They need time to build a bridge towards us. We need time to prepare and we have. But, in the end it might not matter. Hence... Project Kralizec. A last plan to ensure the salvation of Terra.'

'Ensure?' Thomas was not trying to be ungrateful; he was just trying to make sure his desperation was in tune with reality.

Adler smiled a wide smile. Her eyes glimmered with hope and (*could that be...*) satisfaction? 'Not the salvation of our souls. That, as we all agree, will never be guaranteed. No, Thomas, we would ensure something else.' The General shifted her glance to Mira. 'Zapffe, he is your favourite thinker?'

Mira was taken aback for a moment, yet, in typical fashion, immediately regained her composure. 'One of a select few.'

Adler smiled bitterly now. It was a sad thing to see, as her earlier optimism mixed with something else. 'He is most definitely one of *my* favourites.' She shifted her gaze back towards Thomas. 'Inevitability of death. Absence of any structure to the Universe. Inherent loneliness. Responsibility of freedom. The first three are revelations with many answers but no solutions. The fourth is a revelation with many solutions, but no answers.'

'We cannot stop death without ending all life. We cannot order the universe to our liking, for that would turn it into the most boring of hells. We cannot eliminate the loneliness of the individual, for that would mean the dissolution of the self. There are ways around these paradoxes. Project Kralizec is, fundamentally, a potential solution to all of them. However, as individuals, we are responsible and completely free to decide how we choose to live every instant of *this* life.'

'From the lowliest slave of Ancient Egypt, to the greatest king of Babylon, everyone has complete responsibility over their own life. There are consequences to every decision: a slave cannot revolt against his master – at least not alone – without expecting only further misery and punishment. However, if he plays his cards right, the smallest of men can make a deep mark upon the world.'

'Old Earth died during the End Times. Terra endures. This small little world has toppled not one, not two, but three galactic empires. A hundred years ago, we had just barely left the orbit of our own sphere of wet dust. Now, the names of our people echo in whispered tones through halls of power once unfathomable to our forefathers. We have showed the Universe what a little people can do and now we have a chance to drive our point home.'

'Yes. It will mean war. Yes, it might be for nothing. But, in the grand scheme of things, if there really is nothing beyond the veil of death and this universe is all we have, then the only thing that matters is that we strive to make this universe better. A universe in which some fool upon some tall chair dares tell children who they can and who they cannot love is a universe with much room for improvement. All that is needed is one act of defiance. One act deemed impossible to become possible.' Adler's eyes shifted from Thomas' own as she remembered something. 'If you could make God bleed, people would cease to believe in him. There will be blood in the water and the sharks will come.'

'Kralizec will make them bleed.'

Chapter XIII
and then a god wept

The cold arctic wind bit deeply into Thomas, only to find that there was no warmth left for it to claw out of him.

He stood next to Mira and just behind Adler, to the side of a massive a hangar. It was one of many located across the Northern Polar Shield. Terra's hangars were truly gigantic creations, meant to facilitate the docking of most spacecraft. They lay within the two Polar Shields, as well as across the Spines of Terra, covered by massive doors and safeguarded by their own force shields, as well as dozens of towers, artillery batteries and drone patrols. In the distance, about a full kilometre from where Thomas and the rest of the welcoming party were located, the hangar's roof lay open, allowing the frosty Arctic air to creep in. The doors had opened naught but a few moments earlier, as the elven ship above them had signalled that it was commencing its descent.

Two weeks had come and went in a blur following Adler's announcement of Daw al Fajr's arrival. Thomas had left her office in a haze which had continued to cloud his existence in a dark fog ever since. Suffice to say, he hadn't snapped out of it. What's worse was that he had stopped believing he ever would. There was no energy left inside of him. He still had daily sessions with Lakshmi and Fiol, yet they were different now. He just stood there and spat out exhausted criticism at everything, most of which he didn't really believe was valid to begin with. For that was what had happened to him: not only had he lost hope in Project Kralizec and the universe's benevolence, he had also lost hope in himself.

He had lost hope that he would ever traverse this darkness and return to some semblance of his previous life. He had stopped looking for hope. He had stopped trying to construct any meaning beyond that which he already understood. At best, he had fallen into the drought of existentialism, his parched mind only able to surmise that: *I think, therefore I am.* Everything else was subject to interpretation.

Mira had told him a few days before (*or was it a week?*) that he had fallen somewhere she couldn't reach anymore: a pit of nihilism. He still did his duty. He still observed and dissected every little aspect of Kralizec. Yet, he didn't care now. Everything he did was fuelled by the inertia of the life he had before the thoughts had come. What's worse was that he didn't want to care, since, if he cared, he knew that which he cared for would be taken from him. Because if he cared, he cared because he *hoped* and he had learned that all roads led to a place with no hope.

Three months before, if someone would have told him that he would be standing next to Thomas Ashaver, Mira al Sayid, Sorbo Falk, Çingeto Braca, Basenji, Xi Feng, Lakshmi Patel, Laur Pop, Shoshanna Adler, Khalid Minhal, Uma Kaur, Manda Khan, Joji Higashikuni, as well as a score of other champions of Terra, waiting for the arrival of Daw al Fajr, he would've laughed. How could such a gathering deem his presence needed? When Mira had come to him, the day after Adler's revelations, and told him that he would join her, as her ward and aide, for the entirety of Daw's visit, he had merely nodded his irrelevant agreement.

Now, as Daw's ship began to descend into the hangar from the skies above, he stood flanked by the Terran Old Guard, the Vigilant Vanguard, the Wildriders of Kalimaste, the Hajduks, the Ghazis, the Marines, the Jinyiwei and a dozen other Avenger Legions, he felt only the absence of himself, as well as boredom.

Tedious this whole waiting thing was. Waiting around, not doing anything, having life pass you by as it hurdles towards its inevitable demise. It was only in *waiting* where the cheapness of time was truly revealed.

Thankfully, Daw's ship descended rather swiftly and quickly neared them. The massive elven starship barely fit within the hangar. It was a truly gigantic thing, roughly five kilometres in length, three in height and two in width and shaped like beluga whale of the Terran seas. All white it was, with only the milky-grey shades of wear-and-tear, where space travel had left its mark, crisscrossing the pearly white hull. Emerald and sapphire light lined some of the edges of the great ship, where either sensors or windows towards the inside shinned the green of Menegroth and the orange of the Brightguard.

Already, Thomas could hear the telltale sound of massive elven technology: a deep, powerful heartbeat. For so it was that *Nialka* was not a mere ship. She was a life.

Elven ships were rarely machines. They were mostly creatures. Lifeforms somewhere between animal and plant. Brown and green they typically were, though varieties of all colours existed, such as *Nialka* and her milky hide. Biomancers from ages past had first bred the first of the *unialki*, the great voidbeasts of elvenkind. Over time, the elves had refined the original species and had bred them into thousands of subspecies and races, each fashioned for a specific role. Daw's ship was an intergalactic luxury yacht, much smaller than the black behemoths of the elven military and much smaller still than the great yellow and blue tankers which fuelled elven commerce. It was a creature of elegance and proportion, but also speed and expediency. The high elven lords of Gondolin still employed the great palaces of the red and purple unialki, yet Nialka was much smaller than those. A symbol of a god which walked among men, yet also understood humility.

Also, she was less heavily armed. In part, this was a sign of submission, for Nialka was a creature of peace and diplomacy. When Daw's ship could be seen in the skies, it was a sign that, most likely, harmony was coming. Terrans, in particular, would be quite touchy about having an armed *elven* ship making landfall on their precious blue, green, white and iron marble. However, the second reason behind Nialka's lack of weaponry was more than enough to assure her security.

The reality simply was that the greatest defensive capability of the ship was Daw herself.

A goddess. *The Urizen.* Born with the consciousnesses of a thousand kings and queens of elvenkind instilled within her mind. Many were the deep magics which she could conjure up in times of need. Telepathy, telekinesis, teleportation, temporal contraction and dilation, as well as a fair bit of clairvoyance were naught but a few of her more well-known abilities. A thousand other tricks of the mind lay nestled within her, awaiting the perfect moment to be revealed.

As the giant structure neared the hangar's floor, tendrils extended from the belly of the great voidbeast. Over twenty massive pairs of smooth tentacles reached out towards the landing site and proceeded to stretch out, seemingly gripping the surface below. As Nialka rested her neck upon the floor, one could see the edges of a large door begin to glimmer as they began to open. Giant things they were, almost two hundred meters tall, and from their doorframe a great drawbridge began descending, easily more than what was needed to provide a ramp towards the reception below. The inner section of the ramp was brown, green and gold, and structured as a series of steps fashioned, after the preference of the elves, in a natural manner, much like the steps of an old wooden library.

Thomas would have spent some time pondering Nialka's views on mortality, were it not for the figures atop the steps.

The Brightguard.

Though frequently mocked by some of the more martial races of the Alliance, the Brightguard were still a sight to behold. In all frankness, they were not better than the Terran Old Guard, or the Orcish Vanguard, or the Aesir Einherjar or most of the other elite regiments present among the Alliance's members. To be honest, most Terrans would agree that the Brightguard might have been comparable to one of the lower tier Terran Avenger Legions, such as the Maccabians, the Mamelukes or the Irregulars. Yet, they were still an elite regiment and a leader's bodyguard, handpicked by Daw herself from the tens of billions of elves of the Commonwealth. What the elves lacked in the form of a warrior culture, they more than made up with in numbers. Thus, the Brightguard was one of the larger regiments of the Alliance, numbering over ten thousand strong. By comparison, the Terran Old Guard numbered no more than three hundred.

The low elves of the Commonwealth were much smaller than their high elven kin and were usually around a Terran's shoulder in height. Their garb was also far less ornate than that of their former upper caste. While the high elves and dark elves had typically favoured elaborate outfits of supreme craftsmanship, the Brightguard were a much more simple lot, being much more similar to the Vulcans of Star Trek, than to the elves of Tolkien.

Thomas couldn't help but ponder the strangeness of that likeness.

How strange it was that the humans of Old Earth had imagined the elves before the first one had even set foot on Terra. The orcs, the trolls, the remani and the goblins were quite different from their equivalents in Old Earth folklore, but the elves were so spot-on. The high elves were almost mindlessly proud, bordering on an infuriating arrogance. The low elves were strikingly stoic, bordering on downright austere. The high elves were explosively bombastic, bordering on embarrassingly theatrical. The low elves were quietly reserved, bordering on an almost autistic introversion. The high elves were emotional, bordering on hysterical. The low elves were composed, bordering on cold.

There was a strange madness to them though; an underlying sense of instability. Mira had once put it best: 'they're *so* weird'. For the low elves were not as stoic, nor as reserved and definitely not as composed as they had been under high elven domination. Daw herself had seen to that when she had broken them, thus setting them free from the shackles the high elves had made them love. The Brightguard was no exception. As the first ranks began descending the ramp, Thomas was amazed by how bizarre they were, particularly compared to the grim Terrans.

They had a uniform, yet Daw insisted that they strive to both retain and cultivate their own individual identity. Thus, Thomas could see various attempts at individuality scattered awkwardly across the nearing delegation. A ribbon here, a necklace there, a different hair colour over there, a personalized hilt or handle everywhere. Some had scarves and a few had gloves. Many wore hats, and a couple wore caps. One wore boots and another wore sandals. A dozen wore coats and a score spotted belts. While many wore jackets, a few had on hoodies. There were many earrings here and a few bracelets there and yet, they all came together, like birds of a feather that flocked together.

They were like poetry with bad rhythm. However, what they lacked in uniformity, they more than up in pace, as old habits seemed to die hard. They walked in perfect unison, with even their hair seemingly blowing in concordance with the same steps. Their faces were different, but their expressions were the same.

They were a single unit, no doubt about it.

The procession came to a halt just a few yards before them. A hundred men wide and likely a hundred more deep, they stopped in perfect unison and allowed silence to descend upon them. The only sound that broke the silence was the marching of some much heavier footsteps descending the ramp. The source of the sound was evident from the moment the ramp had first descended: a lone human walked among the elves. Bearing the uniform of a Terran, Thomas immediately understood who the man was: Colonel Ramirez, the Head of the Collaborative Section.

A friendly man, with a big hearty smile, Colonel Ramirez strolled towards the welcome party like a pirate sailing back into a friendly port. He was met by Marshal Xi Feng, as well as Tomasz Ashaver himself. The Marshal of Terra was a rotating function, with the position alternating between the various members of the Terran High Command. Feng had previously been a General, distinguishing himself during the Ayve War, in which he had served as a commander of the Terran Extraordinary Force Trishula, alongside the Host, as well as the other Alliance forces which took part in that conflict.

Unlike the jovial Ramirez or the gregarious Ashaver, Feng was a quiet, serious man, never one to speak more than was needed of him. His position, though supreme for the duration of his term, was largely ceremonial during times of peace, with the entirety of his powers being limited to matters of war. Even in that regard, he was subservient to the Warchief of the Alliance, another yearly appointment. Feng had been something of a good peacetime Marshal. He had facilitated the Aesir, Vanir and Hyperborean integration into the Alliance, sent out numerous expeditions to unexplored worlds of the Milky Way, Andromeda and Triangulum and, most importantly, had maintained the secrecy of Project Kralizec. Though, for this last feat, he was not exactly praised publicly.

Thomas found the contrast between him and Ashaver to be emblematic of the Terran hierarchy. If Ashaver would have wanted, he could have crowned himself King of Terra after the War of Vengeance. He had not, however, instead creating the position of Hierarch for retired Warchiefs, a position which could roughly be described as 'parallel-to-the-law'. He was, technically not even a Terran citizen, nor a citizen of any member of the Alliance for that matter. Hierarchs and their Legions stood separate from the conglomerated Alliance structure and were inferior only to the current Warchief in rank. However, together, the Hierarchs were the only system of checks-and-balances put in place to contain the Warchief's authority. If they all agreed, they could remove the current Warchief from power. Furthermore, it was the Council of Hierarchs that elected new Warchiefs, hence assuring the continuous ideological homogeneity of the Hierarchs.

This system, put in place by Tomasz Ashaver, Çingeto Braca and Djibril al Sayid, had been an absolute stroke of genius. It essentially meant that Hierarchs could do whatever they wanted as long as they didn't go against the Warchief's commands, as well as against the will of the Council of Hierarchs. Each Hierarch had basically dedicated themselves to some particular project or strategy. Ashaver, despite having no formal powers, was informally the most powerful man on Terra. He had all the perks of being king, yet none of the responsibilities. At least, he had none of the responsibilities he didn't want.

Daw was a different type of ruler. More akin to a god-queen than to any head of state understood by Terrans, she wielded supreme power over the Commonwealth, with only the Warchief outranking her. There was no system of checks-and-balances in place set up for her, since such a system would be laughable no matter its thoroughness. She always came first.

Except for now, apparently, for she was nowhere to be seen. The solid square of Brightguard stood before them, unmoving, unflinching, unassuming.

Eventually, it was Ashaver that asked, 'Alright, where is she?'

Ramirez's smile grew wider. 'Oh, she's here already. She's just fooling around.'

Ashaver raised an eyebrow, surveyed the assembled elves, and did a double-take as he understood what was happening. 'Daw?' he asked loudly.

'*Yes?*' the elves responded in unison.

'Awww, shit... Where are you?'

'*I am right here, Thomas!*' the block of elves chorused back.

'God fuckin' dammit... well, which one are ya?' Ashaver was getting playfully annoyed.

'*Guess!*'

'Oh, for the love of... that one.' Ashaver pointed at the nearest Brightguard.

'*No!*' the square informed him.

'Pfff, but for fuck's sake... you're in the exact middle!' Ashaver tried again.

'*Wrong again! One more chance!*' the Brightguard told him.

'Jesus Christ... this girl...' Ashaver began scratching his head and genuinely inspecting each individual elf in his vicinity. An awkward moment passed, as some giggles and snickers could be heard from the Terran side.

'Twenty-seven. Thirteen.' Thomas was startled by Mira's piercing voice, as she shouted from right next to his ear. Ashaver turned to look towards her, somewhat confused.

A short silence followed.

In the end, a single elven voice answered. 'From the left or the right?'

Mira answered immediately. 'Right! And from the front!' Her smiled spread from ear to ear. Ashaver's confusion also shifted to a knowing smile, as he turned to observe the disciplined shuffle beginning to occur among the Brightguard ranks. Almost as soon as the movement could be heard, the square of Brightguard split open somewhere close to the front line, to reveal one of them rushing excitedly towards the Terrans. As the sprinting elf passed Ashaver, he extended his hand, as if to greet her, only to have it high-fived as she ran towards Mira.

Mira had barely made a few steps before Daw was all over her. Though a full two feet shorter than her, the little elf jumped into her sister's arms and embraced her. Thomas was left in the middle of a very public display of affection, all the while feeling horrendously out of place and off-beat. Right before he awkwardly moved back into the crowd behind him, he overheard Daw whisper in Mira's ear, 'One for one, Mimi!'

Only for Mira to whisper back. 'I know, Ganga, I know!'

The square of elves broke apart as they came forward to greet the Terrans. There was a certain coldness with which the two sides greeted one another; a testament to wounds healed, yet still aching. These formal salutes stood in contrast to the pure warmth with which Daw and the higher ranking Allies and Terrans greeted one another. After letting go of Mira, Daw had made a beeline for Çingeto Braca, catching the huge mass of orcish muscle and composure in another little bear hug, before insisting on kissing his cheek as she tickled his neck, knowing full well how ticklish orcs were. After she finally let go of him, she proceeded to hug Falk, before grabbing a hold of Basenji and reaching for the root of his tail, right beneath the base of his spine, which she began to scratch. The remani made a little show of attempting to fight her off, right before submitting to the scratch they both knew he would enjoy... with dignity.

As Daw proceeded to greet Feng, Pop and the rest of the assembled Terran hierarchy with much less hugging and more cordiality, Thomas was startled by someone who had managed to sneak up right next to him.

'Do you have a spare cigarette?' a thin, waifish voice asked.

Thomas blinked away his surprise and turned to see someone he had last seen almost in another life.

Toph Pamento.

It took a few moments for him to make sure it was her though. Gone was the Allied Host uniform and the regimental jacket. She now stood before him in the regalia of the Brightguard, her colours now no longer the whites, blues and reds of their old assignment, but amber orange, radiant gold and pure white. At her neck she wore a jade green scarf, the colour of Menegroth, whilst the rest of her costume was complemented by indents of brown and red that could be seen among her insignia, equipment and clothing.

'T-Ta-Toph?'

'Thomas.'

'I, ehm, didn't know you were joining the Brightguard.'

'Well, neither did I.' Her eyes flickered towards Daw, which was all caught up in the act of being a social butterfly. 'I received a call more than a month ago. I had been selected for a place among the Brightguard.' She turned towards Thomas again. 'Mysterious are our Lady's ways.'

Indeed. It was something of a remarkable coincidence, really. The Brightguard might be huge, with its ten thousand members, but there were tens of billions of perfectly viable elves to fill its ranks. Strange how Toph had been selected for such an esteemed position, usually granted only the elite of low elven society. Now, Toph was no helpless creature. Thomas recalled how she was somewhat exceptionally gifted as an reconnaissance infantryman, yet it did seem peculiar how one of the few low elves he had ever had a conversation with would be picked for the Brightguard.

Toph seemed to agree and right before he was about to say more, her eyes shifted, once more, towards her Lady. What she saw seemed to make her stand taller for a second, her posture shifting to one of pride and majesty. Thomas turned just in time to come face-to-face with Daw al Fajr herself.

She was short. Even shorter than Toph, who she was quite short. While most low elves hovered at around one meter and eighty centimetres, a full twenty centimetres beneath the genetically-enforced standard of Terran men and women, Daw herself was maybe one meter and sixty centimetres tall. She had long, pearl blonde hair nestling an elven face with light skin and the sharp features of her kind. Though, her expression was not the mix of quiet innocence and insolent superiority typical of elven faces. Instead, she smiled genuinely and her eyes shone with a warmth that could fill the weariest soul. Moreover, they seemed to be looking right into said soul.

Before he could react to her presence, she spoke, 'You're Thomas, aren't you?'

Thomas was surprised at how friendly her voice was. She waited for him to respond in complete and serene expectation. Mira, who was standing right behind her, could be seen giving Thomas look of insistent expectation.

'Lieutenant Muller, my lady, of the Terran Logistic...' Thomas' resume was cut short as Mira and Daw burst into chuckles.

Whilst still looking straight into him, she said to Mira, 'Did he just call me "my lady"?'

Mira's chuckle broke into a snort. 'Yes. Yes, he did.'

Daw continued. 'No need for titles, Thomas, you can call me Daw.' She reached out and grabbed his hand. It was a gentle gesture. It felt more as if a warm wind had pulled his hand in for a little handshake. 'Mira's told me a lot about you.'

Thomas was confused, but then realised what Mira had been doing. He shot her a glance of utter shock and disappointment. Mira and Daw must have been discussing Kralizec... *over the fucking phone!!!*

Yes, they probably had one of the most secure phone connections in the universe, but still... *over the phone?*

He recollected himself from the paranoia that overcame him. He turned towards Daw and spoke. 'I... uh... don't know what you're talking about... Daw.'

Daw's eyes widened for a moment. Her chin went back towards her neck, as her forehead shot forward and she began leering at him, her short height hiding a mischievous smile. 'Mira?'

'Yes?' Mira had a look like she knew what was coming.

'Could you please introduce me to a fellow keeper, please?' *Holy shit, is she doing this in public?*

'Of course. Lieutenant Thomas Muller, Keeper of Terra, meet Daw al Fajr... Keeper of...' Mira interrupted herself. 'Daw, what kinda keeper are you?'

Daw giggled. 'Just "keeper". I believe that's the relevant nomenclature. You can say "Keeper of Menegroth", if you want, but that's not entirely accurate.'

'Fine. "Keeper of Menegroth" it is.' She looked back towards Thomas.

'Daw al Fajr, Keeper of Menegroth!' She made the announcement and that was it. They had been introduced. Apparently, in this hangar, surrounded by ten thousand elves and almost five thousand Terrans, orcs, remani, as well as an assortment of other allied races and nations, they were all keepers.

Daw leaned in, secretively, yet she spoke rather loudly. 'I've made all the Brightguard keepers. I've been introduced to many Keepers of Terra. I have many more to go. You were one of them, after all. In time, I'll introduce you to a few other keepers.' Her eyes flickered to Toph. 'Starting with Toph Pamento, Brightguard Incumberent and Keeper of Menegroth!'

Thomas and Toph exchanged quick glances and short nods.

'Though you two have met before, have you not?' As Daw spoke, Mira's brow furrowed.

'Yes, milady!' Toph confirmed. 'Thomas was a fellow lieutenant in our brigade during our time with the Allied Host.' Now Daw, Mira and Toph all looked at him for confirmation.

'I... yes! Incumberent Toph was one of us hundred lieutenants in our brigade. She earned promotion – I believe – after the Battle of Musspellheim.'

'... and you earned promotion after the Battle of Astarte. At the end of the war, I believe?' Daw, apparently, knew his resume.

'I – yes...' he confirmed.

'Commandant Giklecoart awarded you the position on grounds of leadership, heroism and diligence, with specific citations for mental clarity, close-quarters weapons combat and administrative excellence, as Commandant Hioktanska awarded Toph her position for leadership, heroism and prowess, with specific citations for operational awareness, subterfuge and attention to detail.'

Daw turned to Mira. 'Sister, remind me, what were you promoted for when you made Lieutenant?'

Mira rolled her eyes. 'Leadership, heroism and efficacy. Specific citations for inspirational presence, melee ability and dedicated rigour. Commandant Sipsi made the promotion.'

'It's good you have this now.' Daw began, speaking to no one and everyone. 'The Host, I mean. I love how it brings people together! Which is something I like doing myself.' She addressed Thomas specifically now, 'I wanted to know more about you. I also needed some more companions. When I found out about Toph, I was super happy!' She now smiled towards Toph. 'I must confess, though, that her presence has been by far the sweetest gift. She has become such a dedicated member of the Brightguard, in such short a time, that sometimes I forget I sought her out for more than her companionship!' She had reached out to hold one of Toph's hands while speaking.

Toph sparkled in the praise, struggling to stay composed.

Daw came in closer to Thomas again. 'I will see you later!' With that, she turned to Mira. 'Let's go say "hello" to everyone, and then let's go hang out until tomorrow morning!!! Bye, Thomas!'

With that they left, leaving Thomas alone with Toph in the crowd. After a moment of quiet contemplation. Thomas heard a strange clicking sound. He turned to see Toph light up a cigarette.

She caught his eye. 'I have my own now.'

They talked. They talked for what at first felt like hours, then later felt as minutes. They spoke mostly of the past, of the war, the Allied Host, the Brightguard, of Terra and of Menegroth. He had even made her laugh when he had told her that the dread Askr squirrels had found employment on Terra.

When General Adler appeared next to them, Thomas couldn't tell if five minutes or an hour had passed.

'Lieutenant Muller. Incumberent...?'

'Pamento, madam!' Toph replied waifishly.

'*Sir*. On Terra we say "sir", like in the Allied Host. Not "madam".' Adler's reply was atypically acidic. *Old wounds never truly heal.*

She turned back to Thomas. 'Tomorrow is Friday.' Thomas understood, dreading what she meant. Their sessions where on Friday. 'It'll be just you. Mira has the day off on account of her birthday.' Adler felt the need to be specific.

'Yes, sir.' Thomas replied.

'Excellent.' Adler paused, seemingly about to depart. She seemed to be considering saying something more. In the end, she just nodded at Thomas and Toph, then left.

'You're busy tomorrow?' Toph asked about the future for the first time.

'Yes. I... have something to do.' He didn't want to go in depth about what the meetings with Adler were about. Neither with Toph, nor with anyone else. At this point, not even with himself. He turned toward the elf. 'I should go, actually. I have to get back to Jerusalem. We were instructed to leave for our usual lodgings and resume our duties tomorrow. The Old Guard, the Sayeret and... you,' he smiled shyly, 'the Brightguard, are to handle security for ... for her.'

Toph nodded. 'Of course.' A look of proud seriousness returned to her. 'I'll see you around, Thomas.'

They parted ways and Thomas left for his shuttle. Mira had told him that they wouldn't be returning to Jerusalem together, so they had each made the journey to the Arctic in their own shuttles. As he flew back to Jerusalem, he felt dread, which was normal at this point. These were his days now: constant tidal storms of numbing dread and cold desperation, with every single moment being one of further torture and terror, as he now knew there was no way out and no certainty to anything.

His cold thoughts, frigid across his beaten mind, weathered him down to some semblance of sleep that night. He woke up as he always did now: tired. He trained unenthusiastically with a non-sentient cyborg for the recommended hour, since Mira also skipped training, then he got in his shuttle and made Mira's hour-long drive to Adler's office in about an hour and a half.

He parked the shuttle, made his way to Adler's office, climbed the stairs to the entrance and... did not find Shang at his usual station. His seat and desk lay empty. Confused, Thomas checked the time and confirmed that he was neither late nor early. Tentatively, he knocked on Adler's door.

The door instantly opened.

Though this was a good sign, Thomas proceeded with care. Adler was a creature of habit, he had realised over the course of their sessions. She was not one to disrupt her routine. At least not without warning. He quickly saw another change in the General's rhythm.

Daw al Fajr was sitting in the antechamber, studying the four horsemen of Adler's painting. As Thomas stood in the doorway, questioning his own sanity, she turned.

'Thomas! You're right on time!' She was dressed differently now. Instead of her traditional garb, she now sported a common Terran outfit, with yellow boots, blue jeans, a white shirt and a green jacket.

'I...eh... Hello, Daw! I wasn't expecting to see you here.'

'Good! I asked Shosho and Mira not to tell you.'

'Not... to tell me about what?' Thomas asked, unsure of what was to happen.

'Well, I know about your sessions with Shosho, Lakshmi and, of course, Mira, and I wanted to have one myself with you.'

'Oh...' Thomas suddenly began to tremble. *Is she really here and saying this? Have I gone completely mad? I should go find Opera and have her investigate me before I become a danger to myself and others.*

'No!' The elf began wagging a finger at him. 'None of *that*! You're not going crazy! I *am* here. I am here to help, as best as I can.' She waved towards the entrance to Adler's office and proceeded to lead the way. Thomas followed suit on trembling legs.

Adler's office was pristine, as always; the only major differences being the absence of both Adler from behind her desk and her teapot from on top of it. This last issue was quickly addressed by Daw. 'Shosho loves her teas. Do you know where she keeps her blends?'

Thomas had seen her, once, during a particularly long session, reach out to one of the walls flanking the office, revealing a hidden compartment full of various teas, kettles, pots and cups (and coasters). He glanced towards the respective wall now.

'Ah, I see! Well, I'll get brewing. Why don't you take a seat, Thomas?' Before finishing her sentence, Daw was already opening the tea compartment and investigating Adler's stash. Thomas stood there, confused for a moment, before deciding to go along with it and proceeding towards his usually seat opposite Adler's chair.

He had barely made two steps before Daw, without turning, asked. 'Do you really like it there? Or is it just habit? The armchairs look so comfy – but the one facing the window is mine!'

He had never really asked himself that question. From the very start, the seat opposite Adler's had been his designated seat. Ashaver and Mira had sat on the couch Adler kept next to the hidden tea compartment, yet the two armchairs flanking the couch, though very comfortable-looking, had always been neglected during his time spent in Adler's office.

She might want me to sit there. She might be using some mind control on me. She might just be honest about it. I might be imagining the whole thing. Fuck it! Might as well go along.

He sat down on the armchair facing towards the room's interior and noticed, for the first time, exactly what Adler faced while sitting in her seat. While to her back lay the cold waters of the restless sea, before her lay a completely different sight. It was a painting. A rather large painting, almost three and half meters tall and around eight across. While the painting in Adler's antechamber was in the classical Terran style of the late middle ages, this one was quite different. The background was black (as could have been expected) but there was so much colour also. Greens, purples, yellows, oranges and blues. It was quite hard to make out what it was that the image portrayed. It seemed to depict two men peering into water, with one of the two just about to impale one of the fish swimming below with what appeared to be some kind of trident. Two women looked on, with one of them appearing to be eating... ice cream?

What struck Thomas the most was how abstract the whole thing was, with the exception of one small detail: the fisherman's hand gripping the trident's shaft. While the rest of the image was an erratic hodgepodge of shapes and colours, the hand was almost perfect in its rendering. It truly seemed to be a vaguely accurate rendition of a human hand.

'Well, we should get to it then!' Daw's voice was subtle, gently lifting him out of his fixation on the hand in the painting. 'How do you normally go about these things?' She came up from just behind him, and placed one of Adler's teacups in front of him. A green tea stared back at him in between wisps of steam. *I didn't hear any noise... Oh my God, she boiled it with her mind!*

'We, uh... We get told how specific mechanics of Olorun, Satya, the Aether, the Orpheus Chamber, Theogenesis and... how other aspects of Kralizec work. We learn these things during the week. And... then I ... I poke holes. Or, at least, I try to. I do that with Colonel Patel and Fiol. Here, with General Adler, it's just a weekly overview where I... I try to piece things together coherently. If something is identified as... incongruent, changes are made.'

Daw had sat down in her seat and now sipped her tea. He noticed that steam had stopped drifting from her cup as she had lifted it to her lips. 'I see. So, what kind of holes have you poked?'

Thomas was quiet for a long time, before letting out a long breath and a truth. 'Well... none, really.'

Daw smiled subtly. 'Oh, I see! Well, Mira tells me you're quite good at your job, so I am assuming there just haven't been any holes to poke up until now?'

'Well, there have been many places to poke... just no holes coming up... just a lot of... dark patches.'

'Which is to be expected. How far along through this process of review of Kralizec are you?'

'We finished about two weeks ago.'

'I see. I understand that none of what you've experienced here has helped you in anyway? You haven't been put at ease?'

'No. Not really.'

'Your acute phase persists?'

Thomas nodded.

'I see.' Daw laid down her teacup on Adler's table, right next to the box of tissue papers that usually stood alone as the table's single adornment. 'You see, Thomas, Mira spent some time explaining to me exactly what you're going through. I can't say that it is entirely unfamiliar. On the contrary, it's *very* familiar. I see it all the time.' Daw paused as she seemed to contemplate the benefits of being blunt versus being gentle. 'I see it all the time in people who are fifty... five hundred... five thousand... fifty thousand years old... or more. But almost never in someone's who's twenty-five. It's actually quite rare, to be honest. Among elves, at least, it's almost non-existent. Among humans... well... Human brains develop differently. Human cultures are also quite different. But, still, what you're describing is something more typical of an older human. Someone... someone nearing the end of their natural lifespan or someone well beyond their *natural* lifespan experiencing the reality of their *unnatural* lifespan.'

She let that sit for a moment.

Which did the trick. 'What do you mean?'

'I mean I don't know why you're still experiencing what you are experiencing.'

A god didn't even know what went wrong with him.

Thomas felt nauseous. No chills gripped him. It was just a sick feeling in his gut, like as if he had just swallowed rotten meat whilst already having a runny bowels. He leaned forward and breathed in some air which simply wasn't fresh enough.

'Can you read my mind?' *Was her assessment final?*

'Yes and no. I can't read Terran minds the way I usually do. You have no wireless interconnection; not with other Terrans, not with anyone or *anything* (well, that I can tell, at least). Your augmentation is quite advanced. I can only pick up on very, very small bursts of brain activity; more like whispers uttered in another building a mile away, than any true transmission. I could likely understand more if I spent enough time with you. With Mira, for example, I pick up on quite a lot, though she is exceptionally gifted at masking her thoughts. With you, I can tell that your mental fortitude, though not as robust as Mira's, is also quite developed. If I'm being honest, it's likely above the Terran average. The only things I am picking up on are simple human cues: your eyes, the tension in your muscles, your posture, your breathing... I actually pick up the most from speech: tone, cadence, inflexions, pauses, choice of words... Traditional, simple things.'

Daw stopped, looking Thomas straight in the eyes. 'I am going to speak in another way. I am curious if you can hear me. If I may, with your permission.'

Thomas knew what she meant and it sent a subtle chill through him. He hadn't heard mindspeech since training at the Academy, where he had first been taught how to mentally condition himself. That mindspeech had come from operators and demani instructors. This mindspeech would come from Daw al Fajr. It would be like catching a boulders as an adult after juggling pebbles as a child. He nodded, his throat dry.

'Good!' she said out loud.

'Terra is the third planet from its sun. Mira's birthday is nineteen days after the eleventh of July. The Terran recipe of *pad thai* is very similar to the goblin recipe of *poiana*.' This she said with her mind. 'Repeat, please!' she instructed, also with her mind.

Thomas was stunned. Her mindspeech was crystal clear. That stuff back at the Academy had been like talking to someone with a bad signal as they shouted into the microphone from across the road.

'Terra is the third planet from its sun. Mira's birthday is nineteen days after the eleventh of July. The Terran recipe of *pad thai* is very similar to the goblin recipe of *poiana*.' He paused, and then added. 'Repeat, please.'

Daw smiled and spoke out loud. 'Even that is a good sign. If something was truly wrong with you, you wouldn't be able to pick that up. At least, not in the way I chose to send it.' She leaned back and griped the armchair's handles in a manner very similar to Mira's. 'How about you tell me everything?'

Thomas blinked. 'What do you mean?'

'I mean the whole trip. Everything. Everything bothering you. You don't have to begin anywhere. You don't have to structure it in any way. You don't have to answer any question. You don't have to touch on any specific points. Just, the whole thing. I have time. Mira's gonna sleep-in for at least six more hours, so we've got at least that much. I could offer to make time go by much slower, but that would really upset a lot of people, so I won't.'

Thomas really couldn't believe his ears. *What would be the point?* What exactly could she–

'Now, you see, that I picked up on. "What would be the point?" That I could *hear*. Can I answer? It'll be the last time I'll interrupt.'

Thomas, a bit startled, nodded.

'Structure might be the problem with you. It might just be that you've never truly had the chance to say everything you're dealing with in one go. It might just be that your mind is full of all of these little thoughts, but no cohesion. Mira told me that you describe it as a house being torn apart by a windstorm while you're trapped inside. Perhaps it might be that you have all the pieces you need for the house, yet have not actually built it. I might be wrong but, even if I am, I think the only way for you to see the light at the end of the tunnel is by not stopping yourself from going through the darkness. Perhaps there is no light at the end of the tunnel. But, if there is, you'll never even see it if you don't move forward. You might think you have travelled the entire length of the tunnel and have seen both the beginning *and* the end of it. Yet, the whole might be greater than the sum of the parts. Travelling the entire length in one go might be the only way to uncover certain sections. Sections that lead towards the outside.'

'That...' *is all very nice, but* '...is not what I meant.' Daw smiled at Thomas' words. 'I meant: how will me telling you everything help with why you're here?' He paused before offering one word as clarification. 'Kralizec.'

Daw smiled very broadly now. 'You really are a Terran, aren't you Thomas? Always all about the practicality of things. Well, it won't. But, then again, I am not here solely for the purpose of Theogenesis. I am also here for my sister and my sister is very, very worried about you. She might not show it, but it bothers her that you are unwell. I don't know if I can help. But, I can try.'

'She... asked you?' *I can't believe it.*

'No. But there was no need for her to. I know she would be very happy if you were better. That's more than enough for me.'

Thomas looked forward blankly. All feeling, both dark and bright, left him. Hope would have sparked inside of him if it would have had any place to catch fire. In a small moment, the quiet, both inside and outside, got to him. Like Ashaver had said in this very room, he felt as if he were a hamster all alone in a vast white room, with naught but his spinning wheel before him.

All that was asked of him was to get on his wheel and run.

Run until the end. Run from rest to exhaustion. Run without pause. Run at all speeds. Run until he and the wheel were one.

Daw was right. He had never really done that. Out loud. Unguided. No direction. No requirement. No pressure. No goal of fixing himself.

Just the run.

He just had one final question before beginning. 'Do...' *How do I put this?*

'I have no answers.' *She might say it's hard to read my mind but she makes it look easy enough.* 'Just talk, Thomas. If you say something crazy, I'll let you know!' she instructed.

So this was it. An audience with a god. Perhaps the closest he would ever get to one.

He began, 'I am twenty-five years old. I am going to die some day. I don't know when. I don't know how. I'd like to believe that day might never come. But, whether it be by war, by accident or due to some simple catastrophe, it is very much unavoidable that there will come a day when I will cease to be alive.'

'I keep doing the math in my head. I can't really say I remember being alive for the first five years. The next ten years are something of a blur. I've only really been alive for the last ten years. Truly alive. Sentient. Conscious. I keep thinking about what I've achieved in that time. What I've seen. What I've done. What I'll leave behind. I think maybe I'll live to be a hundred years old. Maybe. Or maybe more. It's a sign of the times I was lucky enough to live. Probably I'll live for less. That is also a sign of the times I was, perhaps, *un*lucky to live. So, I have about seven sets of ten years left to live a life. To do things. To feel things. To see things. And it feels like so so little.'

'Death never really bothered me until a few months ago. I lived a life were death or (to be more precise) the *act* of death was always present. Most people I know are scared of the act of death. Many even have specific deaths they don't want to experience: drowning, being eaten alive, being burned alive... That sort of thing. I was never really bothered by any single way of dying. I just never wanted to experience death. In a way, I am still not particularly bothered by the act of death. However, I am much more bothered by what comes after.'

'What comes after could be any number of things. It's a lot like the old Fermi Paradox. You might not know that the people of Old Earth thought that the existence of intelligent life on other worlds was almost certain, yet they were confronted with the plain fact that there was no sign of it. Given these two facts, a myriad of potential situations could explain this apparent paradox.'

'The saddest one, I feel, might have been the fact, perhaps, travelling across the vast distances of space was simply impossible. If this would have been the case, we would forever be doomed to a lonely existence. To me, it feels like the prospect of there being no type of existence after death is a lot like this answer to the Fermi Paradox. It is the worst possible outcome.'

'I mean, yes, another answer to the Fermi Paradox was the idea that the universe is full of predatory civilizations who view eternal genocide of any newly discovered species as the only possible way to survive. The equivalent situation, when talking about the afterlife, might be the idea that all that awaits all of us is some type of hell. But... somehow the idea that things just... fade to black when death comes... is even worse to me than the idea of an eternal hell. At least, if there is a hell... you can even draw some solace from the fact that the universe – or the multiverse, for that matter

– has some sort of structure to it. Even if that structure derives meaning from suffering.'

'If the world that comes after is... somehow fair or maybe even *always* a true heaven, as long as I get to experience it... to live it, to remember this life, to have my memories of this life and to be able to be myself... forever, I would be happy. Obviously, I would be. Who wouldn't be? But, that's the problem, isn't it?'

'I'll never know. There's no certainty. Not with Kralizec. Not with whatever the fuck they're up to in the Continuum. Not with whatever happened who-knows-how-fucking-long-ago in a galaxy far away from us. Nor with any other project like Kralizec anywhere in the Known Universe and probably beyond the Known Universe. After all, if no one we know of has come up with a certain solution over the aeons, then how the hell could we expect any creatures bearing the slightest semblance to us to succeed where we have failed?'

'I know we haven't failed yet. But what is our definition of success? Good odds? A fair chance? We'll never know for sure if it works! Just like how elves don't know. Or orcs. Or other humans. No one will know for sure and the ones who claim to are either lying, fanatics, delusional, delusional idiots or... or *well-meaning*! Because that's what's terrifying about it. The fact that... *people are good*. Of course, some are driven by interest, near-sighted, blinded by their own hopes or by the limitations of their own understanding. But... what worries me the most is the fact that people *mean well*.'

Thomas paused, his hands shaking, and steadied himself with a sip of warm tea.

'There used to be something... something on Christmas, before the End Times. Parents would lie to their children and tell them that some bearded man would climb down the chimney and leave them presents. And children would believe it. Even if they didn't have a chimney! They'd say that he would come down through the warm water pipes into the heaters! And, of course, the parents were lying. They were lying because they wanted their children to be happy. To feel the joy of the mystery and the magic and the... the optimism of the unexplainable.'

'There used to be religion on Old Earth. Many, actually. Christianity, Buddhism, Islam, Hinduism and a host of others. All of them insisting blindly that some unexplainable phenomena in the past produced some old wise men or gods which spoke to us mortals of the laws of the unexplainable universe. They spoke of the immortality of the soul and the fairness of the cosmos and the benevolence of whatever force created or ruled over it.'

'Did people believe it? I mean, truly, did they believe it? Is there such a thing as a true fanatic? Someone who *knows* with undeniable certainty that they were fortunate enough to have been born into a faith which had the right understanding of the universe? What's worse is there such a thing as a true atheist? Someone who knows with a zeal indistinguishable from that of a zealot that they are right and that all the stories are either wrong or lies? Because that's the thing about atheism: it's still a form of faith, isn't it?'

'They can hide behind science all they want, but how many of them understand every single scientific fact or reasoning? I have an implant in my hand which runs beneath the metallic plating of my bones and into my nerves – which are coated in a membrane, designed by men, just like me! This implant allows me to communicate with an artificial intelligence, which I carry around on my wrist, like a watch and through it I have access, wirelessly, to the vastness of all knowledge accumulated by my people over thousands of years.'

'I could explain some of that and I do understand how some of that works, but not all of it! To be honest, I've never really met anyone who understood exactly how every single technological development that goes into that system was developed or how it functions. Though, I do believe that there are people who can. But... Kralizec? No one understands the entirety of how it works! *No one!* Everyone just trusts everyone else that everything will come together and it will all work out. But, no one can tell for sure. So...' He breathed a dreadful breath.

'So, after Theogenesis, we'll be left off the same way we started: uncertain. It'll become a thing of faith. Faith that it happened. Faith that it was possible. Faith that it worked. And we will do what many have likely done before in the past on a thousand occasions. We will gather in a room and decide what story we are going to tell. We won't know for sure if we'll be right. No one will know for sure if what we're telling them is true or even accurate and, still, many will *believe*! All will want to believe and most would be happy to spread the belief, even if they themselves do not believe it. Simply out of empathy. Simply so that... that... no one will go through what *I* am going through.'

Thomas felt the tears begin to roll down his cheeks, though he did not sob. His voice never changed. He never reached for the box of tissue paper on the table before him.

'You know... when it first happened. When the thoughts came... I didn't want to tell anyone. Not due to shame. Not due to fear for myself, but for the sake of others. I... I thought it would be like a disease and I might spread it. And I felt so alone! No one I ever talked to ever gave me the feeling that they – or anyone else, for that matter – had ever felt the way I was feeling. Then I thought that maybe this is how crazy people start out. Maybe this is how the weak of mind begin their descent towards madness. Maybe this is how people who kill themselves first stumble upon that path.'

'And, then, in time, it became everything everyone ever wanted to talk about. It turns out that my wildest hopes were not just possible, but imminent! When the thoughts first came, I told myself that there was a chance.'

'A chance that might be a certainty. A chance that civilization *and people* achieve progress by being... well... *good*! I thought that, maybe one day, someone will undo what happened at the end of the Age of Bliss. That a civilization advanced enough would come along and create one heaven to encompass them all or, at least, a heaven for people like me. A good heaven. A heaven with perfect experiential veracity. A heaven which would take care of all that had ever been alive. A heaven which would mend that which was broken! And the civilization which would do such a thing would do so because they were the greatest that ever was. And how else could a civilization become the greatest that ever was without empathy? Without kindness? Without love for all that is and was and would be?'

'It turned out that my civilization might have the ability to do that. Not for all people. Just for ours. Just for those of us who were born of the same stock. Just for those of us on the same side of the cosmic political fence. The deepest hope we have is that, in the end, at the end of time, our side will win and all will be our allies.'

'That though is so... mundane. It is so much less than we could have hoped for. It is so much less than what my mind would have wished to be possible.'

He went on. He went one for hours. He stopped speaking about Kralizec altogether at one point, referring only to the absurdity of sentient existence, in all its tragedies and dramas and comedies. He spoke of the fleeting nature of consciousness itself, of the inexistence of the self. He spoke of the comprehension of infinity and the insignificance of individual actions. He spoke of destiny and fate, of beginnings and endings, of gods and of energies.

He told her everything. He told her things one would have to write an entire library of books to explain. He spoke of it all in almost maniacal craze, driven by that fervour accessible only to someone who was *desperate* to believe but *couldn't*. He wept almost continuously, though it was not a weeping that would reveal itself to anyone who was merely listening to what he was saying. You would have to see his wet cheeks to see that he was crying.

Never did he reach for the tissues.

He would have some of his dignity. If not in front of the universe, the at least in front of himself, for it was he who refused to give up, not the universe!

'The universe doesn't care. The universe just happens. We sit here and we try to order as much of it as possible, not noticing, perhaps that the universe is *already* ordered. In some sense, chaos is the order of the universe. Just that it appears as chaotic *to us*, because we look at things in relation to ourselves. Some things have a positive effect on us, others a negative one.'

'It's not someone's plan! At best, we are God's thoughts! At best, God is trying to figure something out and we are simply living in God's head! We are living his scenarios! We are pieces of his experiment. We are the expression of his theories. And... you know what? Even thought that means God might forget about us once he moves on, I can take some solace in the idea that our isolated and limited existence is nothing more than the hallucination of a random by-product of the universe.'

He was about to go into his interpretation of Nietzsche's eternal recurrence, when he was forced to stop.

There was a noise.

A slight muffling sound. Something between a squeak and a rustle of leaves.

Caught up in his outpouring, Thomas just now realised that he hadn't looked at Daw in a while, having spoken to the empty space in front of him, as if to berate it for its austerity and the oppressive nature of his human condition. He instinctively identified the sound as having come from her direction and looked upon her, for the first time in quite some time.

Tears.

He had spent too long a time questioning his sanity. Now it was time to question his eyes.

Daw al Fajr, the Urizen, Supreme Leader of the United Commonwealth of the Elves, Keeper of Menegroth and a god amongst men... was crying.

It was a subtle thing, with the small noises just barely escaping her. As Thomas caught glimpse of her, she began rubbing her eyes with her hand. *Now... now this is unexpected.* How could she be crying? What happened? For a moment, Thomas wondered if she had received some tragic message or had foreseen some grim future. However, these thoughts quickly passed away as, for the first time ever in his life and, for one of a rare few times, in hers, he saw her for what she likely was.

A person.

A person who seemed to not be... well.

'I'm sorry, but, are you alright?' he asked with genuine concern.

She chuckled. A smile broke through between her wet cheeks, white teeth shinning out from slightly trembling lips. She stopped rubbing her eyes, once more resting her hands on the armchair. She kept her eyes almost closed, yet Thomas could see her peering into the empty space before her, much as he had before.

'Yes. Yes, Thomas, I'm alright.' She let out a breath of air which he could feel lightly brush his knees. It was that warm breath of someone who had been sobbing. That simmering heat of hot sadness that boiled inside those who wept.

She continued. 'You see, Thomas, what you are describing is something everyone has to deal with. Just that you're really good at explaining what it is and how it works. I came here expecting you to be thorough and articulate, but... yeah... you got to me because I, like everyone else, struggle with the exact same thing.'

With that, she proceeded to gingerly reach out to the box of tissue paper on the coffee table before her and, as she gripped the one sheet jutting out from the very top of the box, Thomas heard the sound of her tearing out a couple of sheets.

Pwof!

Pwof!

She proceeded to use the two napkins to wipe her tears and blow her nose.

'Well,' she began, 'please continue!'

Thomas forgot he could do that. He had also forgotten what he wanted to spit out next. Being in an absolutely bewildered state of shock could do that to someone.

'I... eh... I was actually done. I kinda said it all.'

Daw let out a breath of warm weepy air. 'Oh! Well, excellent. Then, I guess, we're done for today!'

Thomas stood immobile for a second, since he didn't know what that meant.

Daw offered instructions and clarification. 'Mira is going to wakes up soon and we have a dinner planned. I recommend you go home and take a nap. I'll see you at the party tonight!' The idea of the evening's planned festivity seemed to cheer her up.

Party? What?

'Ehm... What party?' he asked.

'Oh, Mira's birthday party!' Daw's face changed. Her mood had jumped from that of someone weeping before the madness of existence to that of someone about to present an itinerary.

Now, it changed again to that of someone caught unawares by something unforeseen. 'Did she not invite you?'

Thomas was too rattled by what had just happened to come up with more than: 'Not that I know of.'

Daw shot up and squealed in an exaggerated, childish, manner. 'How rude!!! You've spent every day together for the last months and she didn't invite you *to her birthday party?*'

Thomas felt the impulse to bail Mira out of this strange predicament. 'I guess she thought I wouldn't be in the mood?'

Daw was swiftly threw Mira back under the bus. 'That's no excuse! Well, if Mira didn't invite you, then *I* am inviting you!'

He wasn't quite sure she'd approve. 'But... but it's not *your* birthday party!'

She was having none of it. 'I am her *big* sister! I have every right to invite whomever I want to my little sister's birthday party! So, I will see you tonight at the party or else *I* will be very cross with *you*, Thomas!' With that, she jumped out of her seat. 'Shosho wouldn't like it if I left this place a mess. I'll clean up. You go! Go take a nap! And take the day off tomorrow! And the day after! Me and Mira have planned an absolute ragger of a festivity! She expects everyone to get destroyed tonight and I would hate to have one of *my* guests disappoint her and be a party-pooper.' She paused.

'Thomas, did you get her a present?'

'N-no.' He was ashamed to realise that the thought had never occurred to him.

'Ohhh! But who's a bad friend now? Go! Get her something! Wait a minute... You don't know where it is, don't you?'

Thomas shook his head.

'Well, it would have been very awkward if you left here without knowing that now wouldn't it? It's on Mira's house on Socotra Island. Eight pm local time. You can be fashionably late for around twenty minutes. Now you know! Go!!! Sho!!!'

Daw's cute little elven hand gestures were enough to make him spring out of his chair.

'I... I'll see you tonight!' He made his way to the exit of Shoshanna's office before stopping. He remembered something.

'Thank you!'

'You're welcome. Get a nice present! I'll see you later!'

Thomas left Adler's office in a hurried, orderly fashion. In a matter of mere mental moments, he found himself closing his shuttle's door. As the vehicle began humming and preparing itself for lift-off, he found himself, once more, in a moment of silence.

It was during such times that the thoughts would come.

He breathed in.

Well... let's go... what do you have to say about that?

Silence answered him for a while and then the voice that had spoken to him on Luna – the voice that had set in motion the entire series of events that had brought him here – spoke once more.

Nothing really.

Well, that's strange...

Nothing? Come on, we just saw a god crying about the same thing we've been tortured by for almost three months. That's gotta stir up some morbid existential despair in you.

Right?

The voice answered. Calmly.

Well, actually, like she said: it's something that bothers everyone. Everyone has to deal with it. She's just another person, after all.

And, just like that, it happened.

Thomas snapped out of it.

Chapter XIV
I touched another Voice in the Darkness

'The Book of Revelations, Chapter 7: Verses 16 and 17:
They shall hunger no more, neither shall they thirst anymore and God shall wipe away every tear from their eye.'

Socotra Island had suffered through the standard tsunamis and sea storms of the End Times, yet had avoided the brunt of the more traditional combat of Ragnarok. The island had emerged as a haven for refugees in the closing months of the Fimbulwinter. Yet, in the titanic upheaval of Rapture, as the ground itself tore itself apart and walls of dark waves assaulted the cities of Old Earth, the fickle sea had cleansed the island of those unfortunate souls to have sought out safe haven upon its shores. Today, the island was home to a disparate smattering of households, most of which were perched upon the higher ridges of the southern side, as was the fashion and preference of coastal Terrans.

This was not the case for Mira's house.

Located on the northern side of the island, one could not see the distant lands of Arabia across the vast waters. To the west, the Gulf of Aden began its journey towards the mouth of the Red Sea. The evening twilight hung like a dry mist across the landscape, with the western crags of the islands only now just piercing the golden disc of the departing sun. Thomas quickly identified that there were no parking spots available anymore. There had been around a dozen spots available near the beach, located at the bottom of a stairway which led to the mansion above. Nestled atop a plateau, the mansion sported around two dozen other potential landing sites upon its premises. A few were located upon wide terraces and spacious rooftops, but most located in an inner courtyard, built in the Arabian style, with gold, green and white mosaics lining the inner pillars, as well as the floor beneath. Not that Thomas could see the floor, since it lay beneath eight shuttles, neatly packed and parked within its premises. In between the cars below, Thomas could make out over a hundred people. He could tell that most were Terran, yet a quite large number of elves, orcs and remani were also present.

The most numerous were members of the Ghazis, their green and white scarves adorning many necks, heads and shoulderplates. The second most numerous was the black and orange of the Akali, the Avenger Legion of Khalsa, her mother's homeland. Yet, Thomas also spotted Sayeret, Ashigaru, Keshik, Esho, Akali, Kamayuks and Hajduks. Their garb was informal, with only a few well-placed signifiers of unit appurtenance and designations of rank being present. Like Thomas himself, they were dressed for a party, not a parade, with suits and cocktail dresses, track and bodysuits, as well as both bomber and leather jackets being the norm among his compatriots.

He ultimately realised that his best option was to park his shuttle somewhere on the estate grounds. Clara suggested a clearing on the western side, right next to a crevasse which dropped off to the rocky beaches below. He found a nice place right next to a great dragon tree, picked up the red and gold present box from his passenger seat and got out of his car. After checking his outfit in the shuttle window and making sure his white T-shirt had no creases, his black Logistics Corps bomber jacket had no dust on it, his jeans had no dirt on them, his white sneakers had no blemishes on them, and that his pistol and blade handle were nice and shiny, he made his way towards the front door of Mira's house. The door stood wide open, with a few guests chatting over cocktails whilst many languished on the couches that littered the small ballroom that passed for an antechamber.

Thomas knew that Mira's father had been a member of one of the richest families in Old Earth history, yet this was ridiculous.

The Socotra mansion was part of Mira's grant of the al Sayid family estate. Upon reaching the age of twenty, Mira had inherited about half the island, with the remaining half being split up between several other Arabian families. This prominent piece of Terran real estate, though but a fraction of her family's holdings, was, nevertheless, quite remarkable. The surface mansion itself was roughly twenty times larger than his parents' house in Rosenheim and Thomas could only fathom as to how expansive the underground compound must have been.

From the outside, the mansion was built in the style of an Italian *masseria* and was similar, somewhat, to the design of Laur Pop's residence in Jerusalem, just that it was much larger than any such construction Thomas had seen in Italy or Israel.

Pristine white walls met elaborate Arabian mosaics decorating the inner courtyards. The rooms were all set up in a variety of styles, with the main reception area Thomas had just now entered resembling a simpler, smaller and much more tasteful version of the Hall of Mirrors at the old Palace of Versailles.

And it was crowded and loud.

The sounds of music and conversation filled the cavernous room packed with around a hundred people. Thomas quickly scanned the room, looking for Mira, Daw or at least a familiar face. Which he eventually found, as Opera Bokha made her way through the crowd towards him.

'Hello, Thomas!' she said in her typical cheeky fashion.

'Hello, Opera! Great to see you here!' He really meant that. He felt a little out of place and Opera's familiar presence put him instantly at east.

'Of course.' Opera saw the present he held under his left arm. 'You're going to want to drop that off in one of the present rooms.'

There a room... just for presents? Wait... 'one of'... several? 'Oh, I see.'

'There's one down that hallway.' She pointed to his right. 'Walk to the end. You'll see a painting of a girl with a blue bandana and pearl earring. Take a right at that. Walk down that hallway. You'll reach a big room with lot of couches, tables and chairs. A terrace will be on your left side and pool tables on a platform will be on your right. The present rooms are the first two doors on the right after the pool tables.'

'Got it,' he smiled, 'commandant.'

'Tsk! Thomas! Leave me alone with this bullshit!' She waved her hands in his face, her eyes rolling in her head before fixing upon him. She continued, 'You're early. We are all early, apparently. Mira is still having dinner with the grown-ups.'

'I see.' *Grown-ups?*

'Don't worry about them. Most are leaving afterwards. By edict of the Arabian Princess and the Queen of the Little Pointy-Ears herself, anyone under the age of fifty is ordered to fuck-right-off afterwards.' She was quite expansive in her gesturing, with Thomas blaming a mix of off-duty informality with the influence of some substance or another. Yet, her eyes never left his face.

'Typical Mira...' he said, smirking.

'Huh?' Opera's face wasn't really moving anymore; her eyes still delved into him.

'It's Ashaver, Braca, Adler, probably Pop, Basenji – probably Falk too, since I reckon he's still here.'

'Yes, he's here,' Opera confirmed

'Ah... the King of the Kalimaste himself.' His eyes returned to his doctor's. 'She's literally telling them to fuck off so she can have her fun with her friends.'

'Basenji and Technowolf are staying.'

'You said "under fifty".'

'*Terrans* under fifty,' she specified. 'Perhaps a handful of the elves here are under fifty and most of them will be staying.'

He smiled. 'I see. But, still...'

Opera smiled back. 'Typical, yes.' She seemed to want to confirm her acknowledgement of Mira's antics with more words, not just with a knowing smile. Yet, she paused, before saying something else. 'Thomas?'

'Yes?' Thomas was just about to embark upon the aforementioned trek towards the present rooms.

'How are you?' she said with her most 'professional physician' voice.

Thomas paused. 'I thought we were off-duty.'

Opera smiled only slightly now, seemingly deciding upon the attitude of a friendly professional. 'We are, but – call it an occupational habit – something is different about you today.'

'Oh...' *Oh...* 'I, uh... I, uh, am feeling better about things.'

Opera's face twisted into a smile, which she only tried to suppress with less than half of her willpower. 'I can tell.' She moved in closer, and spoke only so that he could hear. 'Welcome to the other side!'

Thomas didn't flinch. Since she didn't know exactly how to take that.

Opera noticed this and winked. 'Go, Thomas!' She nodded towards the direction of the present rooms. 'I'll see you later in the evening and, if not, I'll see you at work!' She rolled her eyes, subtly this time, only for him to notice. '*Lieutenant* Muller!'

'Commandant Bokha!' *I'm good. Opera's cool.*

He smiled happily at himself, knowing that Opera's diagnostic was correct.

People were already getting into the groove of a night that would be long, but would feel short. Thomas passed by several bands of merry guests engaged in the early stages of what would eventually become fully drunken conversations. A dozen different smells hit his nose as he passed sisha dens, smoking parlours, trap dens, bars and cigar lounges. From the outside he could discern the scents of an ongoing barbecue and the citrusy scents of freshly squeezed fruit.

He heard the music change as he passed by different rooms and hallways. There were the typical Terran tunes and styles, but there was such variety. Chill lounge music. Old-school hip-hop. Classic rock. Early 2000s pop music. EDM festival music.

Everywhere he looked he saw the wealth of Mira's inheritance. It was an opulence derived not from a desire to impress, nor from some need for exaggerated compensation, but from a genuine desire to be enjoyable to those around it. Most Old Earth artwork was stored away in the Shrines of the Lost. The few surviving Old Earth families, such as the al Sayids, had laid claim to a sizeable chunk of the rest. The rest had been distributed among the rest of the oldtimers, with the higher ranking ones claiming some of the more remarkable artefacts. Adler had her desk and her paintings. Pop a vast collection of literature. Even Patel had amassed a collection of artefacts, such as the Delhi Purple Sapphire.

Mira had in her possession a remarkable amount of relics of the past. Outside he saw old Greek and Roman statues. As he reached the big room with the terrace on one side and the pool hall on the other, he saw that in the middle lay an old Terran record player, currently blasting out a Tupac album. Beyond, Thomas could see a large set of wooden doors in front of him and two smaller doors to his right side. A group of Brightguard were engaged in conversation with some Ashigaru on the terrace outside, enjoying some gin & tonics and macaroons. The group that stood to his right, observing a very competitive game of pool, made Thomas' stomach clench.

Jaegers.

Not just any Jaegers. Albrecht Hausser himself was the one currently taking a shot at the eight-ball. The Jaegers were one of the three German Avenger Legions and also the oldest and most prestigious. Unlike the more flamboyant Landsknecht or the dour Rittebruder, the Jaegers traced their heritage to the old German Bundeswehr, the old German army. They were also the dream Avenger Legion to aspire to for a young German Terran.

Thomas had, of course, tried out for membership, having been rejected on account of being found lacking of sufficient experience as an officer. This had not been the case for Commandant Albrecht Hausser. The Hero of Calaiad. The youngest Terran Commandant. The youngest Terran Commandant *of an Avenger Legion*. He was just ten years older than Thomas himself, who had thought it a good idea to bring his Logistics Corps bomber jacket, which included his black, red and yellow German tricolour on it, alongside his rank of Lieutenant.

There was a highly structured hierarchy among Terrans that were part of different units. In short, Hierarch Legions, such as Ashaver's Old Guard, were the most prestigious, containing only the paragons of Terran performance and military excellence. The Avenger Legions, such as the Jaegers, came after. Then came the Republican Alliance's Allied Host. Finally, at the very bottom, lay the Terran Army, which basically included every other living Terran. This was not to say that members of the Terran army were fourth-class citizens, but simply that their units were outranked by the Allied Host and the Legions. The higher a unit's rank, the closer it was to active war. The Hierarch Legions had seen the most war. The Terran Army had seen the least, which sounds like a little, but, you have to bear in mind that the Terran Army had been in a nearly continuous string of conflicts in its almost fifty years of existence, with Terran Army detachments taking part of the War of Vengeance, the Senoyu War, Hellsbreach, the Bloodbrother Crisis and the Ayve War.

Thomas walked briskly towards the present rooms, making an effort to not look at the Jaegers to the left. He was an officer, but a Terran Army officer. These were Jaeger officers. Four in number, with around twenty soldiers around them. He knew what would follow and had no fucking patience for it.

A voice shouted. In German. 'Oh! Hello, Lieutenant!'

Scheisse.

He stopped, turned to Hausser, who eyed him with a suspicious smile, and replied in kind. 'Hello, Commandant!'

'Where are you going?' Hausser interrogated.

'I'm dropping off my present, sir.' He pointed towards the two doors in front of him.

'Ah! You brought a present. That is very nice.' He laid down his pool cue and made his way towards him, coming down the flight of stairs Opera had mentioned. He came up right next to Thomas and spoke. 'I don't believe we've met, Lieutenant...?'

'Muller, sir. Thomas Muller.'

'Ah, I see, Thomas. I'm Albrecht. Albrecht Hausser.' *Not a complete cunt, he wants to go via first names. Sure.*

'I know.' He outstretched his right hand. 'Pleased to meet you, *Albrecht*.'

Hausser took his hand and shook it. 'Pleased to meet you too, *Lieutenant* Muller!' *Aw shit, he's a cunt.* 'I didn't know you were acquainted with Captain al Sayid.'

Of course you don't, you cunt, you didn't even know who I was. 'We work together.'

Hausser smiled, somewhat annoyed by Thomas' subtle insolence. 'Well, we all work together, Thomas.' He turned to the Jaegers at the back. 'We're all in the same military.' They all giggled. He turned back to Thomas. 'Though, could you be a bit more specific?'

Thomas could. 'We work together on the same project.'

'Oh, really? *Uh-hu-hu*! And what might that be?' he asked, in a mood of fake friendly scepticism.

Fuck this guy! 'Me.'

Hausser giggled. Yet, he only giggled after hearing his fellow Jaegers giggle behind him. Up until then, his face had bordered on apoplexy.

'I see you are quite humorous, Thomas! But, no, seriously, what project are you working on?'

'I'm serious. Me!' The deadpan delivery did the trick, again.

'You're the project?' Hausser was somewhat done with toning down his annoyance.

'Well, I'm a lot of work!' *Not anymore I ain't, now I'm just a 'piece of work'.*

The large doors at the end of the room swung open, putting an end to their confrontation, just as Thomas felt Albrecht about to snap. Laughter and loud conversation poured into the room, as Tomasz Ashaver, Çingeto Braca and Sorbo Falk walked out. The three Hierarchs had little time to take in the room before them as they seemed to be caught in a very intense roast session of Falk's 'old man behaviour'. Behind them came several members of the Old Guard, as well as a few orcs and trolls, all seemingly in the process of digesting a particularly delicious meal enjoyed in outstandingly good company.

However, as they neared Thomas and Hausser, both of whom quickly got out of the way, the three Hierarchs noticed them and Ashaver spoke words that made Thomas' heart laugh and Hausser's heart to skip a beat.

'Ah, Thomas!' He turned to Braca and Falk. 'See, Çingeto, he's another Thomas! You told me I'm the only one with the funny name! Well, here's another!'

Thomas basked in the warm smile of Braca, who gave him a gracious bow and was about to introduce himself, yet it was Falk who spoke next. 'This one's much more charming than him!'

The troll turned to Ashaver, who smiled back bearing with a questioning look, which Falk answered. 'We've met before!' Ashaver's eyes widened at the information and the troll turned to Braca, offering clarification. 'He works with Mira on the thing I was telling you about.' Braca's face changed subtly and he bowed to Thomas again. This time much more solemnly. Thomas could feel Hausser getting hot flashes next to him.

'And this is Albrecht!' Ashaver informed Braca and Falk.

'Sirs!' Albrecht nodded.

Ashaver continued. 'He's the mad lad who caused that shithouse at Calaiad!'

Braca spoke. 'Oh, the one with the bomb and the firestorm?'

Ashaver gritted his teeth. 'Nah, that guy's dead. Died at Astarte. Nah, Albrecht is the one who rallied the men and killed all the Einherjar afterwards.'

He turned back to Thomas, noticing the present box he still held. 'Whatcha got there, lad?'

'Mira's present.'

The three Hierarchs all burst into laughter. *Oh, shit, they wanted me to be specific.* It was Braca who managed to speak first. 'He really is a man with a mission, I see!'

'One he treats with the utmost secrecy! No worries, lad, I am certain Mi-' Ashaver began.

'Thomas!' General Adler made her way between the huge frames of Ashaver and Braca, and proceeded to jump onto Thomas, catching him in a warm hug.

Hausser's eyes widened even more.

Ashaver roared in between bouts of laughter. 'Oh, Shosho, easy on the pinot grigio!' He turned to shout at no one in particular, yet to everyone's good-humoured glee. 'She puts two drinks too many in her and now she's going for the younglings!'

'Oh, God, shut up!' Adler attempted to playfully slap Ashaver, who managed to dodge the blow at the last minute. She turned back to Thomas, letting go of him and adjusting her uniform. 'I'm so glad you decided to come.'

Decided? I didn't even have time to decide. I only got invited this morning!

'Uh, why wouldn't I come? I'm happy I could come!' He didn't want people to think he had come out of some sense of duty. He was actually in the mood for a good time. After so many months...

'Well, you know, with all the *work you've been doing*, you are more than entitled to it.' Adler continued. It was only now that she noticed Albrecht. 'Hello, Albrecht!'

'General Adler!' Hausser nodded.

'Great to see you.' She leaned into the two Germans and Thomas realised Ashaver was right. She had had a lot of wine. 'It's perfect you and Thomas are both here. Do you two know each other?'

Thomas responded before Hausser. 'No, we don't.'

Adler went on, regardless. 'Well, then, Albrecht, since you were asking me exactly how a candidate suitable for that role – the one you came over to see me and Tomasz for – looked like, look no further! Thomas is right before you!'

Ashaver stepped in now. 'Ah, Shosho, no roasting of the youth! I am serious! Roast sessions are over! The old people leave now and we roast each other! Let the youth roast each other!'

Adler's annoyed, spicy and tipsy reply was cut short by another sudden hug Thomas had to endure. This one came from Daw al Fajr.

She had also appeared out from behind the three Hierarchs. 'Thomas! You made it and you...' The elf paused as she noticed Thomas protect his giftbox. '... had time to get a present on such short notice!'

Before Thomas could reply, Mira's voice rang out as she appeared form behind Braca. '*Short notice?*'

Once more, he was denied the right to a reply, this time by Daw. 'Yes, Mira, short notice! Why did you not invite him?' she shouted playfully at her sister while Thomas' eyes widened as Hausser's narrowed.

Mira's eyes shuffled between his and Daw's. 'I *did.*'

'*What?*' Daw and Thomas said at once.

Mira looked at them both and repeated herself. 'I did.' Then, suddenly, her eyes narrowed. 'Did... did you forget?'

'Happy birthday, Mira!' he said, lifting the present towards her, only to be met by another explosion of laughter from everyone around, as a well as quick slap on the back from Ashaver. Thomas immediately realised what must have happened. Mira must have invited him. Yet, what had likely happened had been much worse than him forgetting about it. The invitation had likely not even been registered by him, as it had likely come during his darkest hour.

Mira's pokerface changed into a smile and a rare head tilt. She grasped the present in her hands and, in a few expert motions (a hallmark of someone who had been practicing opening present all day) she revealed the bare giftbox.

Her eyes widened as she pulled out the contraption within. The wooden box it came inside of fell to the floor as she took hold of the piece of machinery that had lain within.

Just as she looked up to smile at Thomas, Ashaver blurted out. 'You... is that a *pasta maker*?'

'*Yes*.' Thomas and Mira both replied.

Thomas had taken a quick detour on his way back from the morning's session with Daw and had stopped by the Wolfsburg Forge. It was a place he knew well, for it had been there Thomas had learned his science. While he could perfect the art of chronicling from virtually anywhere, the science of mechanical engineering could only properly be cultivated within one of Terra's many forges, one of the largest of which was in Wolfsburg, were Thomas had spent countless hours learning the secrets of metallurgy. The forgemasters had been a bit surprised to see him arrive unannounced, yet they had granted him access to a work station and the materials needed for him to craft Mira's present.

Ashaver was still somewhat confused. 'It's... it's not even an electric one...'

'*Exactly*!' Mira spoke softly, still studying the device and playing with one of the wooden levers of the adamantine birthday present. Without taking her eyes of her present, she explained. 'Automated ones you can find anywhere, but mechanical ones are rare. Good mechanical ones, like this one, are almost impossible to find.' She looked up at Thomas. 'With this, you can make better pasta than with an automated one... if you know how to use it.'

As those gathered round to observe the unpacking turned to Thomas to shower him with looks of high praise, he felt the need to speak. 'I, eh, made it myself. I, eh, noticed you like doing things by hand so I, eh, thought you'd like one. I found a good design for a stainless steel pasta maker, but I, eh, made it out of adamantine, since I reckoned you would prefer it if the cuts were perfect, so that the pasta would have different texture points on two of its sides.'

'I would.' Mira spoke those words and, then, something miraculous happened. She came close Thomas and gave him a quick little kiss on his cheek.

Ashaver raised an eyebrow, Adler's eyes widened, Falk and Braca both smiled and Daw tilted her head to one side and let out a happy yet surprised little 'huh'.

Mira broke the moment. 'Well, I have to go greet everyone who's come and say goodbye to everyone who's leaving. Thomas, have fun! I'll see you in a while!' She raised the pasta maker a little and smiled. 'Thanks for this! If the other ones are half as good, then it'll be a particularly good birthday!'

With that, the group fractured. Mira, Daw, the Hierarchs, Adler, and the rest of the oldtimers left, leaving a beaming Thomas sitting right next to a stunned Hausser. As they all exited the room, the German Commandant turned towards Thomas and spoke to him. 'Hey, ughhh, me and the guys are gonna go do blow with some Keshik and Sayeret on the north tower in twenty minutes. You wanna come?'

Thomas nodded. 'Yeah. Sure!'

'Great... You play pool?'

'Not really. But I can hang.'

'Ah, ok, let's go. I'll introduce you to the guys!'

Thomas spent the next twenty minutes meeting those few sunriser Jaegers that had been invited to Mira's birthday party. He learned that they had befriended Mira during the Ayve War, as the Jaegers and the Ghazis had fought many battles together during the conflict. He had also learned that he hadn't gotten drunk with Germans in quite some time and that he had forgotten many of the little quirks they had around the ritual.

Terrans didn't really get drunk in the same way as the humans of Old Earth did. Alcohol was a toxin, after all, and their bodies did an excellent job of filtering out toxins. The amount of alcohol needed to cause inebriation in them was quite remarkable by the standards of naturally developed humans. A Terran male needed to drink the equivalent of a litre of pure alcohol in a rather short period of time to truly begin to feel a state reminiscent of an advanced inebriation. If the concentration of alcohol per beverage consumed was less than thirty percent, they would not even have any actual alcohol enter their bloodstream, as it would all be immediately processed by their liver and kidneys, only to be swiftly deposited in their bladders. As a result, alcohols themselves had changed, with most alcoholic drinks produced now bordering on eighty percent, with pure one hundred percent alcohol being considered a legitimate option for a casual drinking session.

Which this was not.

By the time the twenty minutes had passed, Thomas had already had around ten glasses of schnapps and it sure-as-hell was not the schnapps of his ancestors. When they met the eight Keshik in the tower, a quick exchange of airag, schnapps, as well as several other hard liquors followed. By the time the four Sayeret had joined them, the second phase of Terran drinking began.

For such was the case that, in order to get properly inebriated (otherwise known as destroyed, wankered, buzzed, cooked, wasted, smashed, glazed, bashed, stoned, muddled, fuddled, totaled, fucked-up, turnt-up and, or otherwise, drunk) was to combine the excessive alcohol intake with other substances. Cocaine, emdiamay and marijuana were the most common options.

And this is where the real German drinking began since it was traditional for Germans to only be openly drunk after they were about a litre and around five lines into the session. Up until then, they still acted sober, even if they were quite focused on the actual drinking. The Mongols and the Israelis seemed to be quite content with this course of action, as long as they were allowed to drink the same amount in a more gradual fashion.

The north tower, as Hausser had described it, was just one of several towers of Mira's mansion; one which had a currently vacant penthouse at the very top. A marble stairway ascended the tower's six levels and the penthouse seemed to have a jazz theme, with a great black piano being the primary focus. Comfortable couches lay available throughout the room, most of which congregated around the main dinner table, which was were Thomas was located when someone knocked at the door.

One of the Jaegers, a lieutenant named Dieter, got up to open the door to the stairwell, revealing two Hajduks, who quickly walked into the room. They were met with welcoming cheers as Thomas immediately recognized Silvia Murărescu and Nicolae Lăutaru. The two newcomers quickly took up some of the empty seats at the table.

'Oh, Pop let you off the reservation for the day?' Hausser asked.

'Oh, shut up, Hausser!' Nicolae replied. 'Look who's fuckin' talking!' The Hajduk proceeded to look around the table and notice Thomas. 'Hey, kid, what's your name?'

Thomas looked at Nick and realised that it might be possible that the Hajduk didn't recognize him. 'I'm Thomas.'

Nick quickly replied. 'Pleased to meet you, Tom! I'm Nick. Hey!' The Hajduk gestured towards the table in front of him. 'Pass me the plate and the straw, please.'

As Thomas proceeded to do just that, he caught Silvia's eye.

'Pleased to meet you, Thomas!' she said and extended her hand to meet his in a handshake. 'Have you guys eaten?' she asked towards the room.

Hausser replied with a rundown of all the types of food spread around the house.

Silvia had looked on and listened to the selection as she sipped a pina colada and struggled to ignore Nick's very loud snorting. When Hausser finished listing the menu, she spoke, 'Ah, too bad, I kinda felt like having some pho and then, maybe, some paella.' As the last words left her lips, she locked eyes with Thomas for the briefest of moments. It was just enough time for him to get the hint.

The Hajduks had recognized him as someone whom they couldn't justify knowing. This was because the only way they could explain knowing him involved acknowledging the existence of Project Kralizec. Silvia was telling him to play along and not divulge their previous interactions.

'Do you guys know each other?' Hausser had apparently picked up the scent.

Silvia went along. 'He looks familiar, but I can't place him. Nick?'

'No idea.' Nick had found a bowl of Brazilian nuts on the table and began munching down on them.

'Man's mad! He shows up, yeah, is friends with Ashaver, Falk and the lot, then gives Mira al Sayid kitchen utensils and shit. Lad's mad, blud! Mad!' Hausser blurted out.

'Kitchen utensils?' Silvia inquired.

'I, eh, got her a pasta machine.' Thomas clarified.

'Oh! And did she enjoy the gift?' she asked him.

It was Hausser who replied. 'Fucking loved it! I got her a sword sharpener. An automated one! A good one too! Siemens! When I saw the look in her eyes when she saw that thing he gave her, I knew in my heart that I fucked-up.' Hausser began mumbling around about his automated sword sharpener.

'Oh, that's so lovely!' Silvia said, genuinely smiling. 'How did you know?' she addressed Thomas again.

Thomas was confused for a moment. The drinks and the drugs were getting to him a little. 'Know what?'

'That she would love an automated pasta machine?' Silvia was charming, yet, Thomas got the feeling she really wanted him to say why.

'Well, uh, I ate some of her pasta one day and I could tell that she really liked making it and I saw that all her kitchen tools were mechanical. So... I thought she might like a mechanical pasta machine because I saw she didn't have one.'

'Oh, I see!' Silvia informed him. Her eyes flickered for a moment, just enough for Thomas to see what she was doing. 'She made dinner for you in her room?'

Dammit Silvia. This is the price? This is how you're gonna explain to them how I know her? That I was some boyfriend of hers she had picked up in some bar and taken back to his place to fuck and feed?

He saw Silvia look towards one of the Sayeret. Thomas immediately understood what the her glance meant. First, she was telling Thomas that the Sayeret also knew who he really was and, second, she was checking to see if they had observed any indication that Thomas had blown his cover.

The Sayeret in question, Ari, gave a subtle nod confirming Thomas' discretion.

'I, uh, yeah!' *I mean I'll go along with your bullshit alibi, but, seriously?*

'Which reminds me. Hausser, how do you know Mira?' She was masterful, switching the subject just as the cogs of misdirection began turning in the heads of those around them.

Hausser himself had been interrupted from his thought process. 'I, uh, met her during the Ayve War.'

'Nice. So, anyways...' *She clearly didn't really care...*

The conversation moved on to other topics, up until the moment when Silvia, Nick and some of the Jaegers began insisting that they head over to one of the outside courtyards, where the party seemed to be really picking up. Silvia shot Thomas, in particular, a look that insisted that he join them and he obliged.

It was on the stairway that he had found himself right between Nick and Silvia.

'Is everything fine, Thomas?' she asked.

'Yes, ma'am!' He used that word on purpose, to hopefully illicit a response.

'You sure?' She seemed to show genuine concern and ignored the subtle insult.

'I mean it kinda bothered me how you came up with a bullshit excuse that wasn't needed.' *Well, if she wants to keep it real, I can keep it real too.*

She leaned in closer to him and whispered. 'The Jaegers will be introduced to our thing in three weeks. I think we can both agree that we shouldn't drown like the gypsy on the shoreline, especially not with so little time left?'

Thomas had no idea what the expression meant, yet he thought he knew what she meant.

Nick, who had been walking right behind them, leaned in a little closer. 'That's a Romanian expression, Silvia! I don't think the boy knows what it means.'

The boy could speak for himself. 'Oh, I can assume what it means.' He turned to the huge mass of gypsy muscle behind him and whispered, 'It means she's managed to piss both of us off in quick succession.'

Silvia's eyebrow shot up, as Nick let out a burst of laughter he did not even bother to stifle. He replied, 'Boy, if the shit that came out of Romanian mouths bothered gypsies, we would have left them alone a long time ago. They are a simple shepherd people. Their country ways have a certain charm to them.'

Silvia smiled as gracefully as she could allow herself. Yet, she seemed to be studying Thomas more closely now, similar to how Opera had earlier. The conversation was thankfully derailed by the intervention of Hausser, who spent the rest of the way down clearly attempt to impress Silvia, leaving an amused Nick to entertain Thomas with continuous, colourful and comical comments regarding German courtship habits.

As they reached the bottom of the stairs, Silvia announced her desire to do shots at a nearby open bar, before easily convincing the rest of the group to go swimming in the sea. Thus, on unsteady legs, Thomas managed to reach the beach below, together with the two Hajduks, around a dozen Jaegers, as well as some Akali they had befriended at the bar. Silvia set the tone for the beach party, proceeding to get almost fully undressed before jumping into the dark waters of the small bay they found themselves in.

As the rest of the group followed suit, Thomas, who was in no particular mood for swimming, noticed that the bay had a small marina of sorts, including a pontoon deck that featured a phaiser he found to be fully stacked with alcohol. He also found a number of beach chairs, which he immediately slouched on. There was also an unused shisha, which he struggled to turn on.

The day had fully given way to night. Light now came only from Luna, the stars, as well as the many candles and lamps spread out along the beach and the deck. One could hardly hear the festive cacophony of music coming from the mansion up the hill behind them, as the beach itself was awash with old Latino music. While trying unsuccessfully to properly ignite a mix of watermelon, tobacco and marijuana, Thomas was startled by a sloshing sound, accompanied by a shadow appearing next to him.

'Au, *bagamiash*...' Thomas turned to see Nick emerging from the waters of the bay. He was a big, hairy man with dark olive skin, a thick head of hair and a great, big bushy beard which was now soaked in salty seawater. He gave himself a quick shake, spraying water all over the deck. After checking to see that his water-repellent boxers were doing their job, he noticed Thomas' ineptitude at initiating waterpipe percolation.

'I'll take care of that, boy,' he spoke, in the same tone of voice Thomas remembered from the dinner party at Pop's place. A cheerful presence he had been then, always quick to smile and to joke around. He and Silvia were two of General Laur Pop's Commandants, though they were referred to as 'Centurions', as was the fashion of the ranks of the Hajduks. They were the only Romanian-speaking Hajduk Centurions, with the other eight being Serbian, Magyar, Bulgarian, Albanian, Bosnian, Croat, Slovenian and Macedonian. They were also known to be the ones closest to Pop himself. The two were an odd couple, with the warm, yet solemn, and exceedingly graceful Silvia being the complete opposite of the gregarious, loud and burly Nick.

He spoke as he lit up the coals. 'In case you're wondering: not only did we immediately recognize you, we were actually looking for you. Laur saw you give Mira her gift. He told us to hang out with you a little. Check you out.' Nick finally made eye contact with Thomas. 'You know... on account of your... circumstances.'

Thomas nodded, but before he could reply, Nick continued. 'I mean, don't get me wrong, you're a great lad and all that, but I was busy talking up a gorgeous

African girl.' He paused his arrangement of the coals to gesture explicitly towards his chest with both hands wide open. 'I don't even want to get into how her ass looked because... *Lord who is our father in Heaven. Brrr...*' He shook his shoulders as he pretended to be cold.

Now, Thomas could reply, 'No worries! I actually appreciate it. I don't know that many people around here.'

Nick took this as a cue to explain further. 'You see, that was the issue, Laur wanted us to make sure you got your story in order. Which was why Silvia had to... you know, plant gossip and all that. Though, in case you're wondering, I also think she went for some overkill. From what I could tell from Ari and his bunch, you were doing alright. And they're Sayeret! If you think we Hajduks are paranoid fucks, the Sayeret make us look like we don't have a care in the world.' With that, Nick took a strong puff of the water pipe, only to breath out the cool, white smoke of a successful ignition.

'There we go!' He sat down on the beach bed opposite from Thomas and stretched, before passing him the pipe.

Thomas enjoyed a few puffs as he studied the Centurion. A Yin he was, like Silvia and Opera, and one of the older ones at over fifty years of age. He had weathered Doomsday beneath Prague, while Laur Pop and the shattered remnants of over a dozen armies faced annihilation in the red darkness of the Hour of Twilight. The same had been the case for Silvia, as well as many other future Hajduks. They had joined their Avenger Legion not due to their ethnicity alone, but due to the debt, the gratitude and the admiration they had for Pop. Indeed, it had been the case that an argument had been made during the planning of the Last Fitna, that Laur Pop himself should be the last man to be put down. It had been an argument that had been settled by the angry fist of Thomas Ashaver, the hand of Shoshanna Adler and by the fanatical loyalty Pop enjoyed among the Hajduks, which would become an aspiration of the other Avenger legions and their leaders.

'How's it like? Working for Pop?' Thomas just had to know what the man who had put a gun to his head was really like.

Nick seemed to take the question in stride and smiled. 'I often wonder how we pull it off! We represent ten nations – well nine now, since the Magyar left to start the Betyar.'

'The Magyar have a Legion now?' Thomas had no idea. It must have happened recently.

'Oh, yeah. Happened about a month ago. Puskas was shipped off to Triangulum right after,' Nick continued. 'When I joined we were twelve and it was a miracle that that worked out for as long as it did.' The Hajduk turned to look at him. 'I know what he did with you in his office that evening, after dinner.'

No chill went up Thomas' spine this time.

Just a little unexpected rage, which he managed to suppress, somewhat. 'He does that a lot?'

'Yes.' It was Silvia's mouth that spoke these words. They were followed by a loud sloshing sound as she also got out of the sea whilst shaking away some of the water. She then sat down next to Thomas on his seat and put forward her hand. Thomas passed her the waterpipe.

She then continued, 'Most of the time he means it. Sometimes he doesn't. The fact that you're here means that, with you, he didn't.'

'The Law aside?' Thomas asked, wishing to get as close to the truth of the issue as possible.

'Terran Law? No! The Law in his head? Yes!' Nick and Silvia both snorted out a laugh at her words. 'He's very meticulous and he saw *you* – and everyone else in your position – as a variable. Which is something he really hates.' Silvia let out a long puff of smoke. 'If you would have given him an answer he wouldn't have liked, he would have had Opera mindwipe you immediately without further discussion.'

She paused and looked at him. Thomas was stunned by her beauty. He had never truly noticed it before. What a waste to have spent an entire evening next to her, only to not remember exchanging a single word. 'Well, I guess I gave the right answer. Given that I can still remember looking down the barrel of a gun in his office.'

Silvia nodded. 'Yes. Yes, indeed.' She made to speak further, but was interrupted by a noise.

A strange whooshing noise. A noise Thomas had last heard on a battlefield. It was the sound of something closing in very fast in the air, but not as fast as a bullet, or a shell. All of a sudden, a cheerful voice pierced their ears. '*LANDING!!!*'

Within a few moments, the deck shuddered as Daw and Mira landed right next to them. The three Terrans didn't really have any time to react, as Daw quickly jumped right next to Nick and Mira took a seat next to Thomas.

'You know... we could've shot you.' Silvia declared with an astonished look in her eye.

Daw replied. 'No, you couldn't! You left your weapons on the beach! Thomas is the only one here with a gun and he ain't that trigger happy.' In truth, Thomas' hand had reached for his pistol, albeit not as swiftly as it would have if he were sober.

'I see...' Silvia seemed a bit embarrassed about being caught unarmed.

'So, how's everyone?' Daw was incredibly cheerful. Thomas couldn't help but notice that Mira was also in high spirits, as the two jittered and giggled together at the mischief of having Daw catapult them through the air towards the deck.

'Chillin'.' Nick responded. He was the most entitled to such an answer, given that he lay almost fully naked stretched across a literal beach bed, while smoking and drinking.

'I can see! You also went swimming, which is an excellent idea!' Daw jumped off the bed and began taking her clothes off. Thomas, Silvia and Nick were shocked to see that she didn't stop, eventually becoming fully naked. Mira didn't seem surprised at all, though she was massaging her forehead in a moment of cringe.

'You know... there's sharks in the wat–' Nick didn't have time to finish his sentence, as a loud breaking of water cut him off. Daw's head surfaced after a few moments.

'Oh! You're right! There's also dolphins! I love dolphins!' Daw immediately placed her head back into the water. The four Terrans on the beach all felt a disturbance. A low, sharp sound, almost imperceptible, even to their ears.

'Is... is she...?' Silvia began. Yet, she was interrupted by the sound of a distant screeching noise.

'Yup...' Mira answered. 'There's a group of them that hangs out around here. Daw knows them...'

As she spoke, they could see a change in the distant waters, just where the moon could be seen reflected in the sea below. Small white dots of fresh foam glittered in the sea, followed by the sounds of snickering and geeking. To the astonishment of both Thomas and the Hajduks, they saw a pack of around forty dolphins descend upon the marina in general and upon Daw in particular. They began playing with her, as the elf giggled and laughed at their playful pecks and their excited flapping. Very soon, some broke off from the main group, and began playing with some of the other night swimmers.

Just as Thomas could see an ecstatic Hausser attempt to ride one, he heard the sound of footsteps approaching them. The four Terrans turned to see a group of approaching elves. The exact reason behind their arrival swiftly became obvious, as two of them were carrying an excessive amount of bathrobes, towels and slippers.

Thomas heard the sound of a mechanical lighter and didn't even really have to turn to see Mira sparking up a cigarette. She then spoke, in what must have been Menegrothi elven, to the arriving elves. Though he couldn't really tell what she was saying, since he had never had the language learned, he could tell from her tone that she was instructing them to calm the fuck down and relax.

'Oh! And no elvish, we speak English here!' Mira finished, switching to Terran for the last sentence.

'Sure thing, your closeness!' One of the elves replied respectfully.

Mira rolled her eyes. 'Oh, but for fuck sake's, Eang. You've known me since I was a child. Don't you "your closeness" me!'

'Sure, Mira!' Eang seemed to immediately relent. Thomas could tell that informality was actually the norm for their relationship. The elf had been merely trying to be polite in front of Mira's people.

'Good! Now, come over here and drink some more with us!' the birthday girl instructed.

Eang and the other elves immediately froze, their looks being those of typical Menegrothi confusion.

Eang spoke first. 'Mira, we've had enough to drink already!'

Silvia and Thomas both turned to give the elves a closer look. Seven of them they were, with the closest of them appearing to be somewhat too... rigid. As if they were trying really hard to look sober.

A thin, waifish voice rang out. Its tone was humorous. 'Terrans drink to get drunk! Not to get just a little buzz!'

It was only then that an eighth elf revealed herself, stepping out from behind one of the elves carrying towels. Thomas was astounded to see that it was none other than –

'Toph?' he asked, bewildered by what he was seeing.

She had changed completely from her Brightguard uniform and now wore an outfit that could only be described as 'exaggerated Terran party clothes'. While the other elves had managed to piece together outfits that were a mix of elven and Terran garb, Toph was the only one to have gone full native. Albeit, she seemed to have chosen an outfit that was what someone who wasn't from Terra would think a Terran would wear to a Terran party, complete with black stilettos, a black cocktail dress which cut off above her navel and a black bra. Not one of those things that looked like a bra, but was actually just some small corset-like contraption. No. This was an actual black bra. On her shoulders rested a white leather jacket, with the symbols of Menegroth and the Brightguard etched where her Nation and Unit would have been displayed if she were Terran.

She had also done something with her hair. She had puffed it up and had curled it to a point were long, loose circles hung across her shoulders and over her chest. Thomas wasn't sure, but he also thought she might have also changed the colour of her hair. It now seemed to be roughly the same as Mira's shade, who had a particularly dark brunette colour. The contrast with her elvish complexion was startling, yet ... also... interesting.

'Thomas?' she did a little curtsy and giggled.

He didn't catch himself checking her out. He just didn't stop doing it. Ultimately, he remembered to be, at least, courteous. 'Well, you heard her. Come over and have some drinks!'

He felt a shadow shoot up right next to him before he felt the beach bed move as Mira stood up. He turned around to meet her gaze, now fixed upon him. It was a strange look. It could only be described as an extreme version of Mira's inquisitive stare, to which Thomas had grown accustomed to over the last months. However, this one inquired directly into his soul.

Her mouth opened. She made to speak, yet her jaw froze in place. After a few moments, she licked her lips, then moved almost imperceptibly closer to him and asked. 'How?'

How? What? Is... is she jealous?

'What?' he asked back.

Mira's eyes flickered. 'How did it happen?'

Is... is this really happening? 'How did *what* happen?'

That was the last straw. After a moment's pause, Mira slammed her wrist across his temples in a manner that was firm, yet also... playful? '*How* did you snap out of it?'

'Mira!' Thomas and also, surprisingly, Silvia shouted out together.

'Oh, fuck off! They're all too hammered too hear me and we're all keepers here!' She gestured towards the beach and the house behind her, then towards the two Hajduks and the eight elves, before focusing on Thomas once more. She repeated herself, 'How did you snap out of it?'

'I... I'll tell you at work?!' Thomas' answer was met by another hit, this time a slap across the head from her left hand.

'I have been *hoping* and *praying* and *trying* to get you to snap out of your *bullshit*!'

She smacked him with the same playful, yet aggressive, strength.

'*Little*!'

Another smack.

'*Depression*!'

Smack!

'For months now! Sitting around waiting for you to get your shit together and not be so devastated all the time... I tried Thomas! I really tried! And nothing happened! What. Happened. This. Time?'

Thomas was left speechless, but not for too long. 'Her!' She pointed towards the water were Daw was playing with a couple of baby dolphins.

Mira's eyes widened. She immediately made her way to the water's edge and shouted. 'GANGA!!!'

'Oh, shit!' Daw squeaked in the water, seemingly startled. She turned around. '*What*?'

'Did you mind edit him or something?' Mira's voice was more similar to the tone in which she gave orders than to the one she used for friends and family.

'Who? Oh! No! We just talked. He told me what he's dealing with. Why?' she asked.

'He says you snapped him out of it.' Mira replied.

There was a moment of silence, during which the two Hajduks, the eight elves and the two baby dolphins looked from Daw, to Mira, then to Thomas, then back to Daw, then Mira, then Thomas again.

'WHAT?!?!?!' Daw finally squealed, jumping out of the water and right onto the dock. She extended a hand towards one of the Brightguards carrying towels and used some very graceful telekinesis to instantly pull a bathrobe towards and around her.

She came straight towards Thomas and gave him a blank stare. She did so for a few seconds, before speaking. 'Oh, shit! He *has* snapped out of it!'

'No shit!' Silvia muttered, eliciting a raised eyebrow from Nick.

'You... you didn't know?' Mira asked Daw.

'No! I mean I tried, but I honestly thought I failed.' She turned to Mira. 'You were right. He was pretty deep down the hole. I actually thought he might truly be too deep to pull out. I even started crying at the end. He was just so coherent –'

'– That's...' Thomas interrupted, drawing the attention of everyone present. '... that's what did it, actually.'

'The coherency?' Mira looked even more confused.

'The crying.'

The words left Thomas' mouth and entered everyone's ears, causing different reactions. Daw smiled as understanding dawned upon her. The other elves' eyes widened in surprise and worry. Silvia smirked; a warm, friendly glint in her eye. Nick was a little lost. Mira was completely lost.

Thomas continued. 'I, eh... How do I say this...?' He genuinely didn't know how to say it.

'Up until the moment you started crying, I never really realised that, well... the things I was – no – the things I *am* dealing with – and *always* will deal with – are things *everyone* deals with. Everyone has to deal with them in their own way and the vast majority of people do just that. They deal with it! They go about their lives. They enjoy life... You can do that even if you're aware of... *things*.'

Mira's face was one of pure shock.

Eventually she started laughing.

It wasn't a mocking sound. It was actually quite the opposite. Mirth filled her giggles and snorts with joy up to the brim of gleeful ecstasy. By the time others had joined in, she was already clenching her stomach from laughter. After struggling to speak, she managed to spit out the most incoherent of words. 'He.... Me... Cunt... Look who's a cunt... Narcissistic... Idiot...'

The others laughed harder upon hearing the word 'cunt', yet Thomas smiled since he alone understood what she meant. *I didn't ever really apologise for that one.*

Mira laughed so hard she had to sit down. 'Fuck's sake, Thomas, you're gonna make me cry now too. For different reasons...' she finished, laughter overtaking her once more.

The mood grew truly festive after that. Toasts had come immediately in recognition of Thomas' rediscovered peace. Followed by a lot of smoke. The Terrans and the elves spent almost an entire hour together on that dock. Other guests joined them since Mira was, after all, the birthday girl. It was towards the end of this hour that Thomas, Mira and Daw found themselves together. Alone, yet surrounded by people.

'I didn't know that was what he needed. Not that, if I did, I would have been able to summon up the willpower to bear through hours of his bullshit.' She paused, feeling the need to put some extra emphasis into her statement. 'No matter how coherent!'

Thomas rolled his eyes and Daw let out a sigh of mock exasperation. 'Are you sour, Mira?' she asked playfully.

'Sour? I mean look at me: I piss vinegar.' Mira's tone played back.

Her sister put on a face of childish sadness. 'Oh! But now is not the time for that! It's your birthday!'

'No. It ain't. It's not. Well,' Mira stood up, 'I do need to go take a piss though.'

'You're not the only one!' Silvia announced, as she got up. 'I also need to get dressed.'

'You do. Cake's coming soon!' their host informed them of the evening's itinerary.

'Why don't you pee in the sea?' Daw immediately asked, only to be met by disgusted looks from both Mira and Silvia.

'Ew! Daw, that's gross!'

Daw shrugged at Mira's words. 'I'll come too!' was all she added.

Mira turned to Thomas and leaned in, placing a hand on his shoulder. She spoke in such a way that only he could hear. 'There's a bedroom in the southern tower of the inner courtyard. Drink! Dance! Eat! Smoke! Snort! I don't give a fuck! Then, when you're done, you can go there and pass out. It'll be empty and locked with your ID as the key. The door is hidden behind a painting of a dancing lady. Touch the red flower in her hair to open the door. There's breakfast tomorrow at five in the afternoon.'

She paused midstride, just as she was about to leave with Daw and Silvia. 'There's also some éclairs in the phaiser in that room. Mango, pistachio and rose. You'll love them!'

With that she was off.

A few minutes after their departure, Nick informed them that he also needed to 'hit the jakes' and he'd see them around. Thomas was left with the remaining elves, including Toph, as well as a smattering of Terrans.

Just as the music coming from the house grew louder and the beat began to change, he found himself sitting next to Toph, looking up towards the house.

'What kind of music is that?' she asked.

'EDM. Electronic Dance Music.' Thomas paused, remembering something Opera had mentioned earlier. 'Must be Technowolf... Definitely sounds like his type of music.'

They both listened to the music for a few moments, before Toph leaned in closer and whispered. 'I have a question!'

'Shoot!' Thomas met her gaze.

'That night. That night, at the party, when we finished Host service...'

Thomas didn't know where she was going with this '... yes?'

'Was that when you started having the thoughts?'

Thomas shifted slightly. Normally, he would have mulled over her words a little, yet he was not really in the proper capacity for analysis. 'Yes... yes, it was.'

'Ha!' she twitched. 'Knew it!' she said proudly.

'Oh, really?' Thomas was intrigued. 'How?'

'Oh, come on, Thomas!' Toph toyed with him, yet he responded with a blank stare. Eventually, the elf was convinced of his ignorance. She leaned in, much, much more closely this time.

'I wanted to spend the night with you then.' The words were carried across by the chill sea air and yet they burned like hot coals towards his ears. She let the words sink into his chest, which tightened. Then, the words dropped into his gut, which fluttered. Finally, they went lower, and something stirred.

She went on. 'At first, I thought you were rejecting me. But, then, when you started asking me about how long elves lived for, I figured out real quick what was going on.'

'You... why didn't you say anything?' Thomas was quite shocked by what he was hearing.

'I did. I said quite a lot. I answered your questions and I even fanned the flames a little before I left you... until we *met* again!'

She raised a hand to the air. 'My Lady helped me keep the promise. But, also,' her eyes grew more solemn, 'I wasn't someone who was close to you. The type of thing you had... The thing you had up until... a few hours ago, I guess? That thing is something that can be helped only by those close to you. The ones who truly know you and care for you.'

'Huh... well, Daw isn't someone who's close to me and she was the one who eventually got me out of it.' Thomas may have been in overall agreement, yet he still had a problem with factual inconsistencies.

'Daw cares for you because her sister cares for you. Daw knows who you are *from* her.' Toph turned towards the stairs that lead up to the mansion, where Daw and Silvia did their best to get Mira out of as many conversations as quickly as possible, so that they could all finally reach the bathroom. 'She didn't try to help you because you needed help, but because she knew that making you feel better would mean that Mira would feel better.'

She turned to look at him once more. 'I was just some girl who always wondered how it would feel like to get to know you and one for whom you never had time.' She smirked at him and nodded her head towards the three women going up the stairs. 'Though, I do think I know you better than they do in one regard.'

Thomas had a hard time focusing on both his arousal and his gratitude for Mira's friendship. 'What regard would that be?'

She was right next to him now and allowed one of her hands to drift towards his leg. Thomas didn't know if she could feel the deep pumping of blood within him.

'That you're an impulsive little boy.'

No, I'm not!

'That you always try to be the best in every little moment. That you're willing to change who you've been for an entire lifetime, just to do the best thing in a single little moment. That's what makes you formidable: you're capable of things that wouldn't even cross another man's mind and you'll act out the wildest thing that comes to mind in an instant if it feels...' She paused, seemingly short of breath, despite all the heavy breathing they seemed to both be doing. '... *right*.'

She moved away now, no longer whispering sensuously into the goose bumps of his neck, only to caress his eyes with her own. 'It's why they all like you so much, even if some don't know it. It's how you went from just another grumpy young Terran boy to who you are now.' She leaned in within mere inches of his face, eyes exploring the corners of his mouth. 'Is that why it bothers you so much?' Now she looked at him again, and saw his eyes betray his mind's curiosity. 'Death?'

The way her lips moved somehow made the word sound enticing.

'A time when you will not be able to be impulsive? Either within the darkness of non-existence or in some perfectly ordered world of someone else's design and control? A place where every action is fated and your own little moments are not of your own creation?'

Thomas saw his time to play as well. 'Well, that and the inevitability of it all.'

Toph smiled, seeing the little comment for what it was: an impulsive compliment. An admittance of agreement, hidden under the veil of feigned disagreement. 'Yes!' she agreed. 'How can someone be impulsive in the face of the inevitable?'

For the first time in his life, he felt something.

It was a strange feeling. It was a warmth, of sorts. Not the fiery heat of rage or lust, but the toasty warmth of home. It was the feeling a child would feel in a warm house on a cold winter evening. The warmth of being in a place outside the realm of life. Away from the cold. Away from fear. Away from needs and wants. Away from the uncertain and close to the safe. He felt as though he had been a man adrift on a damp raft tossed around across the dark seas up until this single moment, when he had woken up in a warm, dry bed beneath a comfortable blanked in a friendly room with a playful fireplace.

The feeling was closest to him in his chest, though his head also felt lighter as it sat atop a neck of muscles now loose and eased of any strain. His hands felt empty, as they yearned to grip the warmth themselves. Only his eyes trembled in anticipation, seemingly knowing that, right now, today, they were going to see something they had never known they were made for.

'You seem to know a lot about me for someone with whom I've only had three conversations with outside of work.' Thomas sent a hard arrow towards her and his entire being prayed that she would dodge it.

'It takes one to know one.' Toph did more than dodge it. She caught it with her bare hand.

With that, she shot bolt upright.

'I'm gonna go dance, because it feels... right.' She let their gazes kiss each other's bodies for a few second.

Thomas wanted to kiss her in other ways, too. 'What should I do?'

She smiled an inviting smile and answered the predictable. 'What... feels... right!'

With that, she was off.

She had barely managed a few steps before Thomas was up and following her determined steps across the deck of the marina towards the shore. He followed her up the stairs to the mansion, watching her drift into the spaces between people while he shoved his way through the crowd, caring for neither apology nor insult, for his ears could only hear the way her movements matched the sounds of the music playing. He followed her through the gardens leading up to the entrance as she turned to wink and shake looks of excited encouragement for him to catch along the entire way. He followed her in his trance of purpose and yearning as they made their way to the invisible dance floor of the main ballroom. In that mass of people and melody the only attraction they felt was for the quiet of each other's eyes as they danced a dance they had never known before.

They shared that night a memory which they would remember forever in its most minute of details, yet would always feel to have been too short and vague. The type of experience which can weld two lives together, never allowing them to ever twist and turn on their own ever again. The type of moment, this was, that could insist that life could never be the same again, for how can one soul return to the desolate drift of solitude, once it had held another in a moment of togetherness?

Chapter XV
One must imagine Sisyphus happy

The chill breeze of the Arabian Sea and the warm afternoon sun were what woke him up.

He stood up quickly, clenching his entire body, his mind shuffling to remind him of the unusual events of the day before and what had led to him waking up in a bed on Socotra Island, up in one of the towers of Mira's mansion. A strange report flashed before his eyes.

He had snapped out of the darkness.

He had seen a god shed tears at their shared suffering.

He had rushed to craft something in Wolfsburg.

He had found something in the night.

Yet, she was no longer here in this morning.

Thomas stood up straight, studying his surroundings. The bed he found himself in was one of those extravagant oldtimer beds, complete with four posters and a full meter of comfy height, allowing him to peer across the room while he rested his back on the frame behind him. The room was surrounded on three sides by one large balcony that encircled the suite, with a bathroom and dressing room located on the fourth side, right behind him. A large couch stood at the foot of the bed, as well as a few cupboards, armchairs and tables. The way outside was obvious enough: a great oaken door located to the distant right side of his bed. He recalled how much it differed from the secret door downstairs.

He peered across the room and felt loneliness overcome him. *She... she left. I didn't want her to leave. I wished she was still here.* His clothes lay scattered across the room, with only his weapons and utility belt having been thrown onto the nightstand next to him. Thomas turned to the other nightstand for it to reveal hope.

A white leather jacket.

He glanced quickly around the room again and spotted it: a black stiletto in a corner. Another one next to chair. A pair of black shoes on a table.

'What are these?' Thomas was startled as he saw the side of Toph's head rise from the back of the couch in front of him. Her right hand followed, holding up a piece of green... pastry?

'That's... that's an éclair?' He remembered the conversation with Mira from the night before. 'It's green and that means it's probably pistachio flavoured.'

'Yes!' He saw her give him a frustrated little look. 'And *what* is it?'

'Ah... eh... a kind of pastry?' Thomas began to slowly get out of bed.

She shook the éclair in front of her. 'This is amazing! I mean... we have pastry on Menegroth, don't get me wrong. But... this is *amazing*!'

Mira wouldn't have shit food allowed on her property. 'Yeah, I mean it's basically a straight doughnut with toppings.'

'Well, you see, first of all: doughnuts are usually fried in oil or boiled. *This* is a type of dough which we have on Menegroth too, but... not in this shape or with this type of icing! This!' Her eyes fixated on the éclair. '... I'm gonna open up a store with these back home!' She turned to him. 'You want one? There's one left in this box and the phaiser's packed with boxes!'

Thomas sat down on the couch next to her and noticed an almost empty box in front of him. A single orange éclair was left. *Mango.* 'It's–'

His stomach rumbled. *Shit. I need to eat actual food to recover quickly.* 'It's fine. You have it!' he insisted.

'No time!' *What? No! Plenty of time!*

He reached out and grabbed her, kissing her neck and holding her waist. Her body greeted his as if it were an old friend. Her scent now gave life to the air in his lungs.

She kissed him back and giggled. 'Stop! I'm late enough as it is!'

'Late to... where?' *Doesn't today count as a day off?*

Toph sneaked out of his wanting arms and made her way towards her lingerie. 'A maiden of the Lightbringer must always ensure with her own eyes that her Lady is well.' She stopped dressing to look at Thomas, a cheeky smiled on her face. 'The Lady herself would likely also wish to see that I am still in one piece and that I haven't been swallowed up by some hungry Terran beast.

'I... don't think you understand what "maiden" means...' *Though... I've never heard of anyone sleeping with Toph back in the Host...*

'Yes, well, clearly neither do you, judging from your behaviour last night!' She smiled mischievously at him and her eyes revealed a playful wickedness a maiden would have to lose her chastity to understand. He turned her eyes back towards her outfit, leaving Thomas to wonder which specific behaviour she was referring to.

If he would know, he would definitely do it again.

He continued, 'It takes one to know one.' They caught each other's eyes and found in there something they both craved. Acknowledgement. Thomas continued, feeling the moment right enough to ask: 'What are you doing after you check up on each other?' *Could you perhaps come back here to me?*

She came to him, climbing on top of him as he leaned back onto the couch. 'I understand that the party will last for today, as well as tomorrow. So, if you are still interested, we could spend some time together.'

Oh, I'm interested! 'I think we would both be interested?' *Please respond with one of the things...*

'Oh, I think both of us might.' *There you go...*

She got up again and went to get her jacket. 'You sleep deep, for a Terran. I took a shower and dried off and you didn't even stir.'

'You wake up next to a lot of Terrans?' On the one hand, Thomas was being cheeky. But, on the other, he really wanted the answer to be as close to a 'no' as possible.

She smirked. 'No. But I do recall several instances back in Triangulum when we had to sneak around extra quietly through the barracks in case some startled Terran or troll woke up and bashed our heads in.'

'Oh, come on... it's not that bad...' It actually was pretty bad. It happened a lot.

'Well, I can't say it's ever happened to me!' She gave him a little pose as she made her way towards the door leading to the stairway. Thomas noticed she could walk in such a way that her high heels did not make any clicking noise. 'Take a shower and go get some food. You look and like you just rose from a grave. Don't even get me started on the smell!' She giggled as she closed the door behind her.

Terrans allegedly never got hangovers.

Allegedly.

As Thomas managed to get his day going, he slowly realised that there was a limit to how many intoxicants one could ingest until even an enhanced body felt like absolute shit. He knew the remedy: a lot of solid food and even more liquid hydration. Fortunately, both could be found in abundant and varied forms downstairs, on the terrace of the main dining room.

At exactly five in the afternoon he reached the terrace after passing through a house that had just gone through more celebration than it could handle. The terrace had several tables with a myriad of breakfast options on offer ranging from eggs, sandwiches and cereal, to pizza, sushi and barbecue. Though over a hundred people could easily be seated, only about a dozen could be seen at the tables, with a dozen more seemingly enjoying the afternoon sun by the large swimming pool next to the dining area.

Thomas spotted Toph and Daw almost immediately. The dozen people by the pool were all elves. They seemed to be caught in the middle of exchanging stories from the night before, as could be determined from all the talking and giggling. *I hope they're not talking about me.* Not that he cared if they did; he just didn't want to do anything but enjoy some much needed breakfast in good company. As he passed by the poolside debriefing to look for a seat next to the best food, he immediately identified both the best seat for both companionship and gastronomy. After all, he didn't know that many people here, but he did know the birthday girl.

Mira was sitting right next to a selection of sandwiches, enjoying a particularly appetising fried chicken sandwich while wearing sunglasses, slippers and a thin, lose robe. Next to her sat a remani who was likely Technowolf, judging from his outfit. A yellow Hawaiian shirt decorated with black fern leaves sat tightly sealed around a mass of fury muscle. On his feet, Thomas noted, the remani wore not the traditional sandals favoured by his people, but brightly coloured Terran sneakers. Instead of the typical loose trousers, this remani wore tight jeans, with a cowboy belt buckle. The look was completed by a pair of aviator sunglasses. He seemed to be staring off into the distance towards the white-tipped waves of the sea.

For a second, Thomas wondered if perhaps she should leave her alone to enjoy some much needed peace and quiet. Yet, Mira paused mid-bite to gesture that he join them.

'Well, you look like shit!' she said between mouthfuls of bread, coleslaw, breading and chicken.

'Oh, really! You see that through your sunglasses?' *Which you're probably wearing because you haven't healed yet and also look like shit?*

Mira stifled a laugh and almost choked on her food. 'Well, I guess this is who you are then!'

Thomas felt something in her tone. A distant sadness, almost, as well as the tell-tale ring of Mira rage.

Here we go... 'What do you mean?'

Mira paused her meal, leaned back, revealing a belly busy providing urgent replenishment to her body, and took a sip of orange juice. Technowolf stood completely immobile.

'Your actual self. Not who you were when you were going through your *phase*.' She gestured ostentatiously towards him... 'The person you are now... and yesterday.'

He really didn't know how to take that. 'And... how is that person?'

'Ballsy.' She returned to her chicken sandwich. 'You always were. Just that,' she wiped her mouth with a napkin, 'it would always look like you were faking it. Like you were doing it to look confident, while you were all soft inside. Don't get me wrong! I still think you're all mushy on the inside. Just that, now, you don't seem to be faking it.'

'I'll... take that as a compliment.' *A completely arbitrary opinion that is, if ever there was one.*

'You *should*!' Mira's tone sounded familiar again. It was her familiar threatening tone.

'It's, indeed...' Thomas finally sat down on the seat across from Mira. The unmoving Technowolf did not seem to acknowledge his appearance next to him. '... great to finally have a clear head again!'

'Oh.' She turned her face towards the elves by the pool. With the black sunglasses pointed away from him, Thomas could see how bloodshot her eyes were. 'I hear that happens to men.'

Thomas followed her gaze towards the exact elf she had focused on.

Toph.

He didn't really know how to take what she had just said. Yet he was going to address it. 'You... D'you have a problem with that, Mira?'

Mira's eyes flickered back to his. Thomas could see one of her eyes for what it was: a menacing ember. 'You see, Thomas? *That* thing! The way you said *that*! You're not *asking* me to not fuck with you. You're *telling* me not to fuck with you!'

Thomas wasn't sure where she was going with this, but there was one place he sure as hell didn't want her to go. 'You once told me to treat you as an equal.' *I'm pushing it here. She told me to treat her as an equal when no one is around. Technowolf is sitting right there!*

She smiled. A bitter smile almost. Though, also a sweet one. 'I did.'

'Are you angry I took a girl to bed in your house?' *Are you really?*

She answered negatively with her fork, which she had picked up to attack some potato wedges. 'No. I'm not angry. Just surprised. I mean – don't get me wrong – I get it! You're a smart little snack and so is she!' The fork gestures continued. 'I was just surprised by how... *vigorous* you were during the night.'

What the hell is she on about now? 'What do you mean, "vigorous"?'

Her neutral smile shifted to stifled chuckling. 'Vigorous. Full of energy. Creative. Animalistic almost. Potent... '*What the fuck is... oh, no... no fucking way!* 'Virile –'

'– Did you come to the room after me and Toph went in?' *Please say no!*

'... completely removed from your surroundings. No spatial awareness whatsoever...' She paused her rant to look right at him. 'I came over to make sure you were alright, since you missed the cake.' Then she turned her head back to her rant.

'The lifts! The twists! The pounding! The grunting! That thing you did with your mouth and her taint –'

'– *Mira!*' He didn't raise is his voice, yet he did grit his teeth while looking at the still unmoving Technowolf.

Mira saw his concern. 'Oh! Don't worry about him. The comedown from emdiamay is a fucking hammer for remani. He's probably completely out of it now.'

Technowolf nodded.

'See! He doesn't give a shit! Now, back to the literal *fucking* spectacle that went down – in more ways than one – in my house –'

'– I 'm sorry I missed your cake!' *If that's what this is about.*

The comment seemed to work, as she ceased ranting for a moment and her gaze seemed to fixate upon him for a moment, before returning to the plate in front of her. 'The cake was great. You would've liked it.' She went back to assaulting her food, but had to pause, since she couldn't control some maniacal fit of laughter. 'But, I guess her *cake* was better!'

'*Mira!*'

'Fine...' She stifled the laughter. 'It's fine! I really don't give a fuck. Fuck her!' She had dragged a wiener schnitzel onto her plate and began cutting it up. 'Fuck her in my house! *I* honestly don't give a fuck! *You* can give as many fucks as you want, but, please, use them on her! There's time! I'm half-Hindu motherfucker! This party lasts for three days and nights! We're not even halfway –'

'– am I allowed to stay?' *At least do whatever it is you're gonna do already!*

'Yes! Seriously! At my personal insistence! Not Daw's!' She felt the need to emphasize that last bit with an atypical head wobble.

'I will then!' He would really love to.

'You see, that's what I mean about the balls. You're not scared of shit anymore, aren't you?' Mira stopped treating her food as if the schnitzel had been the one that killed her parents. She met his gaze, though her eyes remained hidden. 'You see... I read your file a lot. Not just the part about melee combat. Not just the assessment for promotions. Not just the medals. I, honestly, to this day, cannot tell you what your test scores were, but,' she pinched the air in front of her, 'there was just one thing that didn't fit with the guy I was looking at.'

'Where are this man's guts? This other guy – the one on the paper – is this fucking mountain of determination and confidence... almost mindless he seemed sometimes. Like... you fucking got your promotion for Lieutenant for flanking an entire warband with ten men? What the fuck? The fucking balls on Staff Sergeant Muller! What the fuck happened to this Lieutenant Muller guy in front of me? This pitiful scared little boy whom I have to fucking coddle just to get him through the day?'

'You were fucking terrorized all the time and you let everyone – myself included – walk right over you and use you, on the off-chance that we might actually have the key to bringing you back up. From time to time, I would see little flashes of the man you might have been before and I would wonder: "is there more of this in him?"'

'It clicked after a while. You have balls, but you had never encountered the unknown before. And the unknown frightened you!' Mira leaned back in her seat, truly trying to relax now. 'But, now, after you've survived battling the unknown for so fucking long and after you have built your impregnable house, you're back! And now you *know* that there's nothing that can scare you more than you've scared *yourself* over the last three months.'

Well... that... that's touching. 'I... That's... I need to thank you for that, honestly.'

Mira tilted her head. 'What do you mean?'

'You are the most fearless person I know. The most fearless person I've ever met. Nothing scares you. No enemy. No thought. No punishment. No opinion. As someone who's always been afraid of not being good enough and of not meeting the expectations of those around me, spending time with you taught me that there is no real reason to ever be afraid of anything. After all, I managed to become your friend. Earning your friendship is one of my proudest achievements in life and it's something that's more valuable than anything written on some piece of paper.'

Her wickedness and the rage beneath it seemed to wisp away across the sea breeze as something resembling gratitude flowed across Mira's face. 'I'm not as fearless with my words as you.'

It took fractions of the smallest moments for Thomas to catch her meaning, 'I never did apologise for calling you a "cunt", didn't I?'

Their laughter sealed the peace between them. In that moment, Thomas knew that which he had spent time wondering as he had crafted her present in the Wolfsburg Forge.

Would they still be friends? Now that his crisis was over? He knew they'd still work together on Kralizec. Yet, it mattered more to him that he would continue to spend so much of his day with Mira. He had his answer and, accidental voyeurism aside, their relationship had survived unscathed.

'How's Lorgar?' *Let's talk about things friends talk about. I've always wanted that.*

'He's in a room upstairs, full of food and catnip, with four –very caucasian – elves, whom I convinced to try out some emdiamay.'

Mira noticed Thomas' puzzled look. 'So they'll get all touchy and pet him all day!' she explained.

Their conversation was interrupted by Daw's decision to jump right into the pool with an audible splash. As several of her 'maidens' followed suit, she waved towards Mira, inviting her to join.

'I'm still eating!' she shouted joyfully towards her sister. Seeing Daw reminded him of something he had always wanted to ask Mira.

'Is she really a god?'

'No. There is only one God and we shall never see Him in this life.' He had never heard her speak like that before.

'She is a thousand people, all wrapped into one,' she continued. 'Some of those people I don't even like. The only person I really like is that original "her". The *actual* Daw. The Daw that isn't some ancient king or scholar. The Daw who is... uniquely her.' She took a sip of her juice. 'Some might say that she is very different from us on account of all of the entities that exist within her consciousness. However, once you see that one personality that is just *her*, you immediately understand that she is not a god at all. She's just a person. A very, very complicated person, yet a person nevertheless.'

'More understanding of what the Universe is? Yes. But, is she truly part of the fabric of reality, as only an aspect of the one true God – The God that made everything and *is* everything – could be? No. She is not.'

Thomas realized, to his amazement, that he had actually never asked Mira a crucial question in their line of work.

'Mira, do you believe in God?'

She smiled. 'I believe that there is something at work in the world that we will never truly grasp. Something we can't properly understand. There is... a *presence*. A presence that always was and always will be. A presence that may have been the only thing that ever was and always will be. We may never prove the presence itself exists yet, somehow, we all *feel* it, in some way.'

'You never mentioned that before.' Truly never before and, god knows, there were abundant opportunities.

'You never asked.' She seemed to roll her eyes behind her sunglasses. 'Then again, you always seemed to be too focused on your own perceptions to be concerned with those of the people around you. I was wrong about that. Turns out that making you understand that you weren't the only one struggling with things was actually the way out of the darkness. I'm sorry I didn't figure it out.'

In this little lull in the conversation, Technowolf spoke. 'We should burn this place to the ground.' He finally moved and turned his head towards Thomas. 'Like Burning Man.'

Mira didn't care how the remani had reached this conclusion. 'Uhm... No. This is my house!'

'Ok!' he replied and fell silent, once more.

'Well, on that note,' Mira pulled of her sunglasses, 'is it gone?' She pointed at her face.

Thomas, by this point distracted by a grilled cheese sandwich, containing an excellent mix of gruyere and asiago, looked up to investigate. 'They're clear. Mira, did you cook everything here?' *This is the best grilled cheese I've ever had.*

'What? No! Fucking hell, Thomas, I have operators. I couldn't cook all of this, even if I had a month!' She got up from her seat and stretched. 'The recipes are mine, though.' She finished stretching, picked up an empty glass and began pouring herself pomegranate juice from a nearby pitcher. 'I recommend you get some food in you too. I would be very disappointed if anyone was still sober by nightfall.'

She pointed towards the pool, were Toph seemed to be describing some kind of dessert to her fellow elves. 'The room is yours... and hers, I guess. You can stay until Monday morning, when we both have to get back to Jerusalem.' She looked back towards him now, her eyes bubbling, as two fires of different colours collided within her.

'We will continue the review of the Elocution Protocol. There will likely be changes in the way we go about things. Adler's been wanting us to switch to more active roles for quite some time now. We didn't because some of us are a bit *slow*.' She smirked. 'But, now that we're all aligned and you've managed to snap out of your own little dark night of the soul, things can progress.'

'What does that mean, exactly?'

'Mostly errands Adler will want us to run. We'll find out next Friday, I guess, after she finds out about you.'

'Are you going to tell her?'

'Yes. It'll go in my report.' She smirked again. 'Which, to be honest, I will really enjoy writing this time, in no small part due to the fact that I won't have to document your continuous neurotic musings anymore.'

'Well, I'll miss continuously musing neurotically with you, Mira.' He would. *I hope I can still –*

'– oh, you can still do that. I'll actually enjoy it now that I don't have to write reports every night about it. Plus that now I won't be restricted from calling you out on your bullshit.'

There was a small pause, in which it wasn't clear which one of them would speak.

'*Not that it ever mattered!*' they both said, together, before bursting into laughter.

'Well, I'm off. Two Akali passed out last night and had to be dropped off in the medical room. Gonna go check if they're alive.' She made to leave, then turned. 'Thomas?'

'Yes?' he asked, between mouthfuls of warm falafel.

'I still think mistakes are best accepted, yet not expected.' She said, before gesturing towards a nearby table, where a group of Galloglaich had just finished breakfast. 'I didn't get a chance to talk to you last night! Come! I gotta go check if Sarwan and Japjot are still comatose! We'll catch up on the way. Albrecht, go keep your countryman company!'

Audibly loud grunts of fervent Scottish agreement were followed by dutiful German shuffling, as Hausser and a couple of Jaegers, whom Thomas could tell had just woken up and arrived, joined him for breakfast.

Mira got her wish, as breakfast quickly turned to dinner and, as dusk began to settle, Technowolf stirred and began turning the music louder. The celebration, once more, lasted well into the morning, with Thomas and Toph, once more, waking up in their tower of joy. The cycle continued into Sunday night, with the early Monday morning being the only thing to end the festivities. Clara's alarm woke him up, and the operator also insisted that he eat and hydrate before the drive back to Jerusalem.

He and Mira were the last Terrans to leave the al Sayid estate. Daw left with Mira's shuttle, insisting that she was in the mood for a good *zoom!!!*. A contingent of Brightguard would remain on Socotra, to both help the mansion's operators with the cleanup, as well as in order to take up residence within the vast mansion. They would remain there while their duties would require their presence on Terra.

Toph was not a part of this contingent. Daw had assigned her to the contingent of elves which would reside in Jerusalem. Thomas knew for certain that this had been no coincidence. After all, the Brightguard had been spread out all over Terra, with only around a hundred being gathered in any one place at any given time, to help muddy the waters and obscure the reason for their presence on Terra. What were the chances it would be exactly Toph who would be one of the few assigned to work directly on Kralizec?

They did work. Yes. But they also made love.

They spent every night together, with Toph becoming a fixture of his apartment, as Daw became a fixture of Mira's. Albeit, for completely different reasons. During the day, Toph and the rest of the Brightguard would split their time between guard duty and assisting the Terrans in their excessive checking and re-checking, testing and re-testing, inspecting and re-inspecting, trialling and re-trialling of every minute detail of Kralizec. Daw herself spent many a day within the Orpheus Chamber, locked in deep meditation as she looked over every individual line of code which would trigger the creation of Olorun within the Aether.

Those days were gruelling and tense, as everyone involved in the great Terran plan dedicated themselves fully to its fruition. They barely heard from Adler, as the General was reportedly mired in a thousand different tasks and obligations. Patel and Fiol were constantly in Daw's presence, as they sought her counsel endlessly on a million different assumptions and decisions. Rasmussen and Hos-Hos rarely left their stations anymore, unless directly ordered to by the High Command. Xhisa still slept in the Orpheus Chamber though, with Rasmussen and Hos-Hos joking that they were beginning to understand him. Thomas learned from Silvia that Pop was close to madness, as he and Zaslani struggled to maintain the Project's secrecy. All was madness as the crescendo of labour reached its peak, with Thomas often wondering if Mira's dream of a new Tower of Babel was more prophecy than possibility.

Yet, the nights were sweet and gentle. Time was short and the Thomas and Toph spent their evenings in each other's arms and savouring each other's presence. Thomas would have loved to show Toph the many wonders of Terra, from the pyramids of Cairo, to the Great Bazaar of Samarkand, the Bridge of Istanbul, the Gardens of Babylon, the City of Blackstone, the plains of Zealandia, the Green City of Angkor Wat or the Red City of Marrakesh, the Spires of Chichen Itza or the plateau of Risen Rio, the Maze of Moscow or the Shanghai Dock. It bit into his soul to think that no such time would ever come, as he and Toph discussed their paths once Theogenesis had taken place.

Thomas would stay on Terra for who knows how long, setting in motion the series of events which would follow Kralizec's culmination. Toph would leave with Daw and the Brightguard, as her lady's presence would likely be urgently requested elsewhere the moment she announced the end of her 'friendship tour', as it was officially called. They didn't know how they would meet afterwards, but they had plans. They could go back to the Allied Host and join the same battalion. Thomas could request a transfer to the Terran Commercial Corps and focus on trade with the Commonwealth, Menegroth in particular. Toph could request a discharge from the Brightguard and come to Terra as a *Terran companion*, as Fiol had been before marrying Lakshmi. They could both move to the Allied Host HQ on Luna and find assignments there.

There were plans and possibilities, yet Thomas himself didn't know where his own life would take him. Mira had told him that they would continue to work together and they did. For an entire week, up until their Friday meeting with Adler, they inspected a hundred scenarios. They checked that Hos-Hos' people were accurate in their calculations. They interviewed several of Rasmussen's test subjects, making sure that their experiential veracity was as close to perfection as was possible. By Thursday evening, they were interrogating the Sayeret and Hajduks, just to make sure that they were on top of their game.

Finally, Friday morning came and the two found themselves in Adler's office. Things were... palpably different. Adler even had Xian Shang involved in Kralizec now, with the Sergeant Major taking calls and placing meetings furiously. He didn't even bother pestering Thomas and Mira with questions anymore and just waved them in. They found, for the first time ever, a room in chaos.

Adler's desk was packed full of screens and files. Thomas immediately realized them as Kralizec physical files. These were files that contained information of absolute secrecy, which not even the exceedingly advanced Terran communications system could be entrusted with. They usually contained excerpts of Olorun's actual sourcecode, coupled with detailed reports filed by the highest ranking officers working on the Project. The only free space on the desk was dominated, not by one of Adler's many teapots, but by a gigantic jug of black coffee. Adler herself was a mess. Her hair, usually straightened and well-kept, now hung in an improvised topknot that did a terrible job of holding in about a third of her hair, which hung wildly across her face and shoulders.

Thomas could tell she was exhausted from the way she looked. Her uniform, usually pristine and orderly, now hung across her body like a tired rag. Her tabard unbuttoned all the way down, revealed a wrinkled shirt that had seen far too much cold sweat. Her utility belt, usually tightly bound to her waist, hung on top of her chair, with her pistol resting on one of the piles of files in front of her. As they walked in, she had been coming out of her bathroom, droplets of cold water still visible on her face.

'Ah, Thomas! Mira! Hello! No salutes! Just sit down.' She moved to her seat and collapsed into it, completely ignoring Mira, as she took her usual seat on the couch and Thomas, who sat down across from her, as he always did.

'Glad to see you both! I'm sorry that I haven't been that easy to reach. Just that there's been work and work and work and everyone needs a proofread and approval and editing and checking and everything else. As you can see, I haven't actually had the chance to catch up with everything. I'm actually gonna have to apologise right now. I'm going to have to keep this short. I'm sorry for having you guys come all the way; we could've had this online. Though I'm glad you both came in... How are you?'

She finally looked up from her overdue readings. 'How are you, Thomas?' She turned to Mira. 'How are you, Mira? The birthday was wonderful! Everything was great!'

She turned back to Thomas. 'Have you had time to look over the report on experiential veracity in conjunction with the observation of one's memories? It's quite compelling. Too compelling to be honest. Third person view is fine. First person is where it get's muddy for me. I would love your input, Thomas!'

There was a pause. Thomas wanted to be certain of the truth of what he was about to declare, yet Mira beat him to it. 'She has no idea!'

Adler twitched her head towards Mira. 'Oh, God, what is it now?'

Mira casually pointed towards Thomas. 'Look at him!' She didn't have time to finish her sentence, as Adler's face had snapped back to the young German Lieutenant before her. 'The acute episode is over. He's snapped out of it!'

Adler finally ceased her jittering and seemed to be overcome with stillness. Her eyes looked into Thomas' own, seeking out confirmation of Mira's words. After a few moments, he saw them glaze over and realised what she was doing.

She was conferring with her operator.

'You haven't read Mira's report, General?' he asked.

'I am now. I see that this development also features in General Pop's report. Silvia and Nick both confirm having heard you confess to the end of it.' The corner of her mouth curled up slightly, placing her mouth between a smirk and scowl, and her tone changed. 'I see that you've also acquired a... companion?' Her voice did little to hide her disgust.

'Yes... sir.' He expected that. He had realised during Adler's interaction with Toph in the Arctic that she was most definitely one of those old timers who hadn't ever truly gotten used to the fact that the elves were allies now.

The disgusted expression changed, noting Thomas' own shift in tone. 'Kids these days... Well...' She sat back in her chair, seemingly allowing her body to finally relax. 'It says here,' she tapped the corner of her eyes, 'that it was Daw al Fajr that helped you snap out of it. I assume it happened last Friday, when Daw asked that we cancel our meeting so that she may hold a session with you in my stead. So... '

'How?'

Thomas had anticipated this question, and had prepared a response. 'She had me speak. I spoke for a while.' He pointed to the coffee table and the armchairs next to Mira. 'There! I spent a long time explaining what my thoughts were. I got very into it. At one point I forgot she was there. And then I heard a noise.' Adler raised an eyebrow.

'A sobbing noise. When I looked up, she was crying.' Both of Adler's eyebrows shot up. 'I, eh, asked her what the problem was and she told me that she and likely everyone else in the world struggled with what I was struggling. And always would. And I was, eh, just someone who was good at structuring it. That... did the trick...'

Adler let out a deep breath. '*What?*'

Ok. Gotta be more straightforward. 'I never realised that it wasn't just me who was going through existential dread. Other people do to. Even people like her. And no one has any answers or any certainty. And, yet, they deal with it. Which means that it *can* be dealt with. Knowing that life is fleeting doesn't mean you can't enjoy it anymore. On the contrary, you can only really enjoy it once you become aware that it's limited! When I saw her cry, it hit me that you can be genuinely happy being alive. Like she and – I'm assuming – anyone else who's cheerful all the time.'

Adler's eyes had drifted away as she listened to his explanation. Thomas now realized that she was gazing at the painting behind her. He had never realized that she always did that when deep in thought. Aware of this fact, without turning, he followed her eyes, trying to figure out exactly which part of the painting she always focused on, since she always seemed to be fixated on the same exact place. It took him only a few moments to it figure out: the fisherman's hand. The fingers holding the trident.

The choice.

A few seconds into her silent stare, a smile spread across her face. A genuine smile. It spread from the straight line of her mouth, up until right beneath her eyes, where a glimmer of sincere affection caught flame. She finally spoke and her eyes returned to his. 'Laur was right about you.'

Thomas didn't really know how to take that.

Adler offered clarification. 'He said you were a gentle soul.' She leaned forward into the piles of metal and paper on her desk. 'I'm happy, Thomas. I really am! Seeing you struggle here, in that seat, for so long... it was difficult. I'm ashamed I could never offer you what you needed myself. I must confess... I spent a long time actively trying not to influence you. However, after a while, I began to root for you. It... bothered me when I realized that nothing Kralizec had to offer could help aid you in your struggle.'

Adler smiled for a few moments before taking in a deep breath, a look of determination returning to her face. 'I had the pleasure of welcoming you into Project Kralizec as a participant. Now, I have the pleasure of bringing you on board as a member of the team. Captain al Sayid!'

'Yup?' Mira, who had been sitting forward in hear seat on the couch, her hands clasped together between her legs, straightened up slightly, releasing one hand to have it lean on her thigh.

'You are now relieved of your duty as caretaker of Lieutenant Muller, as well as your duties within the Inception Section. Your new assignment is as a fulltime officer of the Elocution Section. Thus, you are now no longer under Colonel Patel's direct command, but mine. You will maintain your posting in Jerusalem, yet your role will be an entirely different one.'

She rubbed her eyes, seemingly trying to remember some script she had prepared. 'Everything we have worked on for Kralizec is not just going to have an impact in the next life, but also in this one. What lies beyond Theogenesis and Diwali Day is the whole process of revealing Kralizec to as many trusted individuals as possible, so as to assure that some continuity is maintained and that no one ever tries to replicate what we have done here.'

'To do so would not only be pointless, but also a pointless waste of resources. One time is just enough. Then, once the cat will be out of the bag, which, believe me, one day it will, there will be a crisis of faith and identity that shall spread throughout the entire population. But, until we get there, we still have a final hurdle to cross, which is actually taking the project live.'

She exhaled, looking around her desk. 'And that implies a lot of moving documents around. And a lot of editing... which I look forward to, since it'll help clear up my desk.'

She looked up, her eyes seeking out Thomas', then Mira's. 'Your track record so far makes you two excellent candidates for what is to follow. You will assist with organisational matters from now, ranging from the pruning and tweaking of the last details, all the way towards spreading word of Kralizec among selected groups and individuals. You'll get your first set of such tasks soon. Now go back to Jerusalem and wait.'

Chapter XVI
Theogenesis

Ashaver had an apartment in Jerusalem.
An apartment!!!
Thomas had been running around the globe for almost two months now, with his errands taking him to the houses of the most powerful people on Terra. He had been granted entry to the great fortress of the Ghurkhas, high in the Himalayan Mountains. He had seen the Shrine of Amateratsu, the home of the Ashigaru, rising from the Islands of the Shattered Sun. He had been to the home of the Marshal of Terra, on the outskirts of Guangzhou, as well as to the abodes of the Chiefs of the Caucasus clans. He had enjoyed the rights of Pashtuali granted to him by the Mujahedin and the hospitality of the Corsairs of Essaouira. He had even seen the grand Castle of Heidelberg, where it had been he, a mere Army Lieutenant, had made the Jaegers into keepers.

Normally, he would have basked in the wish fulfilment conferred by meeting the famed chieftains of the Terran Nations, walking among the warriors of the Avenger Legions in their Citadels of dark grief, and seeing the preserved relics of the World-Which-Was. Yet, his heart was frequently empty, as duty dictated two things: that he treat his missions with the utmost seriousness and focus... and that he never bring along his 'little elf girlfriend along, so as not to have us kicked into the fucking ground... or worse, laughed at'. This direct quote by Mira had been echoed by Adler herself, who had insisted that Thomas never even mentioned that he spent his nights 'swapping juices' (*ew...*) with an elf.

So it was that every day, Thomas would see the great wonders of Terran martial elitism and speak with the living monuments of the Terran warrior cultures, without being able to truly enjoy a single moment of it. He took in the great sights he beheld and the many artefacts he touched only because he enjoyed the sparkle in Toph's eye when he would describe them to her each night. A lot of things he didn't even have to bother describing to her, since the mansions and fortresses of Terra were littered with items fashioned not by the hands of his people, but by hers. The War of Vengeance had been not only a galactic campaign of unspeakable atrocities fuelled by vindicated rage, but also an absolutely ludicrous exercise in thievery. Terrans had looted elven armouries, universities, banks, museums, hospitals, homes and places of worship with the fevered passion of true kleptomaniacs. Some of the most treasured possessions of the Terran people were gifts from Vigilant, Moria and Pandora, yet most had been jerked from the cold hands of dead elves.

The Axe of Djibril al Sayid, now masterless, lay in the grant repository of Mecca, as it had once sat in the armouries of the high elven nobility, forged by the obedient hands of low elves. Ashaver's own flagship, the *Naglafar*, was merely the repurposed husk of *Marlafior*, one of the great black unialki, the living engines of war of the old Svart fleet. The fabled Armour of Crimson Kali, now in the possession of the General of the Akali, had once belonged to a prince of the high elves, with the mighty panoply of war being claimed Uma Kaur, after she had murdered its previous owner in his sleep.

These were just some of the many wonders that adorned the great halls of Terra and the villas of Terran oldtimers. They sat in vast chambers of dark shades and sombre tones, and acted as a continuous, imposing reminder of the never-ending mourning of their new owners. An ever-present reminder of the might of Terra and the eternal memory of what had happened to the enemies of the World-Which-Was.

Never again!

Yet, here he was, a few streets away from Laur Pop's villa, midway up the hill of Harnof, in a non-descript Terran apartment building. Thomas was no fool, he knew that the building had been occupied by Ashaver's Old Guard and served as their base of operations in Jerusalem. About a third of the Hierarch's legion was known to be in the Israeli Holdfast, with the rest of the Old Guard garrisoning their Citadel on the Isle of Tristan da Cunha or the *Naglafar* in Terra's orbit. However, were it not for the people he knew lay within, the apartment building would not have been in any way remarkable.

Sure, all Terran apartments located outside the Spines were by default beyond reproach. Large rooms, complete with the most advanced healthcare technologies, access to endless amounts of energy, comfortable beds, fully-equipped bathrooms, complementary weapons and munitions, fully-stocked kitchens... These were not the signs of a wasteful culture, consuming itself in mindless excess, but the expectable reaction of a society which had seen the dangers of not being well-prepared. Terran living spaces were built to be apocalypse-proof. Strong structures impervious to earthquakes or bombardment. Food stockpiles in case of a siege or famine. Weapons stashes, in case you ran out of ammo or your gun broke down. A medical capsule in every living room.

These were just the more obvious precautions taken by Terran engineers. Everything had a purpose and that purpose was security. A spirit of survivalism and a deep-seated neuroticism were two of the three muses of Terran design. The third was a desire to be intimidating. This was why Terran Citadels looked like the lairs of vile villains or the dens of malicious monsters.

The dark colours. The imposing designs. The blend of the macabre, the intimidating and the utilitarian usually grew more and more extravagant the higher one was in rank. Adler and her fever-dream paintings. Pop's lavish home, complete with murder zones, hunting trophies and hidden pistols. Lakshmi's home was, in Thomas' experience, the most welcoming oldtimer home he had ever been in, bar perhaps only Ronan's humble abode. In truth, it was not just the oldtimers that embraced this excessively martial style of home decor. Mira's house, despite being visibly less threatening, was nothing less than a tastefully decorated seaside fort. His parents' place, though quaint and simple by comparison, was little more than a mountain stronghold with a luminous living room (his mother's insistence).

The apartment block before him was no different. Thick blastproof walls, bulletproof windows and fireproof doors, standard features of Terran architecture, held together a construction that was essentially an above ground bunker, to go with the actual bunker which likely lay beneath it. As he gained entry from the two Old Guards at the gate, famed and battle scarred veterans of untold horrors, he was shocked by how... *simple* the interior was.

Yes. The Old Guards had made their presence felt, as a half-dozen huddled around two of their number playing backgammon in the lobby. The black and white skull banners of the most morbid of the Hierarch Legions graced the interior with their dark presence. Weapons stolen from a thousand dead foes and armour forged by thousand-year old smiths stood on tables, under seats and hung from the walls, ready to be used at a moment's notice.

He asked the Old Guards inside for the exact location of the Hierarch's abode and was directed to one of the middle floors. *Of course! The penthouse is too exposed and so is the ground floor.* He reached the apartment door in a matter of moments and found himself genuinely worried for the first time since taking up this new assignment with the Elocution Section. In truth, he found Ashaver's simple lodgings to be more intimidating than the most bombastic battlements of the most formidable fortresses.

Behind the door before him was one of the most dangerous men in the Known Universe. A hero of his people and the true power behind the empty throne of Terra. He clutched the file by his side, the reason for his visit. It was a list. A list of people who would be allowed to be in the Orpheus Chamber at the moment of Theogenesis. The audience of the most important show in their people's history.

Like a man about to gamble his life on a mediocre hand of poker, he forced himself to be reckless, allowing himself, in a moment of mindlessness, to knock on the door and the consequences be damned!

After a few moments, the door opened slightly, allowing him entrance inside.

He heard the sounds inside before his eyes could take in the sight. Whistling. Cheering. The sounds of an arena. An English voice. 'Mbappe! Thuram! Mbappe!!!' The cheering reached a thunderous roar and Thomas heard the sound of someone slapping their hands together. '*OH! WOOOW!!! HE IS AN AWESOME FORCE OF NATURE!*'

Too late to turn back now. Thomas entered the room.

Ashaver had been the one slapping his hands in excitement. The Hierarch was seated in the corner of a large couch, with the other neutral being occupied by a particularly neutral-looking Marco Acosta, who seemed much more pleased by the appearance of Thomas, than by the comeback that had just taken place on the screen before them.

'*BRUTAL AND BRILIANT! IT'S TWO EACH IN THE WORLD CUP FINAL!*'

The two stood opposite a giant screen, which danced between images of a jubilant crowd, a worried crowd, people running across a field of grass and a ball being kicked into a net hung between two posts. Thomas recognized the game as football and, judging by the letters 'BBC' highlighted in one of the corners, he could tell that this was old footage from the World-Which-Was. Ashaver, his face marked by a look of renewed optimism, likely due to how the game had just turned, gestured for Thomas to come in.

'Oh-ho-ho! Come in, Thomas! Don't sit in front of the screen! Watcha got there?' He gestured with his chin towards the file Thomas was holding.

'Attendance list, sir! For Diwali Day.'

'Ah! Ok. Good! Everyone's signed off on it?'

'Yes, sir! Awaiting your feedback.'

'Are you on it?' Ashaver was busy looking at a rerun of the goal that had just been scored.

'I... no, sir.' He had felt a little left out when he had first seen the list.

'That's my first comment then. You and Mira to attend! Now, leave it on the kitchen counter! I'll check it out later.'

'Yes, sir!' Thomas started off towards the kitchen.

'Good, good. Ey... Thomas, have you seen this?' He pointed at the screen. '2022 World Cup Final?'

Thomas paused. 'No, sir!' He wasn't really that much of a football fan.

'Ah, great! Leave the thing, then grab a seat!'

Thomas did a double take. 'Sir?'

'D'you got anywhere you gotta be?'

It's eleven in the evening... In my bed? In Toph's bed? He wasn't sure if Ashaver would count any of those two locations as places he *had* to be. He probably meant if he had any duties left, which he did not. Hence, Thomas shook his head.

'Great!' Ashaver pointed at the armchair next to his place on the couch. 'There ya go!'

Thomas had fantasized about such an opportunity as a child, yet wish fulfilment, no matter how deep-seated in one's psyche, could leave one stunned. Thus, after dropping off the attendance list on the counter, he made his way on wobbly, confused legs towards the seat next to Ashaver.

Who was delighted to have him as a guest. 'Oh, wait! Grab yourself a drink from the phaiser! You smoke weed?' Thomas noticed the thick brown blunt in Ashaver's hand.

'I... eh... I...' *I want to say 'yes' so bad...*

'That's a 'yes'! Get a drink and come over!' Ashaver's eyes had never truly left the screen throughout their interaction.

Thomas made his way back to the phaiser, while glancing towards the screen himself. He didn't know anything about football. It had even come as a surprise to him to learn that there had once been a football player with his name. He was, however, good at history, so he was able to realise that, judging from the flags, the match was between France and Argentina. Other than that, he understood very little of what was going on.

Ashaver's phaiser was packed full of what could only be described as 'Terran oldtimer nostalgia'. The companies behind the brands of Old Earth were long gone, with food and beverage production on Terra now being split between imports, rations and artisanal products. Imports were the most varied, as Terrans had acquired a taste for such items as orcish greens, Pandoran game and goblin snacks, yet the bulk of the food available on Terra was indigenous to the planet itself. This indigenous fare usually fell under the designation of 'rations', which was food manufactured and distributed by the Nutritional Department of the Logistics Corps. Rations came in many forms, ranging from the vast stockpiles of non-perishable food stashed away underneath the planet's surface, to the fresh meat and greens grown, harvested and distributed by the Nutritional Department.

It was not bad food by any stretch of the imagination. Sunrisers, such as Thomas, thought of it as the comfort food of their childhood. Yin, such as his parents, usually favoured imported food, for that had been the staple of their childhood. They remembered the days of the War of Vengeance, when Terra had struggled to feed its decimated population, with the orcs and, later on, the goblins shipping over stocks of their own provisions to relieve the starving Terran population.

Oldtimers were notorious for their love of artisanal food.

Artisanal food was produced by Terrans whose chosen art form was either cooking or farming. Some, such as Mira, focused on replicating traditional Terran meals. Others focused more on replicating and improving Old Earth products, particularly food brands. If their products passed the quality standards of their respective guild, they were allowed to package and sell their wares with their Old Earth branding. It was they who now produced the Reese's Peanut Butter Cups, Ferrero Rochere chocolates, Snickers bars, Haribo gummy bears, peanut M&Ms and banana-flavoured Twinkies, but also the Corona beer, Jack Daniel's bourbon, Suntory whiskey and Grey Goose vodka which packed Ashaver's phaiser.

Thomas looked over towards the table next to Ashaver, to see a glass full of an amber liquid. As he looked beneath the table, he noticed a half-empty bottle of a Japanese whiskey. For a moment, Thomas wondered if it would be more polite to not open a fresh bottle, since it would imply that he would remain for the period of time needed to empty it himself, or if it were, perhaps, better to ask politely if he could have a glass from the Hierach's bottle.

Ashaver, it would appear, had an answer. 'Bust open the gin! It's good and I'm feeling a glass myself later!' Thomas complied, fishing out a bottle with an audible clinking sound as it bounced against its neighbours. '... and grab some snacks for the munchies!' Thomas, once more, complied by taking out a box of coconut Raffaello

'Get the Marlenka box!' Thomas awkwardly placed the white and red box back in its place and pulled out the solicited brown and yellow box. '... and some Pringles from the pantry!' Thomas closed the cold section of the phaiser and opened to room-temperature cabinet to reveal an ungodly amount of Pringles and tortilla chips.

'Eh... which flavour?' There were at least a dozen colours.

'I don't give a fuck... Barbecue!' Thomas complied, grabbing a clean glass from the open washing machine before returning to Ashaver's side.

The Hierarch, eyes fixed on the screen, passed him the blunt and grabbed the box of Pringles from his hand. 'D'you follow the *jogo bonito*, lad?'

'Football, you mean, sir?'

'No, cricket... Yes, football!' Ashaver popped about a dozen chips into his mouth in one go.

'I... used to play a little in school, sir. It was part of training. But, I never watched games from before – this game is from before, right?'

'Yup. It's a FIFA World Cup final. See,' Ashaver spoke while chewing, 'I never watched football growing up. I always thought it was stupid. I thought the sport itself was stupid. I thought the people watching it were stupid for watching it. But, then...' He swallowed. '...then I started seeing what was going on...' His words drifted off, as he washed the Pringles down with whiskey.

He didn't continue though, instead focusing on what appeared to be a clear foul in the argentine box. 'Penalty! What? No penalty? Fucking idiots – they had VAR for this game?' he asked Acosta.

The Mexican nodded.

Ashaver went on. 'Fucking pieces of shit... I'm telling you! It's rigged for Messi! They couldn't give it Ronaldo – thank Christ – because the Moroccans were just too good and they didn't give a fuck about the powers that be. Brazil was too weak for Neymar to drag out of the shitter. So, they're going to give it to fucking Messi... fucking bullshit...'

Thomas couldn't help it anymore. 'Uhm, sir?'

'Yes, lad?' The Hierarch asked between chews.

'I... I don't know what happens in this game, but–' he began.

Before he could formulate his question, Ashaver interrupted him. '– neither do I.'

Now Thomas was even more confused. 'Then... but...'

Ashaver figured out his obvious question. 'I may have been alive back then, but I never followed football. The bug hit me a few years ago. I've been catching up ever since. I don't google results or nothing like that, so it doesn't spoil it for myself. I get to watch the games completely oblivious to what's going to happen next.' He gestured to Acosta. 'Marco, here, loves the footie. Always did. But, you know, the reanimation process is weird and he's forgotten a lot. Though, he never tells me what he does remember so I can still root for whomever I want to without knowing what's gonna happen.'

Ashaver paused. 'To be honest with you lad, maybe I did use to watch football every now and then, but whatever memories I had of it went away.' Thomas wasn't sure if the Hierarch was still following the game or if he was gazing off into the distance. 'I spent a good three hours dead the first time and another eight the second time. I lost a lot of shit. Even now, I don't know if I ever watched *The Sopranos* in full, or if I just watched a lot of clips on YouTube. Middle school is gone entirely. I have no idea if I ever went to Disneyland. I'm not sure if I loved pierogi or hated them... A lot is gone.'

Thomas didn't really have time to mull over this surprising moment of openness, since Ashaver snapped out the moment back into something else. 'Anyway, I see it now for what it is.' He pointed his glass at the screen. 'Kinetic intelligence and nationalism. D'you ever hear of Johan Cruyff?'

Thomas shook his head.

'Dutch football player and coach.' Thomas paused. 'D'you know what the "Dutch" were?'

Thomas nodded. 'They lived in the Verdriet Moeras, before the End Times.'

'Aye! A great people they were! And Cruyff! Cruyff was one of their greatest. A genius that man was. In the world before, some looked down upon athletes. Many looked up. Most thought that the ventures of the body were lesser than the exploits of the mind... I guess that still stands true today. You look at these lads here...' He gestured at the screen. '*Phew...* if you only could imagine by what rigour and effort they ended up there, on that pitch on that day. Years of training and testing and competing, ever since they were wee lads and their legs themselves were naught but new toys to them!'

'You see, I think a lot about what they were and what you are now.' He finally glanced at Thomas. 'Sunrisers. You grow up kinda like them. You're born in families or in gardens. We feed you. We love you. We raise you. We dress you. We train you...' Ashaver's tone grew sombre as his mind drifted towards thoughts unsavoury '...we send you off to war... and the ones that survive we call...' He raised a balled fist into the air. 'Men! Women! Terrans! Champions! And then... *again*! We find some other war for you! Every year your cohorts grow thinner, as ours did. One day, if nature is just, it will be you who will be old and I who will be in the ground. Then again, I... eh... huh...' He seemed to smirk at a thought both comical and cruel. 'Then again, I do sometimes get a lil' sad knowing that you will, one day, send children into the grave, as we did with you...'

Ashaver paused to judge a decision by the referee. 'This fucker's Polish and look at him! The cunt! He wants Messi to win too!' The Hierarch stopped talking for a while, taking hearty sips from his whiskey glass.

After a while, Thomas couldn't take it anymore. 'Sir?'

'Yes, lad?' He began refilling his glass.

'What does that have to do with Johan Cruyff?' He was afraid of sounding stupid; perhaps the connection was self-explanatory, but he just didn't get it.

'Oh, yeah, Cruyff! He once said that *football is a simple game, but there's nothing more difficult than playing simple football.*' He brought his fist to his own head, then burst open his hand in an explosive gesture. 'A lot of things in life are like that. Hell... *war* is like that. Sun Tzu ain't got nothing on Cruyff!'

He gestured for Thomas to pass him back the blunt. 'You see, I got into football *after* I actually started doing physical stuff. I mean, don't get me wrong. I wasn't no fatso. I did exercises and tactical, physical training when I was in the Wywiadu – the old Polish intelligence agency – but it was... you know... to get it done and get through with it. I never really, deep down, saw any real merit to it. I just did it because I didn't want to get cut from the program. But, then, I started doing stuff with my body a lot in the Fimbulwinter. I was really good at it, I saw, when I *had* to be good at it. Football? I sucked. But, if they made me play football *for my life*, Jesus Christ, I would have been better than Messi!'

'I was like that. A lot of people weren't. A lot of people collapse under pressure. I was different. To be honest, most of us that survived were like that. Not only did we not break under pressure, we actually got better. One of the ways I got better was by learning how to move. How to dodge, how to strike, how to hold my hands, where to keep my eyes... All of that stuff is kinetic intelligence and some people are visibly better at it.'

He pointed at the sky. 'Cruyff was one of them. Not only was he incredibly good at knowing how to move his own body, but he also knew how to have eleven bodies move perfectly. It's no different in war. The same principles roughly apply. Just that, if you fuck up, most of the time you die... and the kinetic intelligence is just part of why I find this,' he pointed at the screen again, 'this football thing now to be so interesting.'

'Seeing the players on the pitch do their brilliant dance is awesome in itself, I get it! However, there's something else that is really going on. You immediately notice it when you ask yourself: why *did* people watch it? Why did people watch so much of it? Why did they fucking care? Why did they fucking care *so much*? And that... that is what brings me to nationalism!' He took a puff from his blunt. 'You see, I wasn't a big fan of the whole Avenger Legions thing.'

Thomas was unable to stop one of his eyebrows from rising. 'Yes, lad, I wasn't. It was dangerous to me, in my head! I mean, we'd been killing each other for dumb reasons for thousands of years. Now, I don't know who threw the first stone, but I do know that, by the end, everyone lived in glass houses. Everyone's group had done their share of fucked-up shit and they had mostly done it because of the fucked up shit other people did in the past. Now, when we were in the War of Vengeance, we all felt like one people for the first time. No Poles. No Russians. No Americans. No Chinese. For the first time in forever, we were all the same nation. Now, I also wasn't ok with us deleting out cultures. Quite frankly, I think having so many different cultures was what made us so great. It also made us interesting.'

'But, I didn't want it to get too separated. I was worried when I saw Djibril roll only with his Muslims and Georgians. When every General started having their own little group, from their own little ethnicity, around all the time... it bothered me! But, then, it was Laur – of all people – who had the idea. "Let's let people do that, but in a smart way!" Let's do it as a martial elite! I see now what he was thinking. It was basically like this whole football thing: let's have these teams, which would compete with one another by seeing who could be better at making war on someone else!'

'No matter what we do, groups are going to form, so who cares if some of them get built upon their existing history? Let's go further, and have Nations act as football fan clubs and the government act as a football club supporting a team. The people who aren't on the team are still gonna be into football and, if the planet is actually just one big football association, then, over time, not only will the elite teams be better at football, but the entire association!'

He pointed at the screen again and said simply: '*Football*!'

Thomas was rattled, but intrigued. 'But... but you support some teams and not others?'

'I don't support any national football teams from the British Archipelago, the Iberian Peninsula or Latin America.'

'... in football?' *or...*

'In football. Yes! I ain't got no beef with the Redcoats, the Conquistadors or the Barra Bravas, nor with the English, the Spanish or the Brazilians. But, I don't support the English, Spanish and Brazilian national football teams... or the Argentinean one...'

'... from over half a century ago?'

'Oh, not just half a century. I hate teams from two hundred years ago!'

'... and... why those teams in particular?'

'Well, you see, I–' Ashaver was interrupted from his nostalgic little rant by a quick successions of knocks at the door. Before Ashaver could even shout his permission, the door to the apartment opened and Laur Pop revealed himself in the doorway, before casually walking in.

'Hey, Laur! You know the point of knocking is that the person inside has to let you in. Right?' Ashaver quipped at the General.

'You were going to let me in anyway,' Pop responded, as he walked in. The Romanian nodded at everyone in the room, then made his way to the kitchen table, where he dropped off a file, then noticed the file Thomas had just brought over, which he immediately began browsing it. After a few quick page turns, he picked it up and continued to read it as he opened the phaiser and took out a beer.

'This is Shoshanna's list. It's bigger than what I proposed,' he declared.

'Well, it ain't big enough. Mira and Thomas here weren't on it.'

'They're not the issue. The issue is that it's basically half the High Command. Which is a problem, since many should be on the surface, observing Diwali publicly.'

'Are Uma, Deepak–' Ashaver began.

Pop cut him off. 'The South Asians aren't enough. We need at least two thirds of the High Command celebrating it as well. It's not just an Indian thing anymore, Tomasz, people everywhere celebrate it. I even got some candles myself last year.'

'Fine. Make the cuts. But you gotta break the news yourself!' Ashaver waived his agreement.

'I will.' Pop looked up at Thomas. 'You brought it over?' He gestured at the file in his hand.

'Yes, sir!' Thomas replied.

'Hmmm.' Pop acknowledged, his eyes circling between Thomas' eyes, the back of Ashaver's head and the screen before them. 'Let me guess: football was a stand-in for nationalism; Avenger Legions are like football teams; Messi and Ronaldo suck because people worshipped them?'

Thomas laughed nervously, as Ashaver joyously giggled out loud. H turned to whisper loudly to the young lieutenant. 'As you can tell, I've been working on this theory for a while.'

'Well, you're not really the first one to think that, you know?' Pop went back to the list. 'There's like a dozen elves here. That's too many. We *need* Daw there. The rest are fully optional.' Pop paused his browsing for a moment, looking off into space. 'Your girlfriend can't come,' he commented casually, before returning to the file.

Thomas swallowed hard. *Oh, boy! Her name wasn't even on there.*

Ashaver heard the statement. 'Oh, you have a girlfriend now?!' He slapped him on the shoulder. 'Well, where's she from?'

Here we go... 'She, uh...'

Laur let out an audible chuckle, stopping Thomas in his tracks. 'Menegroth,' the General answered.

'Ohhh!!!' Ashaver's eyes were still focused on the screen. 'Good! They fucked our parents up. We fucked them up. Now our children fuck them. I say "God bless"! Love is love, lad, and love is a wonderful thing! Enjoy every moment of it! Bring her on a date with you for the birth of *kingdom come*! I'll bet she's never been to one of those before!'

He turned to Pop, interrupting his viewing. 'What the fuck, Laur? We can have two or three of 'em present. It doesn't matter which ones, give the boy a treat.' Pop shrugged, shook his head then nodded. 'Ah, there ya go lad! The Grinch won't steal Christmas!'

'I... I will! Thank you, sir!' Thomas felt waves of relief course through him,

Pop didn't even have to look up from the file in his hands to see his reaction. 'Oh, don't worry, mate. You won't be the only interplanetary couple there. Lakshmi's bringing her hippy too.'

Ashaver and Thomas both asked. 'Fiol?'

'Yeah, yeah, the hippy with the dirty feet.'

'I like Fiol!' Ashaver commented. *Me too...*

'Oh, he's alright. Good husband.' Pop's acknowledgement came with a complete lack of care.

'Good father to that little girl too. Did you hear she's pregnant again?' Ashaver began elaborating on Fiol's achievements as a husband and a father.

'Of course I did. It's another girl.' Pop's tone suggested that it could have been another duck for all he cared.

'Oh, yeah, then where's all this animosity towards Fiol coming from?' Ashaver's tone had changed now, becoming a frightening mix of coldness and playfulness.

Pop finally looked up from the file. 'Nowhere...' Pop squinted at Ashaver, seemingly searching for the meaning of his words. 'What the fuck? I just think he's ... you know...'

'I know. But you should be happy for Lakshmi. *I* am happy for Lakshmi. *She* is happy with *him* and that makes *me* happy.' Ashaver looked back and forth between Thomas, Acosta and Pop, gesturing towards himself, as well as the absent Lakshmi and Fiol.

'Oh, what the fuck, I'm happy for her too.' Pop did not appear to be in any way intimidated. Just confused.

'Oh, well, then stop being such a shitty friend and be happy!' Ashaver snapped. His voice like that of a proud teacher, having just successfully put down a naughty pupil who knew nothing of human empathy.

'Huh... I will.' Pop finally put down the file. He slowly made his way right behind Ashaver, hands on his hips, eyes on the screen.

'2022 World Cup Final?'

'Yes,' Ashaver answered coldly.

'Argentina–France?'

'Yup,' the Hierarch answered, his tone deadpan.

'Huh...' Pop shook his head, eyes fixated not on the screen, but on the back of Ashaver's head. '... *fucking Messi...*' was all he said as he shook his head.

Ashaver turned around, looking briefly at Pop, then back to the screen, then over to Acosta, who looked somewhere else. His head slowly shifted back towards the screen and he let out an exasperated sigh. '*Motherfucker*!'

'What? You didn't know?' Pop raised his eyebrows in mock surprise.

'Go fuck yourself!' Ashaver let the glass in his hand fall a couple of inches to the table below, making a loud sound as it met the glass table below and a few droplets of whiskey sprayed across the table. One of them connected with the lit blunt resting on Ashaver's ashtray, making a subtle sizzling sound.

'I'm supposed to go fuck myself?' Pop's voice rose, as he began pointing at his chest. 'Fuck you! I'm running around like a maniac trying to keep this shit together and you're sitting here watching games? Fuck you, Tomasz! I'm fucking exhausted! We're all fucking exhausted! You just sit here being all chill and dandy. You throw it into our faces that you're too good to get involved because that would be "Big-Brother-fucking-behaviour" and that shit's "beneath" you!' Pop had been angrily pacing around the room, yet he suddenly changed course and came up close to Ashaver, wagging a finger in his face. 'But you never lose a chance to look like the good guy now, don't you?'

'What the fuck are you on about?' Ashaver's face was now the definition of irritated.

'I come in here and the first thing you do is talk shit about me in front of the kid so you can look cool? Because you're fucking space Jesus and I'm the Bogeyman? Fuck you!'

A long pause formed between the two men. Pop stared down Ashaver with unblinking eyes, as Ashaver's face passed through various stages of confusion. 'You need to get laid more!' the Hierarch proclaimed, before turning back to his game.

'... *Ai nid tu git leid mor...*' Pop shook his head in annoyance at Ashaver's base comments.

'You do! You're on the fucking edge all the time! It's all edgy-ness with you.' He pointed towards Thomas. 'You pointed a gun at this kid's head for no reason, you fucking psycho! You could've just had a conversation with him like a *normal* human being!' *Ashaver knew about that*?!

Now it was Pop's turn to be irritated. 'What the fuck?! He was taking control of the conversation! I had to put him on the spot!' *Well, fuck you too, General Pop!*

'You and your fucking psycho solutions to innocent shit.' He started pointing at the pacing Pop. 'You need to fucking get laid more!' he repeated. 'Can't you see no woman can tolerate you?' He turned to Thomas 'He ain't even gay! He's just creepy like that!'

'Ohhh!' This was the first sound Acosta had made the entire evening.

'Well, he fucking is! Now he's hearing voices and shit. He just squirms in the corner every meeting at High Command only to start speaking like he's travelled to the edge of the light, beyond the dread marshes of oblivion, and there he beheld fucking annihilation and the ghosts of the past come to set things straight!' He turned to Thomas. 'That keeps him fucking up all night! Not heaven! Not doing something constructive! He sits in his little vampire villa like a ghoul and reads which German boy is fucking which elf girl!' Thomas' eyes widened and Pop paused his pacing. Acosta started rubbing his chin in frustration.

'What? It's true!' Ashaver turned to Thomas. 'Ask him! He probably knows everything about her by now! Cup size, pussy hair, how many people she's slept with... If you wanna get the file on this girl, ask him!' He punctuated his words with crude gestures.

Thomas felt a bit compelled to speak now. 'That won't be necess– '

Pop cut him off. 'Shut up, this is national security!' The General looked at Thomas as if he were surprised that he would even dare open his mouth at a moment like this.

'Pfff! "National security". You're just fucking obsessed with shit that's over... I told you to find something productive to do! Not fucking go all fucking tinfoil hat about Hitler still being in Argentina...'

'Fuck you, Tomasz! We've been over this!' Thomas got the feeling that Pop was being honest and they had been over whatever they were talking about now before.

'We have and I understand where you're coming from. I always did! Just that it's been years since we've even had a sighting of one...'

Now Pop cut him off, laying forth an argument which Thomas could tell he had made before. 'Daw says the two are still unaccounted for, plus there's thousands of missing ...'

'I know what Daw says. I also know we burned a lot of ships back then. We never did fucking CSI – that's "Crime Scene Investigation" for you, lad, it's an acronym – on all of them!'

'Oh, but for fuck's sake!' Pop slapped his thighs in frustration and resumed his angry pacing. Thomas could tell he was thinking about the thousandth different way to say the same thing he had said so many times before. The only problem was... what the hell were they talking about?

Ashaver noticed his look. 'Did you ever hear about two elves named Eliafas and Cantor?'

He had. Many times. Dark names they were. 'They were,' he looked towards Pop, 'or they *are* the two highest-ranking Svart who remain unaccounted for? After the War?'

'Aye, lad. We lost them after Gondolin. Them and many others. We hunted them down for years and put a lot of them in the ground. But, we never found Eliafas or Cantor, as well as a few thousand serfs, retainers and courtesans who fled after the War ended. Pop here, *requested* and received the task of continuing the hunt after the rest of us moved on to other matters. Everyone else thinks that the task is done and there's no point obsessing over loose ends. At the end of the day, they might have simply died in the chaos of the war and, if they didn't, they're likely too far or too weak to ever bother us again–'

Pop interrupted. '– *Now!!!* They're too weak *now*. But given enough time–'

'LAUR, I FUCKING KNOW!!!' Ashaver had finally lost his temper. 'BUT I ALSO KNOW THAT YOU BEING A MOODY CUNT ISN'T *FUCKING* HELPING ANYONE!!!'

Pop seethed at his old friend for a long time. The tension in the room was palpable.

'You're right. It's not. I hope I'm wrong.' Just like that, he relented and, as suddenly as he had started the confrontation, he ended it. Pop made his way towards the door and paused before opening it. 'I never said I *knew* that they're still somewhere out there. I just said that we shouldn't behave like we know for sure they're not. I'm sorry about the game...' Pop didn't turn to face Ashaver properly, but he did nod his head towards the screen.

'Don't worry about it, mate. I know where it comes from... but, please, go get laid...'

'Off, go suck my dick!' Pop got annoyed again before saying his goodbyes to the three of them and leaving.

'... or, at least, stop living like a fucking werewolf!' Ashaver shouted after the General as Pop shut the door behind him.

He turned to Thomas. 'I love that man! But what I love about him also makes him insufferable.' Ashaver started downing Pringles again, like nothing had just happened. 'You know what? We live in post-apocalyptic fascist police state where everyone's always a soldier on active duty. I know you don't see it because you're like a fish in water in it. It's all you've ever known. But, I see it and so does Pop. Do you know what the end result of fascism is?'

Thomas did. It was taught in schools. 'They... turn on each other?'

'Yup! In the absence of a big bogeyman lurking in the shadows, ready to genocide them, the people turn on each other, since they are part of a system that can only survive if there is an enemy to destroy. With that in mind, I'm thankful for Laur's obsession and insistence that the Svart are still out there. It keeps people on their toes. It gives them another reason to stick around the fireplace for a little longer. I mean, don't get me wrong, the Continuum is a greater threat of orders of unfathomable magnitude than some surviving dushman cell. But, still, quite frankly, I'm happy Pop's always there with his bell, clinking away that the end is once more nigh.'

'But, sir, do *you* believe that they might still be out there?'

'They might. The Svart were... their arrogance was their weakness always. I think that if any Svart are still around, their arrogance would be gone. In the absence of that flaw, they might one day become formidable once more. But, they would also be a traumatized people, constantly on the run. Desperate. Fearful. The wound we would have enforced on their collective psyche would have truly changed them, making capable of things we never would have thought possible. The Svart we would snuff out in the first decade after the surrender at Gondolin were... changed... more perhaps even than their old High Elven brethren had changed in the same period of time. If a cell would be around today, they would be almost unrecognizable.'

'But, if there was, what could we do about it?' Thomas was beginning to worry that Ashaver's arguments merely supported Pop's apparent obsession.

The Hierarch answered his own question casually and with no emotion. 'Snuff them out, as they tried to do to us. Anyway... I don't know how France goes down, at least not in this world cup, so we might as well enjoy what we can... I guess it'll happen in extra time.'

It didn't happen in extra time, but at the penalty shootout. With an exasperated sigh, Ashaver told Thomas that he would be going to bed and instructed that he do the same with his girlfriend, whom he now knew was named Toph, was thirty-seven and had a sweet tooth, particularly for Terran pastry. After busting out a few jokes about éclairs, apfelstrudel and spring rolls, he insisted that Thomas grab a bagful of sweets from his phaiser before going back to his apartment.

Thomas thus found himself in his shuttle (which he did not drive while inebriated) observing Clara's driving as the operator took him home.

He pondered things. A great many things. He thought about what a truly strange man Ashaver was. He thought about what kind of man Pop was. He thought about football and he thought about nationalism.

In the last months he had darted across his homeworld, meeting more oldtimers than he could count. He had joked to Mira a few days earlier that, at this rate, he would meet all of them. He had grown up with an idea of who they were: dark and brutal men and women. Most carried a madness in their eyes. Some were loud, others were very quiet. Almost all of them were violent in either movement, voice or even just in their very eyes alone. Most enforced the hierarchies of Terra with an almost brutal rigour. Some, like Ashaver, Adler and, to a degree, Pop, swung the other way, however.

Pop was a courteous, civil man, on the outside at least. Yet, right beneath the quiet charm of his cold eyes, lurked a savagery which Thomas himself had beheld in terror once before. However, there was no doubt in his mind that the man had done what he thought had been necessary to know with absolute certainty the strength of Thomas' conviction and the degree of his dedication. He remembered Pop's words from his first night in Jerusalem, which now felt like a lifetime ago.

> *Your trust in those around you and your faith in our way of life are your last line of defence against the void of nihilism and despair.*

He now believed he could see Pop's words for what they were: a confirmation of Thomas' loyalty to the party, to their mission and to Terra itself as an ideal. That must have been what was needed to join Kralizec. After all, did he not judge others in much the same way now? Why did the Jaegers learn of Kralizec before the rest of German Nation? Was it not due to the fact that their dedication to the cause was seen as superior to that of the average German?

Adler was a kind, gentle woman... to Terrans, orcs, remani, trolls, goblins and demani. Beneath her motherly sheen lay a deep disgust, mistrust and disdain for elves. The Aesir and the ursai she could handle, yet one could tell that she still carried a grudge against their former enemies. Nevertheless, her dislike of their former opponent in the Ayve War paled in comparison to her hatred of elves, which she did a horrible and virtually inexistent job of hiding. Many oldtimers were like that, yet Adler was the one in which the contrast was most visible as she was at her core a caring person. Seeing her switch from her usual, empathetic self, to the cold, yet barely composed, attitude she received elves with was the best example of the fascist hatred which worried Ashaver.

It was a hatred that permeated their society.

It was true that Terra still officially hunted the remaining Svart. The Terran population was in a near-continuous state of frenzy when it came to the idea of killing off any surviving dark elves. In his lifetime, he had seen that hatred slowly shift the intensity of its gaze towards the Continuum, with the Aesir having been briefly caught up in the enraged glare of Terran animosity.

He now thought of Ashaver and the conversation he had just had and realised what kept the Hierarch awake at night.

Without an enemy to fight, what would they become? Was there another way? Thomas thought of the World-Which-Was and beheld horror, as he realised that he had no real way of understanding how life had been before. He had studied the histories of the countries of old and many a night he had lost himself in the films of days long gone. Yet, for all its worth, he truly didn't know if the world was better or worse back then. What's worse, he didn't know if the ways of old were even applicable in their new reality.

Yet, in this new, vast world, there were other ways of doing things. Even within the Alliance itself, alternatives existed.

The goblins lived in a true civilian democracy, with checks and balances put in place to control the worst impulses of both the government and the population. They were also the least warlike and the most traditionally democratic of the Alliance races. To put it better: their democracy was the most intelligible to Terrans. They had three branches of government, with each position of power being democratically elected and delimitated by sensible term limits. They greatly respected personal freedoms, especially the right to property. They even allowed for special communes in which individuals, by their own accord, would come together and live under whatever political systems they so desired. Yet, as always, the goblin world served as a cautionary tale for the Terran mind, as many oldtimers remarked that Moria was the world most similar to the World-Which-Was. Moria was fickle, slow and cumbersome. The goblins themselves openly agreed that they would have likely met extinction, were it not for the other Alliance races constantly forcing them to be more... authoritarian.

The remani lived in what was, essentially, a large wolf pack, with one alpha which directed the pack, former alphas that settled disputes and passed laws, and an expansive network of relationships which permeated their decision-making processes, as each remani did what they thought was best for both their pack and for themselves.

The orcs might have been the most militaristic of the peoples of the Alliance, being the paragon which Terrans aspired to emulate, yet they were also quite democratic and liberal in their own right. The lowliest grunt knew well that they may speak their mind right in the face of the Helmsman with no fear of punishment and in full certainty of the fact that their words mattered. They were a people which could live in true peace and harmony, unless threatened or if their code of honour dictated that they come to the aid of another.

The demani did not have a state, in the traditional sense. They had a revolutionary government which, much like the Terrans themselves, sought new meaning in the world into which it had emerged triumphant. While Terra had reached some semblance of stability in the form of its martial society, the demani of the Andromeda galaxy still found themselves in the constant ebb and flow of political soul-searching. Sometimes the state of the demani was quite dictatorial, as was typical of governments birthed by revolution. Other times, it resembled some type of liberal daydream, where the state was more accessory than necessity.

The elves, ursai, Hyperboreans, Aesir and Vanir all dwelt somewhere on the spectrum of democracy and monarchy, with the Aesir and Vanir believing that they had too much freedom, the elves and the believing that they had just the right amount, and the Hyperboreans believing that freedom was a mental construct which only existed as a delusion of the insecure mind. All had banded together under the banner of the Alliance to increase their chances of survival against the Continuum of Humanity.

And what an empire it was...

On Terra, in school, they had a class called *Terran Political Awareness*. Every citizen would have political awareness classes from the age of ten, up until they began their Allied Host service. They studied the political systems of Old Earth, such as the US democracy, Nazi Germany, Ancient Greece, the Roman Empire, the Middle Kingdoms of China, the Empire of the Rising Sun, Napoleonic Europe, Colonial Africa and Dar al Islam. They also studied political systems which had never existed in the World-Which-Was, but might have, such as *Brave New World, 1984, Fahrenheit 451, The Handmaid's Tale, Children of Men, A Clockwork Orange*, as well as a dozen other worlds of oppressive horror.

The Continuum of Humanity was all of the above and neither. A totalitarian domain of a thousand galaxies and untold numbers of singular lives, among which almost none were that different from the other. A dark chasm of oppression, which swallowed up all difference and excreted uniformity. A system obsessed with the natural order of things, never able to behold the affront to nature it had become. A vast and cumbersome military behemoth, which gobbled up beauty and spat out order. A government beyond despotism, fascism or communism in its complete dedication to control and uniformity. An endless army of near-identical drones of the same alien personality, all convinced of their superiority, righteousness and, most disturbingly of all, their individuality.

No... there doesn't seem to be another way..

Terrans could wail at their misfortune of having attracted the ire of the greatest power in the Known Universe all they wanted, for so it was that the horrible truth was that, even if the Terran people vanquished this New Enemy, they would have to find another and they would have to do so quickly. In some way, Thomas saw Ashaver's twisted logic and beheld the horror it revealed. Without the Continuum, there would be no Alliance and likely no Terra. Their alliance with the other races, though built upon a shared history and a well-earned trust, was nevertheless just one big suicide pact, set in motion to protect them all from the Continuum and other threats that might be lurking still within the darkness of the night sky. Terra itself, without the continuous threat of annihilation, might quickly succumb to the infighting of Old Earth. Even if by some miracle this did not come to pass, such salvation could only come about if 'Terra', as a concept, died, yet the humans of Terra survived.

What a horrible thought...

Adler was right. Terra would die. One way or another. Whether it be under the crushing fist of some unstoppable foe, the infighting of fratricide or by the hands of a victorious Terran people realizing that without an enemy to stab their venom into, their culture of war would poison them.

And, yet, Satya would have to be place for all Terrans. Those of the past who had fought each other. Those of the present, who fought their enemies across the stars. Those of the many possible futures even if in some of them they would be non-existent. In some they would be monsters. Most terrifying of all, in some they would not resemble the Terrans of today in the slightest.

He didn't know about Ashaver, but Thomas did know that he himself did not sleep that well that night, despite the warmth of Toph's arms. Just as he was able to drift off into sleep, he dreamt of Ashaver himself, come to torture him with revelations of reality in his sleep. He saw not the great Terran warrior, champion of a thousand battlefields, but a beast in the shape of a man. He had come to Thomas in his parents' house. Yet, his parents were now gone. He did not know were. He just knew they were gone. He and Toph now lay in his living room, as the dark wings of the First Hierarch had filled the room with darkness. He saw Ashaver raise his great blade and cut Toph down in one fell swoop, before looking down at Thomas himself. Adler and Mira, their eyes black and their ears long, had walked into the room at that point and had laughed mockingly at his loss.

It had been the Hierarch's burning eyes that had made him flee from his own dreams to the refuge of reality and the warm Israeli morning. He went about his duties as before, accepting that he had little time to ponder the brutal nature of the World-Which-Was, as long as there was still work to do for the World-Which-Could-Be. If Ashaver lost sleep over the future of Terra and the Alliance, then good! That meant they lived in a world in which people had the time and ability needed to think about making it better!

As Diwali Day neared, their labour reached a frenzy. They raced all across the world and even to Luna and Mars. Everywhere they went, they set in motion the wheels of careful thought, as every man and woman they illuminated was left to bear the task of balancing secrecy with revelation. Thomas had seen many a grim oldtimer cry, rage and become speechless at his words. Many a night he had gone to bed realizing that, in the day passed, he had forced others to rethink their entire lives.

But, it all wore on him. It even wore on Mira. More-and-more callous they became, as exhaustion also overcame them. Sprinting all across the planet didn't help either, as the days and nights began to bleed into one another, and Thomas could no longer remember being in one place for an entire twenty-four hours. He had not realized that it was dusk when he and Mira, now finding themselves in what had once been the Old Earth country of Bolivia, just outside of Ancohuma, the Holdfast of the Kamayuks, received a message from Adler.

'It's done! We've done all we could and all we had to. Stop now! Rest! I'll see you tomorrow!' Without a word spoken between them, the two made their way from where they had parked their shuttle, down towards the rocky coast of Lake Titicaca. They collapsed onto the dry shores, just outside the reach of the water's grasp.

As the distant sun crept towards the edge of the world, they could hear the song of crickets met the soothing sound of restless waves caressing the beach. No aircraft could be seen in the sky. To their backs, the imposing black of the Citadel of Ancohuma was peppered with warm candlelight, as the Kamayuks readied themselves for the night. A friendly wind danced through their hair and rushed past their ears, as the last of the sun's rays bid their goodbyes to their dry skin. Just as the colours of the sky began to change from light blue and bright gold, to a vibrant orange and a warm red, a flock of birds rushed inland above them, chirping tales of their adventures across the waves.

They were both quiet for a long time, as they allowed themselves to finally enjoy a moment of peace. Indeed, they had done all they could, as had everyone else. Tomorrow, the sun would set in this very same place, as it would all across their world, in much the same way as it had before. The world itself would remain much the same, with the earth continuing to cuddle the lake's waters, as it had since times immemorial. A pause had occurred in the days of Rapture, when the high plain of the Altiplano had shattered and the fresh waters of Lake Titicaca had slipped from between the Andean fingers and into the hungering ocean below. It had been the Kamayuks themselves that had mended the cup of the mountains and filled it, once more, with the fresh water of mountain springs, returning this place, once more, to an image of wild tranquillity. Homesteads had sprung up along the new shores and their flickering lights stretched across the waters, mocking the arrival of the sombre darkness.

The sky above them began to blossom, revealing the brilliant garden of the night, as stars unnumbered flowered above them. They would shine tomorrow as well, as they had since the dawn of time and until their distant end. Beneath them, on this world, as on many others across the cosmos, little lights would flicker stubbornly in the face of the impotent darkness, as families would share a meal before the coming of the little death that was the night. Mothers would tell their little treasures that it was time for bed and in tongues uncountable small voices would beg for stories of things that had been, things that were and things that could be. Dancers would emerge from the twilight, their movements too shy to brave the judging light of the sun. They would trust only in the discretion of the pale moon to keep the hundred secrets of their honest movements away from eyes not worthy of such sights.

Some would not sleep that night, their minds awake with an awareness of their condition. For some, it would be the love of others that would keep their eyes fixed upon their ceilings, while, for others, it would be only the love of themselves that would give them little comfort in the empty night. Some would be greedy, wishing to stretch the moment of a wonderful day into the blank canvas of the darkness, while a few planned a better day to follow.

The two Terrans gazed away into the horizon, yet saw no sunset, as their eyes were locked not onto a place, but onto a time. For there would never be a time like this for them again. Tomorrow would change all that they had known before. They knew that which tonight was known to only but a few, but which would soon tie them all together in this world and, perhaps, another.

'Do you think people are watching?' Thomas broke the silence.

'From beyond?' Mira knew what Thomas meant, for such was the way of the dearest of friendships.

'Yes. When I was a kid, I wished I could go back in time and watch the Egyptians build the pyramids. I always wondered how things were like back then. I also would have wanted to see my parents, when they were children. To see in them what I would later discover in myself. To see Yeats, back when he was a puppy, as he cuddled up beneath his mother, with his little eyes closed and his tail beneath his nose. Maybe, I would even watch myself, from behind a one-way mirror, and see my old self be unaware of what lay in the future.'

Mira smiled a distant smile, her eyes never leaving the horizon, as she allowed the breeze to play with her hair. 'Maybe they are. Maybe we also are. Would you do things any different if you knew they were?'

'No,' he smiled now also, 'I've always behaved as if someone was watching.'

Mira chuckled. 'Figures...'

'Well, I have!' He shared the chuckle. 'It's like how Shakespeare said: "all the world's a stage and all men are just actors". You know that presence you feel? The one that's always been and is everywhere? Might as well give it a show. Might as well be entertaining to watch.'

'The presence doesn't see, Thomas. The presence *is*. It doesn't just see you, it is you.'

'Would you do anything different if you knew someone was watching?' he asked.

'I don't know. Would you, if you knew that *no one* was watching?' she shot back.

'No. I wouldn't. Because, even if no one was watching, I would still be watching. Whatever shitshow I put on would be mine to bear and that's worse than being embarrassed in front of anyone.'

Mira's eyes dropped slightly. 'I... I think I would do things different. If someone was watching us.'

'Because they would judge?'

'No. Because I would like to communicate with them.' Her eyes drifted away from the waters of the lake and to the sky above. 'I would like to know how they felt. Who they were! What do they want? Do they want anything at all? I would have questions. I would like to know how the world came to be the way it is. If they watch, why do they watch?'

'The same reason why we would watch. Because we care.'

'We care because it relates to us. Because it's our story.'

'True. But this story takes place on a vast, infinite stage in infinite instalments and timelines. If our story is part of it all, is not all our story?'

'It is... but, does that change anything about it? That we know it is just one of many?'

'It doesn't make it any less than what it is. Seems to me like we're the caretakers of our own story. It's our job to make it great.'

'Why?' she asked.

'For us... for the presence... for those we care about... there are reasons enough.'

'I don't think the presence cares if we do a great job.'

'Do you think the presence cares about anything we do?'

'Anything we *do*? No. I don't.' She took in a deep breath of air and leaned back on her elbows. 'If we die, and all the religious people were right, and I'm brought up before God himself and he announces the commencement of His judgement... I will not be concerned about the things I did. The killing, the stealing, the drinking, the smoking... everything else... I don't think those will be the issue.'

'What would you be concerned about?' Mira had never spoken of these things to him.

'The way I *felt*.' She shared a glance with his him. 'The jealousy. The envy. The pain I caused... to myself and to others... The fact that I wanted people to feel fear... The rage...' She turned back to look upon the waves. 'If you read all those old holy books and really try to understand what the Author really *meant*... He didn't really care that much about what food you ate or what clothes you wore. He cared only about how that made you feel.'

'Would you change the way you felt if you knew that... *that* would be the case?'

'No. The way I see things, if God really made all that is and everything that will be, it's all His will *and* all His responsibility. If God made me, I am the way I am in this world because He wanted me to be... me. He wanted me to want to be what I wanted to be and to feel the way I feel. I can try to control and change it, but... wouldn't my own control over myself simply be just me being me? If I can control something bad about me, isn't that only because God gave me the ability to? If I were evil, would I know it?'

'Sounds awfully nihilistic, Mira.' It both did and didn't.

'It may *sound* nihilistic, but it doesn't *feel* like that. At least, not to me. It sounds to me like I am allowed the sanctity of my own judgement. It means that... who I am is who I am and no one else is truly like me. The presence doesn't care if I do a great job at being me. The presence seems to care only that I *am* me. It's why it made me the way I am.'

'And if you felt bad – or felt evil – a lot?' *I don't think you're going to Hell, Mira.*

'The fact that I'd probably know if that was the case is probably going to be enough to make sure everything's going to be all right. If I don't... if there's ways I've been evil which I never even had the ability to understand, let alone prevent, it changes nothing.'

They both drifted across the chill evening breeze, as it soothed their skin, kissed by the sharp sun of the Andean Mountains over the course of the day. Thomas felt his back muscles finally begin to relax after an entire day of intense conversation. It was hard to tell someone that their brethren had been working on an afterlife program for the last years, without thinking you worthy of involvement, and that tomorrow would be the day when Heaven would begin.

'This whole thing... it changes nothing, doesn't it?'

Mira smiled, understanding the meaning of Thomas' words. 'Oh, it'll change a few things...'

'Intergalactic war, planetwide identity crisis... me and you won't be doing missionary work anymore...' He smiled, realising that they had made many fond memories together.

'Oh, well, that'll be a relief. I find all of it to be very tiring...' She didn't really have a habit of complaining, but now seemed to be one of the times when she had had enough.

Which surprised Thomas. 'Oh, you do? I thought you enjoyed telling stuffy oldtimers that they have no idea how the world works and that you have come to bring the light.'

'I'm tired of pretending that I think it really matters to them spiritually...'

'It... it doesn't?'

'No, it doesn't. You're right... nothing will change. Things will go on as before. People will make up their own minds about what they think is right and wrong. What happened and what didn't. Leaders will move the people by making them believe they all have the same view of what happened, as well as the same desire to do what's right and not what's wrong. There will be people that will twist the words and the facts in ways they see as right. There will be people who we will all agree will just be wrong... Nothing will change in the way people live their day-to-day lives. It will matter little if they believe our version of Heaven is real or not. The great mysteries will probably endure even in Satya, because it is a house built from the ground-up, not from the sky-down. That's all that we're doing, if you ask me: we're just making a house for ourselves. I still want to know who made the mud we made the bricks to build the house out of.'

'Fearless... You always were fearless...' It was at times such as these that Thomas was truly in awe of Mira. He could only hope that perhaps, one day, he himself could be as magnificent as she.

'It's not about *fear*, Thomas. You always speak so much of fear.' Mira's eyes wandered, seemingly looking for something far beyond the horizon. 'In truth, I never understood why you were afraid. I never understood why knowing consciously that which you have known in your heart to be true for your entire life, scared you. I don't understand why anyone is afraid of what might come after. I can understand how you can be afraid of things of this life while being alive. I could even imagine being afraid after death of something within the realm of death. But, I see no purpose in being afraid, in this life, of what comes after death.'

Mira paused, seemingly mulling over her next words. 'I am only afraid of things in this world that would make me think that there is no good in this world. Because, if you don't think that there is anything good in this world, there is no point in living it and that would be such a shame... I have so many wonderful memories of this world. I have felt so many wonderful things. I have seen so many wonderful things. It's... just the fact that I can see the beauty and that makes it all so beautiful and I'd hate to see it all go to waste...'

She smiled and her eyes once more visited his. 'It's why I am so angry at you sometimes. It's why I am so angry with everyone I care about so often... I *will not* allow you to become someone I don't think is wonderful. I won't allow you to make me doubt the beauty of this world and what it can be. It hurt me when I saw that your fear had turned you into someone I could only pity and not admire. And so, I hated your fear and I hated *you*. I hated you for making me care for you; only for you to slip, inch by inch, away from that which I could admire.'

'Well, I'm glad I didn't let you down.'

'Oh, you did... Everyone does, from time to time. When that happens, I tell myself that I am too selfish. That the only love that exists is love that is pure and pure love means loving someone even if they're not who you wanted them to be. Because... that's all we all want, now, isn't it? To be loved for who we are, not for being who someone else wants, just so they can love us. You see, Thomas, I say "I don't care" all the time... but, the truth is, I care a lot. I care a lot about the world being a wonderful place, full of beauty and joy.'

'But, I want it to be true. I want it to be real. I want it to have... experiential veracity. I want people to smile because they feel like smiling. I want them to be nice to one another, because they feel like being nice to one another, not because it's expected. And that means that I have to accept that, sometimes, people will do things I think are reprehensible or foolish. Because, only if I do, can I also accept that my own love for them is real. If I don't... it's just selfishness and selfishness drains all beauty from things. Sometimes instantly and sometimes over a lifetime. When someone I care for becomes someone I don't like, I love them in the only way that it is still possible.

'I love them by leaving.'

Thomas was stunned at what this meant... he could infer her meaning, yet it was her actions that startled him. They pointed towards one single thing. 'You... you don't think it's possible, don't you?'

A pained little smile crossed Mira's face, as she understood what Thomas was asking. 'I think that, if it is possible, it won't resemble anything we saw in Rasmussen's little lab. I don't think it'll be anything like what Fiol and Lakshmi lived through. I think that it's impossible to recreate the conditions of the afterlife in this life.' She smirked. 'Which, from what I recall, was one of your main critiques, now, wasn't it?'

Thomas nodded.

Mira continued. 'In my heart, I hope that it is. But, I'm comfortable not knowing, for now, what'll be the case. I can only hope for the best. For myself and everyone else. Beyond that... I think we've done everything we could. Now we get to live the rest of our lives knowing that we did our best. I don't know about you...but I feel as if, in the grand scheme of things, it matters very little.'

Now was the moment. The moment Thomas had always wondered about. The moment Mira had always avoided. The question he had always wanted to ask her, throughout the entirety of his darkness. 'Mira... can I ask a personal question?'

'I think about my parents every day.'

Wow... I guess there wasn't even a need to speak the words.

Mira continued. 'I still talk to them. In my head. I never met them, but... they're everywhere. I feel as if I got to know them, not as their child, but as their friend, for it was their friends who told me who they were.' Mira sighed. 'I don't know if I will see them in the next life. I don't know if I would even see them as my parents, for they never were my parents in this life. I... I only hope that they are happy, if they are anywhere at all. If they know of me, I hope they're proud.'

'I... I wish that I mattered more...' Mira paused. For the first time in his life, Thomas saw her do something which he never thought she was capable of.

She gulped. She swallowed her words. Then... a rage. A flash of rage crossed her eyes as she looked at the sunset before her. For a fraction of a second, Thomas could swear he saw the sun double its pace, fleeing for safety away from her vengeful glare. She looked at the ground, as if to tell the golden globe in the sky that it wouldn't be safe from her anger if it crossed beyond the horizon.

'I wish I mattered more to them. I wish that they would have chosen to live... for me. I wish they would have found a way... a way out. A way which did not involve them being... being away. I... I look around and all I see are people ready to do what they did. Ready to die for... for Terra. Why? What is the purpose of all of this? Survival? How... how *lame*... what a little nothing that is. I wish they knew... I hope that they know, wherever they are – *if* they are – that if I could chose between this life without them and a life with them... I would make that choice in a heartbeat. My last heartbeat.' The hairs on Thomas' back stood up, as they tried to get away from the chill going down his spine.

'And... yet... Nothing is certain, Thomas Muller... and I choose to live this life. This big, wonderful life and I tell myself that, if my mother wouldn't have thought that life could be beautiful even without her, she wouldn't have given birth to me. She would have taken me with her. I tell myself that if my father would have known that I was alive, he wouldn't have done what he did. He would have lived. I tell myself that he killed himself because he did not want to live in a world without my mother or myself and that, perhaps, if he knew that one of us was alive, he would not have left me alone.'

'And, so... I talk to them. I tell them I wish I would have met them. I tell them I hate them, because they left me here alone. I tell them I love them. I tell them I am grateful. I tell them that I live for myself *and* for them. I look all around me and I see all of these people... so ungrateful to be alive... throwing their lives away into... into nothing. Either a quick death or a long one. It makes me so angry... so fucking angry... Sometimes I wonder if it will ever end or if this is how things will always be. Perhaps they are even like this in the next world. Perhaps people get bored of Heaven. They take it for granted. They turn other people's joys and hopes into suffering and then... then they leave.'

'So, I let people be themselves and I am not afraid. I am not afraid of death or what comes after. If there is life after death, then everyone who would have died will know what it means to lose. To throw something beautiful away. Perhaps that is the only way to make a better world. To have a world where everyone treasures what they have, because they know what it feels like to not have it anymore. To have to...' She paused, her eyes searching for something which her smile found. '... to have to look at a world without you in it anymore and to see the pain your absence causes. To have to see how much your absence can hurt even someone who never met you.'

She never shed a tear. Thomas understood, for the first time since he had met her, why that was the case.

There were no more tears left.

She was right. Thomas saw that now. The world wouldn't change. People had lived hoping that something awaited them beyond the veil of death for a long time. The world they had produced was the one they lived in now. It was a world in which people knew that there was beauty. The expectation of a better existence after it had made no difference to them. Those that could make the world a wonderful place would still do so, while those who would make it miserable would go on and do so further. In the long run, having a place to go to after death did not change the ancient struggle of mankind.

The struggle to make their own world, the one they found themselves in now, a better place.

That meant loving that which was not under your control, for what other way could one describe life, as that which is, by definition, outside of your control? We did not choose to be born. We did not choose when or where we were born. Nor did we choose who we were to be born as. You didn't even have control over what or who you loved in this life. What you did have some control over, was how you loved.

This was how Mira loved. She got angry and raged and acted like a spoiled child, but it was all because she had such high expectations of those around her. It was because only someone like her could know so well how beautiful things could be. She struggled to balance her fury and disappointment with her hope and her genuine love for the individuality of others. All those months she had spent tormenting him hadn't been something she had done for her own amusement. She hadn't used him to achieve some goal. She had done what had stood in her ability to make him better. To have him be someone she could admire and respect. Yet, now he saw her secret.

She would have loved him either way. She had loved him when he had tethered on the edge of madness, even if she did not agree that there was any madness to fall into. She had loved him when he had lashed out at her, after she had, in a moment of weakness, urged him to go against his nature and to rebel, as she did. She had loved him when he had fallen into the darkest pit of depression and resignation. Throughout it all, Mira had stayed true to herself. She had pushed him to be better, yet she loved him even when he faltered.

How did he love?

He found himself in a moment in which he knew was capable of love, but wondered how. He wanted to make things better. He had always wanted to make things better. He had not wanted to be born a burden onto this world; to not be a disappointment to those that had hopes of him. He had wanted to make the world a better place. To make the air sweeter and the days brighter. To leave those he had touched in life with the warm memory of his presence.

How many times had he risked his life in battle for what he saw as the betterment of the lives of those he would never encounter? Had he not been willing to sacrifice everything for that? In the end, though he dare not say it, he understood Mira's parents, in a way she, apparently, did not. He could understand the weight of making things better.

In the end, it was funny.

He had spent so much time in terror at the insignificance of his own life, yet he had always known how small it truly was. He had always known that there were things much greater than his own little existence. In truth, he felt it, in his heart, that his soul could value another more than it did itself. In this moment, on the shores of a lake high in the Andes Mountains, he saw a chance to do what he had always wanted to do. To drink from the waters of life and to create that which he himself had always craved and that which he had always wished he could give to the whole world.

He put forth his hand and reached out to grasp the shoulder next to him.

'Mira, I think everything is going to be alright.'

Chapter XVII
Echoes in Eternity

'Do *you* wanna tell Pop that we fucked up?' Mira asked as Thomas paced around the room. 'Fuck it! Go to Bâlea and tell him we fucked up. But, you're going alone! Me and Daw are having dinner in Mecca tonight and I ain't cancelling. So you might as well pop over to Lakshmi's place now and spare everyone the hassle.'

'Oh, but for fuck's sake, Mira! It's literally on the way!' It really was on the way.

'It is, but if I drop by, I have to come in and say "hello". Lakshmi will want to know how I am doing and why I am popping up by her house instead of her office. Plus, I'll have to decelerate to land. It all adds up to another fifteen minutes and I'm late for dinner as it is. It's half past eight. Dinner is at nine. It's a fifteen minute drive. I need a couple of minutes to get my luggage in my car. I have to get Lorgar in the car. Plus, I gotta pick up Daw from Jeddah. Can't do it.'

'What's Daw doing in Jeddah?' Thomas asked Mira. Daw had been staying in Jerusalem in Mira's apartment for months now.

Yet, it was Toph that answered. 'She wanted to stay in Djibril al Sayid's old house, where she grew up, not in the al Sayid Palace with Mira's relatives.'

'Oh, Christ... can't she just teleport?' Thomas' annoyance grew. 'That'll win you five minutes.'

'It's illegal for her to teleport and you know that!' He did.

Thomas hoped that, perhaps, after all this time, Daw would've earned the right to use her powers unrestrained. If a scanner detected any illegal teleportation on Terra, drones and entire armies would immediately converge on the location, guns blazing. That sort thing would, indeed, derail any dinner party.

He, along with Mira and Toph, were in his apartment in Jerusalem. It had been two weeks since Diwali Day had come and gone. With the purpose of her visit having consummated itself, Daw and her elven companions had been able to extend their stay by only two weeks, which had gone by far too swiftly. In this fortnight, Thomas and Toph had finally had time to themselves. Yet, sweet moments are the most fleeting. He regretted having not been able to show her all that he had planned to. It hadn't helped that the sight they were both most fond of was each other. Many a day had been set aside for Terran tourism, only to be derailed by an unspoken agreement that the precious time they had left should be consummated in the privacy of Thomas' apartment, not on the busy streets of Blackstone, Kathmandu or Ulaanbaatar.

Mira herself had finally been allowed the time she had long craved to spend alongside Daw, as the two had also been nigh inseparable in the last weeks. She and Thomas still had duties, however. One of which being a set of instructions regarding the closing steps of Project Kralizec left by General Pop, who had recently vacated his home in Harnof and returned to the Hajduk Citadel of Bâlea, high in the Carpathian Mountains.

It wasn't a big deal, just some additional set of communication codes and protocols that were to be used by former Section Heads. It was just one of many other things which the Generals and Colonels involved either knew by heart or could easily predict. The last set of such codes was to be delivered by Thomas and Mira to Colonel Lakshmi Patel and they had planned to do just that that very evening, at eight o'clock, approximately half an hour ago. More specifically, *Mira* was supposed to go to Lakshmi's office, within the Kralizec compound in Jerusalem and deliver the code at eight o'clock sharp.

However, Mira, being Mira, had managed to get caught up in packing her luggage and had decided, without telling Thomas, that she would simply catch Patel as she left her office at *eight fifteen*, which was approximately fifteen minutes ago. However, the Colonel had left early that evening and, unawares of Mira's arrival, had simply disappeared without a trace. This normally shouldn't have been an issue, but Thomas and Mira would have to report any delay to Pop, which would be a hassle. More importantly, Lakshmi, Fiol and Sara were moving to Gandhinagar the next day. It had been the Colonel's last day in Jerusalem. She would continue her work directly from her own home station, with her presence no longer being required in the Israeli Holdfast.

Which all meant that someone had to go to Lakshmi and Fiol's house by the Dead Sea, and deliver the file with the codes. Mira, instead of resolving a situation that she had created, had decided to pull rank on Thomas and make *him* deliver the file, since *she* wasn't going to be late to dinner...

'Fucking shit, Mira... Fine! I'll fucking do it.' He took the file out of Mira's hand and proceeded to make his way to the door of his apartment. He stopped to take one of his jackets and his utility belt from his wardrobe. He hadn't even had time to take off his boots yet, as he and Toph had just arrived in the apartment and were about to enjoy a quiet, intimate and *uninterrupted* evening together watching *Princess Mononoke*.

'You're the best!' Mira had been chilling on his couch while explaining to him why he would fix her mess for her since he was 'the best lieutenant ever'. As she got up, she said to Toph in Menegrothi elvish: 'Is he a fucking weeb? Is he making you watch anime and shit?'

'It's a good movie!' Thomas responded in English.

A stunned Mira turned to look at him, as Toph's eyes widened almost as much as her smile. 'You learned elvish?' The young Arab captain asked.

'Oh, Mira, but for fuck's sake, it's a free download! It takes like an hour of sleep.' He had it uploaded to his memory a month before, after having gotten tired of having to listen to Mira, Toph and Daw speaking in elvish together, which they usually did before looking at him and either giggling or sneering.

'Huh... I see!' She turned, once more to Toph and asked, this time in English. 'Did you also learn German?'

'Đúng!' was how one would spell the sound that came from Toph's mouth.

It was Thomas that offered clarification. 'That's.... that's Vietnamese...'

The elf's eyes raced. 'Oh... Es tut mir leid! Ich wollte "jawohl" sagen!'

'Huh... nice...' Mira looked around the room, her eyes taking in the information. 'Well, sorry for fucking up the vibe then... I'm out! I'll see you tomorrow, Thomas!' She turned to Toph, speaking once more in elvish. 'Bye, Toph!'

Mira's apartment was in the opposite direction as the shuttle garage and she gave him a casual wave as she came out the door and made a left towards her place, just before Thomas turned right towards the direction of his shuttle.

Fine. It's only like thirty minutes. If I drive fast, I'll get there in under ten minutes. Spend ten minutes talking to Lakshmi, Fiol and Sara. No Catan. I'll be back home in ten minutes after that... I gotta start packing too soon.

He got his shuttle in the air rather quickly. He had, unfortunately, picked up some bad driving habits after having spent so many hours next to Mira. Thus, he used the maximum acceleration setting allowed for takeoff. More acceleration was possible, just that it would force the passengers to endure G-force which would have been fatal to a human of Old Earth. For a Terran they would be just damn unpleasant. Mira even found the sensation to be 'fun'.

He darted across the long stretch of land he knew so well, homing in on Lakshmi's house. He knew well enough so as to decelerate as he got near the ground, so as not to be rude and make noise in a residential area. As the shuttle reached a silent speed, Thomas caught glimpse of the house. It was quite dark but, then again, Lakshmi and Fiol liked it like that in the evenings. In front of the house, one could see a parked Terran truck shuttle drone, its loading bay doors open. Inside one could see that it almost a quarter of the way full with packages, while another quarter was strewn across the house's driveway and entrance. The remaining half, he could assume, was still in the house.

Oh, crap, they're packing already. They're gonna get annoyed that I'm bothering them for this. Fucking Mira bullshit...

He didn't see anyone though. Which was a little odd. You'd expect to see at least someone in the middle of delivering a fresh batch of freshly packed belongings in the minute it took for Thomas to quietly park the car. *They must have stopped for dinner.*

He got out of his shuttle, file in hand, and proceeded to make his way to the front door, which stood open slightly ajar. As he climbed the stairs towards the door, he announced his presence.

'Lakshmi! Fiol! It's me!'

There was no reply.

Strange, I'm certain they could hear me from anywhere in the house...

'Lakshmi! Fiol! Sara?' he shouted, louder this time. Again, no reply.

'Clara?' he thought

'Yes, Thomas?'

'Are they home?'

'They should be. Colonel Patel has nothing scheduled at this hour. That I know of, at least.'

Strange. Could they have walked down to the beach in their backyard? Perhaps they wanted to go for a salty swim for one last bittersweet time? Thomas walked in, making a big deal of making as much noise as possible. Lakshmi may have been sweet, but she was an oldtimer. He knew how touchy they were about asking for permission before coming into their house. If it weren't for the secrecy required for the sake of the file he held in his hand, he would have simply called her. Instead, he entered the Colonel's living room, as he asked, one more time.

'Lakshmi? Fiol? Sara?' As he caught full sight of the room he had just entered, he saw a figure, which he assumed was Fiol, at first. He couldn't really tell, since the room was lit not by artificial light, but by candlelight, as was always the custom of the Patel household once the sun had set. The dim light was more than enough for Thomas' eyes, as they adapted to the low light conditions easily.

It was when they did that he saw the uniform. A uniform he knew all too well after having seen it strewn across his bedroom floor so many times.

A Brightguard.

The elf stood next to the living room table, holding a book in his hands, as his eyes looked upon the words within. He was tall for an elf, much taller than Toph.

His height neared his own Terran stature. He was lithe of limb, as was typical of his kind. His face looked so elven that Thomas could swear he was likely the most generic looking low elf he had ever seen in his life. His uniform was quite plain. The only addition he had made appeared to be a small bell he had embedded into his front tabard, right above his heart.

It was not his appearance, but his manner which Thomas immediately noticed.

He had a look about him... Thomas couldn't tell what was ... *different* about it.

'Ah, hello!' the elf said, closing the book and looking towards the young Terran. 'Lakshmi mentioned someone might be coming! I presume that would be you!' His voice was warm. His eyes were inquisitive. Curious even, in more ways than one.

Lakshmi didn't know about me or Mira. She knew she had to receive something, though. Perhaps.

'Yes, well, that would be me I suppose.' *Unless anyone else is supposed to come over.*

'Oh, pardon me, I am Incumberent Milui Adrento!' *The most elven-sounding name I've ever heard...*

The elf moved closer, covering the distance between them rather swiftly. His walk was jovial... friendly. He raised his right hand. Thomas saw that within his left one he had been holding a copy of Samuel Huntington's *Clash of Civilizations*.

He responded, 'Lieutenant Thomas Muller. Terran Logistics Corps.

A pause took root between.

'Clara, who is he?' he thought.

'Incumberent Milui Adrento. He appears on the travel journal declaration made by the *Nialka*. He is a passenger.' Clara responded as the handshaking continued.

'Is he a Brightguard?'

'Yes, Incumberent Milui Adrento is a Brightguard. He appears in their records.' The handshaking slowed down now, as the two men smiled cordially at one another. Thomas felt the elf's soft arm ease itself into a lower rhythm, forcing Thomas to do the same.

'I'm sorry to interrupt, but I need to deliver these to Colonel Patel.' He shook the file in his left hand. Something was odd about this elf.

'Oh! I see! Well, Lakshmi, Fiol and Sara are out in the backyard having a swim. I don't like the salty water, so I politely declined to join!' He made it sound as an inside joke. As if he and Thomas were buddies from a while back.

'Ah... I see...' He stood there, looking at the elf's face with great care. He didn't recognize it. 'When did they leave?' Maybe he didn't recognize it because he was so plain-looking.

'Oh, like five minutes ago. It was Lakshmi's idea, actually, she got here from work early and was in the mood for a swim, she said.' He gestured towards a few packages laid out across the living room. 'I guess it's the fact that they won't be so close to it in the future.'

'Did they say how long they would be?' The elf had all the right answers... and he made a point of it.

'Well, Fiol told me that I might as well leave; it would be that long of a while. I politely declined. I didn't want, you see, to pass the opportunity to have one last evening with them before leaving.' *Oh, another dinner party...*

He had no reason to doubt his words. Just that, Lakshmi had never mentioned this elf before. She had mentioned a lot of elves, but not this one. This one was new. No one had mentioned this elf. He wasn't one of the hundred elves working directly on Kralizec.

This elf who was invited to Lakshmi's house for their last supper in Jerusalem.

'Ok,' Thomas said and just stood there, locked in place.

A few peculiar seconds passed. Those seconds seemed to bother the elf. 'If you want you can leave what you brought here, I'll let them know you came over and dropped it off.'

Now that... that's too fishy right there! 'No. It's fine. I'll wait.' *Toph will understand. Hopefully.*

The elf smiled and gave Thomas a knowing look, as if he was about to let him in on a little secret. 'It's fine, Lieutenant Muller!' He leaned in. 'I'm aware of Project Kralizec and its nature. We all are! In the Brightguard, that is!'

Yeah, just that I wasn't aware of you...

Thomas responded with a blank stare. 'Oh, and what *is* that?' He couldn't verify whether or not this elf was a part of Kralizec. That was the problem. There was no database. There was just the *Cosa Nostra* rule: you'll only ever be introduced to one another. No written record existed anywhere. Daw had said that she had made every Brightguard a keeper. But, still, despite the formal commandment, both elves and Terrans were fastidious by nature. Hence, every elf Thomas had met working on Kralizec, had been an elf that had been introduced to him personally. This one was an exception.

The elf broke into laughter. Very elven laughter. No mirth there was in it. 'Oh, I'll never get used to you Terrans and your obsession with rigour!' *Well, I'm German motherfucker, so I pack extra.*

The elf continued. 'Your Great Project, Lieutenant Muller! Your salvation from oblivion! Your afterlife program!' He began to move away from Thomas, nearing the centre of the room, before pausing and turning towards him again. 'The reason why we're here, after all!'

Another, this time shorter, pause followed before Thomas spoke. 'I'm sorry, but I don't recognize you.' *Fuck it... maybe I am overreacting a little.*

'Oh, well, you can't be expected to remember everyone you've met here, can't you?'

Now that! That does definitely make some alarm bells go off!

Still, it was a valid point.

'Mistakes can be made, yes! Yet they're not acceptable.' *For fuck's sake... I probably look racist as a motherfucker... But, on the other hand, something is most definitely wrong here. It's at least different. Fuck it! I'll stay.* 'Don't mind me! I'll just wait here.' With his left hand, he gestured towards Lakshmi's couch, located to his right. His right hand stood, unflinching, an inch away from the pistol on his hip, as was Terran military doctrine.

The elf smiled and his is smile was wide.

But not wide enough... As if he wasn't really paying attention to it.

His pupils, however, were huge and were locked in on Thomas' own.

Thomas felt a little... drained. Not nauseous. Just a bit queasy...

'Clara, call Mira!' he thought.

Something is wrong.

Something was very wrong.

There was movement.

Thomas noticed it, just as he realised it was taking too long for Clara to respond and too long for the elf to keep smiling. The movement came from the elf's left hand, as it dropped the book.

Reflexes took over, as Thomas' right hand, already hovering near his sidearm, jolted towards the pistol's grip, his eyes fixed on the elf. 'CLARA!!!' he shouted with his mind.

He was too slow.

By the time his fingers touched his pistol, the elf had already reached into his own tabard and was pulling something out from within an inner pocket. Thomas knew what those Brightguard inner pockets held.

Pistols.

Normal visitors weren't allowed weapons on Terra, yet the Brightguard were an exception. Hence, Thomas felt no surprise as he saw the elf's hand emerge, holding an elven pistol.

He felt his gut clench as he saw what kind of elven pistol it was.

A whisper pistol.

A quiet weapon. Firing it would not produce a sound that could be heard by someone outside the house. If the elf got the first shot and the long, sharp projectile hit its ideal target, Thomas would be at the very least blinded. Yet there would be no gunshot sound made that could alert anyone nearby.

His own pistol, though, was loud. Very loud. He needed to shot. The sound could definitely alert the neighbours.

Thomas realised he had to gamble.

He had to shoot from the hip, as it were.

He hated shooting like that. He sucked at it. He had been taught the technique, yet had always hated it. However, in this moment in time, necessity trounced preference. The elf was fast and the only way he could counteract his speed was by shooting as quickly as possible. If he got lucky, he might even manage a headshot and end things quickly.

In fractions of a moment, Thomas twisted the pistol towards the elf and pulled the trigger.

He hit the elf right in the chest, right below his collar, with the force of the projectile pushing him back.

However, he was not dead.

The elf's feet reeled back as his heels bit into the ground. He saw the elf manage to regain control of his arm and prepare to shoot.

He wasn't going to let that happen. He had never stopped raising his pistol to his preferred shooting position. As the elf succeeded in aiming his weapon in Thomas' general direction, the Terran managed to let loose another round.

Which missed.

The elf was on the move now, rushing towards Thomas' left. They exchanged rounds of gunfire as Thomas rushed to his right. He managed to hit the elf in the shoulder before the elf managed to hit him in the chest. Thomas reeled as he felt the needle go through his chest and get caught in his ribcage. Elven whisperer pistols couldn't kill him outright. The projectiles themselves were too weak. They travelled very fast and could punch straight through him, if they didn't hit any bone or sinew. Yet, they could not punch through his skull and the elf would have to unload at least a dozen into his chest cavity before Thomas' lungs would collapse or his heart would stop, mangled beyond imagination.

However, they did fucking hurt. The first one hurt. The second one, in his abdomen, hurt like shit, as it had gone right through him. He heard the bullet hit the back of his jacket and felt the small vibration it made, as it hit the floor. The third and fourth rounds hit him in the shoulder. His jacket, covering his shoulder was, thankfully, bulletproof. The impact still fucking hurt though. As he collapsed to the floor, he ducked behind one of the couches. He didn't even have to hear the muffled sounds coming from the front of the couch, since he knew that Terran furniture was usually bulletproof. He checked his pistol. Five seconds had passed since Thomas had made the comment about mistakes and acceptance. He had shot eight rounds and had two more left in the pistol.

He decided to get up and shoot from the couch before switching to his second magazine.

Just that... he didn't fucking have a second magazine. He didn't bring one. There were two or three in the car, but that was too far away. Normally, this wouldn't have been an issue, since he had already put two bullets in his opponent. The problem was... that wasn't going to be enough.

Brightguard uniforms were also bulletproof. They could definitely stop a bullet from his sidearm.

The elf's gun might have been weaker than Thomas', yet the Terran's body armour was definitely the inferior one. He quickly zipped his jacket to protect his torso. His pants were also bulletproof, as were his boots. His only exposed area was his head. Thomas knew that the only chance the elf had was to shoot him in the eyes and blind him. If the elf got lucky, he might even manage to send a bullet into his skull, since the honeybone was weak around the optic nerve.

As he got up, Thomas realized that he would have to rush the elf into close-quarters combat. He didn't know how many rounds his opponent had, but he did know that his opponent had a whole lot more than a whisper pistol on him.

He also had some kind of pulse generator on him, at least. He had likely triggered it the moment Thomas had felt queasy. It was a subtle sign; without his biological augmentation, he likely wouldn't even have noticed it. Thomas had forgotten the feeling and what it meant. It was only now, having realised that it must have been a pulse that had knocked out Clara, that he realized what the elf was doing.

His adversary was isolating him. No Clara meant no communication with the outside world. His heartbeat would eventually recharge and reactivate his operator, but that would take time. Once Clara reactivated, he would have to instruct her to broadcast his position. Help would soon follow. However, Clara wouldn't recharge if the elf kept triggering pulse charges. The neighbours would come, yes, since they would hear the gunshots. However, it would take a while for them to raise the alarm. If he would have had Clara, a drone patrol and an orbital drop pod would already be on their way. By knocking her out, the elf had bought time. Time to escape or time to kill him.

Thomas was in no mood to find out which would be the answer, as he quickly scanned the room for the elf's whereabouts, only to have the elf lunge towards him as he got up from behind Lakshmi's couch.

He was incredibly strong for an elf, successfully knocking Thomas back into the large window behind him, as he clawed at the Terran's pistol with one hand and attempted to shot him with his own sidearm.

It was training that saved Thomas. He caught the elf's right wrist properly and gave it a good twist. Elven wrists were more fragile than human ones. Their bones were thinner. They could be as strong as they wanted to be, which they quite very well were, yet they couldn't fight simple physics. As Thomas twisted, the felt the elf's hand go limp and he managed to knock his opponent's sidearm away, just as his opponent headbutted him. The force was sufficient to wobble his brain which, though reinforced with a lamecular membrane, sloshed into the back of his head, like a wet balloon inside a box.

It was a clever move, since it made Thomas' body loosen for just enough time as was need for the elf to knock his own sidearm away. Thomas recovered his senses just in time to feel the elf's left hand leave his own and rush towards his utility belt. He knew the move and reacted accordingly, reaching out with his right arm, beneath the elf's left arm and towards his right shoulder. His left hand allowed the elf to punch him, but that was alright, since he could grab his adversary's elbow. He kicked the elf in the gut as he began to twist his right arm, catching his opponent's right arm, now holding the hilt of the Terran's shortsword, in something of a vice. The elf's hand released the handle of the Terran's shortsword and he fell to his knees as Thomas twisted his body in such a way that made his opponent's head bash into the window.

Unaltered humans were as strong as elves but a lot slower. Enhanced humans, such as Terrans, were much stronger than even an elf as enhanced as this one. Elves, however, were still much faster than Terrans. This one was no different. The elf managed to swiftly clutch the hilt of his own blade with his free hand, realising Thomas would likely react in kind, though not as swiftly as was needed.

This was when the elf did something remarkable.

Instead attempting to use his blade against Thomas, which was what would have been expectable, the elf used the blade to stab himself in the abdomen.

Thomas' eyes, which had been squinting to stave off any potential attack on them, couldn't help but widen as he realised what was happening.

He has a bag of biophage in there.

Biophage was a catch-all term for a type of poison used throughout the Known Universe. It was made up of nanobots, mechanical or biological in nature, which would dissolve any organic matter they came in contact with. A weapon coated in biophage could quickly turn an entire living enemy into a pile of goo.

It was a dangerous weapon, reserved only for the most brutal of battlefields, as the risk of the biophage accidentally making its way onto to flesh of an ally was a genuine concern which had to be taken into account. Elves, in particular, hated these weapons, as they prevented their consciousness from beyond captured by their soulkeeper discs upon the moment of death. Terrans knew this well and, upon discovering this most disturbing technology, had quickly started using it as a weapon of terror during the War of Vengeance.

Weapons were typically covered in biophage before a battle. However, there was one technique, invented by Terrans during the Senoyu War, which involved hiding bags of biological biophage inside the abdomen, beneath a layer of fake flesh that crafted from a material which resembled skin, yet was not organic. Terran saboteurs and assassins, which there had been many of during the Senoyu War, had employed this method to sneak biophage past the watchful eyes of their enemies. When the time would be right, any weapon forced through the fake flash would become an incredibly potent weapon of murder.

True enough, as the elf's blade withdrew from the stab wound, Thomas could see the metal take on a shiny reddish black sheen, a common colour among biological biophage varieties. He immediately recoiled, disentangling himself from his opponent. He realised that fighting an enemy armed with knife which could kill him with one deep enough cut was too much of a gamble.

With the corner of his eye, he spotted his handgun and jumped towards it, grabbling it as he rolled across the floor. He rolled one more time before jumping towards one of the doors to the house's terrace. The elf gave chase with his knife in hand, but did not have time to catch up to Thomas as he forced the door open and emerged outside, closing the door behind him, just as the elf forced himself against it. The door did not budge, as Thomas kept it closed with the weight of his body.

With his back against the bulletproof door, he knew he just had to aim towards the north, where Lakshmi's neighbours lived. They had a huge living room window, just like the Patels, which Thomas shot at.

The round hit its mark, causing the neighbours' blast doors to seal shut, hiding their living room from view and alerting the Jerusalem Holdfast that someone was shooting at a house near the Dead Sea.

Thomas smiled, knowing that help was on the way. He would have shot Lakshmi's window if it weren't for the fact that he wasn't sure it would've worked, given pulse that had been discharged inside. The blastproof doors would've still gone down, but likely no alert would be sent.

With help on the way, he turned to check up on his opponent.

Which was nowhere to be seen.

Thomas realised what was happening just as he heard the noise.

One small blast, the sound of a mechanical engine being activated to fuel a shuttle.

The second blast, the sound of a shuttle crashing through a dead electrical door.

As Fiol's shuttle burst from its garage, Thomas ducked to prevent it from crashing into him, shooting his final bullet in the shuttle's back to little effect. He was up and running before the shuttle was even past him. He knew he was a five second sprint away from his own shuttle, which he reached in four. The electronic engine was indeed dead, yet Terran shuttles had a special lever which allowed the mechanical engine to activate. The energy produced could be used to restart the normal electrical system...

... but it could also be used to quickly turn the shuttle into a rocket, just as the elf had done with Fiol's car.

As Thomas was pushed against his seat by the sudden acceleration, he immediately began giving chase to the elf. Simultaneously, he reached into one of the inside compartments, pulling out a Terran submachine gun of his preferred HK model.

He switched out the magazine, which he kept stocked with assault bullets and replaced it with the other magazine he kept in his car: the bolt rounds; little artillery shells designed to punch through armour and explode within the soft interior of a machine or a person.

He would need them soon enough but, for now, he placed the weapon in his lap and began directing the engine's power to the electronics. The shuttle had a charging pad he could use to power Clara back up. He just needed to get that part of the shuttle working and he could get Clara back. The operator, once online, could start broadcasting his position and he would have a thousand Terran patrol drones and shuttles on him in minutes or even seconds.

The elf was going directly east, across the Dead Sea, towards where the canyon of Zarqa Main could be seen. He wasn't gaining altitude, which made sense, since attempting to escape through the skies was impossible. The atmosphere was just too heavily monitored. A rogue unannounced shuttle would instantly be identified and immobilized.

Was the elf simply running? Did he have a plan? Thomas was not planning to find out. He would catch up to him and shoot him down.

Just as they entered the canyon, the shuttle regained function of some of its electronics. Thomas placed his hand on the charging point and began thinking of Clara, in anticipation of her reactivating fully. If only he could get her back online–

A strange noise spread through the shuttle as all the electronic lights died and the combustion engine, once more, took over the task of powering their flight.

Another EMP charge. He must be killing my car... But, the EMP is also going to kill his car...

What was the elf's game plan here? Thomas checked the mechanical fuel gauge and saw that his shuttle was just about to run out of fuel. He always kept a full tank. Which meant that Fiol's shuttle would also be just about to run out of fuel. If the elf was fine with running out of fuel that meant that his destination was near.

Thomas was suddenly struck by understanding.

He knew from school that Zarqa Main canyon had once been a skyport, in the days before such operations were moved to the Spines and the Polar Shields. An old fort still lay at the canyon's heart. An old fort which had been abandoned and now served as little more than an old ruin, stripped bare of all inhabitants and equipment.

The perfect place to hide...

The perfect place to hide a small space shuttle...

As Thomas understood the elf's short-term strategy, he failed to see his opponent's immediate strategy, as Fiol' shuttle rose above him and immediately decelerated, right on his trajectory. He saw a shape jump out from the driver's side, just as Thomas rapidly tried to dodge the incoming mass of metal.

He failed. Fiol's shuttle hit the back right-hand side of his shuttle, causing him to spin out of control. Shuttles running on mechanical engines were notoriously hard to manoeuvre and Thomas found himself hitting the wall of the great canyon, before falling to the ground below.

Terran shuttles didn't have airbags, relying on the passenger's enhanced physiology, coupled with the almost indestructible chassis and armoured exterior, to ensure their survival. Which was what Thomas managed to do. He opened the door of the crashed shuttled and realised he was just outside the old fort. He quickly checked his body for injuries, realizing that his wounds, including the gunshots, were more-or-less superficial. He took out his submachine gun and entered the fort through the main gate.

The old gatehouse led straight to the inner courtyard, where Terran ferries had once performed the task of transporting both people and equipment to orbiting battleships. It lay almost completely empty now.

Almost.

By the far eastern wall, Thomas could see an elf floating in the air, which meant two things. The first was that he wasn't actually floating. Rather, he must have been boarding a cloaked starship. It was likely a small ship, probably twenty meters at its longest. Most likely it was a smuggler's ship, meant to swiftly traverse a planet's atmosphere, before making the jump to the Greyspace. It was almost certainly the means by which the elf planned to escape.

The second thing the floating elf meant was that Thomas would have to pull the trigger of his weapon, which he immediately did, peppering the distant shuttle with explosive rounds. He saw, to his satisfaction, that the bolts left behind dark spots, where they had destroyed the cloaking mechanism and interfered with the holographic projection of the environment around the ship.

The elf reached into the starship and pulled out a rifle, forcing Thomas to quickly dodge behind one of the fort's walls. He heard a deep humming sound, followed by the sound of a massive object moving. He turned to see the starship or, more accurately the holes in the cloaking field, almost five meters higher than they had been before. His opponent was now on the ground, advancing towards Thomas and shooting high calibre plasma bolts at him.

They easily broke the fort's walls and Thomas ducked towards the relative safety of the floor behind the shattering masonry. It didn't stop bits of rubble from hitting him as the plasma bolts crashed into his wall next to him. He could tell that the elf was not shooting at him with the intention to kill, but with the intention of keeping him away from the rising starship.

He isn't going to survive this and he knows it.
And he's fine with it.
He just wants that ship to do its thing and get out.
Fuck...

Thomas inhaled slowly, focusing his ears to listen to the sound of his own breathing. He lay out across the ground and focused on what he was sensing. The wound in his abdomen, the bullet in his ribs, the feeling of weightlessness in his head, a sore chest from where the seatbelt had kept him in place during the clash, his sore shoulder, were the elves rounds had hit him. He felt his clothes, where they clung to his body.

Finally, he felt the ground.

He felt nothing in it.

Which meant the elf was sitting immobile, waiting for him to make the first move.

Checkmate. He's played this perfectly... from a tactical perspective.

He couldn't do anything except gamble.

Thomas took out his explosive round magazine and replaced it with his assault bullet one. He twisted on the ground, bringing his machine gun to the edge of the shattered wall. He brought the tip over the edge and began peppering the general area of the elf's last known whereabouts.

He heard a lot clinking, as the assault bullets struck rocks and walls but, then, he heard it.

Thud!

Then he heard that noise... the noise of heels dragging across the ground as the body tried to stay vertical.

I got him.

He dashed from behind the wall and aimed right at the elf. He let loose one round.

Heels dug in.

Two rounds.

Heels digging in again.
Three rounds.
His magazine clinked, indicating that he had five rounds left.
Four rounds.
Heels digging in deeper.
Five rounds.
They all hit the elf, but he couldn't manage to hit him in the fucking head...
Six rounds.
Headshot. He's dead now.
And, then... he heard it again: the sound of heels digging in.
This time Thomas paused to focus, since he couldn't believe it. He could believe what he was seeing. How could he? The elf's forehead was a mass of blood and broken skin but, beneath...
Gold.
Not white. Not the metallic blue of plated honeybone.
Gold...
A dark elf...
Seven rounds.
The elf's neck twisted, blood gushing out. Thomas released his magazine, about to place his explosive round magazine in now.
Eight rounds.
The assault round magazine released. He locked the other one in place and the bolt magazine clicked in place.
He shot one round, then heard the magazine clink.
Five more rounds left.
He aimed for the elf's weapon.
Four more.
The elf's rifle exploded, as the explosive round tore it from his bleeding hands.
Three rounds left.
The elf darted into the air.
The bastard must've gotten a charged jetpack from the fucking ship.
Two rounds left.
Fuck it... I'll shoot the ship.
One round left.
Nothing... it's still moving.
Thomas took a deep breath... What did the elf know? What was in his head? Was it worth the risk of shooting him in the head? If he did, at least whatever the elf knew about Kralizec, that he had not poured into some device on board the fleeing ship above, would be lost to the Enemy. However, if he did shoot him in the head,

they would lose any chance of knowing what he had managed to learn and, more importantly, how?

There were no more rounds left.

He saw the elf's trajectory change, as blood gushed from the back of his head and small explosion occurred... on the outside of his skull...

The golden plating had held... and Thomas was out of ammunition.

Despair filled him, as he realised that the elf was going to get away.

'Clara?' he thought, focusing. 'CLARA!!!'

'Yes, Thomas?' *Finally!!!*

'Tell everyone where I am! Now! Tell them there's a...'

He didn't even see it properly. He just saw a sheen of white and then an explosion as something crashed into the elf's ship. It looked like a white shuttle, but Thomas couldn't tell for sure. The elf himself paused. He turned to observe the ship, now a hundred meters above the ground, begin to slowly pick up speed as it collapsed to the ground.

After a few seconds, the elf's face turned towards Thomas and he was finally able to, once more, see clearly the face of the Enemy.

He saw rage. A deep, boiling rage, as the elf's lips quivered and his face turned into a snarl. Thomas saw the elf, once more, pull out his dagger and plunge it into his abdomen.

Oh, shit! Here we go! Come on motherfucker!

He drew his sword and readied himself for the attack. His pistol, now containing a full magazine, lay at his hip, though its presence mattered little. If the submachine gun hadn't broken through his opponent's defences, the pistol stood little chance. His only hope was that he might best the dark elf in a one-on-one melee match-up, though the biophage tilted such a contest heavily in his adversary's favour.

He breathed in. He forced his eyes to adapt to the lights around him. High above him, he could see the white light of a full moon, as well as the subtle blinking of the stars above; a cold light to match the red flames of the burning starship. Flanking his floating adversary lay the old fort's walls and, beyond, the edges of the canyon's cliffs towered above them both. Dark and solemn they stood, against the madness they now oversaw. Lights flickered around him, yet he focused on the figure above him, much in the same way as the figure focused on him. Which was, in a way, its downfall.

Thomas saw the movement before the elf could react.

Something jumped from the canyon's cliffs. As Thomas focused on the movement, he saw a figure in the moonlight, flying through the air, legs back, chest forward, hands up, clutching something. An axehead glinted at the end of a dark shaft as the figure came within arm's length of the floating elf, which only now turned to face it.

The axe snapped with a loud sonic boom, the hallmark of Terran power weapons. The charged-up weapon moved too fast for the eye to see. Thomas only saw the aftermath as the weapon dug deep into the elf's shoulder. The two figures crashed into the ground together, with the elf being pinned to the fort's shattered floor as the axeman towered above him. It was only then that the identity of Thomas's saviour was revealed.

Mira al Sayid stood above the felled elf, panting as she gathered her breath. Like Thomas himself, she was wearing casual gear, the same outfit she had worn barely twenty minutes ago in his apartment in Jerusalem. For one second, Thomas could swear she was holding the Axe of Djibril al Sayid himself, only to realise that the axe she held, though similar, was another entirely, as her father's relic was still in the Shrine of the Lost in Mecca. She stood fixated upon her quarry and Thomas could tell that she saw now what he had just seen before: a Brightguard uniform, a low elf face of unremarkable quality and the golden bone plating they had all grown up hearing stories about.

A dark elf.

With a hand on a dagger, that he had just plunged into his own abdomen.

She doesn't know.

'PHAGE!!! MIRA!!! PHAGE!!!' he shouted, as he ran towards her.

He saw the elf twist the blade in its gut, tearing open his entire abdomen, allowing the phage to spill into him. With his last ounce of strength, he lunged at Mira, who managed to recoil just in time to avoid the strike. As the elf twisted, belly down, the dagger lodged itself into the stone floor before her, as she stood back, brandishing her axe.

Thomas' instructions changed, as realization came over him. 'HEAD!!! HEAD!!! KEEP THE HEAD.' He hadn't stopped running.

He jumped the last few yards, grabbing the elf's head and pulling it to the side, exposing the enemy's wounded neck.

Mira immediately understood what he meant and quickly raised the axe above her head. As the biophage escaped its compartment, it began dissolving the elf's flesh. Already, his chest had separated from his legs, leaving behind only an empty void beneath a wet uniform and a foul ooze that spilled onto the ground. As Mira brought the axe down, the tendrils of reddish black obliteration neared the base of the elf's neck, as the elf's face contorted in pain.

CLANK!

The axe buried itself in the ground as Thomas popped the head off. He rolled around on the floor before throwing it some distance in front of him. As he got up back on his feet, he checked that the head hadn't dissolved. Then he turned to meet Mira's gaze.

She said nothing, turning back towards what had been their opponent's body.

Black ooze and ichor lay pooled on the ground before her. Nestled in the blackness was the white and orange of the spattered Brightguard uniform. It was where the hands and neck had once stood that she gazed upon now with a look of disbelief in her eyes.

The bones were clearly golden.

Golden otarc plating was quite rare on account of the craftsmanship needed to manufacture it, as well as the fact that the materials needed to forge it were difficult to produce. It was a sign of nobility and wealth and though it was not unheard of for members of many species to afford such a design, within this context, it could only mean one thing.

Before them lay what had been the body of a dark elf. A dushman. A Svart. The Enemy. The bringers of the End Times. The greatest enemy of their people.

Thomas came closer, looking upon the evidence before them as well. As the rush of battle faded, he was struck by the extraordinary nature of what had just happened. A million questions rushed into his mind. Was this truly a dark elf? How did it get to Terra itself? How had it remained undetected for so long? What was it doing here? What was it doing at Lakshmi's house? Where... where was Lakshmi –

'The head?' Mira spoke.

She and Thomas both turned to look at the head on the ground a few yards nearby. It stood with its back towards them. However, from the top, they could see the pointy tip of an elven ear. 'It's saved.'

'Get it!' Mira ordered.

Thomas realised she was right. They had to get it to a stasis field quickly, else the rot would take hold and consume it, spoiling their chances of getting answers to their questions. He walked towards the round lump of black hair and broken flesh. As he picked it up, he checked the site of decapitation, looking for vertebrae.

And, indeed, they were golden. A complete golden plating meant that the brain would likely have survived intact. He turned towards Mira, finding her still gazing upon the dark mess before her.

At least there was one question he could address now. 'How did you know where I was?'

Never taking her eyes off the corpse pond before them, she raised her left hand, pointing towards the west: the entrance to the fort, the canyon, the Dead Sea and beyond... 'That's Israel.' She flexed the index finger of her right hand to point at the ground beneath their feet. 'This is Arabia.' Finally, she turned to look at him. 'Every time you cross national borders, I get a notification.' She paused and her eyes drifted. 'It was in your car. It's why we never took your card anywhere. It had a tracker in it, mine didn't. The tracker told me you where in Arabia like five minutes ago.'

Thomas understood. 'Lakshmi's house isn't in Arabia.'

She nodded. 'I thought it was some fuck-up and I called you to ask what the fuck you were doing. But you were disconnected, which shouldn't happen. I asked your car for your travel log and it was unresponsive.'

'EMP charges,' he explained.

'The thought crossed my mind.' She started looking at the crashed starship. 'I was close. I came close to see what the fuck was happening and then... then I saw *that*,' she nodded towards the wreckage of the elf's ship.

'And *that*! *Shouldn't. Be here!*'

Her eyes began to burn. She moved, aggressively, coming in close to Thomas. 'Where's Lakshmi?' Her eyes glared into him, demanding an immediate answer.

Before Thomas could respond, an explosion of sounds occurred.

Sirens. Footsteps. Drones.

An explosion of light followed, as a hundred pointed weapons turned on their flashlights.

On the tops of the fort's walls, figures had appeared, weapons aimed towards the scene below. Thomas immediately recognized their insignia as Terrans bearing the marks of both the Israeli and Arabian Nation. In their eyes, Thomas could see that which he had seen in Mira's eyes and more.

Shock.

One by one, as each took in the crashed elven smuggler ship, the head in Thomas' hand, the Brightguard uniform covered in black ooze, the bloody axe in Mira's hand and the golden skeleton before them, their faces changed and new expressions emerged.

Disbelief. Anger. Hatred. Fear.

Questions. There would be so many questions.

It was Mira that spoke first.

'I threw my cat in some bushes up there.' She pointed towards the cliffside she had jumped from. 'Please don't shoot him!'

Chapter XVIII
Like the Old Days

Terra was in uproar.

The planet had sealed itself shut within moments of discovering what had transpired on the shores of the Dead Sea. The entire Solar System mobilized. The Terran fleet sprung into action, encircling each planet, moon and station in the Solar System, as the darkness was scanned for potential threats. Every portal to the Greyspace was sealed shut and had grime mines immediately deployed within. The Vigilant, in orbit around Terra, immediately went into Safeguard Protocol, as every orc was mobilized and made battle ready.

The Terrans were no different; if anything, they surpassed their allies in swiftness and fervour. Every Terran on the planet and beyond was immediately mobilized. Leisure time immediately ended and martial law was implemented. The weapon batteries of the Polar Shields and across the Spines of Terra immediately stirred as they activated their defence protocols. Every Avenger Legion Citadel and every Holdfast of the Terran Nations became a bristling fortress, as the men and women of the warrior race of Terra sprang into action.

Homes became forts. Children were immediately sealed in bunkers. Every Terran family immediately began preparations for siege or worse. Avenger Legions launched ships into orbit, as the Terran Navy scrambled every dart and launched every vessel. Armour replaced clothing. Tanks patrolled the streets. Patrols combed the countryside. The oceans came to a standstill, as all of their waves were immediately quelled by the massive web of geomantic control built by a people who still feared the sea, the mountain and the sky.

The very colour of the world changed, as the warm orange lights of Terra-at-Peace were replaced by the violent white lights of Terra-at-War. Yellow and blue lights beamed through the halls of every barracks, hangar and facility, as each branch of the Terran war machine energized in a frenzy of motion. Broadcasting came to a halt, as all communication switched the either cables buried deep under the earth or to the guarded channels used for military communication. Many a message had been sent across those channels and Thomas and Mira were now witnessing the effects of the most secure of those lines of communication.

Thomas had never been inside the Keep of Jerusalem. It lay inside a great turret that protected the very centre of the Holdfast's skyport. A great chamber in one of the middle levels of this turret served as the Jerusalem War Room. It was shaped as a perfect circle, with four entrances spread out across the room. The four entrances converged upon the great table located in the middle of the room around which were now gathered Colonels, Generals and Representatives, all aware of the centrepiece displayed before them upon the table.

The head of the elf slain by Mira and Thomas lay within a transparent cube that glowed with a subtle white light which glistened of the clotting blood and the golden bone beneath. Mira and Thomas had delivered the head themselves, as Mira had ordered the Terran Army soldiers that had found them to immediately secure the area, provide a stasis cube for the head and escort her and Thomas to the Jerusalem Holdfast (after recovering Lorgar, of course). They had delivered the head themselves to Ruben Zaslani. Thomas had expected some great discussion to follow their grizzly presentation to the General, yet their delivery had been met with silence and a slow, concerned nod.

He had never seen Zaslani look worried and he wasn't alone. The entire War Room was slowly filling up, as Terra's elite gathered to see for themselves that which they had not believed to have just happened.

A dark elf had appeared on the very surface of Terra itself and had extinguished the life of an entire family.

That had been the fate of Lakshmi, Fiol and Sara. Thomas still felt his boiling blood mixing with cold tears within his heart, as it had from the moment Master Sergeant Azulai had informed them of what had been uncovered in the Patel household. Israeli Army Sergeants had arrived, as Thomas had hoped, upon receiving word that a house had been shot at near the Dead Sea. They stormed the house and found three pools of biophage ooze. Within one pool was the plated honeybone of a Terran oldtimer, with a few shards of what would become bones where her abdomen had once been. Within another, lay the white bones of a Vanir human male. Within the last, smaller pool, they found the white bones of a Terran child.

Mira boiled next to him, her rage palpable. They had been told to wait and she never liked waiting as it was. Almost every member of the High Command present on Terra would come and they would need them both present, in case questions emerged. Thomas found the idea oxymoronic, since he probably had even more questions than even the most curious member of the High Command. He had learned from Clara, once she had fully recovered and sent a detailed transcript of her memory to the High Command, that the Brightguard had been placed under house arrest, as every Brightguard was now a potential suspect. They had all been shipped over to Mecca, where Daw would verify the identity of each, ensuring that there were no more infiltrators among them.

Clara had also informed him that he was not allowed to message Toph, until Daw had verified her identity. Then, finally, Clara had informed him of that which he had expected ever since he had seen Mira's axe separate the elf's head from his body: he was to connect to one of the mental scanners located in the War Room and provide a recording of the entire evening, to be analyzed by the High Command. The images of the events of the last hour now flashed across some of the screens in the room, with each new arrival staring at them in disbelief.

There was one, however, who did not look as if he had just seen a ghost.

Laur Pop had arrived around two minutes after Thomas and Mira, and had not spared a single look towards anyone in the room, bar the face of the dead man on the table in front of him. He had spent around ten seconds in front of the floating head, before moving towards a nearby bench, upon which he slowly laid down. The Hajduk General had taken out a cigarette and began puffing away, as he stared off into the space before him.

In the time it had taken for Pop to finish his cigarette, the room filled up. Marshal Feng, as well as almost every other member of the High Command had arrived, with the exception of a few that had spread out across the world, acting as designated survivors in the event in which the meeting in Jerusalem would be attacked and its participants slain. Four of the remani had arrived, one of which was Basenji himself. Sorbo Falk had come, followed by Çingeto Braca, who had arrived via an orbital dropship catapulted from the Vigilant above. The three inhumans had all stopped by Mira and Thomas to make sure they were alright. It had actually been at Falk's insistence that Thomas had accepted to allow a medic tend to his gunshot wounds.

He had actually forgotten about them, as they had sealed quite well. His body could heal them on its own, yet medical care from a drone and a physician would help. That physician in question would turn out to be none other than Opera Bokha, who had also arrived, together with Rasmussen, to verify that the two survivors of the fight at Zarqa Main had not been in any way infected, contaminated or manipulated.

One of the last to arrive was Adler, who alternated between glaring at the floating head in pure hatred and questioning Thomas and Mira as to what had transpired in a worried tone. Thomas couldn't help but notice her glancing towards

Pop from time to time. The Romanian never broke from his meditation. It was only the arrival of the last member of the War Council that stirred him, as he looked outside to witness Ashaver's entry.

The Hierarch had apparently been on Luna that evening and, upon getting word of what had transpired, immediately rushed to Terra. It took him thirty minutes to arrive via the sprinting ability of his suit of armour, as well as the quick manoeuvring of the *Naglafar*. Upon arriving in Terra's upper atmosphere, the Hierarch had left his ship, electing to plummet towards the world on his own. As he neared the Jerusalem skyport, his shape changed.

His arrival was heralded by a loud boom as he crashed onto the ground, followed by a sound akin to the burning of a great pyre of dry timber. Fragments of darkness coursed around the menacing shape of the Hierarch, who had arrived regaled in the entirety of his might. Dark wings of liquid shadow covered his body, before spreading out around him, revealing a black and orange suit of armour that had brought down death and terror upon many a battlefield. He began advancing towards the tower of the War Room, as those within beheld him in his macabre grandeur. His helmet lifted itself from his head and took its place on his right hip, revealing a face contorted by a scorching fury and a grim determination, as his dark wings dissipated into wisps of black smoke to be carried off by a chill breeze.

Thomas had never seen the Hierarch in his complete panoply of war with his own eyes before. The jovial man with whom he had watched football was gone, revealing nothing short of a dark beast of pure rage and grim purpose. As he entered the War Room, he made straight for the head in the middle of the chamber. When he came to sit right next to it, as Pop had, he paused and stood there, unflinching, as the room got quiet around him.

After a few moments of heavy breathing and furious glaring, he asked no one in particular. 'Where's Daw?' His voice was more animal than man, resembling more the growling of a wolf than the tone of a human.

It was Zaslani who replied. 'Mecca. She is...'

He didn't have time to finish, as Ashaver roared menacingly. 'I FUCKING KNOW WHERE SHE IS!!! I meant why the *fuck* isn't she here?'

Zaslani, unfazed by the roar, answered again. 'She isn't finished–'

The Hierarch wasn't going to let him finish either. 'If they're all on the same planet as her, she's finished! She isn't here because no one has summoned her and no one has summoned her because everyone's *fucking* suspicious of her for NO. GOD. DAMN. REASON!' He turned to a nearby Commandant bearing the insignia of the Communications Corps. 'Send word to Mecca that Daw is to teleport here *immediately*. Inform the Surveillance Centre that Daw al Fajr has permission to teleport here!'

The Commandant nodded and Ashaver turned to face Thomas and Mira. After locking eyes with both of them, he came towards them. Mira didn't flinch, yet Thomas tensed up.

It was like being approached by a great jungle cat, in the middle of said jungle, whilst fully naked. He knew there was no reason to fear him, yet he couldn't help but tremble before the approaching juggernaut. The Hierarch came up close to the two young Terrans and stopped.

He spoke to Mira. 'He was covering up for you, wasn't he?'

Now it was her that tensed up, as Thomas' heart began to pound. Ashaver continued. 'That's what you were doing at Lakshmi's house, wasn't it?' He turned to Thomas. 'Isn't it?'

'No, sir!' *What the fuck am I doing?*

Ashaver's face froze, as he bore into Thomas' soul with his dead eyes. After a few horrifying moments of agonizing glaring, he smirked and turned to Mira. 'You have your father's gift for attracting undying loyalty, now don't you?'

The two locked eyes and stared at each other. Ashaver moved. He moved with an ungodly speed and Thomas' muscles turned to jelly as he thought he was about to strike Mira.

But he did not.

He hugged her.

'Welcome to the club, girl!' *The elf slayer's club...*

The club of those that had loved ones taken from them by elves.

Mira hugged him back and for a moment Thomas saw that which he had never thought possible. He saw Mira tremble a little, as a child would as a parent's warmth overcame all fear and insecurity. He heard Ashaver whisper to her 'I will miss them also. You did nothing wrong. The past is the past. There is no way to change what happened.' She tensed up and the Hierarch gripped her firmly. 'No! Don't! None of that! It's done! It happened. Don't let anyone – don't let yourself – tell you things could have been different! They couldn't. It happened! There is nothing to regret! There is only... there is only what comes next...'

Mira loosened up and Ashaver let go of her. 'Lad...' He turned to Thomas. 'I haven't looked at what happened thought, make no mistake, I will. But, I must confess that, the very fact that you're here now, breathing, tells me that you are much more formidable than I would have expected.'

Then the Hierarch did the unthinkable.

He saluted him.

Thomas sprang into action, sitting up and saluting back.

'Sit down, lad! You've earned it!' With that, the Hierarch turned to the smoking Romanian on the bench to his distant left. Pop was staring off into the distance again.

'Well...?' Ashaver growled.

Pop's eyes didn't budge, yet his lips moved. 'Do you want this to be like in *Harry Potter*?' He turned to face Ashaver now, eyes locking with his. 'Like when Dumbledore comes in at the end and explains what had been going on during the past school year?'

'We both know you're more of a Snape type of guy, but go ahead. But, please, you know I hate your fucking showmanship...'

Pop nodded, leaned forward on the bench and took the cigarette out of his mouth. '*That* is not Milui Adrento. Daw is going to pop in any moment now and tell us that one of her Brightguard, a certain Milui Adrento, is missing. However, the real Milui Adrento, or whatever is left of him, is probably fertilising some field in the Sahara by now. *That*... is Eliafas Perem Goujnar,' he said, pointing towards the head on the table.

Ashaver nodded slowly, as several other members of the High Command turned to look at the golden head. Most, however, just stood still. It was Adler who spoke next, 'Are you certain?'

'No, I am not. Then again, nothing is ever truly certain. But, I am quite sure.' He took a puff from his cigarette and began gesticulating. 'I've been looking for him thirty-five years. He always slipped right through my fingers. This is the first time I've been in the same room as him.' He turned to Falk.' He is the one who stabbed Caldor at Elocphelion, so I guess that means that it's not the first time someone here has been in his presence. Though... that right there is not the face he was born with.'

The troll's face remained grim, as Thomas recognized the name of Falk's cousin. Pop continued. 'Though, I feel as if I've known him my entire life. You get to know someone very well as you dance in the dark together. You learn things about them. You know things.' He leaned back on his bench, groaning and exhaling. 'He came here on *Nialka*, with Daw and her retinue. With all her might, Daw would not be able to sense him. His otarc plating would make it *difficult* for her to sense him if he was alive. But, if he were dead... his body in stasis somewhere on the ship, waiting to be disturbed by some oblivious Brightguard – such as the real Milui Adrento – Daw would never even know he was onboard even if he was beneath her bed.'

'That ship!' He pointed towards one of the screens, showing the wreckage being examined by members of the Terran Investigative Department. 'That ship is what bothers me or – to put it better – it *bothered* me. You see... it's too big and too heavy to have been smuggled on the *Nialka*. It must have been hailed. He knew he was not getting off-world on the *Nialka*. Daw would eventually sense the absence of the real Adrento and he knew he would be fucked when we would all start looking for him. Everything he would have learned while he was here would be gone too.'

'A ship like that could have breached our defences, unless if there was sufficient activity in the system, as was the case on Diwali Day. If it was lying inactive somewhere outside the Kuiper Belt, he could've hailed it right during the festival's peak and the ship would've been on the surface in less than half an hour – if it got lucky, which it must have, given that it's currently in our possession.'

'You say that so fucking casually...' Adler spat, appalled by how nonchalant he was being about the existence of a gap in their defences, even if said gap would have been created in order to hide something else... something far more vulnerable.

'I'm not saying it casually.' Pop wiped his face with one hand and let out a little laugh between closed lips. 'I'm saying it thankfully.'

Ashaver was right next to him in the blink of an eye, his face inches from the General's eyes. 'I told you to spare the *fucking* theatrics, Laur! Get to the fucking point!!'

Pop blew smoke away from their faces. 'In about thirty seconds, Daw is going to teleport right next to Mira. She's going to walk over to the head and tell you it's Eliafas. Furthermore, she's going to tell you that he had any memory of the whereabouts of the other dark elves deleted from his mind. But, she will also tell you that, in his last moments, he sent a signal to a relay point somewhere beyond the Kuiper Belt. A telepathic signal travelling at lightspeed – so as to avoid our sensors – travelling in a straight line. It will take four hours, maybe a little more, for the signal to get to the relay point. At that point, the relay point will send word to Cantor to flee wherever it is that they're hiding. However–'

Less than thirty seconds had passed and Daw al Fajr appeared with a loud *PFWOP!* right next to Mira. Pop paused as he, and the entire room, turned to look towards the new arrival. Her face was grim, devoid of her usual bubbling emotions. She looked at Mira, then at Thomas, then at Ashaver and Pop, then around the room at all those assembled, until finally seeing the bloody trophy the Terrans had gathered around.

She made straight for it and no one made any effort to stop her. She hadn't even reached the table and her hand was already in the air before her. As she touched the exterior of the stasis field, she paused. Thomas heard her take a deep breath before she swung her hands forwards, putting her thumb on one of the elf's closed eyes, and her index finger on the other.

She stood there for a while. Maybe five seconds. Maybe fifty. Time had a tendency to pass differently in rooms where everyone present was holding their breath. Though her hand had approached the head swiftly, it left it slowly. Daw stood motionless, gazing into the dead eyes before her, before slowly turning around, her own eyes now downcast.

Just before she spoke, she lifted her eyes to meet Ashaver's.

'Eliafas.'

Thomas wasn't sure if his heart was pounding in his ears, or if there were so many rapid heartbeats in the room that all he could hear was the sound of pulsing blood.

'They're all together,' she continued. 'They're all in the same place, on the same world. He was the only one that ever left the world they were on. His mind was purged. Frequently. Much is missing. He deleted any memory of the world's sky or its whereabouts. I do not know where it is.' Daw paused, synthesizing that which she had learned from the elf's dead mind. 'His last thoughts were of their safety. He knew about Kralizec. He wanted to bring evidence of it to the Continuum. He found a way to infiltrate Menegroth. He came here on *Nialka*, with the rest of us. He hid in her gastrointestinal tract. He woke up when Milui – the real Milui Adrento – went down there to perform maintenance. The ship came from the Kuiper Belt two weeks ago. He summoned it. He knew the lights would hide it. He's been running around collecting evidence and storing it on the ship ever since. He killed Fiol first, then Lakshmi... Sara... she had been sleeping... she woke up...'

Daw's cheeks trembled as she lost composure for a moment. 'There is a relay point outside this system. His last action was to instruct it to send word to Cantor to flee their refuge. The signal will reach it in an hour.' She paused, seemingly concentrating on analyzing the rest of the information she had extracted from Eliafas.

Ashaver turned to Pop. 'However?'

'However, thanks to the quick thinking of Lieutenant Muller, we now know the location of the relay point, as well as how to communicate with it.' He pointed at the head. 'It's in there! It has to be. He had to know where he was sending the message to.'

Daw nodded.

Pop smiled. 'The relay point will not communicate directly with Cantor. It will send word to another relay. Then another. Then likely a few more. Until the final relay point will send the message directly to Cantor.' He leaned forward. 'We can follow the message through the Greyspace and reach them. We can even block the final message to Cantor, so they won't know we're coming.'

Ashaver's own eyes had become unfocused as he took in the information 'You knew we would figure that out. Why are you talking so much? What's with this little spectacle?'

Pop's eyes, until this point focused on what lay ahead, shifted back towards his surroundings and fixated upon those of his old friend. 'I am putting on this little spectacle to help you do that which I cannot, as quickly as possible.'

'And what the fuck might that be?' Ashaver's eyes squinted in annoyance.

'Enforce discipline.' He turned and pointed towards Daw. 'You heard her. All our eggs are in the same basket. At least, for the time being.' He turned to Ashaver and swallowed a knot that had formed in his throat.

'I think this is it, Tomasz. I think this might be it. I think we can finally end what they started so long ago. We're going to need men. A substantial force – but not too many, else we might leave Terra vulnerable and attract attention. We will have to move quickly, so we have to make the selection now. Quickly and thoroughly. We both know that... selection will be difficult to enforce.'

Silence.

Pop was right.

Pop was very right. They all knew it. If there was a chance to catch the last of the dark elves, every single Terran on the planet would have to be held down from reaching out and grasping it. If everyone who would have wanted to go would go... Terra would be stripped of almost all its inhabitants.

That could not happen. Not only would Terra remain defenceless, but the movement of so many troops would not go by unnoticed. There were spawn out there, vast swarms of mindless cosmic horror – to not even mention the Continuum and its vast reserves of man and firepower, all waiting to catch the Alliance unawares in a moment of overextension. Furthermore, who knew what other contingency plans the dark elves may have had put in place? These thoughts and more crossed the minds of every single person in the room. One by one, they raised their eyes towards Ashaver, realizing the truth of Pop's words.

It had to be the Hierarch. He may not have been their king. He may not have been the Marshal of Terra. He may not have been their Warchief. He didn't even *want* to be their leader. But it had been he that had turned the tide against the elves. It had been he who had led the Terrans across the starts in their cosmic crusade against the dushman. It had been *him* who had led them to war against the Svart in the War of Vengeance. They would listen to him and *only him* on this matter, for it was he who held legitimacy over the act of vengeance against the elves. It was only he that could decide who would get the chance to shed the last drop of bloody vindication.

Ashaver began pacing.

Erratically.

He started rubbing the back of his head as he walked around with his hand on his hip, his lips moving, yet no words coming out. Until...

'Seven ships! Seven *capital* ships. Seven legions.' He reached towards his chest, where he held the insignia of the Terran Old Guard: a skull-shaped icon of smiling death. He threw it on the table in front of the head. 'The Old Guard and the *Naglafar*...' He began opening the drawers beneath the table, looking for something. 'Çingeto, give me your icon!' He asked of his old friend, as he continued rummaging.

'No!' the orc calmly responded.

Ashaver stopped rummaging and slowly turned to his fellow Hierarch. '*What?*' His look was one of utter shock. Thomas believed that it might have been the only time he had seen Tomasz Ashaver look genuinely worried. In real life, at least; here were a lot of videos online from the old day.

'I will not come.' Çingeto Braca's voice was calm, yet caring. Firm, yet friendly. 'Thomas,' he said, referring to Ashaver, 'I understand why you need to go. I have gladly faced the greatest of challenges by your side in support of your cause, as thus was the great honour of my life: to be your friend. Yet, this has always been your burden to bear, a shadow cast upon your spirit by those uncaring of the value of the lives of others. I have stood by your side, as you stood by mine, when the darkness of mine own people's past returned to taint our present, and I promise you that whenever you shall be in need, I will answer your call with no fear of death nor destruction. Yet, what is set before you today is not a task which requires my aid.'

'I have wished every moment since Gondolin's fall for the strength I needed to even hope to see the day when this burden shall be lifted from your heart. I saw you chip away at it until it was little more than a speck of dust and yet still it weighs heavy on your heart. My heart smiles knowing that, soon, you will be free of this burden and that we may walk together, with lightness of soul, into a future free of the torment of your past. It will be a future in which my only regret shall be that I could not see you shake away the shackles of your past by means other than those of violence. What needs to happen, has no power over me, for I have placed it behind me, as has been the blessing of my condition.'

'I will stay behind and will do that which has been my most beloved duty, one soured only by the necessity of my presence: I will keep your world safe. You go and do what you need to do!'

Ashaver blinked, his hands loose against the edge of the drawer, as he stood amazed at Braca's words. After a few moments, he slowly turned his head back towards the drawer.

'Sorbo?' the Hierarch asked.

His answer came in the form three quick and heavy steps, followed by a loud *clang!* Ashaver's eyes came to rest upon the troll's hand, now spread out on the table.

Falk spoke, his voice like the rumbling of mountains. 'I also have a burden I wish to finally rid myself of.'

Ashaver nodded and his fellow Hierarch continued. 'I have a hundred men. Four wings, as well as the crew of the *Tastostauur*. We will join you today, as we have before and will do again!' Falk took his hand from the table, leaving behind a red wing within a blue circle.

The insignia of the Wildriders.

Ashaver nodded, finally rising from the drawer he had been leaning on, having recovered what he had been looking for: a black cloth bag. He turned to look at the room around him and began drawing in breath to speak. Yet, it was another voice that pierced the silence.

'You'll still need five ships.' Daw al Fajr's rang through everyone's ears like the words of the roiling sea upon the ears of a wary sailor.

Ashaver paused, seemingly understanding her meaning. 'Are you certain?'

'Of course I am. *Nialka* was compromised. I cannot vouch that she carries not in her belly another dagger of the dark, but I *will* vouch for the faithful hearts of the Brightguard.' Her voice had changed. It was... darker now. More ominous. Ancient.

Ashaver began. 'Daw... are you sure you want to–'

'Oh, I won't be coming, Thomas. Cantor and his ilk would sense my presence and scatter away like rats the moment I entered their system, wherever that may be. I will come after, once it is done, to guarantee that it is all finally over. I shall not even send the entirety of the Brightguard. Only half. The rest shall stay with me and *Nialka – here –* safeguarding Terra.' She nodded towards Braca, who beamed and managed to stand even straighter.

Ashaver continued. 'Daw–'

'*I will have none of it!*' Again, her voice changed. It was as if the stars themselves were pronouncing judgement unto the night for strangling their light. 'I am tired, Tomasz! I am *so* tired. I am tired of the looks, I am tired of the whispers and I am tired of the prejudice. Not those which *I* must bear, but the ones *my people* endure. Do you not see what has happened here today? An elf murdered a woman, a man and their *children*! Their children – one born and one unborn – on *Terra*, where that sentence is uttered a thousand times in every moment of every day as you recall your past and what was done to you. My people,' she pointed at her chest, '*my people* drowned under the gilded feet of the Svart for years unnumbered. My people were their tools, their objects and their resource. My people's torment was not the great wound inflicted upon the Humans of Terra or the Trolls of Kalimaste. Ours was the deep death. Ours was to become less that people for years incomprehensible and unbearable.'

'If destiny has arrived in such a way that it did not present Quentyn with the chance to claim redemption unneeded, then it shall be my pleasure to claim my people's right to live in a world where they are *not* remembered by the names of their tyrants. If it was not that Vorclav be here and I away, then so be it! I shall not yield my people's right to gain *closure*! Though it sickens me that our dignity has always come at the cost of our innocence, it is a price every child of the Commonwealth would gladly pay so that *our* children – both born and unborn – not be judged by the failings of their forefathers.'

Daw stood tall, revealing herself for who she had always been: a queen. 'My Brightguard shall join you. They will stand by your side and, they will, once more, make you feel the blessing of their allegiance. Their intention shall be as determined as yours. Their character, as strong as yours. Their hands, as bathed as yours.' She had been walking towards Ashaver and now she gripped his hand in hers, holding it tight. When she let go, it was not just he who could see what he now help in his hand, but the whole room.

A bright orange star.

The insignia of the Brightguard.

He gazed upon it for a moment, then looked upon Daw once more. 'Well... so be it!' Ashaver placed the star next to his silver skull and Falk's red wing. His eyes lingered upon the three icons for a moment, as he recalled their joint history.

The Hierarch broke from his contemplation. 'Laur?' He turned to face Pop, extending his hand.

Pop got up from his bench and began removing the icon on his chest. He passed it to Ashaver, who threw it onto the table behind him. A five-pointed red star upon a black field landed right next to Ashaver's skull.

'The Hajduks and the *Doina* will come.' Ashaver pronounced. 'They were the ones tasked with pursuing any surviving Svart and they have done so for the last thirty years. They know what the Svart have become better than anyone here. They are guaranteed a place.'

He raised the black bag above his head. 'Other than the Hajduks, there are thirty-seven Avenger legions on Terra right now. We need only four. Anything more than that and we'd have a fleet too large to not arouse suspicion.' His eyes looked around the room, finding Marshal Feng's. 'Xi, you cannot leave, for that very same reason and, what's more, Terra needs its Marshal, now more than ever.' Feng nodded. The Jinyiwei would be denied vengeance this day, though the reason was fair.

Ashaver once more addressed the room as a whole, 'Anyone who wants to come–'

He did not have time to finish as the entire room came towards him and the sound of insignias being removed from tabards repeated itself around the chamber.

In less than a minute, thirty-six insignia lay within the black bag in Ashaver's hand. The Hierarch turned to one of the remani in the room. 'Basenji! No one here would doubt you.' He raised the bag towards him. 'You pick!' Ashaver shook the bag before throwing it on the table, where it landed in a chorus of clinking.

The remani nodded and came forward. Without looking, he reached in and pulled out...

A golden horse jumping over a blue field. 'The Keshik of Manda Khan and the *Nisdeg Ger*!' Ashaver announced.

A golden seashell upon a black field. 'The Esho of Kitoye Ogulensi and the Àyàngalú!'

A black lion upon an orange field. 'The Akali of Uma Kaur and the *Vairaag*!'

A white axe upon a green field. 'The Ghazis of... of Khalid Minhal and the *Nasredim*!'

The last insignia lingered in Basenji's hand for slightly more time than the others. The reason for this was not lost on anyone in the room. The insignia had belonged to Djibril al Sayid and the Ghazis had been his legion. Many had been the battles fought by that earliest of legions in the War of Vengeance. All could remember the valour of Djibril al Sayid and his men upon the battlefields of Tbilisi, Trebizond, Bahr Aldhabh and Elocphelion. It was fitting that a force founded so long ago during the End Times, a force that had been there to deliver the first outright victory against the elves, would be there to help deliver the final blow.

He then turned, looking around the room. Almost a hundred eyes looked back. He roared. 'Everyone who wasn't drawn, your duty is far more sacred than ours, as you are to hold Terra safe until we return. The rest of you, I'll see you in orbit. Get your men ready, we make the jump to the relay point's location in an hour.'

Movement immediately commenced, as Pop, Falk, Minhal, Kaur, Khan and Ogulensi immediately rushed towards the door. Ashaver pointed towards another nearby commandant, an American of the Terran Navy. 'Signal the Home Fleet! We're moving out! Our ships will jump beyond the Kuiper Belt. Have a squadron ready to survey our jump site after we leave! We don't want anyone coming in through the door after we close it. We'll jump back near Pluto when we return, so don't be trigger friendly when we come back. Keep everyone on high alert until then! Stop the blockade and reinstate limited trade. We're going to have to send a messenger through.' As he gave out his orders, the room galvanized further, as almost everyone sprang into action, all knowing where they would be needed.

Ashaver turned to look at the bloody head that stood facing the eight insignia before it. 'Did you take everything from in there?' He gestured towards the head.

Daw replied solemnly. 'Yes.'

'Good.' With that he stepped forward and removed the head from the stasis field and threw it on the bare table. 'Cut the brain out and ruin it. Keep the rest of the head for posterity!' he ordered to no one in particular.

The Hierarch's eyes now searched for and found Adler, who had been standing next to Thomas and Mira. He began cutting through the crowd towards them.

As he got right next to the American General, he moved close to almost whisper to her. 'I've informed the Warchief and the other Hierarchs of what has happened here, but someone should bring the news in person. I want you to do it! Take the *Blackbird* and let him know of what we are about to do. It's not that he wouldn't grant his blessing, just that he must also be informed that we do not need it–'

Adler smiled and interrupted. 'This action will fall under the "War of Vengeance"?'

Ashaver drew a quick breath, his mind seeking out the necessary specifics. 'No. This falls under "Operation Eichmann". It counts as a "war", and I have jurisdiction over it, meaning that I can give whatever order I want to anyone I want, if it pertains to it...' Ashaver paused and smirked, from the corner of his mouth. This had been in response to Adler, who had raised an eyebrow. '... I subcontracted it to Laur...'

Adler smirked too now, rolling her eyes. 'Typical...'

'It was more his thing anyway and, plus, he wanted the job!' That was all Thomas could hear, as the Hierarch moved in right next Adler and whispered something in her ear. Over the flurry of sounds in the room, he could not hear Ashaver's words.

The look of utter concern on Adler's face told Thomas that the General, however, had heard everything. Adler nodded. Without a single glance towards Thomas, Mira or anyone else, she made directly for one of the exits, likely about to make straight for the *Blackbird*.

Ashaver turned to Daw, who had followed him to now sit right beside him. 'Can you send the coordinates of the relay point to everyone who was selected?'

Daw's eyes drifted off for one second. 'Done!' she announced.

'Good!' Ashaver seemed to freeze in time for a moment. His movements slowed, as he leaned in close to the elf, in a manner much more familiar as the one he had shown towards Adler. He smiled slightly and honestly, as if he was about to speak to one of his nieces.

'I'll take your guys, Daw. The *Naglafar* is big enough to hold a hundred thousand elves if needed. Five thousand shouldn't be any hassle.' His eyes drifted now, falling to the floor, then back to Daw's. 'I understand why you want this, but–'

'– but you see no need to worry your men?' Ashaver pulled back at Daw's look, now fierce, far fiercer than the one she had given him as she had pled the case of her people. 'Is that it? After all this time? You still do not understand, don't you? Just because *you've* let it go doesn't mean the world has. You think I'm doing this because I don't want the past to come back to haunt the present? Well, you see, Thomas, the past never left. It never left me. It never left you. It never left my people and it certainly never left yours.' She spoke the words coldly, yet their intensity scorched those that heard them.

She continued, '*This* act... this act of being there when the final nail is hammered in... It will remind the world of what it knew already, yet didn't want to admit: my people and yours were victims of the same evil. To believe that we should bear any of the shame in which the Svart must drown in is to deny reality.'

Ashaver waited for her to finish. 'You always did love to interrupt people.'

'Oh, look who's talking...' Daw allowed Ashaver the courtesy of a quick, friendly smile, before continuing to stare him down.

'Fine... I was gonna say that it might be dangerous. Only the Old Guard and the Hajduks have fought elves since the War of Vengeance. Falk's boys are as green as grass. The Keshik, the Akali, the Esho, hell, even the Ghazis haven't fought elves in thirty years. Most will be thrilled at the chance of killing elves one last time, like the old days. The rest will be eager to show their elders that they can kill elves just as well as they could. It'll be brutal. There will be a lot of bloodlust and that can cloud the eyes of some men. Telling friend from foe apart can become... difficult.'

'Are you saying your people are animals?' Daw shot back.

'I am saying that the bloodcraze can make any man an animal.' Ashaver now allowed himself to show genuine concern. 'If I am going to have the lives of your guys on my conscience, I want you to know that you will join me in my regrets.'

'It wouldn't be the first time.' Daw nodded to herself, Ashaver's words seemingly getting to her. 'You are right though. I was going to make the choice of who would go and who would stay a random one. I will not. I will ask those that wish to go to step forward. If those that wish to go are more than half, which I honestly think they will be, I will decide who will go depending on who has had the most taken from them by the Oppressors.'

'That's fair to me. Just make sure they're ready to board in an hour. We'll pick you up in Mecca.' Ashaver's words had barely left her mouth before Daw blinked out of the room.

The Hierarch stared at the empty space where she had been, before moving his gaze towards Mira. 'Should I even bother?'

The young Terran Captain responded immediately. 'No.'

'Fine... I won't. You'll join Brightguard and come with us.'

'WHAT?! NO!!! My men are the Ghazis!' Mira's voice flamed.

'No, Mira, they are not! You renounced that position, remember? The Ghazis, including your old company, belong in their entirety to Khalid. At least for the time being. Your time shall come, but not today. Today you will lead Brightguard. Besides, Khalid wouldn't take you. Neither would Uma. Khalid was glad when you left, since he thought you'd be safer. Uma would rather die than bring Sara's daughter anywhere near danger. But, you already knew that, which is why you didn't bother cantering off after Khalid or Uma. So, you're stuck with me or you can fuck off and let me do the avenging.'

Mira's face twitched in rage and, then, her eyes widened, as something seemed to dawn on her.

Something she seemed to accept. 'Fine.'

It was now, finally, Thomas's chance to speak. 'I am also coming.'

Ashaver froze for a moment, before moving at lightning speed, appearing right next to Thomas in the most menacing manner the young Terran had ever experienced. He leaned in close so that only he could hear his words.

'You can. You have every right to. But, lad, you know you can stay behind, right?'

Thomas' head twitched as he came to look Ashaver straight in the eye.

His first thought came to his mind only after his words had left his mouth. 'I'm not staying behind.'

Cold they were, his words.

Yet, his mind was ablaze. Thomas was a little surprised that he felt not fear, but revulsion at the idea. Revulsion that Thomas 'Three Deaths' Ashaver, the Revenant, Hierarch of the Alliance, Champion of Terra and Hero of the War of Vengeance dared to think he wasn't willing to risk his life for such a cause as the vindication of his people. The fact that he might be able to enact one final act of long overdue retribution was something he had not even fantasized, not even in his wildest dreams.

'Ah…' Ashaver's eyes flickered between what Thomas could see was a brief moment of sincere concern, followed by a strange sadness and a blank stare. A grin formed in the corner of the oldtimer's mouth, as he met Thomas' gaze once more.

'So that's it, eh? You're a zealot now? You ready to die, boy?' Ashaver leaned forward even more into him and laid a hand at the base of his throat, palm on his chest, thumb on his carotid artery. 'One does not have to die to be a martyr. All that is needed is the willingness to become one. Are you willing, boy?'

'No. But, I do accept it.' Thomas spoke the truth, even if it meant admitting that which was taboo in front of a Hierarch. Such had been the journey of Thomas Muller.

Still, Ashaver gave him options. 'You can accept it by staying here.'

Options which were of no interest.

'I know. But, I wouldn't be true to myself if I didn't come.'

'You care more about yourself than about your people?' Perhaps Ashaver wanted to shame him into staying?

'Caring for my people is how I care for myself. Caring for myself is how I care for my people. The two are one and the same. If I achieve just one, I guarantee the other. But I cannot abandon one for the other, since then I would have neither.' He had spent too much time debating people on matters of life and death over the last months to let someone beat him in an argument. Even if that someone had a lot more experience with death and dying than he did.

Ashaver's eyes bore into him and Thomas could not tell what they saw. In the end, the revenant did what he did best: he laughed.

'Mira, Captain Muller will join you as attaché to the Brightguard. The Old Guard will enter the fray first and you will follow us with the Brightguard, which you are to treat as your own men.'

Mira nodded.

'*Lieutenant* Muller, sir.' Thomas' obsession with accuracy, as always, got the better of him.

Ashaver had turned to leave. He paused midstride. 'What?'

'I am a Lieutenant, sir, not a Captain.' *Why the hell did I even have to open my mouth? Like he cares if I'm a Lieutenant of a Captain.*

'Boy, did I stutter?' The Hierarch's decision apparently outweighed his dislike of corrections. He continued his stride towards the door.

Thomas turned, confused, towards Mira. 'I don't understand.' Ashaver opened the door and walked towards the battlements outside.

Mira smirked at him. 'I do...' The orange indents of the Hierarch's suit of armour began to glow.

Thomas waited for Mira to continue, but she simply continued to just smirk at him, not saying a word.

'Well?' *Oh, but for fuck's sake, Mira, just fucking tell me.*

'It means that you can treat me as an equal in public now too.' Black wings sprouted from Ashaver's back, right as the Hierarch jumped off the building.

Thomas' eyes widened as Mira's rolled in her head. 'Come on, the *Naglafar* will land soon. We need to get to Mecca.'

The Hierarch disappeared into the darkness of the black night.

Chapter XIX
Like the Demons are near

'I need my equipment.' Thomas explained.

'You've never been on the *Naglafar* before, have you?' Mira responded as she entered the emergency shuttle they had commandeered to get to Mecca. Since they had both had their cars destroyed that night, they had to use one of the military vehicles provided by the Terran Army in Jerusalem, which were all basically tanks with rockets strapped to them. Thus, Mira was able to fully indulge and excel at her love of high speeds, by managing to make the trip to Mecca in a little under five minutes.

The *Naglafar* was hard to miss, even at night, as it was right in the middle of the Campus of Mecca, just outside city limits. It had to be parked outside the city since it was truly gigantic, even for a Terran capital ship. It had once been the vessel of the infamous high elven general Anteo Perem Svart, acting as his flagship during the End Times. In those days it had known as the *Marlafior* and would have also been alive. The great black behemoth before them was merely the dead husk of *Marlafior*, after the orcish capture of the vessel had claimed the life of the great unialki.

The black *Marlafior* had been a creature far more ancient than the white *Nialka*. Whilst the *Nialka* was merely a young adult, the *Marlafior* had been an elder. He had been large, even for his kind, nearly twice the size of *Nialka* and much larger than most Terran battleships. It had been through reckless ingenuity that the Terrans had brought the ship back to life or, rather, some mockery of life. Whilst *Marlafior* had died, his place had been taken by an artificial intelligence called *Naglafar*, hence the name of the ship they now approached.

Unlike the *Nialka*, Ashaver's capital ship looked less like some graceful cosmic whale and more like a bloated shark of the infinite darkness between the stars. Its surface was a sealed carapace, peppered with a myriad of turrets and weapons platforms. The entrance was minuscule, given the size of the ship. It was located near the back of the leviathan, right beneath the ship's tail and main thrusters, and was roughly a hundred meters wide, and another two hundred meters high. *Marlafior* had many other entrances, yet it had been the desire of the Old Guards that the number be reduced substantially for security reasons. The old entrances had been covered up with giant bricks of weirdplate, a material of such darkness that the *Naglafar* caught the eye's attention even in the night, as its colour was the deep black of the void, not the superficial shade that passed for darkness upon worlds such as Terra.

Across from the *Naglafar* lay the *Nasredim*, the capital ship of the Ghazis. Itself a massive vessel, it was nevertheless dwarfed by the leviathan it sat across from. The *Nasredim* was also the dead husk of an unialki, slain and stolen by Djibril al Sayid from the harbours of the Elocphelion. Unlike the *Naglafar*, however, the *Nasredim* had once been the private yacht of an elven prince, hence it had once been of the white variety, being of the same breed as the *Nialka*. Yet, the vessel they now beheld, though shrouded by the night, was a deep green, with only a few pearl indents remaining across its surface. Its shape was far smoother, as the *Nasredim* had always been used more as a prowler, rather than as a brawler, as was the character and history of the *Naglafar*.

As they began their descent, Thomas could already see the black, green and white colours of the Ghazis boarding their capital ship. He turned to see Mira focused, not on flying, but also on the distant figures of her former comrades. After they parked their shuttle, they began walking up the huge access ramp that lead towards the ship's bowels and beheld the Terran Old Guard.

And what a sight to behold they were...

Dead men walking.

Of the original Old Guard, less than two hundred remained, with the remaining hundred being made up of champions of Terra, selected by Ashaver himself, that had not suffered resurrection at the hands of the Svart. The original Death Knights had been spread out throughout the entirety of the Warhost of Terra, with the largest number of them having always concentrated around their two most famous members: Thomas Ashaver and Djibril al Sayid. The many losses suffered during the War of Vengeance, the Senoyu War and the Ayve War had drastically lowered their number. With Djibril's death, Ashaver had become the sole leader of the Death Knights, which he had summoned to him and formed into the Terran Old Guard.

They stood now before Thomas in their terrible grandeur.

Already they had readied themselves for battle, as a few dozen of them waited at the top of the ramp, with a few dozen more being seen preparing for battle within the ship's bowels. If Terran imagery usually quite grim to behold, the Terran Old Guard were downright macabre. Skulls & bones, spikes and hooks, chains and barbed wire, tengu and clown masks, furs and hides of slain beasts, ornaments of tooth, horn and claw, as well as a myriad of other deathly icons adorned armours and weapons. Ebony weirdplate, shadowy darkplate, dark grey adamantine, cold steel and a hundred other metals, plastics & organics were represented among the vast array of guns, swords, spears, axes hammers, knives, daggers & shields. However, if anything, all they did was take away from true ferocity on display, which lay behind the eyes of the men and women who bore them.

Thomas recognized them all.

The death knights of a shattered world.

A few even recognized him. The man who had feared death now walked towards those who had beheld the oblivion beyond the veil.

Everyone recognized Mira, their niece.

'Well, I guess this gives a certain circularity to everything now, doesn't it?' Kamalutdin Abdulrakhmanov mumbled as Mira walked right by him towards Abhijoy Mukherjee, who lay on top of a giant box of ammunition, loading up a magazine with rounds.

'Abby.' Mira spoke, addressing the Bengali Old Guard.

Abhijoy laid down his magazine, straightened his moustache, then got down from atop the box and adjusted his breastplate before walking over towards Mira.

His eyes were red. 'I'm sorry.' His lips trembled.

Mira's face was harder than his breastplate. She nodded. 'Thomas and I need equipment.'

'Yes. Yes, I heard.' He nodded towards the inside of bay. 'You know where to find it.'

'I do. Thank you.' Mira made towards the *Naglafar*'s interior, yet was stopped by Abhijoy's hand on her shoulder.

'I know better than to boss you around, but there's something you should know now, before our friends come.' Mira's face returned to the Old Guard's, who turned to look at Thomas. 'I hear your actions tonight have earned you a promotion.'

Thomas nodded. He knew he wasn't lying, yet he felt as if he was.

'Congratulations! You *technically* outrank a lot of the Old Guard now. Just so you know: they won't give a shit.' A few chuckles and the *hear! hear!* coming from the surrounding guardsmen punctuated Abhijoy's words. Thomas fought to keep his cheeks from blushing in embarrassment.

His face returned to Mira's. 'Three hundred of us. Five thousand Brightguard and two Army Captains.' He leaned in. 'You know how this is gonna go: we will go in first and carve a path. The Brightguard will be behind us.'

'Where it'll be safer for us to be, as well?' Mira attempted to finish his idea.

'Yyyyyes... But, more importantly, it'll be safer for *them*. I hear we're also going with the Wildriders, the Hajduks, the Keshik, the Akali and the Esho?'

Mira confirmed.

Abhijoy's eyes began scanning the dark horizon. 'There's almost two thousand Hajduks, a thousand Keshik, about five hundred Ghazis, four hundred Akali and maybe four hundred Esho. With us, the Brightguard and the Wildriders, that's around nine thousand five hundred men. The dushman would've had time to grow their numbers, but not by much. If they trained every single teenager capable of holding a gun, maybe they'll have five thousand competent fighters. The rest will be civilians.'

Abhijoy's mourning of Lakshmi and her family had departed his eyes, with an old rage replacing it. 'Laur's theory is that they're all gonna be together in one single den of rats. Somewhere in an empty system. Maybe some orbital defences will be put in place, but nothing more. It'll probably be something hidden. A valley, most likely. Some fortification around a central area. Their style, you know?' Abhijoy waited for Mira to nod. 'The Esho are good in the sky. Not as good as the Wildriders, but no one is going to stop the trolls from coming down onto the planet. So, the Esho will hit any orbital defence, then they'll sweep the system.'

'The Hajduks will go in first and infiltrate them. It'll be quick. They'll also check the planet, to make sure no one else is on it. Then the Wildriders will give them a quick bombing. The Akali... well, you know what they're all about: setting a perimeter and shooting fish in a barrel. Then we go in, together with the Ghazis and the Keshik. We're going to be the first ones to crash into them. Immediately afterwards, the Brightguard will come in.'

'You and the boy are Captains now. You're Terrans. You'll lead the Brightguard into the killboxes we and the Ghazis will set up for you. Do you understand?'

'Has this been confirmed by... *him*?' Mira asked, clearly referring to Ashaver.

'It doesn't have to be. Mira, listen to me! Please!' he spoke softly, yet insistently. 'For you, for him,' he nodded towards Thomas, 'this is your first time fighting them. We've fought them more than we did any other enemy. They were, and always will be, the *Enemy*! We know what is going to happen. We know how it is going to happen. We know *who* will do *what* and *how* they will do it. *That* is how I know that the Brightguard will need you two.'

'Why?' Mira pushed for an answer Thomas thought they both knew the answer to.

'Because they are not like us.' a Mexican voice spoke from the shadows of the *Naglafar*.

Marco Acosta emerged, resplendent in his armour, and walked towards Mira, coming close to her before speaking once more. 'These elves are not good in close fights. They're good from a distance. We are good up close. They need to be good up close. They will need leaders.'

'Done!' Mira spoke as soon Acosta had finished his point.

'Really?' Abhijoy asked, raising an eyebrow and bearing a look of sceptical surprise.

'Yes. Got it. We're Captains. We'll shadow two of their captains. We can cover a thousand men each, as we would do in any other scenario.' Mira was remarkably compliant.

'Well, ok...' Abhijoy raised a hand above his head. 'I thought you'd need more convincing.'

'I don't.' *Strange*. She pointed towards the *Naglafar*'s insides. 'We need to suit up.'

'And *we* need to brood a little.' Abhijoy said and Acosta smirked. 'Go!'

Thomas followed Mira to the ship's interior.

Once inside, they discovered the vast cavern that served as the Old Guard's armoury, training ground and loading bay. It stretched out almost a kilometre into the great ship, with the end being just barely visible, as the giant chamber was remarkably dim lit, even for a battleship. The best source of light was the long glowing row of golden light that ran across the ceiling to the very end of the ship. On the walls, Thomas could see a vast collection of aircraft, tanks and other vehicles, as well as great engines of war and tenacious machinery stocked across the cavern's walls in great lairs forged from weirdplate.

'Why didn't you complain?' he asked her, as they got far enough from the Old Guards.

'Because me wanting revenge for what they did is just as important as making sure we don't lose people we don't have to lose. They're right and everyone knows it. The Brightguard are good, but they're not shock troops. Daw picks them for their abilities as diplomats, administrators, scientists, physicians, therapists, assistants, entertainers... They need martial abilities and experience, sure, but it comes second to them being good at what Daw needs them to be good at and Daw is a literal demigod. She doesn't really need protection services.' She gave him a quick glance. 'They really will need us. Furthermore... you heard him, five thousand Svart... I'm not worried about missing out on any action. There'll be plenty of that to go around.'

It was along the very middle that a long table lay, stretching across the cavern's length and laden with weaponry, ammunition, tools and, most importantly, a lot of Old Guards, all preparing for battle. At the front of the table, near the entrance, Mira led Thomas to a great glass cylinder in which an operator could be seen. His image was that of a black giant whose wrinkles, as well as any other surface of his body where skin folded, lay etched in golden light. His eyes also radiated light, as if they were simple openings to the golden fire within. He wore a black tunic, bearing the silver skull of the Old Guard with matching pants and shoes, giving the impression of a man which burned from the inside out.

'Hello, Naglafar!' Mira tone was the one she used for old friends which she nevertheless found to be a little annoying.

'Hi, Mira! Hello, Captain Muller!' *Oh, it's already official.*

'We need–' she began.

'*Guns!*' Naglafar replied with a voice different from the one he had just used before. As racks of rifles, pistols and machine guns sprang up from the table behind him.

Mira looked annoyed. 'Have you been watching *The Matrix* again?'

'It *is* my favourite movie, after all,' Naglafar teased her.

'Hmmm... Casper?' *Mira's talking to her operator out loud again, looking like a crazy person, like she always does when she does that.* Within a few moments, the avatar of Naglafar was replaced by that of a cartoon version of a ghost.

'I judge that it is now in order?' the ghost spoke.

'Yup! Do the thing!' Mira replied. Instantly, a section of the table almost fifty square meters in size began to rise, revealing underneath it an impressive selection of body armour. Thomas could tell it was female armour, since it seemed to be specifically designed for the thinner sex. Before making her way towards the location of the arsenal, Mira said to Thomas: 'Naglafar is alright, but I am in no mood for him now. Casper's much more quiet and Naglafar won't mind.' She pointed towards the racks of guns, blades and plate. 'Casper, he's a man.' At her words, another section of the table rose, revealing armour fitting of his size. 'Go! Whatever you'll need, you'll find it here.'

Mira seemed to enter a trance. It was similar to how she would move in her kitchen, right before she was about to make beef Wellington or Peking duck. She seemed perfectly at home inside the *Naglafar*, seemingly knowing the available selection by heart. The first thing she did was change into armour. She picked out common Terran Old Guard suit pieces; though Thomas noted that she choose a set-up that was very non-traditional. For her feet, she chose a pair of standard boots, which ran up to her knee, with a large sheet of darkplate sticking out a full hands breadth over the front of her knee. For pants, she went for standard micromail. She seemed to never even court the idea of wearing plate armour on her thighs, though Thomas did note that she had opted for the heavier dissipater variant of pants.

It was a classic choice for women, since they were of much smaller frame. What they lacked in strength, they had to compensate via speed. Mira had chosen lower body armour which would not, in any way, impact her mobility and would also *dissipate* the force of any impact her upper body would have to face. Thus, she was choosing mobility over protection. Which was important information for Thomas, since it meant that Mira expected a lot of melee combat, with heavier weapons such as artillery or missiles being excluded from her foe's arsenal.

She did get decent upper body armour, though.

Her breastplate was a standard Terran variant, though Thomas could tell from the size that it was the female version of a very traditional Terran melee darkplate armour set. There was a solid metal plate that extended from her lower ribcage, up to right in front of her chin. Another plate rose even higher from her back, protecting the back of her head, without impairing her mobility. *Are we worried about being shot in the back, Mira?*

The pauldrons she chose confirmed that she expected a lot of melee combat, as she had chosen a small version of standard Terran female 'parry plates', which was how they were commonly called, as their design was centred around their use in parrying blade swings. Beneath, micromail could be seen protecting her armpits and her throat. Her choice suggested that some light weapons fire was to be expected, but most of the fighting would be up close, versus opponents which could swing a sword.

Her arms she had neglected almost completely. Here rerebraces and vambraces were darkplate, yes. The vambraces extended backwards, protecting her elbow from being slashed or disjointed, yes. She wore micromail, yes. But, her hands were completely bare. It seemed to be her trademark. He had seen it before, during the Battle of Astarte, the last time he and Mira had seen combat on the same battlefield. Mira had worn a much more bulky Terran battlesuit then, yet she had also discarded the idea of a gauntlet in favour of simple micromail gloves. Thomas had noticed this oddity then and he saw it once more now.

It was the mark of an arrogant fighter. It meant that she thought that she didn't need the added protection offered by any real armour, since her skill would keep her safe and was not to be hindered in any way, especially not by light fabric. He did see her spray her hands with anticoating, though, which meant that there was a chance for them to be fighting in the void of space, at the bottom of an ocean or in the middle of a lava field... Thomas glanced around, noticing a box full of the spray, with which he began to efficiently coat every inch of his body.

He was right to do so, since Mira immediately began using entire cans of the stuff on her hair which, apparently, was too important to have catch fire. Then, Mira did something Thomas hadn't seen anyone do in a long while.

She put on make-up.

Not a lot. Some Terran women really exaggerated. A lot of Terran men also exaggerated. Thomas had always thought warpaint to be unnecessary. Mira, however, seemed to favour a light coat of concealer, follow by a slight coat of mascara and some lip-coloured lipstick, on top of the anticoating she had sprayed on her face. It wasn't even noticeable. *What the...? I never knew she was one of those girls.*

He put on a suit of micromail, as Mira had, choosing the version which covered his hands. He choose the same boots as Mira, though he did opt for slightly more rigid darkplate for his groin, backside and thighs, since he liked to expose his lower body a lot during combat. He chose the same upper body armour as Mira, though he did opt for slightly more generous armour for his arms.

It was as he was about to copy her choice of weaponry that Mira broke out of her trance for a moment. 'Bring a grenade launcher.'

'For fortifications?' *Or for–*

'Yes.' Mira gave him a quick glance as she found the words she needed. 'When you told me about that argument Thomas and Pop had – about the Svart still being out there – did Tomasz talk about his theory of how the Svart would be different now?'

He did. 'Yes, he did.'

'The elves didn't go underground back during the War. But, the last time they found a den of them, it was just that: a den. A base dug into the centre of a moon.'

'Rotapple. Yes.' Thomas remembered the name of the moon.

'That's one of our tactics. One which they imitated in the past. Maybe they'll imitate it in the future.'

Which is why she wants me to take the grenade launcher. That and the fact that it's really heavy. More precisely, the ammunition was pretty heavy. 'I'll have one of the incumberents with one next to me at all times.'

Mira gave him a weird look, which he had expected. 'Captains don't carry heavy weapons.' *I mean they do sometimes, but fuck it. It's too heavy and I'm not good with them anyway. Why the fuck do I have to be a walking arsenal just because I'm male!* 'I'll pick up an extra blast charge though.'

Mira looked at him, a smile appearing across her retreating pokerface. 'You know, you don't take success gracefully, Thomas.'

'I'm learning from my mentors.' Thomas quickly replied.

Mira smirked loudly, which was the closest she had come to an actual chuckle the whole evening. She went back to inspecting the arclight spanner she had selected for a few moments. Then, she decided that she had a question that needed an answer. 'Hey... you do understand what is going to happen, right? It's not going to be like Triangulum.' She had spoken in such a way that Thomas understood exactly what she meant.

He didn't have time to respond, though his facial expression gave away part of the answer, as they both turned towards the sounds of rhythmic marching behind him, coming from the bottom of the ramp. Rather, they heard the sound of thousands of bodies running in perfect synchrony up the ramp.

The two Captains turned towards the commotion, both knowing what it likely was.

'Look, lads! The elves arrive at Helm's Deep!' one of the Old Guards joked to his companions.

On the ramp below, Thomas could see the Brightguard approach in one single formation, fifty men wide and almost a hundred deep. They had come ready in complete battle armour, with every single one of them bearing their rifle and at least one type of melee weaponry. Thomas immediately began scanning the faces of the elves for a specific one.

'Samwise!' One of the elves responded, and Thomas remembered his face from Mira's birthday party.

'Eang!' the Old Guard responded. Thomas recognized him as Samwise Metzen, *the Last Man at* Fort Bragg. The *Bearbane.*

'I guess it's gonna be like the old days.' Eang separated himself from the elven column, as the Brightguard began boarding the *Naglafar.*

'Oh, yes, like the demons are near!' Metzen replied, as his eyes spied something in the night. Just as the Old Guard turned his head, over twenty elven aircraft began flying into his ship, all bearing the seal of the Brightguard on their belly.

Eang offered clarification. 'They've just arrived from *Nialka.* Twelve gunships and ten dropships. It should be enough for our contingent.'

'Yeah, I suppose they will be.' He extended his finger, pointing towards one of the vessels in the sky. 'That one yours too?'

'It would appear it is one of yours.' The elf was right. It was one of theirs. It was a Terran Volkswagen shuttle. It was quite a common variety. Thomas' father had the same model. Yet, what was it doing in the Campus of Mecca? It was also going quite fast, having turned on most of its caution lights, as it plummeted towards them. Some of the Old Guards neared their fingers to their triggers. Suddenly, it landed on the top of the *Naglafar's* ramp, right next to the assembled Old Guards, just as Thomas finally caught glimpse of the license plates.

No fucking way...

The passenger door opened first and Ronan O'Malley stepped out of the vehicle clumsily. The old man caught himself on wobbly legs as he got out of the car, taking a moment to catch his bearings, just as the driver got out.

Maximillian Muller moved briskly towards his old commander's side, catching him just as the Irishman was about to fall to the ground. His father was in full uniform and nodded towards Thomas as he gripped Ronan.

'Oh, dammit! I'm fine! I've got it!' The old Terran began walking on his own two feet as Maximillian shadowed him, paying close attention to his frail legs.

'Ronan!' Metzen greeted. 'What, *the fuck*, are you doing here?' the Old Guard asked, his tone one of both surprise and annoyance.

'What am I – are ya fuckin' daft, Sam?' *Well, this isn't the Ronan I meet in Ireland.* Sam's face was more irritated than curious. 'Ya think I live under a fuckin' rock ya fuckin' gobshite lil' yank?' He turned to Max. 'Fuckin' Americans and their shite.' He turned back to Sam and pointed at Thomas, of all people. 'That lad caught an elf that killed a fuckin' paki woman and her fuckin' baby, ya fuckin' eejit!'

'Ya don't say...' Metzen was not amused.

'Oh, but for fuck's sake. Abby!' He gestured towards Abhijoy. 'Go get some crayons, this wagon might need a drawing!'

'Ronan, *I* might need a fucking drawing! What the fuck are you doing here?' Abhijoy's look was entirely one of concern.

The Irishman seemed on the verge of apoplexy. Either that or he was having an actual stroke. His lips moved as he struggled to explain the obvious to people he would have expected to be much more perspicacious.

'He has come to die.' It was Acosta that had spoken. No eyes turned to look at him, as they all seemed to wonder, quietly, if he was right. They all searched Ronan's eyes for an answer.

'Aye... aye, Marco, I've come for that!' He looked around, his eyes resting a moment on Thomas.

'I thought you were a good Christian now, Ronan,' Sam said. 'Isn't suicide on the naughty list?'

'Aye! Aye, it is! And so is killin'!' the Irishman responded as he neared Sam, coming up right next to him. The Old Guard towered almost two feet above his frail frame. 'When you died, Sam, did ya pray for it to be quick?' Sam, who was already tense, now turned to stone, his eyes granting glimpses of the roaring lava that almost spewed out of him. He couldn't respond, for Ronan continued.

'Did you ask God for death, Sam?' he asked again. 'Because, I think ya did. I think that as ya stood there beneath all that rubble, ya prayed to *God* you'd die quick. And what did God do? He granted ya wish and, then, He brought ya back, since He wasn't done with you. Ya know what I prayed for?' He drew even closer to the Old Guard now. 'I prayed for life. I prayed for hope. You know how I did it, Sam? Huh? No?'

His voice had been strained by the effort and now grew hoarse. '*Promises*! I made promises to God. I told Him that, if He'ed let me live, if He'ed make the world right again, I would help. I would help fix the world and praise His name and be a good man. Do ya know what God did, Sam?' The American's face didn't move, nor did Ronan want it to. '*Nothing!* Until... until I started killin'. Until I started killin' the demons myself, with my own hands and their own magics! When I started doing that, God started helping. He started making the world right again.'

'And then there were no more demons to kill and ya know what I did, Sam? I helped the world fix itself. I praised His Name. I tried to be a good man. I did not see that the world God made was a world that would shun Him! I did not see how the world we were making was one in which there was no God in anything we did and, *still*, I tried to help. I praised His Name and loved His Word and still the world moved away from Him. So, I decided to not be part of the new world. I decided to be with God and I *suffered*! I suffered Sam, in ways you cannot even fucking imagine. Punished by my people. Shunned by my friends. Only Max, here, ever calls to see if I'm still alive!'

He gestured towards Thomas' father, who gave Metzen a look of both confirmation and consternation. Ronan continued 'How old were you when you died? Thirty? Twenty? Twenty-five?'

'Twenty-seven,' Sam replied coldly.

'Ah... so ya over seventy now?'

Sam slowly nodded.

'I'm fucking eighty-five and look at me and look at yerself! Do ya know what old age is? Old age is feeling the call of the *ground*, Sam! Old age is to have your body waste away into a pitiful, painful little prison, as you feel your heart begin to yearn to stop beating in ye sleep. Old age is realising, midway through yer day, that you had no reason to get up from bed in the morning. Old age is knowing that you should've died *young*, Sam, yet being thankful for every single moment you lived and still live, while you regret every moment you didn't *live*.'

Ronan caught his breath and continued. 'I prayed for God to take me and He did *nothing*. Now, I see God's desire for me, as I saw it before. I see His Hand now, as I saw it then. I see His kindness and I see His gift. I have come here to go with you and die against the Enemy our Lord always wanted me to die fighting against. I see now the path the Lord put forth for me to take and to have my prayers granted. I...'

He gestured towards his companion. 'I called Max the moment I read the alarm notice. I saw that it was his son and Djibril's girl that caught the *dushman*. Then we heard that Tomasz, Laur and them lot are mobilizing. Ships launching and legions mustering in Bâlea, Eko and Karakorum. The *Naglafar* and the *Nasredim* in Mecca.'

'You've picked up their trail, haven't ya, Sam? Huh? Abby? Marco?' Ronan looked around at the Old Guards in attendance. 'Aye... ya have!' He turned to Max. 'Max was worried about his son – well, not as worried as the lad's mother, God bless her heart, but worried still – so I told him to bring me to Mecca so he could have an excuse to look for his son and I could come over here and tell ya that ya will *not* be leaving without me!'

Sam gave him a long look, as he mulled things over in his mind. 'Ronan, fuck off!"

'Ya fuckin' cunt! Where's Thomas?'

PFWOP!

It was not Thomas Ashaver that appeared, but Daw al Fajr. The Urizen appeared out of thin air, as she had earlier in the day, right next to Mira. She locked eyes with all those around.

'I take it I'm interrupting something? Is that you, Ronan?' she asked, looking carefully at the old Irishman.

'Yes, girl... I apologise for... the time that has passed.' He gestured at his face.

'I know of what happened. I know of the decision you made and I see its effects upon you. However, I take it you have come here to achieve that which you wish you had achieved before you had to make the decision?' *Ronan and Daw know each other?*

'Aye, girl. I have..." he responded solemnly.

She came over and put a hand on his face. The old Irishman seemed to be shocked by her touch. Thomas realised that this must have been the first time someone had touched him like that in a long time. 'I understand your decision now, as I did then." She turned to face Sam and the rest of the Old Guards. 'I take it you are denying him.'

'Yes, Daw, we are,' Sam replied. 'He made a choice and he should keep to it.' He turned to Ronan. 'You expect to sit around for all those years, only to come back at the eleventh hour and set things right? After we called you "brother" and you called us "sinners"? While you built your little church in fucking Ireland or wherever you fucking crawled back to? While we kept everyone safe and good men died so you could chop wood and mix concrete in a hut?"

Ronan sat quietly, his eyes having remained fixed on Daw.

Sam turned to Daw. 'If Thomas lets him come, it's fine by me. But, if not, he should go home and die alone.'

Daw turned from Sam back to Ronan. 'Oh, I don't think he would be alone." Ronan smiled at her, his eyes both shy and grateful. Daw smiled back, before turning towards Sam. 'Luckily, we'll get to find out soon enough.'

It only took a few seconds to pass for Ashaver to appear. He moved quietly in the air and, at night, you couldn't really see him that well, with his armour fully dark, hidden by his shadowy wings. He appeared a few meters in the air above them, before dismissing his wings and landing on the ramp, just a few yards away from the group.

It was at this moment that a small remani shuttle also entered the *Naglafar*, after flashing its presence with its characteristic lights. *The remani have sent someone also.*

Ashaver did not pause his stride to acknowledge the vessel that had arrived with him and began walking quickly towards the group. His eyes looked first to the Brightguard and their vehicles, all of which had boarded his ship, before turning towards the assembled Old Guards, the two army Captains, the one Master Sergeant, the demigod and the old man. He gave Ronan a quick look, before turning towards his Old Guards and showing them his open palms whilst shaking his head subtly.

It was Abhijoy who filled him in. 'We're all set here, sir. Ronan was wondering if we had room for one more.'

Ashaver stopped for one moment, giving Ronan a side glance. 'You gonna fight to the death, Ronan?'

'Like my life depended on it!' the Irishman replied without hesitation, but with a cheeky smile.

Ashaver nodded, his face showing no emotion, before turning to face straight ahead and continuing his walk towards the inside of his ship.

'He can come,' he said, to no one in particular.

No one had time to take in Ashaver's verdict, for the ship's engines began their low, heavy hymn. It was followed by the sound of two hundred square meters of two meter thick metal suddenly lifting their massive weight of the ground, as the ramp began to slowly yet surely rise.

'You heard him, everyone who is cleared to come, get inside! Everyone else...' Sam looked at Daw al Fajr and Maximillian Muller. 'Everyone else... now is the time for goodbyes!'

With that, Abhijoy walked over to Ronan and grabbed him by the shoulders. 'Come on, you old mig! Let's go juice you up.' He began gently leading the Irishman towards the inside, together with Marco, which joined him in essentially carrying their companion.

Thomas rushed to his father, as Daw and Mira rushed towards each other in an embrace and whispering words of encouragement into each other's ear.

His father spoke first. 'You're an Old Guard now?' Thomas could see behind the smile and could tell his father was a little rattled.

'No. He ain't died, yet,' Metzen answered. Before joining his comrades as they prepared the ship for take-off, he said out loud to Maximillian. 'You've got about a minute until the ramp gets too high and you won't be able to fly out anymore.'

His father nodded and the Old Guard turned to leave. Thomas didn't know what to do or what to say. His father didn't seem to know either, though he did try.

'Do you know when you'll be back?'

'No.' He wanted to say so much. He had spoken to his parents every so often in Jerusalem. Yet, never enough. Before he had snapped out of it, he would speak to them to tell them he was alright when he in fact wasn't. After he had snapped out of it, he would speak to them just as often to tell them he was feeling great, which he really was.

But never had he talked to them enough and he really felt that now.

Just that... he really didn't know what to say. Neither was there time, as the ramp became level with the floor of the loading bay. Thomas could see that the ship itself had begun to rise.

His father seemed to understand, as he moved in for a hug. 'I know about what you've been working on, son. I know you can't tell me what it is because I haven't been introduced to you. So, just know that your mother and I know and we're proud of you!'

Now Thomas did know what to say. Not because he could process his father's words, but because he knew the urgency of the moment meant that he should only say the words that mattered. 'I love you, dad!'

'I love you too, Tommy Boy! Go!' With that he broke the hug, nodded at his son, then walked briskly back towards his shuttle. He gave Thomas one last wave, before getting into his car and flying away.

Thomas didn't understand.

His father knew?

Already?

He didn't know he was on the lists...

'Was that your father?' a thin, waifish voice said to him.

By now, he was used to that voice sneaking up on him. 'Yes.' Thomas turned to see Toph by his side, with Mira kneeling behind her, seemingly still hugging the space Daw had occupied before she had teleported away.

Looking back at Toph, he smiled. 'I guess you'll get to meet him next time'

She smiled back. 'I guess I will.'

'Toph... you could've stayed...' he began.

'Hmmm... I could have.' She moved in closer, whispering to him in German, 'I can only trust a quarter of my brothers and sisters to be capable enough in combat.

The way I look at things, if I came, there's one less person I wouldn't want at your side in a fight against the old masters.'

'Besides, it all sounded like a lot of fun!' she continued, as she moved away from him. 'Come! I can tell you're not done with,' she gestured at his outfit, 'that!'

The *Naglafar* entered the Greyspace as soon as it exited Terra's orbit only to emerge, a few seconds later, in the void beyond the Kuiper Belt. As Mira was busying herself with welding axes and chains to her vambraces and just as Thomas was about to decide which rifle model he would equip, they received a summons to the ship's command room. The chamber was located deep within the gigantic vessel, where the great shark's pancreas would have been located, if it were a living creature of Terra's oceans.

Thomas and Mira made the journey together with Eang, the leading elven commander, with their escort comprised of Abhijoy, Marco and Sam. As they entered the great command room of Tomasz Ashaver, Thomas Muller was stunned by how dark it was. Only the cold blues and warm reds of a few lamps truly lit the room, while a myriad of small control lights and screens dotted the great circular chamber. All around the room, Thomas could spot around two dozen Old Guards, some looking over screens, while a few stood preparing their weapons for battle. At the room's centre there lay a great wooden table, above which a hologram of a small, spiky sphere could be seen.

Thomas Ashaver was intently focused on said sphere. On the screens spread around the room, Thomas noted a live feed from the sphere, which seemed to be located about ten kilometres away from the tip of *Naglafar*. Around the sphere, which Thomas realized was barely a few feet across, he recognized the *Doina*, the Àyàngalú, the *Nisdeg Ger*, the *Vairaag*, the *Nasredim*, as well as the hulking *Tastostauur*, itself much larger than even the *Naglafar*.

Next to the wooden table stood a great navigator chair, on which sat Kevin Falk, eldest son of Sorbo Falk. Thomas saw the resemblance to his father now, as he had seen it before when the troll had exited Mira's dining hall together with Mira's senior birthday party guests. He had been blessed with his father's kind face, though not with his relaxed demeanour.

It was tradition for the *Naglafar*'s pilot to be a troll, with the position first being held by the current occupant's father. As they neared Ashaver and his table, Thomas saw Kevin give Mira a quick nod and a nervous smile. Mira smiled back, before acknowledging the other inhuman in the room with another familiar smile. It was this smile that confirmed Thomas' suspicion that the remani sitting next to Ashaver was none other than Basenji. *He must have been the one on that remani ship that flew in.*

'Alright, boss, what's the sitrep?' Sam asked, as they all gathered around the table.

'The Hajduks have accessed the relay point.' He pointed at the sphere. 'In a few minutes, the *Doina* will jump to the next relay location. Once Laur tells us that the next relay point is secured, the *Tastostauur* will follow the *Doina* to the next jump site. Once the *Tastostauur* and the *Doina* are in the same spot, Laur will jump to the next relay point and Sorbo will hail the Àyàngalú, which will jump to the *Tastostauur*'s location. The Àyàngalú makes the jump and Laur confirms the next relay point's location, Falk jumps again, then Kitoye, then Manda and so on. Uma, then Khalid, then us.'

'How long are the jumps?' Acosta asked.

Kevin responded. 'Probably less than eight minutes.'

Eang offered additional information. 'This is an old model.' He gestured towards the sphere. 'They're designed to relay information quietly while remaining hidden. The drawback is that they can't cover large distances. They're short range.'

'That's Laur's assessment also,' Ashaver continued. 'He thinks the next one will still be in the Solar sector, likely perpendicular to the KTM line. But, after that... we can't fucking tell... Though we always assumed they'd still be in the Milky Way. The furthest they might be is Sagittarius, but no further.'

'We don't *know* that.' It was Mira who spoke.

'We don't.' Ashaver confirmed. 'But it's a reasonable assumption.' He turned to the young Arab captain. 'They're not in Triangulum, Andromeda or Shangri. Our contacts in Draco and the Magellanic Clouds tell us that they aren't there either. They have not rejoined the Tribes, since they're exiled. The Continuum sure as hell hasn't taken them in...'

'I know, but that's the North, the Zack and the West –' Mira continued.

'– and the other three directions are crawling with spawn, Atlanteans and Doradi, Mira. If they would've ventured there they'd be lunch, batteries or worse. Plus, we would have detected any intergalactic jumps that big... No, they're still in the Milky Way. So there's no need to worry.' Ashaver smirked. 'They aren't too far away. We only have a couple of days, at most, to wait.'

He drew in a breath of air. 'Which means we do not have too much time to prepare.' He turned to look at Eang. 'Five thousand?'

Eang nodded. 'As well as gunships and dropships.'

'Good! My Old Guards will leave the ship first. The Brightguard will follow. You are to split into five battle groups. You will lead one, alone. The other four will have joint leadership. Basenji will take a thousand. Mira will shadow another thousand. The same goes for Thomas and Ronan will take the last thousand.'

'Ronan isn't a Captain.' It was Sam who spoke.

'Neither is Basenji and you didn't say shit about him now didn't ya, Sam?' Ashaver's tone was firm. He continued, 'Ronan's battle group has the highest priority among the five battle groups, meaning that he will be the first to pick where he wants to go. Given that he has a literal death wish, he will pick the hardest point of their defences, so I recommend that you give him the most experienced of your men.'

Eang nodded.

'You have second priority. Mira third. Thomas fourth. Basenji will act as your rearguard. Is all of that clear?'

They all nodded.

Ashaver pressed a button and the hologram disappeared. He addressed all those in attendance now. 'I want you all to understand something.' The Hierarch looked down on the wooden table before him, as he bit his lower lip, his eyes blank as he looked for the words he needed.

'I wanted them to be dead. I *wanted* them all to be dead and, from what we could tell, they were. I... I wanted us to move on. I wanted us to focus more on dangers that were in the near and distant future, as opposed to the horrors of the past. I wanted us to seek out a future and an identity which no longer revolved solely on what happened forty years ago.'

'However, it would appear that wishful thinking will not warp reality and the reality is this: they're still here. They are still capable of spilling our blood and they're still motivated to seek out our weaknesses and our weakness is now this: Kralizec.'

'I know everyone here knows about it. I know everyone here understood the risk we took when we decided to do it. I know we all acknowledged that it would be a matter of time before the whole universe found it. But, it can't be two weeks. It just can't...'

'Before we left, I told Shoshanna Adler to travel to Nargothrond and tell the Warchief to be ready for a general mobilization of the Allied Host, as well as the Legendary League, the Hierarch Legions and every single member's military. The reason for this is simple: we do not know if Eliafas managed to bring word of Kralizec to the others already.'

'If he did and what young Thomas did was simply stop him from securing some additional *unnecessary* information, it is absolutely paramount that we make sure that we stop them from disseminating that information further. Once we secure their location, Laur and his Hajduks will scour every single one of their records, communication logs – *everything* – to make sure that they have not done so already.'

'However, these people are survivors. *Desperate survivors.* I do *not* think I have to remind anyone in this room what desperate survivors are capable of.' The faces of those gathered confirmed his beliefs. 'We believe they are all in one place. They lack the numbers to defend multiple locations. They lack the resources, the relations, the ability and, dare I say it, *the will* to establish multiple colonies. This *will* be it. This will be their last fortress.'

'But, that doesn't mean it will be their last escape. There will be contingency plans set in place. What that may be, you can all imagine: teleportation, warp jumps, grime mines, a broadcast of Kralizec's meaning to the Emperor's own fucking toilet. *I don't fucking now*. But, there *will* be something.'

'It is imperative for the long term survived of our people – of *all* our people – that they not be allowed to escape. Do I make myself clear?'

'Yes, sir!' confirmed half the room, whilst the other half either nodded or felt no need to.

'Good! Now, go! Ready yourselves and your men! We don't know when, but we will soon be upon them. In the meantime, rest, eat, plan, contemplate... just be ready.'

As Thomas, Mira, Eang, Basenji and many of the Old Guards left the command room, Thomas saw the *Doina* disappear from their screens and sensors.

It begins.

They went back to the armoury and did as instructed, as much as they were able to. The first thing they did was establish which battle group would be joined by which Captain. The Brightguard did not have any unit structures of any nature, unlike the Terran military or the Allied Host. Whereas a Terran Captain would usually lead a battalion of one thousand, the Brightguard's equivalent of Captain (a Pathfinder, such as Eang) could command anywhere from a dozen to two thousand men. Eang himself was merely the most senior of around a hundred Pathfinders that had boarded the *Naglafar*.

A decision was made to split the Brightguard into five battle groups based on different backgrounds and specializations. Ronan would take the most formidable of the Brightguard's warriors: those that could act as shock troopers. He would directly support Ashaver's Old Guard and Falk's Wildriders, as they stormed the enemy stronghold.

Basenji would take the most skilled marksmen and would support the rest of the 'Ratden Expedition', as the group of eight legions had been christened, from afar.

Eang would take those most knowledgeable of the Svart's technology, as well as those that had spent the most time close to their former masters and, thus, were most familiar with their tactics and thinking. His group would seek to support the Hajduks in subduing any of the Enemy's remaining defence systems.

Thomas, it was decided, would take a mix of those Brightguard that had served in the Allied Host, as well as any demolitions experts to be found among the legion's ranks. Their task would be to blast their way through defensive structures set up by the enemy. Toph hadn't even had to insist upon her allocation within Thomas' unit, as the proposal had come from Mira and was quickly supported by both Eang and Basenji. He was glad that he would be able to be close to Toph and help keep her safe.

Mira would take the rest, which meant she would take the weakest among the five thousand Brightguard that had joined the Ratden Expedition. The plan was for her to shadow the Ghazis, since she was very familiar with their tactics and battle doctrine.

It was just as they had finished agreeing upon their strategy, that the *Naglafar* executed its first jump through Greyspace. As had been predicted, they re-entered realspace in just over five minutes.

Then they jumped again.

Then again.

Then again.

Hours passed, with five minutes of jumping always being followed by thirty minutes of waiting.

Thomas even had time to take a nap.

Nine hours later, he awoke to find that the mood onboard the *Naglafar* had changed from one of preparation to one of expectation. The five thousand elves, the three hundred humans, the one troll and the single remani on board all waited for what was to come. Thomas found himself seeking out Mira and finding her in front of the raised ramp squatting, with her hands clasped in front of her face, her index and middle finger extending towards the ramp, while her thumbs cradled her jaw.

He stopped, considering whether or not she wished to be disturbed. She was a berserker after all. He had seen her little rituals performed in the past before their training sessions. Whether it was a strange shake of her head, a peculiar relaxation of her shoulders or the way she played with the hilt of her weapons, Mira always went through her little motions before every sparring session she had ever had with Thomas. He could tell this was something like that, but much more intense.

'It takes longer if you don't do it for a while,' Marco Acosta said, as he came up right next to Thomas. 'Your mind doesn't want you to be in that place. Your mind doesn't want you to be close to that place. If you do it a lot, your mind will keep you close to that place. If you don't do it a lot, your mind keeps you further away.'

'I've heard.' *Many times.*

'You don't have it? The bloodlust?' Marco asked. His tone was solemn, yet curious.

'No.' He glanced towards the Old Guard. 'I... I get *focused*. I do not cross the veil of presence, as it were. I just... see everything clearly.' *At least I try to.*

'Ah, a *focused fighter*. My son, also!' He smiled proudly.

'You? No?' Thomas thought he knew the answer already.

'No.' He nodded towards Mira. 'When I was young, like her. Now, coldblood.' *That's what I heard.* Most Old Guards were coldbloods, men purged of all of the mystery of violence and danger. Resilient men, whose minds had survived untold hours of unspeakable violence, terror and stress. To the untrained eye, it looked as if they felt no difference between the battlefield and the comfort of their own homes. The more thoughtful observer, however, would see through their calm for what it was: their shame.

Deep down, they missed the days from before. The days they used to know fear.

'It's harder now.' Acosta continued, smiling now. 'My son. My wife. I will have another son soon.'

'Congratulations!' Thomas was happy for him. He realised that he had not seen a smile made in honour of life since Toph had smiled at the thought of meeting his parents. Before that, it had been a long string of smiles made at the prospect of death.

'Thank you!' The Old Guard's eyes wandered, not towards the past or the present, but to the future. 'I will make a new escapulario for him.'

Now it was Thomas' turn to smile in gratitude. He reached towards his neck and pulled out something from beneath his micromail. Acosta's eyes widened upon seeing the Virgin Mary etched in white and blue. 'You... you wear it now?'

'I've worn it ever since you gave it to me.' *No lie.*

Acosta didn't have time to express his joy with words, with his expression conveying his appreciation eloquently enough. A strange voice filled the air. 'Oh, lad, I see ya found our Blessed Mary Mother of Christ!'

Thomas and Acosta turned to see a human of Terran height. He was ginger of hair and quite pale of skin. His hair was tied in a topknot giving the appearance of added height, as the red giant towered over them, a look of pious glee on his face. He wore a full suit of Terran armour, complete with a FN FAL model rifle, a sidearm – which was just a shortened version of Winchester model rifle – and, as a melee weapon he had selected a shillelagh, the weapon favoured by the Irish Fianna Avenger Legion.

'Hello, Ronan!' Acosta spoke, as Thomas' eyes widened, realizing he must be right. *That's where he's been. He's been transforming.* 'How are you feeling?' continued Acosta.

'Well, what can I say? Better than I have in ages. That liver cancer was just killing me –'

Ronan did not have time to detail the miracles of modern healthcare, for he was cut off by the sound of alarms.

The Brightguard looked up worried, while the Old Guard didn't even flinch. As the three Terrans behind her either acknowledged, contemplated or interpreted the alarm's meaning, Mira rose from her meditation.

She turned towards them.

'The Hajduks have found Ratden. We're less than thirty minutes away.'

Chapter XX
A Song of Swans

Ratden was a large world almost twice the mass of Terra. Which was quite common for uninhabited worlds; the greater gravity took it outside traditional Goldilocks parameters. However, Ratden was by no means uninhabitable.

It was a world of great canyons, most of which had gone dry, whilst others were still wet. Great rivers dug into the earth across the world, as they raced towards the planet's great oceans. The very peaks of the world, where the canyons began, were cold wastelands, many of which were covered in snow, whilst most were simply red, grey or black. It was beneath the upper plateaus that one could see the blue and white rivers that stood at the bottom of ravines. Some of those blue veins were coated in layers of green.

Their target was very well hidden. Particularly from outer space. Particularly at night. The settlement, roughly five kilometres wide and ten kilometres long was bordered by step ravines on three slides, whilst a wall cordoned it off from the great valley that lay across it in the west. It appeared to encompass the source of one of the world's rivers, as a thin line of blue seemed to spring forward from the settlement's eastern side.

The area appeared to be covered in dense forest which, on closer analysis, served only as cover for the compound bellow. On the three sides which lay protected by the steep cliffs of the great canyon, one could observe the entrances to three large hangars, the largest of which stood next to the source of the river that flowed from the elven stronghold.

A silent scan of the area by the Hajduks revealed the existence of a single large control tower, reaching up from the settlement's western wall. The tower rose almost a kilometre in the air, with manned observation decks present at regular intervals. They also identified a large artificial satellite which stood directly above the control tower, in the upper atmosphere.

The *Doina* had quickly blinded the satellite, as it were, by placing it inside a virtual reality bubble. Thus, the satellite's sensors, as well as its crew, were unaware of what was happening around them, as they saw only the same void they had seen only a few moments earlier. The illusion would only work for a couple of hours, until the satellite's sensors would catch on to what was happening. Though the Hajduks didn't need a couple of hours.

They only needed about forty minutes to land on the world, infiltrate the control tower, as well as several segments of the western wall. At the forty minute mark, Laur Pop phoned the *Doina*, from the last level of the control tower, confirming that the assault could begin in earnest.

By this time, the *Naglafar*, the *Tastostauur*, the *Nasredim*, the *Vairaag*, the *Àyàngalú* and the *Nisdeg Ger* had all arrived in the world's orbit, circling the disabled satellite as wolves would a wounded hare. The *Tastostauur* was the first to hurdle towards the planet's surface, its hangar doors open in preparation for the immediate deployment of its darts. The *Vairaag* began to circle the settlement below, as it released its payload: twelve nuclear warheads. The warheads descended rapidly towards the planet, having been essentially catapulted by the Terran vessel towards the planet below. They would form a circle of fire around the elven settlement, guaranteeing the isolation of their target, whilst also knocking out any electronics.

It was just before the warheads reached their targets that the *Àyàngalú* rammed into the elven satellite above Ratden, making it appear as if an explosion of light had occurred in the night sky. The elves below had little time to contemplate its meaning, as the dozen warheads detonated.

Eight exploded as they hit the upper plateau of the surrounding canyons, causing ash and rubble to rain down upon the settlement below. Four exploded in the air right above the valley beyond the western wall, immediately flooding the settlement in a burst of blinding light, followed by a devastating shockwave.

It was at this point that the trolls of the *Tastostauur* began their own bombardment of the settlement. Napalm poured from the Wildrider's darts as they circled above the compound, setting fire to the upper canopy of the trees and burning alive those few unlucky souls that had the misfortune of being caught in the inferno's path. Missiles hit the buildings below, as machine gun rounds peppered the surface.

By that time, the Old Guards had arrived.

They had jumped from the deck of the *Naglafar* as the Ghazis had jumped from the deck of the *Nasredim* and the Keshik had launched themselves from the *Nisdeg Ger*. The Keshik relied solely on drop pods, which launched groups of ten men towards the surface. The Old Guard relied solely on their suits of armour, as they raced towards their quarry below, followed by the green cloaks of Ghazis. In their wake came the dropships of the Brightguard, bearing in their bellies five thousand elven souls, as well as three humans and one remani.

Around a hundred elves had died at the hands of the Hajduks during their initial infiltration. Maybe a hundred more had died due to the twelve nuclear blasts, whilst another hundred had been blinded by the searing sight of nuclear obliteration. It was many of these poor souls that fell to the falling rubble and the flowing fire of the sky. Many more fell as the trolls pummelled the settlement with raining gunfire and a flurry of explosive blasts, as the trolls brought to them the fury of Kalimaste.

By the time the Old Guards and the Ghazis had landed, a thousand elves already lay dead. It was with their comrades' arrival that the Hajduks revealed themselves and began openly attacking the elven defenders. They were all swiftly reinforced by the arrival of the troll Wildriders of Kalimaste, which had descended from the *Tastostauur*. The legion of Sorbo Falk rode into battle upon the great gryphons of their homeworld and their bone-chilling screeches quickly filled the night. The loud crashes of Keshik drop pods punctuated the chaos, as the elves rallied and readied their last stand.

They were quickly joined in battle by the attackers and the sounds of slaughter roared across the hellish landscape. The fiercest fighting took place in the great courtyard that stood at the heart of the settlement, before the entrance of the largest hangar. As metal met metal, the Hajduks detonated the base of the great elven watchtower, leading to it collapsing across the settlement it had been meant to watch over, splitting the defenders into two desperate halves.

It was then that Ronan O'Malley honoured his vow and met his maker. True to his word, the Irishman had landed in the very heart of the battle, meeting the elven defenders at the very centre of their desperate formation. As the Brightguard tore into their former masters, at their head could be seen a towering red goliath, whose club rushed towards heads that had long scoffed at the impotence of Terra and the sterile minds of their underlings. The giant tore a bloody path through the elven lines, as he sought to escape the protection of his elven allies as he sought out among the horrified defenders the face of he who would have the duty of slaying the great Terran beast.

In the end, Ronan would suffer only partial failure in his endeavour. It had been Khalid Minhal and his Ghazis that had come across the empty husk of the Irishman's armour, perched on top the shattered wreckage of a hastily clad elven suit of battle plate. Around them lay the tabards of many a Brightguard, soaked in the same black ooze as the suit of armour beside them, albeit of a different origin.

On the other side of the collapsed tower, Thomas Ashaver cleaved across the battlefield alongside Sorbo Falk and his beloved gryphon Arrowish. It had been here that the Hierarch finally saw the face that he had long hoped had been lost to the chaos of the void or the ravages of war. The image of Cantor Perem Abrasax appeared before him, rallying the last of his people for one last clash with their nemesis. He wore no longer the bright livery of the court of Gondolin, but the black garb of the elusive dark elves, as was his right, for he was now the sole patriarch of their shattered people.

Ashaver was a menacing sight on the battlefield as it was, but when he saw a face he recognized from the days of a war he had wished behind him, he became truly blinding in his darkness. An avatar of raging shadow came to be where earlier the Hierarch of the Alliance had stood. The dread beast slashed and hacked its way through the elven guard of the last King of the Svart, hurtling towards his quarry.

Cantor met the bane of his people in combat, yet he was far outmatched. As Ashaver sliced through his retinue, the last of the great warriors of old Gondolin, he towered above his hated foe, raising Berlo above him as he struck down upon the elven lord. Some miracle ensured that the elf managed to withstand the first blow with his shield, only to fall to the ground on one knee. Ashaver grabbed the shield's searing edge with one gauntlet and yanked it towards him with such force that he tore the elf's arm off at the elbow. The elven lord attempted to stab the Hierarch with his sword, yet he was no match for the Terran's ferocity.

As his blade raced towards a chink in Ashaver's armour, it met Berlo in a parry. The elf barely clung to the blade, as he readied it for another strike, leaving him unprepared for a kick from the raging shadow before him. Cantor was catapulted several yards across the bloody battlefield. Though his lungs collapsed from the impact, he tried to get back on his feet and raise his blade to defend himself, one last time, as the Hierarch leaped through the air and crash on top of him.

A few of the fallen lord's companions attempted to stop Ashaver from bashing his brains in with his fists, yet they met only the edge of Berlo, the cold fury of the Old Guards and the searing shadows of the Terran warlord's armour. By the time Ashaver rose, nothing recognizable remained of Cantor Perem Abrasax, leaving only a few to hope that he had been reunited with his people in a world much better than that he had departed.

It was in that silence, as the last face of torment was no more, that Ashaver began to hear the screams.

At first, there had been the screams of pain and shock. Then there had been the screams of horror, as the elves realised what was happening. Then there was the weeping, as father, mothers, brothers, sisters, sons, daughters, lovers and friends lay dead or dying in the arms of their unfortunate survivors.

The luckiest ones had died in battle and were spared both a slow death and the torture of having to witness what was happening to those they were leaving behind.

Others had been gunned down by feverish weapons fire, as they had ran for what little remained of their life. Groups of elven civilians were pushed into corners, to be hacked apart by axe and knife. Many non-combatants fled to the relative safety of the surviving structures, only to be trapped inside by the attackers.

The smell of burning flesh began to weigh heavy in the air, as black smoke and white ash filled the air, rising above homes being given to flame and horror. The battle had not even ended, yet the unarmed survivors were already being corralled into large groups, to be brought down by either cold machine gun fire or by frenzied beasts bearing sword, spear, axe and hammer. Many, however, were not granted the blessing of an execution. Too many.

Those trapped under the rubble.

Those that had fought the attackers, only to be left shattered upon the ground, their bodies torn to pieces, yet their minds still aware of the horror around them. Their mouths praying for death to come and spare them the torment that was to be the last thing they would experience.

The mothers and fathers clutching the limp bodies of infants. Their bodies wracked and undeserving of the horrific feelings that coursed through their hearts.

Many had their mouths stuffed with their severed limbs and organs. Others had rods shoved between their lips and down their throat into their bowels, as they were hoisted up in the air. Others joined them on rods of the same fashion, albeit with a different point of entry. A hundred other creative punishments joined them as Ratden became the site of a gallery of the macabre.

The screams began to dwindle. The cries of tortured men died out as the wailing of women grew louder, until only the pained sobbing of a few girls cursed with physical endurance remained to accompany the sound of crackling flesh and breaking bone.

In the end, they begged for death.

The leaves had burned away, yet the charring trees still clawed at the sky, as if to plead with those few that tried to flee the carnage into the heavens above to take them with them. Small elven aircraft, similar in size and design to the ship Eliafas had brought to Terra, attempted to escape from the three hangars built into the cliffside, whilst elven darts attempted to break through the Terran blockade, only to be cut down by the Akali's own aircraft. What few escaped were quickly felled by the might of the seven battleships waiting in the sky above them. A few even attempted jumps, only to be spit out as black debris by the detonation of grime mines planted by the attackers beyond their doorway into the Greyspace.

Basenji had led his contingent atop the battlements of the western wall. Above the carnage of the settlement, his Brightguard came to the aid of the Hajduks, as they wrestled with the defenders for control of the wall and the causeways that lead to the two adjacent hangars. It was as the bodies of a thousand defenders fell towards the uncaring ground below that the last of the Brightguard landed upon the battlefield.

Upon the great stairway that lead to the great middle hangar, the bodies of elves could be seen sliding down. Some of them even bore the emblem of the Brightguard, as Eang had lead his men in their assault upon what appeared to have become the new epicentre of Svart resistance, after the destruction of the forces in the settlement below. It was he who first understood that within the cliff before them there must have been something of remarkable importance. His voice rang out across the general communication channel.

'This is Pathfinder Eang of the Brightguard. We've broken through to the central hangar and are engaged with the enemy within. There is one passage. A freight line. It leads into the mountain.'

'Ship?' Ashaver's voice responded.

'What we see is a railcar. At the other end, we don't know.'

'Can the mines stop it if it's a ship?'

Eang's voice responded. 'Negative, sir! It'd be a warp jumper. They can't stop it once it's ready.'

All knew what the elf was saying: they only had a few minutes to reach any ship inside before it gathered and focused the energy needed to execute its single warp jump, which would allow it to bypass the grime minefield in the surrounding Greyspace. After it launched, it would be almost impossible to pick up its trail. Whomever or whatever was onboard would escape into the vastness of the universe. A few elves might, once more, survive to fight another day or, worse, word of Kralizec might reach the Continuum.

'We're coming!' Ashaver responded.

The dark figure of the Hierarch burst into the air, followed by the gore drenched wings of the Wildriders. On the ground below, the Old Guards rushed towards the central hangar, dashing across the shattered steps of the ascending stairway and leaving behind the Keshik to prevent the surviving Svart from regrouping. Ashaver launched himself upon the beleaguered defenders atop the causeway and across the hangar's floor, slaying dozens of stragglers, before reaching Eang's forward position.

As the Wildriders charged the defenders, the Brightguard, reinforced by their Terran allies, began to advance across the sundered floor of the hangar. They were barely forty yards away when they saw the passageway before them grow dark. At first it appeared as if the elves had shut off the light. Then dust and rubble exploded from the passageway's entrance. The elven defenders now fought with their backs against a wall, with no escape behind them, only the collapsed remnants of what had been the escape of but a few of their brethren. They were cut down in a matter of moments by their enraged enemy.

Ashaver's face twisted into a snarl that was carried across the communication channel. 'Have the *Naglafar* drill into the ground to reach them!'

Falk the Younger answered from the command deck of the *Naglafar*. 'There isn't enough time.'

'Teleport a bomb!' Ashaver already knew that, if that could have been a solution, he would have already felt the mountain tremble as its insides were broken.

'It's shielded,' Eang informed him.

'Collapse the fucking mountain!' It likely wouldn't work from the outside.

'The structure is too strong!' Eang, once more, stated the obvious.

'God *fucking* DAMMIT!!! They've sealed us off, we can't get to them!' Ashaver's shadows seemed to boil as the Hierarch confronted the prospect of an eternal crusade against the Svart.

A voice rang out across the communications channel. The voice of a man with a very high opinion of himself.

'Not from where you are! There are other passages.' Laur Pop made sure his words were clear and his tone was urgent. 'We have access to their schematics. The cliffs are full of tunnels. They all converge upon a large chamber within the mountain. The passage you just saw collapse lead to that chamber. The freight line Eang saw runs nine kilometres into the mountain. We don't know towards what, but it's one hundred percent an escape. We can't get to it from the big hangar anymore. But, we can get to it from the other two hangars. Some of those tunnels are still intact.'

Ashaver turned to seek out the entrances to the other two hangars. He saw quickly the reality before him, as both hangars witnessed heavy fighting, as the Ghazis rushed to reinforce the Brightguard assaults on both sides. The Hajduks bit deep into the defenders, as they rushed across the recently captured causeways. From above, the Akali reigned down hellfire into the large caverns within. However, the Svart were holding. They wouldn't for much longer, yet they would hold for just enough time to allow some of their brethren to escape.

The Hierarch knew his choice was pointless. He was closer to the hangar on the left hand side and Falk was closer to the one the right. With one quick look, the two Hierarchs split, with Ashaver rushing to reinforce Mira's detachment.

The Arabian Captain had swiftly secured her landing zone and, since very few battle plans survived the actual battle, she had decided to not focus on assisting the Ghazis. Instead, she had immediately pushed towards the cliff wall. Once inside the hangar, she had quickly identified the numerous tunnels that reached out from entrances spread out across the great cavern's sides. With care for neither station nor rank, she ordered the elven commander she shadowed to lead the bulk of their forces on an assault on the hangar. Once it was captured, the Brightguard were to link up with the detachments she would take into the tunnels.

She had no need for Ashaver's instruction to enter the tunnels. She knew that there was something in or beyond them that would be of interest. Elves were not practical creatures by nature. They loved to embellish things and to go on tangents. She had seen that many times on Menegroth. The high elves of Gondolin she had seen less, but what she had seen suggested that it had been they that had instilled the love of impractical architecture and useless structures upon their former slaves. These elves were of the same kin as the high elves, yet here they seemed to be different. Ashaver had been correct: these were a changed people. A desperate people.

And desperate people only dig tunnels for a reason.

She knew they had it in them to blow up the tunnels and trap their attackers within the mountain. Yet, she knew she had time to stop them if she moved quickly. Leading a platoon of twenty elves, she made her way through the most promising passage, fighting tooth and nail for every corridor and approaching each corner as if an army lurked behind it.

There were many warriors, yes, but also a great many civilians, including small elven children. Mira knew for certain that she had shot a few by accident, yet most of the little ones that had crossed their path had been put down by the Brightguard behind her.

She knew what she signed up for. But that didn't mean she had to waste her time with the messy details of genocide. She knew that there were many amongst the Brightguard that harboured just as deep a hatred for the Svart as the average Terran oldtimer. It didn't surprise her when she saw one of her men beat an elven woman to death, rather than end her quickly. She was honestly glad that the Brightguard hadn't found it appropriate to provoke even more gruesome and time-consuming act of vengeance at the expense of expediency.

But, she had not come here to slaughter children and piss on corpses. She was here to make sure the Svart never threatened her people again, to avenge the death of Lakshmi, Fiol and Sara, and to keep Daw's people as safe as she could. Thus, she fought like a demon to reach the tunnel's end, which proved to be a large chamber littered with pillars containing vast hoards of what she assumed was genetic, technological and cultural information.

She understood what the pillars were immediately, since they were of elven smartstone, a material she knew well. It resembled Terran marble in a way. The columns before her, clearly built from the material, had become dark, a sign of having been pushed to saturation by the gigantic amounts of information they likely held. They were ridged, much like the columns of ancient Greece, for they were meant to hold long soulkeeper rods within them. It was within these soulkeepers, like many others located in many a vault on an elven world, that the Svart would have kept those dead, but not lost.

Yet, the white rods were gone.

To her left she saw the collapsed remains of a tunnel, likely leading to the large central hangar she had seen outside. Before her, across the forest of pillars, she saw many other entrances to other tunnels, though many had already been sealed shut, rubble now blocking off their entrances To her right she saw the beginnings of another tunnel.

This one was much larger, as it was roughly the same size as the collapsed tunnel to her left. It lay around a eighty meters to her right, beyond around a dozen rows of columns. She could see how it was meant to be traversed, as she could see a large railcar, seemingly stationed at an angle.

She had never seen elves use railcars before. They were primitive contraptions and elves loved to make things complicated. She realised how much these elves had changed the very moment she realised why they had decided upon using railcars: they were reliable. If the elves had to reliably and quickly transport something downhill, deep into the very bowels of the mountain, they were better off allowing gravity to do its thing. Once she saw what the elves were hastily loading into the railcar, she realised what that something was.

Mira knew she had only a dozen men behind when she decided to charge into the great chamber. Yet, she estimated there were only around a forty elves in the entire room. For the moment, at least, since she had seen other elves arriving from the unsealed tunnels. Sure, there were tunnels in the way, not allowing her to quickly see every single elf in the room, but it was a good estimate to go by.

If she hit them hard and quick, they might have a chance of reaching the railcar before it was released downhill.

Which was what Mira did, as she charged into the chamber, immediately eliminating two nearby elves, with her Brightguard quickly bringing down the other five closest to their position. What followed was a quick sprint towards the nearest pillar, as she began shooting towards the elves across the room before they had a chance to shoot back.

There were three major issues with this plan, the first being that there were much more than forty enemy combatants in the room. The more accurate number seemed to be closer to a hundred. Mira felt two shots connect with her armour and she saw another round connect with her rifle, just as a fourth nicked one of the axes attached to her arms. They were being met with a hail of bullets as dozens of elven rifles were aimed in their location.

The second issue, closely related to the first, was the fact that her contingent of elves was almost immediately pinned down. Mira knew that it would take a while for reinforcements to arrive, thus they would have to concentrate on delaying the elves from releasing the railcar. They'd have horrible odds of achieving that if they were hiding behind walls and columns for the entire duration of the firefight.

The third issue was somewhat foreseeable, yet also unexpected. Three elves came up from behind the pillar in front of her. What's worse, she knew she was low on ammunition, as she realised that she only had a couple of rounds left and no time to reload.

She shot the last round just as she let go of her rifle, detaching her left axe from her arm, as her right arm reached towards her pistol, resting on her hip. In one quick motion, she managed to shot the first elf in the head, before succeeding in knocking away the second elf's rifle with her axe. She then let go of her pistol, allowing it to be retracted back into its holster by the long wire attached to the bottom of the sidearm's grip. Mira drew a dagger with her right hand, as she brought her axehead into the second elf's head. She kicked the elf, as she pulled him to the ground. In one movement, she had the second elf on the ground, while she drove her dagger into the third elf, pushing him so hard, he fell backwards. She drew the dagger out, as her body twisted to strike the enemy below.

One good swing was enough to crack the elf's neck, severing his body from his mind. As she pulled the axe out, she looked for her rifle. She saw it laying a couple of yards away, right in the middle of the enemy's line of fire. Her men attempted to counter the enemy, yet their assault was not enough. There was, however, one way she could help with that.

She reached towards her arclight spanner.

A crude weapon, it was essentially a gun that shot what looked like lightning. Though the fact that it would always shoot was quite reliable, since the inherent technology was robustly mechanical in nature, there was no telling where exactly a plasma drill's *lance,* as it was called, would actually shoot. It would usually stick to a particular direction, which roughly coincided with the user's target, yet the lance would twist and turn, as the energy sought to connect with as dense a material as possible, causing it to melt or crumble everything in a relatively wide cone in front of the user.

It was the weapon of someone who considered being surrounded to be a virtue, not a sign of misfortune.

Her men began shooting towards enemies encroaching from all directions now, as they could not stem the tide of elves rushing towards the relative safety of the chamber, which was now the last redoubt left to their people. She quickly identified a viable target just a dozen meters to her right, as she stood with her back against the pillar. She pulled the trigger.

Nothing happened.

Again.

Nothing.

Mira had to duck as a shell hit the pillar, forcing her to the ground. It was only then that she noticed that her right hand was missing. Where it had been but moments before was now only a white, red and blue stump of retreating skin, clotting blood and blue honeybone plating. She must have been hit by a passing shell as she stabbed that third elf, when her hand had overextended beyond the pillar's protection.

She realised the arclight spanner was actually still located in its holster on her lower back

There was no time to really take that in, as Mira griped the hilt of the plasma drill with her left hand and began letting loose lightning towards the enemy positions. By the time she and the Brightguard had managed to eliminate the Svart in front of her, they were down to only seven elves and one maimed Terran.

They achieved nothing, as the elves continued to prepare the railcar for its departure, pilling it with the long white shafts of the last soulkeepers. The elves concentrated their fire, as one projectile managed to break in two the column she had been using for cover. Mira crawled behind the relative safety of the collapsed beam of black smartstone, only to have it struck by another projectile, throwing them both forward and catching Mira's right leg underneath the collapsed pillar.

It was as she sought to free her trapped leg that Mira's ears sealed shut. Her body trembled as it took in the blast of a massive explosion. Smoke and dust filled the room, as the defender's rounds pierced the heavy air.

Only to be met by furious gunfire, as Mira saw the muzzle flash of hot Brightguard rifles, as well as the loud booms of Terran firearms.

Captain Thomas Muller had led his men into the hangar opposite Mira's. Since his contingent was largely made up of former Allied Host soldiers, they were much more disciplined than the regular Brightguard. A full five hundred of Thomas' contingent reached their target hangar above the elven settlement, with Thomas being able to leave three hundred of them to finish off the elves in the large cavern, as he lead the remaining two hundred into the tunnels.

They had been followed into the tunnels by a group of Old Guards led by Marco Acosta, which caught up with them during the heavy fighting in the tunnels. Together, the two forces had fought through the caverns with remarkable efficiency, swiftly nearing the access to the large chamber behind the largest of the three hangars. There they had encountered heavy resistance, followed by a sealed door, which Thomas' Brightguard quickly demolished with some of the blast charges they had brought with them, as per Mira's instruction.

They arrived into the pillared chamber behind a wall of smoke. After identifying the enemy positions towards the far left of the chamber, they quickly advanced towards them. It was then that he noticed that across from them, and much closer to the enemy positions, was a small group of Brightguard, as well as one pinned down Terran Army Captain.

Acosta and the Old Guards advanced upon Mira's position with unbridled fury, with Thomas right next to them, peppering the enemy positions with gunfire. As they reached the collapsed pillar, the Old Guards took up defensive positions around the fallen captain, as Thomas and Acosta lifted the pillar and Mira pulled herself out from underneath it.

He leg was intact, though it lay badly crushed by the pillar's massive weight. She could likely walk, yet she was in no position to run. It was then that Thomas noticed her missing hand.

Shoulda worn those gauntlets Mira...

She got up to use her arclight spanner on the enemy, only for Thomas to grab her and push her to the ground.

'You're staying here!' Mira met his instruction with a look of profound annoyance, as she was clearly ready get up and look for the motherfucker that took her hand. Thomas pushed her down, once more, this time much more firmly. He grabbed an extra machine gun he had brought and placed it in her one good hand, after wresting the arclight spanner from her. If she was to stay behind and provide cover fire, he didn't want her casino gun to score a jackpot in his back.

'Dushman will come from there!' He pointed first towards the open tunnels in the direction of the collapsed passage to the hangar, then towards the machine gun. 'This and twenty Brightguard!'

He hailed a nearby Brightguard Incumberent. 'Stay here with her! Your platoon and Sestoma's! Hold this ground! When our back is secured, take her outside!'

He looked down to see Mira glaring back at him, frustration etched upon her face. After a few moments, she nodded and smirked. 'Hurry!'

With that, Thomas left Mira and joined the Old Guards in their assault upon the remaining defenders. He quickly caught up to Acosta and his three companions, as they led the assault across the pillared chamber. By this point, to their backs were around fifty Brightguards, battering their enemy with rifle bolts and rocket propelled grenades.

Yet, it was the Terrans that dredged through the rubble of fallen columns towards their opponent. It was they who saw the last of the soulkeepers being loaded into the railcar, as the elves began releasing it from its bindings. One of the Old

Guards, whom Thomas identified as Yellow River Charlie, launched a pulse grenade towards the defenders, successfully knocking out their electronics. The elves did not relent, continuing to unlatch the massive cart from its bearings, knowing that gravity would do their work for them.

Without sharing a single look amongst themselves, the Old Guards charged towards their target, naught but twenty yards away, with Thomas in tow. The six Terrans took many rounds, yet their thick armour and heavy build assured that each hit was naught more than a slight impediment. They had to dodge some of the more dangerous projectiles, such as plasma bolts and the larger cannon shells, yet even some of these were mitigated by the shields carried by two of the Old Guards. The pulse grenade knocked out many of the elven weapons systems, as well as the lights, meaning that the already dimly lit chamber was now only lit by muzzle flashes and the roaring fires of destruction.

It was through this hellish landscape that the six Terrans sprinted to reach the railcar, with some of their Brightguard allies right behind them. Two of them stopped behind the last two tunnels, providing cover fire, while another two stopped to engage in melee combat with the defenders.

Thomas and Acosta reached the railcar just as the last of the great latches keeping it in place was freed by a dying elf. The wretched soul had crawled towards the last latch's location, its legs severed from its body by a Brightguard plasma bolt.

The two Terrans quickly began eliminating the railcar's crew, as well as any desperate passengers.

It was just as Thomas was about to find himself overextended whilst tackling one of the last guards, that he saw the muzzle flash of an elven rifle burst from behind him. After running his opponent through the chest with his shortsword, he turned to see the very last of the defenders collapse behind him, his head completely torn off by what had clearly been a blast from a Brightguard's rifle. The elf dropped a pistol from its hand, just as it reached the ground. The bullets within had likely been destined for the back of Thomas' head. He turned his head once more, towards the location of his saviour, only to confirm that one of the Brightguard had managed to reach the railcar as it began its descent into the darkness of the deep mountain.

Toph Pamento's face was lit only be the flames of the burning garments of their fallen foes. Right as he was about to come closer towards her, she was illuminated by the roaring of flames behind her.

Acosta had grabbed Mira's arclight spanner out of Thomas' hand and began shooting the stacks of soulkeepers, which blasted into combustion, burning with a bright white light and lighting up the railcar as it hurdled through the darkness.

With the tunnel now illuminated, the three gazed down the tunnel, as they picked up more and more speed. The railcar was roughly eight yards wide and twenty yards long. Red flames blazed from the front of the railcar, where a grenade had detonated the front section and slain the defenders within the front cabin. The flames revealed the smooth walls of the tunnel, punctuated only by the ancient patterns of the hard rock.

Bodies littered the floor around them, making it both sticky and slippery with blood, gore and wet cloth. Thomas quickly performed a check of his equipment, as he found a large container on which he could lean on. He noted Toph doing the same.

Between the three of them, they had maybe a hundred rounds of ammunition, about five grenades, one functional blast charge, as well as their melee weapons. Their armour had been badly battered, with all of them having discarded their helmets, either in favour of better visibility or simply due to the damage they had taken, which had rendered them little more than flimsy head ornaments. From what he could tell, they were all relatively unharmed.

Acosta walked around the cart, releasing the stacks of soulkeepers into the tunnel behind them. As the shafts fell and shattered in their wake, their shards followed them towards their destination. Thomas and Toph proceeded to do the same.

It was as they were both pushing out one of the last containers on board the cart that they noticed something behind them.

The tunnel was collapsing.

Thomas realized that the elves were likely using the same technique they had used to collapse the other tunnels. Because of all the EMPs, as well as the communications jamming of the Terran ships, the elves below likely didn't know that the railcar rushing towards them had been captured by the attackers. Thus, they had likely followed protocol and destroyed the last tunnel.

This information meant two things. First, the Svart wouldn't expect them to be coming. Second, there was no way out for the three of them. If they managed to survive what was to come downstairs, they would have to wait for their comrades to dig them out, which would likely take a while.

They didn't even have to speak, since they all saw the tunnel's end swiftly nearing before them. They all rose to face their destination. Thomas and Toph gripped their rifles, reading themselves to unleash fire the moment they crashed into their destination. Acosta brandished his sidearm, as well as his sword, preparing to charge into battle first.

The noises were deafening. The sound of the collapsing tunnel behind them. The screeching of the railcar's wheel upon the tracks below. Loudest of all was the sound of wind rushing by their ears. Yet, Thomas could hear something.

Heavy breathing.

He turned to see Toph readying herself for the fight that awaited them. She was using a breathing technique to calm down. He quickly checked to see if she was all in one piece. As he confirmed that she was alright, she turned to look at him and nodded, mouth still slightly open, drawing sweet breaths of air into her lungs. Her face never changed, yet she nodded.

Content that she was alright, he turned to see the end of the tunnel coming ever closer. He braced for impact, yet the cart was caught by a smooth landing pad, dramatically slowing them down, as they docked into their destination.

The elf waiting on the platform in front of them didn't have time to react, his face bearing the same look of horror it had likely expressed in the moment it had become clear that the last stronghold of his people was under attack. Acosta cut his head clean off as he rushed the platform, Thomas and Toph en tow.

Thomas did not know if Acosta paused as he realized what they had stumbled into, but he did sense Toph freeze in her tracks, just as he did.

This wasn't a warp jumper.

This was an Orpheus Chamber.

It bore virtually the same design as the room beneath Terra. Thomas quickly glanced behind him, where he, indeed, saw an observation deck. There must have been no more than twenty elves there alone, with around another twenty spread around the room. As Acosta attacked the latter group, Thomas immediately opened fire, together with Toph, upon the deck, quickly downing many of the elves therein.

Then he heard the great semisphere in the middle of the room begin to hum, as the great empty void of the gigantic screen before him stood quiet, as if bracing itself for the blast of information it was about to receive.

Could it...?

Oh no...

Who knew what Eliafas had stolen from Terra without their knowledge? Who knew how much their Old Enemy knew about the Aether, Satya, Olorun or Yggdrasil?

All Thomas saw was one single horrific scenario.

He remembered a dim lit living room on the shores of the Dead Sea. He remembered what he had learned in that room. He remembered Xhisa's insistence on the connection of Satya to *Yggdrasil*. He remembered his warning that the only danger to Satya would come from other branches of Yggdrasil.

He remembered Diwali Day.

They might access it.

It should be impossible.

We don't know that for certain.

He ran out of rifle bullets and rushed towards the elven Genitrix, using his pistol to eliminate the nearest dushman. Acosta joined him, rushing the last of the Svart, as Toph picked them off from behind them. If he got to the Genitrix device fast enough, he might be able to stop it before it finished its Theogenesis.

Two elves sought to stop him, both in armour. Good armour. Armour they had been wearing before the attacker's arrival in orbit, knowing that there was a chance that such a calamity might occur. He managed to dodge the blade of one as he rushed the other, knocking him to the ground.

He wrestled his opponent on the ground for a few quick moments. He was much stronger than the other ones. A real warrior. A warrior ready for combat.

Thomas broke free from the elf's grip and got up from the floor.

He got ready.

Instincts took hold.

He waited for the great Svart High Guard, the Last Defender of his People, and a hardened veteran of the titanic conflict that had been the War of Vengeance, to rise and strike him.

In a perfect way.

A real warrior's head was severed from his shoulders and struck the ground the same moment as the Svart's knees.

As he regained his footing, Thomas saw another foe closing in from very, very near to him.

Too near.

There was nothing Thomas could do about it.

And then a real warrior's head exploded.

Thomas turn to see the muzzle of Toph rifle behind him, as it quickly turned to help an embattled Acosta, who was struggling against three opponents.

She was too late, as a dark elf blade finally succeeded in separating the Old Guard's head from his body. Acosta's blade would bring one final elf with him into the grave, as Toph finished off the other two with quick shots to the head.

Thomas turned to look at the Genitrix.

It was almost done.

It's all powered up now. It just has to execute the transfer.

He knew what he had to do. He remembered Hos-Hos' explanations as to how it worked. He remembered all the security briefings with Zaslani. He remembered Xhisa explaining the room to him. Fractions of a second were needed for him to sprint towards the semisphere, before it finished its process.

He got to the object in the nick of time, throwing his blast charge right in front of it, as it neared the blank screen. With a subtle thud, the blast charge was caught between the semisphere and the screen.

Thomas didn't hear the explosion. It would have been impossible to. It was too loud to hear. Thomas felt his eardrums explode and warm blood filled his ears. He had kept his eyes closed, hidden by his forearm, allowing himself to not be blinded. His whole body was wracked by the shockwave, which pushed him back several yards across the floor.

Now, he opened his eyes to see what he had done.

They were the only two people left in the room. The light of the Svart had perished into oblivion, with the bodies of the last of their kind laid out across the shattered floor.

The energy stored inside the semisphere was enormous and of such concentrated force, that it had completely destroyed the screen in front of it. Destroyed was an understatement, as Thomas knew that it was not just shattered.

It had virtually been removed from existence.

The explosion had gone only forward, for that had been were the energy had been directed. Thomas saw before him a long, almost endless, new tunnel, its edges brimming red from the heat released as a result of its making. He knew it wasn't endless for it would have likely lead out somewhere hundreds, if not thousands of miles away. The beam of energy would have pierced through the planet's surface, before dissipating into the vacuum of space.

He would never know where it led, for he saw that it had passed through the planet's mantle. Not only that, he saw that the heat had turned the edges of the great circle a bright red. Lava began to drip from the top and pool at the bottom of the new tunnel, coming close to Thomas's feet.

He knew he would not have to fear the fire, for he saw the calamity that neared. He saw the tunnel begin to collapse, as a distant red dot heralded the approach of pressurized magma from beneath the planet's crust right towards him.

Thomas understood what he had done. It was only now that he realized it. Perhaps he had known, somewhere in his subconscious mind, where his instincts ran wild, where the very fibre of his being stood and from where it directed his actions. Perhaps he had taken the decision moments before. Maybe seconds before. Maybe hours. Days. Weeks. Months. Years.

He didn't really know when he had decided his fate, but now he felt it. His heart stopped for a moment, then began to pound with all of its strength. He started tasting the air with the very tip of his nose. Every muscle in his body relaxed, as his fibres loosened in ways they have never had before.

His eyes floated in his head, as all was silent around him. No thoughts spoke within the chamber of his mind. Only, a feeling of acceptance clashed with the spirit of his life. It did so gently, for it knew that, this time, it would win. He felt his mind decide to prepare for what was to come.

Things rushed to him. Not his entire life, but only the things that mattered. Some he had known would matter. Others, he had not. He remembered the sound of his mother's voice, crystal clear, in ways he hadn't realized he took for granted. He remembered the smell of his father's clothes, how it hung around his parent's bedroom in the morning. He remembered going to school. He remembered the children he had grown up with, as they were then, and what they had said and done together. He remembered speaking last to his mother a few weeks before, telling her that he had a feeling everything was going to be alright. He remembered his father's last words to him before coming here. His mind blessed him and did not linger long on contemplating how they would feel when they would hear the news or, even, what they might be feeling now.

The worry of parent's whose child is away.

He remembered the camaraderie of the Allied Host. He remembered the wonders of Triangulum. He remembered the feeling of pride at becoming Lieutenant. He remembered the feeling of the cool waters of a warm beach upon his legs. He remembered a song he liked.

He remembered the *thoughts*, though only subtly, for between the *thoughts* lay Mira. Her face. Her voice. Her food. He remembered that feeling she gave him: that endless possibility might lie just beyond the next door, if only one was brave enough to reach forward an turn the doorknob. He remembered a thin waifish voice.

Toph.

He realized what he had done. He turned quickly towards her. The little elf's heart pounded in her frail chest. Her lungs heaved and begged for more time, as her stomach turned sick with cold pain. In her eyes she saw fear and so much of it. It reminded him of a scarred squirrel he had shot once by mistake and how he had rushed to put it out of its misery, as it had glared at him in mortal pain, knowing what was to come.

He didn't say anything. He just walked towards her. At first she stood still, as she seemed to crave a touch. A hug. An embrace. Then her body grew rigid, as he who had decided to end her approached. He grabbed her shoulder, neither waiting for her permission, nor receiving it, as she pushed him away in horror. Her strength was no match for his, as he grabbed her entire body, holding her in his arms, stopping her from struggling.

With his cheek next to hers, he felt her begin to weep. With his temples he felt her close her eyes tightly shut, so as not to behold what was coming. She stopped fighting him and buried her head in his shoulder, opening her mouth to let out a silent wail. Her arms began to shake and he reached out to hold the back of her head in the cup of his hand. He felt her hold on to him and squeeze him tight.

He kissed her neck, one last time.

Epilogue

The last overdue atrocity of the War of Vengeance had finally come to pass. The Svart had been snuffed out. Their great doom brought upon them by those they had once attempted to snuff out themselves. Some might call us monsters for what we did during the War of Vengeance, including in its final bloody act. Perhaps we are.

Their realm now sits split between those of their brethren that surrendered in the face of those that they had once deemed little more than pests; their former slaves, now ruled by a god far greater than their highest king; and their treacherous kin, whom they had also sought to subjugate. The worlds they had sought to purge, Kalimaste, Terra and Moria, now stand strong in a universe in which they would never again have to fear them. Terra's vengeance had been so absolute, that they were even denied the chance of an afterlife free of the sins of their past. Their dark souls would belong to the *Dancer* now, as they always had and always will. In ways he would see fit he would change them into whatever shape he judged harmonious to all elves. A shape which would not be theirs alone in design.

Daw al Fajr herself, once she received word that the assault had been finalized, appeared in the midst of the ruins of the Enemy's last bastion. With one swift survey of the world, she confirmed with one curt nod that which we had long prayed for. Her presence was to be a brief one, lest she draw the attention of another, much greater Enemy. For that was our fear. That is, still, our fear.

That had been why the closing act of Operation Eichmann had been so rushed. Our fear was that word of our endeavours would reach the dreaded Continuum of Humanity. This had been why we needed to be so thorough in our approach, for we had to make sure that none would ever escape Ratden, lest they somehow manage to bring upon us this new foe, which would punish us for doing that which they would call *blasphemous*, *atrocious* or *heretical*. Only that we call it by other words.

Hopeful.
Just.
Honest.

We took every measure at our disposal to ensure the secrecy of Kralizec, yet we knew that there might be a chance that we fail, and word might reach the Continuum, which was why I, Shoshanna Adler, was sent away from Terra. I travelled to Pandora, the ancient seat of House Uhrlacker. I have always avoided going there. It is a dreadful place, full of wild forests and jungles, all of which teem with the dread beasts the primal elves enjoyed slaughtering oh so much.

Yet, now, I was forced to visit this savage world, since this was now the residence of the Warchief of the Alliance, Vorclav Uhrlacker. Tomasz's words still echoed in my ears as I brought the news to the Lord Commander of the armies of House Uhrlacker. We spent a tense time together afterwards, up until a message arrived from none other than Daw al Fajr, informing us of the attack's success.

I will not lie; I knew Vorclav hated the Svart for what they did to his family. Yet, I did not expect to see him experience such relief that he both laughed and cried. What a justice that all those who had lost so much to the Svart would have some hand to play in the coming and going of their last sunset. Though, I must confess that Daw also brought other news, which made victory seem nothing more than a smaller rendition of the past.

Some had been lost.

Daw had asked the fiery darkness of Ratden how many elven souls there lived still on the world. News reached her mind that there were only four thousand eight hundred and sixty-seven elves alive, of which all were Brightguard. Daw wore the mourning of one hundred and thirty-three lost friends in her eyes, yet it seemed to me that one soul seemed to shine brighter than the rest.

She could not ask the darkness which Terrans or trolls had died. Of them we learned when our legions returned to Terra.

Eleven Hajduks.

Ten Keshik.

Seven Ghazis.

Four Old Guards

And two Terran Army Captains.

One had sought out his death since he had grown to crave it. Ronan O'Malley died the way I could always tell he would, since he died the same way he had lived: on his own terms and with his own beliefs. I cannot say that I understand why he chose to live and die the way he did, though one could never deny that the man represented something that I feel is missing among us in this day and age: the strength of character to be revolted at what we have become.

The other had died in such a way that pains me, for it tears me apart. I am haunted now by the words of Mira al Sayid, as she saw his wrecked body, too shattered to be brought back to life.

'How did he die?' she had asked, only to burst into a wail that shook the very cliffs of the canyon she lay within, upon hearing the answer.

'Crushed. The fire finished the body.'

On the one hand, Thomas Muller died a hero of our people, his name being added to the Great Book of Martyrs, where it stands in the company of the heroes he had looked up to in his young life. I know with certainty that his presence would both humble and honour them, for his valour would put any of them to shame. His entry reads:

'Captain Thomas Muller. Hero of the Ayve War. Last Avenger Incarnate of the War of Vengeance. Beloved son and friend.'

What breaks me is that his entry does justice neither to him, nor his achievements. For none may know the true meaning of his actions, nor the beauty of his soul, nor the importance of our labour together on Project Kralizec. My heart bleeds knowing how wonderful he was and how much he treasured his life and how much he dreaded death.

He did not want to die. Yet, all along, he had the power within him to die for what he believed in. Knowing that will haunt me until the end of my days. For I have only ever had the power to die for those I loved. It's why I, and everyone else I have loved and lost, died for during our wars: the love of our palpable lives, not of our impalpable existence. I look in fear now upon that which we might become once more, ignorant of the value of what we have right *now*. Thus, the Svart did in their last moment as they had always done: they took from us that which we did not know we loved so much and left behind one last wound to ache and torment us.

Our end has not yet come. Our Old Enemy is dead. Our New Enemy leers across the great darkness, ready to erase us from the universe it feels so entitled too. It so may be that our fate has been sealed and that war is coming, bringing with it its fatal certainty. Yet, it may also be that the line of Terra will reach out far into the distant future, into times and places neither of our understanding nor our recognition. I will now live with the burden of knowledge that we too are just as human as those that dwell in the Continuum. The spark of fanaticism can only be buried, contained or embraced. It cannot be denied, no matter how absent it may appear.

In his last moments, I believe Thomas found peace, for that was all I ever wished for him. However, it pains me to acknowledge that, perhaps, he did not. In the end, it does not matter if he saved the heaven we craved for so long. It does not even matter if there is a heaven of any kind awaiting us beyond the veil. What matters is that we bless the ground we walk on now with the gratitude of having felt our touch.

Thus, Terra endures. A grim bastion of sombre determination. A world of heroes and monsters. In our darkest hour, we swore undying loyalty to those that had aided us in our time of need, regardless of whether or not their intervention was requested. We reached out to others across the cosmos, binding ourselves together with the requirements of the same purpose. We accepted the Old Enemy's former servants, partners and even kin into our fold and honoured them as our brethren, even if at times we have doubted their worth. We brought the fight to the very doorstep of our New Enemy, drawing our own line in the sand, beyond which lies our freedom to decide for ourselves what we would do with our lives and our future.

We have lost much and we will lose much more. It is a small prize, considering what we have found along the way.

Though, out of the ruins of Ratden came other news.

It came in the form of an old log the dushman had saved. Within this log were the names of those we called the 'Stolen', since that had been their fate. During the End Times, the Svart spared some of those they conquered. The healthiest of the children they took from us were not granted a death upon Terran soil. They were taken from us, for reasons we would only later understand,

It would be the contents of this log that would lead the Hajduks to the distant world of Shangri, right in the middle of the great void that lies between us and the New Enemy. It was here that we now knew the children passed through, on their way to the Continuum of Humanity. It would be here that the Laur Pop would pick up the trail of the Stolen, as we seek to make new friends and make the line in the sand just a bit deeper.

Appendix I
Cast of Characters

Primary Point-of-View Character

Lieutenant **Thomas Muller**: Terran Human – Nation of Germany

The story's protagonist, Thomas is a young officer who has just finished his Allied Host service and is about to return to Terra to fulfil his dream of joining the Terran Logistics Corps. He is a veteran of the Ayve War in the Triangulum Galaxy and the son of Maximillian and Lisa Muller and, thus, one of the few sunrisers that grew up in a traditional nuclear family.

Occasional Point-of-View Characters

Captain **Amira Parvati al Sayid**: Terran Human – Nation of Arabia

The orphaned daughter of Djibril al Sayid and Sarasvati Singh, two of the greatest Terrans to have ever lived. Mira joined her father's former legion, the Ghazis, following the completion of her Allied Host service. She fought in the Ayve War, where she acquired a reputation for being both exceedingly assertive and ferocious. Her upbringing was unique, as she was raised by both her father's family on Terra and by her stepsister, Daw al Fajr, on the elven world of Menegroth. Goes by 'Mira'.

General **Shoshanna Adler**: Terran Human – Nation of America

A particularly young oldtimer, Shoshanna was born in East Hampton, New York in the old United States of America. She survived the End Times and took part in the Battle of Guyanas on Doomsday. Refuses to have children. She commands the Marines Avenger Legion.

Hierarch **Tomasz 'Thomas' Ashaver**: Terran Human – Nation of Poland

A former Polish foreign intelligence officer, Ashaver emerged as the leader of the surviving humans of Terra after Doomsday. He went on to become the First Warchief of the nascent Republican Alliance after the Second Battle of Terra, going on to lead the War of Vengeance against the elven invaders. Since stepping down from the position of Warchief, he has taken part in virtually every major military operation the Republican Alliance has ever been involved in, continuing to lead his people in his world's post-apocalyptic future as a Hierarch. Is best friends with Çingeto Braca and refuses to have children. He commands the Terran Old Guard Hierarch Legion.

Secondary Characters

Sergeant Major **Abhijoy Mukherjee**: Terran Human – Nation of Bengal
A veteran of every single Terran conflict since the Wars of the Fimbulwinter began on Old Earth, Abhijoy is a member of Ashaver's Old Guard. He is not an original Death Knight and is quite light hearted, especially for an Old Guard. Nicknamed 'Bonegnasher' in memory of his first death.

Basenji: Black Knight Remani
Basenji is a rather young remani, being only around a hundred years of age. He is jet black and has a particularly wolf-like face. He never speaks, despite being completely able to. He is particularly close to Thomas Ashaver and Mira al Sayid. Basenji is the first remani and, by extension, inhuman which Thomas Ashaver ever met. Participated in the Battle of Prague on Doomsday.

Urizen **Daw al Fajr**
A synthetic intelligence created from the merged consciousness of a thousand elven heroes, Daw was created by the Primal Elves of Pandora to instigate a rebellion among the lower caste of elven society. She now acts as the supreme ruler of the recently formed Elven Commonwealth. She considered Djibril al Sayid and Sarasvati Singh to be her parents and now regards Mira al Sayid as her sister. She commands the Brightguard, which act as her bodyguard.

Companion **Fiol Patel**: Vanir Human – Nation of Gujarat
A native of the Triangulum Galaxy, Fiol met Lakshmi Patel during the Ayve War, as he was part of the group of Vanir that introduced the Republican Alliance to their advanced artificial intelligence technologies. He is the husband of Lakshmi Patel and one of the few naturalized extraterrestrial humans present on Terra, thanks entirely to his marriage to Lakshmi. He is the father of Sarasvati Patel.

Colonel **Lakshmi Patel**: Terran Human – Nation of Gujarat
A companion of Sarasvati Singh and a former member of the Pandavas, Lakshmi is now one of the leading Terran experts in the design of complex artificial intelligences. She is married to Fiol Patel and is the mother of Sarasvati Patel. She views Mira al Sayid as her niece.

General **Laur Pop**: Terran Human – Nation of Romania
Nicknamed 'the Lord Inquisitor', Laur is a former Romanian domestic intelligence officer who became the highest ranking member of the Romanian military by the time of Doomsday. He emerged as the leader of the Terran forces that survived the Battle of Prague. He took part in the War of Vengeance and continues to lead the hunt for any surviving dark elves. Masterminded the events of the Last Fitna. Lead the defence of Luna during the Bloodbrother Crisis. Does not like waste. Is regarded as Tomasz Ashaver's right-hand man and refuses to have children. Commands the Hajduk Avenger Legion.

Master Sergeant **Lisa Muller**: Terran Human – Nation of Germany
Ethnically Vietnamese, an infant Lisa Muller (nee Chi Nguyen) ended up in a German orphanage after the conclusion of the End Times, where she met her future husband Maximillian. She would join the nascent Terran Gardener Corps and now assists Gardener families in childbearing and childrearing. She is the mother of Thomas Muller.

Sergeant Major **Marco Acosta**: Terran Human – Nation of Mexico
A veteran of every single Terran conflict since the Wars of the Fimbulwinter, Marco is a member of Ashaver's Old Guard. He is an original Death Knight and the proud father of Eagle Warrior Esteban Acosta of the Otomi Avenger Legion.

Master Sergeant **Maximillian Muller**: Terran Human – Nation of Germany
A veteran of the Senoyu War, where he served under Djibril al Sayid and Ronan O'Malley, now works within the Terran Engineering Corps. He specializes in the implementation and maintenance of the many radar systems that keep watch over the Solar System and Terra itself. Is married to Lisa Muller, a fellow Yin, and is the father of Thomas Muller.

Commandant **Opera Bokha**: Terran Human – Nation of Yoruba
A member of the Terran Medical Corps, Opera is currently stationed in Jerusalem, where she works under Lars Rasmussen and assists Laur Pop in his many vetting processes. She is considered a hidden gem of the Medical Corps, dwelling in the

shadow of her oldtimer superiors, most of whom are keenly aware that she is likely one of the best psychiatrists Terra has to offer.

Infantry **Sarasvati Patel**: Terran Human – Nation of Gujarat
One of the few children of mixed heritage present on Terra, Sara is the daughter of Lakshmi and Fiol Patel and considers Mira to be her cousin, though she refers to her as 'auntie'.

Ronan O'Malley: Terran Human – Nation of Ireland
A survivor of the End Times and a veteran of the War of Vengeance, Ronan reached the rank of Captain under Djibril al Sayid during the Senoyu War, where he also served as a young Maximillian Muller's superior. Found God later in life and decided to abandon military service. He now lives as a mortal hermit in rural Ireland.

Hierarch **Sorbo Falk**: Kalimasti Troll
The leader of the trolls of Kalimaste and the father of three boys and nine girls, Sorbo is an old friend of Ashaver, Braca and the rest of the upper echelons of the Republican Alliance. He considers himself to be Mira's godfather.

Lieutenant **Toph Pamento**: Menegrothi Low Elf
One of Thomas Muller's comrades, the two served within the same Allied Host brigade. Plans to return to Menegroth after completing her service.

Tertiary Characters

Commandant **Albrecht Hausser**: Terran Human – Nation of Germany
A hero of the Ayve War and a member of the Jaegers, Albrecht is the youngest Terran Commandants to currently serve in an Avenger Legion. He is a childhood friend of Mira al Sayid, one whom she never truly liked, yet continues to interact with on account of the good relationship Mira's father's family maintains with his father's family. Despite being Swiss German, he opted to join the Jaegers, as opposed to the Landsknecht, on account of the former's prestige.

Hierarch **Çingeto Braca:** Vigilant Orc
The most famed of the Orcs of Vigilant, he met Thomas Ashaver and Djibril al Sayid during the Hour of Twilight when he lead the Orcish assault upon the Elven flagship Marlafior. He is the best friend of Thomas Ashaver and is the one to whom the Terran entrusted Daw al Fajr during the Fall of Iglarest. It was Çingeto who decided that is was best if Daw be raised by Djibril al Sayid and Sarasvati Singh.

Pathfinder **Eang Linglerfdo**: Menegrothi Low Elf
A former bodyguard in the household of a Svart lord, Eang rose rapidly through the ranks of the elven Commonwealth's military, becoming one of the highest ranking members of the Brightguard, on account of his understanding of military tactics and strategy, which is exceptional among his people.

Lieutenant **Hampstead Tsedenbal**: Terran Human – Nation of Mongolia
A fellow officer in Thomas Muller's Allied Host battalion. Hampstead was raised by a Gardener family in Mongolia and has over twenty brothers and sisters. He is the biological 'son' of two unknown humans from the Old Earth country of England.

Colonel **Hector Ramirez**: Terran Human – Nation of Mexico
An unusually cheerful oldtimer, Hector was born in Omaha, Nebraska and narrowly survived the Rapture thanks to his job working at the US embassy in Madrid. He went on to serve as the premier Terran diplomat (though that's not saying much).

Captain **Ifeanyi Mapupu**: Terran Human – Nation of Hausafulani
A Terran officer of the Medical Corps, Ifeanyi is widely considered to be one of the best Terran physicians on account of his grasp of Hyperborean genetic manipulation, demani healing spells and elven rejuvenation procedures.

General **Khalid Minhal**: Terran Human – Nation of Arabia
Djibril al Sayid's former second-in-command, he now leads the Ghazis Avenger Legion. Has presided over the fracturing of the old Ghazis into the Mujahideen, Mamelukes, Corsairs, Jund and Khevsurs in the years following the death of Djibril al Sayid. Is originally from the Old Earth country of Jordan, where he served in the Royal Army.

Chief Master Sergeant **Kamalutdin Abdulrakhmanov**: Terran Human – Nation of Dagestan
Originally a member of the Ghazis, Kamal joined the Old Guard after the death of Djibril al Sayid together with the rest of the original Death Knights of Islamic heritage.

Navigator **Kevin Falk**: Kalimasti Troll
Oldest son of Sorbo Falk. Navigator of the *Naglafar*.

General **Kitoye Ogulensi**: Terran Human – Nation of Yoruba

A distant relative of Opera Bokha, Kitoye was the son of a prominent Nigerian businessman and survived the End Times, as many of the Yoruba did, by fleeing into the jungles of Western and Central Africa, where he emerged as a leader during the Battles of the Congo. As the leader of the Esho, he pushed towards specializing the Avenger Legion in aerial dogfights, making it one of the premier air forces among the Avenger Legions.

Colonel **Lars Rasmussen**: Terran Human – Nation of Scandinavia
A former radiologist in his native Denmark, Lars has been jumping from one outdated branch of medicine to another for over sixty years. He is one of the last survivors of the European Union Task Force set up to study the physiology of captured elven bodies (living or otherwise) during Ragnarok.

Lorgar Erebus Aurelian: Terran Cat – Nation of Arabia
Lorgar is Mira's pet cat and part of her inheritance, as he previously belonged to her parents. The animal is horrendously prejudiced and is the source of much amusement for Mira, as well as her friends and family.

Lieutenant **Liaco Schvaarei**: Ersatz Orc
A fellow officer in Thomas Muller's Allied Host battalion.

General **Manda Khan**: Terran Human – Nation of Mongolia
Commander of the Keshik Avenger Legion. She is the one who found a newly-born Mira al Sayid outside the gates of the Antarctic fortress, after the death of her mother and father.

Lieutenant **Motley Jallon Ancu Hualoc li Atahualpa Lorem Ibsen da Palma**: Morian Hobgoblin
A fellow officer in Thomas Muller's Allied Host battalion. He is the son of the sister of Kimmie Jimmel's ex-wife.

Centurion **Nicolae Lăutaru**: Terran Human – Nation of Kalo
Born in Pescara, Italy during the Fimbulwinter, Nick was hidden beneath Prague, where he survived the Hour of Twilight. After a remarkable track record during the Senoyu War, he joined the Hajduks, where he now informally commands the Kalo contingent, the smallest faction within the Hajduks. Is recently divorced and is the father of six sons and seven daughters.

General **Ruben Zaslani**: Terran Human – Nation of Israel

An exceedingly paranoid oldtimer General, on par with Laur Pop himself (with whom he frequently insists on working with) Zaslani is a former Mossad officer and was one of the first Terrans to succeed in properly coordinating with the remani of the Black Knight Pride. Commands the Sayeret Avenger Legion.

Sergeant Major **Samwise Metzen**: Terran Human – Nation of America.
A veteran of every single Terran conflict, Sam is a member of Ashaver's Old Guard. He is an original Death Knight. He is the only known survivor of the Battle of Fort Bragg and was reanimated by the Svart in the aftermath of the complete destruction of the American defenders.

Chief Master Sergeant **Shira Cohen**: Terran Human – Nation of Israel
Ragnarok caught Shira during her mandatory IDF service. She is one of the handful of survivors of the Battle of Armageddon. Remarkably well-adjusted for an oldtimer, she has found her calling alongside Themba Xhisa, with whom she has been working with for almost four decades. She is a member of the Sayeret Avenger Legion.

Centurion **Silvia Murărescu**: Terran Human – Nation of Romania
Born in Brașov, Romania during the Fimbulwinter, Silvia was hidden beneath Prague, where she survived the Hour of Twilight. After a remarkable track record during the Senoyu War, she joined the Hajduks, where she now informally commands the Romanian contingent, the largest faction within the Hajduks. She is frequently regarded as Laur Pop's second-in-command, despite being equal in rank to the other Hajduk centurions. Helps run the Brașov orphanage during her spare time.

Technowolf: Black Knight Remani
A middle-aged remani of around two hundred years. His coat is jet black, with the exception of a white patch of fur that extends from his neck to his groin. He is an avid fan of Old Earth techno music and moonlighted as a DJ in the years preceding the Fimbulwinter. Participated in the Battle of Prague on Doomsday.

Colonel **Themba Xhisa** Terran Human – Nation of Nguni
An oldtimer officer of great renown. Has become something of a recluse following his time spent with the Orcs of Vigilant. He previously worked as an engineer in the Old Earth country of South Africa.

General **Uma Kaur**: Terran Human – Nation of Khalsa

A distant relative of Sarasvati Singh, Uma commands the Akali Avenger Legion. As a former member of the now defunct Pandavas, she continues to share Sarasvati Singh's love of weapons of mass destruction, with this fact being reflected in her legion's battle doctrine. She is the closest living relative of Mira al Sayid on her mother's side. She is the wearer of the Armour of Crimson Kali.

Marshal **Xi Feng** Terran Human – Nation of Han
The eldest Han member of the Terran High Command, Xi achieved many great victories during the End Times and the War of Vengeance, yet it was his extraordinary leadership during the Ayve War that earned him the rank of Marshal. He is a quiet man known to downplay his own achievements and is considered one of the greatest Terran commanders alive.

Sergeant Major **Xian Shang**: Terran Human – Nation of America
Xian joined a mercenary company following the conclusion of his time with the US Army Rangers and took part in the Battles of the Guyanas alongside a young Shoshanna Adler, whom he still serves to this day. Despite changing his name to a Han language version, he opted to join the newly formed Nation of America.

Chief Master Sergeant **Xing 'Yellow River Charlie' Ye**: Terran Human – Nation of Han
A hardened survivor of the Chinese Front during the End Times, Xing died during the Battle of Bahr Aldhabh, only to be successfully resurrected by the victorious Terrans. He was later invited to join the Old Guard.

Living Characters Referenced

Eagle Warrior **Esteban Acosta**: Terran Human – Nation of Mexico
Son of Marco Acosta. Member of the Otomi Avenger Legion.

Representative **Joji Higashikuni**: Terran Human – Nation of Japan
Head of the Logistics Corps. Commander of the Ashigaru Avenger Legion.

Hierarch **Kimmie Jimmel Ancu Hualoc li Guardiola Lopez Ibsen da Utgaard**: Morian Hobgoblin
The former head of the Morian intelligence service and a former Warchief of the Republican Alliance. He is the former uncle of Motley Jallon.

Colonel **Mauro Gonçalvo**: Terran Human – Nation of Brazil
A Terran Colonel and former Brazilian Army Engineer.

Warden **Quentyn Andromander:** Nargothrond High Elf
Head of the Gondolin police force. Former prince of the Svart and short-lived King of the Svart following the assassination of his uncle by his own hand during the Assault on Gondolin. Nicknamed 'Jaime Lannister' by the Terrans, for obvious reasons.

Warchief **Vorclav Uhrlacker:** Primal Elf of Pandora
The military leader of the Primal Elves of Pandora and current Warchief of the Republican Alliance.

Deceased Characters Referenced

Hierarch **Djibril al Sayid**: Terran Human – Nation of Arabia
The second Warchief of the Republican Alliance, Djibril was born into a wealthy royal family in what is now Arabia. He was initially ostracized by his relatives on account of his adventurous – yet also excessively warlike – ways, only to eventually become one of the greatest heroes of the End Times and the War of Vengeance. He is known for having achieved the first outright victory against the Svart during the Battle of Tbilisi. His first death occurred during the Battle of Trebizond and he was raised as a Death Knight by the elves, only to successfully break free of their mind-control during the Hour of Twilight. He later fell in love and married future Hierarch Sarasvati Singh. His ultimate death occurred in the Andromeda Galaxy during the later stages of the Senoyu War. Upon learning of Sarasvati's death, as well as that of their unborn child, Djibril walked into a host of Senoyu warriors, fighting them to the death. His former Hierarch Legion became the Ghazis. He is the adoptive father of Daw al Fajr and the biological father of Mira al Sayid.

Hierarch **Sarasvati Singh:** Terran Human – Nation of Hind
The eighth Warchief of the Republican Alliance, Sarasvati was born to a secular Sikh family in Northern India. She became a computer scientist and worked on modernising the Indian nuclear arsenal in the years leading up to Ragnarok. She is famous for being the first to successfully use the Markov trick to destroy elven spacecraft during Ragnarok. She fell in love and married Djibril al Sayid and together they raised Daw al Fajr as their own child. She later became a peacetime Warchief in the aftermath of the War of Vengeance. She died during the events of Hellsbreach, but not before giving birth to Mira al Sayid outside the gates of the Antarctic Shield. Her Hierarch Legion, the Pandavas, was disbanded after her death.

Kernunos: Terran Artificial Intelligence

An artificial intelligence that emerged on the old Terran internet and which ultimately decided that the best possible destiny for the humans of Terra lay under the yoke of the Continuum of Humanity. It opened a portal to the Continuum within the Antarctic Shield, which was successfully closed by the efforts of Sarasvati Singh, who died fighting the infiltrators. Kernunos was later destroyed by Daw al Fajr.

Appendix II
Timeline of Referenced Historical Events

70 000 BB: Rise of the first human civilization on Kalimaste.

50 000 BB: Fall of the first Kalimaste civilization following eruption of the Urshalak supervolcano. Over the next millennia, the survivors evolve into various species of trolls.

15 000 BB: Emergence of early human civilizations on Moria.

12 000 BB: First human civilization emerges on Terra.

5 000 BB: Elves arrive in the Milky Way Galaxy, settle the world of Pandora and adopt a lifestyle in tune with the Primal ideology.

1 500 BB: Nomadic remani prides first become aware of intelligent humanoid life on Terra, Moria and Kalimaste. As part of their non-interventionist culture, they keep their distance from the natives, yet continue to observe their evolution.

1 000 BB: The Svart Tribe of high elves, together with their low elf serfs, acquires an imperial grant of relocation to the Milky Way Galaxy and establish the settlements on Gondolin, Nargothrond, Menegroth and Iglarest within their allocated fiefdom, with the blessing of the Continuum of Humanity.

950 BB: World of Barlog is granted to the Libra Ursai, in exchange for an alliance with the Svart Tribe.

800 BB: Marriage of Scintilla Svart Andromander and Dorian Uhrlacker cements the confederation of the Svart pride and the Pandoran primal elves.

400 BB: Following a devastating solar flare, the humans of Moria begin experimenting with advanced bioengineering. The remani intervene covertly and provide both procedural knowledge and new genetic templates. Over the next hundred years, the humans of Moria evolve into hobgoblins, immune to most forms of radioactivity and illnesses. The intervention causes a rift among the remani, leading to a more decentralised approach to their mission.

100 BB: Remani packs learn that the Svart Elves have begun petitioning both the Tribes of Elvandom and the Continuum of Humanity for the right to claim the entirety of the Milky Way as their fiefdom, insisting that there are no human civilizations present in the galaxy.

50 BB: Some remani begin covert intervention operations on Moria, Kalimaste and Terra, attempting to prepare the oblivious worlds for invasion whilst hiding their existence from the Svart.

20 BB: A catastrophic world war breaks out among the trolls of Kalimaste. The remani begin building giant Arks on the world, since they realise that they will be unable to stop the war and the inevitable Svart invasion.

17 BB: The Svart pride obtains a new imperial grant, covering the entirety of the Milky Way, on the condition that the grant is immediately annulled if unseeded humans are found anywhere in the galaxy and under the condition that the high elves exterminate any other inhumans they might uncover.

15 BB: The Svart pride intervenes on Kalimaste. Majority of trolls are wiped out in either their own world war or the elven invasion. Most survivors escape on board the remani arks. Some cave trolls survive underneath the world and continue to fight a guerrilla war against the elves.

11 BB: Elven colonists discover the Solar System and the human civilization located there. They immediately report back to the High Elf king in Gondolin, who orders the High Elf paladin Anteo Perem Svart to begin the quiet extermination of the humans of Terra. The End Times begin.

10 BB: Fimbulwinter begins on Terra, with unprecedented drought causing crop failures which lead to famine. Deadly illnesses, both old and new, become more virulent, weather becomes incredibly unpredictable and civil unrest begins. Wildfires become frequent, the magnetic poles begin to shift and a global; economic collapse takes place. The Wars of the Fimbulwinter break out among the struggling Terran nations. Selected assassination of potential threats begins by the Svart. Remani commence direct, yet still covert, preparation of Terra for the imminent invasion. Discussions begin between the remani and the orcs of Vigilant concerning a potential intervention in the Milky Way Galaxy.

2 BB: Rapture takes on Terra. The Yellowstone supervolcano, along with other smaller volcanoes, erupts in a catastrophic event. Unprecedented seismic events take place. Almost the entirety of Terra's coastline is devastated by tsunamis. Hurricanes, typhoons and tornadoes become common. Monsoon rains cause unimaginable flooding, landslides destroy Terran cities and infrastructure and storms make the seas unnavigable. Skyfall occurs, as elves divert comets and asteroids towards Terra. The human nations launch nuclear warheads, as a defence, leading to nuclear fallout and partial ignition of the atmosphere.

1 BB: The Apocalypse begins as the elven invasion begins in earnest during the events of Revelation. The remani also reveal themselves to the Terrans, after witnessing their terrible defeats at the Battles of Cairo, Uralvagonzavod, Fort Bragg, Beijing, Kashmir, Paris and Ottawa. The Terran High Command is formed, marking the beginning of Ragnarok. The hiding of the Yin commences, as the Svart begin to kidnap Terran children, to be sold on the black market to Continuum geneticists. Djibril al Sayid achieves first outright victory against elven forces at the Battle of Tbilisi, only to die days later at the Battle of Trebizond. Sarasvati Singh successfully launches India's remaining nuclear warheads, managing to destroy four elven star cruisers with the use of the Markov trick. The Battle of Bicaz takes place, resulting in a rare strategic victory, leading to the First Death of Thomas Ashaver and the escape of millions of refugees across the Carpathian Mountains. Terran and remani infiltrators succeed in stealing substantial amounts of elven weaponry and technology from invading starships in orbit around Terra, igniting some hope for the beleaguered humans. Thomas Ashaver and Djibril al Sayid, together with others, are raised as death knights by the elves, to serve as entertainment during the later stages of the invasion. The remani Black Knight starship enters combat for the first time at the Battle of Armageddon, successfully repelling the invaders, despite the eradication of most of the Terran combatants. The End of Days begins, as the elves deploy lightshunners to block out the sun.

0 BB: Doomsday takes place, as the elves simultaneously attack every remaining Terran stronghold. At the Hour of Twilight for the humans of Terra, the Orc worldship Vigilant arrives, taking the elves by surprise. Thomas Ashaver and Djibril al Sayid manage to break free of their elven mind control and assassinate Anteo Perem Svart. Together with Çingeto Braca, an orc commander, they successfully capture the elven flagship *Marlafior*. The humans, orcs and remani achieve victory against the elves in what becomes known as the First Battle of Terra.

1 AB: The survivors of Kalimaste arrive on Terra, having drifted among the stars on their remani arks for almost 15 years. The Alliance is formed by the Humans of Terra, the Orcs of Vigilant, the Black Knight Remani and the Troll refugees of Kalimaste. The Continuum of Humanity learns of the existence of humans on Terra, yet declares them tainted, due to their remani tutelage. Ivrain Perem Andromander arrives at the head of an elven host, with explicit orders to destroy the nascent Alliance, exterminate the inhumans and deport all Terrans to the Continuum. On the eve of battle, Thomas Ashaver is elected Warchief of the Alliance, and leads the allies in their victory during the Second Battle of Terra.

2 AB: The War of Vengeance begins. The Pandoran primal elves sense weakness and begin plotting against the Svart, due to having long been sidelined by the elven elite, which had attempted to assimilate them as an elven class inferior to the ruling high elves. Many Terrans stay behind on Terra to begin reconstruction.

3 AB: Alliance achieves victory at the Battle of Rivendell. Terran and troll forces slaughter the elven garrison, as well as elven civilians, setting the tone for future atrocities in what would later be called the Crimson Trek across the Stars. Trolls begin constructing settlements on Terra, leading to discontent among the native Terrans, who had begun to view the world as exclusively their own. The remani introduce the hobgoblins of Moria to the Alliance. Thomas Ashaver becomes the most vocal supporter of their ascendancy to the Alliance, even offering them land for bases on Terra, leading to further discontent among the humans.

4 AB: Thomas Ashaver begins to use the elven caste system to the Alliance's advantage by executing only low elves, and offering to release high elf prisoners in exchange for ransoms. Following such an exchange on the world of Lajja, a mutiny takes place, resulting in the Second Death of Thomas Ashaver. The mutineers come to Djibril al Sayid, requesting that he become Warchief. Al Sayid accepts and proceeds to execute the traitors. The Primal elf prince Vorclav Uhrlacker recovers

Thomas Ashaver's body from Lajja, reanimates him, and brings him to Pandora, where the primal elves introduce the Terran to their sedition plot.

5 AB: Kalimaste is reconquered, with the surviving cave trolls joining the Alliance. Siege of Nargothrond begins. The Primal Elves, with help from Ashaver, secretly succeed in birthing a Urizen, using elven soulkeepers, with the high elven leadership becoming instantly aware of this development. The Hobgoblins of Moria officially join the Alliance.

6 AB: Fall of Iglarest takes place. During the ensuing massacre, Ashaver reveals himself to Çingeto Braca and entrusts the Urizen to him. Braca places the Urizen in the charge of Djibril al Sayid, whom he informs of Ashaver's survival. Remarkably, Djibril and Sarasvati Singh, now married, adopt the Urizen as their own child and give her the name Daw al Fajr.

7 AB: Localised low elf rebellions begin, as Daw begins to remove the low elven indoctrination and conditioning, which the Svart had used to control them. The Orcs of Vigilant lead an assault on the ursai world of Barlog. Çingeto Braca challenges the ursai President to a duel and wins. The Libra Ursai pledge to cease hostilities and take no future part in the War of Vengeance. Ashaver and Uhrlacker eliminate all evidence concerning their involvement in the creation of the Urizen. A High Elven delegation arrives on Pandora to investigate potential primal elf involvement in the low elf rebellion. A skirmish erupts and Uhrlacker's sister, Sania, is killed. Enraged, Uhrlacker and Ashaver slaughter the delegation. The primal elves officially blame both Sania's death and the murder of the delegation on Ashaver and pledge themselves fully to the war against the Alliance. Ashaver flees and travels to the world of Ukufa, revealing his survival to his remaining death knights.

8 AB: The primal elf army assembles in full and urges the Svart to meet the enemy in open battle, citing vengeance for the death of Sania Uhrlacker. Thomas Ashaver reveals his return to the Alliance forces on the eve of the Battle of Bahr Aldhabh and leads the charge against the elven forces. As the battle lines meet, the primal elves enact their betrayal, just as the low elven rearguard mutinies, thus encircling the high elf army. A sea of slaughter ensues, with almost the entirety of the high elf military forces being eradicated. The Primal Elves of Pandora formally join the Alliance. Djibril al Sayid steps down as Warchief, with the title returning to Thomas Ashaver. The War of Vengeance changes from a fair fight to a rout, with the high elves now on the run.

9 AB: Low elven revolutionaries successfully take control of Menegroth and numerous other worlds. The remaining worlds are swiftly subdued by allied forces. After breaking the Siege of Pandora, the Alliance begins the assault on the elf capital world, Gondolin. Just as the allied forces break through the orbital defences and bring the fight to the streets of Gondolin, Quentyn Islaz Andromander, one of the last surviving nephews of High King Islaz Filas Andromander, kills his uncle and offers the allies the unconditional surrender of Gondolin, thus quelling the final massacre of the Crimson Trek across the Stars. Siege of Nargothrond ends. Thomas Ashaver passes the mantle of Warchief to Çingeto Braca. War of Vengeance ends.

10 AB: Troll refugees return to Kalimaste. The Vigilant begins orbiting Terra's sun. The remani come together and begin construction of Selena City on Terra's moon, Luna. The low elves, primal elves and surviving high elves establish three separate realms in the ruins of the old Svart Kingdom. The Primal Elves retain full control of their greatly expanded realm, with Pandora at its heart. The low elves form the Elven Commonwealth. The Gondolin system is set aside for the surviving high elves. Partition of Elvandom takes place, with the former low elf servants of Gondolin leaving for the other worlds of the Commonwealth and the surviving high elves, of whom the survivors of Nargothrond make up the greatest contingent, are relocated to the Gondolin system. Some high elves refuse to acknowledge defeat, flee the elven worlds into the dark void and become known as dark elves. A hunt for these fugitives would begin, with the dark elven numbers constantly decreasing due to the fevered efforts of the Alliance. Terran forces return home and attempt an early celebration. Discord brews as the humans begin to ponder their future, having eliminated any immediate threats to their survival. A message from the Continuum of Humanity arrives, calling for a secret conference on the world of Karnak, the northernmost world of the Milky Way Galaxy, and the closest world to the Continuum's dominion. Thomas Ashaver, Djibril al Sayid, Sarasvati Singh, Laur Pop, Shoshanna Adler and others attend. The Continuum offers the Terrans two choices: submit to Continuum rule, become a Continuum outpost and abandon their inhuman allies (pending the certain extermination of latter) or die as part of their Alliance during an inevitable future invasion. The Terrans slaughter the delegation to the last man. On their way back, they piece together a grim plan.

11 AB: On the two-year anniversary of the end of the War of Vengeance, the Last Fitna occurs. The Terran High Command purges all elements of Terran society that would oppose Terran unity, Alliance membership or independence from the Continuum. The Terrans propose a new military system to their allies, with each member maintaining their own defence forces, yet also pooling some of their forces into a joint military force. The proposal passes and the Allied Host, Legendary League and Hierarch Legions are formed, with the office of Warchief ruling over all allied military matters, henceforth known as 'Matters of War'. The title of Warchief also becomes a mandate, with each Warchief serving for only a single Terran year, after which the titleholder became a member of the Council of Hierarchs and is forbidden from ever again bearing the mantle of Warchief. Low elves formally join the Alliance. Sorbo Falk, leader of the trolls of Kalimaste, becomes Warchief. The Republican Alliance is born.

13 AB: Construction begins of the Spines and Shields of Terra.

18 AB: Ursai of Barlog join the Republican Alliance, which begins covert involvement in the Andromeda Galaxy by funding and training a demani insurgency against their human overlords, the Senoyu, which operate under an imperial mandate, similar to that employed by the Svart. Rumours on Terra begin to circulate concerning strange occurrences taking place on the old Terran internet.

19 AB: Hellsbreach takes place. An artificial intelligence named Kernunos gains sentience on the Terran internet, and attempts to allow Continuum military forces access into the Terran High Command's Antarctic citadel. Sarasvati Singh, gives birth to Amira Parvati al Sayid outside of the fortress' gates, then gives her life, together with many others, to seal the portal the machine had opened to a Continuum world. Daw al Fajr arrives in time to destroy Kernunos and the infiltrators. A galaxy away, Djibril al Sayid learns of her death, but not of the survival of his daughter, which was presumed dead, and proceeds to commit suicide by entering lone combat against hundreds of Senoyu. Amira al Sayid is recovered by Manda Khan. The girl is raised by Daw al Fajr and the surviving members of her father's family.

20 AB: The demani successfully revolt against the Senoyu and join the Alliance.

32 AB: The Bloodbrother Crisis occurs. Orcs of Vigilant receive a request from the orcs of Ersatz to assist them against the Jira Spawn, which they are forced by their code of honour to answer. Despite protests from the other members of the Alliance, the orcs teleport the Vigilant away from the Solar System, so as to join their brethren in their struggle. The high elves of Gondolin formally join the Republican Alliance.

36 AB: The Vigilant returns to the Solar System, together with the Ersatz, after years of silence and immediately begins a bombardment of Luna, followed by the commencement of a blockade of Terra, thus marking the beginning of the Siege of Terra and the Siege of Luna. Defector orcs from the Ersatz explain that the war against the Jira had been a ruse, set up by the Continuum of Humanity, to gain control of the orcs of Vigilant and Ersatz by hacking into the joint consciousness which orcs of the same clan shared. They had first achieved this centuries before, in secret, against the orcs of Ersatz, and had decided to exploit this weakness against the orcs of Vigilant. However, some Ersatz orcs had become resistant to the apparent mind control of their hacked joint consciousness. Together with the Terran Old Guard, they attempt to release their brethren from their shackles in an operation which initially failed and resulted in the Third Death of Thomas Ashaver at the hands of Çingeto Braca. However, the plan does eventually succeed and the Orcs of Vigilant are freed. A freshly unshackled Braca also succeeds in storing Thomas Ashaver's consciousness and memories in an orcish soulkeeper, which allows him to be resurrected into a new body. The Orcs of Ersatz join the Alliance.

38 AB: The Orcs of Ersatz join the Alliance.

41 AB: The Alliance intervenes in the Seventh Aesir-Vanir war, together with the humans of Hyperborea.

45 AB: End of Aesir-Vanir War. The Hyperboreans, Vanir and the surviving Aesir formally join the Alliance.

Appendix III
Terran Vernacular

Adamantine: a very standard metal alloy, typically used in the manufacture of bladed weapons, such as swords, knives, spears and axes; it is very light, incredibly durable, can withstand immense temperatures, is not magnetic, requires little maintenance, cannot be eroded by Gallium, and can be folded in such a way that produces incredibly sharp edges;

Allied Host: joint military force of the Republican Alliance;

Ambiguous Terran Monotheism: usually abbreviated to ATM, refers to the informal system of religious beliefs found among the Terran population; though dominated by irreligious, secular, atheistic, agnostic and even nihilistic sentiments, it usually features some belief in a type of higher power, energy, spirit or entity, as well as a propensity for certain superstitions and quirks, depending on the individual, his *Nation* and his personal experiences; the term has some derogatory connotations and is considered to be an insult when used by non-Terrans;

Anticoating: refers to a substance (usually applied as a spray, but also as a cream) that coats the user in a fireproof layer of thermal insulation, whilst also allowing the skin to regulate body heat as it would under normal circumstances; the substance also works as a hairspray, preventing the user's hair from catching fire; in conjunction with common breathing devices, also protects the user from the void of space;

Apocalypse: Refers to the early days of the *End Times*, characterised by the near continuous defeats suffered by the militaries of Terra against the far more advanced elven military;

Arclight Spanner: a type of heavy pistol that shoots an incredibly volatile arc of lightning vaguely in a frontal direction;

Ayve War: Also known as the AV War, is a common way of referring to the Seventh Aesir-Vanir War, in which the Terran military took part in;

Bomber: a manned aerial vehicle, which fulfils roles similar to both an *Old Earth* twenty-first century fighter jet and a bomber; they do not typically carry troops beyond the pilot and the occasional co-pilot(s); depending on model, are sometimes capable of interstellar flight;

Buaram: a type of megafauna present on Pandora, a *buaram* is essentially an omnivorous elk of gigantic size;

Campus: Terran term for the mustering grounds located outside major cities, such as Jerusalem, Mecca, Moscow or Beijing;

Coldblood: the most prestigious Terran fighting style, whereby the practitioner does not enter any state of mind different than his usual one;

Controlled Berserkers: the most difficult Terran fighting style, whereby the practitioner must emulate the trancelike state of a traditional berserker, without ever actually blacking-out or losing control;

To cross the veil of presence: to go berserk, to be claimed by the bloodlust; originally an Orcish expression, now adopted by Terrans;

Dropship: usually refers to special military vehicles that are incapable of interstellar travel and are focused primarily on troop transport;

a **Crowfly**: also known as a *crowing*; describes flying in a straight line; most frequently used to describe a flight path;

Darkplate: the most common material used in the fabrication of Terran plate armour; is incredibly light, yet unimaginably resilient; it is considered to be inferior to *weirdplate*, since it cannot 'heal' itself and its cloaking abilities are not as efficient;

Dart: Typically refers to an autonomous aerial vehicle that fulfils a military role similar to that of an *Old Earth* twenty-first century fighter jet; military use of actual 'darts' also exists, yet those weapons are typically referred to as *blowdarts* (even if they are not propelled by compressed air)

Day of Reckoning: Refers to the day of the attack on Cairo during the *End Times*, the first landfall of the Svart army on Terra;

Director: common term used to describe artificial intelligence with a level of sentience comparable to that of a human; are frequently placed in charge of ships, large facilities or specific programs;

Deeds of Renown: the Terran equivalent of military decorations; are included on a Terran's *rankboard*;

Doomsday: This refers to a specific day during the *End Times* when the elven host culminated their effort to exterminate the remaining humans on Terra; synonymous with the *First Battle of Terra*;

End of Days: Refers to a period of about one week, during which the elven host began employing *lightshunners* during targeted operations;

Day of Revelation: Terran name for the period of them in which the Svart stopped cloaking their presence during the End Times, thus revealing to the population of Old Earth that the catastrophes they had endured up until that point were merely the opening stages of an alien invasion; is frequently shortened to *Revelation*;

Dissipater Micromail: a type of *micromail* that is generally bulkier, yet far more resilient than the regular variety; it is far inferior to plate armour varieties (such *darkplate*) in terms of protection, yet offers much more mobility;

Dushman: a word referring to the Svart elves; now frequently used to describe the dark elves; is considered a racial slur and is sometimes used incorrectly to describe high elves, low elves or primal elves; another term, used much more rarely is *smyrk*; synonymous with *Old Enemy*;

Emdiamay: modern Terran spelling of the psychoactive drug previously known as MDMA, molly or ecstasy; due to advances in Terran biology thanks to the advent of *enhancements*, modern emdiamay is an excessively potent variant of the substance;

Good Ol' Days: common term used to refer to the days before the *End Times*; typically only used by oldtimers;

Great Book of Martyrs: a specific book located within the *Shrine of the Lost* in Samarkand; chronicles the greatest acts of self-sacrifice achieved by Terrans; has two sections: one for the *End Times* and one for the period of time following the *First Battle of Terra*;

Gunship: usually refers to special military vehicles that are incapable of interstellar travel and are focused primarily on providing support to ground troops;

End Times: describes the entire period of time between the first actions undertaken by the Svart to eradicate human life on Terra, up until and including the First Battle of Terra; it is typically split into shorter segments of time, marked by specific events: the *Fimbulwinter*, the *Rapture*, *Skyfall*, *Revelation*, the *Day of Reckoning* the *Apocalypse*, *Ragnarok*, the *End of Days*, *Doomsday* and the *Hour of Twilight*;

Fimbulwinter: The longest period of time of the Terran *End Times*; refers to a period of ten years of global calamities, wars, famines, droughts and plagues;

Focused Fighter: the most common Terran fighting style, particularly among sunrisers, wherein the practitioner enters a state of extreme focus; the use of stimulants to maintain this state is common, yet not universal

Greyspace: common term for *accelerated space*, the universe used by most spacecraft in order to achieve interstellar travel;

Hierarch: former Warchiefs of the Republican Alliance;

Hierarch Legions: military units under the direct command of a Hierarch, most famous examples include the Terran Old Guard and the Vigilant Vanguard;

Hour of Twilight: refers to the closing moments of *Doomsday*, just before the arrival of the orc worldship Vigilant, which turned the tide of battle in the beleaguered human's favour;

ID: also known as a *bio signature*, refers to the specific genetic signature of each individual Terran; it is mostly comprised of an individual's DNA, yet other markers, both natural and artificial, are also taken into account;

Inhuman: a catch-all term for non-humans in the Known *Universe*; some Terrans occasionally use the term to refer to all extraterrestrials, including humans such as the Aesir, Vanir and Hyperboreans; examples include elves, orcs, goblins, trolls, demani, remani, ursai, taori, murin, and mandrakes;

Known Universe: a relative term used to describe the entirety of the universe known to the Continuum of Humanity;

KTM line: refers to the fact that Kalimaste, Terra and Moria are collinear on a star map;

Lightshunner: a type of military technology which involves the blocking of light from a world's star via a massive orbital screen;

Man: used to describe both males and females; Terran *oldtimers* will occasionally use both the terms *man* and *woman*;

Micromail: a fabric similar in use to medieval chainmail armour, yet far lighter; a much more voluminous variant called *dissipater micromail* exists;

New Enemy: common term used to describe the *Continuum of Humanity*;

Old Days: common term used to refer to the *End Times* and the *War of Vengeance*; typically only used by oldtimers;

Old Enemy: common term used to refer to the Svart elves;

Operator: term used to describe artificial intelligences with a level of sentience beneath that of a human;

Otarc plating: a lighter version of *weirdplate*, with similar cloaking abilities, but less durable and much lighter; is typical used to coat the bones of high elves and dark elves in a manner similar to how Terran *honeybone* coating;

Phaiser: a commonplace device which essentially functions as a refrigerator, oven and pantry; operates using the same technology as a *stasis field*

Rapture: the culmination of the *Fimbulwinter*, marks the eruption of the Yellowstone supervolcano;

Ragnarok: refers to the period of time following the formation of the Terran High Command, when Terrans began to cohesively fight the Svart with the assistance Remani of the Black Knight; Terran defeats were still the norm, yet a few rare victories took place during this time, such as the Battle of Tbilisi or the Battle of Bicaz;

Rankboard: Terran term used to refer to the actual document that lists the rank of every single living Terran, regardless of whether or not they are part of the *Allied Host*, a *Hierarch Legion*, *the Legendary League*, an *Avenger Legion* or even the regular Terran military; the rankboard also features the public information of every Terran (age, gender, *Terran Nation*, marital status, units assigned to, a general overview of duties, *deeds of renown*, combat experience, etc.); frequently to describe each individual Terran's profile; essentially functions as a type of social media;

Sir: term by Terrans used for all superiors regardless of gender or age;

Sitrep: slang term for 'situation report';

Shrine of the Lost: a Terran place of remembrance, typically dedicated to those fallen during the *End Times*;

Shuttle: used interchangeably with the word *car*, refers to the mobile aircraft used by Terrans (and many other civilizations) to travel across the surface of planets;

To be stuck: another term for shell-shock, battle fatigue, operational exhaustion, post-traumatic stress disorder; is originally an orcish expression;

Skyfall: A period of time occurring in the aftermath of Rapture, during which asteroids and comments were diverted towards Terra;

Soulkeeping: A type of technology that allows the entire minds, including memories and the actual consciousness, of individuals to be transferred into solid artificial constructs (called *soulkeepers*) where they may either lie dormant (also called *sleeping souls*) or fully awake and conscious, experiencing some type of virtual reality (also called *waking souls*); *soulkeepers* are also used as memory vaults, thanks to their innate ability to encode vast amounts of information; the actual act of *soulkeeping* is usually done by a specialized artificial intelligences called *vault spirits*;

Warchief: refers to the *Warchief of the Republican Alliance*, the supreme military commander of the *Republican Alliance*; the position is granted as a result of an election and carries a one-year mandate;

Warp jumper: a special type of spacecraft that does not use the *Greyspace* to achieve interstellar travel; instead, the warp jumper usually traverses another dimension of our own universe; are typically considered slower, more inefficient and more dangerous to use than vehicles traversing the *Greyspace*; yet, they do see some military use, since they are typically harder to track down, once they successfully undergo a warp jump;

Weirdplate: Terran name for a particularly resilient type of metal; its properties include the ability to 'heal' and mend itself, the ability to achieve an impenetrable layer of insulation, as well as being incredibly resilient in itself; it's only major drawback is its immense weight, resulting in its use being reserved to either fortifications or heavy battleships, such as the *Naglafar*, which makes extensive use of the material; the Armour of Tomasz Ashaver makes heavy use of this material;

Zack & Zont: Terran cosmic cartography term; originates from 2D map terminology in which North and South or on the y-axis, East and West are on the x-axis; thus, *Zack* ('back' and away from the observer) and *Zont* ('front' and towards the observer) refer to the directions of a z-axis in 3D cartography.

Appendix III
Overview of Terran Society

Terran **Civilization**, **Society**, **Culture** and **Ideology**

When attempting to understand the Terrans and who they are, one must understand that the *Terran Civilization* is in equal parts a utopia and a dystopia.

On the one hand, it is a futuristic intergalactic society that has forged alliances with a wide variety of other civilizations and species. They have completely overcome the internal conflicts of *Old Earth* and have established a society in which no individual or group is discriminated against based on their ethnic or sexual identity. They are *functionally immortal*, being immune to all non-military diseases and illnesses, whilst being able to maintain their youth throughout their entire lives without the need for any type of external maintenance. They maintain a highly meritocratic society which places incommensurable value on the quality of their lives and have an internal murder rate of virtually zero.

On the other hand, *Terra* is a post-apocalyptic military dictatorship with clear fascist tendencies, rigid restrictions on personal freedoms and a track record of genocide, war crimes and outright barbarism. It is a society which has achieved technological progress due to either the benevolence of others, heavy-handed political manoeuvrings or through outright theft. The great care they exhibit towards their own people exists simply because they view having a strong, healthy, disciplined, prosperous, independent-minded and well-armed population as a necessary asset, given that they think of themselves as living under a perpetual siege.

Understanding the duality of this identity is key when attempting to relate to the average Terran's mindset. They are a people defined by a profound trauma that is truly incomprehensible in its magnitude to anyone outside of their culture (bar a few exceptions, such as the trolls of *Kalimaste*). A quintessential aspect regarding their existence is the fact that they live in perpetual fear of some other hostile force within *the Dark Forest* that might succeed where their former aggressors failed. It is this very mindset that is both their greatest strength and their greatest weakness. Ironically, it is also what brought them on a collision course with the strongest empire in the Known Universe, since they view assimilation as simply another form of extermination.

A great number of their cultural particularities are explained below. However, a narrative that weaves its way through their story, particularly when *oldtimers* are involved, is the fact that it is a society that copes with old trauma in a multitude of ways. Often times, these coping mechanisms inevitably lead to the emergence of new traumas.

Terra, Old Earth, the World-Which-Was and the World-Which-Is

Though the term *Terra* only officially refers to the name of the eponymous planet in common Terran speech, this term is usually used to refer interchangeably to the Terran state, the Terran government, the Terran military, Terran civilization, as well as the planet itself. The *World-Which-Is* is another term for *Terra*.

Old Earth a term only used by Terrans and (rarely) the remani and the elves, referring to the civilization (of sorts) that existed on the planet of *Terra* before the *First Battle of Terra*. The *World-Which-Was* is another term for *Old Earth*.

The Terran Dominion

Refers to the entirety of the Solar System, including the entirety of the Terran sector (i.e. the collection of systems in the vicinity of the Solar System), as well as a few more distant holdings within the Milky Way Galaxy. It is bordered by the *Morian Dominion* to the West and by the Kalimasti Dominion to the East.

Three special territories exist within the *Terran Dominion*. The first is the world of *Luna*, Terra's sole moon, which functions as the *de facto* capital of the *Republican Alliance*. The second is a section of Terran orbit granted to the Remani of the Black Knight Pride. The third is an entire orbital route around the Sun granted to the Orcs of the Vigilant. Within these territories, Terran jurisdiction is limited, with the above parties essentially renting out these territories from their human allies.

The Terran Military Hierarchy

Every Terran has a specific rank within the Terran military apparatus, regardless of whether or not they serve in the regular *Army of Terra*, the *Allied Host*, an

Avenger Legion or a *Hierarch Legion*. A ceremonial terminology exists for the armies of specific *Nations of Terra* (for example: the *Army of Israel*, the *Army of France*, the *Army of Han*, etc.), though despite having their own names, the *Nations of Terra* do not command any actual army on their own, with the above concepts referring to the to the totality of adults belonging to a specific *Nations*.

Avenger and *Hierarch Legions* usually have their own naming conventions for ranks, yet they all have an equivalent an *Army of Terra* rank. For example, Hajduk *Centurions* roughly correlate with the rank of *Commandant*.

Hierarch Legions belonging to other factions also have Terran equivalents. For example, *Brightguard Pathfinders* roughly correlate to the rank and role of a Terran *Captain*.

Furthermore, the English names of the *Allied Host* ranks are virtually the same as the ranks of the *Army of Terra*.

The *Army of Terra* is split between *soldier* and *officer* ranks, with the primary difference being that officers are selected based on their aptitude for leadership, which is continuously cultivated by their superiors. As a general rule, officers always outrank soldiers. Yet, there is some overlap between certain *soldier* and *officer ranks*, with the rank of *Sergeant Major* roughly correlating to that of *Commandant*, the rank of *Chief Master Sergeant* to that of *Captain* and the rank of *Master Sergeant* to that of *Lieutenant*. For these specific ranks, it is quite common for a Terran to switch between *officer* and *soldier* ranks, depending entirely on the cultivation of their leadership traits.

The officer ranks are in ascending order: *Lieutenant*, *Captain*, *Commandant*, *Colonel*, *General*, *Representative* and, finally, the *Marshal of Terra*. The lowest officer rank, *Lieutenant*, commands a *Company* of one hundred *soldiers*. *Captains* command a *Battalion* made up of ten *Companies* through their *Lieutenants*. *Commandants* command a *Brigade* of ten *Battalions* through their Captains. *Colonels* command a *Regiment* of ten *Battalions* through their *Commandants*. *Generals* command a *Force* of ten *Regiments* through their *Colonels*, as well as their own personal *Avenger Legion*.

Representatives command a *Corps*, as well as their own personal *Avenger Legion*. *Representatives* are somewhat different in nature to *Generals*, since they never truly command armies in the field. Rather, they command the various specialized *Corps* of *Terra* (such as the *Logistics Corps* the *Medical Corps* or the *Gardener Corps*), whose members are spread out across the various *Terran Detachments*. Thus, even though they technically outrank *Generals*, their role is fundamentally different and the two positions could be considered to be roughly equal in practice. Their personal *Avenger Legions* (such as the *Sardaukar* or the

Knights) are also different in nature, since they are typically changed upon a *Representative's* so as to no longer be based around a specific ethnicity.

Finally, the *Marshal of Terra* commands the *Army of Terra*, as well as his own personal *Avenger Legion* and is outranked only by the *Warchief of the Republican Alliance*.

The *soldier ranks* are in ascending order *Corporal, Sergeant, Staff Sergeant, Master Sergeant, Chief Master Sergeant* and *Sergeant Major*. *Sergeant Majors* will always assist a *Colonel*, whilst *Master Sergeants* and *Chief Master Sergeants* will typically do the same for *Captains* and *Commandants*, respectively. Each *Company* is comprised of four platoons of twenty-four men, commanded by a *Staff Sergeant*. Each platoon is comprised of a mix of *Corporals* and *Sergeants*.

Four more *soldier ranks* exist. Terrans under the age of ten hold the *de facto* rank of *Infantry*, Terrans between the ages of ten and fifteen hold the rank of *Cadet*, whilst those between fifteen and twenty years of age hold the rank of *Ensign*. Promotion to *Corporal* is granted automatically upon the age of twenty. These three ranks are not part of the adult Terran military hierarchy, as they are <u>never</u> deployed and are considered a last line of defence, in the case of an absolute calamity on a scale comparable to the *End Times*. The rank of *Companion* also exists, bestowed solely on naturalized Terran citizens (which are few and far between) and is roughly equivalent to a *Corporal*.

The **Terran High Command**, the **Terran Senate** and the **Courts of Terra**

The *Terran State* is loosely based around a traditional three branch system. However, the system itself is very heavily influenced by Terran history, *Terra's* standing within the *Republican Alliance* and the militarized nature of Terran society. Bear in mind that the separation of the executive, legislative and judicial branches is imperfect, at best, though functional within the context of the situation *Terra* finds itself in.

The executive branch is essentially comprised of the entirety of the Terran officer corps (i.e. Lieutenants, Captains, Commandants, Colonels, Generals and Representatives). However, when referring to the executive branch (i.e. the *Terran Government*), most people refer strictly to the *Terran High Command*, which is the entity comprised of Generals, Representatives and the Marshal of Terra. The *High Command* also has legislative duties, for it is only they that can pass *Terran State Laws*. Furthermore, given the fact that Terran society is, essentially, one giant army, the functions of the executive branch are, to a degree, spread out across the entirety of society. Another important aspect is the fact that the position of head of state is split between the *Marshal of Terra* and the *Warchief of the Republican Alliance*, with the former holding supreme jurisdiction over *Matters of Peace* and the latter over *Matters of War*. Furthermore, one might argue that the Terran *Hierarchs* function as heads of state, given the massive amount of informal political power they hold on account of their popularity and their role in the formation of the *Terran State*.

The legislative branch is split between the *National Parliaments* and the *Terran Senate*, and holds very little power relative to the executive branch. The *Terran Senate* is made up of the collective of Terran Colonels and conducts most of its parliamentary sessions online, bar a few formal yearly sessions. The *Senate*'s power is tied to its obligation to assure the uniformity of the Terran system. This refers to a principle of the *Terran Law* that stipulates that no *Nation of Terra* may enforce any State Law or *National Regulation* that either favours or disfavours their own population. The *National Parliaments* virtually include every single adult Terran citizen under the rank of Colonel. Parliamentary sessions, in the traditional sense, do not exist for either of these chamber types. The *parliaments* may meet whenever and wherever they wish, yet in practice conduct most of their deliberations online, with attendance being entirely optional. They can pass *National Regulations*, yet these must be, in turn, reviewed and approved by the *Terran Senate* and the *Terran High Command*. In practice, very few laws and regulation are proposed and almost none ever succeed in being ratified. This is a well-known and accepted fact and is actually a design feature of the Terran legislative system, whose actual role is to ensure that public dialogue continuously exists and that individual and group grievances are always publicly accessible. When situations emerge that highlight the need for new *Terran State Laws* (which are few and far between), the *Terran High Command* formulates said laws, then has them ratified by the *Terran Senate*.

Of note is the fact that *Terran State Laws* are far more important than *National Regulations*.

The Terran judicial system is basically superimposed upon the Terran military hierarchy. If two parties are ever engaged in a legal dispute of any nature, a preliminary judgement is passed by a *Judicator*. A *judicator* is a very advanced artificial intelligence that acts as a judge, prosecutor and legal defence for both parties. Once it passes its verdict, if either of the two sides finds the verdict unjust (which obviously happens quite often, yet not always), the matter is brought to a Terran officer that outranks both of the parties in question, who acts as a judge for the purpose of the trial. If the new verdict overrules the *Judicator's* verdict, the matter is passed on to an even higher ranking Terran officer that acts as a judge for a third and final ruling. However, what can happen (incredibly rarely) is that a specific case can reach levels as high as the *Terran High Command*. There have even been a handful of instances when such divisive legal disputes have been resolved by the soliciting foreign legal experts (mostly Vigilant Orcs) to act as final judges. An important observation is the fact that, both in theory and practice, this system does imply that the *Terran High Command*'s members are, in a way, above the law. The issues that arise from this fact are resolved by an institution known as the *High Court of Terra*, a special tribunal that assembles in order to resolve internal conflicts of the *Terran High Command*.

Terranomics

Initially considered to be a joke term, *Terranomics* has ended up becoming the official academic term used to describe the economics of the Terran society. It is split between Domestic Economics, Community Economics and External Economics. Of note is the fact most societies have no real need for specific raw materials, since most civilizations have achieved some form of transmutation technology, which allows for the production of any naturally-occurring substance. Furthermore, due to several advanced energy-producing technologies, there is also no need for the exchange of energy between different civilizations, since most are more than self-sustainable. Thus, interstellar commerce is usually focused on the exchange of services, information and crafted items that require incredible degrees of specialization.

Terran Domestic Economics refers to the Economics of the *Terran Dominion*. Two currencies exist within this system: *dollars* (also called *money*) and *salaries* (also called *credits*). *Salaries* are the Terran version of universal basic income and are of a purely socialist nature. Every Terran, depending on their rank, receives certain benefits from the *Terran Government*, with these benefits being proportional to their rank. For example, a Terran *Sergeant* receives a house, while a Terran *General* essentially receives a palace. Moreover, they receive a certain amount of fungible tokens known as *salaries*, which they can exchange for non-essential goods. *Dollars* are the actual currency of *Terra* and can be obtained via *deeds of renown*, inheritance (as is the case with Mira al Sayid's vast wealth), gambling or professions (such as painting, writing, cooking, smithing, etc.). *Dollars* are used primarily to purchase goods from *Terran Artisans*. *Salaries* are issued by the *Department of Payments* within the *Logistics Corps*, while *Dollars*, which are based on the principle of artificial scarcity and are capped at one thousand dollars per Terran adult, are regulated by the *Bank of Terra*, itself a subdivision of the *Guild Congress*, one of the few Terran organizations located outside the military hierarchy of the *Terran State*.

Terran Community Economics refers to the main business model and primary revenue stream of the *Terran State*: racketeering. Within the *Republican Alliance*, despite the existence of the *Allied Host*, most member states require additional security assets and forces, in order to protect the integrity of their territory and defend their sovereignty. This fact is, in many ways, the main reason behind the *Republican's Alliance*'s existence, as some members have a defence surplus, which they essentially sell to other members. The *Humans of Terra*, the *Orcs of the Vigilant*, the *Orcs of Ersatz*, the *Remani of the Black Knight* and the *Trolls of Kalimaste* are the main beneficiaries of this protection racket system, due to the highly militarized nature of their societies. The *High Elves of Gondolin*, the *Primal Elves of Pandora*, the *Ursai of Barlog*, the *Humans of Hyperborea* and the *Aesir Humans* also lend their military prowess to the joint might of the Alliance, though their economies are far more diversified. Lastly, despite being the largest of the member states, the *Elven Commonwealth*, the Andromedan *Demani*, the *Vanir Humans* and the *Hobgoblins of Moria* benefit greatly from the protection offered by their allies, whilst in turn offering up their advanced technology, exceptional craftwork and their diversified portfolio of services to their allies as payment. This great exchange is regulated by the *Republican Marketplace*, a free-market entity that sets the value of goods and services among member states.

Terran External Economics is heavily regulated by the leadership of the *Republican Alliance*, since it is, primarily, made up of the raiding and extortion of non-member states, extracommunitary protection racket (as was the case with the *Hyperboreans* and the *Vanir*, before they ultimately joined the *Republican Alliance*), as well as various scavenging, smuggling and espionage activities. The primary targets of such predatory activities are the *spawn* located to the South, as well as the *Continuum of Humanity* located to the North of the Milky Way Galaxy.

The **Nations of Terra** and their **Holdfasts**

The *Nations of Terra* are the subdivisions of the *Terran State*. They lack true political power and exist solely as cultural artefacts meant to instil a sense of both solidarity and variety by evoking some nostalgia for the countries of *Old Earth*. Around one hundred exist, including the *New Nations*, such as Zealandia and Antarctica.

Some of the more numerous *Terran Nations* include Han, Hind, Arabia, Israel, Mongolia, Russia, Bolivaria, Brazil, Mexico, Japan, Germany, France and Persia.

Most Terran nations are quite small, however, numbering far less than one million members. Nations of such average size include Turkey, America, Polska, Ukraina, Carribea, Ireland, Scotland, Nguni, Korea, Romania, Italy, Serbia, England, Scandinavia, Czechia, Spain, Portugal, Armenia, Georgia, Kazakhstan, Khalsa, Gujarat, Tamil, Yoruba, Greece, Egypt, Hausafulani, Igbo, Ethiopia, Sahara, Pashto, Tibet, Uyghur, Maghreb, Tajikistan and Khmer.

Some Terran nations number only in the hundreds of members, such as Hauran, Alawiyah, Bosnia, Tatarstan, Chuvash, Baluchistan, Ganda and Balta.

All Nations have an ancestral territory, in which members of the respective Nation must have their primary domicile. Within this territory lies the Nation's *Holdfasts*. This title is given to a city on Terra that doubles as a capital city, whilst also typically being the largest city in a Nation's territory. The largest of these are the cities of Beijing, Prague, Kathmandu, Jerusalem, Karakorum, Bogota, Mecca, Tenochtitlan, Blackstone and Kinshasa, all Holdfasts of their respective Nations, with their populations numbering in the hundreds of thousands.

The **Avenger Legions** and their **Citadels**

Avenger Legions are elite units of the Terran military which fall under the direct command of a General, Representative or the Marshal of Terra. Unlike the *Hierarch Legions*, membership of an Avenger Legion is usually restricted to members of a specific *Nation of Terra*. Exceptions, such as the *Hajduks*, the *Keshik* and, formerly, the *Ghazis* exist, yet they are few and far between.

Though frequently mistaken for mere honour guards, bestowed upon worthy leaders of Terran society, the reasons behind their creation are far more pragmatic.

First of all, they function as the elite of Terran society, with only members of the *Hierarch Legions* being considered more formidable in their abilities. Though they are technically bodyguards, they are traditionally used as elite shock troops, often being the first forces to enter battle. Furthermore, most Avenger Legions have some degree of specialization. For example, the *Hajduks* specialise in covert operations, the *Keshik* in mobile land combat, the *Esho* in aerial combat, the *Akali* in weapons of mass destruction and the *Kamayuks* in siege warfare. This tendency is not universal, with many legions functioning as a jack-of-all-trades type unit (as is the case with regular Terran Army units), such as the *Jaegers*, while others fully dedicate themselves to their traditional role as shock troops, as is the case of the *Ghazis*.

Restrictions exist regarding their size, with ten thousand being considered the maximum strength they can reach under Terran Law. That being said, most *Avenger Legions* are far smaller, with the *Hajduks*, a particularly large legion, numbering around two thousand members. This is due to a multitude of factors, most prominent of which are the higher than normal rates of attrition (as is the case of the *Vikings* and the *Samurai*), the elitist nature of these units (as is the case of the *Ghazis*), the preferences of individual generals (as is the case of the *Akali* or the *Sayeret*), competition with other *Avenger Legions* recruiting from the same *Nation* (as is the case with the *Jaegers*, the *Landsknecht* and the *Rittebruder*) or simply due to smaller than usual pool of potential recruits (as is the case of the *Cataphracts* or the *Khevsurs*).

A very important lifestyle difference between members of the *Avenger Legions* and regular Terrans is that fact that they are <u>always</u> on active duty <u>and</u> deployed, while regular Terrans are <u>always</u> on active duty, yet are <u>not always</u> deployed. In theory, this means that members of the *Avenger Legions* never benefit from *leisure time*. However, in practice, most of these units have some informal system in play, allowing for their members to experience some downtime to unwind and relax.

Citadels are the headquarters of an Avenger or a Hierarch Legion. They are typically very well fortified. Examples include Tristan da Cunha for the Terran *Old Guard*, Bâlea for the *Hajduks* or Heidelberg for the *Jaegers*.

The *Avenger Legions* feature just under one hundred thousand total members. Of key importance is the fact that *Avenger Legions* do not allow membership to anyone below the rank of *Lieutenant* or *Master Sergeant* and typically have a much more eclectic unit composition.

Their national identity is defined by the nationality of their commander. The national make-up of the *Avenger Legions* as a whole is different to the national make-up of *Terra* as a whole. For example, the Nations of *Germany* and *America* each boast a total of three *Avenger Legions*, while the much larger nation of *Han* also boasts only three.

In the scenario in which a Terran Hierarch dies, his *Hierarch Legion* can become an *Avenger Legion*. This has occurred in the past with the *Ghazis* (which still exist) and the *Pandavas* (which were disbanded).

Certain *Avenger Legions*, such as the *Tuareg* or the *Khevsurs*, are named after ethnic groups of *Old Earth*. In many cases, these Avenger Legions are all that remains of such ancient peoples. In the case of the *Tuareg*, General Tamaklast's ninety strong *Avenger Legion* is all that remains of the Tuareg people.

A partial list of the current Terran *Avenger Legions* includes the *Akali*, the *Akinjis*, the *Ashigaru*, the *Aswaran*, the *Barra Bravas*, the *Boxers*, the *Cataphracts*, the *Caudillos*, the *Condottieri*, the *Conquistadors*, the *Corsairs*, the *Cossacks*, the *Druzhina*, the *Esho*, the *Fianna*, the *Galloglaich*, the *Gbeto*, the *Gendarmerie*, the *Ghazis*, the *Grenadiers*, the *Ghurkhas*, the *Hajduks*, the *Hussars*, the *Hwarang,*, the *Ill Ghazis*, the *Impi*, the *Irregulars*, the *Jaegers*, the *Janissaries*, the *Jinyiwei*, the *Jund*, the *Hulubalang*, the *Kamayuks*, the *Keshik*, the *Khevsurs*, the *Landsknecht*, the *Maccabians*, the *Mamelukes*, the *Marines*, the *Mujahedin*, the *Otomi*, the *Redcoats*, the *Rittebruder*, the *Samurai*, the *Sardaukar*, the *Sayeret*, the *Shaolin*, the *Seals*, the *Sepoys*, the *Maharlika*, the *Tuareg*, the *Vietcong*, and the *Vikings*.

Oldtimers, **Yin** and **Sunrisers**

Terran society and, particularly, interactions between Terrans are greatly influenced by military rank <u>and</u> by age. Within this society, there are three distinct generations, each defined in relation to their connection to the *End Times*. There is no formal hierarchy in place that might dictate that *oldtimers* occupy the top of the pyramid, whilst the *sunrisers* the bottom, yet what has emerged is a society which roughly follows such a distribution of power.

Oldtimers refers to Terrans that were born before the *End Times* <u>and</u> were of fighting age during *Doomsday*. The *oldtimers* are defined by the wars they took part in, namely the *Wars of the Fimbulwinter*, *Ragnarok*, the *War of Vengeance*, as well as the *Last Fitna*. As a result, they are typically exceedingly authoritarian, aggressive and apprehensive towards change. They stand at the top of Terran society on account of having survived a trial by fire of unimaginable proportions and they take the credit for the creation of the highly militaristic society that is Terra. The younger generations typically regard them with a high degree of respect, bordering on outright fear, due to the fact that, unlike the *Yin* and the *sunrisers*, the *oldtimers* bear the taint of fratricide upon them, due to their universal participation in the *Wars of the Fimbulwinter* and the *Last Fitna*. They are also partially responsible for the stagnation of Terran culture, which is deeply mired in the zeitgeist of the decades before the outbreak of the *Fimbulwinter*, to which they currently refer to fondly as *the Good Old Times*. The term *oldtimer* is considered derogatory by most of their number. Examples include Thomas Ashaver, Laur Pop, Shoshanna Adler and Ronan O'Malley.

The *Yin* are those Terrans born before the *End Times*, but who were <u>not</u> of fighting age by the time of *Doomsday*. Their name derives from the Mandarin word for 'hidden' since they were hidden from the elves. At first, this was done simply to protect them from being slain but, once reports of mass kidnappings began to emerge, it was also done to prevent them from being stolen by the invaders. Just as how the *oldtimers* are defined by the wars they fought in their 'youth', the *Yin* are defined by the *Senoyu War*, which took place after their entire cohort reached fighting age. The *Yin* are considered both a highly treasured and a lost generation. They grew up in the shadow of their forefathers' achievements and never truly managed to grow out of their shadow. Though they now occupy many middle management positions within Terran society, they are largely considered to be doomed to live their entire lives unable to match the expectations of those that had sacrificed so much for them. Examples include Maximillian and Lisa Muller, Silvia Murărescu, Nick Lăutaru and Opera Bokha.

Sunrisers refers to Terrans born <u>after</u> *Doomsday*. By far the largest generation, the sunrisers are also defined by the war of their 'youth': the Ayve War. Their name refers to the fact that they were all born after the metaphorical night of the *End*

Times. Unlike the *oldtimers* and the *Yin*, they have lived their entire lives within Terran society. As such, their identity revolves around their joint experience within the Terran educational system, as well as by their *Allied Host* service. Another important aspect is the fact that most sunrisers were not born within traditional family structures as we would know them today. The vast majority were raised by *Gardener Families*, either since birth or at least for some period of time after the deaths of their parents. They are, by far, the most 'normal' and well-adjusted of the Terran generations, bearing the closest resemblance to our own society. Examples include Thomas Muller, Mira al Sayid and Albrecht Hausser.

Honeybone Plating, Lamecular Membranes and other Enhancements

The term *enhancement* retains its old English meaning, yet is usually used to refer to the biological modifications received by Terrans. Most enhancements are the product of gene editing via *genetic templates*, resulting in a population that is virtually immune to disease (as we know it today), whilst also benefiting from increased endurance, strength, speed and even intelligence. The term also includes modifications that can only be made to Terrans after their birth, such as *honeybone* or *eye marbles*, known as *surgical enhancements*.

Some key examples are detailed below.

Honeybone is the term frequently used to describe enhanced Terran bones. In actuality, the actual honeybone refers only to the non-magnetic metallic plating placed on top of an individual's existing bone structure. While appearing simply as a bluish white material, closer analysis reveals the material's structure as a vast network of small hexagonal plates, fused onto the bone, with disparate openings left over, to allow for communication between the bone and the rest of the body. The term is also used to describe enhanced Terran joints and cartilages, despite the fact that those enhancements rely on completely different technologies;

The *Lamecular membrane* is a biological *enhancement* employed by Terrans which provides an additional layer of protection in the form of a coating applied to their nervous system, allowing them to hide their thoughts from potential telepathic espionage, as well as providing an extra layer of protection against telepathic manipulation and blunt force trauma.

Mental conditioning refers to the process by which Terrans receive a great degree of mental resilience and independence. The process itself is quite complex and time-consuming, with the entire endeavour lasting up until late adolescence, when a Terran's prefrontal cortex completely matures. It is split between resilience training, which focuses on increasing an individual's cognitive abilities and their willpower, and independence training, which focuses heavily on making sure that the individual cannot be mind controlled, brainwashed or otherwise nefariously manipulated. *Mental conditioning practices* refers to specific tools, such as breathing exercises, meditation, mantra recitation or sanity checks. The study of philosophy, psychology and politics is frequently seen as a necessary step in achieving complete *mental conditioning*.

Eye Marbles are a *surgical enhancement* that replaces of the cornea and sclera of the human eye with an artificial material which allows for greater protection. The implant also functions in tandem with other *genetic enhancements* made to the eye, allowing for increased vision during low-light conditions, as well increased visual capacity at both long and close distance. Of note is the fact that the old English expression 'to lose your marbles', now refers to one's inability to see something, as opposed to the old meaning of having gone insane.

Additional information regarding *genetic templates* is given in the final appendix: *Notes on Worldbuilding*.

Appendix V
The Dark Forrest

The **Republican Alliance**

Also known as the Alliance of Terra or simply the Alliance is the name of the integrated military alliance formed by the Humans of Terra, the Remani of the Black Knight, the Orcs of Vigilant, the Trolls of Kalimaste, the Hobgoblins of Moria, the Low Elves of the Commonwealth, the Primal Elves of Pandora, the High Elves of Gondolin, the Ursai of Barlog, the Demani of the Andromeda Galaxy, the Humans of Hyperborea, the Vanir Humans and the Aesir Humans.

Overview of **Members** of the **Republican Alliance**
- The **Humans** of **Terra**

The Humans of Terra are what is commonly referred to as 'unseeded', meaning human life did not descend upon Old Earth from among its stars, but emerged from the planet's own soil. The sad truth is that most unseeded worlds go completely unnoticed to the open universe, as human civilization is frail in its infancy. Whether by disease, cataclysm or self-destruction, most unseeded worlds rarely succeed in spreading their stock to other worlds.

Those who do, tend to attract the attention of those peoples that have long mastered interstellar travel. If fortunate, these worlds will encounter friendly forces, of which most preferable is the Continuum of Humanity, the self-styled shepherd of the human race. However, it all so often happens that these worlds encounter hostile entities amongst the stars. This was the case for the Humans of Terra. The Svart, a tribe of elves that split from the Tribes of Elvandom millennia before, had made their home in the Milky Way Galaxy, pushed ever outwards by the Continuum's crusades.

After conquering the Troll world of Kalimaste, the Svart made their way to Terra, as they attempted to cleanse the galaxy of non-Elven life. The ensuing invasion has many names, yet is most commonly referred to as the End Times. With the aid of the Black Knight Pride of Remani, the Orcs of Vigilant and the Troll Refugees of Kalimaste, the Terrans managed to repel the initial invasion and, after the Goblins of Moria entered the conflict, dealt a stunning defeat to the Svart army during the Second Battle of Terra. This victory would mark the beginning of the conflict we now know as the War of Vengeance.

Under Terran leadership, an alliance of humans, orcs, goblins, trolls and remani would wage war on the elves across the stars as the elves were weakened by the Low Revolution and the Primal Betrayal. Following the Surrender at Gondolin, the victorious Alliance would gradually evolve into what is now known as the Republican Alliance.

The Terrans possess a unique standing within the Alliance, as the End Times and the War of Vengeance have had a profound impact on the Terrans. They are the most jingoistic of all the members of the Alliance and, together with the Orcs of Vigilant, make up the backbone of the Allied Host (the Alliance's military component). Terra has been transformed into a fortress world, with some even deeming the most well-defended place in the universe.

However, it is not walls or weapons that keep Terra safe, but its friends. The Milky Way Galaxy is now entirely controlled by the Republican Alliance, which means any foe that seeks to reach the world will have to cross an entire galaxy of hostile forces in order to threaten it.

- The **Remani** of the **Dark Knight Pride**

To the humans of Old Earth, the remani, at first glance, appeared to be some particularly composed race of werewolves, though even a superficial look at them would quickly hint at a more noble nature than that of some mindless lycanthrope. They are not shapeshifters, though they did employ cloaking technologies during their time among the people of Old Earth, as they sought to blend in among their flock. The remani differ from an actual wolfman of myth most noticeably through their very erect body posture, their very humanlike hands, their wet noses, and their prehensile tails (which hint at their true nature).

The remani are a very rare occurrence on the Tree of Man, as they are to lemurs what humans are to apes. They emerged on worlds which, for some reason or another, favoured the development of sentience in the descendants of lemurs, as opposed to those of the higher apes. As such, they retain many of the traits characteristics of their ancestors, in conjunction with many humanlike characteristics, as well as a few other traits which are entirely their own.

The remani of the Black Knight are one of the many nomadic 'prides' (the Terran term used to describe remani ethnic groups) that wander the Universe in search of quiet domains to call their own. They arrived in the Milky Way Galaxy from the West and quickly began observing the development of intelligent life on the worlds of Moria, Terra and Kalimaste. Upon realizing their planned extermination by the Svart and due to reasons far to convoluted to explain here, they ultimately decided to go against their principles and intervene on behalf of the Milky Way natives. They treat the Morians, Terrans and Kalimasti as one would treat their adopted children, continuing to aid them as they navigate a complex universe.

- **The Orcs of Vigilant**

Many have speculated as to Thomas Ashaver's mental state when he decided to call the denizens of the worldship Vigilant 'orcs'. In truth, they do not at all resemble the 'orcs', of Old Earth myth. They are a tall people, with an almost regal posture, with broad shoulders nestling a head that seems to be a bit too small for their body. Their square faces are similar to those of humans (bar their much more brutish appearance) and are flanked by slightly pointy ears. Heavy bones perch upon their visage strong cheeks, a thick brow and a large jaw. Their bodies, again, similar to that of a human, are massive in size, with thick muscles dwelling beneath a thick hide that will slowly change colour to match the orc's environment. They present sexual dimorphism similar to that of humans, with orc females usually being much more muscular than the average Terran female (which, in turn, are generally more muscular than the average human female).

All Orcs derive from a specific breed of man developed after the ancient War at the Gates of Heaven. Their race was created to fill a specialized role as a warrior caste, within the decimated society that survived that great conflict at the beginning of time and elves, orcs and humans all coexisted peacefully, for a time. Yet, with the emergence of the Continuum of Humanity, the Orcs, products of the alteration of the sacred human form, were regarded as abominations, and were exiled away from the ancient worlds of 'seeded humanity'.

Their society is divided into many clans, with each clan usually dwelling upon a gigantic worldship from which the orcs take the name of their people. One such clan is that of the Vigilant Orcs. In their many millennia of traversing universe, they befriended and battled many people, including the remani of the Black Knight Pride, with whom they formed a strong friendship and kept in touch after their paths parted ways. It was the remani who convinced the Orcs of the Vigilant to intervene in the genocides taking place in the Milky Way Galaxy, leading to their arrival during the Hour of Twilight, saving the Terrans from extinction. Following the events of the Bloodbrother Crisis, the orcs of Vigilant no longer employ a shared consciousness, as they did before the disastrous hijacking of said consciousness by the Continuum of Humanity.

- The **Trolls** of **Kalimaste**

The trolls of today's Kalimaste are few in number and many in race. They are a giant people, almost two feet taller than the average Terran and at least a foot taller than the average Orc. Most are of the lithe variety of so-called forest, jungle and desert races, whilst many burly mountain, frost and cave trolls make up the other end of troll physiology. Between them lay the many other variants of their race, such as marsh, hill and plain trolls. Despite their branch lying the closest to that of humans on the Tree of Man, they resemble hobgoblins most in their appearance (with the exception of their eyes, which are generally smaller in proportion to their heads than those of a human), although their general brutish appearance makes them to goblins what orcs are to humans.

Their varied nature is a result of their environment. Whilst elves are what becomes of humans that dwell in the most blessed of worlds, the trolls are the exact opposite. Such is the case of Kalimaste, a world that saw human civilization endure the cataclysmic eruption of the Urshalak supervolcano. Over time, the humans of Kalimaste evolved into the various breeds of modern Kalimasti troll. Their situation was in no way a one-off occurrence, for trolls are quite common within the greater universe, emerging from both seeded and unseeded human populations that suffer some misfortunate or another.

The Svart attempted their eradication while the trolls were caught up in their first true world war, following the industrialization of their people. They partially succeeded in their endeavour, with the only survivors of the Annihilation of Kalimaste being the troll refugees that were evacuated on the arks provided by the Dark Knight remani, as well as a pocket of cave trolls which fought a hopeless guerrilla war against the Svart up until the eventual Reclamation of Kalimaste. They retain a close connection to both the Dark Knight Remani and the Humans of Terra, which harboured them during the War of Vengeance and with whom they are most alike in culture and history.

- The **Hobgoblins** of **Moria**

Goblins are the most diverse branch of the Tree of Man, with trolls coming in at a distant second. Only humans outnumber them across the cosmos, though they do so by a rather large margin. By definition, they emerge as a result of the alteration of the human form by artificial means. This aspect differentiates them from trolls, since the latter emerge from the alteration of the human form by natural means.

This would make orcs a type of goblin, though the specific particularities of their history make such a comparison redundant. Hobgoblin varieties are considered to be the most stable and successful breed of goblin, on account of their race's high levels of both resilience and adaptability. They greatly resemble humans, though they do bear some stark differences, noticeably in the form of their pointy ears, large noses, large mouths, slightly larger eyes and, most noticeably, their skin colour, which ranges from bright greens and reds, all the way to more muted tones of brown and deep blue. Unlike orcs, which can change their skin colour in a matter of hours, goblins do so over many years, depending on their environment.

The humans of Moria became goblins following the intervention of the Black Knight Remani which noticed that they were on the verge of annihilation due to a solar flare that had ravaged their post-modern society, which greatly resembled Old Earth. The remani brought them into the fold of the nascent Republican Alliance and the Hobgoblins of Moria have been stalwart members of the Alliance ever since.

- The **Low Elves** of the **Commonwealth** of **Menegroth**

Elves are variants of mankind that emerge upon blissful paradise worlds after the passing of many generations. It is unclear as to whether or not the first branch of the first sapling of the Tree of Man was elven or trollish, yet Elves are the earliest attested variation of mankind, with the exception, of course, of humans. They are lithe of body and possess features one might describe as conventionally attractive. Their appearance, at first glance, does not seem to differ that much from that of a regular human, yet, on closer inspection, stark differences immediately become noticeable, such as slightly larger eyes, an almost complete absence of body hair, as well as, of course noticeably pointy ears. Sexual dimorphism is far less pronounced than in humans, with males being only slightly bulkier than females.

Low elves are actually the most common variety of elf, given the tendency of elven society to almost always split into an upper and lower caste. The upper caste will typically concentrate upon the development of leadership capabilities, military prowess, as well as cognitive abilities. Meanwhile, the lower caste will typically develop other psychological and cultural traits such as patience, stoicism, diligence, a sublime work ethic, a strong sense of justice, as well as an overall tendency for conformity. They reach maturity much faster than their high elf counterparts, with the age of thirty roughly correlating to their adulthood, whilst high elves typically barely enter early adolescence by that age.

That being said, the Low Elves of the Commonwealth derive from a particularly repressive society. Their former upper caste, the Svart Elves, subjugated them over a particularly long period of time and in an exceedingly thorough manner, including by using various means of mind-control. This has resulted in the common phenomena of recently liberated low elves becoming quite humanlike in the absence of a dominant caste. In time, it is speculated that the low elves of the Milky Way Galaxy will once more diverge into two separate castes, though that day is far into the very distant future.

- ## The **High Elves** of **Gondolin**

Following the end of the War of Vengeance and the partition of the elves of Milky Way Galaxy, the surviving upper caste of elven society was sundered into those that surrendered in the face of annihilation and those that fled into the darkness of the void to become Dark Elves. Unlike their disgraced brethren, the High Elves of Gondolin joined the Republican Alliance and, following the Partition of Elvandom, were relegated to the Gondolin System, where they now dwell.

They are quite stereotypically high elven, being noticeably taller than their Low Elven kin, possessing far pointier ears and, most importantly, a far more infantile demeanour. They differ greatly in terms of temperament and psychology to both the primal and low elves, as they have a childlike temperament, an obsession with hierarchy and social status, excessive ambition, intellectual curiosity, a vindictive nature, as well as being somewhat antisocial and aloof.

Politically, like most other elves, they occupy a peculiar space within the Known Universe, as their branch of the Tree of Man emerges when a human civilization becomes consistently prosperous and successful. Thus, they are typically the only inhuman race that maintains relatively good relations with the Continuum of Humanity, as well their fellow inhumans, thought the Continuum works tirelessly to ensure that none of their population is ever permitted to evolve into elves. Within the Republican Alliance, the High Elves occupy an exceedingly peculiar space, as they are the last survivors of the race that attempted to exterminate three other member races, subjugated two others, coerced a sixth and waged war against two others. Their continued existence and acceptance comes at the expense of many amends made following the conclusion of the War of Vengeance, such as the eradication of any of their race that had any role in the deaths they caused.

- ## The **Primal Elves** of **Pandora**

The third most common and the most peculiar of the elven branches of the Tree of Man, primal elves are elves that emerge within societies that succeed in achieving a prosperous existence whilst in harmony with nature. They are much more muscular than their city-dwelling kin, as well as being far more animalistic in appearance and demeanour. Psychologically, they greatly resemble high elves, though they fundamentally differ from them on account of the absence of any particular sense of belonging to either their nation or their caste. Yet, they are in no way selfish, being simply independent in nature and thought. They do, however, have a strong bond with their immediate family members, much more so than low elves (which are known to be surprisingly ambivalent to their blood), as well as high elves (which are known for their tendency to either compete, undermine or backstab their own kin).

The primal elves of the world of Pandora arrived in the Milky Way Galaxy seeking to escape both the controlling governments of the Tribes of Elvandom, as well as the ever-present threat of genocide at the hands of the Continuum. They settled on the then uninhabited world of Pandora and proceeded to evolve into the modern-day primal elves and lived peacefully and in harmony with the flora and fauna of their new home. They even spread out to other inhabitable worlds of the Milky Way, establishing outposts primarily in the galactic East.

The arrival of the Svart High Elves perturbed their peace and, following centuries of negotiation and tense confrontations, an agreement was ultimately reached, wherein the Primal Elves of Pandora would join with the Svart state within a confederation that was (supposed to be) loose. However, over time, the Svart began to slowly chip away at primal elf freedoms, which in turn caused the people of Pandora to become restless and resentful. The War of Vengeance provided the perfect opportunity for the elves of Pandora to turn on their former partners. Within the Republican Alliance, they express continuous libertarian tendencies, insisting on the complete freedom of their people to live as they see fit.

- The **Libra Ursai** of **Barlog**

The ursai greatly resemble the remani in origin, for they are members of mankind that do not derive from higher apes. Moreover, they do not even descend from primates, for they are actually more akin to intelligent bipedal bears. They are quite independent-minded and are known to obsess over their adherence to their very strict code of honour, as well as their pathological fear of being ashamed. Much of their society revolves around the act of 'saving face', as it is known. As such, they have a tendency to be either withdrawn and reclusive or horribly pugnacious and confrontational.

The Libra Ursai were encountered by the Svart near their initial Urheimat close the borders of the Continuum of Humanity. Following the Svart's land grant in the Milky Way Galaxy, they decided to coerce the Libra Ursai into joining them as military allies. The ursai, burdened by the weight of many burned bridges, gambling debts and blackmailed into cooperation by the elves, agreed, and settled upon the world of Barlog.

They did not initially participate in either the Annihilation of Kalimaste or the Terran End Times, only entering the War of Vengeance in the aftermath of the

Second Battle of Terra. Ultimately, through clever political manoeuvring, successful acts of espionage and a duel fought on Barlog, the Libra Ursai eventually exited the War of Vengeance, only to later join the nascent Republican Alliance. They maintain good relations with the city-state of Shangri, were they maintain a strong presence through a number of their kin that decided to leave Barlog and the Svart Elf domination of their people.

- The **Demani** of the **Andromeda** Galaxy

Though technically a branch of goblinkind, the Demani differ drastically in both nature, appearance and origin to regular goblins. In short, while goblins emerge when a human population purposefully alters their form with the use of advanced bioengineering, demani emerge when a human population alters their form in such a way as to better interact with a specific technology. As one might imagine, this leads to a plethora of new and strange forms, though the demani of the Andromeda Galaxy typically retain a great degree of physical similarity to baseline humans. They generally resemble humans, though stark differences are present when it comes to skull shape, the extremities of their limbs, as well as their skin colour. Most Andromedan Demani have elongated skulls that jut out from the backs of their heads. Their feet are either humanlike, even-toed ungulate hoofs, odd-toed ungulate hoofs, paws (similar to remani), froglike, or even birdlike claws in some subspecies, while their hands bear either five, four or even just three digits. Their skin colour varies wildly, from humanlike pinks, whites and browns, all the way to golden, bright red, ultramarine blue or even jet black colours.

Most demani are thought of as failed branches of the Tree of Man, since their commanding feature is that they usually emerge when a society reaches a point where their technology is quite advanced but their understanding of said technology becomes crippled, as they usually forget how it works. What typically follows is a failure to replicate, use or contain it. Thus, their technology appears downright magical to both themselves and others. This is the case of the entire Andromeda Galaxy, which is permeated by one overreaching magical energy web designed and implemented by the demani's ancestors. The existence of this web has lead the demani to become quite primitive to external eyes, with their technology becoming the object of religious worship, as opposed to scientific understanding.

It was this primitivism that lead to the enslavement of the demani at the hands of the Senoyu, a corporate contractor of the Continuum of Humanity. The Senoyu used the demani as labourers and extracted the magical energy of their galaxy for either the betterment of their own standard of living or for trade with the Continuum. The Republican Alliance intervened in the Andromeda Galaxy with the purpose of both weakening the Continuum's presence in the region, as well as with the goal of drawing the demani and their technology into the fold of the Republican Alliance. The liberated demani are currently in the middle of a cultural renaissance, seeking to redefine their own existence within the context of their newly regained freedom.

- ## The **Orcs** of **Ersatz**

The Orcs of Ersatz are an orcish clan of the Republican Alliance and the denizens of the great worldship Ersatz. They are identical to the Orcs of Vigilant in nearly every way, yet they are culturally quite distinct. Whilst the Orcs of Vigilant are a rather optimistic lot, the Orcs of Ersatz are typically a grim, dour and fatalistic people.

Just like the Orcs of Vigilant, they previously shared a joint consciousness among themselves, yet they fell victim to enslavement by the Continuum, which employed this web of consciousnesses to control them. Some of their number succeeded in breaking free of said mind-control and managed to assist the Republican Alliance in liberating both their brethren and the Orcs of Vigilant.

In the aftermath of the Bloodbrother Crisis, they joined the Republican Alliance and now dwell within the Milky Way Galaxy, where the Ersatz now orbits a star located to the galactic South.

- ## The **Humans** of **Hyperborea**

The Humans of Hyperborea are seeded humans of the Continuum of Humanity that arrived in the Triangulum Galaxy sometime before the Aesir and the Vanir. They are essentially religious sect that fled persecution within the Continuum. Their core tenet is the belief that though the human shape and essence should not be altered, the make-up of the human body is an incomplete work of art and should be improved upon.

They are identical to baseline humans on the outside, yet their physiology is the result of millennia of careful development. Thus, they are far stronger, faster and more resilient than any unaltered human. Their intelligence, memory and senses are also greatly improved, making the eldest of their people almost truly inhuman on account of being able to store gigantic hoards of perfect memories both within their own heads, as well as within external storage units.

Though they lived for millennia as religious hermits upon the world of Hyperborea, they saw within the Republican Alliance a group of like-minded peoples among which they might be able to survive within a hostile universe. They remain the only people to have ever approached the Alliance on their own accord and insist that they join. In exchange for membership, they pledged their military to the service of the Alliance and, most importantly, they shared with the humans of Terra their perfected genetic template. This now serves as the fundamental basis on which the Hyperborean economy functions: in exchange for security provided by strength in numbers and diversity, they provide the other races of the Alliance, as well as other parties, with the fruits of their zealous scientific advancements.

- ### The **Aesir** and **Vanir Humans**

The story of the Aesir and Vanir is one that encapsulates both the best and the worst of humanity. They are in essence two feuding families, jokingly referred to by Terrans as the Hatfields and McCoys, that have oscillated for millennia between engaging with each other in alliances of convenience and warring against each other as bitter enemies. Their origins lie as refugees fleeing the ancient *War at the Gates of Heaven*, arriving within the Triangulum Galaxy over a million years before the rise of the Republican Alliance. It is unknown how the two groups first came at odds, though a common folktale says that the great conflict stems from a an argument between the wives of two twin brothers. One argued that a salad made from chopped parsley, tomatoes, onions and mint leaves should also contain pomegranate seeds, while the other argued that it should not.

What followed were aeons of brutal internecine violence during which both groups successfully beat each other into stone age levels of civilization on numerous occasions. Accounts of these great conflicts survive in the oral traditions of both groups, with the last conflict, known to Terrans as the Ayve War, having begun at least a thousand years before the Terran End Times.

The Republican Alliance intervened in the Ayve War, with the goal of drawing one of the two groups, the Vanir, into the fold. One incentive behind this decision was the Vanir's possession of advanced eschatological technology, yet another one was to prevent the Continuum from taking advantage of the conflict and turning the Triangulum Galaxy into a bridge to Andromeda and the Milky Way. In the end, both factions joined the Republican Alliance, though the Aesir only did so after being beaten into submission by the coalition of Allies, Vanir and Hyperboreans.

The **Sphere of Influence** of the **Republican Alliance**

This group of states is comprised of peoples located in the vicinity of the Milky Way, Andromeda and Triangulum Galaxies, which have traditionally either been affiliated, aligned or simply on friendly terms with the Republican Alliance, despite not becoming outright members.

They include the realms of the:

Humans of **Avalon**: an unruly vassal of the Continuum of Humanity encompassing the Phoenix Dwarf Galaxy;

Humans of **Dorado**: a spacefaring civilization of unseeded humans living in the Bootes Dwarf Galaxy;

Humans of **Erebor**: a city-state of seeded humans, formerly of the Human Confederation, located in the Large Magellanic Cloud;

Humans of **Liliput**: a group of seeded humans (that are close to becoming elves) that dwell within the Small Magellanic Cloud;

City of **Shangri**: a multiracial city-state located between the Continuum and the Triangulum Galaxy in the Pisces Dwarf Galaxy;

Trolls of **Atlantis**: sea troll survivors of an ancient catastrophe that dwell within the Sextans Dwarf Galaxy;

Draco Mandrakes: a coven of mandrakes that lay within the Draco Dwarf Galaxy;

Various remani prides known to roam the Local Cluster;

Countless potential troll and primitive human civilizations scattered throughout the Local Cluster;

At least one orc worldship rumoured to be hiding somewhere in the intergalactic void between Andromeda and the Milky Way;

A herd of taori of unknown origin that is believed to have assisted the Terran Expedition to the Andromeda Galaxy during the Senoyu War.

The **Continuum of Humanity**

Occasionally referred to as Leviathan, the Continuum is the primary antagonist of the Republican Alliance, the Others Unaligned, as well as the Spawn. The Continuum of Humanity is the largest known civilization in the Universe. Its primary domain is referred to as the Continuum Realm, a vast totalitarian realm of countless worlds entirely populated by mortal humans under the role of a single despot. The Continuum also maintains a Near Domain comprised of vassals (such as Camelot) and contractors (such as the Senoyu).

It is the successor state of the Old Realm of Mankind, the first true superpower of the Known Universe

The **Others Unaligned**

Opposite the Continuum lies a vast assortment of smaller states which together rival the Continuum in size and population. They are typically confederations of the larger branches of the Tree of Man, banding together around their shared evolutionary heritage. An uneasy peace exists between the two groups, centred on the Others Unaligned vowing to respect certain criteria set forth by the Continuum, which in turn is forced to curb its expansionist ambitions.

The Others Unaligned are not an integrated alliance, such as the Republican Alliance. On the contrary, when they're not fighting the Continuum, they tend to battle each other in smaller transgalactic conflicts. However, it is the interplay between these two great factions that allows the Republican Alliance to exist, since the Continuum cannot risk overextending its reach, for that might incur conflict with the Others Unaligned.

The most dominant groups among the Others Unaligned are the Human Confederation, the Clans of Ork, the Tribes of Elvandom, the Goblin Corporation, the Prides of the Remani and the Demani Cabals.

Spawn

Spawn is a catch-all term referring to intelligent life outside the Tree of Man. Spawn are at best disinterested in mankind and at worst downright hostile. Most are part of collective consciousnesses with no true individuals being present among their race (if they could even be considered one). They resemble insects the most, living in hives at the behest of a single dominant entity. When the Others Unaligned and the Continuum of Humanity are not busy fighting each other, they are usually fighting spawn of one origin or another.

Appendix VI
Notes on Worldbuilding

The setting of *The Keepers of Terra* should be somewhat intuitive in its comprehension for most readers. Most of the aspects that have to do with how things work and how the setting came to be are explored and explained throughout the text, in places where such information is key to the reader's understanding of specific situations, decisions and the context in which they occur. The more subtle aspects that have to do with the various worldviews and mindsets present in this fictional setting, despite being the very substance of the book, are never truly detailed, neither within the text, nor within any appendix. They are left, purposefully, to the interpretation of the reader.

However, there are certain concepts and worldbuilding decisions which do actually warrant additional clarification. With this in mind, it must be underscored that the purpose of these notes is not to be an essential tool for deciphering the text. Rather, it is meant to serve as a readily available companion, helping the reader achieve better immersion into the universe of Terra.

Ultimately, *The Keepers of Terra* is written in the spirit of rewarding the reader for their attention, without meaning to punish lack of awareness of one detail or another. If you ever find yourself uncertain as to how one thing or another functions within the context of this story's setting, you may refer to this section and, hopefully, achieve a greater degree of clarity which will allow you to better enjoy the story.

Some of the below concepts don't even feature within the story directly (such as farsight visions), though they are part of the same fictional universe. From a literary perspective, the below notes exist primarily to assure both the reader and the writer of the absence of those most dreaded of errors: plot holes. A casual reader might not really be interested in why it takes four hours for a signal encoded within a burst of light to reach the Kuiper Belt from the surface of Earth, while a Terran spacecraft can traverse the same distance in a few seconds. However, some readers, such as myself, prefer to not have our immersion perturbed by ambiguous texts with lazy worldbuilding and hazy rules.

One very important aspect to highlight is that you will find no information below regarding the technologies used for Project Kralizec. Those are addressed heavily within the novel itself. If any information concerning this technology appears to be missing from the novel's body, then please understand that such omissions are by design, not by mistake.

Greyspace Spaceflight

Most science fiction stories set in universes populated with spacefaring civilizations need to address the issue of *fast* space flight. The warp drives of *Star Trek* or *Warhammer 40k*, the hyperspace of *Star Wars*, the slipstream of *Andromeda*, and the spacefolding of *Dune*, are all prime examples of how a non-spacefaring civilization could imagine fast spaceflight being possible. Within the world of *Keepers of Terra* there is not one single means of space travel, but many.

The humans of Terra have experimented with many types of space travel, most of which obtained by either receiving or stealing alien technology. The most common means of space travel employed is the accelerated space warp drive. Essentially, spaceships have warp drives which allow them to transfer themselves to another universe (i.e. the accelerated space, also referred to as the *Greyspace*) where the rules of physics are slightly, yet profoundly different, from those of our universe.

Let's say that we are in point A of our universe and wish to get to point B, also in our universe, and the time that would take going at a comfortable cruise speed would be 47 million years. An accelerated space warp drive functions by transporting our vessel from point A, in our universe, to point A-quick in the Greyspace. From point A-quick, we can travel to point B-quick in the Greyspace, which is the equivalent of point B, in our universe. Such a journey would take around 24 hours. From point B-quick, we can return to our universe, finding ourselves in point B, our destination in our own universe.

The Greyspace is not something crafted by any intelligent life, at least not in the sense we could ever identify, but simply a naturally occurring phenomena within the multiverse. Furthermore, there are several Greyspaces. The worldship Vigilant, home of the orcs of Vigilant, also achieves spaceflight through Greyspace. However, the Greyspace entered by the Vigilant is so – for lack of the better word – *quick*, that transportation appears to be almost instantaneous. The Vigilant, and ships of its kind, can jump from one galaxy to another in a matter of moments. However, the Vigilant's Greyspace requires such a vast amount of energy to access, that it has to spend rather long periods of time charging itself for jumps. Terran warships, which use the same Greyspace as that used by the remani, can travel the same distance as the Vigilant, albeit much slower, yet at a much lower energy cost.

The Vigilant is solar powered, using stellar energy to charge itself, both to power its jumps, and also to maintain its ecosystem and defence systems. If the Vigilant wanted to jump from the Milky Way galaxy to the Andromeda galaxy, the closest galaxy to our own, it could do so in about 4 seconds. However, such a jump would consume over a month's worth of solar energy. If a Terran or remani ship was to traverse the same distance, it could do so without any charging time, yet the journey itself would take over a week.

Another piece of information which is relevant is the fact that Greyspaces are, for lack of a better term, empty. There is a very basic energy web present, which is important for navigation purposes. Yet, by and large, Greyspaces are a dark, black void of feeble entropy. What little energy and mass enters the Greyspaces very quickly latches onto the passing ships from our universe. This allows for the Greyspaces to remain free of 'pollution'. However, this also allows for the deployment of grime mines.

Grime mines are, simply put, mines placed within an area of Greyspace, which will instantly attach to any ship traversing it, with catastrophic effect. They are frequently employed in sieges, espionage or general sabotage.

Greyspace travel is not the only means of space travel which functions within the universe of *Keepers of Terra*. However, it is the most prevalent type of space travel in the corner of the universe in which the story takes place. Hence, understanding the basic way in which this type of transportation occurs is rather important for the reader.

In regards to interplanetary travel, this is achieved through advanced means of propulsion, which do not usually involve extradimensional travel. Using propulsion systems commonly found on Terran warships, one can travel from Mercury to Pluto in under twenty hours.

Greyspace Communication

Communication of information between two points also takes place with the employment of technology similar to that of Greyspace. In short, messages are broadcast into another Greyspace universe and are directed towards a specific destination within the Greyspace universe. At said destination, the information is transported back into our universe and interpreted.

Keep in mind that these communication Greyspaces are usually different from travelling Greyspaces, yet this is not a rule.

Furthermore, just as how grime mines can be used to isolate an area of Greyspace, grime noise can be used to jam communications in areas of Greyspace.

Languages

Technology exists that allows for people to learn other languages instantaneously. Said technology comes in various forms. Of these forms, two warrant mention.

The first involves technology implanted in either the ears or the brains of speakers and hearers, which instantly translates languages unknown to the hearer into a language understood by the hearer. If two people were talking face-to-face, while speaking two different languages and employing such technologies, they would each hear words in the language they understood. However, if they were to look at the mouths of the other speaker, they would see that the movements did not match the sounds they were hearing. This type of technology is frequently employed by peoples and civilizations which do not wish to *pollute* their minds with the thinking patterns employed by other languages. The most widespread use of this type of technology is within the Continuum of Humanity, which holds purity, be it spiritual or physical, above all else. This type of technology is known as Externally Processed Messaging (EPM).

The second type of translation technology is the one employed by Terrans and the members of the Alliance as a whole and is known as Internally Processed Communication (IPC). This is the type of technology which Thomas Muller and the people he interacts with use. In essence, everyone speaks English, yet the way they learn English is fundamentally different. Some people, mostly Terrans, are native English speakers. A large number of people, particularly Terrans, many Kalimaste Trolls, a few Vigilant Orcs and most Black Knight Remani, speak English as a second language. However, most people in the Alliance learn English with the use of IPC technology. That is to say that they artificially learn this language using IPC machine which encodes the language into their brains.

This does not mean that the speaker forgets their own language. On the contrary, the speaker still *thinks* primarily in their own language, yet is now able to communicate, as well as think, in the IPC-learned language. Two goblins from Bowieville on Moria would still be able to speak the goblin language of Bowian among themselves. Yet, if they received IPC English, they could also speak English among themselves or with a third participant, be they elves, orcs or humans.

This type of language learning is considered to be both more efficient, but also more intrusive. It is efficient because no time or meaning is lost in the process of external translation. Yet, it is also somewhat intrusive, since the IPC language has a tendency to flow over into the everyday thinking of speakers in subtle ways, leading to situations where goblins will begin to think in English and elves will use troll words for objects and concepts which have no equivalent word in their native language.

Another characteristic of IPC languages is that speakers will often develop accents or specific speaking styles within the process of learning a language. One of the clearest examples is the tendency of all Vigilant orcs to speak with a posh English accent, referred to as Received Pronunciation. Another is the fact that goblins, regardless of their native language, will typically have either a Spanish, French or Italian accent when speaking IPC-learned English. Terrans themselves have a tendency to develop speech mannerisms that go far beyond regular accents. The most famous and noticeable example occurs with Terran death knights, who have a tendency to speak in hodgepodge of accents and erratic speech patterns, a reflection of the changes undertaken by their mind during the process of death and reanimation.

The reason why English is the main language of the Alliance is fairly simple. English was the *lingua franca* of Old Earth and was the language most commonly used by Terrans when coordinating the battles of the End Times. The remani, which had watched over the people of Old Earth for almost a century, already had a strong grasp of English. When the Orcs of the Vigilant arrived, they decided to learn English, as opposed to obliging their new allies to go through the shock and difficulty of having to learn a new language, particularly orcish. When the troll refugees of Kalimaste arrived, they took to learning English to better communicate with their human hosts. As such, English emerged as the language of the Alliance more due to circumstance rather than anything else. Later additions to the Alliance, such as the Hyperboreans or the Aesir and Vanir, also picked up English as the language of Allied communication.

Terran Naming Conventions and **Terran English**

Every name presented within the story of *Keepers of Terra* is the Terran version of said name. As an example: Çingeto Braca and Sorbo Falk are not actually named as such in their native orcish and troll languages. In the case of the former, his English name derives from a nickname made up by Thomas Ashaver for his orcish friend, while the latter's name is a phonetic translation of Sorbo's actual troll name into English.

Furthermore, many names, particularly Terran names, are derived from old nicknames, titles and *nomes de guerre*. The best example of this is Thomas Ashaver, whose name is actually the *nome de guerre* taken up by the Terran Hierarch took up during his time with the Primal Elves of Pandora, with his real name being quite different. Some Terran names are alterations of names given before the End Times. This is the case with Mira al Sayid's last name, which is an altered version of her family's old name.

In regards to locations, bear in mind that the names of many locations are actually the names given by Terrans to said locations. These names draw inspiration from a variety of sources. A prime example of this are the names of the elven worlds of Gondolin, Nargothrond & Menegroth, which are derived from the writings of the J.R.R. Tolkien. The elven name for each of these worlds is quite different yet, they are referred to, in English at least, by these names, given to them by Terrans based on their similarity to the cities of the fictional land of Beleriand.

The above concept may be extrapolated to the names of peoples and races. With this in mind, elves, for example, are named *elves* due their physical resemblance to the elves of Old Earth fairy tales and cinema (Tolkien, World of Warcraft or Warhammer 40k). Other names are given quite comically, as is the case with orcs, which bear some resemblance to certain Terran ideas of 'orcs', yet, in actually, are entirely different in demeanour and essence.

Functional Immortality and **Genetic Templates**

The peoples of the Alliance are functionally immortal, meaning that they do not die of old age and are immune to a vast range of ailments and diseases, including a great degree of resistance to radiation poisoning. This is due to the existence of widespread technologies allowing for organic optimization and maintenance through the implementation of various genetic templates onto different species.

For example, the humans of Terra used to employ a chimaeric genetic template, spliced together from orcish, remani, elven and human genetic templates, which allowed for increased survivability. Coupled with advancements in medicine provided by the remani and orcs, this led to an increased human lifespan, bordering on functional immortality.

However, when the Hyperboreans joined the Alliance, they brought with them their most prized possession, the Hyperborean genetic template, which was quickly distributed among the Terran population. The hyperborean genetic template is one of the highest quality genetic template available to humans in the Known Universe.

Apart from ensuring a reliable form of functional immortality, the Hyperborean genetic template includes various other additions which make it legendary among humans. Apart from providing noticeable boosts to strength, speed and intelligence, it also introduced new metabolic concepts to Terran biology, such as the Borean Sleep, a type of comma which can be triggered by a human body with a Hyperborean genetic template, which encapsulates the brain when death is imminent. This makes reanimation much easier, if the brain survives whatever caused the destruction of the body.

However, these changes, though profound, do little to change human physiology from an external perspective. Nevertheless, the average Terran does look healthier and more athletic than the typical human of Old Earth, with the most distinct difference being that Terrans are, by large, much more muscular than their forefathers. They are also taller, with the average height being around 2 meters tall and a Terran of under 1.9 meters being considered short, regardless of gender. Yet, they still look distinctly human, meaning they maintain the human shape.

An important aspect of genetic templates is that they are species-specific, meaning that humans can only use human genetic templates, while trolls can only use troll genetic templates and so on and so forth. An exception to this are chimaeric genetic templates, which are primitive and unstable mixes of genetic templates.

Furthermore, genetic templates, if designed as such, can be passed down to offspring, meaning that there is no need to administer genetic templates to subsequent generations, due to the templates already being passed down from the parents.

One last aspect concerns the prevalence of genetic templates among the civilizations and species of the universe. Orcs, hobgoblins and elves are functionally immortal due to their own inherent genetics. Remani, demani, taori, ursai and, most famously, trolls, are not. As such, these species often have to implement or develop their own genetic template in order to achieve immortality. This implementation is widespread and generally accepted among the members of these species. This is not the case for humans.

Most of the humans in the Known Universe live in the Continuum of Humanity, which explicitly forbids the attainment of functional immortality, with the penalty being the execution and damnation of those individuals who attempt to attain such immortality. This mindset is, again, a result of the Continuum's obsession with the purity of the human mind and body. If nature intended humans to grow old and die, then it was an abomination to not allow the body to age. Terrans, Hyperboreans, Aesir, Vanir and others, are, for this reason and sometimes others, considered to be traitors to humanity, since they openly allow, encourage and even enforce (as is the case with Terrans) functional immortality within their populations.

The **Tree of Man** and **the Forest of the Shapers**

Humans are the most widespread and basic form of intelligent life to develop within the Known Universe. They emerge via the process of evolution on worlds that bear resemblance to Old Earth over the course of millions of years of evolution from primordial soup and eventually become primordial man. Bear in mind that the words *mankind* and *humanity* are not interchangeable within this setting, as *humanity* refers solely to *homo sapiens* and other, near-humans, while *mankind* refers to all the different variations of humanoid life, regardless if said life is human or not.

It must be underlined that the human form is not the final destination of the journey of mankind. Nor is it the only path of evolution taken by intelligent life. Human beings can evolve naturally into different types of humanoids, such as elves and trolls. Human beings can also be artificially changed into creatures such as orcs or one of the myriad goblin races. Furthermore, animals such as wolves, dragons, bears, aurochs and even cats can become man-like due to long-term exposure to mankind. They can also develop humanoid shapes and minds on their own or be genetically manipulated into humanoid shapes by higher powers. Such processes are how the remani, ursai, mandrakes, taori and other such branches of mankind came to be.

Lastly, technology itself can change humans into new forms. A prime example are the demani, whose prolonged use of incredibly advanced technology changed their actual physiology. However, technology itself can become humanoid, as is the case with cyborgs.

This diverse family web, encompassing that which we know as mankind, is referred to as the *Tree of Man*. However, not all intelligent life is humanoid in nature, with the *Forest of the Shapers* being populated by other families of intelligent life, albeit not as prevalent or dominant as those of mankind. The most common examples are known as *spawn*, which is a catch-all term for various insectoid civilizations, most of which are either isolationist or openly hostile to humanoid life. Some exceptions to this rule exist, yet they are few and far between.

Magic Webs, **Relative Magic** and **Technology**

The simplest way to explain how magic works within the universe of *Keepers of Terra* is to reference Arthur C. Clarke's statement that 'any sufficiently advanced technology is indistinguishable from magic'. In short, everything that looks magical within the context of the setting is actually the result of incredibly advanced technology beyond the understanding of the writer, the reader and, frequently, to the characters within the story itself. It is often the case in the Known Universe for something which someone might consider to be some technology or another to be something which someone else might consider to be magic.

Relative magic is a concept employed by many in the Known Universe to explain the difference between perceptions of what is magic and what is technology. For example, for a human of Old Earth, a fair amount of technology employed by the Humans of Terra might seem to be simply very advanced technology. They might not understand exactly how it works, however they can wrap their head around how it *might* work. However, most demani technology would appear to be downright magical to the average human of Old Earth, while appearing only to be simply very advanced technology to the average Orc of Vigilant. This gap in understanding is what is referred to as 'relative magic'.

Furthermore, particularly in reference to the demani, the concept of a 'magical web' must be explained. This is, simply put, a region within the universe where certain type of magic is possible. This possibility is a result of the construction of a very advanced technological web that has been encoded into the very fabric of reality. The most well known example for the Humans of Terra is the Andromeda Galaxy, the home of demani which, long ago, had such a web encoded in a significant number of regions of space within the Andromeda Galaxy. Within these regions, a certain type of magic, as it were, is accessible to certain skilled users who have both been trained in the magical are capable of magical feats of, primarily, energy manipulation.

Another important example is Daw al Fajr, known to many *the Urizen*. Daw is, to put it as simply as possible, a type of artificial god. Her abilities are not relative magic only to Terrans, goblins and trolls, but also for advanced peoples such as the demani, the majority of elves and almost all orcs. While a demani sorcerer can practice his or her form of magic only within the confines of magical webs such as or similar to those of the Andromeda Galaxy, Daw is capable of feats such as teleportation, telekinesis, farsight, telepathy and energy manipulation almost anywhere in the Known Universe. Daw is, nevertheless, a product of technological innovation, having been constructed using ancient elven knowledge passed down over the millennia from the days of the Age of Bliss.

Artificial Intelligence and **Natural Intelligence**

Artificial intelligences are quite abundant in the world of the *Keepers of Terra* and come in many shapes and sizes, ranging from simple operators, to entities such as Daw al Fajr.

Operators are the simplest form of AI, functioning primarily as assistants or pets to either natural life forms or to other AIs. They are both conscious and sentient. However, their level of sentience, intelligence and consciousness is far less developed than that of most people.

Directors are AIs with sentience, consciousness and general intelligence comparable to that of most natural intelligences. They are frequently employed by the Alliance and placed in command of various facilities, such as starships, satellites and various other complex systems.

Warfare

Despite unimaginably advanced technology being omnipresent, the actual warfare of the setting might come off as remarkably primitive, given the abundance of melee combat, simple firearms and frequent infantry battles. However, this is not *despite* of the advanced technology available, but *due* to it. The primary family of technologies responsible for this are called *negation* or *pulse weapons* or *charges*, with Terrans frequently referring to them as EMP weapons, despite the fact that they are not all based on Electro-Magnetic Pulse technology.

Pulse charges are commonplace and they are frequently used to disable advanced enemy technology during combat. Thus, most of the truly spectacular weaponry one might expect from hyper-advanced intergalactic civilizations is typically neutralized during the early stages of combat, with only sharp sticks, boom sticks, as well as the occasional power-regenerating weapon surviving to see actual use.

Some technologies, such as Thomas Ashaver's armour, are biological in nature and hence can withstand the effect of pulse charges. The reason why such suits of armour and weapons are not commonplace is due to a combination of the costs needed to manufacture them, the skills required to craft them, the understanding of technology needed to produce them, the fact that they are quite difficult to use (let alone master) and due to the fact that they depend (in part) on leeching off the energy of the user, making them potentially dangerous to the wearer.

Farsight Visions

This is a fairly esoteric phenomena which has some impact on both how Terrans view the greater universe and how they plan their future actions. That being said, *farsight visions* are not specific to Terrans, with almost all civilizations bearing individuals which have some capacity for such visions.

To put it simply, people's thoughts can travel, in very subtle and unimaginably imperceptible ways, across the vastness of space and can be sensed by the minds of other individuals located in faraway corners of the universe. These thoughts manifest themselves as visions for the receivers of said intergalactic thoughts. The most defining characteristic of these visions, however, is their vagueness and malleability, which is the result of having to traverse the vast melange of energy and matter of the universe, coupled with the inherent subtlety of such burst of information. They often manifest themselves as dreams and are frequently blended together with the seers' own thoughts and identity. As a result, it is often quite impossible to determine exactly when a farsight vision occurs, or when it is simply a figment of a person's own imagination.

Most technology accessible to Terrans has, insofar, proven to be ineffective in detecting farsight visions experienced by its own population. Many events through which the Humans of Terra have gone through were, to some degree, predicted or, at least, hinted at by such farsight visions, such as the existence of humanoid alien life resembling werewolves, bulky orcs, pointy-eared elves and long-nosed goblins. A correlation has even been made between the heightened 'fear of impending doom' felt by many Terrans in the days leading up to the End Times. Though widely suspected of being related, the connection between the two events is predominantly agreed to be quite exaggerated.

However, some individuals have proven to be particularly susceptible to experiencing farsight visions. The clearest example is that of Daw al Fajr, whose farsight nears omniscience when it comes to matters of elvenkind, and extends into a form of clairvoyance in which she is capable of seeing several potential futures with remarkable clarity, based on the information she accumulates from the fragmentary farsight visions she experiences. Among the Terrans, Thomas Ashaver and Sarasvati Singh (the deceased mother of Mira al Sayid) are two well-known examples of human Terrans particularly gifted at receiving and interpreting such visions. However, perhaps the best example of a mortal farsight seer is Sorbo Falk, the unofficial leader of the trolls of Kalimaste and a Hierarch of the Alliance. Sorbo's visions have proven to be of a surprising clarity, with Daw al Fajr herself often expressing surprise as to how receptive Sorbo is in interpreting and understanding even the minutest and fragmented stray signals sensed by his mind.

A simple rule to understanding how farsight visions work is to always remember that most people in the universe, even the most receptive seers, wouldn't be able to sense anything emanating from the mind of a person located in the same room as them, unless if they possessed actual telepathic abilities which they have honed and cultivated. However, if enough people (and by 'enough' we are referring to trillions of individuals) have similar thoughts, then a sufficiently gifted farsight seer might be able to, at least, estimate what that thought might be. Farsight is a numbers game which can never truly be mastered. Even individuals of immense farsight capacity, such as Daw al Fajr, almost never produce visions of greater complexity than mere feelings, hazy images or vague concepts.

Appendix VII
About the Author

Vlad Adam was born and raised in Bucharest, Romania. He graduated from Leiden University in the Netherlands with a degree in International Relations, before pursuing a career in corporate finance. *Keepers of Terra* is his first novel, part of his *Saga of the Days After* series, together with *The Many Names of Cain*, *Here and There* and *The Lives of the Children*. He lives with his fiancé and their two cats, Caesar and Oscar.

Printed in Great Britain
by Amazon